.... DANGLING MAN ......

.... THE VICTIM ......

.... SEIZE THE DAY ......

.... DANGLING MAN .....

.... THE VICTIM ....

.... SEIZE THE DAY .....

BY SAUL BELLOW

Saul Bellow

DANGLING MAN

The Vanguard Press, Inc.

NEW YORK

T O   A N I T A

Printed in the United States of America

December 15, 1942

There was a time when people were in the habit of
addressing themselves frequently and felt no shame at
making a record of their inward transactions. But to keep
a journal nowadays is considered a kind of self-indulgence, a weakness, and in poor taste. For this is an era of
hardboiled-dom. Today, the code of the athlete, of the
tough boy—an American inheritance, I believe, from the
English gentleman—that curious mixture of striving, as-
ceticism, and rigor, the origins of which some trace back
to Alexander the Great—is stronger than ever. Do you
have feelings? There are correct and incorrect ways of
indicating them. Do you have an inner life? It is nobody's
business but your own. Do you have emotions? Strangle
them. To a degree, everyone obeys this code. And it does
admit of a limited kind of candor, a closemouthed straight-
forwardness. But on the truest candor, it has an inhibitory
effect. Most serious matters are closed to the hard-boiled.
They are unpracticed in introspection, and therefore badly
equipped to deal with opponents whom they cannot shoot
like big game or outdo in daring.

If you have difficulties, grapple with them silently, goes
one of their commandments. To hell with that! I intend to
talk about mine, and if I had as many mouths as Siva has
arms and kept them going all the time, I still could not do
myself justice. In my present state of demoralization, it
has become necessary for me to keep a journal—that is,

9

to talk to myself—and I do not feel guilty of self-indulgence in the least. The hard-boiled are compensated for their silence; they fly planes or fight bulls or catch tarpon, whereas I rarely leave my room.

In a city where one has lived nearly all his life, it is not likely that he will ever be solitary; and yet, in a very real sense, I am just that. I am alone ten hours a day in a single room. As such places go, it is not bad, though there are the standard rooming-house annoyances: cooking odors, roaches, and peculiar neighbors. But over the years I have become accustomed to all three.

I am well supplied with books. My wife is always bringing new ones in the hope that I will use them. I only wish I could. In the old days, when we had a flat of our own, I read constantly. I was forever buying new books, faster, admittedly, than I could read them. But as long as they surrounded me they stood as guarantors of an extended life, far more precious and necessary than the one I was forced to lead daily. If it was impossible to sustain this superior life at all times, I could at least keep its signs within reach. When it became tenuous I could see them and touch them. Now, however, now that I have leisure and should be able to devote myself to the studies I once began, I find myself unable to read. Books do not hold me. After two or three pages or, as it sometimes happens, paragraphs, I simply cannot go on.

Nearly seven months have gone by since I resigned my job at the Inter-American Travel Bureau to answer the Army's call for induction. I am still waiting. It is a trivial-seeming thing, a sort of bureaucratic comedy trimmed out in red tape. At first, I took that attitude toward it myself. It began as a holiday, a short reprieve, last May, when I was sent home because my papers were not in order. I have lived here eighteen years, but I am still Canadian, a British subject, and although a friendly alien I could not be drafted without an investigation. I waited five weeks and then I asked Mr. Mallender at Inter-American to take me back temporarily, but business had so fallen off, he told me, that he had been obliged to lay off Mr. Trager and Mr. Bishop, in spite of their long years of service, and could not possibly help me. At the end of September I was informed by letter that I had been investigated and approved and again, in accordance with the regulations, I was instructed to present myself for a second blood test. A month later I was notified that I was in 1A and was told to hold myself ready. Again I waited. Finally, when November came, I began to inquire and found that through a new clause affecting married men my induction had been postponed. I asked for reclassification, pleading that I had been prevented from working. After three weeks of explaining, I was transferred to 3A. But before I could act (in a week, to be accurate), I was summoned for a new blood test (each holds good for only sixty days). And so I was shifted back. This tedious business has not ended yet, I am sure. It will drag on for another two, three, four months.

Meanwhile, Iva, my wife, has been supporting me. She claims that it is no burden and that she wants me to enjoy this liberty, to read and to do all the delightful things I will be unable to do in the Army. About a year ago, I ambitiously began several essays, mainly biographical, on the philosophers of the Enlightenment. I was in the midst of one on Diderot when I stopped. But it was vaguely understood, when I began to dangle, that I was to continue

11

with them. Iva did not want me to get a job. As a 1A I could not get a suitable one anyhow.

Iva is a quiet girl. She has a way about her that discourages talk. We no longer confide in each other; in fact, there are many things I could not mention to her. We have friends, but we no longer see them. A few live in distant parts of the city. Some are in Washington, and some in the Army; one is abroad. My Chicago friends and I have been growing steadily apart. I have not been too eager to meet them. Possibly some of our differences could be mended. But, as I see it, the main bolt that held us together has given way, and so far I have had no incentive to replace it. And so I am very much alone. I sit idle in my room, anticipating the minor crises of the day, the maid's knock, the appearance of the postman, programs on the radio, and the sure, cyclical distress of certain thoughts.

I have thought of going to work, but I am unwilling to admit that I do not know how to use my freedom and have to embrace the flunkydom of a job because I have no resources—in a word, no character. I made an attempt to enlist in the Navy last time I was reclassified, but induction, it seems, is the only channel for aliens. There is nothing to do but wait, or dangle, and grow more and more dispirited. It is perfectly clear to me that I am deteriorating, storing bitterness and spite which eat like acids at my endowment of generosity and good will. But the seven months' delay is only one of the sources of my harassment. Again, I sometimes think of it as the backdrop against which I can be seen swinging. It is still more. Before I can properly estimate the damage it has done me I shall have to be cut down.

I HAVE begun to notice that the more active the rest of the world becomes, the more slowly I move, and that my solitude increases in the same proportion as its racket and frenzy. This morning Tad's wife in Washington writes that he has flown to North Africa. In all my life I have never felt so stock-still. I can't even bring myself to go to the store for tobacco, though I would enjoy a smoke. I will wait. And simply because Tad is now landing in Algiers or Oran or already taking his first walk in the *Casbah*— we saw *Pepé le Moko* together last year. I am honestly pleased for his sake, not envious. But the feeling persists that while he rockets to Africa and our friend Stillman travels in Brazil, I grow rooted to my chair. It is a real, a bodily feeling. I will not even try to rise. It may be that I could get up and walk around the room or even go to the store, but to make the effort would put me in a disagreeable state. This will pass if I ignore it. I have always been subject to such hallucinations. In the middle of winter, isolating a wall with sunlight on it, I have been able to persuade myself, despite the surrounding ice, that the month was July, not February. Similarly, I have reversed the summer and made myself shiver in the heat. And so, also, with the time of the day. It is a common trick, I suppose. It can be carried too far, perhaps, and damage the sense of reality. When Marie comes to make the bed, I shall get to my feet, button on my coat, and go to the store, and that will be the end of this feeling.

As a rule I am only too anxious to find a reason to leave my room. No sooner am I in it than I begin to cast around for one. When I do go, I do not go far. My average radius is three blocks. I am always afraid of running into an acquaintance who will express surprise at seeing me and ask questions. I avoid going downtown and, when I must go, I carefully stay away from certain streets. And I think I have carried over from my schooldays the feeling that there is something unlawful in being abroad, idle, in the middle of the day.

However, I am poor at finding reasons. I seldom go out more than four times a day, three times for meals and the fourth on a contrived errand or on some aimless impulse. I rarely take long walks. For lack of exercise, I am growing heavy. When Iva objects, I point out that I shall lose weight quickly enough in the Army. The streets at this time of year are forbidding, and then, too, I have no overshoes. Occasionally I do take a longer excursion, to the laundry or to the barber shop, to Woolworth's for envelopes, or even farther, at Iva's request, to pay a bill; or, without her knowledge, to see Kitty Daumler. And then there are obligatory visits to the family.

I have fallen into the habit of changing restaurants regularly. I do not want to become too familiar a sight in any of them, friendly with sandwich men, waitresses, and cashiers, and compelled to invent lies for their benefit.

At half-past eight I eat breakfast. Afterward I walk home and settle down to read the paper in the rocker by the window. I cover it from end to end, ritualistically, missing not a word. First come the comic strips (I follow them because I have done so since childhood, and I compel myself to read even the newest, most unpalatable ones), then I read the serious news and the columnists, and, finally, the gossip, the family page, the recipes, the obituaries, the society news, the ads, the children's puzzles, everything. Reluctant to put it aside, I even reread the comics to see if I have missed anything.

Re-entering waking life after the regeneration (when it is that) of sleep, I go in the body from nakedness to clothing and in the mind from relative purity to pollution. Raising the window, I test the weather; opening the paper, I admit the world.

I am now full of the world, and wide awake. It is nearly noon, time for lunch. Since eleven I have been growing restless, imagining that I am hungry again. Into the silence of the house there fall accentuating sounds, the closing of a door in another room, the ticking of drops from a faucet, the rustling of the steam in the radiator, the thrum of a sewing machine upstairs. The unmade bed, the walls, are brightly striped. The maid knocks and pushes open the door. She has a cigarette in her mouth. I think I am the only one before whom she dares smoke; she recognizes that I am of no importance.

At the restaurant I discover that I am not hungry at all, but now I have no alternative and so I eat. The stairs are a little more difficult this time. I come into the room breathing hard, and turn on the radio. I smoke. I listen to half an hour of symphonic music, disturbed when I fail to catch the announcer before he begins to advertise someone's credit-clothing. By one o'clock the day has changed, has taken on a new kind of restlessness. I make my effort to read but cannot key my mind to the sentences on the page or the references in the words. My mind redoubles its efforts, but thoughts of doubtful relevance are straggling in and out of it, the trivial and the major together. And suddenly I shut it off. It is as vacant as the street. I get up and turn on the radio again. Three o'clock, and nothing

15

has happened to me; three o'clock, and the dark is already setting in; three o'clock, and the postman has bobbed by for the last time and left nothing in my box. I have read the paper and looked into a book, I have had a few random thoughts. . . .

"Mr. Five-by-five,
He's five feet high
An' he's five feet wide . . ."

and now, like any housewife, I am listening to the radio.

The landlady's daughter has cautioned us not to play it too loudly; her mother has been bedridden for more than three months. The old woman is not expected to live long. She is blind and very nearly bald; she must be close to ninety. I see her at times, between the curtains, as I go upstairs. The daughter has been managing the house since September. She and her husband, Captain Briggs, live in the third-floor apartment. He is in the Quartermaster Division. A man of about fifty (much older than his wife), he is solid, neat, gray, and quiet-spoken. We often see him walking outside the fence, smoking a last cigarette before retiring.

At four-thirty I hear Mr. Vanaker next door, coughing and growling. Iva, for some reason of her own, has named him the "werewolf." He is a queer, annoying creature. His coughing, I am convinced, is partly alcoholic and partly nervous. And it is also a sort of social activity. Iva does not agree. But I know that he coughs to draw attention to himself. I have lived in rooming houses so long that I have acquired an eye for the type. Years ago, on Dorchester Avenue, there was an old man who refused to shut his door but sat or lay facing the hall and watched

16

everyone, day and night. And there was another on Schiller Street in whose washbasin you could always hear the water running. That was his manner of making himself known to us. Mr. Vanaker coughs. Not only that, but when he goes to the toilet he leaves the door ajar. He tramps down the hall, and a moment later you hear him splashing. Iva lately complained about this to Mrs. Briggs, who thereupon tacked a notice on the wall: *Occupant please close door when using and wear bathrobes to and fro.* So far it hasn't helped.

Through Mrs. Briggs we have learned a number of interesting facts about Vanaker. Before the old woman took to bed he was continually urging her to go to the movies with him. "When it should be plain to anybody Mamma can't see a thing." He was formerly in the habit of running down to answer the phone in his pajama trousers only—the reason for the bathrobe warning. The Captain had to step in and put an end to that. Marie has found half-smoked cigars ground out on the floors of unoccupied rooms. She suspects Vanaker of snooping through the house. He is no gentleman. She cleans his room, and she knows. Marie has high standards for white conduct, and her nostrils grow wider when she speaks of him. The old woman, Mrs. Kiefer, once threatened to put him out, she claims.

Vanaker is energetic. Hatless, he hurries in his black moleskin jacket up the street and between the snowy bushes. He slams the street door and kicks the snow from his boots on the first step. Then, coughing wildly, he runs up.

At six, I meet Iva at Fallon's for supper. We eat there quite regularly. Sometimes we go to the "Merit" or to a cafeteria on Fifty-third Street. Our evenings are generally short. We turn in before midnight.

IT IS a narcotic dullness. There are times when I am not even aware that there is anything wrong with this existence. But, on the other hand, there are times when I rouse myself in bewilderment and vexation, and then I think of myself as a moral casualty of the war. I have changed. Two incidents in the past week have shown me how greatly. The first can hardly be called an incident. I was leafing through Goethe's *Poetry and Life* and I came upon the following phrase: "This loathing of life has both physical and moral causes. . . ." I was sufficiently stirred by this to read on. "All comfort in life is based upon a regular occurrence of external phenomena. The changes of the day and night, of the seasons, of flowers and fruits, and all other recurring pleasures that come to us, that we may and should enjoy them—these are the mainsprings of our earthly life. The more open we are to these enjoyments, the happier we are; but if these changing phenomena unfold themselves and we take no interest in them, if we are insensible to such fair solicitations, then comes on the sorest evil, the heaviest disease—we regard life as a loathsome burden. It is said of an Englishman that he hanged himself that he might no longer have to dress and undress himself every day." I read on and on with unacccustomed feeling. Goethe's heading on the next page was "Weariness of Life." Exactly. *Radix malorum est* weariness of life. Then came the statement: "Nothing occasions this

18

weariness more than the recurrence of the passion of love." Deeply disappointed, I put the book down.

Nevertheless, I could not help seeing how differently this would have affected me a year ago, and how much I had altered. Then, I might have found it true but not especially noteworthy. I might have been amused by that Englishman but not moved. But his boredom threw that "passion of love" in the shadow and he instantly took his place for me beside that murderer Barnardine in *Measure for Measure* whose contempt for life equaled his contempt for death, so that he would not come out of his cell to be executed. To be so drawn to those two was proof that I had indeed changed.

And now the second incident.

My father-in-law, old Almstadt, came down with a bad cold, and Iva, knowing how inept her mother is, asked me to go there and help out.

The Almstadts live on the Northwest Side, a dreary hour's ride on the El. I found the house in great disorder. Mrs. Almstadt was trying to make the beds, cook, attend her husband, and answer the telephone all at the same time. The telephone was never idle for more than five minutes. Her friends kept calling, and to each she repeated the full story of her troubles. I have always disliked my mother-in-law. She is a short, fair, rather maidenish woman. Her natural color, when visible, is healthy. Her eyes are large, and they wear a knowing look, but since there is nothing to be knowing about they only convey her foolishness. She powders herself thickly, and her lips are painted in the shape that has become the universal device of sensuality for all women, from the barely mature to the very old. Mrs. Almstadt, nearing fifty, is already quite wrinkled, much to her concern, and she is forever on the watch for new packs and face lotions.

When I came in, she was busy talking over the telephone to someone, and I went to my father-in-law's room. He was lying with his knees drawn up and his shoulders raised, so that his head seemed joined without a neck directly to his body. Through an opening in his pajamas his flesh showed white and fatty under graying hair. He looked unfamiliar in the high-buttoned tunic with the crest on the pocket, and a little ludicrous. This was Mrs. Almstadt's doing. She bought his clothes, and she had dressed him for bed like a mandarin or a Romanoff prince. His broad knuckles were joined on the silken quilt. He greeted me with a not wholly ungrudged smile, and also as though it might be considered unmanly or unfatherly to fall sick. At the same time, however, he tried to make it plain that he could afford to spend a few days in bed; he was far enough ahead of the game; the business (this he told me with conflicting nonchalance and defiance) was in good hands.

The phone rang again, and Mrs. Almstadt once more began to tell her story to one of her innumerable connections (who knows who they are?). Her husband had come down yesterday, and they had had the doctor in, and the doctor had said there was a regular epidemic of grippe this winter. She was worn out, just worn out, trying to keep house and take care of Mr. Almstadt. You couldn't leave a sick person alone . . . and what could you do without a maid? Her words showered down upon us like little glass pellets. Old Almstadt gave no indication that he heard; at times he seemed automatically deaf to her. But, of course, it was impossible not to hear her; she has a high, atonal voice which penetrates everywhere. And

20

what I now became curious to know was whether he was unaffected or whether she was a nuisance to him. In the five years that I had been his son-in-law I had heard neither criticism nor defense of her from him, save on two occasions when he said, "Katy's still a child; she never grew up."

Before I was aware of it I was saying, "How did you ever manage to stick it out so long, Mr. Almstadt?"

"Stick out? What?" he said.

"With her," I plunged on. "It would get me, I know it would."

"What are you talking about?" the old man asked, perplexed and angry. I suppose he thought it dishonorable to allow anyone to say such things to his face. But I could not help myself. It seemed, at the moment, not an error but a very natural inquiry. I was suddenly in a state of mind that required directness for its satisfaction. Nothing else would do. "I don't know what you mean; what are you talking about?" he said again.

"Well, listen to her."

"Oh," he said, "you mean the telephone."

"Yes, the telephone."

He appeared somewhat relieved. "I don't pay any attention to it. All women are talkers. Maybe Katy talks more than most, but you got to allow for that. She . . ."

"Never grew up?" I said.

I doubt that this was what he intended to say, but since the phrase was his he could not dissent. With lips tightly drawn together, he nodded. "Yes, that's right. Some people just turn out different than others. Everybody isn't alike." He spoke stiffly; he was still angry. He had to make allowances for me, too, once in a while. My behavior was not always what it should be, he thus, indirectly, gave me to understand. His color had thickened furiously; it was slow to recede. Harsh and red his face shone under the branched brass fixture whose light had a singular hue, like tea. Was he deliberately covering up an opinion which, it must be conceded, he had every right to hold privately, or did he believe what he said? The latter was the more likely explanation. Babble, tedium, and all the rest were to be expected; they came with every marriage. There was still another possibility to consider, and that was that he was not resigned and that he did not ignore her as he pretended but—and there was every likelihood that he was unaware of this—heard and delighted in her, wanted her slovenly, garrulous, foolish, and coy, took pleasure in enduring her. His face, as we looked at each other, took on a doglike aspect. I was perturbed, and rebuked my imagination.

The doctor had left a prescription which the old man asked me to take to the drugstore. As I went out I heard Mrs. Almstadt saying, "My Iva's husband Joseph is here to lend a hand. He isn't working now, he's waiting for the Army, so he has all the time in the world." I started and turned, full of indignation, but she, pressing the black, kidney-shaped instrument to her cheek, smiled at me all oblivious. I wondered whether it was possible that she should not have said it intentionally, that she should be blameless; whether her thoughts were as smooth and contentless as counters or blank dominoes; whether she was half guile and half innocence; or whether there worked through her a malice she herself knew nothing about.

There was a sharp wind outside; the sun, low and raw in a field of coarse clouds, ruddied the bricks and windows. The street had been blown dry (it had rained the day before), and it presented itself in one of its winter aspects, creased and with thin sidelocks of snow, all but deserted. A block-long gap lay between me and the nearest walker—out on some unfathomable business—a man in a long, soldierly coat which the sun had converted to its own color. And then the pharmacy where I waited, sipping a cup of coffee under the crepe-paper lattice till my parcel, wrapped in green Christmas paper, was handed to me.

As I was going back, an exhibit in a barbershop attracted me: *"Fancy articles from kitchen odds and ends by Mrs. J. Kowalski, 3538 Pierce Avenue."* And there were laid out mosaic pictures, bits of matchstick on mats of leaf from old cigar butts, ash trays cut from tin cans and shellacked grapefruit rind, a braided cellophane belt, a letter opener inlaid with bits of glass, and two hand-painted religious pictures. In its glass case the striped pole turned smoothly, the Lucky Tiger watched from a thicket of bottles, the barber read a magazine. Turning with my parcel, I went on and, through the gray pillars and the ungainly door which clanked on the mailboxes, entered the sad cavern of the hall.

Upstairs, I worked energetically on the old man. I had Mrs. Almstadt make a pitcher of orange juice, dosed him with the medicine, and rubbed him down with alcohol. He grunted with pleasure during the massage and said that I was stronger than I looked. We were on better terms by this time. But I would not be drawn into a conversation. If I kept silent, I could not make another mistake. If I began to talk I would soon find myself explaining my position and defending my idleness. Old Almstadt did not bring up the subject. My own father, I must say, treats

23

me less considerately in that respect. He would have asked me, but Almstadt said nothing about it.

I rolled down my sleeves and was preparing to go when my mother-in-law reminded me that she had poured a glass of orange juice for me in the kitchen. That was not lunch, but it was better than nothing. I went to get it and found on the kitchen sink a half-cleaned chicken, its yellow claws rigid, its head bent as though to examine its entrails which raveled over the sopping draining board and splattered the enamel with blood. Beside it stood the orange juice, a brown feather floating in it. I poured it down the drain. Wearing my hat and scarf, I wandered to the living room where I had left my coat. Mr. and Mrs. Almstadt were conversing in the bedroom. I looked out of the window.

The sun had been covered up; snow was beginning to fall. It was sprinkled over the black pores of the gravel and was lying in thin slips on the slanting roofs. I could see a long way from this third-floor height. Not far off there were chimneys, their smoke a lighter gray than the gray of the sky; and, straight before me, ranges of poor dwellings, warehouses, billboards, culverts, electric signs blankly burning, parked cars and moving cars, and the occasional bare plan of a tree. These I surveyed, pressing my forehead on the glass. It was my painful obligation to look and to submit to myself the invariable question: Where was there a particle of what, elsewhere, or in the past, had spoken in man's favor? There could be no doubt that these billboards, streets, tracks, houses, ugly and blind, were related to interior life. And yet, I told myself, there had to be a doubt. There were human lives organized around these ways and houses, and that they, the houses, say, were the analogue, that what men created they also

24

were, through some transcendent means, I could not bring myself to concede. There must be a difference, a quality that eluded me, somehow, a difference between things and persons and even between acts and persons. Otherwise the people who lived here were actually a reflection of the things they lived among. I had always striven to avoid blaming them. Was that not in effect behind my daily reading of the paper? In their businesses and politics, their taverns, movies, assaults, divorces, murders, I tried continually to find clear signs of their common humanity.

It was undeniably to my interest to do this. Because I was involved with them; because, whether I liked it or not, they were my generation, my society, my world. We were figures in the same plot, eternally fixed together. I was aware, also, that their existence, just as it was, made mine possible. And if, as was often said, this part of the century was approaching the nether curve in a cycle, then I, too, would remain on the bottom and there, extinct, merely add my body, my life, to the base of a coming time. This would probably be a condemned age. But . . . it might be a mistake to think of it in that way. Mists faded and spread and faded on the pane as I breathed. Perhaps a mistake. And when I thought of the condemned ages and those unnamed, lying in their obscurity, I wondered. . . . How did we know how it was? In all principal ways the human spirit must have been the same. Good apparently left fewer traces. And we were coming to know that we had misjudged whole epochs. Besides, the giants of the last century had their Liverpools and Londons, their Lilles and Hamburgs to contend against, as we have our Chicagos and Detroits. And there might be a chance that I was misled, even with these ruins before my eyes, sodden, themselves the color of the fateful paper that I read daily. . . . The worlds we sought were never those we saw; the worlds we bargained for were never the worlds we got.

I have spoken of an "invariable question." But the fact is that it had for many months been not in the least invariable. These were things I would have thought last winter, and now, in their troubled density, they served only to remind me of the sort of person I had been. For a long time "common humanity" and "bring myself to concede" had been completely absent from my mind. And all at once I saw how I had lapsed from that older self to whom they had been so natural.

FOR LEGAL purposes, I am that older self, and if a question of my identity were to arise I could do nothing but point to my attributes of yesterday. I have not tried to bring myself up to date, either from indifference or from fear. Very little about the Joseph of a year ago pleases me. I cannot help laughing at him, at some of his traits and sayings.

Joseph, aged twenty-seven, an employee of the Inter-American Travel Bureau, a tall, already slightly flabby but, nevertheless, handsome young man, a graduate of the University of Wisconsin—major, History—married five years, amiable, generally takes himself to be well-liked. But on close examination he proves to be somewhat peculiar.

Peculiar? In what way? Well, to begin with, there is

something about his appearance, something wrong. His is a long, straight-nosed, firm face. He wears a little mustache, which makes him look older than he really is. His eyes are dark and full, rather too full, a little prominent, in fact. His hair is black. He does not have what people call an "open" look, but is restrained—at times, despite his amiability, forbidding. He is a person greatly concerned with keeping intact and free from encumbrance a sense of his own being, its importance. Yet he is not abnormally cold, nor is he egotistic. He keeps a tight hold because, as he himself explains, he is keenly intent on knowing what is happening to him. He wants to miss nothing.

His wife does not remember him without a mustache, and he had just turned seventeen when they met. On his first visit to the Almstadts, he had smoked a cigar and talked loudly and fairly expertly (he was then a Communist) about the German Social Democracy and the slogan "United Front from Below." Her father had taken him for twenty-five and had angrily ordered her not to invite grown men to the house. It amuses Mr. Almstadt to tell this story, now a family joke. He says: "I thought he was going to carry her away to Russia."

To turn now to Joseph's dress (I am wearing his cast-off clothes), it adds to his appearance of maturity. His suits are dark and conservative. His shoes, it is true, are pointed and rather dandyish, but that is possibly intended as a counterbalance. A broader toe would give you a man in his middle thirties. As he is in most things, Joseph is conscious of a motive in his choice of clothes. It is his answer to those whose defiant principle it is to dress badly, to whom a crumpled suit is a badge of freedom. He wants to avoid the small conflicts of nonconformity so that he can give all his attention to defending his inner differences, the ones that really matter. Furthermore, he takes a sad or negative satisfaction in wearing what he calls "the uniform of the times." In short, the less noteworthy the better, for his purposes. All the same, he manages to stand out.

In things of this sort his friends sometimes find him ridiculous. And, yes, he says, he admits he is on "the funny side" in many ways. But that can't be helped. The appearance and behavior of reflective men is seldom comparable to that of the less reflective, who unhesitatingly entrust all they stand for to their looks and gestures. What he is trying to do is not easy, and it is not unlikely that the more he succeeds, the more odd he may seem. Besides, he says, there is an element of the comic or fantastic in everyone. You can never bring that altogether under control.

"An element of the comic or fantastic . . ." such phrases have a queer ring; and people who have begun by taking him for a clerk at Inter-American, a fairly nice chap, begin to look at him with changed eyes. But even his oldest friends, those who like John Pearl and Morris Abt have been close to him since boyhood, often find it hard to make him out. And, despite his anxiety to be understood, he cannot always help them.

Joseph, since leaving school, has not stopped thinking of himself as a scholar, and he surrounds himself with books. Before he interested himself in the Enlightenment he made a study of the early ascetics and, earlier, of Romanticism and the child prodigy. Of course, he has to earn his living, but he tries to strike a balance between what he wants and what he is compelled to do, between

28

the necessity and the wish. A compromise exists, but then men's lives abound in such compromises. He is proud of the skill with which he manages both sides and—albeit somewhat mistakenly—likes to refer to himself as a Machiavellian. He keeps his roles successfully distinct and even goes out of his way to be an excellent employee, simply to prove that "visionaries" can be hardheaded.

Everyone admits, however, that Joseph has a close grasp on himself, that he knows what he wants and how to go about getting it. In the last seven or eight years he has worked everything out in accordance with a general plan. Into this plan have gone his friends, his family, and his wife. He has taken a great deal of trouble with his wife, urging her to read books of his choosing, teaching her to admire what he believes admirable. To what degree he has succeeded he does not know.

It should not be thought that Joseph, when he speaks of the "less reflective" or of his "element of the comic," is being harsh. He is not severe toward the world. He calls himself a sworn upholder of *tout comprendre c'est tout pardonner*. Theories of a wholly good or a wholly malevolent world strike him as foolish. Of those who believe in a wholly good world he says that they do not understand depravity. As for pessimists, the question he asks of them is, "Is that all they see, such people?" For him, the world is both, and therefore it is neither. Merely to make a judgment of that kind is, to representatives of either position, a satisfaction. Whereas, to him, judgment is second to wonder, to speculation on men, drugged and clear, jealous, ambitious, good, tempted, curious, each in his own time and with his customs and motives, and bearing the imprint of strangeness in the world. In a sense, everything is good because it exists. Or, good or not good, it exists, it is ineffable, and, for that reason, marvelous.

But for all that, Joseph suffers from a feeling of strangeness, of not quite belonging to the world, of lying under a cloud and looking up at it. Now, he says, all human beings share this to some extent. The child feels that his parents are pretenders; his real father is elsewhere and will some day come to claim him. And for others the real world is not here at all and what is at hand is spurious and copied. Joseph's feeling of strangeness sometimes takes the form almost of a conspiracy: not a conspiracy of evil, but one which contains the diversified splendors, the shifts, excitements, and also the common, neutral matter of an existence. Living from day to day under the shadow of such a conspiracy is trying. If it makes for wonder, it makes even more for uneasiness, and one clings to the nearest passers-by, to brothers, parents, friends, and wives.

December 20

PREPARATIONS for the holiday. I went out yesterday to do some shopping for Iva. Downtown there were bell ringers on every corner, in beards of soiled cotton and red Santa Claus costumes. For love of the poor, for dear charity, clang-clanging away in the din. Immense wreaths were mounted on buildings in the green, menacing air; the thousands upon thousands of shoppers ground through the stores and the streets under the smoky red façades and in the amplified roar of carols. The holly berries flashed on the tarred poles in thick drops. The jukeboxes in the

30

taverns were playing "I'm Dreaming of a White Christmas." Everyone prays for snow, and the thought of rain or sleet brings panic.

Vanaker is restless these days. He keeps moving the furniture around his room. Marie complains more than ever. By changing the position of the bed he makes it hard for her to clean the room. The door is blocked. She doesn't like to go in anyway. He doesn't keep himself clean, she claims. Instead of sending his linen to the laundry, he airs it at the window. He hangs up his underwear at night and forgets to take it down in the morning. Mrs. Briggs tells me that he is engaged to marry a lady of sixty who insists that he be converted to the Catholic faith and that he goes every evening to the church of St. Thomas the Apostle for indoctrination. At the same time, I notice that he receives large quantities of mail from the Masonic Scottish Rite. It may be this conflict of principle that drives him to get up at two in the morning to change the position of his bed.

We have two invitations to Christmas dinner, one from the Almstadts and another from my brother Amos. I am for refusing both.

December 22

An unusual explosion of temper this afternoon, when I was with Myron Adler. I behaved unaccountably, greatly surprising myself and, of course, bewildering Myron altogether. He had phoned me about a temporary job which would consist of asking people questions for a poll he is conducting. I hurried down to meet him at the Arrow for lunch. I arrived first, took a table toward the back, and immediately fell victim to depression. I had not visited the Arrow for a number of years. It was at one time a hangout for earnest eccentrics where, at almost any hour of the afternoon or evening, you could hear discussions of socialism, psychopathology, or the fate of European Man. It was I who had suggested that we eat there; for some reason it had been the first place that came to my mind. Now it depressed me. Then, as I looked around at the steam tables and the posters of foundering ships and faces of Japanese, I suddenly saw Jimmy Burns sitting at a table with a man I did not know. Since the days when we had been Comrade Joe and Comrade Jim, we had seen each other no more than two, perhaps three, times. He looked changed; his forehead had grown higher and his expression more severe. I nodded to him, but got no recognition for my pains; he looked through me in the way which is, I suppose, officially prescribed for "renegades."

When Myron came in a few minutes later and started at once to talk about the job, I said impatiently, "Wait a second, now. Just hold on."

"What's the matter?"

"Something very special," I said. "Wait till I tell you. You see that man in the brown suit over there? That's Jimmy Burns. Ten years ago I was privileged to call him Comrade Jimmy."

"Well?" said Myron.

"I said hello to him, and he acted as if I simply wasn't there."

"What of it?" said Myron.

"Does that seem natural? I was once a close friend."

"Well?" said Myron.

32

"Stop saying that, will you!" I said in exasperation.

"I mean, do you want him to throw his arms around you?" asked Myron.

"You don't get the point. I despise him."

"Then I don't get the point. I confess I don't get it."

"No. Listen. He has no business ignoring me. This is always happening to me. You don't understand it because you're a person of no political experience. But I know what this means, and I'm going to go up to him and say hello whether he likes it or not."

"Don't be a fool. What do you want to make trouble for?" said Myron.

"Because I feel like making trouble. Does he know me or doesn't he? He knows me perfectly well." I was growing angrier by the minute. "I'm surprised that you shouldn't be able to see it."

"I came here to talk to you about a job, not to see you throw a fit," he said.

"Oh, a fit. Do you think I care about *him?* It's the principle of the thing. It seems to escape you. Simply because I am no longer a member of their party they have instructed him and boobs like him not to talk to me. Don't you see what's involved?"

"No," Myron said carelessly.

"I'll tell you what's involved. I have a right to be spoken to. It's the most elementary thing in the world. Simply that. I insist on it."

"Oh, Joseph," said Myron.

"No, really, listen to me. Forbid one man to talk to another, forbid him to communicate with someone else, and you've forbidden him to think, because, as a great many writers will tell you, thought is a kind of communication.

And his party doesn't want him to think, but to follow its discipline. So there you are. Because it's supposed to be a revolutionary party. That's what's offending me. When a man obeys an order like that he's helping to abolish freedom and begin tyranny."

"Come, come," said Myron. "You're making too much fuss over it."

"I should be making twice as much fuss," I said. "It's very important."

"But you've been through with them for years, haven't you?" Myron asked. "Do you mean to say you've just discovered this now?"

"I haven't forgotten, that's all. You see, I thought those people were different. I haven't forgotten that I believed they were devoted to the service of some grand flapdoodle, the Race, *le genre humain*. Oh, yes, they were! By the time I got out, I realized that any hospital nurse did more with one bedpan for *le genre humain* than they did with their entire organization. It's odd to think that there was a time when to hear that would have filled me with horror. What? Reformism?"

"I've heard of that," said Myron.

"I should think so. Reformism! A terrible thing. About a month after we parted company, I sat down and wrote Jane Addams a letter of apology. She was still alive."

"Did you?" he said, looking at me curiously.

"I never mailed it," I said. "Maybe I should have. Don't you believe me?"

"Why shouldn't I?"

"I changed my mind about redoing the world from top to bottom à la Karl Marx and decided in favor of bandaging a few sores at a time. Of course, that was temporary, too. . . ."

"Was it?" he said.

"Oh, for heaven's sake! You know that, Mike," I said loudly.

The man who was sitting with Burns turned around, but the latter still pretended not to see me. "That's right," I said. "Look the other way. Go on. That boy is mad, Myron. He's never been sane. Everything has changed, he's been left far behind, but he thinks it's as it used to be. He still wears that proletarian bang on his earnest forehead and dreams of becoming an American Robespierre. The rest have compromised themselves to the ears, but *he* still believes in the revolution. Blood will run, the power will change hands, and then the state will wither away according to the in-ex-or-able logic of history. I'd gamble my shirt on it. I know his mind. Let me tell you something about him. Do you know what he used to have in his room? I went up with him one day, and there was a large-scale map of the city, with pins in it. So I said, 'What's this for, Jim?' And then—I swear this is true—he started to explain that he was preparing a guide for street-fighting, the day of the insurrection. He had all the critical streets marked in code for cellars and roofs, the paving material, the number of newsstands at each corner that could be thrown into barricades (the Parisian kiosks, you remember). Even abandoned sewers for hiding arms. He traced them through City Hall records. At that time I didn't know how crazy it was. The things we used to accept as natural—why, it's unbelievable! And he's still in that. I'll bet he still has the map. He's an addict. They're

35

all addicted people, Mike. Hey, Burns! Hey!" I called out.

"Shut up, Joseph! For God's sake. What are you doing? Everybody's looking at you."

Burns glanced briefly in my direction and then resumed his conversation with the other man, who, however, turned again to examine me.

"What do you know about that! Burns won't give me a tumble. I can't arouse him. I'm just gone. Like that." I snapped my fingers. "I'm a contemptible petty-bourgeois renegade; could anything be worse? That idiot! Hey, addict!" I shouted.

"Have you gone mad? Come on." Myron pushed back the table. "I'm going to get you out of here before you start a fight. I think you would start a fight. Where's your coat, which is it? Why, you're a madman! Come back here!" But I was already out of his reach. I halted squarely before Burns.

"I said hello to you before, didn't you notice?"

He made no reply.

"Don't you know me? It seems to me that I know you very well. Answer me, don't you know who I am?"

"Yes, I know you," Burns said in a low voice.

"That's what I wanted to hear," I said. "I just wanted to be sure. I'm coming, Myron." I pulled my arm away from him, and we strode out.

I was aware that this had made a bad impression on Myron, but cared to do little to rectify it beyond explaining in a few short words that I had not been myself lately. But I did not say this until we had come to our second course in another restaurant. I became very quiet. I did not, and still do not, know where this outbreak came from.

I suspect that it originated in sheer dishevelment of mind. But how could I explain this to Myron without becoming entangled in a long description of the state I was in and its causes? I would make him squirm and I myself would squander my feelings in self-pity.

We talked about the job, and he promised to recommend me to his superiors. He hoped, he said (he had sounded more positive on the phone), that I would get it. Myron likes me, I know he does. But he has worked hard to reach his present position and, realist that he is, it cannot have taken him long to decide that he could not afford to be responsible for me. I might prove unreliable, raise a cry about "the principle of the thing," and with one quirk or impulse, undo him. I could not blame him after what had just happened.

But still, I could not condemn myself altogether for it. It was wrong to make a scene but, after all, it was not so wrong to be indignant at Burns. To have invented a letter to Jane Addams was, however, clearly wrong. Why on earth had I done that? I had a point to make, yes; but I should have thought of a better way. For a moment, in the interest of elementary honesty, I thought of confessing. But if I told him that and no more (and I did not want to say more), he would become even more confused and distrustful. And why bother?

And so I said, as we were about to separate, "Mike, if you have anyone else in mind for that job, feel free to suggest him. I can't tell how long I'll be around. They may notify me any day, and then I'd be forced to walk out in the middle of things. That wouldn't do. But thanks for thinking of me. . . ."

"Oh, now, Joseph, look. . . ."

"Never mind, Mike. And I really do mean that."

"I'll put your name up. And, Joseph, we ought to get together. I want to talk to you. One of these days."

"Well, all right. But the fact is, I'm not fit company. I'm all up in the air. And forget about the job." And I walked away quickly, certain that I had lifted a burden from him and, by so doing, had acquitted myself decently.

Later, thinking these incidents over, I felt less inclined to shoulder all the blame. It seemed to me that Myron might have been somewhat less worried about the spectacle I had made of myself and the attention I had drawn to him and more concerned about the cause of my outburst. If he had thought about it, he would have seen that there were reasons for my behavior, reasons that might well prove disquieting to a friend. And, moreover, he might have found that what I was driving at was not without importance. For the insolence of Burns figured the whole betrayal of an undertaking to which I had once devoted myself, and my chagrin—though it seemed to find its object in Burns—was actually aimed at those who had perverted it.

But then, I may be expecting too much from Myron. He has the pride of what he has become: a successful young man, comfortable, respected, safe for the present from those craters of the spirit which I have lately looked into. Worst of all, Myron has learned, like so many others, to prize convenience. He has learned to be accommodating. That is not a private vice; it has ramified consequences—terrible ones.

For months I have been angry with my friends. I have thought of them as "failing" me. Since the Servatius party,

38

last March, I have been brooding over this failure. I have made it look like a major catastrophe, whereas it was nothing of the sort, and have made an obsessional grievance of betrayal where, in fact, only my shortsightedness was at fault—that and the inflationary, grandiose, tasteless attitudes I dissociate myself from by pinning them on Joseph. In reality, the Servatius party merely forced on my attention certain defects in the people around me which, if I had been as astute as I should have been, I would have recognized long before, and of which I think I must have been partly aware all the time.

Partly, I say. And here I feel it necessary to revive Joseph, that creature of plans. He had asked himself a question I still would like answered, namely, "How should a good man live; what ought he to do?" Hence the plans. Unfortunately, most of them were foolish. Also, they led him to be untrue to himself. He made mistakes of the sort people make who see things as they wish to see them or, for the sake of their plans, *must* see them. There might be some justice in the view that man was born the slayer of his father and of his brother, full of instinctive bloody rages, licentious and unruly from his earliest days, an animal who had to be tamed. But, he protested, he could find in himself no such history of hate overcome. He could not. He believed in his own mildness, believed in it piously. He allowed this belief to interfere with his natural shrewdness and did both himself and his friends a disservice. They could not give him what he wanted.

What he wanted was a "colony of the spirit," or a group whose covenants forbade spite, bloodiness, and cruelty. To hack, to tear, to murder was for those in whom the sense of the temporariness of life had shrunk. The world

39

was crude and it was dangerous and, if no measures were taken, existence could indeed become—in Hobbes' phrase, which had long ago lodged in Joseph's mind—"nasty, brutish, short." It need not become so if a number of others would combine to defend themselves against danger and crudity.

He thought he had found those others, but even before the Servatius party he (or rather I) had begun to have misgivings about the progress that was being made. I was beginning to see that a difficult plan or program like mine had to take into account all that was natural, including corruptness. I had to be faithful to the facts, and corruptness was one of them.

But the party shocked me.

I did not want to go. It was Iva who insisted, out of loyalty to Minna Servatius and because she knew what it was to be a disappointed hostess. It was a long time since a party, any party, had given me pleasure. I liked nothing better than to see my friends singly or in pairs, but when they came together in a large group they disheartened me. You knew what to expect beforehand. If there were jokes, you knew how they would be told; if there were exhibitions, you knew who would make them and who would be hurt or shamed or gratified by them. You knew what Stillman would do, you knew what George Hayza would do, you knew that Abt would make fun of everyone and that Minna would have difficulties with her husband. You knew there was bound to be mischief, distortion, and strain, and yet you went. And why? Because Minna had prepared a party; because your friends were going to be there. And they were coming because you were going to be there, and on no account must anyone be let down.

When the heat and stridency of the party burst upon us through the open door, I began to regret that I had not been more firm in refusing, this once. Minna met us in the entry hall. She was wearing a black dress with a high, silver-trimmed collar; her legs were bare, and she had on high-heeled, red sandals. It was not immediately apparent how drunk she was. She appeared, at first, self-possessed and grave; her face was white, her forehead full of creases. Then we noticed how she was perspiring and how unsteady her eyes were. She looked first at Iva and then at me, saying nothing. We did not know what to expect. Then, with alarming suddenness, she cried, "Sound the gong; they're here."

"Who?" said Jack Brill, putting his head out of the door.

"Joseph and Iva. Always last to show up. They come when everybody's high so they can stand around and watch us make fools of ourselves."

"It's my fault," Iva murmured. We were both taken aback by Minna's outcry. "I have such a cold, and . . ."

"Darling," said Minna. "I was only joking. Come in."

She led us into the living room. There, both doors of the phonograph were open, but the guests talked; no one seemed to listen to the music. And here was the scene, predictable to the last detail, hours, days, weeks before—the light furniture in the popular Swedish style, the brown carpet, the Chagall and Gris prints, the vines trailing from the mantelpiece, the bowl of Cohasset punch. Minna had invited a number of "strangers—" acquaintances, that is, who did not belong to the inner circle. There was a young woman to whom I had once been introduced. I remembered her because of her downy, slightly protuberant lip.

41

She was quite pretty, however. Her name escaped me. Did she work in Minna's office? Was she married to the fat man in the steel-rimmed glasses? Had I also met him? I would never know. And in this noise I could not help being indifferent about it. So it was with these strangers. Some, like Jack Brill, you came to know well, in time. The others remained grouped together indistinctly and were recalled, if the need arose, as "that fellow with the glasses" or "that pasty-looking couple."

One by one, the friends came forward—Abt, George Hayza, Myron, Robbie Stillman. They were the center of the party; they performed. The others looked on, and who could tell whether they were amused or resentful at their exclusion, or even if they were aware of being excluded? The party went on around them. If they were aware of what was happening, they made the best of it.

And so did you. Your first tour of the room done, you moved aside with a glass and a cigarette. You sat—if you could find a place—and watched the performers and the dancers. You heard Robbie Stillman tell a story he had told any number of times about the mishaps of a stuttering girl, or about a hobo with a new portable radio he had met one day on the steps of the Aquarium. You did not like him less for telling it. You felt, somehow, that he, too, was forced to endure it, that he began unwillingly and was under a compulsion to finish what no one wanted to hear finished. You could not blame him.

Minna went around the living room from group to group, unsteadily, as if in danger of falling from her high heels.

Finally she stopped before George Hayza. We heard

them arguing. It turned out that she wanted him to record on the machine a poem he had made popular years ago when he had played at being a surrealist. To his credit, he refused. That is, he tried to refuse, reddening and smiling anxiously. He wanted to live it down. Everybody was tired of it, he most of all. Others came to his support. Abt said, with an edge of impatience in his voice, that George ought to be allowed to judge whether or not he should recite it. And since everyone had heard it—a dozen times . . .

"Everyone has not heard it," said Minna. "Besides, I want to make a record of it. It's clever."

"It used to be considered clever."

"It still is. It's very clever."

Abt gave up the argument, for a sense of a special situation was arising. Abt had once been engaged to Minna, but for reasons none of us knew, she had suddenly decided to marry Harry Servatius. There was, therefore, a complex history of injured feelings between Abt and Minna, and, in a gathering atmosphere of embarrassment, Abt withdrew, and Minna had her way. The poem was recorded. George's voice came out strangely high and unsteady.

"I am alone
And eat my hair as a calendar of regrets—"

George, with a grimace of apology, backed away from the phonograph. Only Minna was satisfied; she played the record again.

"What's wrong tonight?" I asked Myron.

"Oh—it's Harry, I guess. He's in the study with Gilda Hillman. They've been there all evening. Talking."

"Joseph," said Iva from her chair near by, "will you get me some more?" She held out her glass.

"Iva," said Jack Brill, with a warning laugh. "Go slow."

"With what? The punch?"

"It tastes mild, but it isn't mild at all."

"Maybe you shouldn't drink any more of it," I said, "since you're not feeling well."

"I don't know why I'm so thirsty. I haven't eaten anything salty."

"I'll bring you some water if you like."

"Water." She drew back the glass contemptuously.

"I wish you wouldn't drink tonight. It's a strong punch," I said. My tone was unmistakable. I did not mean to be disobeyed. Yet a little later I saw her at the bowl and frowned at the quick motion with which she raised her arm and drank. I was irritated enough to consider, for a moment, striding up and snatching the glass away.

Instead I started a conversation with Abt on the first subject that came to hand, the war in Libya. We wandered into the kitchen, talking.

Abt is one of my oldest and best friends. I have always been much attached to him and have valued him perhaps more than he has valued me. That does not make much difference; he certainly has great affection for me, and some respect. At college we roomed together for a while. We were temporarily estranged because of a political matter. When we returned to Chicago we resumed our friendship, and while he worked for his doctorate—until last June he was an instructor in political science—he practically lived with us.

"We owe a lot to the Italians," Abt was saying. "They have a sensible attitude toward the war. They want to go home. And that isn't our only indebtedness. Capitalism never made them the victims of addition and subtraction. They remained a thoughtful people." (He spoke slowly, so that I knew he was improvising, an old habit of his.) "And they never became swashbucklers. They have better taste and less false pride than the heirs of Arminius. Of course, that was an Italian mistake. Tacitus inflated the Germans. . . ."

My irritation with Iva faded. I found myself listening, amused, to his praise of the Italians. "So that's our debt," I said, smiling. "Do you think they're going to save us?"

"They won't do us any harm. It begins to look as though civilization may start its comeback from the Mediterranean, where it was born."

"Have you tried that on Dr. Rood?"

"He'd take me seriously and try to steal the idea."

Dr. Arnold Rood, or Mary Baker Rood, as Abt liked to call him, was the head of his department and a dean of the college.

"How is the old man?"

"Still oily, still the highest-paid Reader in the city, and just as ignorant as ever. I have become his favorite problem in conversion and I have to see him twice a week to discuss *Science and Health*. Some fine afternoon I'll stick a knife into him and say, 'Pray yourself out of that, you bastard.' That's a vulgar refutation, like Johnson's kicking the stone to triumph over Berkeley. But I can't think of any other way to deal with him."

I laughed, and at the same moment another, shriller laugh, almost an outcry, came from the front of the house. I stared down the hall.

"Minna," Abt said.

"I wish something could be done. . . ." It appalled me

45

to hear that cry and to recall the look on her face when she had greeted us in the entry hall. The party blared on inside, and I began to think what a gathering of this sort meant. And it came to me all at once that the human purpose of these occasions had always been to free the charge of feeling in the pent heart; and that, as animals instinctively sought salt or lime, we, too, flew together at this need as we had at Eleusis, with rites and dances, and at other high festivals and corroborees to witness pains and tortures, to give our scorn, hatred, and desire temporary liberty and play. Only we did these things without grace or mystery, lacking the forms for them and, relying on drunkenness, assassinated the Gods in one another and shrieked in vengefulness and hurt. I frowned at this dreadful picture.

"Oh, yes," said Abt, "she's having a bad time."

It reassured me to hear him say this; he felt as I did about it.

"But she shouldn't allow herself. . . ." Rapid footsteps came toward the kitchen. "There's such a thing as . . . ." But again he did not finish. Minna came in accompanied by George.

"What's such a thing?" Minna said.

"Was that you yelling?" said Abt.

"I wasn't yelling. Stand aside from the refrigerator. George and I have come for ice cubes. Say, what are you hiding in the kitchen for, anyway? There's a party on. These two," she said to George, "are always in a corner together. Him in his undertaker's suit, and this one . . . with rings under his eyes. Like a couple of plotters." She walked out unsteadily. George, with a set and disapproving face, carried the ice-filled bowl.

"Having a wonderful night, isn't she?" said Abt.

"Is Harry drunk, too? What's the matter with them?"

"He may be a little soused. I think he knows what he's doing," said Abt. "But it's really not our business. . . ."

"I thought they were getting along."

"There's trouble of some sort. But, ah!" he made a grimace. "It's very unlovely."

"It certainly is," I said.

"I've had my share, too, tonight. That business of George's damned poem."

"Oh, I know."

"I'm going to keep my nose clean."

I felt increasingly disturbed. Abt looked and sounded exceptionally unhappy. Not that it was unusual for him to be unhappy; he was seldom otherwise. But tonight there was a much larger degree of harshness in his customary mixture of levity and harshness. I had noticed that and, though I had laughed, I had also winced a little when he spoke of stabbing Dr. Rood. I sighed. Of course he was still in love with Minna. Or would it be better to say that he had never recovered from his disappointment in her? But there was more to it than that, I knew—a fundamental discontent which would not yield its meaning to such easy formulations as "love" and "disappointment." Still more, I was disturbed at myself because I knew that at heart I was tired of Abt's unhappiness and of seeing him rise to it like a jaded but skillful boxer. I did not want to admit that. I urged my sympathies to work for him. He *was* unhappy, after all, wasn't he?

We came back to the living room. Iva was sitting beside Stillman on the piano bench. Servatius and Gilda Hillman had appeared at last; they were dancing. Her face was lowered against his chest; they hung together, moving slowly.

"Nice-looking couple, aren't they?" Minna said. She was standing behind us. We turned uneasily.

"Well, they are," she said. "Harry dances well. She's not bad, either." We did not reply. "Oh, you're a couple of fish." She started to walk away but thought better of it. "You needn't have such high opinions of yourselves. You're not the man Harry is, and you're not, either."

"Minna," I said.

"Minna yourself!"

We turned from her. "She's getting worse and worse," I said awkwardly. "We ought to leave." Abt answered nothing.

I told Iva that I was going to get her coat. "What for?" she said. "I don't want to go yet." She regarded the matter as settled. She looked around calmly; she was mildly drunk.

I persisted. "It's getting late."

"Oh, don't break up the party," said Stillman. "Stay a while."

Red-faced and smiling broadly, Jack Brill came up to us a few minutes later, saying, "Minna's looking for you, Morris."

"For me? What does she want?" said Abt.

"Search me. But I'm pretty sure she'll get it."

"Morris!"

"Morris!"

"I told you. Here she comes," said Brill.

"Morris," said Minna, putting her hand on his shoulder, "I want you to do something for the party. It's got to be livened up, it's going dead."

48

"I'm afraid I can't help you," said Abt.

"Yes you can. I have a marvelous idea."

No one asked what this idea was. Jack Brill, after smiling at everyone's discomfiture, said, "What's your idea, Minna?"

"Morris is going to hypnotize somebody."

"You're mistaken," said Abt. "I've given up amateur hypnotism. You'll have to ask someone else to liven up your party." He spoke coldly and without looking at her.

"It's not a good idea, Minna," I put it.

"You're wrong; it's a wonderful idea. Keep out of this."

"Oh, drop it, Minna," said George Hayza. "Nobody wants to see it done."

"You shut up, too, George. Morris," she said beseechingly, "I know you're mad at me. But, please, this once. The party'll break up if something doesn't happen soon."

"I've forgotten how. I can't hypnotize anyone any longer. I haven't done it for years."

"Ah, you haven't forgotten. You can do it. You have a strong mind."

"Go away, Minna," I said.

"She'll get her way," Jack Brill chuckled. "Wait and see."

"You encourage her," I said severely.

"She does everything without encouragement. Don't blame me." He still smiled, but back of his smile there was a resentful and inimical coldness. "I just like to see how she goes about getting her way."

"Morris, please do it."

"Get someone else to do tricks. Get Myron, here."

"He's too stiff for tricks. He doesn't know any."

"Thank God for that," Myron said.

"Now, to get you a subject," said Minna.

"I don't want a subject."

She rapped for attention on the piano. "Announce‑ment," she called out. Servatius and Gilda did not inter‑rupt their dancing. "We need someone for Morris, here, to hypnotize. Judy, how about you?" Judy was the girl with the man in the steel-rimmed glasses. "No? Afraid you'll give yourself away? This takes a little courage. Stillman? These people are against it. Does anybody want to volunteer?" There were no volunteers. "Oh, what a lot of wet blankets."

"There," I said, "nobody's really interested. So you see. . . ."

"Then I'll be your subject myself," Minna said, turning to Abt.

"That's the silliest proposal yet," said George.

"Why shouldn't I be his subject?"

We waited to hear what Abt would say. He had so far given no indication of what he thought of her proposal. He regarded her with raised brows like a doctor who is considering how fully to answer a layman's question while, with quizzical, concealing eyes, he keeps him waiting. The indirect ceiling light gave the side of his face the look of a sheet of thick paper, artfully folded at the eye and pierced, high on the forehead, by straight, black hairs.

"I'll be damned," Jack Brill said softly to me. "He'll take her up on it, too."

"Oh, impossible," I said.

Abt hesitated.

"Well?" Minna said.

"All right," he said. "Why not?"

"Morris."

He disregarded me.

And the others also protested. "She's drunk," said Stillman. And George said, "Are you sure you know what you're up to?" But he disregarded them, too, and made no attempt to explain or justify himself. He and Minna started off toward the study.

"We'll call you. I mean, Morris will call you," Minna said. "Then you can all come in."

When they left, the rest of us fell silent. The dancing had stopped. Jack Brill, leaning one shoulder against the wall, smoked his pipe and seemed to relish watching us. Harry Servatius and Gilda were together on a narrow seat in the corner. They were the only ones talking; no words, however, were audible, only his heavy burring voice and her occasional choppy laughter. What on earth could he be saying that she found so funny? He was making an idiot of himself, and if Abt were correct in saying that he was not too drunk, then he was doubly idiotic. Iva still kept her glass on the piano ledge and took a small sip every so often. I did not like the aimless absorption with which she smoothed out the paper napkin on her knee, nor the rapid yet vague way her eyes moved around the room.

She remained behind with Harry and Gilda when Abt called us. The rest of us crowded into the study and, in embarrassed silence, stood looking down at Minna on the couch. I could not believe at first that she was not pretending; the change seemed too great. I was soon convinced that this was real enough. She lay loosely outstretched, a strong light behind her turned against the wall. One of her sandals had come unfastened and swung away from her heel. Her hands lay open at her sides. One noticed how narrow and bony her wrists were and the mole between two

51

branches of a vein on her forearm. But, for all the width of her hips, and the feminine prominences, her knees under the dress, her bosom, the meeting of her throat and collar-bones, she looked less specifically like a woman than a more generalized human being—and a sad one, at that. This view of her affected me greatly. I was even more prejudiced against Abt's performance.

He sat beside her and talked to her soothingly. Her breathing was regular, but touched with hoarseness; her upper lip was drawn away slightly from her teeth.

He began by making her feel cold. "Someone must have turned off the heat. I'm chilled. Don't you feel cold, too? You look cold. It is cold here; it's almost freezing." And she gasped a little and drew up her legs. He went on to tell her that when he pinched her hand she would feel no pain, and so she felt none, though the skin, where he had twisted it, remained white long afterwards. He deprived her of the power to move her arm and then ordered her to raise it. She struggled until he released her. The rest of us, half-tranced ourselves, eager to see and yet afraid of what we were seeing, concentrated on her face with its lifted lip and creased eyes. He let her rest, but only for a moment. Then he asked her to recall how many glasses of punch she had drunk. He would give a series of numbers and she was to make a sign at the right one. At this, her eyes moved or flinched under her lids, as though in protest. He began counting.

I was standing at a corner of the couch in such a position that her bare heel, the one from which the sandal hung, grazed my trouser-leg. I had an impulse to touch the mole on her arm with my finger. All at once, looking at her face and her closed lids, my impatience with Abt turned into anger. Yes, I thought, he *likes* this. I tried to think what I could do to stop it. Meanwhile he was counting. "Six? Seven?" She tried, but was unable to answer. Perhaps she was aware of the insult. "So you can't remember?" said Abt. "No?" She rolled her head. "Maybe you've forgotten how to count? Let's see if you have. I'm going to tap your cheek a few times. You count and tell me how many. Ready?"

"Bring her out of it, Morris, we've all had enough," I said.

He did not seem to hear me. "Now I'm beginning," he said. He struck her lightly four times. Minna's lips began to form the first "f" but dropped away, and the next instant she was sitting up, open-eyed, exclaiming, "Harry! Oh Harry!" Then she began to cry, her face fixed and bewildered.

"I told you you were going too far," I said. Abt reached his hand out to her in surprise.

"Let her alone!" someone said.

"Oh Harry, Harry, Harry!"

"Do something, Morris!" Robbie Stillman shouted. "Slap her, she's having a fit!"

"Don't touch her. I'll get Servatius," said Jack Brill. He ran, but her husband was already at the door, staring in.

"Harry, Harry, Harry!"

"Get out of the way, she doesn't see him," George said.

"Let's clear the room." Jack Brill began herding us out. "Go on, don't stand there." Abt pushed Brill's hand away and muttered something to me which I did not hear.

Iva was no longer in the living room. I went looking for her and found her on the porch off the kitchen.

"What are you doing here?" I said roughly.

"Why, it was warm. I wanted to cool off."

I pulled her inside. "What's the matter with you tonight?" I said. "What's got into you?"

I left her in the kitchen and strode back to the study. I found Brill guarding the door.

"How is she now?" I asked.

"She'll come out of it," said Brill. "George and Harry are in there with her. What a wow of a finish."

"My wife's gone and made herself drunk, too."

"Your wife. You mean Iva."

"Yes, Iva." He was right. I was still treating him like a semi-stranger and he resented it. He had irritated me before when I had thought that he was goading Minna on; but I saw now that, after all, he was no worse than any of the others.

"Well, the party turned into a terrible mess, didn't it?"

"Yes," I agreed.

"Do you ever wonder what's the matter with these people?"

"I've been wondering," I said. "What do you think?"

"So you want my opinion," Brill said, smiling. "You want to see this as an outsider sees it?"

"You're not exactly an outsider, Jack."

"I've only been around five or six years. Well, if you want to know how I feel about it. . . ."

"You're being a little hard on me," I murmured.

"That's right. I am. This is a tight little bunch. I like some of the people in it. I like Minna a lot. Others lean to the snob side. They're not very agreeable. They're cold. Even you, if you don't mind my saying so."

"I don't. . . ."

"You're all fenced around. It took me some time to find

out you weren't such a bad guy. At first I thought you wanted people to come up and sniff you, as if you were a tree. You're a little better than that. Not Abt, though, he's a bad case."

"Maybe he needs more study."

"I wish I could give him what he needs more of. No, there's something wrong. And then you people all seem satisfied to settle down to a long life of taking in each other's laundry. Everybody else is shut out. It's offensive to people like me."

"What makes you come around then?" I said.

"I don't know," said Brill. "I guess it interests me to watch you carry on."

"Oh, I see."

"You asked."

"It's perfectly all right. So long, Jack." I offered him my hand; after a moment of surprise (perhaps it was an ironic surprise), he took it.

"So long, Joseph."

Iva was in no condition to walk. I got a cab, helped her in, and held her head on my shoulder all the way home. When we stopped at an intersection I looked down at her shadowed face. The yellow traffic light fell on her temple, where I saw a single vein near the surface of the skin, crooking with the slight groove of the bone. I responded to this almost as I had to Minna on the couch. The cab continued down the black street, which was streaked with the remnants of that afternoon's snowfall waning under the changed warm wind.

What could I say to all this? I asked myself fitfully and as though I, too, were a little drunk. I thought that with one leap "nasty, brutish, and short" had landed in our midst. All my feelings, what I had felt in looking at Minna, what I had felt at Jack Brill's words and at Iva's disobedience, now attacked me together. What could I say? I repeated, but in the midst of the question perceived my purpose in asking it. I was looking for a way to clear Abt or protect him, and, through him, what was left of the "colony of the spirit." But then, how much was he to be blamed?

For let us admit the truth. One was constantly threatened, shouldered, and, sometimes invaded by "nasty, brutish, and short," lost fights to it in unexpected corners. In the colony? Even in oneself. Was anyone immune altogether? In times like these? There were so many treasons; they were a medium, like air, like water; they passed in and out of you, they made themselves your accomplices; nothing was impenetrable to them.

The cab stopped. I helped Iva into the house, undressed her and put her to bed. She lay on the blankets, naked, shielding her eyes from the light with her wrist. I turned off the switch and in the dark took off my own clothes.

What sort of barrier could one put up against them, these treasons? If, in Abt, cruelty and the desire for revenge were reduced to pinching a woman's hand, what would my own mind give up if one examined its tiniest gaps and runnels? And what about Iva?—and the others, what about the others?

But suddenly I felt that none of this excused Abt and that I had only cunningly maneuvered to achieve the very end I had begun by rejecting. No, I could not justify him. I had been revolted by the way he had pinched her. I could find no excuse for him, none whatsoever. I was beginning to understand what it was that I felt toward him. Yes, I had

56

been revolted by the rage and spite which emerged in the "game"; it had been so savage because its object could not resist. It was some time before I could bring myself to fall asleep. I would think of this more sanely tomorrow, I promised myself, wiping my forehead on the edge of the sheet. But I already knew that I had hit upon the truth and that I could not easily dispel it tomorrow or any other day. I had an uneasy, dream-ridden night.

This was only the beginning. In the months that followed I began to discover one weakness after another in all I had built up around me. I saw what Jack Brill had seen, but, knowing it better, saw it more keenly and severely. It would be difficult for anyone else to know how this affected me, since no one could understand as well as I the nature of my plan, its rigidity, the extent to which I depended on it. Foolish or not, it had answered my need. The plan could be despised; my need could not be.

I have not visited Minna or Harry since the party. I do not know what sort of aftermath there was; I suppose their troubles were eventually ironed out. Abt has gone to Washington. He writes occasionally, usually to ask why he so seldom hears from me. He is doing well as an administrator, one of the "bright young men," though I understand he is not satisfied. I don't think he ever will be satisfied. I should perhaps write oftener; he is, after all, an old friend. It isn't his fault that I am disappointed in him.

December 23

SLEPT until eleven o'clock; sat around all afternoon and thought of nothing in particular. We are going to

57

have Christmas dinner with Amos. Iva accepted his invitation.

MYRON ADLER phoned to say that his agency had decided to hire women to make the survey; there is less possibility of their being taken away, leaving things in mid-air. But he did try to get me in, Myron says. He has kept a copy of the memorandum he sent recommending me and he is sending it on as proof that he kept his word. I told him it wasn't necessary to send it; I believed him. He is sending it anyway. He wants to have a talk with me in the near future. We have agreed tentatively to meet during the holiday. He feels, I daresay, that I need to be taken in hand by someone and straightened out. It's good of him, but I don't think I could allow him to do much for me.

We got "Season's Greetings" cards from John Pearl and from Abt. One of these days I'll have to get around to the dime store to buy envelopes. Iva put in a supply of cards a week ago but she forgot to buy envelopes. Can't convince myself that it's worth the bother. But I suppose we ought to keep up our end of the amenities.

Vanaker is drinking heavily these days. He disposes of his empty pints by throwing them into the neighboring yards. This morning I counted eighteen in the snow.

Iva insists that we keep our door locked. Some of her things are missing. Ethel Pearl sent her five small bottles of perfume for her birthday; two of these are gone from the basket on the dresser, and Iva says in her positive way:

"He's a kleptomaniac." She means Vanaker, of course. She is indignant about the loss of her perfume and means to talk to Mrs. Briggs about it. I shall have to start wearing my room key on a chain.

I SEEM to be unable to stay out of trouble. Disgraced myself at my brother's house last night. I can take it lightly, but Iva feels it very keenly.

My brother Amos, who is my senior by twelve years, is a wealthy man. He began his career as a messenger on the Exchange and before he was twenty-five had become a member of that body, with a seat of his own. The family is very proud of him, and he, in turn, has been a reliable son, very much alive to his duties. Toward me he took a protective attitude at first, but he soon gave up, confessing that he did not know what I was after. He was hurt when I became a radical, relieved when he assured himself I was one no longer. He was disappointed when I married Iva. His own wife, Dolly, had a rich father. He had urged me to follow his example and marry a wealthy woman. He was even more disappointed when, instead of accepting the position he offered me in his business, I took what to him seemed a menial job at Inter American. He called me a fool, and for nearly a year we did not see each other. Then he and Iva arranged a reconciliation. We have been on fairly good terms since, however strange he thinks my choice of occupation and my ways. He tries not to disapprove of me too openly; but he has never learned that I resent his way of questioning me when we meet. He is

59

often tactless and sometimes rude. For some reason he has not been able to accept the fact that it is possible for a member of his family to live on so little.

"Haven't they given you a raise yet? How much are you making? Well, do you need money?" I have never accepted any.

Now that I have been out of work since May, he has become more pressing. Several times he has sent me checks for large amounts, which I have returned immediately. The last time this happened he said, "*I'd* take it, by golly. *I* wouldn't be so proud and stiff-necked. Oh, no, not Brother Amos. Some day you just try offering me money, and see if I pass it up."

A month ago when we visited him (he invites us for meals frequently, thinking, presumably, that we do not get enough to eat), he made such a scene when I refused to take some clothes he was thrusting on me that Iva at last whispered pleadingly, "Take it, Joseph, take the stuff!" and I gave in.

Dolly, my sister-in-law, is a pretty woman, still slender, large-bosomed, but attractively so, dark, with fine hair combed upward in a way designed to make the most of her neck. She has a very graceful neck; I have always admired it. It is one of the traits my fifteen-year-old niece Etta has inherited. To me it has always been one of the exquisite characteristics of femininity; I can well understand why it provoked the prophet Isaiah to utter the words: "Because the daughters of Zion are haughty, and walk with stretched forth necks and wanton eyes, walking and mincing as they go, and making a tinkling with their feet: therefore the Lord will smite with a scab the crown of the head of the daughters of Zion, and the Lord will discover their secret parts."

It astonishes me that the same association should be in both our minds, though with a different cast. Certainly it is the "stretched forth necks," or delicacy in conjunction with the rugged ancient machinery of procreation, that has for a long time been identified in my imagination with feminine nature. Here the parallel ends, for I am the very opposite of vindictive in regard to this duality and have, indeed, found pleasure in recognizing it.

My niece and I are not on good terms; there is a long-standing antagonism between us. Ours was not a rich family. Amos tells frequently how he struggled, how badly he was dressed as a boy, how little my father could give him. And he and Dolly have brought up Etta to identify poverty not so much with evil as with unimportance, to feel that she, the daughter of a wealthy man, is worlds apart from those who live drably, in ill-furnished flats, without servants, who wear inferior clothing and have so little pride as to be debtors. She prefers her mother's people. Her cousins have automobiles and summer homes. I am in no way a credit to her.

In spite of our antagonism, I had until lately tried to influence the girl, sending her books and, on her birthday, record albums. I knew I could have little effect on her. But when she was twelve I undertook to tutor her in French as a means of broaching other subjects. (Her father, naturally, wanted her to be accomplished.) I was unsuccessful. My missionary eagerness betrayed itself too soon, before I had her confidence. She told her mother that I was teaching her "bad things." And how was I to explain to Dolly that I was trying to "save" Etta? It would have been insulting. Etta hated the lessons, by simple extension she hated me, and if I had not given her an excuse for discontinuing them, she would soon have found one.

Etta is a vain girl. I am sure she spends a great many hours before the mirror. I am sure, also, that she must be aware of the resemblance she bears to me. It goes beyond the obvious similarities pointed out by the family. Our eyes are exactly alike, and so are our mouths and even the shape of our ears, sharp and small—Dolly's are altogether different. And there are other similarities, less easily definable, which she cannot help recognizing and which—our enmity being what it is—must be painful to her.

At dinner the talk, in which I scarcely took part at first, was of the hardships of rationing. Dolly and Amos are coffee drinkers but, as patriots, they tempered their complaints with resignation. They turned next to shoes and clothing. Dolly's brother, Loren, who represents a large Eastern shoe firm, had warned them that the government intended to limit the sale of leather goods.

"We couldn't get along on four pairs a year," said Dolly.

But that was unpatriotic, wasn't it? The contradiction was too plain to be unnoticed.

"You have to take into account what people are accustomed to," said Amos; "their standard of living. The government overlooks that. Why, even charities don't give the same amounts to any two families. It would cause too much hardship."

"Yes, that's what I meant," said Dolly. "You couldn't call it hoarding."

"No," I replied. She had addressed herself to me.

62

"Later on there'll be a run on clothes, too," asserted Amos. "That's the way the consumer market is when people are earning."

"Of course, Joseph won't have to worry. The Army will take care of him. But we poor civilians . . . ."

"Joseph would be indifferent, anyway," said Iva. "It wouldn't affect him. He never buys more than one pair of shoes a year."

"He isn't on his feet much," said Etta. Her mother gave her a sharp look.

"I do lead a sedentary life," I said.

"That was all I meant, Mother," said Etta.

"He doesn't worry about any of those things too much, was what I meant," Iva continued, speaking quickly. "He doesn't particularly care what he eats, either, just so it's food. It was no problem pleasing him when I used to cook."

"It's a blessing to be that way. Amos is so hard to suit. You wouldn't think they were brought up by the same mother."

"He wasn't so easy to raise in all respects," Amos said with a smile across the table.

"When are you going into the Army, Joseph?" asked Etta.

"Now, Etta," said Amos reprovingly.

"*Uncle* Joseph, I'm sorry. When are you going?"

"I don't know. Whenever God wills."

This amused them.

"He's certainly taking His time about it," said Dolly.

"There's no hurry," Iva interposed. "The longer the better."

"Oh, of course," Dolly said, "I know how you feel."

"But Joseph doesn't feel that way about it, do you, Joseph?" Amos looked pleasantly at me. "I'm sure he'd like to find out how to hurry Him up. It isn't only the waiting, but he'll miss out on his chances for advancement. He ought to get in there and become an Officer Candidate."

"I don't think I want to try to make an officer of myself."

"Well, I don't see why not," said Amos. "Why not?"

"As I see it, the whole war's a misfortune. I don't want to raise myself through it."

"But there have to be officers. Do you want to sit back and let some cluck do what you can do a thousand times better?"

"I'm used to that," I said, shrugging. "That's the case in many departments of life already. The Army's no exception."

"Iva, do you intend to let him go in with that attitude? A fine Army we'd have."

"It's my conviction," I said. "Iva couldn't change it, and I'm inclined to think she wouldn't want to. Many men carry their ambitions over from civilian life and don't mind climbing upon the backs of the dead, so to speak. It's no disgrace to be a private, you know. Socrates was a plain foot soldier, ⌐ hoplite."

"Socrates, eh?" said Amos. "Well, that's a good and sufficient reason."

A little later in the evening, Amos, calling me aside, led me up to his bedroom and there, producing a hundred-dollar bill, thrust it like a handkerchief into my breast pocket, saying, "This is our Christmas present to you."

64

"Thank you," I said, pulling it out and laying it on the dresser; "but I can't take it."

"Why can't you take it? Nonsense, you can't refuse it. I tell you, it's a present." He picked up the bill impatiently. "Be a little more hardheaded, will you? You're always up in the air. Do you know what I paid in income taxes alone last year? No? Well, this isn't a drop in that bucket. I'm not depriving myself of anything to give it to you."

"But what will I do with it, Amos? I don't need it."

"You are the most obstinate jackass I've ever seen. You can't stand being helped even a little, by anyone."

"Why, this is your shirt I'm wearing, and these are your socks. I appreciate them, but I don't want anything else."

"Joseph!" he exclaimed. "I don't know what to do with you. I'm beginning to think you're not all there, with your convictions and your hop—! I wish I knew how it was going to turn out with you. You'll ruin yourself in the end. Think of Iva sometimes. What's her future going to be like?"

"Oh, the future."

"That's what I said."

"Well, who the devil has one?"

"Everybody," Amos said. "I have."

"Well, you're in luck. I'd think about it a little if I were you. There are many people, hundreds of thousands, who have had to give up all thought of future. There is no personal future any more. That's why I can only laugh at you when you tell me to look out for my future in the Army, in that tragedy. I wouldn't stake a pin on my future. And maybe I wouldn't have yours . . . ." Toward the end my voice had begun to shake.

Amos faced me quietly for a while. Then he said, "Take

the money, Joseph," and left. I heard him going downstairs.

I sat on the bed groggily, holding my head. There was a weak lamp burning in one corner; from its copper slot one band of light crossed the curtain; the rest of the room was nearly dark. The ceiling had become a screen for the accidental motions of the greenish street beyond, and across half its width was thrown intact a reflection of the Venetian blind, like the ribs of some immemorial fish. What sort of impression had my words made on Amos? It was impossible to tell. What could he think? Perhaps he considered me more hopeless than ever. But what did *I* think? Was what I had said half as true as it was impetuous? His neat vision of personal safety I disowned, but not a future of another kind. Still, how could I reason with him? He was a distance beyond reckoning from the craters of the spirit, so that they were no more than small pits on his horizon. But in time they would draw closer. Yes, everyone came to face them when those horizons shrank, as they could not fail to shrink. I went to the bathroom and washed. The crammed feeling at my heart began to wear off, and when I hung the towel back on its glass rod I was less confused. I picked up the hundred-dollar bill from the dusk of the carpet where it had fallen. If I tried to hand it back now there would be a scene; I knew better than to try. I searched the top of Amos's dresser for a pin or clasp of some kind. Not finding one there, I opened one drawer after another until, in Dolly's dressing table, I came upon a pincushion. I went to the bed and stuck the bill to the counterpane over the pillow. Then, in the hall, I stood for a while, hearing the husky voice of

66

the radio speaker below and the laughter and comment of the others. I decided not to join them.

Instead, though I knew it meant working a hardship on Iva to leave her to Dolly, Etta, and Amos, I climbed to the third floor. There, in what had once been an attic, Dolly had furnished a music room. One entire side of it was taken up by a broad monster of a piano which crouched on bowed legs, awaiting use. It was, however, seldom touched, for it had been replaced downstairs by a more jaunty and stylish instrument that showed its teeth like a darky entertainer. On the opposite side of the room was a phonograph with a shelf of records above it. I began to look for a record I had bought Etta a year ago, a Haydn divertimento for the cello, played by Piatigorsky. To find it, I had to hunt through a dozen albums. Here Dolly and Etta, for all their sense of property, were careless; there were numerous broken records. But I found mine whole and, thankfully—my dejection would have doubled if it had been cracked or missing—I started it, and sat down facing the piano.

It was the first movement, the adagio, that I cared most about. Its sober opening notes, preliminaries to a thoughtful confession, showed me that I was still an apprentice in suffering and humiliation. I had not even begun. I had, furthermore, no right to expect to avoid them. So much was immediately clear. Surely no one could plead for exception; that was not a human privilege. What I should do with them, how to meet them, was answered in the second declaration: with grace, without meanness. And though I could not as yet apply that answer to myself, I recognized its rightness and was vehemently moved by it. Not until I was a whole man could it be my answer, too.

And was I to become this whole man alone, without aid? I was too weak for it, I did not command the will. Then in what quarter should I look for help, where was the power? Grace by what law, under what order, by whom required? Personal, human, or universal, was it? The music named only one source, the universal one, God. But what a miserable surrender that would be, born out of disheartenment and chaos; and out of fear, bodily and imperious, that like a disease asked for a remedy and did not care how it was supplied. The record came to an end; I began it again. No, not God, not any divinity. That was anterior, not of my own deriving. I was not so full of pride that I could not accept the existence of something greater than myself, something, perhaps, of which I was an idea, or merely a fraction of an idea. That was not it. But I did not want to catch at any contrivance in panic. In my eyes, that was a great crime. Granted that the answer I was hearing, that went so easily to the least penetrable part of me, the seldom-disturbed thickets around the heart, was made by a religious man. But was there no way to attain that answer except to sacrifice the mind that sought to be satisfied? From the antidote itself another disease would spring. It was not a new matter, it was one I had frequently considered. But not with such a desperate emotion or such a crucial need for an answer. Or such a feeling of loneliness. Out of my own strength it was necessary for me to return the verdict for reason, in its partial inadequacy, and against the advantages of its surrender.

As I began to play the record for the third time, Etta came into the room. Without speaking to me, she went to the shelf and, taking down a bright-colored album, waited, an impatient frown on that fresher and somewhat harder or unworked version of my own face. I now scarcely heard the music. I was already braced for a struggle, the inevitability of which I recognized at once. I groped inside the cabinet of the phonograph for the lever.

"Just a minute. What are you doing?" she said, coming forward a step.

I turned with an aggressive movement. "What?" I said.

"I want to use the machine, Joseph."

"I'm not finished with it yet."

"I don't care," she insisted. "You've had it to yourself all this time. It's my turn. You've been playing that thing over and over."

"You snooped, didn't you?" I said accusingly.

"I did not. It was so loud everybody heard it downstairs."

"You'll have to wait, Etta."

"I will not," she said. "I want to play these Cugat records Mama gave me. I've been wanting to hear them all day."

I did not step aside. At my back the turntable whirred, the needle making a dull scrape among the last grooves. "As soon as I play the second part of this I'll go."

"But you've had the phonograph since dinner. It's my turn."

"And I say no," I replied.

"You have no business saying no to me," she said.

"No business!" I exclaimed with an abrupt, raw jerk of anger.

"It's my phonograph; you're keeping me from my phonograph!"

"Well, if that isn't small!" I said.

"What you call me or think about me doesn't matter."

Her voice rose above the *tac-a-tac* of the machine. "I want to listen to Cugat. I don't care."

"Look," I said, making a strong effort to control myself. "I came up here with a purpose. What purpose it isn't necessary to tell you. But you couldn't stand to think that I was here alone, no matter why. Maybe you thought I was enjoying myself, ah? Or hiding away? So you hurried to see if you could spoil it for me. Isn't that true?"

"You're such a clever man, Uncle!"

"Clever man!" I said, mimicking. "Movie talk. You don't even know what you're saying. This is absurd, quarreling with a stupid child. It's a waste of time. But I know how you feel toward me. I know how much and how genuinely you hate me. I thank God, child that you are, that you have no power over me."

"You're crazy, Uncle," she said.

"All right, that's said and over, there won't be any more of it," I said, and believed that I was succeeding in checking myself. "You can listen to the conga, or whatever it is, when I leave. Now, will you go or sit down and let me play this to the end?"

"Why should I? You can listen to this. Beggars can't be choosers!" She uttered this with such triumph that I could see she had prepared it long in advance.

"You're a little animal," I said. "As rotten and spoiled as they come. What you need is a whipping."

"Oh!" she gasped. "You dirty . . . dirty no-account. You crook!" I caught her wrist and wrenched her toward me.

"Damn you, Joseph, let go! Let me go!" The album went crashing. With the fingers of her free hand she tried to reach my face. Seizing her by the hair fiercely, I snapped

70

her head back; her outcry never left her throat; her nails missed me narrowly. Her eyes shut tightly, in horror.

"Here's something from a beggar you won't forget in a hurry," I muttered. I dragged her to the piano bench, still gripping her hair.

"Don't!" she screamed, recovering her voice. "Joseph! You bastard!"

I pulled her over my knee, trapping both her legs in mine. I could hear the others running upstairs as the first blows descended and I hurried my task, determined that she should be punished in spite of everything, in spite of the consequences; no, more severely because of the consequences. "Don't you struggle," I cried, pressing down her neck. "Or curse me. It won't help you."

Amos pounded up the last flight of stairs and burst in. Behind, breathless, came Dolly and Iva.

"Joseph," Amos panted, "let her go. Let the girl go!"

I did not release her at once. She no longer fought against me but, with her long hair reaching nearly to the floor and her round, nubile thighs bare, lay in my lap. Whether this was meant to be an admission of complicity and an attempt to lighten my guilt, or whether she wished them to see and savor it fully, I did not know at first.

"Stand up, Etta," Dolly said curtly. "Straighten your skirt."

Slowly, she got to her feet. I wonder if any of them were capable of observing how exactly alike we looked at that moment. "And now, if you can, Joseph," said Dolly, turning her dilated eyes on me, "explain what you were doing."

"Mother," Etta suddenly began to sob. "I didn't do anything to him. He attacked me."

"*What!* In the name of God, what are you talking

about?" I exclaimed. "I spanked you because you had a spanking coming."

What unspeakable inference or accusation was that in Dolly's widened eyes? I returned her look steadily.

"Nobody has ever laid a hand on Etta for any reason whatsoever, Joseph."

"Whatsoever! Is calling her uncle a beggar a sufficient 'whatsoever'? There's something ambiguous in your mind. Why don't you speak out?"

She turned to Amos as though to say, "Your brother is going insane. Now he's springing at me."

"I put her over my knee and gave her a hiding, and it wasn't half of what she deserved. She swore at me like a poolroom bum. A mighty fine job you've done with her."

"He pulled me by the hair, that's what he did," Etta cried. "He nearly twisted my head off."

Iva, after turning off the phonograph, had seated herself near it in the background and did her best to efface herself. Which signified to me that she was acknowledging my shame. But there was no "shame." She, too, now came into the sphere of my anger.

"What else did he do?" Dolly demanded.

"Oh, so you think she's covering something up! I spanked her. What else are you fishing for? What are you hoping she'll say? What sort of vulgarity. . . ."

"Stop acting like a wild man!" Amos said peremptorily.

"It's your fault, too," I retorted. "Look how you've brought her up. It's might fine, isn't it. You've taught her to hate the class and, yes, the very family you come from. There's a whatsoever for you. Are people to be null because they wear one pair of shoes a year, not a dozen? Try your teeth on that whatsoever!"

72

"You had no right to raise your hand to the child," said Dolly.

"Why doesn't he tell you what he was doing in your room?" said Etta.

I could see Iva sit up in her chair rigidly.

"What?" said Dolly.

"He was in your room."

"I went there with Amos. Ask him," I said.

"Daddy wasn't there when I saw you. You were looking in Mama's dressing table."

"You little spy!" I shouted, glaring at her. "You hear?" I said to the others. "She accuses me of being a thief."

"What were you doing?" Etta said.

"I was looking for something. You can go down and see if anything's missing. There's nothing missing. Or you can search me. I'll let myself be searched."

"Tell us, what was it? Nobody says you're a thief."

"It's what you're thinking. It's clear enough to me."

"Well, tell us," Dolly insisted.

"It was only a pin. I needed one."

In the darkened corner near the phonograph Iva lowered her head into her hands. "Hey! what are you acting up for back there?" I called out to her.

"A pin, is that all?" Dolly said. She allowed herself, despite the seriousness of the moment, to smile.

"Yes. And it happens to be true." They did not answer. I said: "This, I suppose, makes my shame complete. I'm not only rash and stiff-necked, a beggar" (I bowed to Etta, who scornfully turned away her tear-smeared face) "and" (to Amos) "a jackass, but really an idiot." Iva left the room without looking at me. "You, Amos," I continued, "can begin living me down. You, too, Etta. Dolly is not

73

a blood relative so she's absolved, of course. Unless I bring disgrace on the whole family. Convicted of theft, or assault, or worse. . . ." Neither Dolly nor Amos undertook to reply.

I followed Iva downstairs.

She did not speak to me on the streetcar and, when we got off, she hurried home ahead of me. I reached the door of our room in time to see her drop to the edge of the bed and burst into tears.

"Dearest," I shouted. "It's so nice to know that you at least have faith in me!"

December 27

Amos CALLED us up this morning; I sent Iva down to talk to him. She returned and wanted to know why I hadn't spoken out, why I had wanted to give my brother's family a wrong impression. I replied that as long as they were satisfied with the impression they had of themselves I didn't care what impression they had of me. Iva rubbed mercuric oxide into her red lids before leaving for work. Her crying had continued for several hours.

I felt relieved on one score; I had been uneasy about the money, believing that Etta was not above taking it. But she went away without waiting to see what I was doing in Dolly's dressing table. She did not know about the money. She might have stolen it to spite me.

But I have been wondering, now, what it can mean to Etta that she so closely resembles me. And why should I, furthermore, have assumed that our physical resemblance was the basis for an affinity of another kind? The search for an answer takes me far into my earlier history, a field I do not always find agreeable but which yields a great deal of essential information. And there I discover that the face, all faces, had a significance for me duplicated in no other object. A similarity of faces must mean a similarity of nature and presumably of fate.

We were a handsome family. I was brought up to think myself handsome, though not by any direct process that I can recall. It was conveyed to me by the atmosphere of the household.

Now I recall an incident from my fourth year, a quarrel between my mother and my aunt over the way in which she (my mother) dressed my hair. My aunt, Aunt Dina, claimed it was high time my curls were cut; my mother refused to hear of it. Aunt Dina was a self-willed woman; she had arbitrary ways. She took me to the barber and had him cut my hair after the fashion of the time, in what was called a Buster Brown. She brought the curls back in an envelope and gave them to my mother, who thereupon began to cry. I bring this up not simply to recall how the importance of my appearance was magnified in my eyes, but also because during adolescence I was to remember this in another connection.

In a drawer of the parlor table where the family pictures were kept, there was one to which I was attracted from earliest childhood. It was a study of my grandfather, my mother's father, made shortly before his death. It showed him supporting his head on a withered fist, his streaming beard yellow, sulphurous, his eyes staring and his clothing shroudlike. I had grown up with it. And then, one day, when I was about fourteen, I happened to take it out of the drawer together with the envelope in which my curls had been preserved. Then, studying the picture, it occurred to me that this skull of my grandfather's would in time overtake me, curls, Buster Brown, and all. Still later I came to believe (and this was no longer an impression but a dogma) that the picture was a proof of my mortality. I was upright on my grandfather's bones and the bones of those before him in a temporary loan. But he himself, not the further past, hung over me. Through the years he would reclaim me bit by bit, till my own fists withered and my eyes stared. This was a somber but not a frightening thought. And it had a corrective effect on my vanity.

Only by this time it was not so simple as that, it was not merely vanity. By this time my face was to me the whole embodiment of my meaning. It was a register of my ancestors, a part of the world and, simultaneously, the way I received the world, clutched at it, and the way, moreover, in which I announced myself to it. All of this was private and never spoken of.

But, still more, while I was conscious of being handsome I was not a little suspicious of it. Mortality, I've explained, played its part, making inroads on my vanity. Suspicion undermined it further. For I kept thinking, "There's something wrong." I meant that there was a falseness about it. And then this incident occurred:

In high school I became friendly with a boy named Will Harscha, a German. I used to visit him at home and I knew his sister and his younger brother, as well as his mother. But I had never met his father, who kept a store in a distant neighborhood. However, when I came to call one Sunday morning, the father happened to be at home, and Will took me in to meet him. He was a fat man, black-haired and swart, but kindly-looking.

"So this is Joseph," he said as he shook hands with me. "Well. *Er ist schön*," he said to his wife.

"*Mephisto war auch schön*," Mrs. Harscha answered.

Mephisto! Mephistopheles? I understood what she had said. I stood frozen there. Mr. Harscha, observing me, must have grasped that I knew what she had referred to, for he began glaring at his wife, who, with her lips pressed together, continued to look at me.

I never saw them again. I avoided Will at school. And I spent sleepless hours thinking of what Mrs. Harscha had said. She had seen through me—by some instinct, I thought then—and, where others saw nothing wrong, she had discovered evil. For a long time I believed there was a diabolic part to me. Later, I gave that up. It was "poor devil," if any devil. Not me, specifically, just the general, poor, human devil. But meanwhile I had the confirmation of people like Mrs. Harscha for my suspicion that I was not like others but (and I now know that it is an old belief and at the heart of what we call "Romantic") that I concealed something rotten. And perhaps it is world-wide, such a conviction, and arises because we know ourselves too well to accept the good but, rather, embrace the bad opinions others have of us. Mrs. Harscha may have disliked me because I was too "well-behaved," or because of a way of mine in boyhood of making, or attempting to make, a compact with the adult relatives of my friends, particularly mothers, over the heads of their sons. She may have thought I had no business being unboyish. Many people resented that.

I have long ago freed myself from this morbidity. It

is because of Etta that I undertook to trace it back. But there is no reason to believe that there is any parallel between us. It may be that grandfather's head hangs over both of us, but if and when it devours us it will be devouring two people who have nothing else in common.

I have also been considering Dolly. Of course, I knew that she was no saint; but now, reviewing her part in last night's affair, I find her farther on the hellward side than ever. Here I have additional proof of my inability to read people properly, to recognize the likelihood of baseness in them—as natural in some as a blink, a nod, a flip of the hand. I make theoretical, that is, unreal, allowances for it. I shall have to begin schooling myself in shrewdness.

December 28

WHAT would Goethe say to the view from this window, the wintry, ill-lit street, he with his recurring pleasures, fruits, and flowers?

December 29

SLEPT until one o'clock. Out at four for a walk, I lasted ten minutes and then retreated.

December 31

I SHAVED in honor of the holiday. But we are not going out. Iva has some sewing to do.

78

MR. VANAKER observed the birth of the new year with large quantities of whisky, with coughing, pelting the yard with bottles, with frequent, noisy trips to the lavatory, and ended his revels with a fire. At about ten o'clock I heard his growls, unusually thick, and repeated thumps in the corridor and looked out to see him shambling through the smoke, feeling his way along the wall. Iva ran to summon Captain Briggs while I thrust open Vanaker's door. The armchair was burning. He hurried in with a cup of water, which he poured over it. He was wearing sleeveless pajamas, and his bare arms were marked with sooty fingerprints. His large, fleshy, somewhat concave face, with its high forehead overarched with gray curls in a manner that suggested a bonnet, was red and distressed. He did not speak; he ran to fetch another cupful.

By this time other roomers were on the scene, for the smoke had spread through the house: Mrs. Bartlett, the middle-aged practical nurse from the large room in the rear; Mrs. Fessman, the pretty Austrian refugee; and Mr. Ringholm, who shares the third floor with Captain and Mrs. Briggs.

"Tell him to carry out that chair," Mrs. Bartlett said to me.

"He's trying to put the fire out," I replied.

Hasty slapping sounds came from Vanaker's room.

"With his hands."

"He'd better take it out. This is a frame house. It's dangerous." Mrs. Bartlett came closer to me in the smoke, a tall figure in a kimono; her head was bound in a handkerchief, a black cotton sleeping mask hung around her neck.

"Someone should tell him to. Take it out, mister." But the smoke was too much for her. She retreated to the stairs. I, too, was coughing and rubbing my eyes. I stepped back into our room to recover. Throwing open the window, I cleared my head in the frigid air. Loud knocks began outside. Iva looked in.

"He locked himself inside. He must be afraid of the Captain," she said.

I joined her in the hall. "Damn," said the Captain, amused and vexed. "What'd he start running for? How'm I going to get at the fire?" He doubled the tempo of his knocks. "Open up, Mr. Vanaker. Come on, now."

"It's a wonder you don't lose your temper, Sir," said Mrs. Bartlett.

"Mr. Vanaker!"

"I'm awright," Vanaker said.

"He's ashamed, that's what it is," Mrs. Bartlett explained to us.

"Well, I want you to let me in," the Captain said. "I have to see if the fire's out."

The key turned, and Vanaker, with streaming eyes, stood in the doorway; the Captain passed by him into the ragged smoke. Mr. Ringholm, touching his head, complained that this was doing his hang-over no good.

"We're lucky not to be in ashes," said Mrs. Bartlett.

And now the Captain, also coughing, reappeared, dragging the chair. He and Mr. Ringholm together carried it down. The carpet had caught fire in several places. I brought a double handful of snow from the window sill, and Mrs. Briggs joined me in stamping out the sparks and wetting down the burned spots. Vanaker had fled to the bathroom, where we heard him washing, splashing in the sink.

A little later we heard Vanaker explaining: "It was a cigarette, Cap-tain. See? I put ah on the saucer. Then ah rolled off. . . ."

"You must be careful, old-timer," the Captain said. "With cigarettes you must be careful. They're dangerous; cigarettes are dangerous."

"Awright, Captain."

That was our only New Year's Day diversion and a rather poor substitute for observing the holiday. It did give us a feeling of being set aside to let the entire day slip by. Children ran past in the morning blowing horns; in the afternoon, families in their Sunday clothes went promenading. The Captain and his wife drove off in their car early in the day and had just returned when the fire broke out.

But what such a life as this incurs is the derangement of days, the leveling of occasions. I can't answer for Iva, but for me it is certainly true that days have lost their distinctiveness. There were formerly baking days, washing days, days that began events and days that ended them. But now they are undistinguished, all equal, and it is difficult to tell Tuesday from Saturday. When I neglect to look carefully at the newspaper I do not know what day it is. If I guess Friday and then learn that it is actually Thursday, I do not experience any great pleasure in having won twenty-four hours.

It is possible that that is one reason why I have been creating agitation. I am not sure. The circumstances at the Arrow and at Amos's house were provoking enough, but I could have avoided making scenes if I had wished. It may be that I am tired of having to identify a day as "the day I asked for a second cup of coffee," or "the day the waitress refused to take back the burned toast," and so want to blaze it more sharply, regardless of the consequences. Perhaps, eager for consequences. Trouble, like physical pain, makes us actively aware that we are living, and when there is little in the life we lead to hold and draw and stir us, we seek and cherish it, preferring embarrassment or pain to indifference.

January 3

A JEFFERSON FORMAN is listed as having crashed in the Pacific. His home is given as St. Louis. The Jeff Forman I knew came from Kansas City, but his family may have moved in the last few years. The name is not common; it must be the same Forman. I had heard that he was in the merchant marine. Probably he had himself transferred when the war broke out. I heard a rumor that he had been arrested in Genoa about four years ago for shouting *A basso* in a public place. No name, simply *A basso*. According to Tad, the consulate had great difficulty in getting him released, though nobody claimed that he had added anything to his *A basso*. Jeff was in love with excitement. He was expelled from the University for some misdemeanor or other. I never learned the facts about it. It is surprising that he was not thrown out during his first year. One night he knocked George Colin down on the street; he never tried to explain why, merely apologized to Colin before the Dean. And his inspiration for waking me early one winter morning was to throw snowballs mixed with ashes into my bed.

His rank was given in the paper as ensign; his ship was a Catalina. I suppose the submarine danger was not enough for him. I always suspected of him that he had in some fashion discovered there were some ways in which to be human was to be unutterably dismal, and that all his life was given over to avoiding those ways.

January 4

WITH ALL the respect we seem to have for perishable stuff, we have easily accustomed ourselves to slaughter. We are all, after some fashion, the beneficiaries of that slaughter and yet we have small pity for the victims. This has not come with the war, we were ready before the war ever started; it only seems more apparent now. We do not flinch at seeing all these lives struck out; nor would those who were killed have suffered any more for us, if we, not they, had been the victims. I do not like to think what we are governed by. I do not like to think about it. It is not easy work, and it is not safe. Its kindest revelation is that our senses and our imaginations are somehow incompetent. The old Joseph who, in view of the temporariness of life, was opposed to hacking and tearing, said that he regretted that with the best will in the world one must deal out his share of bruises. . . . Bruises! What a piece of innocence! Yes, he recognized that even those who meant to be gentle could not hope to escape whipping. And that was modest enough.

Yet we are, as a people, greatly concerned with perishability; an empire of iceboxes. And pet cats are flown hundreds of miles to be saved by rare serums; and country neighbors in Arkansas keep a month's vigil night and day to save the life of a man stricken at ninety.

Jeff Forman dies; brother Amos lays up a store of shoes for the future. Amos is kind. Amos is no cannibal. He cannot bear to think that I should be unsuccessful, lack money, refuse to be concerned about my future. Jeff, under the water, is beyond virtue, value, glamor, money, or future. I say these things unable to see or think straight, and what I feel is less injustice or inhumanity than bewilderment.

Myself, I would rather die in the war than consume its benefits. When I am called I shall go and make no protest. And, of course, I hope to survive. But I would rather be a victim than a beneficiary. I support the war, though perhaps it is gratuitous to say so; we have the habit of making these things issues of personal morality and private will, which they are not at all. The equivalent would be to say, if God really existed, yes, God does exist. He would exist whether we recognized him or not. But as between their imperialism and ours, if a full choice were possible, I would take ours. Alternatives, and particularly desirable alternatives, grow only on imaginary trees.

Yes, I shall shoot, I shall take lives; I shall be shot at, and my life may be taken. Certain blood will be given for half-certain reasons, as in all wars. Somehow I cannot regard it as a wrong against myself.

January 5

THIS AFTERNOON I emptied the closet of all its shoes and sat on the floor polishing them. Surrounded by rags, saddle soap, and brushes—the brown light of the street pressing in at the windows, and the sparrows bickering in the dead twigs—I felt tranquil for a while and, as I set Iva's shoes out in a row, I grew deeply satisfied. It was a borrowed satisfaction; it was doing something I had done as a child. In Montreal, on such afternoons as this, I often asked permission to spread a paper on the sitting-room floor and shine all the shoes in the house, including Aunt Dina's with their long tongues and scores of eyelets. When I thrust my arm into one of her shoes it reached well above the elbow and I could feel the brush against my arm through the soft leather. The brown fog lay in St. Dominique Street; in the sitting room, however, the stove shone on the davenport and on the oilcloth and on my forehead, drawing the skin pleasantly. I did not clean shoes because I was praised for it, but because of the work and the sensations of the room, closed off from the wet and fog of the street, with its locked shutters and the faint green of the metal pipes along the copings of its houses. Nothing could have tempted me out of the house.

I have never found another street that resembled St. Dominique. It was in a slum between a market and a hospital. I was generally intensely preoccupied with what went on in it and watched from the stairs and the windows. Little since then has worked upon me with such force as, say, the sight of a driver trying to raise his fallen horse, of a funeral passing through the snow, or of a cripple who taunted his brother. And the pungency and staleness of its stores and cellars, the dogs, the boys, the French and immigrant women, the beggars with sores and deformities whose like I was not to meet again until I was old enough to read of Villon's Paris, the very breezes in the narrow course of that street, have remained so clear to me that I sometimes think it is the only place where I was ever allowed to encounter reality. My father blamed himself bitterly for the poverty that forced him to bring us up in a slum and worried lest I see too much. And I did see, in a curtainless room near the market, a man rearing over someone on a bed, and, on another occasion, a Negro with a blond woman on his lap. But less easily forgotten were a cage with a rat in it thrown on a bonfire, and two quarreling drunkards, one of whom walked away bleeding, drops falling from his head like the first slow drops of a heavy rain in summer, a crooked line of drops left on the pavement as he walked.

January 6

ABT HAS sent me a copy of a pamphlet he wrote on the government of the Territories. He expects a flattering comment, no doubt, and I shall have to rig one up. He will want me to tell him that no one else could have written such a pamphlet. Suppose I were to try to tell him what I thought of him. He would reply coldly, "I don't know what you're talking about." He has a way of turning aside everything he has no desire to understand.

Abt, more than anyone I have known, has lived continually in need of being consequential. Early in life he discovered that he was quicker, abler, than the rest of us, and that he could easily outstrip us in learning and in skills. He felt he could be great in anything he chose. We roomed together in Madison as freshmen. He was very busy that first year keeping up all his accomplishments, his music, his politics, his class work. Living with him had a bad effect on me, for I withdrew from any field he entered. People came from other campuses to consult him on doctrinal matters; no one had as much out-of-the-way information as he; he read foreign political journals the rest of us had never heard of, and reports of party congresses, those dun, mimeographed sheets on international decisions in France and Spain. No one was so subtle with opponents. Nor did many students get as much attention as he got from his teachers. A few were afraid of him and learned to avoid challenging him publicly. Late afternoons, he played the piano. I would often stop by for him at the music building on the way to dinner and spend half an hour listening. He did not waste time maturing, he did not make any of the obvious mistakes. His hold was too good. That winter he was Lenin, Mozart, and Locke all rolled into one. But there was unfortunately not enough time to be all three. And so, in the spring, he passed through a crisis. It was necessary to make a choice. But, whatever it was he chose, *that* would be the most important. How could it be otherwise? He gave up attending meetings and practising the piano, he banished the party reports as trash, and decided to become a political philosopher. There was a general purge. Everything else went. *Anti-Duhring* and *The Critique of the Gotha Program* sank to the rear of the bottom shelf of his bookcase and were supplanted at the top by Bentham and Locke. Now he had decided, and in dead earnestness he followed greatness. Inevitably, he fell short of his models. He would never admit that he wanted to become another Locke, but there he was, wearing himself thin with the effort of emulation, increasingly angry at himself, and unable to admit that the scale of his ambition was defeating him.

He is stubborn. Just as, in the old days, it disgraced him to confess that he was not familiar with a book or a statement that came under his jurisdiction, he now cannot acknowledge that his plan has miscarried. But then, it bothers him to be found guilty even of small errors. He does not like to forget a date or a name or the proper form of a foreign verb. He cannot be wrong, that is his difficulty. If you warn him that there is a fissure at his feet, he answers, "no, you must be mistaken." But when it can no longer be ignored he says, "Do you see it?" as though he had discovered it.

Of course, we suffer from bottomless avidity. Our lives are so precious to us, we are so watchful of waste. Or perhaps a better name for it would be the Sense of Personal Destiny. Yes, I think that is better than avidity. Shall my life by one-thousandth of an inch fall short of its ultimate possibility? It is a different thing to value oneself, and to prize oneself crazily. And then there are our plans, idealizations. These are dangerous, too. They can consume us like parasites, eat us, drink us, and leave us lifelessly prostrate. And yet we are always inviting the parasite, as if we were eager to be drained and eaten.

It is because we have been taught there is no limit to what a man can be. Six hundred years ago, a man was what he was born to be. Satan and the Church, representing God, did battle over him. He, by reason of his choice, partially decided the outcome. But whether, after life, he went to hell or to heaven, his place among other men was given. It could not be contested. But, since, the stage has been reset and human beings only walk on it, and, under this revision, we have, instead, history to answer to. We were important enough then for our souls to be fought over. Now, each of us is responsible for his own salvation, which is in his greatness. And that, that greatness, is the rock our hearts are abraded on. Great minds, great beauties, great lovers and criminals surround us. From the great sadness and desperation of Werthers and Don Juans we went to the great ruling images of Napoleons; from these to murderers who had that right over victims because they were greater than the victims; to men who felt privileged to approach others with a whip; to schoolboys and clerks who roared like revolutionary lions; to those pimps and subway creatures, debaters in midnight cafeterias who believed they could be great in treachery and catch the throats of those they felt were sound and well in the lassos of their morbidity; to dreams of greatly beautiful shadows embracing on a flawless screen. Because of these things we hate immoderately and punish ourselves and one another immoderately. The fear of lagging pursues and maddens us. The fear lies in us like a cloud. It makes an inner climate of darkness. And occasionally there is a storm and hate and wounding rain out of us.

January 7

ADLER'S bureau is sending him to San Francisco for two weeks. He is leaving tomorrow. Our talk will have to be put off.

JOHN PEARL writes of an exhibit of his pictures at a women's club in New York. It was not a success. For want of space they crowded his things into the dining room, then held so many Red Cross luncheons that no one could get in. He sold nothing. A lady who admired a still life wanted to order a flower painting for her daughter's bedroom—three flowers in a blue vase. "Only three? A fourth flower will cost you twenty-five dollars more. It'll fill the picture out. That's very reasonable." She pondered this but in the end she decided three would be enough. Her husband grew peonies; she would have the flowers and a vase sent over. "I'm sorry," Johnny said. "I thought we were talking about roses. Peonies are too big for the price. I'll have to charge ten dollars extra for each flower. It's the standard rate for flowers with a three-inch diameter. A lemon will be ten dollars more, unpeeled. Half-peeled, fifteen dollars."

"Are there rates for everything?" she said. She had become suspicious.

"In a manner of speaking, there are. They're a little lower than the ones I quoted you. The Jones Street Convention of 1930 set them lower. But, with inflation. . . ." Here she fled.

"Ethel said it was nasty of me, but the woman was so serious I could not resist joking. I didn't think it would lose me the commission."

He still has his job with the advertising agency, drawing "cartoon faces of bilious men and headachy office girls." And that, he goes on, serious all at once, "is the adult, commonsense, wise world. I am exhilarated by the tremendous unimportance of my work. It is nonsense. My employers are nonsensical. The job therefore leaves me free. There's nothing to it. In a way it's like getting a piece of bread from a child in return for wiggling your ears. It is childish. I am the only one in this fifty-three-story building who knows how childish it is. Everybody else takes it seriously. Because this is a fifty-three-story building, they think it must be serious. 'This is life!' I say, this is pish, nonsense, nothing! The real world is the world of art and of thought. There is only one worth-while sort of work, that of the imagination."

It is an attractive idea, it confers a sort of life on him, sets him off from the debased dullness of those fifty-three stories. He is not making this up. I know him. He has no reason to lie to me. He is telling me what he feels: that he has escaped a trap. That really is a victory to celebrate. I am fascinated by it, and a little jealous. He can maintain himself. Is it because he is an artist? I believe it is. Those acts of the imagination save him. But what about me? I have no talent for that sort of thing. My talent, if I have one at all, is for being a citizen, or what is today called, most apologetically, a good man. Is there some sort of personal effort I can substitute for the imagination?

That, I am unable to answer. But certainly he is better off. There he is in New York, painting; and in spite of the calamity, the lies and moral buggery, the odium, the detritus of wrong and sorrow dropped on every heart, in spite of these, he can keep a measure of cleanliness and freedom. Besides, those acts of the imagination are in the strictest sense not personal. Through them he is connected with the best part of mankind. He feels this and he can never be isolated, left aside. He has a community. I have this six-sided box. And goodness is achieved not in a vacuum, but in the company of other men, attended by love. I, in this room, separate, alienated, distrustful, find in my purpose not an open world, but a closed, hopeless jail. My perspectives end in the walls. Nothing of the future comes to me. Only the past, in its shabbiness and innocence. Some men seem to know exactly where their opportunities lie; they break prisons and cross whole Siberias to pursue them. One room holds me.

When the Italian General Bergonzoli (I think it was Bergonzoli) was captured in Libya, he would not discuss military matters or the strategy that led to his defeat, but said, "Please! I am not a soldier. I am primarily a poet!" Who does not recognize the advantage of the artist, these days?

January 11

THE OTHER night Iva was searching through the shelves for a book she had put away months before and was musing aloud about its disappearance.

I was trimming my nails, listening absently, guiding the tiny crescent shears away from the quick, and was, as I can become in small matters, preoccupied with the gathering up of the clippings, when suddenly I remembered that I had lent Kitty Daumler a book.

"What did you say you were looking for?"

"Didn't you hear me before? A small, blue book, *Dubliners*. Have you seen it?"

92

"It must be around."

"Help me look."

"It's probably buried among the others. Why don't you read another book? There're plenty."

But Iva would not be so easily dissuaded. She went on searching, piling books on the floor near my chair.

"You won't find it," I said after a time.

"Why not?"

"These things have a way of dropping out of sight and turning up months later. It may have fallen behind the case."

"Let's move it."

"Not I. Next time Marie holds a general cleaning." I picked up the clippings in pinches and threw them into the wastebasket. "I ought to bury them, by rights."

"Those? Why?" She stood up, in her blue figured wrap, to ease her back against the wall. "I can't stay bent over very long. Old age."

"Nails, hair, all cuttings and waste from the body. Fear of sorcery."

"The door's been locked for days; *he* couldn't have taken it. Anyhow, what would he do with *Dubliners?*"

"Vanaker?"

"Yes." Iva was still sure he was responsible for the disappearance of her perfume bottles.

"I'll dig the book up tomorrow," I said.

"But it *should* be here."

"Very well, it should. But if it's not, it won't appear, no matter how determined you are."

"You mean it isn't in the room?"

"I'm not saying that."

"Then what do you mean?"

"I mean you'd rather waste an evening looking for it than read another book."

She said indignantly: "You told me to read it yourself. You insisted."

"But that was long ago, months and months ago. You should have read it in a few hours."

"Yes," she said. "And it's months and months since you took an interest in me. Lately, for all you care, I might just as well not be here. You pay no attention to what I say. If I didn't come home for a week you wouldn't miss me."

I received this charge in silence.

"Well?" she said aggressively.

"Ah, that's all foolishness."

"That's no sort of answer."

"Iva, it's this situation we're in. It's changed us both. But it isn't permanent."

"You mean you'll go away soon, and that'll be the end of it."

"Oh," I said, irritated, "don't nag. It is the situation. You know it is."

"It certainly has changed you."

"Of course it has; it would change anyone."

Rising, I took my coat from the hanger and went to the door.

"Where are you going?"

"To get some air. It's stuffy here."

"Can't you see it's raining? But I suppose even that's better than spending the evening with a nagging wife."

"Right, it is better!" I exclaimed. I had no more patience. "For ten cents they'll bunk me in a flophouse, no questions asked. You needn't expect me back tonight."

"That's right, advertise to the entire house. . . ."

"It's just like you to worry about the house. Damn the house. It's more shameful to act this way than that the house should know. I don't give a bloody damn about the house!"

"Joseph!" she said.

I shut the door with a crash, already aware, under my anger, that this was beneath me and altogether out of proportion to the provocation. I pulled my hat down against the rain. Our windows, with their glowing shades, set two orange rectangles, trade-marks of warmth and comfort, against the downpour and the dark, the glitter of the trees, the armor of ice on the street. The intense cold of the past week had lifted. Fog had succeeded it, rising in spongy gray blooms from the soaked walks, hovering in the yards and over the hollows blinking with rain and changes of color from the muffled signal lights—green, amber, red, amber, green, shuttering down the street. Mr. Vanaker's window went up. He threw a bottle, using the neck as a hilt. It landed softly into the clay, beside the others; there were dozens of bottles among the bushes, their high shoulders streaming as though drops of mercury were falling on them from the withes. The window was run down hastily.

My shoes, their once neat points scuffed and turned up, squashed, as I walked, through half-a-dozen leaks. I moved toward the corner, inhaling the odors of wet clothes and of wet coal, wet paper, wet earth, drifting with the puffs of fog. Low, far out, a horn uttered a dull cry, subsided; again. The street lamp bent over the curb like a woman who cannot turn homeward until she has found the ring or the coin she dropped in the ice and gutter silt. I heard behind me the clicking of a feminine stride and, for a moment, thought that Iva had come after me, but it was a stranger who passed at the awning of the corner store, her face made bleary by the woolly light and the shadowy fur-piece at her throat. The awning heaved; twists of water ran through its rents. Once more the horn bawled over the water, warning the lake tugs from the headlands. It was not hard to imagine that there was no city here at all, and not even a lake but, instead, a swamp and that despairing bawl crossing it; wasting trees instead of dwellings, and runners of vine instead of telephone wires. The bell of an approaching streetcar drove this vision off. I hailed it and, paying my fare, remained on the platform. It was not far to Kitty's. If my shoes had been watertight, I would have walked.

My purpose was not to retrieve the book—though, of course, I might as well ask her to return it while I was there —but to see Kitty.

I don't recall how she came to ask me for the book, nor how it was that I volunteered to give it to her. She would not have heard of it, and I cannot conceive in what con- nection I mentioned it. Here was one more conflux I could not trace or interpret. Kitty—but I do not say this in dis- praise—is not an intelligent or even clever girl. She is sim- ple, warm, uncomplicated, and matter-of-fact. Two years ago I had mapped out a Caribbean tour for her, and she had come in later to tell me what a good time she had had and to ask me to appraise some of the things she had bought. For that purpose I went to her apartment. She accepted my verdict of her tourist stuff so casually and treated me with such marked friendliness that I began to think—not without a touch of pleased excitement—that she was less interested in the appraisal than in me. At the first opportunity, I mentioned Iva, but it was apparent from her reaction or lack of reaction that she had taken my being married for granted. For her, she said, marriage as such did not exist. There were only people. Then began a conversation on marriage and love which I don't care to remember in detail. I made it abundantly plain that while I would talk of such matters I would not venture beyond talk. I was, however, flattered that such a handsome woman should be drawn to me. She was saying that some of the others on the cruise had made themselves absurd with the guides and beach boys. She could not stand that kind of looseness, and the pretty, characterless romantic Latin faces filled her with aversion. They were such vapid-looking men.

As I was leaving, her friendly hand somehow finished a gesture on my shoulder. She hoped I would come again for a talk. Next time I should do the talking. She was also a good listener.

I did not see her again for a month. Then one day she walked up to me at Inter-American and, without preliminaries, asked why I had not visited her. I answered that we had been busy.

"But you can break away one evening, can't you?"

"I can, certainly, if I want to."

"Why not come Thursday, then? We can have supper together."

Iva and I had not been getting along well. I don't think the fault was entirely hers. I had dominated her for years; she was now capable of rebelling (as, for example, at the Servatius party). I did not at first understand the character of her rebellion. Was it possible that she should not want to be guided, formed by me? I expected some opposition. No one, I would have said then, no one came simply and of his own accord, effortlessly, to prize the most truly human traditions, the heavenly cities. You had to be taught to struggle your way toward them. Inclination was not enough. Before you could set your screws revolving, you had to be towed out of the shallows. But it was now evident that Iva did not want to be towed. Those dreams inspired by Burckhardt's great ladies of the Renaissance and the no less profound Augustan women were in my head, not hers. Eventually I learned that Iva could not live in my infatuations. There are such things as clothes, appearances, furniture, light entertainment, mystery stories, the attractions of fashion magazines, the radio, the enjoyable evening. What could one say to them? Women—thus I reasoned—were not equipped by training to resist such things. You might force them to read Jacob Boehme for ten years without diminishing their appetite for them; you might teach them to admire *Walden* but never convert them to wearing old clothes. Iva was formed at fifteen, when I met her, with likes and dislikes of her own which (because, for some strange reason, I opposed them) she set aside until the time when she could defend or simply assert them. Hence our difficulty. There were nervous quarrels. She, in brave, shaky, new defiance, started to enjoy her independence. I let her alone, pretending indifference.

Now I began to visit Kitty Daumler frequently. She lived in a rooming house similar to the one where Iva and I had stayed the first two years of our marriage, before we could afford a flat. I partly blamed the flat for the change in Iva and so took some pleasure in Kitty's

98

rooms. Her furniture was soiled, the wallpaper next to the mirror was smeared with lipstick, clothes were flung about, the bed was always unmade, and she was careless about herself, trying to rule her hair with a single comb, pulling it back constantly from her solid face with its large brows and large mouth. An affectionate, worldly, impudent, generous face.

We talked about all kinds of ordinary things. My friends were leaving the city, one by one. I found no comfort in them anyway. I would not have held these conversations with anyone but Kitty. But I had learned to discern the real Kitty, the lively, plump, high-colored, scented, gross girl, behind the talk. I liked her. Beyond talk, however, Kitty and I did not go. She freely admitted that she "liked being with men" if they were the kind that interested her. I did interest her. We were amiable toward each other and were continually smiling. And the burden of the amiability and the smiles, as we both understood, was twofold: the intention and its check; the smiles checked us. I continued to smile.

Until, one wet and prematurely cold evening in early fall, I came in to find her in bed, drinking rum and tea. She had been caught in the rain and chilled. I sat by the bedside, holding a cup of whisky that was daubed along the rim with lipstick (her mark: towels, pillowcases, spoons, napkins, forks, all bore it). The room, in its usual state—the bronze-leafed lamp, the tissue paper of shoe boxes, the doll with the telephone concealed in its petticoat, the framed Venetian scene, the drying slip hung from an elbow of the steampipe—was no longer, for some reason, the usual comfortable anchorage. I was not smiling. I had not smiled since entering. She sipped her drink, her head raised between the cleft of the raised pillows; her chin, when she lowered the cup, nestled above the other cleft, the world's most beautiful illustration of number, tender division of the flesh beginning high above the lace line of her nightgown. The blood charged quickly to my face. I was overcome when she spoke to me, stammered my answer. I had not heard. "What?"

"I said, will you bring my bag? It's in the next room."

I got up, gracelessly.

"I want to powder."

"Oh, sure."

My shoes had made a large gray stain on the round rug.

"Tracked your mat up. I'm sorry," I said.

She shifted and looked, balancing the cup.

"I should have asked you to take your shoes off."

"My fault. You have it cleaned; I'll pay," I said. My flush grew deeper.

"Why, that isn't what I meant at all. You poor thing, you must be drenched. Pull them off this minute and let me see your socks."

I bent to unlace my shoes, my head suddenly gorged with blood. "Wet through and through," she said. "Give them here, and I'll hang them up for you." I saw my socks appear beside the slip. She was standing before me, holding out a towel. "Dry yourself. Do you want to catch pneumonia?" As I lowered myself to the chair, her hand passed over my head and grasped the chain of the lamp, yanking it rudely. I could hear it in the darkness, beating against the shell of the bulb. I waited for the sound to subside, then reached upward. She intercepted my fingers. "It would only be putting it off, Joey," she said. Withdrawing my hand, I hurriedly began to undress. She groped her way around the chair and sat on the bed. "I knew you'd see it my way sooner or later."

"Darling!"

I "saw it her way" for two months, or until she began hinting at my leaving Iva. She claimed that Iva did not treat me well and that we were not suited to each other. I had never given her cause to think so, but she said she could tell. I have no real appetite for guile; the strain of living in both camps was too much. And I was unlike myself. I was out of character. It did not take me long to see that at the root of it all was my unwillingness to miss anything. A compact with one woman puts beyond reach what others might give us to enjoy; the soft blondes and the dark, aphrodisiacal women of our imaginations are set aside. Shall we leave life not knowing them? Must we? Avidity again. As soon as I recognized it, I began to bring the affair with Kitty to a close. It died in the course of a long conversation, in which I made it clear that a man must accept limits and cannot give in to the wild desire to be everything and everyone and everything to everyone. She was disappointed but also pleased by my earnestness, the tone I took, and felt honored to have her mind, her superior nature, thus addressed. We agreed that I was to continue visiting her on a friendly basis. There was nothing wrong in that, was there? Why not be sensible? She liked me, liked listening to me; she had already learned a great deal. Did she understand, I asked, that my motives had nothing to do with her, personally? In many ways I was reluctant . . . I . . . was not the kind who could keep too many irons in the fire, she finished for me good-naturedly.

It was a great relief. But the matter was not ended. I felt

101

obliged to visit her, at first, as though to assure her that I valued her as much as ever. Had she thought my interest in her was at an end, she would have been deeply offended. But my visits were not long obligatory and one-sided, for with the onset of the dangling days it was a positive relief to drop in now and then to smoke a few cigarettes and drink a glass of rum. I was comfortable with Kitty.

The missing book reminded me that I had not seen her for some weeks, and I thought I would spend the rest of the evening with her and avoid bickering with Iva and going to sleep in raw temper.

The transom over Kitty's door appeared dark, but the room was not unoccupied. I heard her voice before I knocked. There was a brief silence. I took off my glove and knocked again. Kitty's transom has been lacquered over because, from the staircase, one can easily peer into her apartment. It was not easy to tell, therefore, whether the lights were out. And even if they were, it was still possible that she might be in the adjoining room, the kitchen. But at my third knock light suddenly shone through the scratches and uneven brush strokes in the transom. I could hear her conferring with someone, and then the knob turned and Kitty appeared, tying the cord of her dressing gown. She was not, of course, delighted to see me and I, too, was somewhat put out. I said that I was passing by and had decided to drop in for my book. She did not ask me in, though I mentioned with inappropriate irony that my feet were wet.

"I—ah, can't look for it now. The place is such a mess. Suppose you stop by again tomorrow?"

"I don't know whether I can tomorrow," I replied.

"Busy?"

"Yes."

It was her turn to look ironical. She began to relish the situation and, her arm casually stretched across the door, smiled at me and now did not seem at all displeased at having been found out.

"Are you working?"

"No."

"Then what keeps you busy?"

"Oh, something's come up. I can't come. But I have to have the book. It isn't mine, you see. . . ."

"It's Iva's?"

I nodded. Glancing into the room, I caught sight of a man's shirt hanging on the back of a chair. Had I edged over a few inches, I know I would have seen a man's arm on the coverlet. The room was always kept overheated and, through the haze, the thick, comfortable yet stirring scent I had come to associate with her was diffused. It reached me here in the hall, arousing nostalgia and envy in me, and I could not resist feeling that, like a fool, I had irrevocably thrown away the comfort and pleasure she had offered me in an existence barren of both. She looked behind, and then turned to me with a smile, but half in contempt, as much as to say, "It isn't my fault that that isn't your shirt hanging on the chair."

I said angrily: "When can I get it?"

"The book?"

"It's important that I get it back," I said. "Can't you locate it now? I'll wait."

She seemed surprised. "I'm afraid not. Suppose I mail it tomorrow, will that be all right?"

"It'll have to be, from the looks of it."

103

"Well, good night then, Joseph." She closed the door. I stood looking up at the transom. The streaks of light flashed out. It was left a tarnished dull brown. I started down the stairs, breathing the staleness of cabbage and bacon and of the dust sifting behind the wallpaper. As I approached the second floor, I saw in the apartment below, through the open bar of the doorway, a woman in a slip, sitting before the mirror with a razor, her arm crooked backward, a cigarette on the ledge of the radio beside her, and from it two curling prongs of smoke rising. The sight of her held me momentarily; then, possibly because the sound of my steps had ceased, or sensing that she was being watched, she looked up, startled—a broad, angry face. I hurried down the remaining stairs into the vestibule, with its ageless, nameless, rooming-house hangings, its plush chairs, high, varnished, sliding doors, and, on the grained oak board, the brass nipples of call bells. From various parts of the house there were sounds: of splashing and frying, of voices raised in argument or lowered in appeasement or persuasion, singing popular-songs:

> Dinner in the diner
> Nothing could be finer
> Chattanooga choochoo. . . .

of chiming telephones, of the janitor's booming radio one floor below. On a pedestal a bronze Laocoön held in his suffering hands a huge, barbarically furred headpiece of a lampshade with fringes of blackened lace. Buttoning my gloves, I passed into the outer hall, thinking, as I did so, that by this time Kitty had slipped back into bed and that she and her companion had (I sought a way to say it) fallen together again, his appetite increased by the intrusion. And, while I could objectively find no reason why she should not do as she pleased, I found myself nevertheless ambiguously resentful and insulted.

Fog and rain had gone, abolished by a high wind, and, in place of that imagined swamp where death waited in the thickened water, his lizard jaws open, there was a clean path of street and thrashing trees. Through the clouds the wind had sunk a hole in which a few stars dipped. I ran to the corner, jumping over puddles. A streetcar was in sight, crashing forward, rocking on its trucks from side to side and nicking sparks from the waving cable. I caught it while it was in motion and stood on the platform, panting; the conductor was saying that it was bad business to flip a car in the wet, you wanted to be careful about such tricks. We were swept off with quaking windows, blinking through floods of air, the noise of the gong drowning under the horn of the wind.

"Reg'lar gale," said the conductor, gripping the hand rail.

A young soldier and a girl got on, both drunk; an elderly woman with a pointed, wolfish face; a seedy policeman, who stood with his hands buried in his pockets so that he seemed to be holding his belly, his chin lowered on the flaps of his collar; a woman in a short skirt and fur chubby, her stockings wrinkling over her knees, her eyes watering, and her teeth set.

"You'd think," said the conductor pityingly as she worked her way through the car, "that a woman like that, who ain't no youngster, would stay home close to the steam on a night like this, instead of knockin' around on late cars. Unless," he added to the policeman and me, "she's out on business," and showed his yellow teeth in a smile.

"Do'ch'ster next. Do'ch'ster!"

I jumped off and struggled homeward against the wind, stopping for a while under the corner awning to catch my breath. The clouds were sheared back from a mass of stars chattering in the hemispheric blackness—the universe, this windy midnight, out on its eternal business.

I found Iva waiting up for me. She did not ask where I had been, taking it for granted, I suppose, that I had followed my custom after quarrels, of walking along the lake shore. In the morning we had a short talk and were reconciled.

January 13

A DARK, burdensome day. I stormed up from sleep this morning, not knowing what to do first—whether to reach for my slippers or begin immediately to dress, turn on the radio for the news, comb my hair, prepare to shave. I fell back into bed and spent an hour or so collecting myself, watching the dark beams from the slats of the blind wheeling on the upper wall. Then I rose. There were low clouds; the windows streamed. The surrounding roofs —green, raw red blackened brass—shone like potlids in a darkened kitchen.

At eleven I had a haircut. I went as far as Sixty-third Street for lunch and ate at a white counter amid smells of frying fish, looking out on the iron piers in the street and the huge paving bricks like the plates of the boiler-room

106

floor in a huge liner. Above the restaurant, on the other corner, a hamburger with arms and legs balanced on a fiery wire, leaned toward a jar of mustard. I wiped up the sweet sediment in my cup with a piece of bread and went out to walk through large melting flakes. I wandered through a ten-cent store, examining the comic valentines, thought of buying envelopes, and bought instead a bag of chocolate creams. I ate them hungrily. Next, I was drawn into a shooting gallery. I paid for twenty shots and fired less than half, hitting none of the targets. Back in the street, I warmed myself at a salamander flaming in an oil drum near a newsstand with its wall of magazines erected under the shelter of the El. Scenes of love and horror. Afterward, I went into a Christian Science reading room and picked up the *Monitor*. I did not read it. I sat holding it, trying to think of the name of the company whose gas stoves used to be advertised on the front page of the *Manchester Guardian*. A little later I was in the street again, in front of Coulon's gymnasium, looking at photographs of boxers. "Young Salemi, now with the Rangers in the South Pacific." What beautiful shoulders!

I started back, choosing unfamiliar streets. They turned out to be no different from the ones I knew. Two men were sawing a tree. A dog sprang from behind a fence without warning, yapping. I hate such dogs. A man in a mackinaw and red boots stood in the center of a lot, throwing boxes into a fire. At the high window of a stone house, a child, a blond boy, was playing king in a paper crown. He wore a blanket over his shoulders and, for a scepter, he held a thin green stick in his thin fingers. Catching sight of me, he suddenly converted his scepter into a rifle. He drew a bead on me and fired, his lips moving as he said, "Bang!"

107

He smiled when I took off my hat and pointed in dismay to an imaginary hole.

The book arrived in the noon mail. I will find it tonight. I hope that will be the last deception imposed on me.

I MET Sam Pearson, Iva's cousin, on Fifty-seventh Street today. He said, "Well, I didn't expect to see you, are you still among us?" He knew I was.

I said, glumly, "I'm not in Alaska."

"What are you doing with yourself?"

"Nothing."

He smiled, allowing me my joke. "Who was it that told me you were taking a course in a trade school . . . ?"

A: "That's just a rumor."

Q: "What are you doing, then?"

A: "Just living off Iva."

Again he smiled, but he was no longer sure of himself.

Q: "I heard you were studying, or something."

A: "No, I just sit at home all day and do nothing."

Q: "Nothing?"

A: "Absolutely nothing."

Q: "Oh, well, I suppose we'll all be going soon, won't we?" (Sam has three half-grown children).

A: "If the man power shortage becomes any more acute."

It's time I was uncivil to Sam. He has always, by his questions, exercised a social or family tyranny over me, checking on my suitability for Iva. No doubt he will report this to the Almstadts.

108

LOOK out for yourself, and the world will be best served.

Yesterday I had a talk with Mr. Fanzel, the tailor, an Alsatian gentleman. Last spring he bought some Lille thread, about two hundred spools, at a bargain. He paid twenty-five cents a spool; today the price is seventy-five cents. He does not intend to sell any of it. The increase goes into the garments he sews, and he is busier now than he was in his best year, 1928. One of his customers has just ordered six new suits and two sport jackets. "Pretty soon I maybe won't have material. I got to look ahead. So I make higher the price," says Mr. Fanzel. Which is his kind of wisdom, business wisdom. If everybody takes care of number one, the general welfare is assured. A year ago Mr. Fanzel sewed a button to my coat gratis; this year he charged fifteen cents. Perhaps he used precious Lille thread, or perhaps the value of his time has increased, now that he has so many customers. Mr. Franzel is frightened. He makes an outward show of confidence and of riding the wave but in many ways manifests his terror. The tenants of his building who were on relief four years ago now have become highly paid defense workers, and one of them, to his consternation, last week came down and ordered a suit costing eighty dollars. Heretofore Mr. Fanzel's customers have been the rich of the Kenwood district. He could not stop talking about his tenant whom he was once on the verge of evicting, and who now earns a hundred and ten dollars a week. Mr. Fanzel is master only of his scissors and needles, not of the greater fate that makes such changes, and, in his fear, with wars and transformed tenants and, it may be, even the shadow of

Jeff Forman's falling plane crossing his security, he re-
solves to protect himself by charging eighty dollars for
suits worth forty and fifteen cents for a button he formerly
sewed out of kindness. Mr. Fanzel is innocent. I blame the
spiritual climate. In it we enjoy our gobber of Jeff Forman
without a thought for him, let alone a word of gratitude.
Supply is supply, and demand is demand. They will be
satisfied, be it with combs, fifes, rubber, whisky, tainted
meat, canned peas, sex, or tobacco. For every need there
is an entrepreneur, by a marvelous providence. You can
find a man to bury your dog, rub your back, teach you
Swahili, read your horoscope, murder your competitor.
In the megapolis, all this is possible. There was a Parisian
cripple in the days of John Law, the Scottish speculator,
who stood in the streets renting out his hump for a writing
desk to people who had no convenient place to take their
transactions.

What can poor Mr. Fanzel do? He must make money
while he can; he is one of the little people. He barely
managed to hold on to his property during the crash.
Though he knows I am not working, he must charge fifteen
cents for sewing the button. Otherwise, through his very
kindness, he may find himself among the hindmost, where
the devil, who is so far among the foremost he has doubled
his trail, can snatch him up. And then who, if he keeps
down his prices and allows himself impulses of charity,
will furnish Mr. Fanzel his roast, his cabbage, his roll
and coffee, his bed, his roof, his morning *Tribune*, the
price of his movie, and his Prince Albert tobacco?

He showed me an article by former President Hoover
which advocated the abolition of all control over prices,

110

thus encouraging manufacturing initiative in the interests of increased armament production.

"What do you think?" he said.

"What do *you* think of it, Mr. Fanzel?"

"Such a plan would save the country."

"But should we pay them to save the country? Have they no other reason to manufacture these things?"

"They are in business."

"Aren't they making lots of money now?"

"More will be better for everybody. It's business. Ah," he laughed, waving his hand at me, "you don't understand it. They will work harder and we will win the war faster."

"But the prices will go up, and then more money will be like less money."

"Oh, oh, you don't understand it," he said, snuffing with laughter through the ginger-colored hairs of his nose and mustache.

"Mr. Fanzel, when you sew a dress for your wife, do you charge her for it?"

"I make only men's garments, not ladies'."

I laid three nickels on the counter and picked up the coat.

"You think it over," he called to me. "They don't make a man the president for nothing."

I walked away, fingering the button which had been threatening for weeks to drop off, weighing the value of its stability against that of the fifteen cents, representing three cups of coffee, or three cigars, or a glass-and-a-half of beer, or five morning papers, or something less than a package of cigarettes, or three telephone calls, or one breakfast. Iva's check at the library having been held up,

I went without breakfast. Money has been scarce this week. But it does not disturb me to miss a meal now and then. I do not use as many calories as an active man and I have fat to spare. Mr. Fanzel, I am sure, would have been appalled to learn that he had deprived me of my toast and coffee, despite the fact that he has every theoretical right to a clear conscience. I should be taking care of myself. He can't be responsible for me. I recall the words of the suitor Luzhin in *Crime and Punishment*. He has been reading the English economists, or claims he has. "If I were to tear my coat in half," he says, "in order to share it with some wretch, no one would be benefited. Both of us would shiver in the cold." And why should both shiver? Is it not better that one should be warm? An unimpeachable conclusion. If I were to tell this to Mr. Fanzel (without mentioning breakfast), he would certainly agree. Life is hard. *Vae victis!* The wretched must suffer.

January 16

FAIRLY quiet day.

January 18

I SAT WATCHING Marie this morning as she changed the sheets and dusted and washed the windows. To see her at the windows fascinated me especially. It was merely her work, but even she seemed to derive a sober pleasure from it, following the rag over the glitter with her eyes, pulling the frames back and forth on their resonant cords, moving the curved water line further and further across the spotted glass.

To make a dirty surface clean—a very simple, very human matter. I, while shining shoes, grew partly aware of it. In those moments at the window, how different Marie was, how purely human as she rubbed the glass. I sometimes wonder if it can be entirely a source of pleasure to clean. There is too much urgency in it; sometimes it becomes a preoccupation of body and heart. "Ah, in anxiety I lie, thinking, what surface tomorrow?" But it has its importance as a notion of center, of balance, of order. A woman learns it in the kitchens of her childhood, and it branches out from sinks, windows, table tops, to the faces and hands of children, and then it may become, as it does for some women, part of the nature of God.

January 19

SUSIE FARSON came over in tears to ask Iva what to do about her husband. I withdrew and left them to talk. Susie and her husband wage an endless fight. He, Walter, is a ruddy, big-jawed, blond Dakota boy of the kind city girls are often attracted to. Susie, who was a schoolmate of Iva's, is six years older than he. He resents this difference in their ages, he resents having been trapped into marriage, and, most of all, he resents the baby, Barbara. Recently Iva indignantly wanted me to punch his head for gagging the child with a handkerchief because she disturbed his sleep. Last week he pressed her jaws together for the same reason, almost suffocating her. This week he bruised Susie's face. Iva advised Susie to leave him, and Susie says she intends to.

Iva and I met downtown at six. The occasion was our sixth wedding anniversary. She had decided that we deserved a celebration. We had had none New Year's Eve. It had been a bad year—all the more reason for a good dinner and a bottle of French wine. She was determined that this was not to be just another evening.

I came down on the El, getting off at the Randolph and Wabash station. There were crooked streaks of red at one end of the street and, at the other, a band of black, soft as a stroke of charcoal; into it were hooked the tiny lights of the lake front. On the platform the rush-hour crowds were melting under the beams of oncoming trains. Each train was followed by an interval of darkness, when the twin colored lamps of the rear car hobbled around the curve. Sparks from the street below were caught and blanked in the heavy, flat ladder of ties. The pigeons under the sooty, sheet-iron eaves were already asleep; their wadded shadows fell on the billboards and, with every train, fluttered as though a prowler had sprung from the roof into their roost.

I walked along East Randolph Street, stopping to look at the rich cakes and the tropical fruits. When I came to the smoky alley alongside the library where the south-bound cars emerge, I saw a man sprawl out in front of me, and at once I was in the center of a large crowd and, from a distance that could not have been as great as it seemed, a mounted policeman standing before a Cottage Grove car was gazing down.

The fallen man was well dressed and above middle age. His hat lay crushed under his large bald head, his tongue had come forward between his lips, his lips seemed swollen. I stooped and tore at his collar. A button sprang away. By this time the policeman had pushed his way forward. I drew back, wiping my hands on a piece of paper. Together, we stared at the fallen man's face. Then my attention was drawn to the policeman's own face. It was long and as narrow as a boot. His features were sharp, red, wind-scarred, his jaws muscular, his sideburns whitish, intersected by the straps of his stiff blue cap. He blew his steel whistle. The signal was not necessary. Other uniformed men were already coming toward us. The first to arrive was elderly himself. He bent and reached into the fallen man's pockets and produced an old-fashioned strap-fastened wallet like my father's. He held up a card and spelled the name. The victim's broad coat was hitched up behind, his chest and belly rose hugely together as he labored, snoring, for breath. A path was cleared for the approaching ambulance. Its bell beat rapidly; the on-lookers moved away, reluctant to disengage themselves. Would the red face go gray, the dabbled hands stop their rowing, the jaw drop? Perhaps it was only an epileptic fit.

As I withdrew with the others, I touched my forehead; it had begun to smart. My finger tips searched for the scratch Aunt Dina had left on it the night of my mother's death. The nurse had called us. From all parts of the house we came running. My mother may still have been alive, though her eyes were shut, for when Aunt Dina threw her-self upon her, her lips seemed to move crookedly in a last effort to speak or kiss. Aunt Dina screamed. I tried to pull her from the body, and she lashed at me, clawing with enraged fingers. In the next blurred moment, my mother was dead. I was looking at her, my hand pressed to my face, hearing Aunt Dina cry, "She wanted to say something! She wanted to talk to me!"

To many in the fascinated crowd the figure of the man on the ground must have been what it was to me—a prevision. Without warning, down. A stone, a girder, a bullet flashes against the head, the bone gives like glass from a cheap kiln; or a subtler enemy escapes the bonds of years; the blackness comes down; we lie, a great weight on our faces, straining toward the last breath which comes like the gritting of gravel under a heavy tread.

I mounted the library stairs and from there saw the tall blue ambulance slip from the narrow passageway, the calm horse stepping away from the car.

I mentioned nothing of this to Iva; I wanted to spare her. But I could not spare myself, and several times during dinner the image of the fallen man came between me and my food, and I laid down my fork. We did not enjoy our celebration. She thought I was ill.

January 21

Susie Farson came by in great excitement and said that she and her husband were going to Detroit. He has been offered a radio training course by the War Department. She hopes to be admitted to the same school. They are leaving the baby with Farson's sister, who is a "twenty-six" girl in a downtown restaurant. "She'll look after her; Janey adores the kid. I'll write and tell you how we're getting along. And, Iva, you'll stop by once in a while and see how she's getting along. I'll give you Janey's address."

"Of course," said Iva, but coldly. And after Susie had

116

rushed away, she said, "That fool! What if something should happen to the baby?"

"She doesn't want to lose her husband," I said.

"Lose him? I would have shot him by now. Besides, she's only making things worse. He'll blame her if anything goes wrong. And she believes she's doing it for love. Oh, be quiet, you!"

Mr. Vanaker was raking his throat, coughing, halting with a fleshy catch and coughing again. Any disturbance in our room sets him off. He did not stop until Iva, with a show of temper unusual for her, banged on the wall with her slipper.

January 22

I ATE a large breakfast, intending to go without lunch. But at one o'clock, intensely hungry, I tossed aside Abt's pamphlet and went out for lunch. On the way back I bought several oranges and a large bar of chocolate. By four o'clock I had eaten them. Later, at Fallon's, I had a large dinner. And a few hours later, in the movies, I added to all this a whole package of caramels and most of a bag of mints. Now, at eleven, I am still hungry.

January 24

WE HAD supper with the Almstadts yesterday. Cousin Sam has not reported me. I had prepared Iva by telling her of our conversation, but nothing was mentioned. Old Almstadt dominated the conversation, telling of the profits he could make if there were no shortage of supplies. My

117

mother-in-law also is kept busy these days. Last week she baked a cake for the Russian Relief Bazaar. This week all the ladies of her club are contributing blood to the Red Cross. She knits a muffler a week. She tried gloves but had no success with them. She could not do the fingers. And the girls, Alma and Rose, complained that all the young men were disappearing into the Army and that only high-school boys were left. Mrs. Almstadt again mentioned that she would like to have Iva with her when I was drafted. I said there was time enough to decide. I love Iva too much to turn her over to them.

Next week we are going to my father's. We have been declining my stepmother's invitations for weeks; she is becoming offended.

January 26

IN BED with a cold. Marie made tea for me in the morning. Iva came home after lunch to nurse me. She brought a box of Louisiana strawberries and, as a treat, rolled them in powdered sugar. The coverlet was starred with the green stems. She was at her most ample and generous best. She read to me for an hour, and then we dozed off together. I awoke in the middle of the afternoon; she still slept. I gazed up at the comfortable room and heard the slight, mixed rhythm of her breathing and mine. This endeared her to me more than any favor could. The icicles and frost patterns on the window turned brilliant; the trees, like instruments, opened all their sounds into the wind, and the bold, icy colors of sky and snow and clouds burned strongly. A day for a world without deformity or threat

118

of damage, and my pleasure in the weather was all the greater because it held its own beauty and was engaged with nothing but itself. The light gave an air of innocence to some of the common objects in the room, liberating them from ugliness. I lost the aversion I had hitherto felt for the red oblong of rug at the foot of the bed, the scrap of tapestry on the radiator seat, the bubbles of paint on the white lintel, the six knobs on the dresser I had formerly compared to the ugly noses of as many dwarf brothers. In the middle of the floor, like an accidental device of serenity, lay a piece of red string.

Great pressure is brought to bear to make us undervalue ourselves. On the other hand, civilization teaches that each of us is an inestimable prize. There are, then, these two preparations: one for life and the other for death. Therefore we value and are ashamed to value ourselves, are hard-boiled. We are schooled in quietness and, if one of us takes his measure occasionally, he does so coolly, as if he were examining his fingernails, not his soul, frowning at the imperfections he finds as one would at a chip or a bit of dirt. Because, of course, we are called upon to accept the imposition of all kinds of wrongs, to wait in ranks under a hot sun, to run up a clattering beach, to be sentries, scouts or workingmen, to be those in the train when it is blown up, or those at the gates when they are locked, to be of no significance, to die. The result is that we learn to be unfeeling toward ourselves and incurious. Who can be the earnest huntsman of himself when he knows he is in turn a quarry? Or nothing so distinctive as quarry, but one of a shoal, driven toward the weirs.

But I must know what I myself am.

It was good to lie in bed, awake, not dreaming. Hemmed in all day, inactive, I lie down at night in enervation and, as a result, I sleep badly. I have never known dreamless sleep. In the past, my dreams annoyed me by their prolixity. I went on foolish errands, and held even more foolish debates, and settled and arranged the most humdrum affairs. But now my dreams are more bare and ominous. Some of them are fearful. A few nights ago I found myself in a low chamber with rows of large cribs or wicker bassinets in which the dead of a massacre were lying. I am sure they were victims of a massacre, because my mission was to reclaim one for a particular family. My guide picked up a tag and said, "This one was found near. . . ." I do not remember the name; it ended in *Tanza*. It must have been Constanza. It was either there or in Bucharest that those slain by the Iron Guard were slung from hooks in a slaughterhouse. I have seen the pictures. I looked at the reclining face and murmured that I was not personally acquainted with the deceased. I had merely been asked, as an outsider. . . . I did not even know the family well. At which my guide turned, smiling, and I guessed that he meant—there was not enough light in the vault to make his meaning unambiguous, but I thought I understood—"It's well to put oneself in the clear in something like this." This was his warning to me. He approved of my neutrality. As long as I took the part of the humane emissary, no harm would come to me. But it offended me to have an understanding with this man and to receive a smile of complicity from his pointed face. Could I be such a hypocrite? "Do you think he can be found?" I said. "Would he be here?" I showed my distrust. We continued up the aisle; it was more like the path of a gray draught than anything so substantial as a floor. The bodies, as I have said, were lying in cribs, and looked remarkably infantile, their faces pinched and wounded. I do not remember much more. I can picture only the low-pitched, long room much like some of the rooms in the Industrial Museum in Jackson Park; the childlike bodies with pierced heads and limbs; my guide, brisk as a rat among his charges; an atmosphere of terror such as my father many years ago could conjure for me, describing Gehenna and the damned until I shrieked and begged him to stop; and the syllables *Tanza.*

Some of the other dreams have been only slightly less dreadful. In one I was a sapper with the Army in North Africa. We had arrived in a town, and my task was to render harmless the grenade traps in one of the houses. I crawled through the window, dropped from the clay sill and saw a grenade wired to the door, ridged and ugly. But I did not know where to begin, which wire to touch first. My time was limited; I had other work before me. I began to tremble and perspire and, going to the far end of the room, I aimed my pistol long and carefully at the ridges and fired. When the din subsided, I realized that if I had hit the mark I would have killed myself. But I had scarcely a moment to feel relieved. Pincers in hand, I went forward to cut the first wire.

I recognize in the guide of the first dream an ancient figure, temporarily disguised only to make my dread greater when he revealed himself.

Our first encounter was in a muddy back lane. By day

it was a wagon thoroughfare, but at this evening hour only a goat wandered over the cold ruts that had become as hard as the steel rims that made them. Suddenly I heard another set of footsteps added to mine, heavier and grittier, and my premonitions leaped into one fear even before I felt a touch on my back and turned. Then that swollen face that came rapidly toward mine until I felt its bristles and the cold pressure of its nose; the lips kissed me on the temple with a laugh and a groan. Blindly I ran, hearing again the gritting boots. The roused dogs behind the snaggled boards of the fences abandoned themselves to the wildest rage of barking. I ran, stumbling through drifts of ashes, into the street.

Could the fallen man of last week have seen, had he chanced to open his eyes, his death in the face of that policeman who bent over him? We know we are sought and expect to be found. How many forms he takes, the murderer. Frank, or simple, or a man of depth and cultivation, or perhaps prosaic, without distinction. Yet he is *the* murderer, the stranger who, one day, will drop the smile of courtesy or custom to show you the weapon in his hand, the means of your death. Who does not know him, the one who takes your measure in the street or on the stairs, he whose presence you must ignore in the darkened room if you are to close your eyes and fall asleep, the agent who takes you, in the last unforgiving act, into inexistence? Who does not expect him with the opening of the door; and who, after childhood, thinks of flight or resistance or of laying any but ironic, yes, even welcoming hands on his shoulders when he comes? The moment is for him to choose. He may come at a climax of satisfaction or of evil; he may come as one comes to repair a radio or a faucet; mutely, or to pass the time of day, play a game of cards; or, with no preliminary, colored with horrible anger, reaching out a muffling hand; or, in a mask of calm, hurry you to your last breath, drawn with a stuttering sigh out of his shadow.

How will it be? How? Falling a mile into the wrinkled sea? Or, as I have dreamed, cutting a wire? Or strafed in a river among chopped reeds and turning water, blood leaking through the cloth of the sleeves and shoulders?

I can safely think of such things on a bright afternoon such as this. When they come at night, the heart, like a toad, exudes its fear with a repulsive puff. But toward morning I have a way, also, of holding court on myself, and that is even more intolerable. Half-conscious, I call in a variety of testimony on my case and am confronted by the wrongs, errors, lies, disgraces, and fears of a lifetime. I am forced to pass judgment on myself and to ask questions I would far rather not ask: "What is this for?" and "What am I for?" and "Am I made for this?" My beliefs are inadequate, they do not guard me. I think invariably of the awning of the store on the corner. It gives as much protection against rain and wind as my beliefs give against the chaos I am forced to face. "God does not love those who are unable to sleep soundly," runs an old saying. In the morning I dress and go about my "business." I pass one more day no different from the others. Night comes, and I have to face another session of sleep—that "sinister adventure" Baudelaire calls it—and be brought to wakefulness by degrees through a nightmare of reckoning or inventory, my mind flapping like a rag on a clothesline in cold wind.

We had an enormous sunset, a smashing of gaudy colors, apocalyptic reds and purples such as must have appeared on the punished bodies of great saints, blues heavy and rich. I woke Iva, and we watched it, hand in hand. Her hand was cool and sweet. I had a slight fever.

January 28

WE DID not have a bad time at my father's house. My stepmother was cordial; my father did not pry. We left at ten o'clock. Iva did not tell me until today that, as she was preparing to go, my stepmother gave her an envelope containing a card congratulating us on our anniversary and a check.

"Now, Joseph, don't be angry," Iva said. "We can use the money. We both need things."

"I'm not angry."

"They wanted to give us a present. It was nice of them. You need a new shirt. And some shorts. I can't keep darning them." She laughed. "There's no place for another patch."

"Whatever you like," I said, putting a strand of hair behind her ear.

I was glad enough to have escaped the usual interview with my father, which begins, as a rule, with his taking me aside and saying, "Have I told you about Gartner's boy, the youngest, the one who was studying chemistry? They've taken him out of school. He has an excellent job in a war plant. You remember him."

Indeed I do.

This means that I, too, should have been a chemist or

physicist or engineer. A nonprofessional education is something the middle classes can ill afford. It is an invest-ment bound to fail. And, in the strictest sense, it is not necessary, for any intelligent man can pick up all he needs to know. My father, for instance, never went to college, and yet he can keep up his end of a conversation with a quotation from Shakespeare—"Pause, now, and weigh thy values with an equal hand," "A loan oft loses both itself and friend," the passage beginning, "Yes, young boy," from *King John*.

My accomplishments, he acknowledges, are wider than his; my opportunities were greater. But bread and butter come first. Besides, professional men are also sometimes cultured. Take George Sachs, now (our family doctor in Montreal), who was a scholar and even wrote a book in his spare time. (A pamphlet for the Quebec Musical Society: *The Medical Facts about Beethoven's Deafness*.) My father's justification is, however, that I have prepared myself for the kind of life I shall never be able to lead. And, where my abiding obsession formerly was to carry out my plans, I know now that I shall have to settle for very, very little. That is, I shall have to accept very little, for there is no question of settling. Personal choice does not count for much these days.

January 29

As I was passing Vanaker's favorite dumping yard, I saw on a bush, amid the bottles, a pair of socks that had a familiar look. I took one of them off and examined it. It was mine. There could be no doubt about it; I had bought

125

several pairs in this pattern about a year ago. To make doubly sure, I took one of the socks home and compared it with the others. It was the same in every detail. Perhaps he did steal Iva's perfume. I had been unwilling to believe it before. Vanaker, Mrs. Briggs tells me, has a good job in a garage. Sunday mornings, when we see him leaving for church, he is well dressed. What can have inspired this theft of my worn socks? I said nothing about it to Iva, but wrapped the evidence in a piece of paper and threw it away.

January 30

I WROTE to Abt without mentioning his pamphlet. He is sure to be angry.

January 31

SLIGHT letup in the cold. The fury of cleanliness. One of my shirts came back from the laundry without a single button. I must complain.

February 1

NEAR Sixty-third and Stony Island I ran into Alf Steidler, whom I hadn't seen in years. He had heard that I had been drafted, and I had heard the same news about him. "They turned me down," he said. "Bad teeth, bad heart, and emotionally unsuitable. Mostly the last. Jack Brill was bait, though."

"Did they take him?"

"In December. He's going to be a bombardier."

"What are you doing so far from Huron Street?"

"I've been up to see my brother in the hospital. He smashed his cab last Thursday."

"Too bad. Is he hurt much?"

"Oh, no, he damaged his looks a little, that's all."

I said I was sorry to hear it.

"That's the way the breaks run," said Steidler. "Doesn't make much difference, now that he's married. It won't interfere with his wolfing around."

"I didn't know he was married."

"How would you? It didn't make the front pages."

"I'm trying to say that I'm surprised. Who . . . ?"

"Wilma. He married the kid."

"The girl I saw him with at the Paxton?"

"That's the one."

Whenever I meet Steidler, I think of Rameau's nephew, described by Diderot as ". . . *un* (*personnage*) *composé de hauteur et de bassesse, de bon sens et de déraison.*" But, less emphatic, more sentimental (after his own fashion), and not nearly as shrewd.

He carried a match to the stump of his cigar, sucking. His black hair, freshly cut, was combed back in the usual way, as though painted on, flush against the rising hump of his head. It gave his face, with its contrasting long cheeks, jutting bones and fleshy nose and lips, a curious bareness. He looked very pale, almost limy in the dusty sunlight under the El pillars. He was shaved and powdered, and he wore a new striped tie. But his once natty coat was frayed, the brown belt looked greenish.

"How's our old school chum Morris?" he asked.

"Abt? He's doing very well; he's in Washington."

"And what about you?"

"I'm waiting for the Army call. What are you doing, Alf?"

"Oh, the same. Still trying to lead a genteel life. WPA folded, you know. It was good going for a couple of years. I was an honored artist of the republic. First I was in the theater, you remember. Then I organized a water ballet for the parks system, and after that I led a chorus in a settlement house. Say, but I started at the bottom. My first job was digging up a street. I had to explain to the people who asked me what I was working at that I was a geologist. Ha, ha! Then I was a smoke watcher."

"I don't understand."

"Up in the West Side factory district I sat on a roof with a chart of six shades of smoke and watched the chimneys eight hours a day. Then the theater project. Anyway, the whole business folded up, and I went out to the Coast. Say, there's a Thompson's down the way. How about a cup of coffee? Good. It's been years since I saw you. The gay old Coast. I went out with some ideas and tried to get in to see Lubitsch, but I couldn't find anyone to introduce me. Christ, it's mad out there. It's the world's greatest loony-bin. Ever been on the Coast?"

"Never."

"Christ, stay away from it, it's murder. But then, if you want to see what the life of the country can wash up, take the trip. I've been around a little bit. But in L.A. they conned me for my fifty bucks as though I'd been a baby. Of course, I'm drawn into different circles than you. Well, I was broke, so I wired my mother and got twenty bucks and a note about how slow the beauty-parlor business was. That was a tricky week. I had to go to work for a while, to raise some money." He looked at me somberly, a decayed Spanish prince with a splayed nose and a long upper lip covered with bristles. His blue eyes grew darker. "I didn't have it easy.

"One nice thing about the Coast, though," he added, brightening, "the nooky situation is awfully good where there aren't too many soldiers. You whistle for it. Did you read about that silly trial? Now, there was something really funny. If we were more civilized we'd put it on the stage. This Canadian officer kept that girl in a hotel. But it was just brotherly, she said. He called her his little strumpet. 'Crumpet, you mean,' said the prosecutor. Right then and there he must have known his case was gone. 'No,' she insists, 'strumpet. It's a kind of biscuit the British like.' " Alf laughed, holding the sugar shaker and spoon suspended over his cup. "Well, they wouldn't convict anybody on *that* sort of evidence." He reached forward to hand me the sugar, revealing a rolled copy of *Variety* in his coat pocket. He was lulled by the joke; musing, smiling, he stirred and sipped, and then wet a fresh cigar along his underlip.

At twenty-eight, he was old-fashioned. He had all the ways of a theatrical generation that was already at the point of death when, in his high-school days, he had cut classes to admire its aging comedians in the mangy splendor of the Oriental. He grew up behind his mother's beauty shop. When I knew him well, at sixteen, he was already a stage gentleman, and rose at two every day to breakfast on tea and sardines. He spent his evenings at the Arrow, amid amateur talk of *Magda* and *Desire Under the Elms*. He played in all the local productions, was Joxur in *Juno and*

129

the Paycock and did *Cyrano* for a triumphant week (which he never forgot) at the school auditorium.

"I wouldn't have come back from the Coast," he said. "But my number came up; the board called me. It's a good sign for the country that I was rejected. They'd deserve to lose if they put me in their Army. The psychiatrist asked me what I did, and I replied, 'To be perfectly frank, I've been a deadbeat all my life.' He said, 'How do you think you'll get along in the Army?' and I answered, 'Now, what do you think, doctor?'"

"You said that?"

"Sure, I was being honest. I'd never be any damned good to them. I'd set an all-time record for gold-bricking. It's up to you normal bastards to do the fighting. I said, 'What do you think?' and he took another look at my papers and said, 'They've got you down for a bad heart, here. Well, this will make it final.' And he wrote down, 'Schizoid Type.' That would mean I was in the split-pea soup, wouldn't it? I looked it up. You think a guy can tell by looking at you? Or because you tell him you're a deadbeat? That isn't enough, is it?"

"No," I said, "they need more evidence than that; it isn't enough. Don't worry about it."

"Oh, I'm not worried, don't kid yourself." His glasses duplicated the triangular flame of another match. "They wouldn't know what to make of me, because I'm not your average guy. I know that. Why, I couldn't fight. It isn't my line. My line is getting by."

"How do you get by, Alf?"

"It's a wonder to me. But every January swings around, somehow, and there I am; I've come through. But I don't know how. I work a little, sponge a little, gamble a little.

I suppose I am a deadbeat. Or will be till I am what I want to become. Well, I entertain the people I sponge from. That's something, anyhow."

"You expect me to pay for your coffee?" I said.

"*You*, Joseph? This is Dutch treat. What a corny joke!" He looked offended.

"I was referring to the entertainment."

"Oh. One of these days I expect an opening. . . ."

"I didn't mean anything by that," I said.

"Forget it. Who holds your bad jokes against you? Did you see me in any of the Federal productions?

"I wasn't bad. A big improvement over the old days. *Roxanne!* Remember? Ha, ha! Well, it's in the family. Have you ever heard my old lady sing, were you ever around when that happened? Oh, you've missed something. My brother writes songs, too. He just wrote one for the United Nations. It's called 'Let's Link Hands Across the Ocean.' He keeps bothering me to do something about it. He's sure it would make the Hit Parade. Now he wants me to go to New York on the insurance money. Wilma's against it."

"Do you intend to go?"

"A year ago I would have gone like a shot. But since Wilma's against it . . . I owe the girl a good turn. I got her into trouble a few years ago. Phil hung a shiner on her when they were living together for taking twenty dollars out of his pocket. Only she didn't take it. I took it."

"Did you confess?"

"Confess! It would spoil my credit with him forever. I was sure they'd make it up by and by. He gave her an awful pasting. She cried. . . ."

"Were you there when it happened?"

"Right in the room. I couldn't butt in."

"What about the money?"

"I pinned it on a false hope. I suppose you think that's terrible, huh? Well, this may sound hard, and you may not believe it, but they're more human when they're fighting. Besides, it was like a movie. He suffered remorse, she forgave him because he was her man, and so on. They got a big kick out of it. I know. I was their go-between. But now she says she's the one who should take the song to New York, if anyone goes. I guess she sees herself in Tin-Pan Alley, her face streaked with tears. . . ."

"Oh, it can't be that bad."

"Can't it, though? You don't know the type. Let me show you. She hides overnight in a publisher's broom closet and surprises Mr. Snaith-Hawkins himself in the morning. 'What are you doing here?' 'Oh, for my sake, Sir, listen to this. My husband wrote it.' As he sternly refuses, she throws herself at his feet, and he says, 'Come now, my girl.' Not a bad man, you see. 'It's not only for my sake, but for Democracy and . . .'; as she goes on, he relents. 'You shouldn't be lying on the floor, my dear. Here, take this chair. I'll have Mr. Trubshevsky run through it' (the score)—Just wait" (I had tried to interrupt)—"Trub-shevsky plays; Snaith-Hawkins frowns, strokes his beard. His expression changes. Trubshevsky pounds in ecstasy. They sing together, 'Let's link hands,' et cetera. 'This is great, positively!' exclaims Snaith-Hawkins. And Trub-shevsky, enthusiastically, his eyes shining, 'Your husband is a genius, Madam, positively.' 'There, don't cry, my dear,' says Snaith-Hawkins. 'Oh, Sir, you can't understand. All those years of struggle, driving a cab, working at his music after supper.' They're overcome. You see?"

132

said Steidler. "That's how they think. She'll probably go. It's money thrown away. Well, he won't be satisfied otherwise."

"What a shame."

"It's not a shame at all. It's just as well. Just think what the world would be like if their dreams came true."

Or if yours came true, I was tempted to say.

I had a full day of this. He walked home with me and stayed until five o'clock, talking incessantly and smoking so many cigars I had to ventilate the room when he left. I was as tired as though I had spent the day in dissipations of a particularly degrading sort with Steidler as my accomplice. I did not tell Iva of the visit. She disapproves of him.

February 2

STILL no fruits and flowers. I have been too lazy to stir out. But I know I am not lazy. Here is an incalculable deception. Lazy we are not. When we seem so, our cyclonic wishes are baffled, and pride requires us to be indifferent.

The Egyptians were right to make one of their gods a cat. They, the worshipers, knew that only a cat's eyes could see into their interior darkness.

The papers say no husbands have been drafted from Illinois since last summer. But now the supply of men is lower, and married men without dependents will soon be called up. Steidler asked me how I was using my liberty. I answered that I was preparing myself spiritually, that I was willing to be a member of the Army, but not a *part* of it. He thought this a very witty answer. He believes I am a natural comedian and laughs at everything I say. The more serious I become, the harder he laughs.

He now reveals that he lived in the County Hospital for three months, last year, in the internes' quarters. The officials knew nothing about it. His friend Shailer, who was then in residence, took him in, and the other internes agreed to keep his secret. He ate in the cafeteria, and his clothes were washed in the hospital laundry. He made his pocket money at cards; there were escapades and jokes; he was introduced to patients as a specialist; he gave advice. The internes were genial and admiring; he was hilarious. Shailer's room was crowded all night long. He was given a party right in the hospital before he left for California. And I suppose it is all true. He exaggerates, but he does not lie.

February 3

AN Hour with the Spirit of Alternatives.

"Let's have a talk, shall we, Joseph?"

"Glad to."

"We'll make ourselves comfortable."

"You can't be very comfortable here."

"Perfectly all right. I thrive on small hardships."

"You'll find all you need."

"Don't worry about me. You're the one who's uneasy."

"Well, the fact is, though I'm glad to have this opportunity, I can't quite place you."

"By name?"

"That doesn't matter."

134

"Of course not. I go by several."

"Such as?"

"Oh—'*But on the Other Hand*,' or '*Tu As Raison Aussi*.'
I always know who I am; that's the important thing."

"An enviable position."

"I often think so."

"Have an orange."

"Oh, thanks, no."

"Take one, go on."

"They're so expensive now."

"To please me."

"Oh, well. . . ."

"I've grown fond of you. I like your manner."

"We'll each take half."

"Good enough."

"So you like me, Joseph?"

"Oh, yes."

"That's flattering."

"No, really I do. I appreciate you."

"Do you take quick likes and dislikes?"

"I try to be reasonable."

"I know you do."

"Is that wrong?"

"To Understand?"

"You want me to trust Unreason?"

"I want nothing; I suggest. . . ."

"Feelings?"

"You have them, Joseph."

"Instincts?"

"And instincts."

"I know the argument. I see what you're after."

"What?"

"That human might is too small to pit against the unsolvables. Our nature, mind's nature, is weak, and only the heart can be relied on."

"What a rush you're in, Joseph. I didn't say that."

"But you must have meant it. Reason has to conquer itself. Then what are we given reason for? To discover the blessedness of unreason? That's a very poor argument."

"You're inventing a case against me. You're to be congratulated on your conclusions, but they're off the point. However, you've had a hard time."

"Am having."

"Quite so."

"And will continue to have."

"Of course. You must be prepared for it."

"I am. I am."

"It's sensible of you to expect so little."

"But it's sad, you must admit."

"It's a matter of knowing how much to ask for."

"How much?"

"I'm talking about happiness."

"I'm talking about asking to be human. We're not worse than the others."

"What others?"

"Those who proved it possible to be human."

"Ah, in the past. '

"Listen, *Tu As Raison Aussi*. We abuse the present too much, don't you think so?"

"You're not so fond of it."

"Fond! What a word!"

"Alienated, then."

"That's bad, too."

"It's popular."

"There's a lot of talk about alienation. It's a fool's plea."

"Is it?"

"You can divorce your wife or abandon your child, but what can you do with yourself?"

"You can't banish the world by decree if it's in you. Is that it, Joseph?"

"How can you? You have gone to its schools and seen its movies, listened to its radios, read its magazines. What if you declare you are alienated, you *say* you reject the Hollywood dream, the soap opera, the cheap thriller? The very denial implicates you."

"You can decide that you want to forget these things."

"The world comes after you. It presents you with a gun or a mechanic's tool, it singles you out for this part or that, brings you ringing news of disasters and victories, shunts you back and forth, abridges your rights, cuts off your future, is clumsy or crafty, oppressive, treacherous, murderous, black, whorish, venal, inadvertently naïve or funny. Whatever you do, you cannot dismiss it."

"What then?"

"The failing may be in us, in me. A weakness of vision."

"Aren't you asking too much of yourself?"

"I'm serious."

"Where shall I put these pips?"

"I'm sorry; have you been holding them? Here, in this ash tray. I'm telling you. It's too easy to abjure it or detest it. Too narrow. Too cowardly."

"If you could see, what do you think you would see?"

"I'm not sure. Perhaps that we were the feeble-minded children of angels."

"Now you're just amusing yourself, Joseph."

137

"Very well, I would see where those capacities have gone to which we once owed our greatness."

"That would be tragic."

"I don't say it wouldn't be. Have you any tobacco?"

"No."

"Or paper? If I had paper I could roll a cigarette out of these butts."

"I'm sorry I came empty-handed. If you're not alienated, why do you quarrel with so many people? I know you're not a misanthrope. Is it because they force you to recognize that you belong to their world?"

"I was wrong, or else put it badly. I didn't say there was no feeling of alienation, but that we should not make a doctrine of our feeling."

"Is that a public or a private belief?"

"I don't understand you."

"What about politics?"

"Do you want to discuss politics with me? With *me?* Now?"

"Since you refuse to subscribe to alienation, perhaps you might be interested in changing existence."

"Ha, ha, ha! Have you any ideas?"

"It's really not my place, you know. . . ."

"I know, but you started it."

"My position. You don't understand."

"Oh, I do."

"So, about changing existence. . . ."

"I never enjoyed being a revolutionary."

"No? Didn't you hate anyone?"

"I hated, but I didn't enjoy. As a matter of fact—"

"Yes—"

"You're so attentive—. I regarded politics as an inferior activity. Plato tells us that if everything were as it should be, the best men would avoid office, not vie for it."

"They did once vie for it."

"They did. Public life is disagreeable. It's forced on one."

"I often hear that complaint. But all this is neither here nor there as far as measures to be taken are concerned."

"But with whom, under what circumstances, how, toward what ends?"

"Ah, that's it, isn't it? With whom."

"You don't believe in the historic roles of classes, do you?"

"You keep forgetting. My province is . . ."

"Alternatives. Excuse me. With whom, to go on. A terrible, unanswerable question. With men dispersed into separate corners, incommunicado? One of their few remaining liberties is the liberty to wonder what will happen next."

"Still, if you had the power to see. . . . Here you are willing to say that it is weakness of imagination that leads to alienation but not, it seems, that a similar weakness is impairing you politically. If you could see it over-all. . . . Where are you going?"

"Just to look in my coat for a cigarette; I may have left one there."

"If you could see it that way."

"There isn't a smoke in the house."

"Over-all. . . ."

"You mean, if I were a political genius. I'm not. Now what do you face?"

"What to do under the circumstances."

"Try to live."

"How?"

"*Tu As Raison Aussi,* you're not giving much help. By a plan, a program, perhaps an obsession."

"An ideal construction."

"A German phrase. And you with a French name."

"I have to be above such prejudices."

"Well, it's a lovely phrase. An ideal construction, an obsessive device. There have been innumerable varieties: for study, for wisdom, bravery, war, the benefits of cruelty, for art; the God-man of the ancient cultures, the Humanistic full man, the courtly lover, the knight, the ecclesiastic, the despot, the ascetic, the millionaire, the manager. I could name hundreds of these ideal constructions, each with its assertions and symbols, each finding—in conduct, in God, in art, in money—its particular answer and each proclaiming: 'This is the only possible way to meet chaos.' Even someone like my friend Steidler is under the influence of an ideal construction of an inferior kind. It is inferior because it is loosely made and little thought has gone into it. Nevertheless it is real. He would willingly let go everything in his life that is not dramatic. Only he has, I am afraid, a shallow idea of drama. Simple, inevitable things are not dramatic enough for him. He has a notion of the admirable style. It is poor stuff. Nobility of gesture is what he wants. And, for all his boasted laziness, he is willing to pursue his ideal until his eyes burst from his head and his feet from his shoes."

"Do you want one of those constructions, Joseph?"

"Doesn't it seem that we need them?"

"I don't know."

"Can't get along without them?"

"If you see it that way."

"Apparently we need to give ourselves some exclusive focus, passionate and engulfing."

"One might say that."

"But what of the gap between the ideal construction and the real world, the truth?"

"Yes. . . ."

"How are they related?"

"An interesting problem."

"Then there's this: the obsession exhausts the man. It can become his enemy. It often does."

"H'm."

"What do you say to all this?"

"What do I say?"

"Yes, what do you think? You just sit there, looking at the ceiling and giving equivocal answers."

"I haven't answered. I'm not supposed to give answers."

"No. What an inoffensive career you've chosen."

"You're forgetting to be reasonable."

"Reasonable! Go on, you make me sick. The sight of you makes me sick. You make me queasy at the stomach with your suave little, false little looks."

"Joseph, look here . . . !"

"Oh, get out. Get out of here. You're two-faced. You're not to be trusted, you damned diplomat, you cheat!" Furious, I flung a handful of orange peel at him, and he fled the room.

February 4

THE landlady, Mrs. Kiefer, had another stroke yesterday that paralyzed her legs. According to Mrs. Bartlett, whom

Mrs. Briggs has engaged as a nurse, she can't live more than a few weeks. The windows are kept darkened; the halls and stairways smell of disinfectant, so that, going up to the landing with its stained-glass window, one imagines oneself in the hospital of a religious order. Except when Vanaker comes or goes, the house is quiet. He still is noisy; he has not learned to close the door when he goes down the hall. To stop him, I have to come out and march threateningly toward the bathroom. Thereupon he slams it shut. I have several times made general but loud and menacing remarks about decency and politeness. But he is either too drunk or too witless to change. When I do these things, I make myself ill. When I step out of the door to reprimand and stop him I am merely a nervous or irascible young man and I feel the force on me of a bad, harsh mood which I despise in others—the nastiness of a customer to a waiter or of a parent to a child. Iva is the same way. She gasps, "Oh, the fool!" when I go into the hall with a cross pull at the door. I suppose she means Vanaker; but may she not also mean me?

February 5

MY PRESENT ill temper first manifested itself last winter. Before we moved out of our flat I had a disgraceful fist fight with the landlord, Mr. Gesell.

That fight had been on the horizon a long time. Throughout the summer we had been on good terms. We exerted ourselves to be courteous to Gesell and to Mrs. Gesell, who made a daily racket in her shop downstairs with a machine-powered chisel. She was an amateur sculptress. Often the house trembled. Then she borrowed our books, and brought them back with stone dust on the pages. We did not complain.

But, when the frosts began, the house was underheated. We could not bathe at night; in December we had to go to bed at nine, when the radiators turned cold. Then, during one week in January, the furnace broke down. Mr. Gesell was an electrician himself; to save money, he undertook the repairs. But he had his job to attend to, so he worked at the furnace evenings and Sundays. The fireplace stifled us when we tried to use it, it was blocked with bricks. Below, Mrs. Gesell, surrounded by heat lamps, worked away at the figure of a sand hog she was designing for the new subway—she was going to enter a competition. When we went down to complain, she did not answer the bell. We ate supper with our sweaters on.

The gas stove in the kitchen, which was now our only source of heat, began to give us headaches. We lived with Myron for a week, the three of us in one bed. I caught Mr. Gesell at last, when he was airing the dog. He joked about the cold, and said I was so strapping I could bear it. He pounded my arms playfully, exciting the dog, from whom I shrank. Gesell said. "You'll do. You're pretty husky for a guy that leads such a soft life. Even though you couldn't stand up a day in my line." He was a strongly built man, about forty years old. He dressed in old trousers and flannel shirts. His wife wore the same costume—jeans, shirt, and neckcloth. He began to relate how near the two of them had come to freezing, during the depression, in a bare studio on Lake Park Avenue. They burned orange crates while waiting for the Relief to deliver coal. They took down the curtains and stuffed them in cracks against the wind. "The depression's over," I said. He laughed so hard he had to take hold of my arm to keep himself up. "Say, you're all right, you are." The dog, with rueful red eyes, watched the snow wreathing back and forth over the street. "We'll see what we can do about you," said Gesell.

A little heat began to seep up, but the house was not really warm. Iva hit upon the plan of holding up the rent. On the fifth of the month, Gesell made belligerent representations. Iva retorted angrily. She didn't expect an artist to make a good landlord. "But *you*, Mr. Gesell!" "An artist!" I snorted, thinking of that poor sand hog with his nose and thick legs. Gesell probably carried this back to Beth Gesell, for she stopped speaking to me. There were hard feelings.

But in February things took a turn for the better. In our encounters, as we went in and out of the house, we began to greet one another once more. The rent was paid, the heat rose, the hot water returned. I entered one day, with a check, to find the Gesells having breakfast at a table you might expect to find in a log cabin. The Dalmatian came and rubbed himself against me embarrassingly—poor animal, he was an adjunct and had no life of his own. Gesell took the check with thanks and began to write out a receipt. Beth, resting her chin on the back of her hand, was looking out of the window, watching the snow. She was a fat woman, with red hair cut in square, boxlike, masculine fashion. I began to think she was still angry and did not want to speak to me, but she was watching the fall of soft, heavy flakes, and all at once she said:

"When we were kids in Montana, we used to say they were plucking geese in heaven. I wonder if they still say that."

"I never heard it before," I said, entirely willing to make peace.

"Maybe the saying's gone out. It was long ago."

"Couldn't be so long," I said generously, and won a saddened smile.

"Oh, yes, long enough."

Gesell wrote on, also smiling, thinking, perhaps, of his wife's girlhood or of similar myths of his own early days. The yawning dog closed his jaws with a snap.

"Then there was rain," said Beth.

"I know," said Gesell. "Angels?"

"Oh, get along, Peter." She laughed, and the color from her hair seemed to spread along her cheeks. "Placer mining."

"I never heard of that, either," I said.

"And here you are," said Gesell, fluttering the receipt.

We were smiling broadly, all three.

Not long afterward, however, on a Sunday afternoon, the house began to go cold, and at two o'clock the electricity was shut off. It was a mild day; we might easily have borne the chill. But we had been listening to a Brahms concerto. I hurried downstairs and rang at Gesell's door. The Dalmatian threw himself in a rage against it, clawing the glass. I ran around to the basement entrance and, without knocking, went in. Gesell stood at his workbench, a length of pipe in his hand. A pistol would not have deterred me. I strode toward him, kicking rods, board-ends, pieces of wire, out of my way.

"Why did you turn off the current?" I said.

"I had to work on this stoker, that's why."

"Why the devil do you wait until Sunday? And why couldn't you tell us beforehand?"

"I don't have to get your permission to work on this stoker," he said.

"How long are you going to keep it off?"

Ignoring this question, he turned sullenly back to his bench.

"Well, how long?" I repeated. And, when I saw that he was not going to reply, I took him by the shoulder and, forcing him round, pushed aside the pipe and struck him. He fell, the pipe clattering under him on the cement. But instantly he was up again, brandishing his fists, shouting, "If that's what you want!" He could not reach me. I carried him to the wall, hitting repeatedly into his chest and belly and cutting my knuckles on his open, panting mouth. After the first few blows, my anger vanished. In weariness and self-disgust I pinned him against the bricks. Hearing his thick, rasping shouts, I said pacifyingly, "Don't get excited, Mr. Gesell. I'm sorry about this. Don't get excited!"

"You damned fool!" he cried. "You'll get yours! You damned crazy fool!" His voice quivered with terror and anger. "Beth, Be-eth! You wait!" Twisting him away from the wall, I shoved him from me. "I'll get out a warrant. Be-eth!"

"You'd better not," I said. But I felt the emptiness of my threat and, more ashamed than ever, I went upstairs where I bandaged my hand and sat down to wait for the police. Iva laughed at my fears and said I would have a long wait. She was right, though I was prepared all week to go to court and pay a fine for disorderly conduct. Iva guessed that Beth was unwilling to invest in a warrant. We moved a month later. Iva and Beth made all the arrangements. We forfeited several weeks' rent to make our escape.

146

This was "not like" me; it was an early symptom. The old Joseph was inclined to be even-tempered. Of course, I have known for a long time that we have inherited a mad fear of being slighted or scorned, an exacerbated "honor." It is not quite the duelist's madness of a hundred years ago. But we are a people of tantrums, nevertheless; a word exchanged in a movie or in some other crowd, and we are ready to fly at one another. Only, in my opinion, our rages are deceptive; we are too ignorant and spiritually poor to know that we fall on the "enemy" from confused motives of love and loneliness. Perhaps, also, self-contempt. But for the most part, loneliness.

Iva, though she concealed it at the time, was surprised; she later told me so. This was a rebellion against my own principle. It alarmed me; and the treasons I saw at the Servatius party were partly mine, as I was forced at the time to acknowledge.

February 8

THE thermometer still wavers around zero. The cold is part of the general malignancy. I think of its fitness, as the war news comes in. You are bound to respect such a winter for its unmitigated wintriness. "I tax not you, you elements, with unkindness," Lear yells. He invites their "horrible pleasure." He is quite right, too.

February 9

I FEEL I am a sort of human grenade whose pin has been withdrawn. I know I am going to explode and I am continually anticipating the time, with a prayerful despair crying "Boom!" but always prematurely.

The sense in which Goethe was right: Continued life means expectation. Death is the abolition of choice. The more choice is limited, the closer we are to death. The greatest cruelty is to curtail expectations without taking away life completely. A life term in prison is like that. So is citizenship in some countries. The best solution would be to live as if the ordinary expectations had not been removed, not from day to day, blindly. But that requires immense self-mastery.

February 10

STEIDLER has been here twice in the past week. He seems to find me congenial. Which means, I venture to say, that he assumes we are in the same boat. I would not mind the visits nor the assumption if it were not for the fact that I still feel, at the end of a few hours, that we are practicing some terrible vice together. We smoke and talk. He tells me about his adventures on the Coast, in the hospital, and about his present affairs. I have learned that he receives ten dollars a week from his mother and five more from his brother. Budgeting himself strictly, he manages to live on twelve, and the rest he spends on horses. Occasionally he wins, but he estimates that he has lost four or five thousand dollars in the last ten years.

He does not care to speak of such things. He mentions them only in passing. He is not at all blind to their meanness. He simply takes it for granted that they are bound to be mean. There is no dignity anywhere, nothing but absurd falsehood. It is no use trying to bury this falsehood.

148

It would only rise again, to laugh at you. He says this in so many words. When you ask him about the details of his life, he gives you a look of surprise. He is not offended; but that such admittedly shabby things should interest you surprises him genuinely. He would rather tell you the story of a bet lost or won, a fraud, a clever reply, an interesting reprisal, an insulting letter he sent a creditor, a love affair.

Last time, he told me a tortuous, long story about his attempts to conquer a Norwegian girl who lives in his hotel —Laird Towers. He had met her on Thanksgiving Day, in the lobby. Hartly, the night clerk, had given him the wink, and so he set about the siege. She didn't like him, of course. It always started that way. Around Christmas she started to look at him more encouragingly. Unfortunately he was pinched, had no money. It came to his notice that other men in the hotel were making headway with her. Hartly kept him only too well informed. "He didn't have to tell me. I could see from the beginning she was dynamite."

During the holiday he made a killing on a little pony called Spotted Cow; it romped home two lengths ahead of the field. He asked the Norwegian out to the Fiorenza for a spaghetti dinner.

"I thought we were getting along pretty well, and when she excused herself for a few minutes at eleven o'clock I sucked tranquilly at my Perfecto Queen and said to myself, 'It's in the bag.' She had been drinking Pink Ladies, and she was running over. She went away unevenly. I waited. At eleven-fifteen there was no sign of her, so I thought, 'Maybe she's sick in the powder room?' And I went to get the matron to have a look. But I got as far as the orchestra, and there was the girl sitting in some guy's lap.

149

Well, I tried not to seem injured, and I suggested that it was getting late, we ought to start for home. But she wouldn't get up, and I didn't want to make a fool of myself. So I beat it."

He sent her letters for two weeks. She did not answer. When he had almost spent the last of his winnings, he met her in the Loop. It was her birthday, she said. He offered to buy her a drink. They went to the Blackhawk and had four. By-and-by a few handsome, well-dressed fellows came up to the bar, one in a naval uniform. Alf rose, paid for the drinks, put the rest of his change on the table, and said, "I know when I'm outclassed." Without a cent in his pocket, he walked back to the hotel.

The story wandered to its inevitable conclusion—the conquest, with the Norwegian learning at last to distinguish between his superior worth and his appearance, giving in to him jokingly and condescendingly while drunk, and then finding that she had more than she had bargained for, et cetera. It would have shocked Alf to know that he was boring me, for he considers himself a first-class entertainer. Any night club would be lucky to have him. He can be original in several dialects. But I would rather not be entertained. I welcomed him at first, and I still rather like him. But I wish he would not come so often.

February 11

MYRON ADLER is back; he called this morning and said he was coming to visit me as soon as he could break away. Robbie Stillman has come in after six months in Officers' School. He has become an engineer. His business will be

150

to construct airfields. Army life, he says, is not hard when you accustom yourself to discipline. You have to learn to submit.

His brother Ben is somewhere in the interior of Brazil. He hasn't been heard from since October.

February 14

No SIGN of Myron or of anyone else. Even Steidler seems to have deserted me. Two days without visitors, talk, interest. Nothing. A pair of perfect blanks punched out of the calendar. It's enough to make one pray for change, merely change, *any* change, to make one worship experience-in-itself. If I were a little less obstinate, I would confess failure and say that I do not know what to do with my freedom.

February 15

LETTER from Abt, rich in Washington gossip and explanations of current policy. Why we act as we do in North Africa and toward Spain, De Gaulle, Martinique. It amuses me to catch the subtle pride with which he mentions his familiarity with important figures. (I assume they are important in official circles; I have never heard of them.)

February 16

OLD MRS. KIEFER is, as Mrs. Bartlett puts it, "sinking PDQ. She can drag along for a week or two weeks, but this"

—in dumb show she sank a needle into her arm—"can't keep her going forever." We walk through the house gingerly. Captain Briggs no longer goes out for his evening smoke. It is too cold.

February 17

IVA AND I have grown closer. Lately she has been remarkably free from the things I once disliked so greatly. She does not protest against this rooming-house life; she seems less taken up with clothes; she does not criticize my appearance or seem disturbed because my underwear is in such a state that in dressing I often put my leg through the wrong hole. And the rest: the cheap restaurant food we eat, our lack of pocket money. Yet she is as far as ever from what I once desired to make her. I am afraid she has no capacity for that. But now I am struck by the arrogance with which I set people apart into two groups: those with worth-while ideas and those without them.

February 18

YESTERDAY, passing the bush on which I found the stolen socks, I saw a second pair. Vanaker must have taken several. I pointed them out to Iva as we passed this evening. She, too, recognized them. She says we should find a way of showing that we are aware of the theft.

February 19

ANOTHER letter from John Pearl, asking for news of Chicago. As if I had any to give him. I know no more about it

152

than he does. He wanted to go to New York but now sounds nostalgic and writes with deep distaste about his "peeling environment."

"Peeling furniture, peeling walls, posters, bridges, everything is peeling and scaling in South Brooklyn. We moved here to save money, but I'm afraid we'd better start saving ourselves and move out again. It's the treelessness, as much as anything, that hurts me. The unnatural, too-human deadness."

I'm sorry for him. I know what he feels, the kind of terror, and the danger he sees of the lack of the human in the too-human. We find it, as others before us have found it in the last two hundred years, and we bolt for "Nature." It happens in all cities. And cities are "natural," too. He thinks he would be safer in Chicago, where he grew up. Sentimentality! He doesn't mean Chicago. It is no less inhuman. He means his father's house and the few blocks adjacent. Away from these and a few other islands, he would be just as unsafe.

But even such a letter buoys me up. It gives me a sense of someone else's recognition of the difficult, the sorrowful, in what to others is merely neutral, the environment.

February 22

IF I HAD *Tu As Raison Aussi* with me today, I could tell him that the highest "ideal construction" is the one that unlocks the imprisoning self.

We struggle perpetually to free ourselves. Or, to put it somewhat differently, while we seem so intently and even

153

desperately to be holding on to ourselves, we would far rather give ourselves away. We do not know how. So, at times, we throw ourselves away. When what we really want is to stop living so exclusively and vainly for our own sake, impure and unknowing, turning inward and self-fastened.

The quest, I am beginning to think, whether it be for money, for notoriety, reputation, increase of pride, whether it leads us to thievery, slaughter, sacrifice, the quest is one and the same. All the striving is for one end. I do not entirely understand this impulse. But it seems to me that its final end is the desire for pure freedom. We are all drawn toward the same craters of the spirit—to know what we are and what we are for, to know our purpose, to seek grace. And, if the quest is the same, the differences in our personal histories, which hitherto meant so much to us, become of minor importance.

February 24

HEAVY snowfall last night. I skipped lunch, to avoid wetting my feet three times in one day.

February 27

ONLY twenty-two days until spring. I swear that on the twenty-first I will change from my winter clothes and, no matter what the weather is like, even if there is a blizzard, I will walk through Jackson Park hatless and gloveless.

ADLER showed up, at last. He came in the middle of the afternoon, when I was not expecting him. Mrs. Bartlett had let him in and, I gathered, cautioned him against making noise, for when I saw him on the landing he was walking on tiptoe.

"Who's sick, Joseph?" he asked with a look back at Mrs. Bartlett, who was softly monitoring the street door. The pneumatic arm that shut it was out of commission.

"The landlady. She's very old."

"Oh-oh! And I rang twice," he said guiltily. I motioned him into the room. He was much disturbed. "Do you think I shouldn't have?"

"Everybody rings the bell. How do you suppose people get in here? Don't worry about it."

Adler was very spruce, in a wide-shouldered coat and a tweed suit, new style, without cuffs. He looked fresh and healthy. His hat with its blunt crown was new also, and very stiff. It had cut a red line into his forehead.

"Sit down, Mike," I said, clearing a chair for him. "You've never been here before, have you."

"No," he said, and he inspected the room, hardly able to conceal his surprise. "I thought you had an apartment."

"Our old apartment? We gave that up long ago."

"I know. But I thought you were living in one of those furnished flats."

"It's snug here."

It's true, the room did not look its best. Marie had cleaned it, after a fashion, but the coverlet was wrinkled, the towels on the rack looked as though they had not been changed for weeks, Iva's shoes under the bed showed a crooked line of heels. The day, too, was not altogether favorable. The sky hung low, loose, with blemished clouds that spotted the street from curb to horizon with shadows. And the weather intruded into the room. The walls above the radiator were as dirty as the snow in the yard, and the linen—the dresser scarf and the towels—seemed spun out of the same material as the sky.

"You've been here since last fall, haven't you?" he said.

"Since June," I corrected. "Nearly nine months."

"Is it that long?" he said unbelievingly.

"Almost the tenth."

"And there's nothing new?"

"Do I look as if I were concealing something new?" I exclaimed. This startled him. I relented and said, "Nothing's been changed."

"You don't have to take my head off because I ask."

"Well, you see, everybody asks the same question. You get tired of answering. I have this routine to do, over and over and over. Questions are fired at me, and I'm supposed to scramble like a retriever, fetching answers. Why? Well, if I don't I won't get a certificate of politeness. Hell!"

Adler's color changed, so that the dent the hat had made above his eyes showed white.

"You're not very generous, Joseph."

I did not reply. I looked down at the street, the yards, at the masses of snow like dirty suds.

"You've changed a lot. Everybody says so," he went on more calmly.

"Who?"

"Why, people who know you."

"I haven't seen anyone. You mean that business in the Arrow."

"No, no, that was only one case."

"I wasn't all wrong in the Arrow."

"You're becoming bad-tempered."

"Good! I am. Now, what do you want me to do? Did you come to tell me that I was bad-tempered?"

"I came to see you."

"That's mighty handsome of you."

In rising anger, he stared at me, his mouth pursing. I began to laugh, and at that he rose and made for the door. I pulled him back.

"Here, don't go, Mike. Don't be a fool. Sit down. I wasn't laughing at you. I just happened to think that I'm always hoping a visitor will come. When he does come, I insult him."

"I'm glad you see it," he muttered.

"I do see it. Certainly I see it."

"Why jump on people? Good Lord. . . ."

"It just turns out that way. As the French say, *'c'est plus fort que moi.'* Does that prove that I'm not happy to see you? Not at all. It's not really a contradiction. It's natural. Almost a welcome, one might say."

"What a welcome," he said; but he seemed somewhat mollified.

"I see people so seldom, I've forgotten how to act. I don't want to be bad-tempered. But, on the other hand, the people who accuse me of that haven't exactly been beating the woods in searching parties. Things have changed, Mike. You're busy and prosperous—best of luck to you. But we may as well be honest about this."

"Now what's coming?"

"We're temporarily in different classes, and it has an

157

effect on us. Oh, yes, it does. For instance, the way you took in this room, the way you looked around . . ."

"I don't get what you're driving at," he said in perplexity.

"You get it. You're not stupid. Don't act like Abt, saying, 'I can't follow you.' We *are* in different classes. The very difference in our clothes shows it."

"What a change," he said. "What a difference." He shook his head in regret and reminiscence. "You used to be an absolutely reasonable guy."

"I was sociable."

"Now you sound so wild."

The subject would bear no more discussion. "How was your trip?" I asked.

He stayed all afternoon and tried to make an old-time visit of it. But, after such a start, that was impossible. He was hale and businesslike, wanting no further trouble with me. So, haltingly, we covered a variety of subjects—public opinion, the war, our friends, and again the war. Minna Servatius was about to have a baby. I had heard something about that. George Hayza was expecting a naval commission. I had heard about that, also. There was a rumor that Abt was to be sent to Puerto Rico. Adler said he would find out definitely next week. He was going East.

"You see, Joseph," he said at four o'clock, "there's nothing we'd rather do than come and chat with you as we used to. But that's all gone now. We're busy. You'll be busy yourself, one of these days, busier than you'd ever care to be."

"Yes, things change. *C'est la guerre. C'est la vie.* Good old punch lines."

"What a Frenchman you've become."

158

"Say, do you remember Jeff Forman?"

"I read about him. He got a posthumous medal. Poor Jeff."

"*C'est la vie.*"

"That's not funny," said Adler disapprovingly.

"I was just quoting from the last war. I didn't mean to be funny. We can't do anything for Jeff, anyway, by pulling a long face. Can we?"

"I guess not."

And, in this manner, the visit drew to a close.

"When you're in the East," I said, "look up John Pearl. He needs a breath of Chicago. You ought to stop in and see him, I think." I added, with a laugh, "You might run into another Chicagoan in New York. Steidler. He hasn't been here for a long time. My guess is he took his brother's money."

"Alf?"

"His brother wrote a song and wanted Alf to take it to New York for him. He's looking for a publisher."

"If I thought there was a chance of running into Steidler, I wouldn't see Pearl. Why isn't he in the Army?"

"He's leaving the war to us normal bastards, he says."

"You've been seeing him. I wouldn't. He's not your kind. Stay away from him."

"Oh, oh, now! He can't hurt me. Besides, beggars can't be choosers. I'm quoting my niece. Lines addressed to me."

"Really? Amos's girl?"

"Oh, yes," I said. "She's quite grown-up."

And so Myron left, plainly dissatisfied with the results of his call. I went down with him into the street. We tramped to the corner over the discolored snow. While we waited to cross to the car stop, Myron offered to lend me money.

"No," I said, and gently moved his hand away. "We have enough. We get along very well." He put the money back in his purse. "Here comes the Fifty-five car. Better run for it." He gave me a final pat on the shoulder and sprinted across, whipping off his hat as he went, to hail the motorman.

March 3

DOLLY phoned to ask us to dinner next Sunday. I said we had already accepted another invitation.

The Farsons have returned from Detroit, their training over. Susie dropped in to see Iva at the library. The baby had grippe; not a serious case. They have decided to send her to Farson's parents in Dakota, while they themselves go to California to work in an aircraft factory. Susie is in good spirits and is delighted at going to California. Walter missed the child more than she did. They intend to send for her as soon as they settle down.

March 5

THERE is a woman who goes through the neighborhood with a shopping bag full of Christian Science literature. She stops young men and talks to them. Since we cover the same streets, I encounter her often, but she keeps forgetting me, and it is not always possible to avoid her. For her part, she has no understanding of the art of stopping people. She rushes to block you with her body clumsily, almost despairingly. If she misses, she is incapable of following up, and if you succeed in eluding her—if you want to elude her, if you have the heart to continue doing so time after time—she can only stand, defeated, staring after you. If you do stop, she takes out her tracts and begins to speak.

She must be nearly fifty, a tall and rather heavy woman. But she has a sickly face—thin chapped lips, square yellow teeth, recessed brown eyes which you vainly read and reread for a meaning. The skin under her eyes reveals tiny, purple, intersecting vessels. Her hair is grizzled, her forehead is broad and blazed with a scar that resembles an old bullet wound. She speaks in a rapid whisper. I listen and wait for an opportunity to disengage myself.

Her speech is memorized. I watch her chapped lips through which the words come, so dry and rapid, often pronounced as though she did not understand them. The words, the words trip her fervor. She says she has talked to many young men who are about to go to war, who are going to face destruction. Her duty is to tell them that the means of saving themselves is at hand if they want it. Nothing but belief can save them. She has spoken to many others who have come back from the jungles and the fox holes, surviving the maiming fire only because of their faith. The doctrines of the science are not superstitions but true science, as has been proved. She has a pamphlet of testimonials, written by soldiers who know how to believe.

Meanwhile her face and the hard brown shells of her eyes do not change. She writes on a pad while she is talk-ing. When she is done, she hands you the paper. It con-tains the names and addresses of the various churches and

Reading Rooms in the neighborhood. And that is all. She is now at your mercy. She waits. Her lips come together like the seams of a badly sewn baseball. Her face burns and wastes under your eyes; the very hairs at the corners of her mouth seem already to have shriveled. When, after a long pause, you do not offer to buy one of the tracts, she walks away, her run-down shoes knocking on the pavement, her load swinging as heavily as a bag of sand.

Yesterday she was sicker than ever. Her skin was the color of brick dust; her breath was sour. In her old tam that half-covered the scar, and her rough, blackened coat buttoned to the neck, she suggested the figure of a minor political leader in exile, unwelcome, shabby, burning with a double fever.

She addressed me in the usual whisper.

"You spoke to me two weeks ago," I said.

"Oh. Well . . . I have a pamphlet here about the beliefs of Science. And testimony by . . ." She groped. Then I felt sure it had taken her these extra minutes to hear what I had said. I was about to ask, "Don't you feel well?" but, from fear of offending her, I held back. Her lips were more badly chapped than I had ever seen them. On the protruding point of the upper, a scab had formed.

"The men from Bataan," I said. "The one you told me about last time."

"Yes. Five cents."

"Which would you rather sell me, this or the other?"

She held out the one with the veterans' testimony.

"You're going to the Army, too? This is the one." She took the coin and slid it into her pocket, which was edged with a sort of charred fur. Then she said, "You're going to read it."

162

I don't know what prevented me from saying yes.

"I'll try to find time for it," I said.

"No, then you aren't going to. I'll take it back."

"I want to keep it."

"You can have your nickel. Here it is back."

I refused it. She shook her lowered head as a child might, sorrowing.

"I'm going to read this," I said. I thrust the pamphlet into my coat.

"You mustn't be proud," she said. She misunderstood my smile. At that moment she looked very grimly sick; though her eyes retained their hard brown centers, the whites had lost their moisture and, in each, a dry streak of vein had appeared.

"I give you my word, I'll read it."

She had held out her hand with a stiff movement of her arm to receive the pamphlet back. Now her hand went back to her side. For a while, as I watched her face with its small chin and large, marred forehead, I thought she had lost all sense of her whereabouts. But she soon picked up her bag and walked away.

March 10

RAIN, yesterday, that turned into snow overnight. Cold again.

March 12

RECEIVED a note from Kitty, asking why I hadn't stopped by lately. I tore it up before Iva could see it. I haven't thought about Kitty lately. I can't be missing her much.

SUNDAY was warm, hinting at spring. We visited the Almstadts. In the evening I walked in Humboldt Park, around
the lagoon, across the bridge to the boathouse where we
used to discuss *Man and Superman* and where, even
earlier, with John Pearl, I pelted the lovers on the benches
below the balcony with crab apples. The air had a brackish
smell of wet twigs and moldering brown seed pods, but it
was soft, and through it rose, with indistinct but thrilling
reality, meadows and masses of trees, blue and rufous
stone and reflecting puddles. After dark, as I was returning, a warm, thick rain began falling with no more warning than a gasp. I ran.

ANOTHER Talk with the Spirit of Alternatives.

"I can't tell you how much I appreciate your coming
back."

"Yes?"

"And I'd like to apologize."

"That's not necessary."

"And explain."

"I'm used to abuse. It's in the line of duty."

"But I want to say—I'm a chopped and shredded man."

"Easily exasperated."

"You know how it is. I'm harried, pushed, badgered,
worried, nagged, heckled. . . ."

"By what? Conscience?"

"Well, it's a kind of conscience. I don't respect it as I

do my own. It's the public part of me. It goes deep. It's the world internalized, in short."

"What does it want?"

"It wants me to stop living this way. It's prodding me to the point where I shall no longer care what happens to me."

"When you will give up?"

"Yes, that's it."

"Well, why don't you do that? Here you are preparing yourself for further life. . . ."

"And you think I should quit."

"The vastest experience of your time doesn't have much to do with living. Have you thought of preparing yourself for that?"

"Dying? You're angry because I threw the orange peel."

"I mean it."

"What's there to prepare for? You can't prepare for anything but living. You don't have to know anything to be dead. You have merely to learn that you will one day be dead. I learned that long ago. No, we're both joking. I know you didn't mean that."

"Whatever I mean, you get it twisted up."

"No. But I'm half-serious. You want me to worship the anti-life. I'm saying that there are no values outside life. There is nothing outside life."

"We're not going to argue about that. But you have impossible aims. Everybody else is dangling, too. When and if you survive you can start setting yourself straight."

"But, *Tu As Raison Aussi*, this is important. And what's the rush? There are important questions here. There's the whole question of my real and not superficial business as a man."

"Oh, now, really. What makes you think you can handle these things by yourself?"

"With whom can I start but myself?"

"Nah, foolishness!"

"No, but the questions have to be answered."

"Aren't you tired of this room?"

"Weary of it."

"Wouldn't you rather be in motion, outside, somewhere?"

"Sometimes I think nothing could be better."

"Do you really think you can handle all your own questions?"

"I'm not always sure."

"Then your position is weak indeed."

"Look, there are moments when I feel it would be wisest to go to my draft board and ask to have my number called at once."

"Well?"

"I would be denying my inmost feelings if I said I wanted to be by-passed and spared from knowing what the rest of my generation is undergoing. I don't want to be humped protectively over my life. I am neither so corrupt nor so hard-boiled that I can savor my life only when it is in danger of extinction. But, on the other hand, its value here in this room is decreasing day by day. Soon it may become distasteful to me."

"There, you see it yourself."

"Wait, I'm collecting all my feelings and my misgivings. I am somewhat afraid of the vanity of thinking that I can make my own way toward clarity. But it is even

166

more important to know whether I can claim the right to preserve myself in this flood of death that has carried off so many like me, muffling them and bearing them down and down, minds untried and sinews useless—so much debris. It is appropriate to ask whether I have any business withholding myself from the same fate."

"And the answer?"

"I recall Spinoza's having written that no virtue could be considered greater than that of trying to preserve oneself."

"At all costs, oneself?"

"You don't get it. *Oneself*. He didn't say one's life. He said oneself. You see the difference?"

"No."

"He knew that everyone must die. He does not instruct us to graft new glands or to eat carp's intestine in order to live three hundred years. We cannot make ourselves immortal. We can decide only what is for us to decide. The rest is beyond our power. In short, he did not mean preservation of the animal."

"He was speaking of the soul, the spirit?"

"The mind. Anyway, the self that we must govern. Chance must not govern it, incident must not govern it. It is our humanity that we are responsible for it, our dignity, our freedom. Now, in a case like mine, I can't ask to be immune from the war. I have to take my risks for survival as I did, formerly, against childhood diseases and all the dangers and accidents through which I nevertheless managed to become Joseph. Do you follow that?"

"It's impossible, every bit of it."

"We are afraid to govern ourselves. Of course. It is so hard. We soon want to give up our freedom. It is not even real freedom, because it is not accompanied by comprehension. It is only a preliminary condition of freedom. But we hate it. And soon we run out, we choose a master, roll over on our backs and ask for the leash."

"Ah," said *Tu As Raison Aussi.*

"That's what happens. It isn't love that gives us weariness of life. It's our inability to be free."

"And you're afraid it may happen to you?"

"I am."

"Ideally, how would you like to regard the war, then?"

"I would like to see it as an incident."

"Only an incident?"

"A very important one; perhaps the most important that has ever occurred. But, still, an incident. Is the real nature of the world changed by it? No. Will it decide, ultimately, the major issues of existence? No. Will it rescue us spiritually? Still no. Will it set us free in the crudest sense, that is, merely to be allowed to breathe and eat? I hope so, but I can't be sure that it will. In no *essential* way is it crucial—if you accept my meaning of essential. Suppose I had a complete vision of life. I would not then be affected essentially. The war can destroy me physically. That it can do. But so can bacteria. I must be concerned with them, naturally. I must take account of them. They can obliterate me. But as long as I am alive, I must follow my destiny in spite of them."

"Then only one question remains."

"What?"

"Whether you have a separate destiny. Oh, you're a shrewd wiggler," said *Tu As Raison Aussi.* "But I've been waiting for you to cross my corner. Well, what do you say?"

168

I think I must have grown pale.

"I'm not ready to answer. I have nothing to say to that now."

"How seriously you take this," cried *Tu As Raison Aussi*. "It's only a discussion. The boy's teeth are chattering. Do you have a chill?" He ran to get a blanket from the bed.

I said faintly, "I'm all right." He tucked the blanket round me and, in great concern, wiped my forehead and sat by me until nightfall.

March 17

WASHED and shaved and rode downtown to meet Iva. I walked from Van Buren to Randolph Street on the park side of Michigan Boulevard, past the Art Institute lions and the types enjoying cigarettes in the watery sunlight and the shimmering exhaust gas, after a long winter in the interior. The leached grass is beginning to take on a weak yellow in some spots, and there are a few green stubs of iris showing, nearly provoking me into saying: "Go back, you don't know what you're getting into."

March 18

No MAIL in the box. Except for the paper that lies scrambled over the bed and the passing of an occasional soldier or military truck in the street, we are insulated here from the war. If we chose, we could pull the blinds and fling the paper into the hall for Marie to gather up, casting it out utterly.

NEVERTHELESS, spring begins on Sunday. I always experience a rush of feeling on the twenty-first of March. "Thank heavens, I've made it again!"

I CARRIED out my threat and walked in the park in my spring coat, and suffered for it. It was a slaty, windy day with specks of snow sliding through the trees. I stopped at a tavern on the way back and treated myself to a glass of rye.

Because of Mrs. Kiefer, we could not listen to the Philharmonic in the afternoon, so, after lolling on the bed eating oranges and reading the magazines and the Sunday features, we set out at four o'clock for the movies. As we stood buttoning our coats in the hall, in came Vanaker in his bowler and polka-dot muffler, carrying a bag in which bottles rattled.

"*Sacre du Vin Temps,*" I smiled.

We had a late dinner and turned in at eleven. Vanaker coughed boozily all through the night and awakened me near dawn, banging doors and making his customary splash.

MR. RINGHOLM moved out last week. His room has been rented by a Chinese girl. Her trunk came from Interna-

tional House this morning. I read the tag—Miss Olive
Ling.

A PICTURE postcard of Times Square from Steidler on the
hall table this morning, with the message: "I am thinking
of stopping here indefinitely." Probably he has already
run through his brother's money.

Mrs. Bartlett was beckoning to me as I was going upstairs; she asked if I would help her carry up a cot from
the storeroom. She was going to sleep downstairs with Mrs.
Kiefer henceforward. I descended with her. She had
already pulled the folding bed from the musty wood closet
across half the length of the cellar. In the hot light of the
furnace grating, her face, the face of an overgrown country girl, with large, slightly protruding front teeth that
lent it a kind of innocence, was rather prepossessing. I was
glad she had asked me to help her. "Take it from the bottom, that's it. Now. Up. I'll go first." She puffed out her instructions. "Lord, they should make these contraptions of
wood." We struggled up with it and carried it into the
room where the old woman lay, her white hair arranged in
a fringe that nearly met her brow. Kitty wore hers that
way. Mrs. Kiefer's cheeks were collapsed and her face was
moist. It reminded me of a loaf, before the baker puts it in
the oven, smeared with white of egg. I went into the hall
quickly.

"Thanks," Mrs. Bartlett whispered loudly from the
dark square inlet of the lower hall. "Thanks loads." And
her teeth shone up at me good-naturedly.

171

MORNING began dull and numb, then brightened miraculously. I tramped the neighborhood. It was warm in earnest at one o'clock, with a tide of summer odors from the stockyards and the sewers (odors so old in the city-bred memory they are no longer repugnant).

In the upper light there were small fair heads of cloud turning. The streets, in contrast, looked burnt out; the chimneys pointed heavenward in openmouthed exhaustion. The turf, intersected by sidewalk, was bedraggled with the whole winter's deposit of deadwood, match cards, cigarettes, dogmire, rubble. The grass behind the palings and wrought-iron frills was still yellow, although in many places the sun had already succeeded in shaking it into livelier green. And the houses, their doors and windows open, drawing in the freshness, were like old drunkards or consumptives taking a cure. Indeed, the atmosphere of the houses, the brick and plaster and wood, the asphalt, the pipes and gratings and hydrants outside, and the interiors—curtains and bedding, furniture, striped wallpaper and horny ceilings, the ravaged throats of entry halls and the smeary blind eyes of windows—this atmosphere, I say, was one of an impossible hope, the hope of an impossible rejuvenation.

Nevertheless, a few large birds, robins and grackles, appeared in the trees, and some of the trees themselves were beginning to bud. The large rough cases cracked at the tip, showing sticky green within, and one tree was erupting in crude red along its higher branches. I even saw in a brick passageway an untimely butterfly, out of place both

172

in the season and the heart of the city, and somehow alien to the whole condition of the century.

And there were children, on skates and bicycles, or scouting along the curbs for salvage, playing ball or hopping after bits of glass in chalk squares. There was a showing of ice-cream cones, despite the inroads of rationing, and a sprinkling of spring articles, though infants still wore wool leggings and the elderly were fully buttoned and somberly hatted. Sound was magnified and vision enlarged, red was rough and bloody, yellow clear but thin, blue increasingly warm. All but the sun's own yellow that ripped up the middle of each street, making two of everything that stood—object and shadow.

The room, when I returned to it, was as full of this yellow as an egg is of yolk. In honor of the transformation in the weather, I decided to clean up for supper and, as I stood changing my shirt in the unaccustomed brilliance of the mirror, I observed new folds near my mouth and, around my eyes and the root of my nose, marks that had not been there a year before. It is not pleasant to find such changes. But, tying my tie, I shrugged them off as inevitable, the price of experience, an outlay that had better be made ungrudgingly, since it was bound in any case to be collected.

March 26

WE HAD been short of funds for several days. Iva received her check on Thursday but, instead of cashing it, brought it home and left it in my bureau drawer with instructions to take it to the bank. The reason she gave for not taking it to the currency exchange downtown, as usual, was that this week she was working evenings in the reference room and did not want to risk carrying such a sum home. She had heard rumors of holdups.

But I refused to go to the near-by bank with it.

I had had several experiences there with Iva's checks. I had been turned down twice last fall; once because I had insufficient identification and, again, when the vice president, looking from my cards to me and from me to my cards, once more said, "How do I know you're this person?"

I replied, "You can take my word for it."

He did not smile; I did not rate a smile. But the indications were that under different circumstances—say, if I had been clean-shaven and my shirt had not been frayed, or if bits of torn lining had not shown from my coat sleeve —my words would have evoked one. He sat back seriously and considered the check. He was a plump man, about thirty years old. *Mr. Frink* stood in brass letters on the wooden block at his finger tips; his clean sandy hair was already fading back in two broad freckled arches. He would be bald within a few years, his bare head spotted with those blackish freckles.

"That's a city check, Mr. . . . Frink, is it?" He acknowledged the name. "Certainly there isn't much risk in accepting a city check."

"If you know who the endorser is," said Mr. Frink, unclasping his pen and shuffling professionally through my cards with one hand. "Now, where do you work, Joseph?"

In such cases I generally answer that I am working at Inter-American; it is an impressive reference and not a

174

wholly false one; Mr. Mallender would stand behind me, I am sure. But because he addressed me by my first name, as though I were an immigrant or a young boy or a Negro, I said—dismissing diplomacy without a second thought—"I'm not working anywhere now. I'm waiting for my draft call."

Of course, that finished my prospects. He immediately said, reassembling his pen, that the bank did not make a practice of cashing the checks of nondepositors. He was sorry.

I gathered up my cards.

"Here, you'll notice that I have a surname, Frink," I said, holding one of the cards up. "I realize it's difficult to deal with the public efficiently and still politely. All the same, people don't like to be treated like suspicious characters and patronized at the same time." I made an effort to control myself as I said this, but when I ended I saw that several bystanders were looking at me. Frink seemed more alarmed by my tone than by my words. I am not sure he understood them, but he faced me as if to show that in him I menaced a courageous man. It was a foolish incident. A year ago I would have accepted his explanation politely and have moved away.

Too late, I stuffed the check into my pocket and, without another glance at Frink, I walked off.

Naturally, when I came to explain my reasons for not going back to the bank I could not tell Iva all of the story. I said merely that I had been turned down twice and did not want it to happen a third time.

"Oh, now, Joseph, why should there be any trouble about it? I've cashed hundreds of checks."

"But they turned me down. And it's as embarrassing as anything can be."

"I'll give you my identification disk. All you have to do is show it."

"I won't do it," I said.

"Then go somewhere else. Go to the currency exchange, the one near Lake-Park Avenue."

"Before they do business with you there, they make you fill out a long, long form. They want to know everything . . . where you're employed. If I say I'm not working, they'll laugh me out of the place. 'What? Not working? Anybody can get a job these days.' No, I won't go. Why don't you cash it downtown?"

"I'm not going to carry all that money late at night. It's out of the question. If I'm held up, we'll have to borrow from your father or mine, or from Amos."

"Have you ever been held up?"

"You know I haven't been."

"Then why have you suddenly begun to worry about it?"

"You read two papers a day, from front to back. You ought to know. There've been holdups."

"Pooh! Two people. And not near here, either, but miles away, up on Sixtieth Street."

"Joseph, are you or are you not going to cash this check?"

"No," I said.

Perhaps I should have told her about my experience with Mr. Frink. Then, at any rate, the reason for my re-fusal would have been clear. But she would have been just as angry. She would have been in the right, hence very severe. And, although she would have excused me from re-

176

turning to the bank, it is likely that she would have made things hard for me in other ways. Therefore I said nothing about it.

"All right," she said. "The check will stay in the drawer. We won't eat."

"I can stand it if you can."

"I'm quite sure you can stand it. You'd have to be as weak as . . . as Gandhi before you'd give in. You're mulish."

"I don't think you have much right to call *me* mulish. As if you weren't twice as stubborn. I don't feel like fighting about it, Iva. That's the truth. I can't go. I have my reasons."

"You always have reasons, and with principles. Capital *P*," she said, tracing the letter on the air with her finger.

"Don't be a fool. Do you think it's pleasant to walk up to a bank window and be turned away?"

"Are you sure you didn't get into a fight of some kind over there?" she asked shrewdly. "I have a suspicion. . . ."

"Your suspicion is wrong. You always jump to the worst conclusion you can think of. If I wanted to do that . . . well."

"Well?"

"I'd say plenty."

"For example."

"You want me to do all kinds of things I was never expected to do before. Now, why this sudden fear of being robbed? I could say you trumped it up. You've been carrying money for years, and larger amounts, too. Suddenly it frightens you. Well, the reason is that you want me to run errands."

177

"Errands?"

"Yes."

"Let's have the whole thing. You must have a principle hidden somewhere."

"Don't make fun of me, Iva. Things have changed. You've become the breadwinner, and whether you know it or not you resent the fact that I stay at home while you go to work every morning. So you think up things for me to do. You want me to earn my keep."

"Of all the things to say." Iva grew white. "I never know what you're going to do. You go along quietly and all of a sudden you come out with something, something . . . it's a terrible thing to say."

"It happens to be true."

"It isn't."

"You aren't aware of it yourself, Iva. I'm not blaming you. But you are the provider. After all, it's bound to have an effect on you. . . ."

"*You're* having an effect on me. You're making me sick."

"No, listen to me, Iva," I persisted. "I'm not making this up. I see it and feel it constantly. I know you don't want it to be true, but it is, nevertheless. You take it for granted that I have nothing to do. Every morning you leave half a dozen orders for me. And just a while ago you mentioned that I read the papers."

"How you twist everything around," Iva said bitterly.

"Not as much as you think."

She reached for her handkerchief.

"Just as soon as I take up a subject you don't like, you begin to cry. Don't you want me to say anything about this?"

178

"I can depend on you not to keep quiet when you think you're being wronged. You think everybody's trying to take advantage of you. Even I . . ." and she could not continue.

"This is what happens whenever I bring up a disagreeable subject. I'm just trying to point out something I don't think you're aware of. I thought you wanted me to tell you such things. You never used to object."

"You never used to be so mean and ugly-tempered. You . . ." Now she broke off and began to cry.

"Jesus, Jesus! Can we never have a talk without a flood of tears? It's easy for you to cry. But what can I do? I'm getting out. I should get out for good. This is no sort of life. Stop that crying!" She did try to stop; her efforts ended in a grotesque sound brought up from her throat. She rolled over on the bed and concealed her face from me.

Up to this point in our quarrel, Vanaker had given several protesting coughs, and now I heard his footsteps in the hall as he went to the bathroom and then, just as I had expected, the sound through the open door, of his splash, growing louder as he trained his stream to the center where the water was deepest. Shuffling off my slippers, I stepped out stealthily and advanced on his silhouette. When he turned, hearing me, my foot was already in the door. He had neglected to turn on the light, but I could see perfectly clearly by the small bulb outside. In the semidark, a look of panic sprang to his moist, drunken eyes, and he pushed against me, but I was solidly planted on the threshold.

"Took you in it at last, didn't I!" I exclaimed. "You damned old whisky-head. By God, I've had more than I can stand. There's a dying woman downstairs, and you slam around here all boozed up, raising as much hell as you please."

"Joseph," Iva called in a strained voice. She had come into the hall. "Joseph!"

"It's about time I told him off. I'm fed up. Completely. Do you think you can get away with it forever?" I shouted at him. "Kicking up a racket in the middle of the night, hoicking, forcing us to listen when you make your business, you crowbait? Didn't you ever learn to shut the door when you went to the toilet? By God, you kept it shut tight enough the night you set the house on fire!"

"Mister!" I heard Mrs. Bartlett cry from the stairs. A door closed. Iva had gone back into the room, and similar sounds told me that either Mrs. Fessman or Miss Ling had come out to listen and then had quickly retreated. There were further noises from Captain Briggs' apartment. I heard a man's tread in the passage above.

"And stealing, besides," I went on.

"Steal?" he said weakly.

"Stealing," I repeated. "Then going before the priest at St. Thomas the Apostle and standing in my socks and stinking of my wife's perfume. I've got a good mind to go and tell them about it there. How would you like that?" He stared dumbly, his head a long blob of shadow in the pewter gleam of the mirror on the medicine chest. Then he came forward a pace, hopefully, for the Captain was behind me in his dressing gown.

"What are you doing?" he said sternly. Mrs. Briggs appeared at his side. "Fasten yourself up," he ordered Vanaker, who thereupon took shelter behind the door.

"Either he moves, or my wife and I. . . . We refuse to put up with him," I said.

"Now," said the Captain. "You've done enough shouting. Calm down. They can hear you all over the house."

"It's an outrage," his wife breathed. "With my mother downstairs."

"I'm sorry, Mrs. Briggs," I said in a lower voice. "But I had as much as I could stand from him. I admit I lost myself."

"I should say."

"Just a minute, Mil," the Captain interrupted. And then to me: "We can't allow behavior of that sort here, and . . ."

"What about his behavior?" I said excitedly. "It seems he can do as he pleases, but if I protest I am the one who's blamed. Why don't you ask him about it? What's he skulking in there for?"

"If you had complaints, you should have brought them to me or to my wife instead of making a row. This is not a tavern. . . ."

"I put up with his indecency. I don't care. It's that kind of inconsiderateness," I said disconnectedly.

"This is terrible, shameful," said Mrs. Briggs.

"We can't have this," said the Captain, "we can't have it. It's the worst kind of rowdyism!"

"Howard," remonstrated Mrs. Briggs.

"You're the one that's shouting now, Captain," I said.

"Don't tell *me* how to talk," the Captain exploded.

"I'm not your subordinate. I'm a civilian. I don't have to take this from you."

"By Jesus, I'll take a swing at you in about a minute!"

"Try it!" I said, stepping back and tightening my fists.

181

"Howard, please. Howard," said Mrs. Briggs.

"Joseph," said Iva, appearing in the doorway. "Come here. Come into the room." I edged by them, guardedly. "Get in," commanded Iva.

"If he touched me, I'd murder him, soldier suit or no soldier suit," I growled as I went in.

"Oh, keep quiet," said Iva. "Mrs. Briggs, please, just a moment." She hurried toward them.

I put on my shoes, snatched my street clothes from the closet, and flung out of the house. I walked rapidly through the drizzle. It was not late, certainly not more than ten o'clock. The air was dense and black and pressed close on the hourglass figures the street lamps made. I could not have slowed my walk; I was not sure of my legs. So I went on for some time, until I came to an open place, a lot with a wire backstop for baseball games. The ground was flooded, a wind-blown sheet of water, utterly dark. Behind the backstop was a white drinking fountain and water from it flurring into the warm air. I drank and then I went on, not so fast as before but just as aimlessly, toward the static shower of lights in the street ahead, a spray of them hanging in the middle distance over the shine of the pavement. Then I turned back.

I could not even imagine what Iva's misery must be, nor the state of the house. Iva must be trying to explain; Mrs. Briggs, if she was listening at all, was listening frostily; while Vanaker was making his way to his room, meek but vindicated, and probably wondering what had happened. Once more he seemed to me, as in the early days, simple-minded, perhaps subnormal.

I walked over the cinders of a schoolyard and came into an alley approaching our windows. I looked for Iva's shadow on the blind. She was not there. I had halted near a fence against which a tree leaned, freshly budding and seething under the rain. I made an effort to dry my face. Then it occurred to me that the reason I could not see her was that she was lying on the bed again. My skin was suddenly as wet with perspiration as it had been a moment ago with rain. I turned and started back along the schoolyard fence. A steel ring on a rope whipped loudly against the flagpole. Then, for a moment, a car caught me in its lights. I stood aside for it and followed its red blur. It was gone. Something ran among the cans and papers. A rat, I thought and, sickened, I went even more quickly, skirting a pool at the foot of the street where a torn umbrella lay stogged in water and ashes. I took a deep breath of warm air.

I believe I had known for some time that the moment I had been waiting for had come, and that it was impossible to resist any longer. I must give myself up. And I recognized that the breath of warm air was simultaneously a breath of relief at my decision to surrender. I was done. But it was not painful to acknowledge that, it was not painful in the least. Not even when I tested myself, whispering "the leash," reproachfully, did I feel pained or humiliated. I could have chosen a harsher symbol than that for my surrender. It would not have hurt me, for I could feel nothing but gratification and a desire to make my decision effective at once.

It couldn't be later than half-past ten now. The draft board often held late sessions. I set out for its office in the Sevier Hotel. As I was walking across the old-fashioned lobby, trying to remember on which side the office was, the clerk called me over. He guessed what I wanted.

"If it's the board you're after," he said, "everybody's gone home."

"Can I leave a note? Oh, never mind, I'll mail it."

I sat down at a desk in a corner, near one of the portieres, and wrote on a sheet of stationery:

> "I hereby request to be taken at
> the earliest possible moment into
> the armed services."

To this I added my full name and call number, and across the bottom:

> "I am available at any time."

After I had posted this, I stopped at a tavern and spent my last forty cents on a drink.

"I'm off to the wars," I said to the bartender. His hand hovered over the money. He picked it up and turned to the cash register. The place, after all, was full of soldiers and sailors.

March 27

THIS morning I told Iva what I had done. She made only one comment, namely, that I should have consulted her. But I said, "I'm doing myself no good here." There was no answer to that. She took the check downtown to cash. I waited for her on the library steps, sitting among the pigeons, reading the paper. She came down at noon, and we had lunch together. She did not look well. There was a blemish on her face that always shows up when she is disturbed. I felt weak myself, standing in the sunlight.

Mrs. Briggs had asked both parties to yesterday's disgrace to move.

"You can stay on alone," I said to Iva. "She won't object."

"I'll see about it. When do you think you'll be called?"

"I'm not sure. I think in about a week."

"I don't think you ought to spend your last week moving," she said. "We'll stay on for a while. I'm sure Mrs. Briggs will let us."

About her own plans she said nothing.

March 29

MRS. KIEFER died during the night. When I went out to breakfast I saw her door thrown open, her bed empty, the curtains in the room pinned back, the window open. Later, Mrs. Briggs appeared in black. In the afternoon other mourners came, gathering in the parlor. At five o'clock they began to pour out of the house. They went up the still street to the undertaker. The odor of coffee drifted up from the kitchen.

That evening, as we came out of the restaurant, we saw Mrs. Bartlett across the way. She had changed her white uniform for a silk dress and a short fur coat. Her hat was a strange affair with a flat top and a curtain or wimple that fell about her neck—a fashion that disappeared many years ago. We guessed that she was on her way to the movies after her long confinement with Mrs. Kiefer. Her shiny, long, black pocketbook was clasped under her doubled arm; she walked in a heavy-hipped, energetic stride toward the brightly lit avenue.

TODAY, the funeral. The Captain drove up with a wreath in his car; to him came a woman in a blue cape and feathers and short legs in ribbed hose. Her foot was set on the running board as though she were standing at a' bar. Then she sprang in, and they drove off together. Telegraph messengers kept coming all morning. I don't know how many children the old woman had. There was a son in California, Marie had once said. The family gathered on the porch. The women's faces were mottled with crying; the men looked morose. They returned from the funeral at noon and had lunch at a long table in the parlor. I saw them when I went down for the midday mail. The Captain caught me looking in, and frowned. I withdrew quickly.

The postman was putting a letter in the box next door and he pointed vigorously at me and drew his finger across his throat. I had received my notice. "A committee of your neighbors. . . ." I was summoned for the ninth. My blood test was to be on Monday. I took the papers out of the envelope and propped them up on the dresser where Iva could see them when she came in.

Later in the day, as I sat reading, Marie came to the door with fresh towels. She, too, was dressed in black. She went about the house somber and unapproachable, as though she shared with Mrs. Kiefer and the mourners

186

some unusual secret about death. I took this opportunity
to tell her that I was going away.

"Your wife going to stay?" she said.

"I don't know."

"Uh-huh. Well, good luck." She gloomily wiped her
cheeks with a black-edged handkerchief.

"Thanks," I said.

She took the soiled towels and shut the door.

April 2

UNIVERSAL relief. As old Almstadt put it, since I had to
go, it was better to go and get it over with. And my father,
too, said, "Well, at least you don't have to wait any more."
Amos, when I spoke to him yesterday, asked me to have
lunch with him at his club. I told him I was going to be
busy. I know he would have introduced me to his friends
as "my brother who is going into the Army," and would
thereafter be known as a man who was "in it."

April 4

VANAKER moved this morning. I heard Marie in his room
after he had gone and went in. She had found two empty
perfume bottles in his wastebasket. I was right. He left
an interesting lot of goods behind, lying in the stale closet.
Bottles, of course—those he had not seen fit, for some
reason, to throw into the yard—picture magazines with
photos of nudes, gloves, soiled underwear, the bowl of
a pipe, a grease-stained handkerchief, a copy of *Pilgrim's*

Progress and a school edition of *One Hundred Great Narrative Poems,* a carton of matches, a felt hat, a necktie with some matter dried into it. The whole collection went into a box which Marie carried down to the basement.

Spent several hours putting my things away in the trunk.

April 5

WHILE it was still dark, I left the house this morning to go for my blood test. I had not been out so early for many months. The cars were jammed with factory workers. When I asked the conductor about my destination, a small park which I had never heard of, he said, "Stick around, I'll fix you up." We plunged up the broad street for a mile or two, and then he nudged me and said, "Here y'are; comin' up." And with a sort of playfulness he pushed me toward the door, while the others looked on gloomily, sleepy and dark-faced.

I waited in line at the field house, under the thin trees. In the gymnasium I took off my clothes, marched naked around the floor with the others, examining their scars and blemishes as they did mine. There were few boys; most of the men were in their thirties. The cripples were swiftly weeded out. A doctor felt us in the groin; another, an aging man with a cigar, said perfunctorily, wielding the needle, "Clench your hand; open; that's it." Holding a swab to your arm, looking curiously at your blood in the tube, you filed out and were dismissed.

It was eight o'clock, morning, full and brilliant; my

usual hour for rising. I stopped at a cafeteria for breakfast, went home, and read all day.

Iva has put together a few things she thinks I'll need in the Army—my razor, a few handkerchiefs, a fountain pen and a block of note paper, my shaving brush. I am not going to take the usual ten-day furlough. I would rather save the time and use it later, if that is possible. Iva, of course, thinks it a sign of coldness on my part. It is merely that I do not want any more delays. She is going back to the Almstadts'. Her father is coming on the tenth to move her things.

When I visited my father yesterday, I went upstairs to my old room. For a time after my marriage the maid had occupied it. It was unused now, and I found in it many of the objects I had kept around me ten years ago, before I left for school. There was a Persian print over the bed, of a woman dropping a flower on her interred lover— visible in his burial gown under the stones; a bookcase my mother had bought me; a crude water color of a pitcher and glass done by Bertha, some nearly forgotten girl. I sat in the rocking chair, feeling that my life was already long enough to contain nearly forgotten periods, a loose group of undifferentiated years. Recently, I had begun to feel old, and it occurred to me that I might be concerned with age merely because I might never attain any great age, and that there might be a mechanism in us that tried to give us all of life when there was danger of being cut off. And while I knew it was absurd for me to think of my "age," I had apparently come to a point where the perspectives of time appeared far more contracted than they had a short while ago. I was beginning to grasp the meaning of "irretrievable." This rather ordinary and, in some ways mean, room, had for twelve years been a standard site, the bearded Persian under the round stones and the water color, fixtures of my youth. Ten years ago I was at school; and before that. . . . It was suddenly given me to experience one of those consummating glimpses that come to all of us periodically. The room, delusively, dwindled and became a tiny square, swiftly drawn back, myself and all the objects in it growing smaller. This was not a mere visual trick. I understood it to be a revelation of the ephemeral agreements by which we live and pace ourselves. I looked around at the restored walls. This place which I avoided ordinarily, had great personal significance for me. But it was not here thirty years ago. Birds flew through this space. It may be gone fifty years hence. Such reality, I thought, is actually very dangerous, very treacherous. It should not be trusted. And I rose rather unsteadily from the rocker, feeling that there was an element of treason to common sense in the very objects of common sense. Or that there was no trusting them, save through wide agreement, and that my separation from such agreement had brought me perilously far from the necessary trust, auxiliary to all sanity. I had not done well alone. I doubted whether anyone could. To be pushed upon oneself entirely put the

190

very facts of simple existence in doubt. Perhaps the war could teach me, by violence, what I had been unable to learn during those months in the room. Perhaps I could sound creation through other means. Perhaps. But things were now out of my hands. The next move was the world's. I could not bring myself to regret it.

Amos and Dolly and Etta and Iva were at the table when I came in to dinner. My father presented me with a watch. Amos gave me a suitcase which, he said, would be handy for overnight trips when I came back. From Etta and Dolly I got a leather sewing kit, complete with scissors and buttons.

April 9

THIS is my last civilian day. Iva has packed my things. It is plain that she would like to see me show a little more grief at leaving. For her sake, I would like to. And I am sorry to leave her, but I am not at all sorry to part with the rest of it. I am no longer to be held accountable for myself; I am grateful for that. I am in other hands, relieved of self-determination, freedom canceled.

Hurray for regular hours!

And for the supervision of the spirit!

Long live regimentation!

THE VICTIM

by Saul Bellow

AUTHOR OF "DANGLING MAN"

The Vanguard Press, Inc.

New York

To my friend

Paolo Milano

Printed in the United States of America

It is related, O auspicious King, that there was a merchant of the merchants who had much wealth, and business in various cities. Now on a day he mounted horse and went forth to recover monies in certain towns, and the heat oppressed him; so he sat beneath a tree and, putting his hand into his saddle-bags, he took thence some broken bread and dried dates and began to break fast. When he had ended eating the dates he threw away the stones with force and lo! an Ifrit appeared, huge of stature and brandishing a drawn sword, wherewith he approached the merchant and said, "Stand up that I may slay thee even as thou slewest my son!" Asked the merchant, "How have I slain thy son?" and he answered, "When thou atest dates and threwest away the stones they struck my son full in the breast as he was walking by, so that he died forthwith."

"The Tale of the Trader and the Jinni"
from *Thousand and One Nights*

Be that as it may, now it was that upon the rocking waters of the ocean the human face began to reveal itself; the sea appeared paved with innumerable faces, upturned to the heavens; faces, imploring, wrathful, despairing; faces that surged upward by thousands, by myriads, by generations. . . .   DE QUINCEY, *The Pains of Opium*

1

ON SOME NIGHTS New York is as hot as Bangkok. The whole continent seems to have moved from its place and slid nearer the equator, the bitter gray Atlantic to have become green and tropical, and the people, thronging the streets, barbaric fellahin among the stupendous monuments of their mystery, the lights of which, a dazing profusion, climb upward endlessly into the heat of the sky.

On such a night, Asa Leventhal alighted hurriedly from a Third Avenue train. In his preoccupation he had almost gone past his stop. When he recognized it, he jumped up, shouting to the conductor, "Hey, hold it, wait a minute!" The black door of the ancient car was already sliding shut; he struggled with it, forcing it back with his shoulder, and squeezed through. The train fled, and Leventhal, breathing hard, stared after it, cursing, and then turned and descended to the street.

He was bitterly irritated. He had spent the afternoon with his sister-in-law, his brother's wife, in Staten Island. Or, rather, he had wasted it because of her. Soon after lunch she had phoned him at the office—he was an editor of a small trade magazine in lower Manhattan—and immediately, with terrible cries, she implored him to come out, to come at once. One of the children was sick.

"Elena," he said as soon as he was able to make himself heard, "I'm busy. So I want you to control yourself now and tell me: is it really serious?"

"Come right away! Asa, please! Right away!"

He pressed the tip of his ear as if to protect himself from her shrillness and muttered something about Italian excitability. Then the connection was broken. He hung up, expecting her to ring again, but the phone remained silent.

He did not know how to reach her; his brother was not listed in the Staten Island directory. She was calling either from a store or from a neighbor's house. For a long time, Leventhal had had very little to do with his brother and his brother's family. Only a few weeks ago he had received a card from him postmarked Galveston. He was working in a shipyard. At the time, Leventhal had said to his wife, "First Norfolk, now Texas. Anything is better than home." It was the old story; Max had married young and now he was after novelty, adventure. There were plenty of shipyards and jobs in Brooklyn and Jersey. Meanwhile Elena was burdened with the care of the children.

Leventhal had told her the truth. He was busy. A pile of unchecked proofs lay before him. He moved away the phone after waiting a few minutes and, making an impatient noise in his throat, picked up a piece of copy. No doubt the child was sick, probably seriously sick, or she wouldn't have carried on so. And, since his brother was away, it was somewhat in the nature of a duty to go. He would go this evening. It couldn't be so urgent. It was just beyond Elena's power to speak calmly about anything. He told himself this several times; nevertheless her cries continued to sound in his ears together with the windy thrum of the long-stemmed electric fans and the tick of typewriters. What if it were really critical? And suddenly, impulsively, meanwhile condemning himself for it, he got up, pulled his jacket from the back of the chair, went to the girl at the switchboard, and said, "I'm going in to see Beard. Buzz him for me, will you?"

With his hands in his hind pockets, pressing against his chief's desk, bending toward him slightly, Leventhal announced quietly that he had to go out.

Mr. Beard's face, a face enlarged by baldness, with a

[4]

fierce bony nose and a veined forehead, took on an incredulous, sharp look.

"With an issue to get ready?" he said.

"It's a family emergency," said Leventhal.

"Can't it wait a few hours?"

"I wouldn't go if I thought it could."

Mr. Beard made a short, unpleasant answer to this. He slapped his metal ruler on the pages of the type-book. "Use your own judgment," he said. There was nothing further to be said, but Leventhal lingered beside the desk hoping for something more. Mr. Beard covered his blemished forehead with a trembling hand and studied an article silently.

"Goddammed fish!" said Leventhal to himself.

A thundershower began when he approached the outside door. He watched it for a while. The air was suddenly as blue as siphon glass. The blind side wall of the warehouse on the corner was streaked black, and the washed paving stones and tar seams shone in the curved street. Leventhal returned to the office to get his raincoat, and as he was going down the hall he heard Mr. Beard saying in that nagging, prosecuting voice of his, "Walks out right in the middle of everything. Right in a pinch. With everybody else swamped."

Another voice which he identified as that of Mr. Fay, the business manager, answered, "It's funny that he should just pick up and go. There must be something up."

"Takes unfair advantage," Mr. Beard continued. "Like the rest of his brethren. I've never known one who wouldn't. Always please themselves first. Why didn't he offer to come back later, at least?"

Mr. Fay said nothing.

Expressionless, Leventhal put on his raincoat. His arm caught in the sleeve, and he pushed it through violently. He walked out of the office with his rather hulking stride, halting

[5]

in the anteroom to draw a drink from the glass cooler. While waiting for the elevator, he discovered that he was still holding the paper cup. Crumpling it, he threw it with an energetic swing between the bars into the shaft.

The trip to the ferry was short, and Leventhal did not take off his rubber coat in the subway. The air was muggy; his face grew damp. The blades of the fan turned so slowly in the gloomy yellow light that he could count the revolutions. The shower was over by the time he reached the street, and when the boat rode out of the slip over the slight swell, the sun came out again. Leventhal stood in the open, his coat slung over his shoulder, the folds gathered in his hand. There was a slow heave about the painted and rusted hulls in the harbor. The rain had gone out to the horizon, a dark band far overreaching the faint marks of the shore. On the water the air was cooler, but on the Staten Island side the great tarnished green sheds were sweltering, the acres of cement widely spattered with sunlight. The disembarking crowd spread through them, going toward the line of busses that waited at the curb with threshing motors, in a shimmer of fumes.

Max lived in a large apartment building. His flat, like Leventhal's own on Irving Place, was a high walk-up. Children were running noisily through the foyer; the walls were covered with childish writing. A Negro janitor in a garrison cap was washing the stairs and looked angry at Leventhal's tracks. In the court, the wash swung stiff and yellow in the strong sun; the pulleys were creaking. Elena had not answered Leventhal's ring. The elder of his nephews came to the door when he knocked. The boy did not know him. Of course, Leventhal reflected, how should he? He glanced up at the stranger, raising his arm to his eyes to screen them in the sunny, dusty, desolate white corridor. Behind him the flat was dark; the shades were drawn and a lamp was burning amid the clutter of the dining-room table.

"Where's your mother?"

"She's in here. Who are you?"

"Your uncle," said Leventhal. Coming into the hall he unavoidably pushed against the boy.

His sister-in-law hurried toward him from the kitchen. She had changed; she was heavier than when he had last seen her.

"Well, Elena?" he said.

"Oh, Asa, you're here?" She reached for his hand.

"Sure I'm here. You asked me to come, didn't you?"

"I tried to call you again, but they told me you were gone."

"Why again?"

"Phillie, take Uncle's coat," said Elena.

"Doesn't the bell work?"

"We disconnected it because of the baby."

Leventhal dropped his raincoat into the boy's arms and followed her into the dining room where she busied herself with clearing a chair for him.

"Oh, look at the house," she said. "I haven't had time to clean up. My mind is just miles away. It's already three weeks that I took down the curtains and I haven't got them back yet. And look at me." She put down the clothes she had lifted from the chair and showed herself to him with outspread arms. Her black hair was in disorder, she was wearing a nightgown under her cotton dress, her feet were bare. She smiled mournfully. Leventhal, impassive as usual, merely nodded. He observed that her eyes were anxious, altogether too bright and too liquid; there was a superfluous energy in her movements, a suggestion of distraction or even of madness not very securely held in check. But he was too susceptible to such suggestions. He was aware of that, and

[7]

he warned himself not to be hasty. He looked at her again. Her face, once florid and dark, was softer, fuller, and more pale, a little yellow. He was able to picture her as she had once been when he glanced at his nephew. He resembled her strongly. Only his slightly outcurving nose belonged to the Leventhals.

"Now, tell me, what's the matter, Elena?"

"Oh, Mickey is sick, he's terribly sick," said Elena.

"What's he got?"

"The doctor says he doesn't know what it is. He can't do anything with him. He runs high fevers all the time. It started a couple of weeks ago. I give him to eat and he doesn't keep it down. I try everything. I don't know what I should do with him. And today I got such a scare. I went into the room and I couldn't hear him breathe."

"No, what do you mean?" said Leventhal.

"Just what I'm telling you. I couldn't hear him breathe," she said with intensity. "He wasn't breathing. I put my head on the pillow by his. I couldn't hear a thing. I put my hand over his nose. I couldn't feel anything. I got cold all over. I thought I was going to die myself. I ran out to call the doctor. I couldn't get him. I called his office and everywhere. I couldn't find him. So then I called you. When I got back he was breathing. He was all right. Then I tried to phone you."

Elena's hand was resting on her bosom; the long, pointed fingers were dirty; beneath them her skin was white and very smooth.

So that was the crisis. He might have guessed it was something like that.

"He was breathing all the time," he said somewhat roughly. "How could he stop and start again?"

"No, no," she insisted. "He wasn't."

[8]

Leventhal's composure was not perfect; it was tinged with fear. He thought, looking away from her toward a corner of the ceiling, "What superstition! Just like in the old country. The dead can come back to life, too, I suppose, and all the rest of it."

"Why didn't you feel his heart?" he said to her.

"I should have, probably . . ."

"You certainly should."

"You were busy, weren't you?"

"Well, sure, I had work. . . ."

She expressed such contrition at this that he told himself to be kinder. He might as well be; he was here, the harm was done. He assured her that he had an afternoon coming. He had been with the firm six years, and if he couldn't take a few hours off on a personal matter after six years, he might as well give up. He could go away every afternoon for a month without coming close to the number of hours of over-time without pay that he had put in. After he stopped talking his mind ran on in the same strain. In the civil service it was different. There you had your sick leave and you went home with a headache. And you had tenure. . . . But he did not want to dwell on this. He got up and turned his chair, as if to change the subject of his thoughts by changing his position.

"You should raise the shades," he said to Elena. "Why do you keep them down?"

"It makes the room cooler."

"It cuts off the air. . . . And you have to keep the lamp on. That gives off heat."

She had moved the clothing from his chair to the table, pushing back dishes, bread, milk cartons, magazines. He guessed that she kept the shades down for no other reason than to hide her slovenliness from the neighbors across the court. He looked at the room with displeasure. And Max drifted around from Norfolk to Galveston to God knows where. Perhaps he preferred living in rooming houses and hotels.

Elena gave Philip a dollar and sent him down for beer. She took the money from her dress pocket, which was filled with change. When he had gone, Leventhal asked to see Mickey.

He was lying in Elena's hot, shadowy, close room, dozing in the large bed that stood against the wall, the sheet pulled down to his waist. His short black hair seemed damp; his mouth was open. He was wearing a sleeveless undershirt. Leventhal carefully put the back of his hand to his cheek; it was burning. In withdrawing he knocked his ring against the bedpost. The look Elena shot him startled him. He found himself raising the same hand apologetically and felt his face flush. She, however, was no longer looking at him; she was drawing the sheet over the child's shoulder. Leventhal withdrew to the hall and waited for her. She shut the door slowly, with such care that it seemed to him whole minutes passed. He gazed into the room; it grew darker about the figure on the bed partly hidden from him by the bulge of the chiffonier. At last she released the knob and they returned to the dining room.

He sat down, depressed and gloomy. He began at once to argue that Mickey should be taken to a hospital. "Who is this doctor of yours?" he said. "What's wrong with him that he lets you keep the boy at home? The hospital is the place for him." But he soon realized that Elena, not the doctor, was to blame. She said, with great obstinacy, that he was better off at home, where she could take care of him herself. She showed such a dread of hospitals that at last he exclaimed, "Don't be such a peasant, Elena!" She was silent, though she appeared more distressed than offended and probably did not understand him. He was annoyed with himself for being so vehement, but everything here oppressed him—the house, his sister-in-law, the sick child. How could the boy get well in such a place, in that room? "Well, for goodness sake, Elena," he argued in a different tone, "a hospital is nothing to be afraid of." She shut her eyes and shook her head; he began to shape another sentence but stopped and lay back in the mohair armchair.

Suddenly she said brightly, almost happily, "Here's Philip and the beer." She rose to bring glasses. There was a hunt for the bottle opener; it was not found, and Philip pried off the caps on the handle of a metal cabinet in the kitchen. Elena wanted to make sandwiches, but Leventhal said he was not hungry. "Oh, it'll be dinnertime soon. Your missis won't like it if your appetite is spoiled. How is she? She's such a pretty girl." Elena smiled warmly. She did not even know his wife's name. They had met only once or twice. He hesitated to tell her that Mary had gone South for a few weeks to be with her mother. Elena would have insisted that he stay.

To change the subject, he asked about his brother. Max had been in Galveston since February. He wanted the family to join him, but the city was so crowded it was impossible to find a flat. He looked for one whenever he had time to spare.

"Why doesn't he come back to New York where he's got a flat?" said Leventhal.

"Oh, he makes good money down there; he works fifty, sixty hours a week. He sends me plenty." She did not appear to feel abandoned or even greatly concerned about Max's absence.

Hurriedly drinking down his beer, Leventhal rose, saying that he might still go back to the office for an hour to clear up some things. Elena gave him a neighbor's phone number; he copied it into his book and told her to ring in a day or two if Mickey did not get better. At the door, he called Philip and gave him a quarter for a soda. The boy took it, muttering "Thanks," but with a look that refused obligation. Probably a quarter did not mean much to Philip. Elena's pocket was full of change; she must be free with it. Leventhal drew his finger along the boy's cheek. Philip dropped his head, and, somewhat disappointed and dissatisfied with himself, Leventhal left the house.

He had to wait long for a bus, and it was dusk when he reached Manhattan. Too late to be useful at the office, he nevertheless debated at South Ferry, in the tenebrous brown heat, whether to return. "Ah, they'll get along without me today," he finally decided. Beard would interpret his coming in now as an admission that he was in the wrong. Moreover, it might seem that he was trying to establish himself as one of the "brethren" who was different. No, not even a hint of that, thought Leventhal. He would have an early dinner and go home. He felt dry, rather than hungry, but he must eat. He made an abrupt start and walked toward the train.

2 LEVENTHAL'S FIGURE was burly, his head large; his nose, too, was large. He had black hair, coarse waves of it, and his eyes under their intergrown brows were intensely black and of a size unusual in adult faces. But though childishly large they were not childlike in expression. They seemed to disclose an intelligence not greatly interested in its own powers, as if preferring not to be bothered by them, indifferent; and this indifference appeared to be extended to others. He did not look sullen but rather unaccommodating, impassive. Tonight, because of the heat, he was disheveled, and he was even ordinarily not neat. His tie was pulled to the side and did not close with the collar; his shirt cuffs came out beyond his coatsleeves and covered his thick brown wrists; his trousers sagged loose at the knees.

Leventhal came originally from Hartford. He had gone through high school there and after that had left home. His father, who had owned a small drygoods store, was a turbulent man, harsh and selfish toward his sons. Their mother had died in an insane asylum when Leventhal was eight and his brother six. At the time of her disappearance from the house, the elder Leventhal had answered their questions about her with an embittered "gone away," suggestive of desertion. They were nearly full grown before they learned what had happened to her.

Max did not finish high school; he left in his second year. Leventhal graduated and then went to New York, where for a time he worked for an auctioneer named Harkavy, a friend of his Uncle Schacter. Harkavy took Leventhal under his protection; he encouraged him to go to college at night and even lent him money. Leventhal took a prelegal course, but he did not do well. Perhaps the consciousness that he was attempting to do something difficult overweighed him. And the school itself—its atmosphere, especially on blue winter nights, the grimness of some of the students, many of them over fifty, world-beaten but persistent—that disturbed him. He could not study; he had never learned how, in the room behind his father's store. He finished the course, but without distinguishing himself, and he was not encouraged to go on to law school. He would have been satisfied to remain Harkavy's assistant, but the old man caught pneumonia and died. His son Daniel, then a junior at Cornell, left school to take over the business. Leventhal still remembered how he had come into the shop after the funeral in a bearskin coat, tall, blond, serious, saying emotionally to each of the clerks, "Let's dig in and hold the line!" Leventhal, virtually the old man's ward, was too dispirited by his death and trusted himself far too little to be of much use to Daniel. The shop was soon shut down. Going back to Hartford was out of the question (his father had remarried), and Leventhal, beginning to drift, was in a short time, a few months after Harkavy's death, living in a dirty hall bedroom on the East Side, starved and thin. For a while he sold shoes on Saturdays in the basement of a department store. Later he found steady work as a fur dyer, and after that, for about a year, he clerked in a hotel for transients on lower Broadway. Then his turn came on a civil-service list and he put himself down for "assignment anywhere in the United States." He was sent to the Baltimore customhouse.

The life he led in Baltimore was considerably different; it was not so solitary. It came to him slowly that in New York he had taken being alone so much for granted that he was scarcely aware how miserable it made him. During his first winter in the customhouse he was invited to join a party that went to the opera in Washington on Saturdays. He sat through five or six performances with a kind of alien, skeptical interest. But he began to go out regularly. He learned to like seafood. He bought himself two suits and a topcoat—he who from October to April had sweated in a heavy camel's-hair coat old Harkavy had given him.

At a picnic on the Chesapeake shore one Fourth of July, he fell in love with a sister of one of his friends. She was a tall, heavy-moving, handsome girl. With his eyes, he followed her in the steady, fiery sparkle of the bay when she climbed to the dock from the excursion boat and started arm in arm with her brother toward the grove and the spicy smoke of the barbecue clouding in the trees. Later he saw her running in the women's race, her arms close to her sides. She was among the stragglers and stopped and walked off the field, laughing and wiping her face and throat with a handkerchief of the same material as her silk summer dress. Leventhal was standing near her brother. She came up to them and said, "Well, I *used* to be able to run when I was smaller." That she was still not accustomed to thinking of herself as a woman, and a beautiful woman, made Leventhal feel very tender toward her. She was in his mind when he watched the contestants in the three-legged race hobbling over the meadow. He noticed one in particular, a man with red hair who struggled forward, angry with his partner, as though the race were a pain and a humiliation which he could wipe out only by winning. "What a difference," Leventhal said to himself. "What a difference in people."

He ran in the egg race, he swam, he felt his spirits thawed out that day. He was with Mary most of the afternoon. They took their sandwiches to the beach, walking half-shoe over in the white sand to find a place to themselves. From sundown, when they started back, till they came into the heat of the sluggish harbor among the heels of tankers, and through the yellow film spread over the water and in the air by the mills and piers, they sat together on the fantail of the little steamer. Her brother was waiting for her in the crowd at the gangplank, and they said good night in the noise of the steam plunging loosely skyward.

By autumn they were engaged, and Leventhal's success amazed him. He felt that the harshness of his life had disfigured him, and that this disfigurement would be apparent to a girl like Mary and would repel her. He was not entirely sure of her, and, in fact, something terrible did happen a month after the engagement. Mary confessed that she found herself unable to break off an old attachment to another man, a married man. In the pain of the moment, Leventhal almost lost his power to speak. He looked at her—they were in a restaurant. Then he asked if she had gone on seeing this man during the engagement. She said that she had and only at that moment seemed to realize how serious the matter was. He started to leave, and when she tried to hold him back, he pushed her, and she lost her footing in the booth and fell. He helped her rise; her mouth had gone white, and she averted her eyes from him. They left the restaurant together—she even waited while he paid the check—but outside they instantly separated without speaking.

About two years later she sent him a friendly letter. He did not know how to reply. It stood on his dresser for more than a month, confronting him nightly and overriding all his other concerns. He was still deliberating when he received a second letter from her. In it she asked him directly to consider how harassed she had been; she admitted that she had tried to end her infatuation by becoming engaged to him but that that was not the only reason; she had not chosen him indiscriminately. Leventhal found this letter easier to answer. They began to correspond. At Christmas he went down to visit her, and they were married by a justice of the peace in Wilmington.

He had meanwhile moved back to New York, having left Baltimore a few weeks after the engagement was broken. Daniel Harkavy had somehow landed on a trade paper. Leventhal, who had been editing a book of departmental regulations, thought that he, too, could handle that kind of job. He got in touch with Harkavy, and Harkavy wrote back that he was sure he could place him on a paper if he wanted to come to New York. Harkavy had many connections. Leventhal packed his trunk one week end and sent it to Harkavy's rooming house. He could not bear to stay in Baltimore; he was too wretched. He could not think of it later without flushing and wincing. A man brought up on hardships should have known better than to cut himself adrift. Even then he had realized that it was foolhardy to throw up his job and worse than that to put faith in Harkavy, and he told his chief that he was resigning to take another position. He was ashamed to tell him the truth.

He found Harkavy looking a little different. He was losing his hair and he had grown a red mustache. There was a certain swagger about him; he had taken to wearing large bow ties and black suede shoes. But he was essentially the same. He had written about his connections, but he could think of only one man to call on. This was a middle-aged Kentuckian by the name of Williston, short and ruddy, with a broad head across which his brown hair was brushed with a sort of backwoodsman's Sunday care. He was one of those people who keep their regional traits after twenty years in New York. It was a cold fall day, and he had an electric

heater beside his desk. He sat back in his swivel chair, occasionally raising a foot to warm it over the coils.

No, he said, there was no vacancy in his office. An experienced man might find something even now, in bad times.
An inexperienced one didn't have a chance. Unless by a
freak—his shoe shone over the burnished heater—unless
he knew someone very influential.

"We don't," Harkavy said. "We have no pull. And how
will he get experience?"

He wouldn't suggest, said Williston, that Leventhal try
to get a job running copy with a pack of boys at six bucks
a week. Even such jobs were scarce. He would suggest that
he stick to his trade. Leventhal's face grew dark, more with
self-condemnation than with resentment. He might have
asked for a transfer instead of quitting the civil service outright and waited it out, no matter how long it took. He
imagined that Williston partly divined what had happened.
It stupefied him, what he had done. But, Harkavy was saying, speaking of himself, he had gotten his job by luck,
without experience. Oh, no, Williston answered, his father's
name counted for something in the antiques field—Harkavy
worked on a paper for auctioneers and antique dealers.
"Leventhal was with my father and me for a long time,"
Harkavy told him. And Williston lifted his shoulders and
gazed into the face of the heater as if to say, "In that case,
nothing's too good for him." He seemed to regret this when
he saw Leventhal's pained, lowering look. Of course he
would do what he could, he said, but he didn't want them
to believe that much could be done. He would phone some
people, and meanwhile Leventhal could begin making the
rounds.

He began in a spirit of utter hopelessness. The smaller
trade papers simply turned him away. The larger gave

him applications to fill out; occasionally he spent a few minutes with a personnel manager and had the opportunity to shake someone's hand. Gradually he became peculiarly aggressive and, avoiding the receptionists, he would make his way into an inner office, stop anyone who appeared to have authority, and introduce himself. He was met with astonishment, with coldness, and with anger. He often grew angry himself. They were frightened, he observed to Harkavy, when you got out of line, out of the proper channel. But the channel led out of the door. How could they expect you to stay in it? He discussed it reasonably enough with Harkavy, but the provocations and near-quarrels continued, and in the heat of these provocations he frequently lost sight of his real object. He might remind himself while shaving or when he entered the bank to draw on his savings that he was after all defeating his own purpose, that anyone who, on an outside chance, had a job to give would not give it to him. But he did not change.

This queer condition lasted for about two months. Then, since Harkavy was becoming increasingly difficult to live with (several nights a week he entertained a woman friend and Leventhal, turned out of the room, went to a movie or sat in a cafeteria), and since his money was running low, Leventhal decided to take any job at all, the next that came his way—he was thinking of trying his old hotel on lower Broadway—when he received a note from Williston asking him to come in. One of his men was sick and had to go to Arizona for the winter, and Leventhal could fill his place till he came back.

So it was through Williston that Leventhal got his start in the profession. He was grateful and worked hard for him, and he discovered he had a knack for the job. From June until the end of summer he was idle again—that, too, was a difficult period. But now he had a season's experience and he found a place at last with Burke-Beard and Company. Apart from his occasional trouble with Beard, he was satisfied. He was really better off than in the civil service.

He said occasionally to Mary, revealing his deepest feelings, "I was lucky. I got away with it." He meant that his bad start, his mistakes, the things that might have wrecked him, had somehow combined to establish him. He had almost fallen in with that part of humanity of which he was frequently mindful (he never forgot the hotel on lower Broadway), the part that did not get away with it—the lost, the outcast, the overcome, the effaced, the ruined.

3

LEVENTHAL'S FATHER-IN-LAW had recently died, and his mother-in-law had been persuaded by the family to give up her house in Baltimore and to live in Charleston with her son. Mary had gone to help her move. In her absence Leventhal had been eating in an Italian restaurant in the neighborhood. It was in the basement of an old tenement. The stucco walls were almost black. It had a damp, woody smell from the sawdust sprinkled over the plank floor. But it suited him; the meals were cheap, and he generally did not have to wait for a table. Tonight, however, there was only one available. The waiter led him to it. It was in the corner behind a projecting wall which cut off the breeze of the fan. He was about to protest and opened his mouth impatiently, but the waiter, a dark man with thin hair curved over his perspiring forehead, anticipated him with a tired and rather insincere shrug, indicating with a motion of his toweled arm that the place was filled. Leventhal tossed his hat down, moved aside the dishes, and leaned forward on his elbows. Near the kitchen step, the proprietor and his wife were finishing their dinner. She gave Leventhal a look of recognition which he acknowledged, making a stir in his chair. The waiter brought his meal, an omelet in a chipped, blackened enamel dish with tomato sauce hardened on the rim, a salad, and some canned apricots. He ate, and his mood gradually improved. The coffee was sweet and thick; he swallowed even the sediment and put the cup down with a sigh. He lit a cigar. There was no one waiting for the table and he sat awhile, bent backward and puffing, clasping his hands on the densely growing hair on the back of his neck. From the tavern across the way came the slow notes of a guitar, the lighter carried away, the deeper repeated tranquilly.

Presently he shoved a tip under the saucer and went out.

There was still a redness in the sky, like the flame at the back of a vast baker's oven; the day hung on, gaping fierily over the black of the Jersey shore. The Hudson had a low luster, and the sea was probably no more numbing in its cold, Leventhal imagined, than the subway under his feet was in its heat; the trains rushing by under the gratings and along the slanting brown rock walls seemed to set off charges of metal dust. He passed through a small park where the double circle of benches were jammed. There were lines before each drinking fountain, the warm water limping and jetting into the stone basins. On all sides of the green square, the traffic of cars and cabs whipped endlessly, and the cumbersome busses crawled groaning, steering down from the tall blue oblong of light at the summit of the street through a bluish pallor. In the bushy, tree-grown corners, children played and screamed, and a revivalist band sang and drummed and trumpeted on one of the sidewalks. Leventhal did not stay long in the park. He strolled homeward. He thought he would mix a cold drink and lie down beside an open window.

Leventhal's apartment was spacious. In a better neighborhood, or three stories lower, it would have rented for twice the amount he paid. But the staircase was narrow and stifling and full of turns. Though he went up slowly, he was out of breath when he reached the fourth floor, and his heart beat thickly. He rested before unlocking the door. Entering, he threw down his raincoat and flung himself on the tapestry-covered low bed in the front room. Mary had moved some of the chairs into the corners and covered them with sheets. She could not depend on him to keep the windows shut and the shades and curtains drawn during the day. This afternoon the cleaning woman had been in and there was a pervasive odor of soap powder. He got up and opened a window. The curtains waved once and then were as motionless as before. There was a movie house strung with lights across the street; on its roof a water tank sat heavily uneven on its timbers; the cowls of the chimneys, which rattled in the slightest stir of air, were still.

The motor of the refrigerator began to run. The ice trays were empty and rattled. Wilma, the cleaning woman, had defrosted the machine and forgotten to refill them. He looked for a bottle of beer he had noticed yesterday; it was gone. There was nothing inside except a few lemons and some milk. He drank a glass of milk and it refreshed him. He had already taken off his shirt and was sitting on the bed unlacing his shoes when there was a short ring of the bell. Eagerly he pulled open the door and shouted, "Who is it?" The flat was unbearably empty. He hoped someone had remembered that Mary was away and had come to keep him company. There was no response below. He called out again, impatiently. It was very probable that someone had pushed the wrong button, but he heard no other doors opening. Could it be a prank? This was not the season for it. Nothing moved in the stair well, and it only added to his depression to discover how he longed for a visitor. He stretched out on the bed, pulling a pillow from beneath the spread and doubling it up. He thought he would doze off. But a little later he found himself standing at the window, holding the curtains with both hands. He was under the impression that he had slept. It was only eight-thirty by the whirring electric clock on the night table, however. Only five minutes had passed.

"No, I shouldn't have gone," he said to himself. He was suddenly full of misgivings. It was a mistake to run out of the office like that. If he had considered the thing sensibly, he would have waited till evening. Five minutes more and Elena would have called him again. Then why hadn't he waited? Did he actually want to stand Beard up for once, was that why he had left the office? No, and Beard's remark was disgusting, besides. It did not come as a surprise. He had known all along that he was capable of making it. If a man disliked you, he would dislike you for all the reasons he could think of. It was not important, merely disgusting. All the same, he shouldn't have gone. He washed his face, put on his shirt, and left the apartment. His difficulty, he reflected, was that when he didn't have time to consider, when pressure was put on him, he behaved like a fool. That, mainly, was what troubled him. For instance, last week at the press Dunhill, the linotyper, sold him a ticket he didn't want. He protested that he didn't care for shows and had no use for one ticket—this was before Mary left. But because Dunhill had insisted, he bought the ticket. He gave it to one of the girls at the office. Now if only he had been able to say at the outset, "I will not buy your ticket. . . ." He muttered, "Well, what do I do it for?" frowning. One of his neighbors appeared, bare-chested and in tennis shorts, and deposited a clinking bag of bottles to be removed by the janitor.

The Porto Rican superintendent, Mr. Nunez, in a straw hat, his dark feet in Chinese straw slippers, was sitting on the stoop. Leventhal asked him whether he had noticed anyone ringing his bell, and he answered that he had been on the stoop for half an hour and that no one had gone out in the last fifteen minutes or come in. "Maybe you heard the radio," he suggested. "Sometimes I think somebody is in the house talking to me, but it's the radio somewhere."

"No, the bell rang," Leventhal said positively; he looked

seriously at the superintendent. "Was it the dumb-waiter bell, you think?"

"If somebody was fooling around the basement. I didn't touch it tonight."

Leventhal set out for the park. Perhaps it was a radio, though he did not think so. Perhaps something in the wiring, affected by the heat—he did not know much about electricity—or the dumb-waiter. What really concerned him was that perhaps his nerves were to blame and that he had imagined the ring just as he had imagined that he had slept. Since Mary's departure his nerves had been unsteady. He kept the bathroom light burning all night. Somewhat ashamed of himself, he had yesterday closed the bathroom door before getting into bed, but he had left the light on. This was absurd, this feeling that he was threatened by something while he slept. And that was not all. He imagined that he saw mice darting along the walls. There actually were mice in the apartment. The building was old; there were bound to be some nesting under the floors. He had no dread of them, and yet he had begun to jerk his head around at the suspicion of a movement. And now he had been unable to fall asleep. Heat had never hitherto interfered with his sleep. He was sure he was unwell.

The park was even more crowded than before, and noisy. There was another revivalist band on the corner, and the blare of the two joined confusingly above the other sounds. The lamps were yellowed, covered with flies and moths. On one of the paths an old man, sunburned, sinewy, in a linen cap, was shining shoes. The fountain ran with a green, leaden glint. Children in their underclothing waded and rolled in the spray, the parents looking on. Eyes seemed softer than by day, and larger, and gazed at one longer, as though in the dark heat some interspace of reserve had been crossed and strangers might approach one another with a kind of recognition. You looked and thought, at least, that you knew whom you had seen.

Some such vague thing was in Leventhal's mind while he waited his turn at the drinking spout, when suddenly he had a feeling that he was not merely looked at but watched. Unless he was greatly mistaken a man was scrutinizing him, pacing slowly with him as the line moved. "He seems to know me," he thought. Or was the man merely lounging there, was he only a bystander? Instantly Leventhal became reserved, partly as a rebuff to his nerves, his busy imagination. But it was not imagination. When he stepped forward, the man moved, too, lowering his head as if to hide a grin at the thin-lipped formality of Leventhal's expression. There was no hint of amusement, however, in his eyes—he was now very close; they were derisive and harsh.

"Who's this customer?" Leventhal said to himself. "An actor if I ever saw one. My God, my God, what kind of a fish is this? One of those guys who want you to think they can see to the bottom of your soul." He tried to stare him down, only now realizing how insolent he was. But the man did not go. He was taller than Leventhal but not nearly so burly; large-framed but not robust. "If he starts something," Leventhal thought, "I'll grab his right arm and pull him off balance. . . . No, his left arm and pull towards my left; that's my stronger side. And when he's going down I'll give him a rabbit punch. But why should he start anything? There's no reason."

He was squared and resolute; nevertheless there was a tremor in his arms, and during all of it he felt that he himself was the cause of his agitation and suspicion, with his unreliable nerves. Then in astonishment he heard the stranger utter his name.

"What, do you know me?" he asked loudly.

"Do I? You're Leventhal, aren't you? Why shouldn't I know you? I thought you might not recognize me, though. We met only a few times, and I suppose I look a little different than I used to."

"Oh, Allbee, isn't it? Allbee?" Leventhal said slowly, with gradual recognition.

"Kirby Allbee. So you do recognize me?"

"Well, I'll be damned," said Leventhal, but he said it rather indifferently. What if it were Kirby Allbee? And he certainly looked changed, but what of that?

Just then several people in the line pushed against him. It was his turn at the spout and, as he took a swallow of the warm water, he looked sidewise at Allbee. The woman who had preceded him—she was painted heavily and looked like a chorus girl who had slipped out of the theater for a breath of air—was in Allbee's way, and while he was trying to step aside, caught in the circle around the spout, Leventhal walked off.

He had never liked this Allbee, but he had never really thought much about him. How was it, then, that his name came to him so readily? He had a poor memory for names; still he saw the man and recognized him in a moment. "What a box, the mind," Leventhal thought with something approaching a smile. "You'd just as soon expect hair to grow in your hand as some of the things that come out of it."

"Hey, wait!"

Allbee was dodging through the crowd after him. "What does he want?" Leventhal irritably asked himself.

"Wait, where are you going?"

Leventhal did not answer. What business was it of his?

"Are you going home?"

"Yes, by and by," he said distantly.

"Well, now you've found out that I still exist and you're going home, is that it?" He had a curious smile.

"Why should I doubt that you exist?" Leventhal was smiling also, but without much mirth. "Is there any reason why you shouldn't? I'm afraid I don't get it."

"I mean that you just wanted to have a look at me."

"Pardon?" said Leventhal. He drew up his brows. "To have a look?"

"Yes, I think you did want to, to see how I've made out. The results."

"I came out to cool off a little." He was beginning to be really annoyed. "What makes you think you've got anything to do with it?"

"Well, I didn't expect this," Allbee said. "Of course, I didn't know what to expect. I wondered what line you were going to take with me." He brought his lips together as if to hold back laughter, slightly jeering, presumptuous, and drew his hand down his cheek over the blond bristles, and all the while his deeply ringed eyes looked angrily into Leventhal's. He appeared to be saying that he knew perfectly well what he was saying and that it was effrontery and bad acting to deny it. "Just like a bad actor to accuse everyone of bad acting," thought Leventhal, but he was troubled nevertheless. What was he after? He studied Allbee more closely; until now he had not noticed how seedy he looked, like one of those men you saw sleeping off their whisky on Third Avenue, lying in the doorways or on the cellar hatches, dead to the cold or the racket or the straight blaze of the sun in their faces. He drank, too; that was certain. His voice was thick. He had fair hair parted in the center over his large forehead, moist in the lamplight. He wore a flimsy shirt of material that must have been imitation

[28]

silk; it opened on the chest on the dirty hem of an under-shirt; his light cotton suit was soiled.

"The fact remains that you wanted to see me," he resumed.

"You're mistaken."

"Well, you got my letter, didn't you? And I asked you to meet me here tonight . . .?"

"You wrote me a letter? What in the world for? I never got a letter from you. I don't understand this."

"Neither do I; if you didn't get it, this would be quite a coincidence. But," he went on, smiling, "of course you're pretending you didn't get the letter."

"Why should I pretend?" said Leventhal excitedly. "What reason have I got to pretend? I don't know what letter you're talking about. You haven't got anything to write me for. I haven't thought about you in years, frankly, and I don't know why you think I care whether you exist or not. What, are we related?"

"By blood? No, no . . . heavens!" Allbee laughed.

Leventhal stared into his laughing face and then began to walk away, whereupon Allbee thrust his arm straight before him and held him back. Leventhal grasped it, but he did not jerk according to his plan. He felt no resistance to his grip. It was he rather than Allbee who was off balance, and he removed his hand; he appeared to scowl—in reality he was clearing his throat—and he said, not at all loudly, "What do you want?"

"Oh, that's more sensible." Allbee straightened his shoulders and pulled down his cuffs. "I don't want to wrestle. I'm probably no match for you. I wanted to talk. I didn't think there would be any physical violence. That's not how you people go about things. Not with violence."

"What people are you talking about?" asked Leventhal.

Allbee did not reply to this. "I wanted to take up a few things with you, which is why I wrote," he said.

"I tell you again, I never got a letter from you."

"So you're sticking to that." Allbee smiled deprecatingly as though wondering why Leventhal refused every opportunity to get rid of this clumsy pretense. "Then why are you here? You wanted to see but not be seen, and you're mad because you got caught."

"I'm here because I live down the street a way. Why don't you own up instead that you wanted to catch me. God only knows what for and what you've got to say."

Allbee moved his large face from side to side in denial. "It's the other way around. You knew I was here . . . well, it's immaterial. As for what I have to say to you, I've got plenty to say. But you know that."

"That's news to me, too."

Allbee grinned at him with an intimation of a shared secret that aroused and vexed Leventhal, and sickened him.

"Let's sit down," Allbee proposed.

"Damn him, he's got me, he's got hold of me," Leventhal thought. "He's become some kind of a crank. I shouldn't have gone out. I should have tried to sleep, after the day I've had."

They found a place on a bench.

"I haven't got much time. I get up early. What do you want?"

Allbee regarded him. "You've become stouter," he said. "Darker, too. How much do you weigh?"

"About two hundred and ten."

"That's too much. It's bad for your heart to carry so much weight. Don't you feel it in this weather? I'll bet your heart takes a beating from it. You have a lot of stairs to climb."

"How do you know that?"

"Oh, I happen to know that you live on the fourth floor."

"How do you know?" Leventhal insisted.

"I just happen to. Is it some kind of a secret? Isn't anybody allowed to know that you live on the fourth floor?"

"What else do you know about me?"

"You work for the Burke-Beard people. You put out one of their sheets."

"Any more?"

"Your wife is away. She is . . ." he glanced over as though to see if he was entirely right, "down South. Went a few days ago. These things aren't hard to find out."

"Did you ring my bell before?"

"Did I ring it? No, why should I?"

Leventhal grimly looked at him in the light that came through the leaves. He had been spying on him, and the mystery was why! How long had he been keeping watch on him and for what reason—what grotesque reason? Allbee returned his look, examining him as he was examined, in concentration and seriousness, his lower jaw slipped to one side, his glum, contemplative eyes filled with a green and leaden color. And in the loom of these eyes and with the warmth of the man's breath on his face, for they were crowded together on the bench, Leventhal suddenly felt that he had been singled out to be the object of some freakish, insane process, and for an instant he was filled with dread. Then he recovered and told himself there was nothing to be afraid of. The man was a crank and irritating, and certainly it was creepy to think of being observed secretly. But there was nothing so alarming about this Allbee. He had become a bum and a drunk and he seemed to have an idea or a twist about him, a delusion; perhaps it was even invented. How could you tell about these drunks? There must be reasons, but they were beyond anybody's ability to find out—smoky, cloudy, alcoholic. Allbee had taken him by surprise. It was

[31]

surprising. And in his present state of mind he was, more-over, easily carried away by things. He felt unwell, and that didn't help. He gave a steadying, wary pull to his shoulders.

Still looking at him, Allbee said, "It's hard to know what kind of a man you are, personally."

"Oh, it's me you want to talk about?"

"Now, you see? There's an example. You're outspoken, but are you leading away from the main thing? You are. It's a maneuver. I don't know whether you're smart or crude. Maybe you don't even care much about the main thing."

"What don't I care about?"

"Ah, come on, drop it, Leventhal, drop it! You know what it is."

"I don't."

There was a pause; then Allbee said with an effort at patience, "Well, if that's the way it's got to be—I guess you want me to go over the whole business. I thought it wouldn't be necessary, but all right. *Dill's Weekly*. You remember *Dill's Weekly?* Mr. Rudiger?"

"Of course I do. Sure. Rudiger. I have it written down in an old appointment book I've been hoping to run across; his name keeps getting away from me. Oh, Rudiger," he said reminiscently and began to smile, but with a line of con-straint about his mouth.

"So you do remember?"

"Naturally."

"Now what about the rest of it? No, you won't go on to the rest of it. You'll make me do it. Okay, I will. It was through Rudiger that you got at me."

"Got at you?" said Leventhal, astonished. He turned his hot face to Allbee, and his scalp seemed to descend toward his brows.

"Got back at me. Got even with me," Allbee said with

great distinctness. His lower lip came forward, it was dry and cracked; his nose looked swollen, all at once. His eyes were open to the full.

"No, no," Leventhal muttered. "You're mistaken. I never did."

Allbee passed his hand before him in a movement of denial and shook his head slowly. "I couldn't be mistaken about this."

"No? Well, you are."

"Did I get you an appointment with Rudiger? I fixed you up with an interview, didn't I?"

"Yes, you did. Yes. . . ."

"Then you went in and deliberately insulted Rudiger, put on some act with him, called him filthy names, deliberately insulted him to get me in bad. Rudiger is hot blooded and he turned on me for it. You knew he would. It was calculated. It worked out just as you thought it would. You were clever as hell. He didn't even give me a week's notice. He turned me out."

"That's all wrong. I heard you weren't with Dill's any more. Harkavy told me. But it couldn't have been my fault. I'm sure you're mistaken. Rudiger wouldn't blame you for the run-in we had. It was his fault, too."

"Rudiger did," said Allbee. "He was plenty clear about it. He almost killed himself blowing his top at me. And that was what you wanted."

"All I wanted was a job," Leventhal declared, "and Rudiger was tough and nasty. There's something wrong with that man. Hot blood isn't the word for it. He's vicious. I didn't exactly keep my temper down. I admit that. Well, if that's the reason I may be to blame in a way, indirectly. But you say. . . ."

"I say you're entirely to blame, Leventhal." He opened

his mouth and appeared to hold his breath an instant as he smiled. Leventhal's attempt to keep a clear head came to nothing; he felt himself slipping into confusion.

"And why did I do it, do you say?"

"For revenge. Damn! You want to go over the whole thing to make sure that I'm really on. I really am on, Leventhal. Jesus, do you think I still haven't figured it out? Give me a little more credit than that; I was on a long time ago. But if you want me to pull it all out, I'm willing. I'll start farther back: Williston's house. There was a party."

"Yes, that's where we met, at Williston's."

"Ah, well, you recall it. I thought you'd balk all along the line and refuse to remember. Fine. Your friend was there too, another Jewish fellow—you mentioned his name before."

"Harkavy."

"That's the one, Harkavy. We're making headway." He laughed aloud. "Well, that's the key. A Jewish fellow. Lord, you want to draw the whole business out. Does it have to be drawn out? I suppose it has to. You were sore at something I said about Jews. Does that come back to you?"

"No. Yes, it does. It does, too," he corrected himself, frowning. "I also remember that you were drunk."

"Wrong. I was liquored up but not drunk. Positively not. You Jews have funny ideas about drinking. Especially the one that all Gentiles are born drunkards. You have a song about it—'Drunk he is, drink he must, because he is a Goy ... *Schicker*.' " He had ceased laughing; he looked morose.

"Bah!" Leventhal said contemptuously. He pushed at the bar of the bench and got to his feet.

"Where are you going?"

"I had nothing to do with your losing that job. It was probably your own fault. You must have given Rudiger a plenty good reason to fire you, and I can imagine what it was. I'm not the sort of man who carries grudges. It's all in your mind. I remember all about that night at Williston's, but you were drunk and I didn't hold it against you. Besides it was a long time ago, and I don't see your object in looking me up just to remind me of it. Good night!"

He walked away. Allbee stood up and shouted after him, "You wanted to get even. You did plan it. You did it on purpose!" People turned to look at them, and Leventhal increased his pace.

"If he follows me now I'll punch him in the jaw. I'll knock him down," he thought. "I swear, I'll throw him down and smash his ribs for him!"

He opened the mailbox when he got home and found the note. It was signed "Sincerely, Kirby A." and said that he would be in the park at nine. Why the park? Well, why such an accusation? What an idea! The one made about as much sense as the other. There was no stamp on the envelope; Allbee must have delivered it himself. Chances were it was he who had rung the bell.

"Some judge of time, that Nunez," Leventhal growled, starting up the stairs.

4

HE FELL ASLEEP without difficulty and slept deeply. The alarm clock on the night table awoke him, and he seized it and clapped down the catch. Then he crouched down at the window—he was naked—and looked over the sill. Already, at half-past seven, the street looked deadened with heat and light. The clouds were heavily suspended and slow. To the south and east, the air was brassy, the factories were beginning to smolder and faced massively, India red, brown, into the sun and across the hot green netting of the bridges. There was a hard encircling rumble of trucks and subterranean trains. Nunez was out in front, cleaning the sidewalk with a bucket of water and the stub of a broom. His wife was busy at the window boxes. New white strings stretched up to the lintel; she was leaning out, training vines on them.

Leventhal washed and shaved. Allbee's note was lying on the kitchen table. He reread it and threw it into the pail beside the sink. He was about to slam down the lid but checked himself—he was behaving as he would have yesterday when he was at the end of his patience—and, almost smiling at himself, he set it in place lightly and pushed the pail toward the wall with his foot. Well, he could have been forgiven yesterday for losing his patience or even his head. What a day! With all that he had weighing on him already, this Allbee shows up to add his little bit. He must have brooded over the affair for years, until he convinced himself that Rudiger had fired him because of that interview. Of course, it was true enough that Rudiger had a rotten bad temper, probably was born bad-tempered, but not even he would fire an employee, not for what the man himself had done but because of someone he had recommended. "How could he?" Leventhal asked himself. "Not a good worker;

never." It was absurd. Allbee must have been **fired** for drunkenness. When could you get a drinking man to acknowledge that he had gotten into trouble through drinking? Especially when he was far gone? And this Allbee was far gone.

He put on the wrinkled brown summer flannels he had thrown over the foot of the bed last night, and a pair of white shoes. He remembered to shut the windows and draw the drapes. The room was darkened. He took a handkerchief from the dresser and came across a statement on tax deductions for the year, a gloomy reminder of Mr. Beard and the office. Instead of keeping such things in the desk where they belonged, Mary had the habit of putting them under the linens. Irritated, he buried the paper deeper and roughly shoved the drawer shut. He went out with a frown. Beard would probably send for him and call him down, ostensibly for some mistake which he would dig up. Or he would delegate someone—he had done that before; perhaps that pinch-nosed, knob-faced little Millikan, his son-in-law. "If he sicks him on me . . ." he thought. But he did not know what threat to make. And now it seemed to him that he had rested badly. His legs were tired, his head ached, and his eyes—he examined them in the long mirror in the pillar before the coffeeshop—were bloodshot; he looked drawn. He shook his head in concern. The corners of the glass were flaming with the blue and red of the spectrum.

For a while he was so preoccupied with what awaited him at the office that he forgot about Allbee. He did not think of him again until he was on the subway. He was even less amused than before. From a sober person—that is, from a normal person, someone you would have to reckon with—such an accusation would be no trifle. With Allbee it came out like a stunt: the note, the bell ringing, the acting. And

[37]

not quite a stunt, for a stunt was done deliberately, whereas it was questionable whether this queer, beaten, probably suffering Allbee was in control of his actions. Suffering? Of course, suffering, Leventhal told himself gravely: down and out, living in a moldy hotel somewhere, hanging out in bars, sleeping whole days, picked up off the streets by the paddywagon or the ambulance, haunted in his mind by wrongs or faults of his own which he turned into wrongs against himself; and that stirring around of the thoughts and feelings, that churning—everybody experienced it, but for a man like that it must be ugly, terrible, those thoughts wheeling around. It was something like this that Leventhal was thinking of when he occasionally said that he had gotten away with it. But (without taking credit for it; he might have fallen in another way) his character was different. Some men behaved as though they had a horse under them and went through life at a gallop. Or thought they could, at any rate. He was not that way.

He had met Allbee several times at Williston's house. In those unsettled days when he was jobhunting, the Willistons used to give parties frequently. Perhaps they still did; he had not seen them in several years. Because they were roommates, he and Harkavy were usually invited together. Allbee had shown an antipathy toward Harkavy, and Leventhal recalled that he, as a matter of fact, had been offended by several of Allbee's remarks and by his attitude generally. Mrs. Allbee was a quiet blonde. He wondered what had become of her; had she left him, divorced him? He found that he retained a distinct image of her, of the firmness of her face and the form of her eyes, gray eyes. He had thought her much too good for the husband lounging beside her with a glass, staring at the other guests and smiling. He might have been asked by Williston to classify them, he eyed them

[38]

so, spread out there on the sofa, large-limbed, his face swelling with smiles. From time to time he made a comment to his wife, fixing his look on someone so that it was uncomfortably evident whom he was talking about. He frequently picked out Harkavy, which Leventhal resented, Harkavy himself seemingly unaware that he was being stared at.

It had to be admitted that Harkavy attracted stares. He liked to talk and at these parties he was easily kindled, for some reason. Any trifle made him enthusiastic, and when he spoke his hands flew and his brows slanted up, sharpening the line of his nose. His eyes were light, round, and depthless, his fair hair was fading back, the curls thinning. Allbee studied him, grinning and curious; Harkavy appeared to delight him. He must have had some witty things to say about him for he sometimes made his wife smile, and as a rule she did not respond to his remarks. Harkavy may have noticed this. Leventhal had never asked him about it, but perhaps it did light on his consciousness, for all his traits, the Jewish especially, became accentuated. He carried on, giving imitations of auctioneeers, in reality burlesquing his father. Leventhal watched, unsmiling and even forbidding. The laughter and the somewhat ambiguous applause, sometimes led by Allbee, seemed to excite Harkavy, and he would start again, working up the bid. The Willistons laughed with the guests, though more moderately and with a trace of anxiety about Allbee. Leventhal himself, at times, could not help joining in. But he was annoyed.

The incident Allbee had referred to occurred one night when Harkavy and a girl he had brought to the party were singing spirituals and old ballads. It was late, and everyone else was silent, rather tired. That evening Harkavy had been a little more restrained than usual. He sang poorly, but at least he did not provoke laughter and was not trying to. Nor did the girl sing well; she hesitated over words. It was pleasant, however. Halfway through a ballad Allbee interrupted; regardless of his denial, he was drunk.

"Why do you sing such songs?" he said. "*You* can't sing them."

"Why not, I'd like to know?" said the girl.

"Oh, you, too," said Allbee with his one-cornered smile. "It isn't right for you to sing them. You have to be born to them. If you're not born to them, it's no use trying to sing them."

His wife spoke up. "Don't pay any attention to him," she said. "You sing it very nicely."

"Aaah, yes he does," he said contemptuously.

"Why, thank you, Mrs. Allbee," said Harkavy. "It's a lovely song."

"Go on, Dan, go on with it," Phoebe Williston urged him. And Leventhal said, "Sing the rest of it."

"I'm going to," Harkavy replied, and began over.

"No, no, no!" Allbee broke in again. "You shouldn't sing those old songs. You have to be bred to them."

His wife colored and said, "Kirby, don't be like that."

"Oh, I don't mind, ma'am." Harkavy drew in his chin and crossed his arms, his round eyes glimmering.

"Sing, Dan," said Leventhal.

"Sing a psalm. I don't object to your singing. Sing one of the psalms. I'd love to hear it. Go ahead. I would," said Allbee.

"I don't know any psalms."

"Then any Jewish song. Something you've really got feeling for. Sing us the one about the mother." And with a drunken look of expectancy he bent forward, leaning on his knees, and pretended to prepare to listen. It was apparent to everyone that he was deeply pleased; he smiled at Harkavy and the girl, and he had a glance for Leventhal, too. His wife seemed quietly to dissociate herself from him. The Willistons were embarrassed. Allbee was not merely an acquaintance but a friend, and Williston later tried to make excuses for him and explain away the insult.

That was what had happened. Leventhal had naturally been angry, but not for long. He had shrugged it off. Did Allbee think something like that would make him go to such lengths for revenge? He was an idiot if he did. He over-estimated the magnitude of the insult and his power to be insulting. Or did he think that on that night he had revealed something that was not plain before? Then he was twice as idiotic. "And if I were mad, is that what I would do?" thought Leventhal. "He gives himself an awful lot of credit for nothing. Who does he think he is?"

That he had afterwards asked Allbee for an introduction to Rudiger should have shown how much importance he attached to the incident. At that time, Williston's man had returned from Arizona and Leventhal was looking for another place. Williston gave him a very good reference letter which made it easier to get interviews. However, several months went by before Leventhal was hired by Burke-Beard and Company, and during those months he was despondent and became quarrelsome once again, difficult, touchy, exaggerating, illogical, overly familiar. Reports of this reached Williston, who called him in and lectured him. Leventhal was bitter and suspicious of him and he offered to return the letter—foolishly, he now realized. But he thought that Williston regretted writing it.

It was his own idea to approach Allbee about a job at *Dill's*. Williston endorsed it and may have been instrumental in getting Allbee to introduce him to Rudiger. Or perhaps

Allbee agreed in order to make up for his unpleasantness. Williston tried continually to explain it away. You had to know Allbee when he was sober, he said; he was intelligent and decent. His New England upbringing was behind his drinking; there were ministers in his family, influences to throw off, and once he threw them off he would be another man. Leventhal indifferently acknowledged that that might be so; he had no particular grudge against him. "I'll be much obliged to him if he gets me the introduction. What a break if I could land a job with an outfit like that."

The interview at *Dill's* still troubled him.

Rudiger kept him waiting for nearly an hour in the reception room and for a few minutes more in his office. He was watching several tugs shouldering a huge liner up the river and his back was turned. But as soon as he faced about, Leventhal knew at once that he had nothing to hope for; he saw even before Rudiger uttered his first word that he did not want him. He was a short man, broad featured and red; his hair was intensely red. He had a mustache of short golden hairs overspread by a powerful nose with the cartilages widely separated at the tip. He spoke energetically, peremptorily, quickly, in a husky tone. At the outset Leventhal thought, "I've hit him at a bad time." Later he could not decide whether he had come upon him in an unusual mood of great stress and aroused cruelty or whether Rudiger had only treated him as he generally did people whom he didn't want to hire and who were wasting his time. In telling Harkavy about it that same afternoon, Leventhal said, "He was burning like a boiler. I never saw anything like it."

"Well?" Rudiger said, putting his hands on the desk. He might have been arresting momentarily a swing back to the window. Leventhal began to speak, and he cut him off with, "No vacancies, no vacancies here. We're filled. Go somewhere else."

Leventhal said stumblingly, "I thought there might be an opening here. I didn't know. . . . Didn't Mr. Allbee say what I wanted?"

Rudiger looked at him awhile. They were on the sixtieth floor of the Dill Building. The sun was far behind the dull, black, tarnished spikes and pinnacles of the skyscrapers below.

"What's your experience?" he said.

Leventhal told him.

"No, never mind that stuff. What newspapers have you been on?"

"No papers," Leventhal said rather nervously.

Rudiger burst out, inflamed, "Then what in the name of hell are you taking up my time for? What are you doing here? Get out. By Jesus, you come pestering around here when I'm busy without a goddam thing to offer."

"I'm sorry to bother you." Leventhal spoke stiffly, not to reveal his alarm.

"This is a news magazine. If you have no news experience, you've got no business here. Do you think we run a vocational school?"

"I thought I could do the work. I've read your magazine, and I thought I could." He labored at the words, stalling, and bent his head.

"Oh, did you? Did you?"

"Yes. . . ." He was beginning to recover his presence of mind. "I didn't know my experience wasn't the right kind for you. I have a letter from Mr. Williston. He says he knows you." Leventhal reached into his pocket.

But Rudiger exclaimed, "I don't want to see it."

"Well, Mr. Williston said he didn't see why I shouldn't be able to handle a job here. . . ."

"Nobody asked him. I don't care what he said."

"I think he knows what he's talking about. I respect his opinion."

"I know my own business. Never mind about Williston. I ought to know what I need here. You're not it."

"You probably know your business," Leventhal said stolidly, evenly, hunching his head forward. "I'm not saying you don't. But there's nothing so special about your magazine. I've read it, as I said." He put a cigarette in his mouth and, without asking Rudiger's permission, reached for a packet of matches on his desk, tore out one, struck it, and threw it into a tray. Angry and tense, he managed to present a surface of dry, uncaring calm. "Anybody who can write English can write for it. If you gave a man a try and then thought he couldn't make the grade, I'd say you knew your business a lot better. That's a prejudice, Mr. Rudiger, about newspaper experience."

Rudiger shouted, "Oh, is it?" Leventhal saw that he was not invulnerable, and by now a spell had been created, an atmosphere of infliction and injury from which neither could withdraw.

"Sure it is," said Leventhal rather easily. "It's a guild. Any outsider hasn't got a chance. But as a matter of fact you ought to think of your paper first and hire people because they can do the work. It wouldn't hurt."

"You think you could improve the paper?"

Leventhal replied that not his only but any fresh point of view wouldn't hurt. His confidence was enormous, so radically unusual that, despite his calm, it was like a seizure or possession, and he said things which his memory, limited by what was habitual, could not retain. So he did not know

[44]

now exactly what followed. He recalled something like, "Well, you buy an article in the grocery and you know what you're getting when you buy a standard brand. You open up the can and the product is inside. You're not disappointed and you're not overjoyed. It's standard." He shrank from the recollection as from a moment of insanity and he flushed roughly; he surmised that he might be making it worse than it had been, but even one tenth of the reality was calamitous.

Then, glaring at him crazily, Rudiger said, "What did you want to be here for if it's so bad!"

And he answered, "I need a job, it so happens."

The air between them must have shaken, it was so charged with insult and rage. Under no circumstances could he imagine doing now what he had done then. But he had determined not to let his nose be pulled. That was what he told himself. "He thinks everybody who comes to him will let his nose be pulled." Too many people looking for work were ready to allow anything. The habit of agreement was strong, terribly strong. Say anything you like to them, call them fools and they smiled, turn their beliefs inside out and they smiled, despise them and they might grow red, but they went on smiling because they could not let themselves disagree. And that was what Rudiger was used to.

"Get out!" Rudiger cried. His face was aflame. He rose with a thrust of his stocky arm while Leventhal, evincing neither anger nor satisfaction, though he felt both, rose, smoothed the groove of his green velours hat, and said, "I guess you can't take it when people stand up to you, Mr. Rudiger."

"Out, out, out!" Rudiger repeated, pushing over his desk with both arms. "Out, you case, you nut, you belong in the asylum! Out! You ought to be committed!"

And Leventhal, sauntering toward the door, turned and

retorted, made a remark about two-bit big shots and empty wagons. He didn't believe he had said more than that—notwithstanding Allbee's charge that he swore. He had said something about empty wagons being noisy. His present mortification would not be greater if he had sworn. He did remember, and very clearly, too, that he was elated. He congratulated himself. Rudiger had not pulled his nose.

He went at once to see Harkavy and, over a cup of coffee in a corner cafeteria, told him the whole story. It delighted him.

"You said that to Rudiger? Oh, golly, that must have been something. Really something, Asa my boy. He's a bull, that man. I've heard stories about him. A regular bull!"

"Yes. Well, you've got to remember one thing, Dan." Leventhal's spirits dropped suddenly. "Someone like that can make trouble for me. He can have me black-listed. You've got to realize . . . Eh, can he?"

"Never, Asa," Harkavy said.

"You don't think so?"

"Never. Who do you think he is?" Harkavy looked at him severely with his round, clear eyes.

"He's a big shot."

"There isn't a thing he can do to you. Whatever you do, don't get ideas like that into your head. He can't persecute you. Now be careful. You have that tendency, boy, do you know that? He got what was coming to him and he can't do anything. Maybe that Allabee, what-do-you-call-him, put him up to it, wanted to play you a dirty trick. You know how it goes: 'There's a fellow bothering me. Do me a favor and give him the works when he comes around.' So he does it. Well, he fouled his own nest. You follow me, boy? He fouled his own nest. So by now he realizes it was his own fault and he had it coming. How do you know it wasn't rimmed?"

"You really think they did? I don't know. And I didn't bother that Allbee. I only asked him once."

"Maybe he didn't put him up to it. But he might have. It's a possibility. Something like that happened to another friend of mine—Fabin. You know him. They gave him the works, and it was a put-up job. Only he didn't talk back the way you did. He just let them fling it at him. No, you did right and you haven't got a thing to worry about."

Nevertheless, Leventhal was not reassured. And on after-thought he had misgivings about Harkavy's reference to persecution. Harkavy used such words whether they fitted or not. Rudiger's anger was not imaginary, and he was a man to fear. There were black lists; that was well known. Of course, he had not actually worked for Rudiger and Rudiger could not black-list him as a former employee. In the nature of it, it must be a secret process, passing through many connections, private and professional. After all, Rudiger was influential, powerful. And who knew how these things were done, through what channels? It was downright silly of Harkavy to speak of imaginary persecution.

Leventhal suspected, in the days that followed, that the black list was real enough, for firm after firm turned him down. It was only when he found his present job that his suspicions faded and he ceased to fear Rudiger.

Beard did not send for him; Leventhal's apprehensions were unfounded. The old man, when they met in the lavatory in the afternoon, was not affable, but he was not so disagreeable as Leventhal had anticipated. He even asked about the family troubles. It was Leventhal himself that was distant.

"Was it as urgent as you thought?" said Beard.

[47]

"Oh, absolutely," Leventhal replied. "And my brother is away. I have to look out for his family."

"Yes, I see. Naturally. Your brother is a family man, is he?"

"He has two children. He's married to an Italian woman."

Mr. Beard said with a look of mild inquiry, "Oh, a mixed marriage."

Leventhal nodded slightly. Mr. Beard shook his dripping hands and dried them on the towel he carried over his shoulder. He did not use the paper towels in the tin box. In words hardly above a whisper, he made some comment about the heat, wiped his wan forehead, and went out, tightening his belt, pulling down his white vest, a round-shouldered figure with bald head and large elbows. The old man's mildness made him feel easier. They had met the deadline without him. It hadn't been so catastrophic; Fay and Millikan stayed an hour overtime. He would have done the same in a similar emergency. Had done it. And what if he himself had been sick? A man wasn't made of metal parts. Damn him, old Beard might have let him off a little more pleasantly. It gratified Leventhal, however, to have made that remark about Elena. Mixed marriage! It had come out instantaneously. He wondered how to hint to the old man that he had heard him yesterday, or that he was under no illusions, at any rate. He wanted him to know.

On the way to his desk he met Millikan, nervous, narrow-faced, sallow, with his scrap of mustache. He carried a towel, too, and approached, signaling with it. How he aped his father-in-law!

"Telephone, Leventhal. Miss Ashmun's been looking for you. Some party on your line."

"Who?" Leventhal was filled with anxiety, suddenly. He went rapidly to his desk.

[48]

"Asa?" It was Elena.

"Yes, what's the matter? Anything wrong?"

"The baby is worse. Mickey . . ." he heard her say. Her voice shot up and she became incoherent.

"Slower, slower Elena, please. I can't follow you. What's happening over there?" He guessed, his heart sinking, that she, too, was growing worse. "Now tell me slowly what's the matter."

"I want to get a specialist."

"Why don't you send the boy to the hospital?"

"I want a specialist to come to the house."

"What does your doctor say?"

"He didn't come today. Let him stay away. What good does he do him anyway? He doesn't do any good. He doesn't come even when he knows Mickey is so sick. Asa, do you hear me? I want a big man."

"All right. But if you took my advice about the hospital . . ."

Again she cried out incoherently, piercingly. He made out phrases of exclamation and question but scarcely any words except the persistent "No! No, no, no!" He attempted to interrupt. It was the operator, depositing the coin with a mechanical whirr, who put a stop to it. Elena, in fear, shrieked, "Asa!"

"Here. We haven't been cut off yet. I'm still on the wire. Listen, I'll get another doctor and be out myself after work."

"A specialist . . . I don't want anybody else."

Twice the operator demanded another coin. "Shut up!" Leventhal at last said, exasperated. "Can't you wait another second." But he was already talking on a dead line. He banged the instrument and jolted it aside with his elbow. Miss Ashmun seemed astonished. He gazed at her gloomily and presently picked up the phone again. He called the

Harkavys. Harkavy's sister Julia had a child and should be able to recommend a good doctor. Harkavy's mother answered the phone. She was extremely fond of Leventhal and spoke to him cordially, asking about his wife. "But I guess it's Dan'l you want to talk to. 'Dan'l!' " she called. "He's home today."

Leventhal at once explained it was Julia he wanted. Afterward he regretted that he had not taken the opportunity to ask Harkavy about Kirby Allbee. But what a time it was to have thought of him!

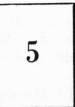

5

AFTER A HURRIED SUPPER of a sandwich and a bottle of soda at a stand near the ferry, Leventhal crossed to Staten Island. He walked onto the deck with his hands in the pockets of his fully buttoned, wrinkled jacket. His white shoes were soiled. Posted beside a life ring, his dark forehead shining faintly under his ill-combed, thick hair, he gazed out on the water with an appearance of composure; he did not look as burdened as he felt. The formless, working, yellowish-green water was dull, the gulls steered back and forth, the boat crept forward into the glare. A barge was spraying orange paint over the hull of a freighter, which pointed high, lifting its bow out of the slow, thick cloud. Surely the sun was no hotter in any Singapore or Surabaya, on the chains, plates, and rails of ships anchored there. A tanker, seabound, went across the ferry's course, and Leventhal stared after it, picturing the engine room; it was terrible, he imagined, on a day like this, the men nearly naked in the shaft alley as the huge thing rolled in a sweat of oil, the engines laboring. Each turn must be like a repeated strain on the hearts and ribs of the wipers, there near the keel, beneath the water. The towers on the shore rose up in huge blocks, scorched, smoky, gray, and bare white where the sun was direct upon them. The notion brushed Leventhal's mind that the light over them and over the water was akin to the yellow revealed in the slit of the eye of a wild animal, say a lion, something inhuman that didn't care about anything human and yet was implanted in every human being too, one speck of it, and formed a part of him that responded to the heat and the glare, exhausting as these were, or even to freezing, salty things, harsh things, all things difficult to stand. The Jersey shore, yellow, tawny, and flat, appeared on the right. The Statue

of Liberty rose and traveled backwards again; in the trembling air, it was black, a twist of black that stood up like
smoke. Stray planks and waterlogged, foundering crates
washed back in the boat's swell.

The specialist was coming. But what he could do depended
on Elena. Contagious cases were hospitalized; the health
authorities were called in. But the first doctor seemed to
have given up the struggle with Elena, and presumably he
knew the law. With unconscious grimness, Leventhal prepared himself to struggle with her. As long as she held out,
all the specialists in the world were futile. The prospect of
interfering, rushing in to rescue the boy, was repugnant to
him; it made him feel, more than ever, that he was an outsider. But what could you do with Elena? To begin with,
ordinary good care might have kept the child from falling
sick, and judging from what he had seen . . . well, her fear
of the hospital was an indication of her fitness to bring up
children. Some people would say that she loved them and
that her love made up for her shortcomings—not to look
too closely at those shortcomings. Love, by all means. But
because the mother and the child were tied together in that
way, if the child died through her ignorance, was she still
a good mother? Should someone else—he thought of it
seriously—have the right to take the child away? Or should
the fate of the two of them be considered one and the same,
and the child's death said to be the mother's affair only
because she would suffer most by its death? In that case
the child was not regarded as a person, and was that fair?
Well, that was the meaning of helplessness; that was what
they meant when they said it. Now with that in mind you
could understand why little children sometimes cried the
way they did. It was as if it were in them to know. Unfair,
thought Leventhal, not to say tragic.

He began to consider his own unfortunate mother whose large features and black hair he could summon up very faintly. Invariably he saw her wearing an abstracted look, but he was not in fact sure that her look was abstracted. Perhaps he attributed it to her. And when he examined his idea of her more closely he realized that what he really meant by abstracted was mad-looking; a familiar face and yet without anything in it directed toward him. He dreaded it; he dreaded the manifestation of anything resembling it in himself. A period of coolness toward Harkavy had followed the latter's remark about persecution. Knowing his history, how could Harkavy say that to him? But eventually he satisfied himself that Harkavy was merely thoughtless and didn't sufficiently understand what he was saying. Until he spoke, he himself didn't know what was coming. So he had forgiven Harkavy, but he was left more conscious of his susceptibility to remarks of that kind. He was afraid the truth about him was so apparent that even Harkavy might see it.

He had spoken of his fears to Mary late one night in bed. She laughed at him. Why did he accept his father's explanation of his mother's illness? And he had never really learned the facts about it, it was true. He had only his father's word for it that she died insane. Many of the things that terrified people lost their horror when a doctor explained them. Years ago everyone spoke of brain fever; now it was known that there was no such sickness. "For my own peace of mind," Mary said. "I would try to find out what she had." But, although Leventhal then promised that he would go into the matter soon, make a real inquiry, so far he had done nothing about it. As for his fears, he was too ready, Mary told him, to believe anything and everything about himself. "That's because you're not sure of yourself. If you were a little more sure you wouldn't let yourself be bothered," she said with all the firmness of her own confident strength. And she was probably right. But, my God, how could anyone say that he was sure? How could he know all that he needed to know in order to say it? It wasn't right. Leventhal felt the presumption of it without, however, blaming Mary; he knew she expressed truthfully what she felt.

"The only proof there is of anything wrong with your mother is that she married that father of yours," Mary had ended. This remark brought tears into Leventhal's eyes as he sat in the dark, cross-legged, bending away from the pillow at his back. Nevertheless Mary's words were beneficial on the whole. Till he had better evidence, his fears were the fears of hypochondria. The word was helpful; it gave them an amusing aspect. Still the fact remained that when he called up his mother's face at some moment it was, for all of that, abstracted.

He gazed down at the dented deck brass. For the present he preferred to be cautious about Elena and assume that her nerves were overworked. She gave way without control to what any parent with a sick child was liable to feel. But when he allowed himself to go further, to think of more than overworked nerves and Italian emotions, he saw the parallel between her and his mother and, for that matter, between himself and Max and the two children. The last was not so important. But it gave him a clearer view of each of the women to consider that they were perhaps alike. At least you could say of them that they were both extraordinary when they were disturbed (he had not forgotten his mother's screaming)—whatever the right word for it was.

The winches began to rattle, a gate dropped resoundingly in the green wooden cove of the slip. The water turned yellow and white under the bows like stale city snow. The boat started back and then, with shut engines, glided in, bumping the weedy timbers. On the long hill beyond the arches of the sheds, the house fronts were suddenly present, and Leventhal, moving ashore in the crowd, heard the busses throbbing before the station.

Philip again let him in. Recognizing his uncle he stood aside for him.

"Where's Elena. Is she here?" Leventhal said, striding into the dining room. "How's the boy?"

"He's sleeping. Ma's downstairs using Villani's telephone. She said she'd be up right away." He turned to the kitchen, explaining from the doorway, "I was eating supper."

"Go ahead, finish," said Leventhal. He walked restlessly round the room. Mickey was asleep; the second alarm seemed to be like the first. Touching the hall door, he debated whether to go into the child's room alone. No, it would be wiser not to; there was no telling how Elena would take it.

It was shortly before sundown, and there were lights in the flats giving on the airshaft where the walls, for a short distance below the black cornice, were reddened by the sky. Leventhal went into the kitchen where Philip sat beside the table on a high stepstool. He had a bowl of dry cereal before him and he poured milk over it, digging up the flap of the milk carton with his thumbnail; he peeled and sliced a banana, sprinkled sugar over it, and flipped the skin into the sink with its pans and dishes. The paper frills along the shelves of the cupboard crackled in the current of the fan. It ran on the cabinet, sooty, with insectlike swiftness and a thrumming of its soft rubber blades; it suggested a fly hovering below the tarnish and heat of the ceiling and beside the scaling, many-jointed, curved pipes on which Elena hung rags to dry. The boy's knees were level with the tabletop, and he bent almost double as he ate, spreading his legs. Leventhal reflected that he had taken the stool instead of a chair because he felt the need to do something extreme in his presence. "I used to do stunts, too, when there was a visitor," he reminded himself. "And that is what I am here, a visitor."

"Is this your whole supper?" he asked.

"When it's hot like this, I never eat a lot." The boy had a rather precise way of speaking.

"You ought to have bread and butter, and so on, and greens," said Leventhal.

Philip interrupted his eating to look at his uncle briefly. "We don't cook much during the heat wave," he said. He set his feet on a higher rung and bent even lower. His hair had been newly cut, roughly clipped on top and shaved high up the back of his neck to a line above his large but delicately white ears.

"What kind of a barber do you have?"

Philip looked up again. "Oh, Jack McCaul on the block. We all go to him; Dad too, when he's home. I told him to cut it this way. I asked for a summer haircut."

"They ought to take away the man's license for giving you one like that." He said this too forcefully and overshot his intended joke, and he paused and made an effort to find the right tone.

"Oh, McCaul's all right," said Philip. "He takes care of us. I was waiting for the kid to get better so's we could go together. But Ma said I should go and have a trim before she had to buy me a fiddle to go with my hair. This haircut is all right for the weather. Last summer I got a baldie—all off."

"Well, it's really okay." Leventhal watched him eat, penetrated with sympathy for him. "An independent little boy," he thought. "But how they treat him."

He sat down by the window, unbuttoning his creased jacket, and glanced at the sky through the airshaft's black square. In one of the other flats, a girl in a parlor chair was brushing a dog that yawned and tried to lick her hand. She pushed its muzzle down. A woman in a chemise passed through the room, back and forth from kitchen to hall. Mickey's window gave on the shaft; it was on the corner, and if he were awake now he might be able to see his brother and his uncle.

"The doctor's going to be here any minute." Leventhal was suddenly impatient. "I thought Elena was in such a hurry for him to come. What's keeping her?"

"I'll go and see." Philip sprang from the stool.

"Don't leave your supper. Tell me where she is and I'll find her." But Philip was already in the corridor. Leventhal, however, instead of footsteps, heard voices through the open doors. Had he met Elena coming up the stairs? The light went on in the dining room, under the green glass panes of the shade, and Leventhal had a glimpse of a woman in a black dress moving beside the table.

"Boy?" he called out. "Say, Phil?"

"Here. Come on in."

"Who is it?" he inquired in a low voice. He tried to see beyond the lamp to the other end of the room.

"My grandmother."

"The old woman?" said Leventhal in surprise. He had heard something about her from Max but had never seen her. He started from the doorway and, looking confused, went toward her around the dining-room table, changing his direction when she turned and sat down in the mohair armchair.

"This is Dad's brother," Philip said to her. Leventhal was conscious of prolonging his nod almost into a bow; he

[57]

wanted to be prepossessing. The old lady gave him only a brief sharp glance. Taller than Elena, she was gaunt and straight-backed, and the carriage of her head was tense. She wore large gold earrings. The hair came out short and white at her temples; toward the back of her head it was black and tightly knotted. Her dress also was black, a·black silk, and despite the heat she wore a shawl on her shoulders.

Since she remained silent, Leventhal stood undecided; it seemed inadvisable to say more; to sit down without being answered would embarrass him. But, also, it might be impolite to return to the kitchen. Maybe he misunderstood her taciturnity. However, she seemed to avert her head from him, and he had to struggle with an angry urge to compel her to face him. Nevertheless she had not spoken, and he could not be sure. It was possible that he was mistaken.

"I thought you were going to fetch your mother," he said to Philip somewhat impatiently. And when Philip started to leave, he said hastily, "I'll go with you." He had decided that the grandmother's look was unfriendly, though in the dusty green-tinged light that came through the lampshade it was difficult to get a definite impression. But he felt her antagonism. In a shambling gait—the heat made him heavy —he followed Philip down several turns of the stairs to the neighbor's flat. Philip knocked, and in a few seconds Elena came hurrying out to them, eager and fearful.

"Oh, Asa, you," she said. "And the specialist? Did you bring him?"

"He said between seven and eight. He ought to be here soon."

The neighbor, Mr. Villani, smoking a twisted stogie, appeared in the hallway and cried out to her, "You let us know right away what he says about the boy up there." He looked at Leventhal, perfectly unconstrained in his curiosity. "How do?" he said to him.

"This is my husband's brother," said Elena.

"Yes, sure," said Villani taking the cigar out of his mouth. Leventhal impassively looked back at him, his eyes solemn and uncommunicative, only a little formally inquiring. A drop of sweat ran down his cheek. Villani, one hand in his pocket, spread his trousers wide. "You look like Mr. Leventhal, all right," he said. He turned to Elena. "And what the doctor tells you, you do it, missis, you hear? We're gonna pull that boy through, so don't worry. What I think is he's only got summer fever," he said to Leventhal. "It ain't serious. My kids had it. But this missis is the worrying kind."

"It's plenty serious," said Elena. She spoke quietly, but Leventhal, watching her closely and paying particular attention to the expression of her eyes, felt a pang of his peculiar dread at their sudden widening.

"Ah, ah, how do you know? Are you a doctor? Wait a while."

"The man is right, I think, Elena," said Leventhal.

"Sure I am. You got to have confidence in the doctor." An impassioned, sharp sound caught in his throat and he flung his arm out in a short, stiff, eloquent curve. "What's the matter! Sure! You listen to me. That boy is all right." The cigar glowed in his fingers.

"She'll have confidence," Leventhal assured him.

They started upstairs. On the fourth floor Elena stopped and with an excited escape of breath, "Phillie, what did you tell me—Grandma's here?"

"She just came."

"Oh my!" She turned with anxious abruptness to Leventhal. "What did she say to you, anything?"

[59]

"Not a single word."

"Oh, Asa, if she does. . . . Oh, I hope to God she doesn't. Let her say what she wants. Just let it pass."

"Oh, sure," he said.

"She's a very peculiar type of person, my mother. She acted terrible when Max and I got married. She wanted to throw me out of the house because I was going with him. I couldn't bring him in. I had to meet him outside."

"Max mentioned once or twice. . . ."

"She's an awfully strict Catholic. She said if I married anybody but a Catholic she wouldn't have any more to do with me. She would curse me. So when I left the house she did. I didn't even see her until Phillie was born. I still don't see her much, but since Mickey is sick she's here pretty often. If Max is home she won't even come in. She's very superstitious, my mother. She has all the old-country ways. She thinks she's still in Sicily." Elena spoke in a near-whisper, covering the side of her face with her hand.

"Don't worry, I'll know how to take her."

"She just is that way," Elena explained, smiling helplessly.

"You can stop worrying."

The old woman met them in the hallway and she began immediately to speak to her daughter, her eyes occasionally moving to Leventhal's face. Her voice had what to him was a characteristic Italian hoarseness. Her long head was drawn back rigidly on her black shoulders. He observed how she turned down her underlip, exposing her teeth as she lingered on a syllable. Elena, dejected, shook her head and answered in short phrases. Leventhal tried to seize a word here and there. He understood nothing. Suddenly Elena interrupted her mother, crying out, "Where? Why didn't you say so right away, Mamma? Where is he? The man is here!" she exclaimed to Leventhal. "The specialist!" She ran in. Leventhal, walking behind the grandmother in the hall leading to the bedroom, contorted his face in an unusual release of feeling. Ugly old witch! To make her daughter wait and listen to her complaints before telling her the doctor had arrived. "Parents!" he muttered. "Oh, yes, parents! My eye, parents!" He was tempted to jostle her.

They entered the bedroom. The doctor had pulled up Mickey's shirt and was listening to his heart. The child seemed scarcely awake; he was dull and submitted to the examination, listless with the fever, lifting his eyes only to his mother, identifying rather than appealing to her. Philip leaned on the bedpost to see him.

"Phil, don't shake, stay off it," Elena said.

The doctor turned a glance over his shoulder. He was a young man with a long, rosy face and thin, gold-rimmed lenses over his close-set eyes. While he pressed the stethoscope on the child's chest and shoulders, he looked steadily at Leventhal, evidently taking him for the father. At first Leventhal was bothered by this error. Soon, however, he grasped the fact that the doctor was trying to tell him the illness was serious. Unobserved by Elena, who was folding back the counterpane, he gave him a gloomy nod to show that he understood. The doctor let the earpieces of the instrument fall around his neck and felt the boy's arms with his clean red fingers. In the yellowish, stiff web over the blackness of the window, the ferns and the immense moths were shot with holes and gaps. The kitchen air and the noises of the court entered the room. The boy was raised and his pillow turned over.

"You should sponge him every few hours," said the doctor.

"I did it this afternoon. I'll do it again soon," said Elena. She had been whispering to him from time to time and

[61]

now she spoke up eagerly, almost joyfully. She seemed to
feel there was nothing to fear any longer. "I trust him so
much," she said to Leventhal, gazing at the doctor. Leventhal's hands were damp and chill. He was beginning to feel
ill from the sudden doubling of his tension. He wiped his
face, passing the handkerchief over the bristles on his cheek
and leaving a piece of lint on them. He was sure he had
interpreted the doctor's silent communication correctly.
Elena's hopefulness stunned him. He turned, careworn, looking at her and at the children, and a few moments passed
before it came to him that this burden after all belonged to
his brother. At once he was furious with Max for being
away. He had no right to go in the first place. Leventhal felt
for his wallet; he had put Max's card in it. He would wire
him tonight. Or no, a night letter was better, he could put
more into it. He began to form the message in his mind.
"Dear Max, if you can tear yourself away from what you're
doing . . . if you can manage to get away for a while . . ."
He would not spare him. The harsher the better. Just look
at what he left behind him: this house, a tenement; Elena,
who might herself need taking care of; the children they had
brought into the world. Leventhal returned to the composi-
tion of the night letter. "You are needed here. Imperative."
That it was he, almost a stranger to the family, who was
sending the message, should show Max how serious the
matter was. Ah, what a business! And the grandmother?
If anything happened to the boy she would consider it in
the nature of a judgment on the marriage. The marriage
was impure to her. Yes, he understood how she felt about
it. A Jew, a man of wrong blood, of bad blood, had given
her daughter two children, and that was why this was happening. No one could have persuaded Leventhal that he
was wrong. Hardly hearing what was being said in the room,

[62]

he contemplated her grimly, her grizzled temples, the thin straight line of her nose, the severity of her head pressed back on her shoulders, the baring of her teeth as she opened her lips to make a remark to her daughter. No, he was not wrong. From her standpoint it was inevitable punishment—that was how she would see it, a punishment. Whatever else she might feel—and after all the boy was her grandson—she would feel this first.

He just then observed great agitation in Elena and began to pay attention to the conversation. He heard the doctor speaking of the hospital and he thought, "She can't keep the kid here any more. She'll have to give in."

"I told her yesterday she ought to send him to the hospital," he said.

Elena still resisted. "But why isn't it just as good for him at home? Better. I can look after him better than a nurse."

"He's got to go if you want me to take the case."

"But what's the matter here?" she pleaded.

"Has to be done," said the doctor knocking up the clips of his bag.

"Should I go for a cab?" Philip softly asked his uncle.

Leventhal nodded. Philip ran from the room.

6

THE DOCTOR told Leventhal on the way back to Manhattan that he thought—though he needed more evidence to confirm the diagnosis—Mickey had a bronchial infection of a rare kind. He named it two or three times, and Leventhal tried to fix it in his mind but failed. Such cases were serious; not necessarily fatal, however. "You think you'll be able to help him, doctor?" he asked in great eagerness, and the doctor's word of hope raised his spirits. The boat moved out; the immense golden crowns of light above the sheds now had space to play on the water between the stern and the shore. "I was going to wire my brother to come," said Leventhal—he had already explained that he was not the father. The doctor answered that he didn't think it was necessary at present. It was enough to tell him to stand by. Leventhal accepted this as sensible advice. Why create a scare now? It wasn't so critical after all. He would send Max a night letter and let him decide for himself whether to come or wait. The ferry crawled in the heat and blackness of the harbor. The mass of passengers on the open deck was still, like a crowd of souls, each concentrating on its destination. The thin discs of the doctor's spectacles were turned to the sky, both illumined in the same degree by the bulb over his head. Leventhal wanted to ask him more about the disease. It was rare. Well, did medicine have any idea how a thing like that singled out a child in Staten Island rather than, say, St. Louis or Denver? One child in thousands. How did they account for it? Did everyone have it dormant? Could it be hereditary? Or, on the other hand, was it even more strange that people, so different, no two with the same fingerprints, did not have more individual diseases? Freed from his depression by the doctor's encouragement, he had a great desire to talk. He would have liked to discuss this but he had already asked the name of the disease several times and failed to retain it, and so the doctor must have a poor opinion of him. And maybe he would be condescending to a layman. Accordingly, Leventhal was silent and thought, "Well, let it ride." But he continued to wonder about it. They said that God was no respecter of persons, meaning that there were the same rules for everybody. Where was that? He tried to remember.

They were in the middle of the harbor when the heat was suddenly lifted by a breeze. High and low between the shores, the lights of ships, signals, and bridges drifted and ran, curved, and stood riding on the swell, and the sonorous, rather desolate bells rang from the water when the buoys were stirred. The breeze blew a spray to the deck, and the boat now and then seemed to tremble to the pull of the ocean beyond the islands. As they neared the Manhattan side, people began to get up from the benches in the salon; there was a great press when the chains were dropped. Leventhal was separated from the doctor.

He went home on the subway, pushing through the revolving steel gate at his station and breathing the cooler air of the street with deep relief.

He was expecting a letter from Mary—one was about due —and he opened the mailbox swiftly while Nunez' dog sniffed at his legs. Instead of a letter, Mary had sent two post cards closely covered with writing. She and her mother were starting for Charleston on Friday. The house was sold. They were both well and she hoped he was, too, in spite of the heat. It was fine old Baltimore summer weather—it simply drugged you. The second card was different; there were intimate references on it. Only Mary could write such things on cards for everybody in the world to read. Amused, proud, pleased with her, pleased rather than embarrassed at the possibility that postal clerks had read the cards, he put them in his pocket. "Do I pass inspection?" he demanded of Nunez' dog. "Blow now." Stooping he caught the dog's head and rubbed it. He started up stairs and the animal came after him. "Blow now, I say." He barred the way with his leg, then whirled inside and slammed the hall-door. "Go home!" he yelled, and laughed uproariously. "Go on home!" He pounded the glass, and the dog barked raucously and leaped at the pane. Leventhal told one of the neighbors, whom he hardly knew, "The super's dog is having a fit. Hear him?" An elderly, guarded, pale face gave him an uncertain smile and seemed to listen in awe to the racket in the foyer. Leventhal hurried up with thumping steps, whipping his hat on the banister and entering his flat with a commotion. Dear Mary! If she were only here now to put his arms around and kiss. He flung away his hat and his jacket, pulled off his shoes, and went to open the windows and push aside the curtains. It had turned into a beautiful night. The air was trembling and splendid. The moon had come out; there were wide-spaced stars, and small clouds pausing and then spinning as the cool gusts broke through the heat.

He lit the lamp on the secretary and began to write to his wife. Gnats fell and rose again from the illuminated green blotter. He gave her an account of himself, forgetting that he had felt nervous, restive, and unwell. He said nothing about what had happened at the office. It did not seem worth saying. He wrote swiftly and exuberantly; he discussed the weather, he mentioned that Wilma had drunk the beer, that the parks were terribly crowded. Then he found himself telling her about his nephew, writing with sudden emotion, the words beginning to sprawl as his hand raced. In a changed tone he described Elena. He had been afraid to look at her, he confessed, when she got into the cab and he laid the bundled-up child—she had him in two blankets although the temperature must have been over ninety—on her lap. All the impressions of the moment returned to him—the boy's eyes with the light of the meter on them, the leathery closeness of the back seat, the driver's undershot jaw and the long peak of his black cap, Philip's crying, Villani keeping back the children on the sidewalk. The beating of Leventhal's heart rose and his tongue became dry. As for his brother . . . But when he had written Max's name he stood up and leaned over the paper. He had meant to send the night letter before coming up. The pen was staining his fingers. He dropped it and began looking for his shoes outside the circle of lamplight. He had just found them and was forcing his feet into them without bothering about the laces when his bell rang, piercingly and long. Leventhal straightened up with a grunt of annoyance and surprise. "Now who in the name of hell would ring like that?" he said. But he already knew who it was. It was Allbee. It must be. He opened the door and listened to the regular sibilance and knocking of the footsteps in the hollow stair well. It occurred to him that he could escape Allbee by going to the roof. If he went out stealthily he could still get away. And if he were followed, the next rooftop was only a matter of six inches away, an easy step over. Then he could get into the street and good-by. He could go even now. Even *now*. Yet he stood firm and strangely enough he felt that he had proved something by doing so. "I won't give ground," he thought. "Let him. Why should I?" He promptly went back to his letter, leaving the door open. He finished it abruptly with a few perfunctory sentences and read it over. He wrote "All my love," signed his name, addressed the envelope, and by that time Allbee was in the room. He knew that he had come in; nevertheless he controlled his desire to turn.

[67]

He stamped the envelope first, sealed it, momentarily guessed at its weight, and only then did he appear to take notice of his visitor, who smiled at him without parting his lips. To enter without a knock or invitation was an intrusion. Of course the door was open, but it was taking too much for granted all the same not to knock. Leventhal thought there was a trace of delight in the defiance of Allbee's look. "I *owe* him hospitality, that's how he behaves," passed through his mind.

"Yes," he said tonelessly, indifferently polite.

"You're well fixed up here," said Allbee taking in the room. He might have been comparing it with his own place. Leventhal could imagine what that was like.

"As long as you're here, sit down," Leventhal said. "What's the use of standing?" He would not get rid of him without hearing him out, and it might as well be now as another time.

"Much obliged," said Allbee. His head came forward courteously and he seemed to read Leventhal's face. "It's a long pull up those stairs. I'm not used to these high walk-ups." He drew a chair close to the desk, crossed his legs, and clasped his knee with somewhat rigid fingers. His cuffs were frayed, the threads raveled on the blond hairs of his wrist. His hands were dirty. His fair hair, unevenly divided on his scalp, was damp. It was apparently true that the climb had been hard for him. "It's quite a height, this," he smiled. "And for me, well . . ." he caught his breath, "I'm used to low places." He pointed his finger at the floor and worked it as though pulling a trigger.

"Are you here to give me the same song and dance as the last time? Because if you are let me tell you once and for all . . ."

"Oh, hold on," said Allbee. "Let's be sensible and open.

I didn't come to complain to you. Why should I? I only said what's obvious. Nothing to wrangle about. I'm on the bottom. You don't want to deny that, do you?" He extended his arms as if to offer himself for examination, and although he did it wryly Leventhal saw that he was really in earnest. "Whereas you . . ."

He indicated the flat. Leventhal said, "Oh, please," and shook his head. "Don't give me that stuff."

"It's a fact, a hard fact," said Allbee. "I'm the best judge of the facts. I know them intimately. This isn't just theoretical with me. The distance between you and me is greater than between you and the greatest millionaire in America. When I compare myself with you, why you're in the empyrean, as they used to say at school, and I'm in the pit. And I have been in your position but you have never been in mine."

"What do you mean? I've been down and out."

Allbee gave him a tolerant smile.

"Stony broke, without a nickel for the automat," Leventhal said.

"Ah, go on. You don't know anything about it, I can tell by your talk. You've never been in my place. Nickels for the automat . . . temporary embarrassment. That . . ." and he ended with his head to one side nearly touching his shoulder, and with his outstretched arm and open hand he made a gesture of passing the comparison away. There rose immediately to Leventhal's mind the most horrible images of men wearily sitting on mission benches waiting for their coffee in a smeared and bleary winter sun; of flophouse sheets and filthy pillows; hideous cardboard cubicles painted to resemble wood, even the tungsten in the bulb like little burning worms that seemed to eat up rather than give light. Better to be in the dark. He had seen such places. He could still smell the carbolic disinfectant. And if it were *his* flesh

[69]

on those sheets, *his* lips drinking that coffee, *his* back and thighs in that winter sun, *his* eyes looking at the boards of the floor. . . ? Allbee was right to smile at him; he had never been in such a plight. "So I'm mistaken," he reflected. "Why do I have to match him in that? Is it necessary? Anyway, what does he want?" For a time he forgot about the night letter. He waited for Allbee to reveal what he had come for. He did not know just what to expect, but he considered it very likely that he would repeat his charge despite his saying that he was not here to complain.

"Well," he said, prefacing his remark with a short laugh. "It's a peculiar statement to begin a visit with."

"Why, no. What could be better. It's the height of politeness to admire your host's house. And the contrast between us should please you very much. It should give you a lot of satisfaction to have done it all yourself."

"Done what myself?" said Leventhal suspiciously.

"Raised yourself up, I mean," said Allbee quickly. "You were just telling me you were once broke, which is to say that you're a self-made man. There's a lot of satisfaction in that, isn't there? And when you see somebody that hasn't made out so well it adds something to your satisfaction. It's only human. Even if you know better."

"I didn't say I was a self-made man or any such thing. That's a lot of nonsense."

"I'm glad to be corrected then," Allbee replied. "I must have had the wrong impression. Because, you know, the more I think about it the more I feel it's bunk, this self-made business. The day of succeeding by your own efforts is past. Now it's all blind movement, vast movement, and the individual is shuttled back and forth. He only thinks he's the works. But that isn't the way it is. Groups, organizations

[70]

succeed or fail, but not individuals any longer. Don't you agree?"

"Oh, it's not that way, exactly," Leventhal said. "No, I don't."

"You don't agree that people have a destiny forced on them? Well, that's ridiculous, because they do. And that's all the destiny they get, so they'd better not assume they're running their own show. That's the kind of mistake I wouldn't care to make. There's nothing worse than being confused, too, in addition to being unlucky. But you find people who have their luck and take the credit for it, too—all brains and personality, when all that happened was that they were handed a bucket when it rained."

"Let's have this cleared up right now, if you please," said Leventhal coldly. "We might as well be open and aboveboard. What does all this lead up to?"

"Oh, it doesn't lead to anything. It's just discussion, talk. Talk, talk, talk, talk, talk!" he exclaimed grinning, flinging up his hands. His eyes began to shine.

Leventhal impassively looked at him. "And what's that for?" he asked.

Allbee now appeared to be very depressed, perhaps at his own unsteadiness, and Leventhal was a little sorry for him. His alternation of moods, however, affected him unpleasantly. It was clear that the man was no fool. But what was the use of not being a fool if you acted like this? For instance, there was his language, did he have to speak like that, make himself sound so grand? Because he needed something to brace himself on? Oh, there was a smashup somewhere, certainly, a smashup and a tragic one, you could be sure of that. Something crushing, a real smash. But the question that remained uppermost with Leventhal was, "What does he want?" And notwithstanding his insistence on being above-board, he was unable to ask it.

"Is that your wife?" Allbee looked over Leventhal's head at a framed photograph on the secretary.

"Yes, that's Mary."

"Oh, say, she's charming. Ah, you're lucky, you know?" He stood up and bent over him, turning the photograph to the light. "She is charming."

"It's a good picture of her," said Leventhal, not liking his enthusiasm.

"She has that proud look that's proud without being hard. You know what I mean. It's a serious look. You see it in Asiatic sculpture."

"Oh—Asiatic!" said Leventhal scoffing.

"Certainly, Asiatic. Look at the eyes, and those cheek-bones. You're married to a woman and don't know she has slant eyes?" He made a descriptive turn of his thumb. "She's positively Asiatic."

"She comes from Baltimore."

"First generation?"

"Her mother is native-born, too. Further back than that I don't know."

"I'm willing to bet they came from Eastern Europe, originally," said Allbee.

"Why, that's not so stupendous. You wouldn't get any takers."

"I know I wouldn't get any takers in your case."

"No? Maybe since you investigated me and found out so much about me, you took the trouble to find out what part of Europe my parents came from."

"It's apparent enough; it doesn't need any investigating. Russia, Poland . . . I can see at a glance."

"You can, ah?"

"Well, of course. I've lived in New York for a long time. It's a very Jewish city, and a person would have to be a pretty sloppy observer not to learn a lot about Jews here. You know yourself how many Jewish dishes there are in the cafeterias, how much of the stage—how many Jewish comedians and jokes, and stores, and so on, and Jews in public life, and so on. You know that. It's no revelation."

Leventhal refrained from answering. It was, after all, no revelation.

Allbee once more turned his attention to Mary's picture. As he studied it and nodded, his eyes, to Leventhal's amazement, filled with tears, and he took on an expression of suppressed grief and injury.

"*Your* wife . . . ?" Leventhal ventured in a low voice.

"She's dead," replied Allbee.

Leventhal's tone fell even lower as he said, with a resonance of horror, "Dead? Oh, too bad. I'm sorry. . . ."

"So you should be. So you should." The words seemed to have been brought up from Allbee's chest as if they had been stored there and were now dislodged and uttered irregularly before he could hold them back.

Leventhal concentrated on them, averting his face—a characteristic of his when he was puzzling something out. He did not understand what Allbee meant.

"Of course I should be," he murmured, not quite aware that he was acknowledging a charge. The things that had happened to him in the last two days had made him acutely responsive, quick to feel. "What a shame!" he said in deep emotion, recalling the woman's face. "She was much too good for him, much too good," he thought. "But why should I say that? He was her husband, so that doesn't enter in now. He has to be considered. She's dead, but he's alive and feels.

That's what brought him down. He wouldn't be like this otherwise."

"So you're alone, now," he said.

"Yes, I'm a widower, have been for over four years. Four years and about three weeks."

"And how did it happen?"

"I don't know exactly. I wasn't with her. Her family wrote the news. She was hurt in an automobile accident. They thought she would recover, but she died suddenly. That's all I know. She was buried before I had a chance to get to Louisville."

"They didn't wait till you came?"

"Well, to tell you the truth I didn't want to be there. It would have been a terrible business. The family would have relieved itself by being angry with me. I would have tried to relieve myself by sneaking out to a bar, probably sat in the bar and missed the whole thing. That would have made it ten times worse for everybody. I was in that condition. And it was hot then. Louisville in hot weather. For *that!* Oh no, brother, I holed up where I was. It would have been brutal. She was dead. I wouldn't have been going to see *her* but *them*, her people. Dead is dead. Finished. No more. You long for your wife when she goes, if you love her. And maybe sometimes if you don't love her so much. I wouldn't know. But you're together, she bends to you and you bend to her in everything, and when she dies there you stand, bent, and look senseless, fit nothing. That's my personal feeling. Of course, I'm the first kind. I loved her. Well, I say, you long for her . . . but everything inanimate is the same to me. I'm not sentimental."

He was acting, lying, Leventhal decided. His moment of genuineness had passed and once more he had taken up his poise, mystifyingly off center and precarious. When he had

[74]

announced his wife's death, he had sounded wrathful, but Leventhal had felt himself come nearer to him or to something clear, familiar, and truthful in him. Now he was repelled again. He wondered whether Allbee was not actually a little drunk.

"But," said Allbee, "that's not all there is to it."

"No? There's more, eh?"

"Somewhat. We were separated before she died. That's why my relations with her family weren't good. Naturally, from their standpoint . . ." He paused to rub his eyelid and when he stopped it was red and appeared to have gone lower than the other. "They were prejudiced against me, wanted to shove the whole blame on me. I could blame them, if I wanted to. Her brother was driving the car; got off with scratches and a few bangs. The way those Southerners drive. Pickett's charge over and over again. Well . . . we were separated. Do you know why?"

"Why?"

"Because after Rudiger fired me, I couldn't get a job."

"What do you mean? You couldn't find any jobs? No jobs at all?"

"Not in my line. What could I have earned at any job? Not enough to keep going. After a man spends years in one line he doesn't want to change. He isn't in a position to do much. In something else he has to start at the bottom. What was I going to do, become a peddler? Salesman? Besides, I'd have to stop looking for what I wanted by taking any job."

"I would have taken anything before I let my wife go."

"We're made of different stuff, you and I." Allbee grinned. "And I didn't let her go. She left me. I didn't want her to go. She was the one."

"You're not telling me all there is to tell."

[75]

"No, no," he said, almost delightedly. "I'm not. And what's the rest? You tell me."

"Didn't your boozing have something to do with it?"

"Oh, there you go, there you go," said Allbee, smiling at the floor and swaying his large frame slightly. "My vice, my terrible vice. She left me because of my drinking. That's the ticket."

"A woman doesn't leave her husband for anything—just for a trifle."

"That's perfectly true, she doesn't. You're a true Jew, Leventhal. You have the true horror of drink. We're the sons of Belial to you, we smell of whisky worse than of sulphur. When Noah lies drunk—you remember that story?—his gentile-minded sons have a laugh at the old man, but his Jewish son is horrified. There's truth in that story. It's a true story."

"Watch your talk," said Leventhal stiffly. "You sound like a fool. I don't know what you're after, but you're not doing yourself any good with talk like that. I tell you that straight."

"Well . . ." he began; but he arrested himself. "All right, never mind. But it's unfair to try to put the blame for my wife's death on me. It's worse than unfair; it's cruel when you consider what she was to me and what I've been through. I don't know how you look at it, but I take it for granted that we're not gods, we're only creatures, and the things we sometimes think are permanent, they aren't permanent. So one day we're like full bundles and the next we're wrapping-paper, blowing around the streets."

"But I warn you I won't stand for such talk. Get that!" Leventhal spoke curtly, and Allbee seemed to lose his presence of mind and lowered his head, grieved and incapable of answering. It was hard to tell whether he was looking for the strength to continue, conniving something new, or disclosing his true state without pretense. Leventhal saw the side of his face, deeply indented at the lid and mouth, his cheek and chin covered with golden bristles, the blue of his eye fixed in brooding. The skin of his forehead, even-grained by the light of the lamp, was wet, and that of his jaw and throat was creased in a way that made Leventhal think of gills. Allbee's remark about creatures had touched his imagination in a singular way, and for an instant he was no more human to him than a fish or crab or any fleshy thing in the water. But only for an instant, fleetingly, until Allbee moved and looked at him. He appeared discouraged and tired.

"You'll excuse me," said Leventhal with somewhat provocative politeness, "but I have a wire to send. I was about to go send it when you came." Did that sound like an invention? Allbee might think so and interpret it as a maneuver to get rid of him. However, he had seen him writing when he entered, so why shouldn't it be true? He might have been drafting the message. Anyhow, why should he care? And besides, it was absolutely a fact that he was going to wire Max. Allbee could come along and check up on him if he wanted to. He studied his face to see how he was taking it. Allbee had risen. Suddenly Leventhal twisted about and his heart sprang. He thought he had seen a mouse dart into the corner and he hurried after it, lit a match, and examined the molding. There was no hole. "Ran away!" he thought. Or was it his fancy? "We have mice here," he explained to Allbee, who was at the door in the dark vestibule. He seemed to turn his head away, unresponding.

When they reached the lower hall, Allbee stopped and said, "You try to put all the blame on me, but you know it's true that you're to blame. You and you only. For everything. You ruined me. Ruined! Because that's what I am, ruined!

You're the one that's responsible. You did it to me deliberately, out of hate. Out of pure hate!"

He had clutched Leventhal's shirt and he twisted it as he spoke.

"You're crazy!" Leventhal shouted in his face. "You're a crazy stumblebum, that's what you are. The booze is eating your brain up. Take your hands off me. Off, I say!" He pushed Allbee with all the force of his powerful arms. He fell against the wall with an impact that sickened Leventhal. Allbee stood up, wiped his mouth, and stared at his hand.

"No blood. Too bad. Then you could say I spilled your blood, too." Leventhal cried.

Allbee answered nothing. He dusted his clothes unskillfully, stiff-handedly, as though beating his arms. Then he went. Leventhal watched his hasty, unsteady progress down the street.

Mr. Nunez, who had seen the incident, started up astride the striped canvas of his beach chair, and his wife, who lay on the bed near the window in a white slip, whispered, *"Que pasa?"* Leventhal looked at her in bewilderment.

7

"The nerve of him, that damned clown!" said Leventhal fiercely. His high, thick chest felt intolerably bound and compressed, and he lifted his shoulders in an effort to ease his breathing. "Ruined! I'll ruin him if he comes near me. What a gall!"

The letter to Mary was crumpled in his hand. It was impossible to send it like this. He would have to get another envelope and stamp, and for a moment this inconvenience grew overwhelmingly into the worst consequence of the scuffle. He tore the letter open, crushed the envelope, and threw it over the balustrade. Nunez had gone into the house and he was alone on the stoop. His glance seemed to cover the street; in reality he saw almost nothing but was only aware of the featureless darkness and the equally featureless shine of bulbs the length of the block.

Then his anger began to sink. He drew in his cheeks, somberly enlarging his eyes. The skin about them felt dry and tight. To think up such a thing! The senselessness of it perturbed him most of all. "Why me?" he thought, frowning. "Of course, he has to have someone to blame; that's how it starts. But when he goes over everybody he knows, in that brain of his, how does he wind up with me?" That was what was puzzling. No doubt the Rudiger business had a bearing on it; for some reason it caught on, and worked on a deeper cause. But that alone, out of hundreds of alternatives, had snagged.

In a general way, anyone could see that there was great unfairness in one man's having all the comforts of life while another had nothing. But between man and man, how was this to be dealt with? Any derelict panhandler or bum might buttonhole you on the street and say, "The world wasn't made for you any more than it was for me, was it?" The error in

this was to forget that neither man had made the arrangements, and so it was perfectly right to say, "Why pick on
me? I didn't set this up any more than you did." Admittedly
there was a wrong, a general wrong. Allbee, on the other
hand, came along and said *"You!"* and that was what was
so meaningless. For you might feel that something was owing
to the panhandler, but to be directly blamed was entirely
different.

People met you once or twice and they hated you. What
was the reason; what inspired it? This Allbee illustrated it
well because he was too degenerate a drunk to hide his feelings. You had only to be yourself to provoke them. Why?
A sigh of helplessness escaped Leventhal. If they still believed it would work, they would make little dolls of wax and
stick pins into them. And why do they pick out this, that, or
the other person to hate—Tom, Dick or Harry? No one can
say. They hate your smile or the way you blow your nose or
use a napkin. Anything will do for an excuse. And meanwhile this Harry, the object of it, doesn't even suspect. How
should he know someone is carrying around an image of
him (just as a woman may paste a lover's picture on the
mirror of her vanity case or a man his wife's snapshot in his
wallet), carrying it around to look at and hate? It doesn't
even have to be a reproduction of poor Harry. It might as
well be the king of diamonds with his embroidery, his
whiskers, his sword, and all. It doesn't make a bit of difference. Leventhal had to confess that he himself had occasionally sinned in this respect, and he was not ordinarily a malicious person. But certain people did call out this feeling.
He saw Cohen, let us say, once or twice, and then, when his
name was mentioned in company, let fall an uncomplimen-
tary remark about him. Not that this Cohen had ever offended
him. But what were all the codes and rules, Leventhal re-

flected, except an answer to our own nature. Would we have to be told "Love!" if we loved as we breathed? No, obviously. Which was not to say that we didn't love but had to be assisted whenever the motor started missing. The peculiar thing struck him that everything else in nature was bounded; trees, dogs, and ants didn't grow beyond a certain size. "But we," he thought, "we go in all directions without any limit."

He had put the letter in his pocket and he now took it out and debated whether to climb up to the flat for a stamp and envelope, or to try to buy them in a drugstore. He might not be able to obtain a single envelope. He did not want to buy a box of stationery.

Then he heard his name called and recognized Harkavy's voice.

"Is that you, Dan?" he said looking down the stairs at the dim, tall figure on the sidewalk. The shifting of the theater lights across the way made his vision uncertain. It was Harkavy. There were two women with him, one holding a child by the hand.

"Come down out of the clouds," said Harkavy. "Are you asleep, or something, on your feet?"

Nunez returned to his deck chair. His wife was in the window, resting her head on the sash.

"Do you go into a trance when the little woman is away?" Harkavy's companions laughed.

"Dan, how are you?" said Leventhal, descending. "Oh, Mrs. Harkavy, so that's you?"

"Julia, Julia, too." Harkavy pointed at his sister with his cigarette holder.

"Julia, Mrs. Harkavy, glad to see you both."

"And my granddaughter Libbie," said Mrs. Harkavy.

"Oh, this is your girl, Julia?"

"Yes."

Leventhal tried to make out the child's features; he saw only the vivid pallor of her face and the reddish darkness of her hair.

"Very active, Libbie," said Harkavy. "A little too energetic, at times."

"Oh, she runs me ragged," Julia said. "I can't keep up with her."

"It's the food you give her. No child should have so much protein," said Mrs. Harkavy.

"Mother, she doesn't get more than others do. It's just her nature."

"We came to call on you," Harkavy said to Leventhal. "But it looks as if you're stepping out."

"I have a couple of errands," said Leventhal. "I was going to send a wire."

"We'll walk you to Western Union, then. Are you wiring Mary? I suppose you want her back already." Harkavy smiled.

"Daniel, it's not a thing to joke about, if a couple is devoted," his mother said. "It's nothing to ridicule. These days when marriages are so flimsy it's a real pleasure to see devotion. Couples go to City Hall like I might go to the five-and-dime to buy a hinge. Two boards on a hinge, and clap, clap, clap, that's a marriage. Wire your wife, Asa, it's the right thing and it's sweet. Never mind."

"It's my brother I've got to send the wire to, not Mary."

"Libbie, come here to me, here!" Julia furiously exclaimed, pulling the child's arm. "I'll tie you in the middle with strings!"

"Oh, your brother?" said Mrs. Harkavy.

Leventhal flushed, inexplicably. "Yes, it was his boy I called Julia about. My nephew."

"Did you get hold of the doctor?" Julia asked. "Doctor Denisart, mother."

"Oh, he's a fine doctor, Asa; his mother is a lodge sister of mine and I've known him since he was a boy. You can have confidence in him. They gave him the very best education. He studied in Holland."

"Austria, mother."

"Abroad, anyway. His uncle put him through. He was in jail afterwards, the uncle, for income taxes, but that wasn't the Denisarts' fault. They used to send him pheasant to Sing Sing and they say he was allowed to have card parties in his cell. But they really learn in Europe, you know. That's because their slums are worse; they get complicated cases in their clinics. Our standard of living is so high, it's bad for the education of our doctors."

"Why, who says so?" said Harkavy, looking at his mother with interest.

"Everybody. Why, all the medical books Papa used to bring home from the salesroom were full of European cases —Fraülein J. and Fraülein K. and Mademoiselle so and so. The best medical education is foreign."

"And how is your nephew?" Harkavy said.

"They took him to the hospital today."

"Oh, very sick, does that mean? I'm sorry to hear it," said Julia.

"Very."

"But you can depend on Doctor Denisart. He's a fine young man—brilliant. I'll talk to his mother tomorrow. He'll take more interest in the case."

"I'm sure he'd do his best without being spoken to," said Julia. They were walking, and she pressed her daughter's head to her side.

"Influence is a good thing," Mrs. Harkavy said. "You

mustn't forget it. If you don't use it, you're left behind in the race of the swift. Everything depends on it. Of course, the doctor would do his best because of his ethics and so on, but if I talk to his mother he'll pay special attention to the case and do his very best. People are bound not to take things too much to heart, for their own protection. You've got to use influence on them."

"Take it up with Mrs. Denisart, then. It can't hurt," said Harkavy.

"I will."

"Dan," said Leventhal, drawing his friend behind, "do you remember a fellow called Allbee?"

"Allbee? Who? What's his last name?"

"Allbee is his last name. Kirby Allbee. We met him at Williston's. A big man. Blond."

"I suppose I could remember him if I put my mind to it. I have a pretty good memory."

They had come to the telegraph office, and Leventhal, standing at the yellow pine counter, wrote out a message to his brother entirely forgetting the sharp words he had intended to use. When he came out, he took Harkavy aside.

"Dan, could we have a private conversation for a few minutes?" he said.

"Why, I should say so. What's the matter, old fellow? Wait a minute. Let's ditch the women."

Mrs. Harkavy, Julia, and Libbie were waiting at the corner.

"Ladies, excuse us," said Harkavy with a pleased smile, fitting a cigarette into his holder. "Asa wants to talk over something with me."

"I'll see Mrs. Denisart for you tomorrow. Don't you worry," Mrs. Harkavy said.

Leventhal thanked her, and he and Harkavy crossed the street.

"Now what's the trouble, did you get into a scrape?" asked Harkavy. "You know you can trust me. It's safe to tell me anything. You can bank on it. Anything you confide in me will never come back to you through a third party, not any more than if you whispered it in the confession box. So let's have it."

"There's no secret to keep. It's nothing like that." Glancing at his friend, he hesitated, dissatisfied. Would it be worthwhile to explain the whole matter to Harkavy? He was warmhearted and a sincere friend, but he frequently put emphasis on the wrong things. He was already on the wrong track, suspecting a scrape. He probably meant an intrigue, a scrape with a woman. "It's this Allbee," Leventhal said. "He's been giving me a headache. You must remember him. He made fun of your singing one night at Williston's. You and that girl. Sure you can recall him. He worked at Dill's. . . ."

"Oh, *him*. That bird." It seemed to Leventhal that Harkavy listened more gravely, though perhaps it was his own wish to have something so troubling to him taken seriously that was behind this impression. He described his first meeting with Allbee in the park. When he told him how amazed he was at Allbee's spying, Harkavy murmured, "Well, isn't that the limit? Isn't that disagreeable? Nervy. Disagreeable."

"I thought you wouldn't forget how he went for you over that song."

"Oh, no, I have him definitely placed now. So that's the man?" He drew his head back with a restrained rearing motion and, from the stretching of his clear eyes, Leventhal saw that a connection of the utmost importance had been established in his mind.

[85]

"Dan, do you know any facts about him that I don't?"

"What do you call facts? It depends. I think so. I mean, I've heard. But was he around again? Let's have the rest of it."

"What have you heard?"

"You tell me first. Let's see if it's all one piece. Maybe it isn't. It may not be worth bothering about—loony all of it, and we ought to tie a can to it?"

He would not speak, and Leventhal hurriedly set forth all that Allbee had done and said, and, despite his haste and his eagerness to find out what Harkavy knew, he interrupted himself from time to time to make scornful, almost laughing comments which in his heart he recognized to be appeals to Harkavy to confirm the absurdity, the madness of the accusations. Harkavy, however, did not respond to these appeals. He was sober. He continued to say, "Disagreeable, disagreeable," but his manner did not give Leventhal much comfort.

"He makes out a whole case that I'm responsible for his wife and everything . . . !" said Leventhal, his voice rising nearly to a cry.

"His wife? That's far-fetched, far-fetched," said Harkavy. "I wouldn't listen to stuff like that."

"You think I do? I'd have to be crazy too. How could anybody? Could you?"

"No, no, I say it's far-fetched. He's overstraining the imagination. He must have a loose screw." Harkavy twisted a finger near his head and sighed. "But the story went round that he was canned, and then I heard that he couldn't get another job. They canned him at quite a few places before."

"Because of drinking. . . ."

Harkavy shrugged. His face was wrinkled and he was half turned away from Leventhal. "Maybe. He wasn't in good anywhere, as I heard it, and he was just about running out of breaks when he got the job with Dill's."

"Who told you that?"

"Offhand I don't recollect."

"Do you think there's a black list, Dan? When I talked over that Rudiger thing with you, you laughed at the idea."

"Did I? Well, I don't believe in such stuff in general."

"All right, here's proof. You see? There is a black list."

"I'm not convinced. This man of yours wasn't steady, and the word got around. It just got to be known he wasn't reliable."

"Why did he lose the job at Dill's? It was because he boozed, wasn't it?"

"Why, I can't say," Harkavy replied, and Leventhal thought that he looked at him anxiously. "I haven't got the inside information on it. As it came to me, the reason was different. In these cases, though, you get all kinds of rumors. Who knows? The truth is hard to get at. If your life depended on getting it, you'd probably hang. I don't have to tell you how it is. This one says this, and that one says that. Y says oats, and Z says hay, and chances are . . . it's buckwheat. Nobody can tell you except the fellow that harvested it. To the rest it's all theory. Why? He was skating on thin ice and he had to skate fast, faster and faster. But he slowed up. . . . and he fell through. As I see it . . ." Harkavy himself was discontented with this explanation; it was obviously makeshift. He faltered and his glance wandered. He had, unmistakably, information that he was trying to hold back.

"Why did he lose the job? What do they say?"

"There's no 'they'."

"Dan, don't try to give me the runaround. This is something I won't rest easy about till I know. It's no trifle. You must tell me what they say."

"If you don't mind, Asa, there's one thing I have to point out that you haven't learned. We're not children. We're men of the world. It's almost a sin to be so innocent. Get next to yourself, boy, will you? You want the whole world to like you. There're bound to be some people who don't think well of you. As I do, for instance. Why, isn't it enough for you that some do? Why can't you accept the fact that others never will? Figure it on a percentile basis. Is it a life and death matter? I happen to have found out that a young lady I always liked said I was conceited. Perhaps she didn't think it would get to me, but it did. Too bad people everywhere don't know what I'm really like. Or you. It would be a different universe. Things are too subtle for me; I have to knock along on common sense. What about this girl? I know she has reasons that she doesn't understand herself. All I can say is, 'Lady, God bless you, we all have our faults and are what we are. I have to take myself as I am or push off. I am all I have in this world. And with all my shortcomings my life is precious to me.' My heart doesn't sink. Experience has taught me to expect this once in a while. But you're so upset when somebody doesn't like you, or says this or that about you. A little independence, boy; it's a weakness, positively."

"I want you to tell me," Leventhal persisted. "I'll stick to you till you do. Considering what I'm being blamed for, it's natural that I should want to find out."

Harkavy gave in to him. "Williston thought you made trouble for this fellow when you went to Dill's and you acted up. He kind of hinted that it was intentional."

"What? Williston says that? Did he say that?"

"Well, something like it."

"How could he? Is he such an idiot?" Pale, his lips tight, making a great effort to hold back his anger and the unaccountable fear that filled him, Leventhal put his hand to his throat and stared frowningly at Harkavy. He said loudly, "And did you stand up for me?"

"Naturally I said he was mistaken and did all I could. I told him he was wrong."

"You ought to have said that I came to you immediately with the whole story about Rudiger. You even thought that it might be rigged up, that Allbee and Rudiger wanted to make a fool of me and it was hatched out by the two of them. Did you bring that up?"

"No, I didn't take the trouble."

"Why not!" He swiftly clenched his fist as though catching at something in the air. "Why not!" he demanded. "It was your duty if you're a friend of mine. Even if you didn't know the facts you should have defended me. And you did know the facts. I told them to you. You should have said it was a slander and a lie. If anybody repeated such a lie to me about you, you'd see how fast I'd take him up on it. It's not only loyalty but fairness. And how did he know what I did at Dill's? Why were you such a stick? Were you afraid to hurt his feelings by contradicting him?"

"I was not," said Harkavy. His marveling eyes took Leventhal in, but he answered quietly. "I didn't think it would benefit you if I argued with Williston. I just said that he was wrong."

"My friend!"

"Yes, if you ever had one. I am your friend."

"He might have asked me, before he said a thing like that, given me a chance to defend myself. He'd rather take that drunk Allbee's word for it. Where's their Anglo-Saxon fairness . . . fair play?"

"It's hard for me to understand Williston's side of it. I had an idea he was pretty level."

"Is it so hard?" Leventhal said bitterly. "I told you why

Allbee said I was out for revenge. And if Williston believes that I went to Dill's to make trouble, he must think what Allbee does, all around."

"Who, Williston? Oh, you're way off, boy, way off."

"Oh, am I? Well, you don't know what it's all about, I can see that. Williston is too nice a fellow, you mean. Talk about being innocent! Talk about a man of the world! Any child knows more about these things than you do, Dan. If he has it in him to think it was that insult . . . the insult to you, too, Dan, come to think of it. If that's what he believes . . ."

"Williston *is* a nice fellow," said Harkavy. "Remember, he was nice to you."

"I do remember. What makes you think I don't? That's exactly it. That's what makes it so bad, horrible. That's the evil part of it. Of course he helped me. So now if he wants to believe this about me he has the right? Can't you see how it stacks up?" He groped. "Certainly he helped me."

"You can be sure he doesn't know what your Mr. Allbee is up to and wouldn't like it if he did. Regardless. I mean that he couldn't believe that he says . . . that you ruined him. The man is off his trolley, sleuthing after you like that. He's disturbed in his mind. Haven't you ever seen such a case before? It's very pitiful. It happened in the family. My father's sister got strange during the change of life—said all the clocks were warning her to look out, look out, look out. Oh, she was just off. It was a calamity. She claimed that somebody was stealing out of her mailbox, taking letters. Oh, all kinds of things. I couldn't begin to tell you. Well, obviously that's the kind of case you're up against. It's disagreeable, but it's nothing to be alarmed about. She started telling people that she was Krueger the match king's widow, though my uncle was still living. Sometimes she said Cecil Rhodes, not Krueger. My grandfather fought in the Boer

War. Where else could she have gotten that? She went to an institution, poor thing. How those ideas get into their heads only Heaven knows."

Leventhal nodded inattentively. He could only brood over Williston. How could Williston believe that of him? Was it possible to know him and yet think him capable of deliberately injuring someone? For a reason like that? For any reason, even strict self-defense? He could not have imagined and carried out such a plan. Leventhal was deeply roused. He turned away from Harkavy, wrinkling up his eyes. Williston had helped him. He was indebted to him. Would he deny it? Harkavy had in his way rebuked him for seeming to forget it. He had not forgotten. But it was only natural to ask how much he owed Williston and how far gratitude should be expected to stretch. He had used the word "evil" a while ago, and what had given rise to it was a feeling that Williston had made the accusation under an influence against which he could not help himself. If he was ready to believe that he was such and such a person—why avoid saying it?—that he would carry out a scheme like that because he was a Jew, then the turn he always feared had come and all good luck was canceled and all favors melted away. He looked hopelessly before him. Williston, like himself, like everybody else, was carried on currents, this way and that. The currents had taken a new twist, and he was being hurried, hurried. His heart shrank and he felt faint for a moment and shut his eyes.

"I'll get it from him straight," he muttered, recovering himself a little. "I won't take somebody else's word for it. That would be doing what he did." He pulled out his handkerchief and mopped his face.

8

BUT THE WEEK PASSED and Leventhal made no move to get in touch with Williston, though he promised himself every day to clear up the whole business. Allbee did not appear, and Leventhal hoped that he had seen the last of him without really believing that he had. But at least matters in Staten Island were going better. Mickey was by no means out of danger; still he was improving, and Leventhal felt less worried about him. Max had wired back that he was ready to leave as soon as the doctor gave the word, and Leventhal wrote to say that while he thought Max ought to come home where he was needed, the decision was his own to make.

On Friday night Leventhal felt Mary's absence keenly. Before going to bed, he was tempted to put in a call to Charleston. He even went to the telephone, lifted it, and turned it, untangling the cord, but he set it down and went on undressing. He put on a white cotton robe she had given him on his last birthday, smoothing the lapels lightly and glancing down. She would be sure to feel if he called her now, at the beginning of the week-end, that he found being alone unendurable and was appealing to her to come home. And that would be unfair, since she could not come as long as her mother needed her. Also, when he hung up and she was inaccessible again, he would miss her even more than he did now. And she him.

There were several glasses on the sink. He washed them and turned them upside down to dry. Then he went into the dining room which had been shut since her departure. He left all the doors in the flat standing open; it made him feel easier.

He did not sleep well. Most of the night he could hear the motor of the refrigerator shuddering and rocking as it started and stopped. Several times he opened his eyes because of it. The light was burning in the bathroom. There was a short downpour and mist floated at the window. Toward morning he was aware that someone was speaking loudly in the street and he listened, breathing heavily. There was enough light to see by. He had gone to bed in the cotton robe and he lay, both pillows under his head, his hands joined on his chest; his feet and outspread legs were visible beside the deep shadow of the wall. The air was gray and soft in the long defile of the street.

A woman's voice cried out, and he flung himself up, brushing aside the curtains with a clatter of rings. There was a commotion at the corner. He saw a man start a crazy rush at one of two women; another threw himself in his way, shrieking, and held him off. Across the street two soldiers stood watching. They had been with the women, it was clear enough, and then the man had caught them—perhaps a husband, a brother, probably the former—and they drew off. The man circled with short, sidling steps, and the woman hung back dumbly, with horrible attentiveness, ready to run. Her high heels knocked on the pavement. He had reached her once, her dress was ripped from neck to waist. She shook her head and pulled back her hair. He darted in again, grabbing at her, and the friend, uttering her begging, agonized cries, caught his arms and was swung round by him. The soldiers had an air of being present at an entertainment especially arranged for them, and seemed to laugh to themselves from time to time. The husband's soles scraped on the pavement as he pushed toward his wife, and this time she ran away. She ran up the street awkwardly but swiftly, her soft figure shaking, and the soldiers started off at once in the same direction. The husband did not chase her; he stood still. The other woman with her hands on his arm spoke to him urgently,

[93]

thrusting forward her face. The rain was rapidly, unevenly drying from the street. Leventhal growled under his breath and wound the robe around himself more tightly. There was a gleam, as if a naked copper cable was lifted from the water and rose quickly, passing over masonry and windows. The sun was forcing its way through a corner of the gray air. The woman was still speaking to the man, imploring, pulling him the other way. She wanted him to go with her. Leventhal drew the shade and dropped into bed.

He was up at ten o'clock with a free week-end before him. The day had changed its look since dawn; it was warm, singularly beautiful. The color of the sky was strong; the clouds were as white as leghorn feathers rolling before a breeze that blew into the curtains and hauled at the strings of Mrs. Nunez' flower boxes. Leventhal bathed, dressed, and went down for breakfast. In the restaurant he took a booth instead of sitting at the counter as he did on weekdays. He found a copy of the *Tribune* on the seat and read, propping the paper on the sugar shaker while he drank his coffee. Afterward he took a walk uptown, enjoying the weather and looking into shopwindows.

The scene on the corner remained with him, however, and he returned to it every now and then with the feeling that he really did not know what went on about him, what strange things, savage things. They hung near him all the time in trembling drops, invisible, usually, or seen from a distance. But that did not mean that there was always to be a distance, or that sooner or later one or two of the drops might not fall on him. As a matter of fact he was thinking of Allbee—he was not sure that he had stopped spying on him—and with the thought came a faint sick qualm. Once more he reminded himself that he had to call Williston. But gradually the qualm passed, and his intention slipped to the back of his mind. And

later, when he took some nickels out of his pocket to pay for
a drink and saw an empty phone booth at the rear of the store,
he reconsidered and decided, for the time being, not to make
the call. He had not seen Williston for three years or more,
and to ask him, out of a clear sky, about something so difficult and obscure, perhaps forgotten, might appear strange.
Besides, if Williston was capable of believing he had injured
Allbee on purpose, he would be cold to him. And perhaps
Harkavy was right. Perhaps he would be trying to get Williston to assure him that he still liked him, to demand that assurance of him more than fairness. He pictured Williston
sitting before him in a habitual pose, at ease in his chair,
his fingers in the pockets of his vest, red-cheeked, his blue
eyes seeming to say, "So much frankness and no more," the
exact amount remaining in doubt. In all likelihood Williston
had made up his mind that he was responsible for what had
happened to Allbee and while he would listen—if Leventhal
knew him—with an appearance of courtesy and willingness
to suspend judgment, he would already be convinced. To
imagine himself pleading with him filled Leventhal with
shame. Didn't he know, he himself, that he had never con-
sciously wanted to harm Allbee? Of course he did. It was
for Williston, even if he was his benefactor, to explain why
he was ready to believe such a thing. And when you said that
someone was your benefactor, what did it actually mean?
You might help a man because he was a bother to you and
you wanted to get rid of him. You might do it because you
disliked him unfairly and wanted to pay for your prejudice and then, feeling that you had paid, you were free and
even entitled to detest him. He did not say that it was so in
Williston's case, but in a question like this you couldn't be
blamed for examining every possibility, or accused of being
cold-blooded or heartless. It was better to think well of peo-

[95]

ple—there was a kind of command that you should. And on the whole it was Leventhal's opinion that he had an unsuspicious character and preferred to be taken advantage of rather than regard everyone with distrust. It was better to be genuinely unsuspicious; it was what they called Christian. But it was foolish and miserable to refuse to acknowledge the suspicions that came into your mind in an affair like this. Because if you had them you should not put on an innocent front with yourself and deny that you did.

At the same time Leventhal was reasonable enough to admit that he might be trying to release himself from a sense of obligation to Williston by finding fault with him. He had never been able to repay him. Was he looking for a chance to cancel the debt? He did not think so. He wished he could be sure. Ah, he told himself, he was sure. He had never felt anything but gratitude. Again and again he had said—Mary could testify—that Williston had saved him.

But then, as he dwelt on it, the whole affair began to lose much of its importance. It was, after all, something he could either take seriously or dismiss as an annoyance. It was up to him. He had only to insist that he wasn't responsible and it disappeared altogether. It was his conviction against an accusation nobody could expect him to take at face value. And what more was there for him to say than that his part in it was accidental? At worst, an accident, unintentional.

The morning, with its brilliance and its simple contrasts, white and blue, shining and darkened, had a balancing effect on him of which he was conscious. He looked up, and a slight smile appeared on his face, swarthy in the sunlight. His clean white shirt was crookedly buttoned and tight at the neck; he put his fingers inside the band and tugged at it, drawing his chin up, and he straightened his shirt front clumsily, his gold wedding ring clicking on the buttons.

At noon he was in the west Forties. He ate a bowl of chili in a place opposite a music shop where a man in shirt sleeves, standing at one of the broad-swung windows on the second floor, blurted out an occasional note, testing a horn, one arm embracing the shining roundness of the brass. He was blowing erratically rich impatient notes and deep snores whose resonance Leventhal felt somehow entering his very blood as he gazed into the sun and dust of the peaceful street. He broke a cigar out of its wrapper, making a ball of the cellophane small enough to squeeze into the band. He felt along his thigh for matches and, when he had blown out his first puff, he walked into a booth and phoned Elena. One of the Villani children was sent to fetch her. Leventhal's eyes remained fixed on the horn player during the conversation.

Elena sounded quieter than usual. She was going to visit Mickey at three o'clock. He asked her about Philip and while Elena, after she had said, "Oh, Phillie? He's upstairs," went on talking about the hospital, Leventhal conceived the idea of spending the day with him and interrupted her to propose that Philip come over to Manhattan.

"I'll meet him at South Ferry. If you want me to, I'll come for him."

"Oh, I'll send him," said Elena. "That's fine. He'll like it. No, he can go on the ferry himself. What's there to it?"

Already full of plans, Leventhal hurried into the street. They would take a ride along the Drive on an open bus. The boy might enjoy that. Perhaps he would prefer Times Square, the shooting galleries, the penny arcades and pinball games. He congratulated himself on having thought of Philip; he was delighted. He would have passed the time tolerably well, he reflected, until some time toward evening when he realized he had not spoken three words to a living soul and the blues descended on him. And Philip, too, would have been left alone when his mother went to the hospital. Leventhal took the train downtown and sat in the small square on a bench commanding the ferry gates.

He kept his swarthy, unimpassioned face turned to the exit. The strain of waiting made him almost tremble, yet it was pleasurable, a pleasurable excitement. He wondered why it was that lately he was more susceptible than he had ever been before to certain kinds of feeling. With everybody except Mary he was inclined to be short and neutral, outwardly a little like his father, and this shortness of his was, when you came right down to it, merely neglectfulness. When you didn't want to take trouble with people, you found the means to turn them aside. Well, the world was a busy place—he scanned the buildings, the banks and offices in their Saturday stillness, the pillars ribbed with soot, and the changeable color of the windows in which the more absolute color of the sky was darkened, dilated, and darkened again. You couldn't find a place in your feelings for everything, or give at every touch like a swinging door, the same for everyone, with people going in and out as they pleased. On the other hand, if you shut yourself up, not wanting to be bothered, then you were like a bear in a winter hole, or like a mirror wrapped in a piece of flannel. And like such a mirror you were in less danger of being broken, but you didn't flash, either. But you had to flash. That was the peculiar thing. Everybody wanted to be what he was to the limit. When you looked around, that was what you saw most distinctly. In great achievements as well as in crimes and vices. When that woman faced her husband this morning after he had most likely tracked her all night from joint to joint and finally caught her catting, too red-handed to defend herself; when she faced him, wasn't she saying, silently, "I'm being

[98]

up to the limit just what I am"? In this case, a whore. She may have been mistaken in herself. You couldn't expect people to be right, but only try to do what they must. Therefore hideous things were done, cannibalistic things. Good things as well, of course. But even there, nothing really good was safe.

There was something in people against sleep and dullness, together with the caution that led to sleep and dullness. Both were there, Leventhal thought. We were all the time taking care of ourselves, laying up, storing up, watching out on this side and on that side, and at the same time running, running desperately, running as if in an egg race with the egg in a spoon. And sometimes we were fed up with the egg, sick of it, and at such a time would rather sign on with the devil and what they called the powers of darkness than run with the spoon, watching the egg, fearing for the egg. Man is weak and breakable, has to have just the right amounts of everything—water, air, food; can't eat twigs and stones; has to keep his bones from breaking and his fat from melting. This and that. Hoards sugar and potatoes, hides money in his mattress, spares his feelings whenever he can, and takes pains and precautions. That, you might say, was for the sake of the egg. Dying is spoiling, then? Addling? And the last judgment, candling? Leventhal chuckled and rubbed his cheek. There was also the opposite, playing catch with the egg, threatening the egg.

Boats from the island were arriving every few minutes, and, after the crowds had several times poured out and dispersed, Leventhal saw Philip standing at the gates. He got up and beckoned him, grunting, "Here, this way," and, waving his arm, advanced to the curb. The noise of the busses made shouting useless. "Here, here!" He motioned, and at last the boy saw him and came over.

[99]

"Well, was it nice crossing?" were Leventhal's first words. "It's a swell day. You can smell the sea here." He breathed deeply. "Fish and clams."

He observed approvingly that Philip's short hair was wetted and brushed, and that his shirt collar, which lay over the collar of his coat, was fresh and clean. He himself was wearing a seersucker suit that had just come back from the laundry; it made him feel set for the holiday.

"Now, how will we go uptown? On the bus?" He touched the boy on the shoulder. "There isn't much to look at on a Saturday from the Broadway bus."

"Oh, I get over to Manhattan," said Philip. "I know what it looks like. Let's take the subway."

They walked down, Leventhal guiding him through the turnstile and the gloom of the curved platform. A distant, rapid concussion of cars, like hammer blows, came to them in the tunnel.

It was fortunate that Philip was talkative, for, if he had been shy, Leventhal would have thought he was being reproached for his past neglect, not to be made up for in a single afternoon. He had read such a reproach into his silence last week, when he gave him the quarter. But there was no cause for misgiving. Philip talked on fluently, and Leventhal, though his mind sometimes appeared to be elsewhere, was secretly minutely attentive. The emotions Philip raised in him deepened his ordinary stolidity. But he glanced frequently at the slope of his cropped, handsome long head and into his face, and he thought that Elena's blood might show in his features but not in his nature. There they had something in common. The boy seemed to see it, too, Leventhal told himself.

Philip put his hand on a chocolate slot machine on one of the pillars, and Leventhal hastily went through his pockets for pennies and put in five or six, turning the knobs. The train rolled in while he was getting the chocolate out of the metal trough, and they abandoned the machine and ran.

"What do you say we walk a little?" Leventhal suggested at Pennsylvania Station. They got out and started up toward Times Square.

The air was stiller here in midtown, and they walked, Leventhal listening to Philip's chatter, often a little puzzled by it. Philip was curious about the foundations of the skyscrapers. Was it true that they had to have shock absorbers? They must have something to ride out the vibrations of the subway and to take in the play at the top, the swaying. They all swayed. Max had told him that in a ship the plates were arranged in parts of the deck to give when there was bad weather to ride out.

"It sounds reasonable," said Leventhal. "Of course, I'm no engineer."

Philip went on, speculating about what there was under the street in addition to foundations: the pipes, water pipes and sewage, gas mains, the electrical system for the subway, telephone and telegraph wires, and the cable for the Broadway trolley.

"I suppose they have maps and charts at City Hall." Leventhal stopped. "What about a drink?"

They had a glass of orangeade at a bamboo stand where the paper grass bristled on the walls. The woman at the tank clapped down the pull with her wrist, holding her fingers with their cameo rings rigid. The drink was slightly bitter with ground rinds.

Coming out of the stand they walked into a crowd that had formed around a man selling toy dogs that skittered and barked. The peddler, in a flecked sweat shirt and broken shoes, a band with Indian figures on his forehead, pushed them with his wide toe whenever they slowed down. "Run three minutes, guarantee," he said. To wind them he clasped them by the head; his fingers were too big to get at the key easily. "Three minutes. Two bits. They cost me eighteen. That's the con." He made his joke sullenly. His cheeks were heavy, his gaze unconciliating. "Three minutes. Don't pester, don't *shtup*. Buy or beat it."

There was laughter among the bystanders. "What's he saying?" Philip wanted to know.

"He's telling them in Yiddish not to push," Leventhal replied. He was reminded of what Allbee had said about Jews and New York. "Come on, Phil," he said.

On Forty-second Street the boy stopped often to look at the stills outside theaters, and Leventhal reluctantly—he did not care for movies—asked whether he wanted to take in a show. "I'd certainly like to," Philip said. Leventhal surmised that Mickey's illness had probably interfered with his Saturday movie-going.

"Any one you want," he said.

Philip chose a horror picture, and they bought tickets and passed over the brown rugs of the sunless lobby, between the nebulous lamps in their shattered, dust-eaten silk shades, and the long brocaded chairs, into the stifling darkness. They sat down in the leather seats.

On the screen an old scientist was seen haunting the dressing room of a theater where he had murdered his mistress many years ago. He had hallucinations about a young star who resembled her and he attempted to strangle the girl. The flaring lights hurt Leventhal's eyes, the music was strident, and, after half an hour of it, his nerves jarred, he went down to the lavatory. He found an old man there, leaning against a yellow sink, picking clean the end of a rolled cigarette.

"The stuff they put Karloff in," he said. "A man of his ability."

"You like him?" said Leventhal.

"In his line, he's a genius." He offered Leventhal a light, holding the match vertically pinched between limy white nails; his fingers were raw; he must be a dishwasher. "Here he's horsing around. It's an inferior vehicle. Even so, he shines. He really understands what a mastermind is, a law unto himself. That's what he's got my admiration for."

Leventhal threw away his cigarette; the smell of disinfectants interfered with the taste of it. He rejoined Philip, sliding into the seat. He shortly fell asleep. The efforts of the man next to him to push out of the row woke him up. He rose suddenly and heard the music of the newsreel.

"Phil, let's go. There's no air in the place," said Leventhal. "It's a wonder anybody stays awake."

The street was glaring when they emerged. The lights in the marquee were wan. There was a hot, overrich smell of roasting peanuts and caramel corn. A metallic clapping sound came to them from a shooting gallery. And for a time Leventhal felt empty and unstable. The sun was too strong, the swirling traffic too loud, too swift.

"Well, where next?" he asked. "What about the park? We can take in the zoo. A little fresh air wouldn't be bad, would it? Out in the open? We'll have a sandwich first and then walk down."

Philip agreed, and Leventhal could only guess whether the idea pleased him, or whether, having had his way about the movies, he felt obliged to acquiesce. "I'm out of touch with kids," he thought. "Maybe he's too sophisticated for the zoo. But I don't know why he should be." His earlier confidence in the understanding between them was fading.

"Is there anything you'd rather do instead?" he said to the boy. "You don't have to be afraid to speak up."

"The only thing I can think of is the Dodgers against Boston. But it must be about the fifth inning by now. I'm not afraid to speak up."

"Good. We'll get the ball game another time. When you've got something on your mind, I want you to tell me. Meanwhile let's have a bite."

The restaurant they went into was an immense place, choked with people. There were several lines before each counter. Leventhal sent Philip to buy soft drinks; he himself went for sandwiches. They found a table and Leventhal began to eat, but Philip went in search of a mustard jar. Leventhal sat sipping out of his bottle. Suddenly there was a stir in the crowd at the front of the restaurant; voices rose sharply. Several people stood up on chairs to see what was happening. Leventhal, too, lifted himself up and looked around for Philip, frowning, beginning to feel troubled. He entered the crowd and pushed forward.

"Here's my uncle. Uncle!" shouted Philip, catching sight of him. His arm was held by a man whose back was turned but whose blond head and cotton jacket Leventhal immediately recognized.

"What are you doing?" he said. In his astonishment he spoke neither to Philip nor to Allbee, but, as it were, to them both.

"I took the mustard from the table and this man grabbed me," Philip cried.

"That's right, I did. You put it back."

Leventhal flushed and pulled Philip away from Allbee.

"Oh, so this is your uncle?" Allbee smiled, but his eyes did not rest long on Leventhal. He was playing to the crowd and, standing there, his head hung awkwardly forward, he

[104]

could hardly keep from laughing at the sensation he was making. And yet there was the usual false note, the note of impersonation in what he did.

"I asked if I could have the mustard. I asked a lady and she said it was all right," said Philip. "Where is she?"

"That's right, mister." Leventhal met the distressed eyes of a young girl. White-faced, she pressed her pocketbook to her breast.

"What did I tell you?"

"You sneaked the mustard jar away. It doesn't belong to this young woman. It belongs to the table."

"I didn't see you at the table," she cried.

"You keep on following me around," said Leventhal in a low voice, tensely, "you keep it up and see what happens. I'll get out a warrant. I'm not joking."

"Oh, I could get a warrant out for you on a battery charge. Very easily. There was a witness."

"I should have broken your neck," Leventhal muttered. His large head twitched. Because of the boy he dissembled his anger.

"Oh, you should have. I wish it was broken." Allbee moistened his lips and stared at him.

"Come on, Phil." Leventhal led him out of the crowd.

"Who is he?" asked Philip.

"He's a nuisance. I used to know him years ago. Don't pay any attention to him. He's just a nuisance."

They sat down. Philip smeared mustard on his sandwich and looked silently at his uncle.

"It didn't upset you, did it?"

"Well, I jumped when he grabbed me, but I wasn't afraid of him."

"He's nothing to be afraid of." He pushed his plate across

the table. "Here, eat this half of mine, Phil." His heart was pounding. He gazed at the entrance. Allbee was out of sight for the moment.

"I won't stand it," he thought. "He'd better stay away from me."

9

IN THE THRONGED ZOO, Leventhal kept an eye out for Allbee. Defiant and alert at first, he soon became depressed. For if Allbee wanted to trail him how could he prevent it? Among so many people he could come close without being seen. Frequently Leventhal felt that he was watched and he endured it passively. Half out of fear of being mistaken, he made no effort to catch Allbee. He tried to put him out of his thoughts and give all his attention to Philip, forcing himself to behave naturally. But now and then, moving from cage to cage, gazing at the animals, Leventhal, in speaking to Philip, or smoking, or smiling, was so conscious of Allbee, so certain he was being scrutinized, that he was able to see himself as if through a strange pair of eyes: the side of his face, the palpitation in his throat, the seams of his skin, the shape of his body and of his feet in their white shoes. Changed in this way into his own observer, he was able to see Allbee, too, and imagined himself standing so near behind him that he could see the weave of his coat, his raggedly overgrown neck, the bulge of his cheek, the color of the blood in his ear; he could even evoke the odor of his hair and skin. The acuteness and intimacy of it astounded him, oppressed and intoxicated him. The heat was climbing again, and the pungency of the animals and the dry hay, dust, and manure filled his head; the sun, overflowing above the topmost twigs and bent back from bars and cages, white and glowing in long shapes, deprived him for a moment of his sense of the usual look of things, and he was afraid, too, that his strength was leaving him. But he felt normal again when he forced himself to walk on.

Leaving the zoo, he and Philip went into the park. Philip wanted to rest and went toward a bench. But Leventhal said,

"We'll find a place with more shade," because this was at a crossing of two paths and exposed to all directions. They sat down on a slope where no one could approach unseen. At the crossing, about fifty yards distant, there was a knot of people, one of whom might have been Allbee. Evening was coming on, and a new tide of heat with it, thickening the air, sinking grass and bushes under its weight. Leventhal watched. He even thought of turning the tables on Allbee, lying in wait for him somewhere. But what if he did trap him, what use was it? Would he embarrass him? He was beyond being embarrassed. Beat him? With pleasure. But he felt that he ought to beware, for his own sake, of countering absurdity with absurdity and madness with madness. And of course he did not want to make another scene while Philip was with him. He did not know what effect Allbee had had on him in the restaurant. He believed that Philip realized how much the incident had disconcerted him and therefore tactfully hid his feelings. He had a mind to talk to him about it. But he did not want to betray his anxiety; furthermore, he was afraid to begin a conversation without knowing in advance where it would lead. And maybe he was giving the boy credit for too much discernment. But the mood of the outing had changed. Philip looked pensive; he had nothing to say; and it would have been natural for him to mention the incident once, at least. Certainly he hadn't forgotten it.

"What's up, Phil," he said.

"Nothing. My feet are tired," he answered, and Leventhal remained in the dark as to what Philip really felt.

He decided to take a taxi to the ferry and he stood up, saying, "Let's go, Phil. Time to get you back." He set a rapid pace toward Fifth Avenue. Philip appeared to be somewhat puzzled by his haste but he enjoyed the ride in the open-roofed cab. Leventhal accompanied him to Staten Island and put him on the bus. Then he returned to Manhattan.

About nine o'clock, after a seafood dinner he barely tasted, he was on his way home without a thought of going elsewhere. He wandered into a cigar store, glanced round at the shelves beyond the flame on the counter, and bought a package of cigarettes. He took the change absent-mindedly, but, instead of putting it in his pocket, he began to look through it to find a nickel with which to phone Williston. For all at once he had a consuming need to get an explanation from him, tonight, immediately. He could not understand why he had put it off all week. He leafed through the directory quickly, copied the number out, and went into the booth.

Phoebe Williston answered, and the sound of her voice gave him an unexpected stab; he was reminded of the many times he had called to ask a favor of Williston, to get advice from him, or an introduction. The Willistons had been patient with him, usually, and he had often rather helplessly and dumbly put his difficulties in their hands and waited, sat in their parlor or hung on the telephone, waiting while his problems were weighed, conscious that he was contributing nothing to their solution, wishing he could withdraw them but powerless to do so. Inevitably there had been times when his calls were unwelcome and the Willistons' patience overdrawn. Whenever he rang their bell, or dropped a nickel in the slot and heard the dial tone, the question in his heart was, "How will it be this time?" And now, too, it was present, despite the fact that the circumstances were altogether different.

"This is Leventhal," he said. "How are you?"

"Leventhal? Oh, Asa Leventhal. How are you, Asa?" He thought she didn't sound unfriendly. It was too much to ask that she should be positively cordial, considering that this was his first call in three or four years.

"I'm good enough."

"You want to talk to Stan, I suppose."

"Yes."

He heard the instrument being laid on the table with a knock and then, for several minutes, the sound of a conversation carried on at a distance. "He doesn't want to talk to me," thought Leventhal. "He must be telling her that she should have said he was out." Presently the phone was picked up.

"Hello, there."

"Yes, hello. Is that you, Asa?"

Leventhal said without preliminaries, "Say, Stan, I want to see you. Can you give me a little time tonight?"

"Oh, tonight? That's pretty short notice."

"Yes, I know it is. I should have asked if you were going out."

"Well, we were planning to later, as a matter of fact."

"I won't stay. About fifteen minutes is all I want."

"Where are you now?"

"Not far. I'll grab a taxi."

It seemed to him that Williston did not conceal his reluctance. But when he said, "All right," Leventhal did not even bother to say good-by. He did not care how Williston consented to see him, just so he consented. He went into the middle of the street and flagged a cab. Of course, he observed to himself getting in, Williston was displeased by his phoning and blurting out his request, dispensing with the usual formalities. But there was much more than that to be concerned about, assuming that Williston really did side with Allbee. There was fairness, a man's reputation, honor. And there were other considerations as well.

The cab raced uptown, and Leventhal suddenly felt his face burning, for he had just recalled a verse his father had liked to repeat:

Ruf mir Yoshke, ruf mir Moshke,
Aber gib mir die groschke.

"Call me Ikey, call me Moe, but give me the dough. What's it to me if you despise me? What do you think equality with you means to me? What do you have that I care about except the *groschen*?" That was his father's view. But not his. He rejected it and recoiled from it. Anyway, his father had lived poor and died poor, that stern, proud old fool with his savage looks, to whom nothing mattered save his advantage and to be freed by money from the power of his enemies. And who were the enemies? The world, everyone. They were imaginary. There was no advantage. He carried on like a merchant prince among his bolts and remnants, and was willing to be a pack rat in order to become a lion. There was no advantage; he never became a lion. It gave Leventhal pain to think about his father's sense of these things. He roused himself to tell the driver to hurry. But the cab was already in Williston's block, and he grasped the handle of the door.

He recognized the elderly Negro who took him up in the elevator. Short, broad-shouldered, and slow, he stooped over the lever, handling it with the utmost deliberateness. They rose and stopped smoothly on the fourth floor. The knocker on Williston's door was also familiar—a woman's head cast in copper that surprised you by its heaviness.

Phoebe Williston let him in. Leventhal shook hands with her and she preceded him along the high-walled gray corridor into the living room. Williston stood up from his chair in the bay window, a newspaper falling from his lap and

[111]

spreading around the base of the lamp. He was in his shirt sleeves, the cuffs turned back on his smooth, reddish forearms. He hadn't lost any of his ruddy color. His brown hair was brushed sideways and his dark green satin tie hung unknotted from his buttoned collar.

"Pretty much the same, eh?" he said in his pleasant, deep voice.

"Yes, just about. You, too, I see."

"A couple of years older all around," Phoebe remarked.

"Well, it goes without saying."

Williston brought another chair forward in the bay window and the two men sat down. Phoebe remained standing, resting her weight on one foot, her arms folded, and Leventhal thought that her look was fixed on him longer than it need have been. He submitted to this prolonged look with an air of allowing her the right, under the circumstances, to inspect him.

"You seem to be all right, filled out," she said. "How's your wife?"

"Oh, she's out of town for a while, down South with her mother and family. She's fine."

"Lord! South in this weather? And are you still in the same place?"

"Address or job? Both the same. The same job, Burke and Beard; same people. I guess Stan knows."

The maid came in to ask Phoebe a question. She was a pale, slow-spoken girl. Phoebe listened, inclining her head and twisting her necklace in her fingers. She went back with her to the kitchen. Williston explained, "That's a new girl learning her way around." Leventhal, as in the past, felt conscious of a household that had more of the atmosphere of established habit than any he had ever known. Williston lay loosely in his chair, crossing his feet, his fingers pushed

[112]

under his belt. Within the metal guard of the semicircular window were several flowerpots with blossoms coarse as bits of red ore. Looking at them, Leventhal considered how he should begin. He was unprepared. It had seemed simple enough; he came with a grievance and he wanted an explanation. Perhaps he had counted on finding Williston roused against him; he certainly had not expected him to sit back and wait while minute after minute of the time he had requested ran out. He had not foreseen the effect Williston was having on him; he had forgotten what he was like. More than once, in the old days, he had mistrusted him. He had been full of rancor toward him when he thought Williston was uneasy about the reference letter. But on that occasion and others he had changed his opinion; he invariably did when he was face to face with Williston. He came to him complaining, but soon, without quite knowing how it happened, he began to feel unsure of his ground. So it was now, and he was unable to start. He sat in the bay window looking down, over the heads of the flowers, at the sprinting headlights in the depth of the park below the net of trees, as they turned on a curve and illuminated the boulders and trailing bushes of a steep hillside, one beam after another passing through an immobility of black and green.

"I wanted to talk to you about your friend Allbee," he said at last. "Maybe you understand what he's up to."

Williston was immediately interested; he lifted himself up in his chair. "Allbee? Have you seen him?"

"I sure have."

"I lost track of him years ago. What's he doing? Where did you see him?"

But Leventhal would answer no questions till he knew where he stood with Williston. "What was he doing last time you saw him?" he said.

"Nothing. He was living on insurance money. His wife was killed, you know."

"I heard."

"It hit him hard. He loved her."

"All right, he loved her. He didn't go to her funeral. And why did she leave him?"

Williston raised his eyes to him curiously. "Why," he said with a certain reserve, "I can't say for sure. That was something between them."

Leventhal was quick to feel the rebuke in this and he changed his tone somewhat. "Yes, I guess a third party never really gets the true story. I thought maybe you knew." He sensed that he ought to explain himself further. "I'm not trying to find out something that's none of my business. I have a good reason. Maybe you have an idea what it is . . . ?"

"Well, I think I do," Williston replied.

Leventhal's heart ran hot. "I understand that you take his side," he said. "You know what about. You think I'm responsible for everything, just as he does."

"Everything takes in a lot of territory," said Williston. "What are you driving at? I'd be more specific about something I was going to land on a man for." He was not quite so composed and genial, now; his voice was beginning to sound taut, and Leventhal thought, "Better, much better. Maybe we'll get somewhere." He bent his heavy, dark face forward.

"I didn't come to accuse you of anything, Stan. I'm not landing on you. I came to ask why you said certain things about me without hearing my side of the case?"

"Unless you tell me exactly what you're talking about, I can't answer."

"You want me to believe that you don't know? You know . . ." he made an ill-defined pushing gesture. "I want you to tell me right out if you think it's my fault that Allbee was fired from *Dill's Weekly*."

"You do? You want to?" Williston asked this grimly, as if offering him the opportunity to reconsider or withdraw the question.

"Yes."

"Well, I think it is."

A hard stroke of disappointment and anger went through Leventhal and drove the breath from his body. His limbs were empty; his thighs felt hollow and rigid as brass, and he could not stir his hands from them. He hardly knew what expressions were crossing his face.

"It is . . . It is?" he said, struggling. "I don't see why."

"For definite reasons."

Leventhal, his glance bitter and uncertain, said stumblingly, "I wanted to know. . . ."

Williston did not treat this as needing an answer.

Leventhal continued more surely, "I asked you, so you were bound to give me your opinion. If it's right, fair enough. But what if it's wrong? It might be wrong."

"I'm not infallible."

"No. When you say it's my fault, you're as good as telling me that I set out to make trouble for Allbee because of the way he acted toward Harkavy that night at your house, here. It must mean that I wanted to get even with him because of what he said about Jews." Williston's frown told him that this was something he didn't want to hear. Ah, but he would hear it, Leventhal said to himself fiercely. "That's what Allbee claims, that I wasn't going to let him get away with it and I made a plan to get him kicked out of his job. So, now, do you think that too?"

"I didn't say so."

"But if you blame me you must have the same idea. I

[115]

don't see any difference. And what if it is wrong? Isn't it awful if you're wrong? Doesn't it make me out to be terrible without giving me a chance to tell my side of it? Is that fair? You may think you have a different slant on it than Allbee has, but it comes out the same. If you believe I did it on purpose, to get even, then it's not only because I'm terrible personally but because I'm a Jew."

Williston's face had flamed up harshly. At either corner of his mouth there was a white spot of compression. He looked at Leventhal as though to warn him of the dangerous strain on his self-control. "I shouldn't have to tell you, Asa, that that wouldn't enter into it with me," he said. "You misunderstand me. I hope Allbee didn't tell you that I agree with him about that. I don't."

"That sounds fine, Stan. But it adds up to the same thing, as far as I'm concerned. You think that he burned me up and I wanted to get him in bad. Why? Because I'm a Jew; Jews are touchy, and if you hurt them they won't forgive you. That's the pound of flesh. Oh, I know you think there isn't any room in you for that; it's superstition. But you don't change anything by calling it superstition. Every once in a while you'll hear people say, 'That's from the Middle Ages.' My God! We have a name for everything except what we really think and feel."

"Looks like you're pretty sure of what I feel and think," Williston said stingingly, and then he shut his teeth and seemed to fight off his exasperation. "The Jewish part of it is your own invention. You take it for granted that I think you got Allbee in trouble purposely. I didn't say that. Maybe you aimed to hurt him and maybe you didn't. My opinion is that you didn't. But the effect was the same. You lost him his job. He might have lost it anyway, eventually. He was shaky at *Dill's*; they had him on probation."

"How do you know?"

"I knew it then and I had a talk with Rudiger about it later. He told me so himself."

Leventhal's black eyes went vacant. "Go on!" he said.

"That's the story. I would have told you right away but you wanted to jump all over me first. Rudiger claimed that Allbee brought you up to Dill's on purpose and that he either gave you instructions or knew you would act as you did. They had it in for each other. I guess Rudiger isn't an easy person to please. He was giving Allbee a last chance but he was more than likely hankering for him to make a false step so that he could land on him. He must have been on his tail all the time and he knew best whether Allbee had reasons for wanting to get a lick in at him."

"The whole thing is crazy. You can't answer for everybody you recommend. You know that. . . . But that's what Rudiger told you?"

Williston nodded.

"And didn't Allbee's boozing have anything to do with it?"

"He lost quite a few jobs because he drank. I won't deny it. His reputation wasn't good."

"Was he on a black list?" Leventhal said, intensely curious.

Williston was not looking at him. His face was directed reflectively toward the flowers, rough and crumbling in the warm night air.

"Well, as I say, he was on probation at *Dill's*. I asked Rudiger about the drinking. He had to admit Allbee had stayed on the wagon. He wasn't fired because he drank."

"So . . ." Leventhal said blankly. "In a way it really seems to be my fault, doesn't it?" He paused and gazed abstractedly at Williston, his hands still motionless on his knees.

"In one way. Of course I didn't mean to get him in trouble. I didn't know what this man Rudiger was like. . . ."

"No, you didn't."

There was something more than agreement in this reply. Leventhal waited for Williston to make it explicit but he waited in vain.

"How was I supposed to know what I was walking into?" he said. "This Rudiger . . . I don't see how anybody works for him. He's vicious. He started right away to tear at me like a dog."

"Rudiger said that never in all his experience had he had such an interview."

"Nobody ever talked back to him. He's used to doing whatever he likes. He . . ."

Williston whose color had deepened again to a hard red interrupted. "Don't let yourself off so easily. You were fighting everybody, those days. You were worst with Rudiger, but I heard of others. You came to ask him for a job and he wouldn't give you one. He didn't have to, did he? You should have had better judgment than to blow up."

"What, wipe the spit off my face and leave like a gentleman? I wouldn't think much of myself if I did."

"That's just it."

"What is? What I think of myself? Well . . ." He checked himself, sighed, and gave a slightly submissive shrug. "I don't know. You go to see a man about work. It isn't only the job but your right to live. Say it isn't his lookout; he's got his own interests. But you think you've got something he can use. You're there to sell yourself to him. Well, he tells you you haven't got a goddam thing. Not only what he wants, but nothing. Christ, nobody wants to be cut down like that." He suddenly felt weak-headed and confused; his face was

[118]

wet. He changed the position of his feet uneasily on the soft circle of the carpet.

"You were wrong."

"Maybe," Leventhal said, drooping. "My nerves were shot. And I never was any good at rubbing people the right way. I don't know how to please them."

"You're not long on tact, that's perfectly true," said Williston. He seemed somewhat appeased.

"I never intended to hurt Allbee. That's my word of honor."

"I believe you."

"Do you? Thanks. You'd do me a favor if you'd tell Allbee that."

"I don't see him. I told you before that I haven't seen him for years."

Allbee was ashamed to show himself to his old friends, Leventhal thought. Of course it was only natural.

"He thinks I'm his worst enemy."

"Where did you run into him? What's he doing? I didn't even know he was still in New York. He sank out of sight."

"He's been following me around," Leventhal said. And he told Williston about his three encounters with Allbee. Williston listened with a gravely examining expression and a modified but noticeable disapproving tightness at the corners of his mouth. Leventhal concluded, "I don't see what he's after. I can't find out what he wants."

"You ought to," said Williston. "You certainly ought."

"Does he mean that I ought to do something for him?" said Leventhal to himself. That, unmistakably, was what he implied. But what and how? It was not at all clear. He felt that he had not said everything he had come to say. The really important things, the deepest issues, had not been touched. But he saw that it was necessary for him to accept

[119]

some of the blame for Allbee's comedown. He had contributed to it, though he had yet to decide to what extent he was to blame. Allbee had been making a last great effort to hold on to his job. . . . However, it was time to go. He had taken up much more than his fifteen minutes. He stood up.

Williston said at the door that he expected to hear from him about the matter; he was very much interested in what was happening to Allbee.

Leventhal pressed the button for the elevator. It started up with a subdued meshing and locking of the metal doors and rose with measured slowness.

In bed later, lying near the wall, his knees pulled up and his face resting on the striped ticking of the mattress, Leventhal went over his mistakes. Some of them made him wince; others caught at his heart too savagely for wincing, and he stifled his emotion altogether and all expression, merely moving his lids downward. He did not try to spare himself; he recalled them all, from his attack on Williston tonight to the original scene in Rudiger's office. When he came to this, he turned on his back and crossed his bare arms over his eyes.

But even as he did so, he recognized one of those deeper issues that he had failed to reach before. He was ready to accept the blame for losing his head at *Dill's*. But why had he lost it? Only because of Rudiger's abuse? No, he, he himself had begun to fear that the lowest price he put on himself was too high and he could scarcely understand why anyone should want to pay for his services. And under Rudiger's influence he had felt this. "He made me believe what I was afraid of," Leventhal thought, and he doubted whether Williston could have understood this. For he belonged to the professional world and was loyal to it. There was always a place for someone like him, there or elsewhere. And another man's words and looks could never convert him into his own worst enemy. He did not have to worry about that.

Williston had not tried to justify Rudiger, true, but to Leventhal it was apparent that he himself was considered the greater offender. And looking at the incident from Rudiger's standpoint and taking Allbee's character into account, too, it was, after all, plausible that he, Leventhal, had been sent with instructions to make a scene. Harkavy had suspected Allbee and Rudiger of rigging it up in the first place. It had seemed reasonable to him and it seemed reasonable also to Rudiger. Only to Rudiger the suspicion was instantly true, true because it occurred to him, probably. That was the kind of man he was.

There was still another consideration—he ran his hand down his throat and through the hair of his chest which began with the shaven line above his collarbone. Had he unknowingly, that is, unconsciously, wanted to get back at Allbee? He was sure he hadn't. The night of the party he was angry, of course. But since then, no. Truthfully, no. Williston had said that he believed him; he wondered, however, whether he really did. It was hard to tell where you stood with Williston.

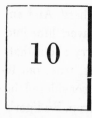

10 LEVENTHAL ran into Harkavy early Sunday afternoon in a cafeteria on Fourteenth Street.

He had come in as much to escape the hot wind as to eat. The glass door shut on the dusty rush behind him, and he advanced a few steps over the green tile floor and paused, opening his mouth a little to take in the coolness of the place. The trays were on a stand nearby, and he picked one up and started toward the counter. The cashier called him back. He had forgotten to pull a check from the machine. She smiled. "Sunday hangover, or what?" But Leventhal did not respond. He turned from the machine and found Harkavy standing in his path.

"Are you hard of hearing this morning? Man, I called you three, four times."

"Hello. Oh, the cashier was yelling too. I can't hear everything at once."

"You're not very alert today, are you? Anyway, come sit with us. I'm here with some people. My brother-in-law—you know Julia's husband, Goldstone—and some of his friends."

"Do I know them?"

"I think you do," said Harkavy. "Shifcart's one of them."

"That musician? The trumpeter?"

"Not any longer. Give the woman your order or you'll never get waited on. No, he's not in that line any more. He's with a big Hollywood outfit, Persevalli and Company, the impresarios and talent farmers, or whatever you call them. And you remember Schlossberg."

"Do I?"

"Oh, sure you do. The journalist. He writes for the Jewish papers."

"What does he write?"

"Whatever comes to hand, I think. Nowadays, theater reminiscences—he used to be a theatrical man. But science, too, I hear. You know, I can't read Yiddish."

"Let me have a Swiss on rye," said Leventhal over the counter. "Elderly man, isn't he? Didn't I meet him at your house with someone else?"

"That's right; his son, whom he still supports at thirty-five."

"Is he sick?"

"No, just looking around; hasn't made up his mind about a vocation. There are daughters, too. Worse yet."

"Loose?"

"Here's your sandwich," said Harkavy. The woman sent the plate across the counter with a spin and a rattle, and Harkavy hurried Leventhal to his table. The three men shifted their chairs to make room.

"This is an old friend of mine, Leventhal."

"I think I used to know Mr. Shifcart," said Leventhal. "—How are you?—When I roomed with Dan, we met."

"In the bachelor days," Harkavy said. "Goldstone—no introduction needed. And this is Mr. Schlossberg."

Shifcart was bald and high-colored, his neck was thick and his lips small but fleshy. He said amicably, "Yes, I think I place you," and with a spanning hand pressed on the round gold rims of his glasses. Schlossberg repeated his name sonorously but obviously did not remember him. He spoke in deep tones, not always distinctly because of his heavy breathing. He was a large old man with a sturdy gray head, hulking shoulders, and a wide, worn face; his eyes were blue and disproportionately small, and even their gaze was rather worn. But he was vigorous and he must once have been (some of his remarks evoked him, for Leventhal, as a younger man) sensual, powerful, flashy, a dandy—as his double-breasted vest and pointed shoes attested. He wore a knitted tie which had lost its shape with pulling and was made up with a bold, broad knot. Leventhal felt himself strongly drawn to him.

"We were just talking about an actress Shifcart sent out West a few years ago," said Goldstone bringing his long, bony, hairy hand to the back of his head. "Wanda Waters."

"Persevalli is the one that makes them," Shifcart said. "He's a great showman."

"But you picked the girl."

"I didn't know she was your discovery, Jack," said Harkavy.

"Yes, I saw her singing with a band one night."

"You don't say."

"At the shore in New Jersey. I was on vacation."

"She's very appealing," said Goldstone.

"You might not like her much, in person."

"Why, she certainly looks like a gingery piece in the pictures," said Harkavy.

"Yes, she has magnetic eyes. But you'd pass her on the street any day and not notice her."

"Oh, I don't know," Harkavy said. "You have a professional attitude in this, seeing so many beauties. I'm still unspoiled. I suppose you can do a lot with paint and cameras, but there has to be something to start with. You can't fake those gorgeous sex machines, can you? Or is it the gullible public again? They look genuine to me."

"Some really are. And if the rest take you in, that's what they're supposed to do."

"It must be quite a knack to pick them," Goldstone remarked.

"It isn't all guesswork. You can't go and run a screen test

for every girl you see. But I myself, personally, don't care for some of the best successes I sent into Hollywood."

"Which do you like?" asked Goldstone.

"Oh," he said slowly, thinking, "there's Nola Hook."

"You don't mean it," said Schlossberg. "A little cactus plant . . . skinny, dry. . . ."

"I think she has a kind of charm. Or what's the matter with Livia Hall?"

"Such a discovery!"

"She is. I'll stand up for her."

"Oh, a firebrand." The old man's countenance was too large for fine degrees of irony. Only Shifcart, his lips open to begin his reply, did not join in the laughter.

"What's the matter; hasn't she got anything?"

"She's got!" Schlossberg waved him down. "God made her a woman, so who are we to say? But she isn't an actress. I saw your firebrand last week in a picture. What is it? She poisons her husband."

"In *The Tigress*."

"What a lameness!"

"I don't know what your standards are. A perfect piece of casting. Who else could have done it?"

"Wood, so help me. She poisons her husband and she watches him die. She wants the insurance money. He loses his voice and he tries to appeal to her she should help him. You don't hear any words. What is she supposed to show in her face? Fear, hate, a hard heart, cruelness, fascination." He shut his eyes tightly and proudly for a moment, and they saw the veins in his lids. Then he slowly raised them, turning his face away, and a tremor went through his cheeks as he posed.

"Oh, say, that's fine!" Harkavy cried, smiling.

[125]

"That's the old Russian style," said Shifcart. "That doesn't go any more."

"No? Where's the improvement? What does she do? She sucks in her cheeks and stares. A man is dying at her feet and all she can do is pop out her eyes."

"I think she was marvelous in that show," said Shifcart. "Nobody could have been better."

"She is not an actress because she is not a woman, and she is not a woman because a man doesn't mean anything to her. I don't know what she is. Don't ask me. I saw once Nazimova in *The Three Sisters*. She's the one whose soldier gets killed in a duel over a nothing, foolishness. They tell her about it. She looks away from the audience and just with her head and neck—what a force! But this girl . . . !"

"Terrible, ah?" Shifcart said sardonically.

"No, isn't it? And this is a success? This is your success, these days. You said you could pass this Waters on the street and not recognize her. Imagine!" the old man said, making them all feel his weighty astonishment. "Not to recognize an actress, or that a man shouldn't notice a beautiful woman. It used to be an actress was a woman. She had a mouth, she had flesh on her, she carried herself. When she whispered tears came in your eyes, and when she said a word your legs melted. And it didn't make any difference; on the stage or off the stage you knew she was an actress."

He stopped. They considered his words gravely.

"Say," began Harkavy. "My father used to tell a story about Lily Langtry, the English actress, when she was presented at court by Edward the Seventh. Old Victoria was still alive, and he was the Prince of Wales."

"That's the one they call the Jersey Lily, isn't it?" said Shifcart.

"I've heard this." Goldstone got up and took Leventhal's

tray. "Does anyone want coffee? I'm going to the counter."

"Is it good, Monty?"

"My late father-in-law's favorite." He strode off to the steam table.

"Pop told me this one after I was old enough to vote. He saved up all his best stories till I was of age. Before that . . . But of course you pick up everything yourself and they know it. It's only off the record. Well, you know that Edward was a sport. And when he fell in love with Langtry he wanted to present her at court. They say people in love want to be seen together in public. Proud to have it known. I suppose it has a dangerous outcome, sometimes. Well, he wanted to present her. Everybody was scandalized. What was Lily going to say to the old woman, and wouldn't Victoria be angry at having her son's mistress in St. James or Windsor or wherever? All the reporters were waiting after the ceremony. She came out, and they asked her, 'Lily, what did you say to Her Majesty?' 'I was worried that I would say the wrong thing,' said Lily. 'But the last moment the right one came to me. I kissed the hem of her dress and said, *"Ich dien'!"* ' "

A smile went around the table. Goldstone, carrying the tray, pulled his chair aside with his foot.

"The motto of the King of Bohemia in the Hundred Years War," Harkavy explained, his round eyes shining at them. "They found it on his helmet after the Battle of Poitiers."

"I doubt very much if she would kiss the queen's dress," said Leventhal. "Is that a part of the ceremony?"

"Curtsy," Goldstone laughed, pulling his napkin open to demonstrate."

"All right, I tell it as my father did. I haven't changed a word."

[127]

"The old woman being a German, she figured she'd understand her," Schlossberg said.

"What? No, that's the Hanoverian motto," Goldstone said.

"That was a deal. A German queen, a British Empire, and an Italian Jew for prime minister."

"Disraeli an Italian?" said Goldstone. "Wasn't he English born?"

"But his father."

"Not even his father. His grandfather. He was an authentic Englishman, if citizenship stands for anything."

"He wasn't an Englishman to the English," Leventhal said.

"Why, they loved him," said Goldstone.

"Then who said he was the monkey on John Bull's chest?"

"He had enemies, naturally."

"I understand they never took him in," Leventhal declared.

"Wrong!" Harkavy cried. "He was a credit to them and to us."

"I don't see that," Leventhal slowly shook his head. "It didn't make any difference to them that Victoria was a German. But Disraeli . . . ?"

"He showed Europe that a Jew could be a national leader," said Goldstone.

"That's Leventhal all over for you," exclaimed Harkavy. "That shows you where he stands."

"Jews and empires? Suez and India and so on? It never seemed right to me."

"To teach the world a lesson with empty hands—I know that stuff by heart." Harkavy stared at him with shocked, reprimanding eyes. "The Empire was certainly his business. He was an Englishman and a great one. Bismarck admired him. *Der alter Jude, das ist der Mann!*"

"Is there such a difference between an empire and a department store?" asked Shifcart. "You're managing a business."

"And he was managing the firm?" said Goldstone. "Bull and Company. The sun never sets on our stores. B. Disraeli, chief buyer."

Leventhal at the outset had been a little reluctant to speak and had a fleeting feeling that it was a mistake to be drawn or lured out of his taciturnity. Nor had he thought, with his first remark, that he had much to say on this subject. But now, to his surprise, he was unable to hold back his opinions —they were his, of course, but he had never before expressed them, and they sounded queer to him.

"You bring up Bismarck," he said. "Why did he say *Jude* instead of Englishman? Disraeli was a bargainer, so he was a Jew to him, naturally."

"Don't misrepresent Bismarck on the Jews," warned Harkavy. "Be careful, boy. He lightened their load."

"Yes, he had something to say about making a great race. What was it, now? 'A German stallion and a Jewish mare.' "

"A regular Kentucky Derby," said Schlossberg. "Hay for everybody."

"Don't be down on a man for a figure of speech," said Goldstone. "He was an old cavalryman. That was just his way of talking about the best qualities of both."

"Who needs his compliments?" Schlossberg said. "Who wants them?"

"Does it sound like flattery to you?" Leventhal raised his hand from the top of his head questioningly.

"I see what's on your mind," Goldstone answered. "You're blaming him for the Germans of today."

"I don't," cried Leventhal. "But why are you so glad to

[129]

have one word of praise from Bismarck, and cockeyed praise too?"

"Why do you have it in for Disraeli?" demanded Harkavy.

"I don't have it in for him. But he wanted to lead England. In spite of the fact that he was a Jew, not because he cared about empires so much. People laughed at his nose, so he took up boxing; they laughed at his poetic silk clothes, so he put on black; and they laughed at his books, so he showed them. He got into politics and became the prime minister. He did it all on nerve."

"Oh, come on," Harkavy said.

"On nerve," Leventhal insisted. "That's great, I'll give you that. But I don't admire it. It's all right to overcome a weakness, but it depends how and it depends what you call a weakness. . . . Julius Caesar was sick with epilepsy. He learned to ride with his hands behind his back and slept on the bare ground like a common soldier. What was the reason? His disease. Why should we admire people like that? Things that are life and death to others are only a test to them. What's the good of such greatness?"

"Why, you're succumbing yourself to all the things that are said against us," Harkavy began in an upbraiding tone.

"No, I don't think I am," said Leventhal. He declined to argue further. He had already said too much and he gave notice by the drop of his voice that he intended to say no more.

A Filipino busboy came to clear the table. He was an old man and frail looking, and his hands and forearms were whitened by immersions in hot water. The cart loaded, he bent his back low over it, receiving the handlebar in his chest, and pushed away slowly. Behind the steam tables, one set of white-lettered menu boards was hauled down and another sent up in the steel frame with a clash.

"I have seen only one actor do Disraeli," said Goldstone. "That was George Arliss."

"Made for the part, that man," Shifcart asserted.

"Him I liked in that," said Schlossberg. "You're right, Jack, he was made for it. He had the right face to play it, with his thin lips and long nose."

"Somehow I've passed up all the Victorias," remarked Goldstone. "I haven't seen a single one."

"So what have you missed?" said Schlossberg. "A successful Victoria I have yet to see."

It was a slow hour in the restaurant. On all sides there were long perspectives of black-topped tables turned on an angle to appear diamond-shaped, each with its symmetrical cluster of sugar, salt, pepper, and napkin box. From end to end their symmetry put a kind of motion into the almost empty place. At the rear, under the scene of groves painted on the wall, some of the employees sat smoking, looking toward the sunlight and the street.

"I have seen good ones," Shifcart contended. "Don't you like any of them?"

"No. One thing is why there should be so many Victorias. Maybe it's because she was so plain. An ordinary-looking queen has a lot of appeal these days. Everything has to be pulled down a little. Isn't it so? Why is she so popular?" He held out his hands to them as though soliciting a better answer. "She loved Albert; she was stubborn; she was a good housekeeper. It goes over."

"I thought Eunice Sherbarth was a good Victoria," said Harkavy.

"She's a healthy, beautiful lady; it's a pleasure to look at her," said Schlossberg.

"So what's the matter?" asked Shifcart. "She can't act? You only wish you had her contract, Schlossberg."

"Why not?" Schlossberg admitted. "As long as I'm wishing, I'd like to be thirty years old today with death a little farther off than it is. Besides, my pants are shiny. And who can't use money? She must make plenty, I can imagine. And partly she has it coming because she's good to look at. But act? I could play a better Victoria myself." And indeed he could, thought Leventhal with more respect than amusement, if his voice weren't so deep.

"Yes, in skirts you could be a hit," said Shifcart.

"Anybody could be a hit today," Schlossberg replied. "With the public so crazy to be pleased. It's a regular carnival. Everybody is on the same side with illusion. Tell me, Jack, do you think you have ever discovered a good actress?"

"You mean an artist, I suppose, not a little type like Waters."

"I mean an actress."

"Then I say Livia Hall."

"You mean that?"

"Yes, I do."

"Impossible," said Schlossberg. "A pair of chopsticks."

Shifcart's stout neck grew red in patches and he said, a shade away from anger, "She is not a cheap success. Not everybody is so hard to satisfy, Schlossberg. It looks like it's a big job to entertain you and maybe nobody does."

"You are a tough critic, Marcus," Goldstone said.

"Do I make up the specifications?" said Schlossberg. "*Narischer mensch!* I'm speaking for you, too. This is not the public. Between ourselves we can tell the truth, can't we? What's the matter with the truth? Everything comes in packages. If it's in a package, you can bring the devil in the house. People rely on packages. If you will wrap it up, they will take it."

"I didn't claim the woman was Ellen Terry. I only said

she was a good actress. You have to admit, Schlossberg, she's got some ability."

"For some things, maybe. Not too much."

"But some?"

"Yes, some," Schlossberg carelessly granted.

"*Something* at last pleases him, thank God!" Shifcart said.

"I try to give everybody credit," declared the old man. "I am not a knocker. I am not too good for this world."

No one contradicted him.

"Well," he said. "And what am I kicking for?" He checked their smiles, holding them all with his serious, worn, blue gaze. "I'll tell you. It's bad to be less than human and it's bad to be more than human. What's more than human? Our friend—" he meant Leventhal, "was talking about it before. Caesar, if you remember, in the play wanted to be like a god. Can a god have diseases? So this is a sick man's idea of God. Does a statue have wax in its ears? Naturally not. It doesn't sweat, either, except maybe blood on holidays. If I can talk myself into it that I never sweat and make everybody else act as if it was true, maybe I can fix it up about dying, too. We only know what it is to die because some people die and, if we make ourselves different from them, maybe we don't have to? Less than human is the other side of it. I'll come to it. So here is the whole thing, then. Good acting is what is exactly human. And if you say I am a tough critic, you mean I have a high opinion of what is human. This is my whole idea. More than human, can you have any use for life? Less than human, you don't either."

He made a pause—it was not one that invited interruption —and went on.

"This girl Livia in *The Tigress*. What's the matter with her? She commits a murder. What are her feelings? No love, no hate, no fear, no lungs, no heart. I'm ashamed to mention what else is missing. Nothing! The poor husband. Nothing is killing him, less than human. A blank. And it should be so awful the whole audience should be afraid positively to look in her face. But I don't know if she's too pretty or what to have feelings. You see right away she has no idea what is human because her husband's death doesn't mean to her a thing. It's all in packages, and first the package is breathing and then it isn't breathing, and you insured the package so you can marry another package and go to Florida for the winter. Now maybe somebody will answer me, 'This sounds very interesting. You say less than human, more than human. Tell me, please, what is human?' And really we study people so much now that after we look and look at human nature— I write science articles myself—after you look at it and weigh it and turn it over and put it under a microscope, you might say, 'What is all the shouting about? A man is nothing, his life is nothing. Or it is even lousy and cheap. But this your royal highness doesn't like, so he hokes it up. With what? With greatness and beauty. Beauty and greatness? Black and white I know; I didn't make it up. But greatness and beauty?' But I say, 'What do you know? No, tell me, what do you know? You shut one eye and look at a thing, and it is one way to you. You shut the other one and it is different. I am as sure about greatness and beauty as you are about black and white. If a human life is a great thing to me, it *is* a great thing. Do you know better? I'm entitled as much as you. And why be measly? Do you have to be? Is somebody holding you by the neck? Have dignity, you un-derstand me? Choose dignity. Nobody knows enough to turn it down.' Now to whom should this mean something if not to an actor? If he isn't for dignity, then I tell you there is a great mistake somewhere."

[134]

"Bravo!" said Harkavy.

"Amen and amen!" Shifcart laughed. He drew a card out of his wallet and threw it toward him. "Come and see me; I'll fix you up with a test."

The card fell near Leventhal, who seemed to be the only One to disapprove of the joke. Even Schlossberg himself smiled. The sunlight fell through the large window over their heads. It seemed to Leventhal that Shifcart, though he was laughing, looked at him with peculiar disfavor. Still he did not join in. He picked up the card. The others were rising.

"Don't forget your hats, gentlemen," called Harkavy.

The musical crash of the check machine filled their ears as they waited their turn at the cashier's dazzling cage.

11

"I saw williston last night," Leventhal mentioned to Harkavy outside.

"How is Stan? Oh, yes, about that thing you were telling me." Harkavy would perhaps have said more, but the others were waiting for him. "Say, one of these days let me know how you're making out with it, will you?"

"Sure," Leventhal said. And Harkavy loitered off eastward on Fourteenth Street with Goldstone and his friends. He was the tallest among them. His yellow hair drifted flimsily, silkily over his bald spot. Leventhal watched him go. He would not admit to himself that he felt deserted. "Maybe it's a good thing he isn't interested," he thought. "I don't know if I could explain it anyhow. It's getting too complicated. And he'd give me all kinds of useless advice—the usual. Anyhow I'm glad. I don't think I really wanted to talk about it." He remained aimlessly in the same place for a while and then walked off, pressing the bulky Sunday paper under his arm. He did not have a conscious destination and was distantly under the dread of being the only person in the city without one.

In the next block he remembered that he had neglected to call Elena to make sure Philip had gotten home safely and to ask about Mickey. He stopped at a cigar store and dialed Villani's number. He sat in the booth, one leg stretched out of the door. No one answered. Leaning out, he looked at the clock cut squarely into the patterned tin of the wall. It was half-past two, and Elena had probably left to visit Mickey. He phoned the hospital, though he understood well enough that the information given about patients wasn't reliable. He heard that Mickey was doing nicely, which was what he had expected to hear. There were upward of three thousand beds in the hospital. How could the girls at the switchboard be expected to know anything but the bare facts about each patient—whether he was alive or dead, that is? The word "dead," dissociated from what he had thought, accompanied him ominously out of the store, and he made haste to get rid of it, simultaneously realizing, in another part of his mind, how superstitious he was becoming. All he had meant was that the hospital was too vast, and suddenly he had to erase an incidental word. Why, everyone born was sick at one time or another. Nobody grew up without sickness. He had had pneumonia himself and an ear infection, and Max had been down, too—he couldn't recall with what.

He began to wonder how long Max was going to put off coming home. "Maybe he's afraid of being tricked into returning," he thought. "I'll have a thing or two to say to him when I see him. For once in our lives. It's time somebody called him down. Elena won't, so he's used to doing whatever he wants." And what would Max have to say for himself? Something simple minded and foolish, he was certain. Because he was foolish. Philip already had more common sense than his father. Leventhal visualized his brother's strongly excited face and imagined his incoherencies. "He sends them money and that makes him a father. That's the end of his responsibilities. That's fatherhood," he repeated to himself. "That's his idea of duty."

From the dark staircase and hall, he entered the brilliantly sunlit front room. He sat on the edge of the bed and pushed off his shoes. The sheets were warm to his touch. The heavy folds of the curtain, the brown door, the fine red flowers in the carpet slowly consumed into a light smoke of dust, gave him a feeling of suspension and quietness. There was a long spider's thread on the screen, quivering red, blue, and deeper blue against the wires like the last pliant, changeable thing in the stiffening, fixative heat. With one stockinged foot set on the other, his shoulders drooping, Leventhal sat watching, his face somnolent, his hands looking as if it would require a great effort to unclasp them.

Presently he went into the kitchen. He absent-mindedly rinsed a few dishes under the rumbling tap and, returning to the front room, unbuckled his belt, drew the curtains, and, with the Sunday paper unheeded under his legs, went to sleep.

A deep rolling noise awakened him. He thought at first that it came from below, out of the subway. But there was no accompanying tremor through the building. He soon placed the sound outside and above him. It was thunder. He looked out. There had been a storm. The screen was still clogged with raindrops. The street was softly darkened by the clouds and the wet brownstone. In one of the rooms across the way a two-branched green lamp was shining. A woman lay on a sofa, one arm bent over her eyes. At the next sound of the retreating thunder she moved her legs.

Leventhal glanced again into the mist and water of the street and then went to the phone and tried Villani's number. There was still no answer. Apparently they were out somewhere, making a day of it. He poised the receiver over the hook, aimed it, and let it fall into place.

He worked his feet into his shoes, treading down the heels, and went down to the restaurant for an early dinner. The waiter, the same bald, lean man who last week had anticipated his protest about the bad table with a gesture of insincere helplessness, appeared to be occupied with thoughts of his own. His black suit looked damp, and his leather bow tie was not fastened but hung on its elastic from a buttonhole. He brought Leventhal a veal cutlet and a bottle of beer and hurried away with a muscular swing, softly—his soles were padded with sawdust—to wait on a long table of *boccie* players whose game had been rained out and who were drinking wine and coffee. The odor of wet wood was very noticeable. Leventhal did not linger over his meal. He was soon outside again. The air was dimmer than before, and hotter. He turned west on Eighteenth Street and saw Allbee waiting for him on the corner. He had to look twice in the wavering, longitudinal grays and shadows of the watery street to identify him.

Leventhal did not halt until Allbee detained him, stepping in his way. He dropped his head diffidently and clumsily, as though asking Leventhal to understand that he was compelled to do this.

"Well?" Leventhal said after a moment's silence.

"Why didn't you stop? You saw me. . . ."

"And if I did? I'm not looking for you. You're the one. You follow me around."

"You're mad about yesterday, aren't you? That was a coincidence."

"Oh, it was for sure."

"I wanted to talk to you yesterday, it so happens. You won't hunt me up. If I want to talk to you, I have to find opportunities."

"Is that the way you describe it?"

"But when I remembered it was Saturday—you people don't do business on Saturday—I postponed it." The saying of this appeared to delight him. But then his expression changed. He seemed to recognize and even to be depressed by the poorness of his joke. He looked somberly and earnestly at Leventhal, who understood that Allbee wanted him to know of the feelings that gave rise to it, and to know also that since those feelings were dire and powerful the joke dissembling them was actually a courtesy.

[139]

"I don't observe the holiday," said Leventhal deliberately and dryly.

"Oh, of course not," said Allbee, and he again began to smile. He added, a second later, "As far as 'following' is concerned, that's not the way to put it. I have a perfect right to see you. You act as if I had some kind of game, whereas you're the one that's playing a game."

"How do you figure that?"

Allbee raised his hand. "You pretend that I haven't got a grievance against you. That's playing." His fingers brushed over his chest, and then he covered his mouth and cleared his throat.

"Say . . . with the kid—stuff like that has got to stop."

"I didn't know he was with you."

"Not much! Well, I'm telling you. Besides, I told you the first time, I never wanted to do you any harm."

"We differ about that. And there was a second time, too." He gave an illustrative push that stopped short of Leventhal's shoulders. "That was a little too much game for me. Or were you trying to scare me off?"

"If I was, you mean that I can't, huh?"

"Well," Allbee suggested, "you might have sent me to the hospital and gotten rid of me that way for a while." He grinned. "You said you should have broken my neck."

Leventhal said contemptuously, "But otherwise . . . to scare you? It's impossible to scare you, isn't it?"

"A year ago I wouldn't have come to you. But now that I've done it, made up my mind, it is impossible."

"What was different a year ago?" asked Leventhal.

"Then I was getting by, somehow, and I wouldn't have thought of coming near you," he said quite seriously.

"And now?"

"My wife left me some money. It wasn't a lot, but I

[140]

stretched it. As long as it lasted—why, if I were still getting by you'd never hear from me. I'll say it again. But maybe I don't have a real sense of honor or I wouldn't put myself in such a position. I mean real honor. There's no getting away from it, I suppose, honor is honor. Either you've got it up to here," he drew a line across his throat, "or you haven't got it. It doesn't make you any happier to tell yourself you ought to have it. It's like anything else that counts. You have to make sacrifices to it. You know, I'm from an old New England family. As far as honor's concerned, I'm not keeping up standards very well, I admit. Still, if I was born with my full share of it, in New York I'd have an even worse handicap. Oh, boy!—New York. Honor sure got started before New York did. You won't see it at night, hereabouts, in letters of fire up in the sky. You'll see other words. Such things just get swallowed up in these conditions— modern life. So I'm lucky I didn't inherit more of a sense of it. I'd be competing with Don Quixote. Now with you it's different, altogether. You're right at home in this, like those what-do-you-call-'ems that live in the flames—salamanders. If somebody hurts you, you hit back in any way and anything goes. That's how it is here. It's rugged. And I can appreciate it. Of course, the kind of honor I'm familiar with doesn't allow that. Mine tells me not to ask for damages, and so on. But I have it in diluted form; that's obvious."

Allbee said this conversationally, in a factual manner; nevertheless Leventhal heard the spiteful ring in it. But he evinced no feeling and made no comment.

"I have an idea that it's one of those things that's bound to go."

"You went through the money," Leventhal said, disregarding the rest. "Why didn't you get a job?"

"What did I want to work for? What sort of a job could

I get anyhow? Nobody would give me what I wanted. And do you think I could take a leg job, like a high-school kid? An errand boy? Besides, I was in no hurry. Why should I be?"

"Were you black-listed?" Leventhal was unable to conceal his concern. "Is that the reason?"

Allbee did not reply to this directly. "Why, Rudiger wouldn't have taken me back even to empty his ash trays."

After this they were both silent for a while. Under its flat rim the ball of the lamp nearby began to shine in the gray and blue depth of the air, revealing suddenly the perspiration on Allbee's face. The rings under his eyes gave him an aspect of suffering anger and hate. Yet he seemed unaware of any exposure and spoke evenly.

"No, I didn't want to work," he said. "I had a hell of a time after my wife was killed and I decided to take myself off the market for a while. I lived like a gentleman."

Leventhal said grimly to himself, "Oh, gentleman. It looks like it. A marvelous gentleman."

"Well, what do you want from me?" he asked Allbee. "You lived like a gentleman. I guess that means getting up at eleven or twelve every day. I get up at seven and go to my job. You've had a long vacation. Still you want me to do something for you. I don't know what you want. What do you want?"

"I could use some help. The vacation's lasted a little too long."

"What sort of help?"

"I don't know what sort. I wanted to take that up with you. You could help me if you wanted to. You must have connections. I'd like to get away from my old line, something new, a complete change."

"For example?"

"Do you think you can get something for me in a bank?"

"Oh, you want to go straight where they keep it, where the money is," said Leventhal.

"Or a brokerage firm?"

"Stop your joking," Leventhal said somewhat sharply. "I don't care for the sort of jokes you make. I'm not under an obligation to you. I'll do something for you if I can. And just remember, it doesn't mean I admit anything. I think you're crazy. But Stan Williston thinks I ought to help you, and out of respect for him I'll try."

"What!" exclaimed Allbee. "You discussed me with Williston? What did you tell him about me?"

"Oh, you don't like that? No, I see you don't," said Leventhal. "I didn't make anything up."

"What did you tell him?" he said again, in agitation.

"What do you think I could tell him? Are you afraid I blackened your character? Are you touchy about your reputation? I thought you had lost your sense of honor?"

"You had no business—no damned business!" Allbee cried out in a flash of hatred and with an intensity of shame that disturbed Leventhal in spite of himself.

"Well, you're a crazy, queer bastard," he said. "What's the matter with you? You come to me with this hokum about being too down and out to have any pride left—you can even come to me, and this and that. I knew it was all fake. One minute you're on the bottom, couldn't be any lower, and the next you're a regular Lord Byron."

There was an interval of silence during which Allbee appeared to be struggling for control over himself. Then he said in a low voice, "Williston is an old friend of mine. I just happen to have special feelings about him and Phoebe. But I guess it really doesn't make much difference." He gradually recovered his smile and he remarked, withdraw-

[143]

ing his eyes from Leventhal and beginning a protracted, glittering study of the street behind him, "I should have expected you not to miss still another chance to get at me."

"Are you in your right mind?" Leventhal demanded. "Are you straight in the head? Is it the booze or what? God almighty! Every day I see new twists." He looked heavenward and gave way to a short laugh. "So help me, it's like a menagerie. They say you go to the zoo to see yourself in the animals. There aren't enough animals in the world to see ourselves in. There would have to be a million new feathers and tails. There's no end to the twists."

Allbee, preoccupied with the dwindling violets and grays of twilight and the swarms of light, seemed also to find this comical.

"Well, you've got nothing on me," he said.

"You think not?"

"You're just as much of a monster to me."

"I am?"

"Hell, yes. Well, you look like Caliban in the first place," Allbee said, more serious than not. "But that's not all I mean. You personally, you're just one out of many. Many kinds. You wouldn't be able to see that. Sometimes I feel— and I'm saying this seriously—I feel as if I were in a sort of Egyptian darkness. You know, Moses punished the Egyptians with darkness. And that's how I often think of this. When I was born, when I was a boy, everything was different. We thought it would be daylight forever. Do you know, one of my ancestors was Governor Winthrop. Governor Winthrop!" His voice vibrated fiercely; there was a repressed laugh in it. "I'm a fine one to be talking about tradition, you must be saying. But still I was born into it. And try to imagine how New York affects me. Isn't it preposterous? It's really as if the children of Caliban were running everything. You go down in the subway and Caliban gives you two nickels for your dime. You go home and he has a candy store in the street where you were born. The old breeds are out. The streets are named after them. But what are they themselves? Just remnants."

"I see how it is; you're actually an aristocrat," said Leventhal.

"It may not strike you as it struck me," said Allbee. "But I go into the library once in a while, to look around, and last week I saw a book about Thoreau and Emerson by a man named Lipschitz. . . ."

"What of it?"

"A name like that?" Allbee said this with great earnestness. "After all, it seems to me that people of such background simply couldn't understand. . . ."

"Of all the goddamned nonsense!" shouted Leventhal. "Look, I've got things to attend to. I have a phone call to make. It's important. Tell me what in the name of hell you want and make it snappy."

"I assure you, I wasn't trying to be malicious. I was only discussing this. . . ."

"I assure you, you were trying, I assure you!" Leventhal flung out. "Now what are you after? Probably a few bucks for whisky."

Allbee laughed aloud. "They say drinking is only another kind of disease," he said. "Like heart disease or syphilis. You wouldn't be so hard on anyone with heart disease, would you? You'd be more sympathetic. They even say crime is only a sort of disease and if you had more hospitals you'd need fewer prisons. Look how many murderers are let off and get treatment instead of execution. If they're sick it's not their fault. Why can't you take that attitude?"

[145]

"Why?" Leventhal involuntarily repeated. He was bewildered.

"Because you've got to blame me, that's why," said Allbee. "You won't assume that it isn't entirely my fault. It's necessary for you to believe that I deserve what I get. It doesn't enter your mind, does it—that a man might not be able to help being hammered down? What do you say? Maybe he can't help himself? No, if a man is down, a man like me, it's his fault. If he suffers, he's being punished. There's no evil in life itself. And do you know what? It's a Jewish point of view. You'll find it all over the Bible. God doesn't make mistakes. He's the department of weights and measures. If you're okay, he's okay, too. That's what Job's friends come and say to him. But I'll tell you something. We do get it in the neck for nothing and suffer for nothing, and there's no denying that evil is as real as sunshine. Take it from me, I know what I'm talking about. To you the whole thing is that I must deserve what I get. That leaves your hands clean and it's unnecessary for you to bother yourself. Not that I'm asking you to feel sorry for me, but you sure can't understand what makes a man drink."

"All right, so I can't. What then? What did you stop me for, to tell me that?"

"No, you never could and I'll tell you why. Because you people take care of yourselves before everything. You keep your spirit under lock and key. That's the way you're brought up. You make it your business assistant, and it's safe and tame and never leads you toward anything risky. Nothing dangerous and nothing glorious. Nothing ever tempts you to dissolve yourself. What for? What's in it? No percentage."

Leventhal's expression was uncomprehending and horrified. His forehead was wrinkled. His heart beat agonizingly, and he faltered out, "I don't see how you can talk that way.

That's just talk. Millions of us have been killed. What about that?"

He seemed to be waiting for a reply, but before it could be given he turned and walked away rapidly, leaving Allbee alone under the lamp.

12

LEVENTHAL strode home blindly and rapidly, his stout body shaken by the unaccustomed gait. Perspiration ran from his bushy, lusterless hair over his dark skin. He was thinking that he should have done something, slammed Allbee on the head, not let him off. He felt he had answered stupidly, although he did not know what he should have told him; he was unable to remember all that had been said. But as the first throbs of anger began to pass into soreness, it began to appear to him that he had known all along, all through the conversation, what to do and had failed to do it, that he had been unequal to what was plain, clear, and necessary. "I ought to have done it," he thought, "even if it meant murdering him."

Just then, the blink of a yellow light in the middle of the street started him into a trot. An eddy of exhaust gas caught him in the face. He was behind a bus. A tearing of gears carried it forward, and he came up on the curb, breathless. He rested a moment and then went on, gradually slowing to his ordinary pace. His head ached. There was a spot between his eyes that was particularly painful; the skin itself was tender. He pressed it. It seemed to have been the dead center of all his staring and concentration. He felt that his nerves were worse than ever and that his rage had done him harm, affected his very blood. He had an impression of bad blood as something black, thick, briny, caused by sickness or lust or excessive anger. His heart quickened again. He cast a glance behind. Several people were going in the other direction. "Let him better not come near me," he muttered. His brain was clearer, and the single thought of murder that had risen in it was gone. However, he regretted not having hit Allbee and would almost have welcomed another chance. What was the use of wasting words on such people?

Hit them! That was all they understood. A woman in the movies whom Mary had asked to remove her hat, two or three years ago, had turned around and uttered some insult about "the gall of Jews." Woman or no, Leventhal had had a powerful desire to drive his fist into her head, tear the hat off. He had afterwards argued with Mary that there were times when that should be done. "Where would it get you?" was Mary's answer. Practically, she was right, no doubt; she knew the value of staying cool. But he regretted it. Oh, how he sometimes regretted not slapping off that hat. With his father it had at least been *"gib mir die groschke,"* a potentially real compensation. "But what about me?" Leventhal asked with an arrested upward glance of his large meditative eyes. There was a murky redness in the clouds, absorbed from the neon lights and the clock tower on Fifth Avenue. His father had believed in getting his due, at any rate. And there was a certain wisdom in that. You couldn't say you were master of yourself when there were so many people by whom you could be humiliated. As for Mary, she must have been thinking, in answering, of the night he had pushed her, years ago in Baltimore. Perhaps she wanted to remind him of it. Of course, there was no excuse for that. But he still felt that the woman's hat should have been snatched off and hurled away.

And he uttered a low, unwilling laugh when he recalled how he had stood, just stood, without the presence of mind to realize that he was being insulted. It did have to do with presence of mind, exactly as in the case of Dunhill, the lino-typer who sold him the unwanted ticket. With Allbee there was the added confusion that he brought off his insults with an air of discussion. When he started out, even though he made a crooked joke here and there, he seemed to be speaking impersonally. But all at once he said something in earnest that was terrible. Of course, he was sick. He himself had brought up the subject of disease, so he must be aware of it. But did his sickness, whatever it was, account for what he said, or would good health only have given him the strength to keep it to himself? Some people, gentle to begin with, were kind when they were sick. Leventhal said to himself, impatiently, "There are two billion people or so in the world and *he's* miserable. What's he so special?"

Mrs. Nunez was standing on the brownstone stoop. She and her husband had just returned from a Sunday outing. She carried gloves and a red patent-leather bag. Her hat was a white straw with cherries on the brim. Her Indian face was small, but she had an ungainly, full-hipped figure. She wore a close-fitting striped suit, her shoulders were raised, her bosom was high, and her lips were parted as if at the end of a long breath. Mary, whom nothing escaped, had once said about Mrs. Nunez' suits, "I don't see why she wears them. She could look very pretty in silk prints." Till then Leventhal had scarcely noticed her. Now, when she said good evening and he nodded to her, he remembered this and had a moment of intense longing for his wife.

"Were you caught in the rain?" said Mrs. Nunez.

"No, I slept through the whole storm."

"We were in Prospect Park to see the flowers. My brother works in the hothouse. My, it was terrible. A tree fell down. The lightning hit it."

"That must have been frightening."

"Terrible. We were inside. But I was scared. Oh, awful," she said with a release of breath. "Your missis coming back already?"

"Not yet."

She drew the gloves out and worked them with her long

brown fingers whose size and strength he noted in absent-minded surprise.

"Coming soon?"

"I don't think so."

"Oh, too bad, too bad," she said in her light, flat, rapid way. Leventhal had often paused at the Nunez' door to listen, entertained, to their quick-running Spanish, not a word of which he understood. "Too bad," she repeated, and Leventhal, with a glance of surmise at her small face under the white brim, wondered what hint her sympathy might contain. There was a burst of music above them; a window was thrown open.

"I'll be a bachelor for a month or so yet," he said.

"Oh, maybe you enjoy yourself anyhow; makes you a change for a while."

"No," he said bluntly.

He went into the foyer where Nunez' dog scampered at him, jumping up. He bent and clasped the animal, and rubbed its head. It licked his face and pushed its muzzle into his coat under his sleeve.

"She's crazy about you," said Nunez from the doorway. "I think she smells you coming." He was polishing his glasses with a flowered handkerchief of his wife's. Beside the bed, in his room, there were beer cans and newspapers.

"That's a friendly dog. I have a soft spot for dogs myself."

"Up, Smoke," said Nunez. "Do hounds ever faint, Mr. Leventhal? Sometimes I think this one is going to faint when you rub her belly."

"I don't know. Do animals faint? Does anyone faint from pleasure?"

"Somebody," Nunez joked. "A lady with a weak heart, maybe. Look a' that, on her back. Look a' that chest on her." He put on his glasses and held the edge of the door.

[151]

The red of the foyer and the yellow of his flat were drawn on its black panels. His sport shirt was open, and a religious medal swung over the twist of hair between the muscles of his dark, reddish breast.

"Come in and have a beer," he said.

"I can't, thanks, I have something to do." Leventhal remembered that he had not yet reached Elena. It occurred to him, moreover, that Nunez had been a witness to his scuffle with Allbee in the hall. He looked at him uncomfortably and moved toward the stairs.

For the third time he got no answer at Villani's and he began to be anxious. The Villanis had young children, and young children had to be put to bed. It was already after eight. "Maybe I'd better go out and see Elena and Phil," he said to himself. "I don't have anything to do tonight." But his concealed thought was that Villani's absence was a bad sign. He set out again, nodding to Mrs. Nunez on the stoop as though he saw her for the first time.

He found Villani and the old woman sitting with Philip and Elena in the parlor. They had just returned from the hospital, and he gathered that Mickey was worse. He appeared to be losing weight. Villani betrayed his misgivings by the pitch of his optimism. He cried, "Don't worry about them, out there. They make them eat. There's no such thing in a hospital, not eating. They see to it. They can handle the kids; they got experience." Elena was coldly silent. Evidently she had accused the hospital of not feeding the child. Her look was waxen. Everything—her black hair, dark nostrils, and white lips; her lack of stir at his arrival; even the fact that she was dressed for the street and not in her gingham with the nightgown under it—made Leventhal uneasy.

"Give them time," said Villani. "He ain't been there long. What do you say?"

Leventhal gave out a sound of confirmation and glanced from Elena to the old woman in her dark colors. Her lean wrists, marked with raised, dull blue veins, rested in her lap. He observed that her ankles, above her unfashionable black shoes, were swollen—probably from walking the long hospital corridors. Her mouth was thin, the underlip not quite matching the expressionless upper because her chin was sunk. The tilt of her body in the Morris chair, her crossed feet, suggested rest, and yet rest was what she seemed to be resisting, drawing off her shoulders from the cushion behind her. Her eyes, whenever her lids went up, disclosed a fierceness as piercing as a rooster's. Leventhal, in spite of himself, was arrested by her face. Other people might change themselves still; it was hard, it might not work, but they could try. This woman, as she was, was finished forever.

He took the first opportunity to whisper to Villani that perhaps Max ought to be sent for now, and Villani shut his eyes in agreement. It was serious, then. He would phone the doctor in the morning and get a report. Denisart had promised to tell him when to send for Max.

He got away to the kitchen for a while, ostensibly for a glass of water. Actually he was afraid that if he sat opposite Elena much longer he might lose control of himself. His face might twitch, perhaps, or his voice crack. Worst of all, he might ask her why she thought he was to blame, and that would be utterly wrong and possibly dangerous. She did hold him responsible, plainly. He had urged her to send the boy to the hospital. But the doctor had done that, too. And what could he look for later, if she blamed him now? This was only the beginning, judging from the signs Villani gave; there was more to expect. They themselves, the parents, were responsible insofar as anyone was. Especially Max. Why did he postpone coming home? Because he thought he could

[153]

get by? He could get by, though, only if Mickey, hanging on in the hospital, got by. Not that Max's being at home now could make a real difference to the child, but at all events he might not seem so given up to that enormous hospital, and on Max's side an acknowledgment would be made. After all, you married and had children and there was a chain of consequences. It was impossible to tell, in starting out, what was going to happen. And it was unfair, perhaps, to have to account at forty for what was done at twenty. But unless one was more than human or less than human, as Mr. Schlossberg put it, the payments had to be met. Leventhal disagreed about "less than human." Since it was done by so many, what was it but human? "More than human" was for a much smaller number. But most people had fear in them—fear of life, fear of death, of life more than of death, perhaps. But it was a fact that they were afraid, and when the fear was uppermost they didn't want any more burdens. At twenty they had vigor and so were careless, and later they felt too weak to be accountable. They said, "Just let me alone, that's all I ask." But either they found the strength to meet the costs or they refused and gave way to dizziness—dizziness altogether, the dizziness of pleasures before catastrophes. Maybe you could call it "less than human" to refuse; he liked to think "human" meant accountable in spite of many weaknesses—at the last moment, tough enough to hold. But to go by what happened in the majority of cases, it was the last dizziness that was most typical and had the best claim to the name.

He went back to the parlor for a while. When he announced that he was leaving, Elena looked at him but did not say good night.

Philip, heavy eyed and dejected, sat outside the circle of

adults, his arms wound around the back of the chair. His shirt was pulled out at the sides and his shoes untied.

"Tired from trotting after them all day," Leventhal observed to himself. He was filled with tenderness toward him. "Go to sleep, Phil," he said.

"I will."

"Did you have a good time yesterday?"

"Yes, swell."

"When the kid gets out we'll take one of those boat excursions around the island. I understand they're really beautiful."

Philip laid his cheek on the top rung of the chair in a way that fatigue alone could not have explained. Leventhal passed his hand over his short hair, saying, "All right, boy." But beyond that he could bring nothing out. He foundered, the thread of reassurance lost, the very breath with which to make reassurances driven out of him by his pity for the children. He hurried down the dirty tile stairs. A bus loomed up, half a block away, and he ran across the street. Though there were empty seats around him he stood up, supporting himself on the shining pole, hardly hearing the escape of air from the brakes and the pneumatic doors, and seeing only chaotically shapeless colors with his brimming eyes. Philip must have noticed him whispering to Villani. But probably he had begun to understand earlier. He knew, Leventhal was convinced. And perhaps even little Mickey in the hospital comprehended it all, after a fashion, affected as a candle flame is by varying amounts of air, as all that wants to be what it was made responds to whatever feeds or endangers it.

Looping and swerving the bus reached the waterfront. The smell of the harbor and the flash of the arcades came to

Leventhal. He made his way through the dim space of the shed to the bow of the boat and looked out on the water, the sharp stars, and the crimson and yellow spots hung from the cranes and hulls swinging between the slip and the incandescent low crust of the shore.

13

THE WEEK that followed was a miserable one for him. Dr. Denisart was not optimistic on Monday, and, since he had proved before that he was anything but an alarmist, Leventhal saw that in his professional way he was giving notice that there was very little hope. On Tuesday he said he thought it advisable that Max should come home. Leventhal cried into the phone, "What do you mean? Is this it?" The doctor answered, "The father ought to be on hand." "It's the showdown, in other words," Leventhal said. He sent the wire, and that evening and the next he went out to the hospital, making every effort to avoid meeting Elena. Mickey was now unconscious, and they fed him intravenously. Hot and grimy after his long trip, Leventhal bent over the bed. The boy's face was darkened with fever; the needle was taped to his arm with strips broad enough for a grown man. The level of the liquid in the flask held by a clamp on the long stand did not seem to change. Leventhal moved to the window and lifted the edge of the shade an inch or two with his forefinger, peering down at the stone jars of vines and geraniums, too massive for the small sunken court. Then he went out, with a hesitation at the foot of the bed. He traveled two hours in order to spend ten minutes in Mickey's room.

He kept telling himself, "The showdown is coming"— guiltily, for at heart he had no hope. The word itself was an evasion, and he, not the doctor, had introduced it. But it was a comprehensive word; it embraced more than Mickey's crisis, or Elena's, or his own trouble with Allbee. These were included; what had been going on with Allbee, for example, could not be allowed to continue indefinitely. But what he meant by this preoccupying "showdown" was a crisis which would bring an end of his resistance to something he had no right to resist. Illness, madness, and death were forcing him to confront his fault. He had used every means, and principally indifference and neglect, to avoid acknowledging it and he still did not know what it was. But that was owing to the way he had arranged not to know. He had done a great deal to make things easier for himself, toning down, softening, looking aside. But the more he tried to subdue whatever it was that he resisted, the more it raged, and the moment was coming when his strength to resist would be at an end. He was nearly exhausted now.

It was nearly midnight when he came home on Wednesday. Even before he unlocked the door, he heard the refrigerator panting as though it were trying to keep up a charge of energy in the air of the empty flat. He turned on the lights in the front room and in the bathroom where he undressed and put on pajamas. Opening the medicine chest, he stared like someone who has forgotten what he is looking for; in reality, his mind was empty. His hand touched his razor and, unthinkingly, he changed the blade and set it back in the red velvet groove of the case. Barefooted he walked into the front room. There was paper on the desk, and it occurred to him to send a note to Mary. He sat down, twisting his legs around the legs of the chair, wrote a few words, and stopped to consider what he ought or ought not to say. There was plenty to choose from. That he missed her? That it was still hot? He put down the pen and leaned on the desk, pressing his chest against the edge of the leaf. Dumb and motionless in the silent room, he heard the slamming of car doors and the racing of motors outside. Suddenly there was a prolonged, tearing peal of the bell. A finger screwed the pusher mercilessly in the socket. Hurrying to the door he shouted, "Yes?" He heard his name pronounced several times and called back, "Who is it?" Stooping over the banister, he caught sight of Allbee on the landing below and he withdrew into the vestibule and shut the door. Presently the handle was turned, turned again quietly, and then shaken.

"Yes, yes, what do you want now? What do you want?" he said.

Allbee knocked. Leventhal jerked the door open and saw him with his knuckles raised, ready to knock again.

"Well?"

"I want to see you," said Allbee.

"Well, you're seeing me." He made as if to close the door, and Allbee brought his head forward quickly in a movement of melancholy protest, looking at Leventhal without rancor, however.

"That isn't fair," he said. "I work up my courage to come and see you. It takes me nearly a day to do it."

"To cook up something new."

Allbee's expression was serious. The insane element usually manifested in his smiles was absent.

"The other night—last week—I was getting around to something," he said. "There was something I wanted to say to you."

"I don't want any more discussions. I won't stand for any. Anyhow, it's after midnight."

"Yes, I know it's late," Allbee conceded. "But there was something important to say. We were sidetracked."

"You were," Leventhal said heavily. "I wasn't even in it."

"I guess I know what you're referring to. But whatever I did say, I didn't intend to be personal. You shouldn't consider . . ."

"What? It was all theory, theoretical?" he said sarcastically.

"Well, partly. It was partly joking," Allbee explained

[159]

painfully. "That's an ingrained habit with me. I know it's bad."

"I'm sorry, but I don't understand you. Maybe I don't understand Emerson either. It goes together."

"Please . . ." he said despondently.

There was a hush in the hall under the dull spokes of the skylight and the filmy glass.

"You take it all in the wrong spirit," he went on.

"How should I take it?"

"You ought to realize that I'm not entirely . . ." he stumbled, "that I'm not entirely under control." The slant of the shadows on his pale, fleshy face made it look infirm. The marks beneath his eyes brought to Leventhal's mind the bruises under the skin of an apple. "Things get away from me. I'm not trying to excuse myself. But you wouldn't believe how much . . ."

"Say, nowadays you can believe almost anything," Leventhal said, and he laughed a little but without relish.

With a grave look, Allbee appealed to him not to persist in this. His brows went up, he pushed his fingers through his dirtyish blond hair, and Leventhal remarked to himself that there was an element of performance in all that he was doing. But suddenly he had a strange, close consciousness of Allbee, of his face and body, a feeling of intimate nearness such as he had experienced in the zoo when he had imagined himself at Allbee's back, seeing with microscopic fineness the lines in his skin, and the smallest of his hairs, and breathing in his odor. The same sensations were repeated; he could nearly feel the weight of his body and the contact of his clothes. Even more, the actuality of his face, loose in the cheeks, firm in the forehead and jaws, struck him, the distinctness of it; and the look of recognition Allbee bent on him duplicated the look in his own. He was sure of that.

Nevertheless he kept alive in his mind the thought that Allbee hated him, and his judgment, although it was numbed by his curious emotion of closeness—for it was an emotion—did not desert him. His burly, keen-set figure did not budge from the doorway any more than the spokes in the skylight moved.

"Will you let me in?" Allbee said at last.

"What for?"

"I want to talk to you."

"I told you, it's late."

"It's late for you, but it's all the same to me what time it is. You said you'd help me."

"I don't want to start discussing your future now. Go away."

"It's the present, not the future."

Leventhal felt inexplicably weak against him. "Am I forgetting all the things he said to me, how mad I was, all that ugly stuff?" he asked himself. And it was true that his sense of injury had not remained sharp; his self-reproach did not make it any sharper. The hall was airless, just as Mickey's room had been. He was starved for a free breath of air. His eyes were hot and tired, and the feeling of closeness seemed to have superseded and made faint all other feelings.

"What, the present?" he said.

"Well, you can go in, turn off the lights, and go to sleep," said Allbee. "It's nothing you have to think about. But I have nowhere to go. Not for the last few nights. I was put out."

Leventhal studied him silently. Then he moved aside and said, "All right. Come on." He let Allbee precede him into the front room and pointed to a chair. He himself went to the window and put his head out, getting a glimpse of the

[161]

reddened and darkened heavy forms of the street as he drew a long breath. He sat down on the creaking bed. It had not been made for a week, and papers and cardboard crescents the laundry put inside his collars were scattered over it. In crossing his legs, Allbee gave a twitch to his stained, loose-hanging trousers. His manner in some things was persistently gentlemanly. He knit his fingers around his knee.

"Now let's have it again. What happened, you were thrown out? Where were you, in a hotel, a room?"

"A furnished room. My landlord confiscated my stuff. Not that there was much of it." Allbee's smile crept for a moment into the corners of his mouth and then was gone. "But such as there was."

"For back rent?"

"Yes."

"Was it much?"

"I have no idea what I owed him. Or them. There's a landlady, too. In fact she's the whole works. The Punts. They're a couple of Germans. She's a fat old woman with snag teeth. The nephew's a longshoreman. He's not so bad. It's that smelly old woman's fault. She kept after him. Old people, especially old women, are the hardest customers. They've made it, so to hell with everybody."

"Made what? What are you talking about?"

"Lived so long. Pulled through. A long life," said Allbee. "All the hardships. The rich are rough on the poor for the same reason. The veteran is rough on the tenderfoot. All the way down the line. You know that yourself. . . ."

"How much do you owe them? Ten dollars, twenty . . . ?" said Leventhal stopping him impatiently.

"More like forty or fifty. To be honest with you, I can't even make an estimate. I gave them a little on account, now

[162]

and then. I don't know. Less than they say, you can be sure of that."

"Didn't they say?"

"I don't remember."

"Don't tell me!"

Allbee did not speak.

"Don't you want to go back there, pay them a little? If it's forty dollars, I haven't got that kind of money on hand, but if you give them something . . . ?"

"No, thanks, the whole house smells. Pardon me, but that old Mrs. Punt—I can't stand uncleanliness like that."

"I'll bet you're a model roomer, too."

"I'm not the worst."

"Excuse me, but I forgot you were an aristocrat," Leventhal muttered with a short laugh. Allbee looked at him simply, without a touch of reproof.

"Well, where have you been staying?"

"Fortunately the weather's been nice. I slept out. In the open. I could have gone to a shelter or a mission. I thought if the weather turned bad that I would. I'd go religious for a while. But it's been beautiful."

"I don't know how you could let things get that bad. If you're telling me the truth."

"If I told you the whole truth, it wouldn't sound plausible, so I'm only telling you part of it. I'm cutting it short. I suppose I shouldn't have let things get out of hand like this. Last week I kept warning myself to hurry up and do something, but I didn't pull myself together for some reason, and then Punt threw me out and there I was." He turned his hand inward in a gesture of self-presentation. "The way I look, pearl diving is about the only work I could get."

"How much money did your wife leave you?" Leventhal asked suddenly.

[163]

Allbee colored. "What business is it of yours?" he said.

"Why, man, you should have done something with it instead of just living it up."

"You can't bring the world to its knees with a little insurance money. . . ." He hesitated and added, "I don't owe you any explanation, do I?"

"You don't owe me anything. I don't owe you anything, either."

Allbee did not accept this, but he confined his disagreement to a shrug. Then he examined Leventhal at length. "I had my reasons for doing what I did," he said. "I was in a peculiar state of mind and I wanted to get off the merry-go-round. Your wife is away, now. What if she were killed in an accident? Then you'd have the right to ask me such a question."

"You're an idiot!" said Leventhal.

"I'm only saying that we're not in the same boat. Wait till we're in the same boat."

"God forbid!"

"Of course. Who wants to see harm come to anyone? But accidents happen. You ought to realize that."

"Look," said Leventhal, "it's as I say. I don't owe you anything. But I'll give you a few bucks. Go to your rooming house or to a hotel."

"I can't go back. It's impossible. I can't ring Punt's bell at this time of the night. Besides, they have somebody else in the room. That's why they threw me out. And what sort of hotel would take me in? Like this? Without a bag? Unless you're suggesting a flophouse?"

"Well," said Leventhal. "Why beat around the bush? I see you've got your heart set on sleeping here tonight. I could see that all along."

[164]

"Can you suggest a place for me to go?"

"You're just inviting yourself in. It's after one, do you know that?"

Allbee did not answer.

"After the way you've acted I should throw you out. And if you really believe half the things you said to me, you shouldn't want to stay under the same roof. You're a lousy counterfeit."

"Why, you have the whole place to yourself. You can put me up," Allbee said quietly smiling. "I wouldn't be inconveniencing you. But if you want me to do this in the right spirit . . ." And to Leventhal's astonishment—he was too confounded when it happened to utter a sound—Allbee sank out of his chair and went to his knees.

Then he shouted, "Get up!"

Allbee pulled himself to his feet.

"For Christ's sake, stop this damned clowning! What do you think this is?"

With a look of amusement, his eyes appearing fixed and large, Allbee seemed to taste first one lip and then the other.

"I warn you," said Leventhal, "I won't stand for your monkeyshines. Your jokes!" His disgust was passionate. "You know they're not jokes; they're not supposed to be funny. You're trying to work something on me. You think you'll throw me off and I won't know what's happening."

"You don't understand. I only wanted to do what was appropriate."

"That's all right," said Leventhal grimly, refusing to hear. "I want you to get this—as far as I'm concerned, I'm letting you sleep here tonight to return a favor, and that's all. Do you hear me?"

"Oh, you *do* owe me something."

[165]

"Am I the only one that does? Haven't you ever done anybody else a favor? It looks as if I'm the only one. And what do I owe you? You've pestered enough out of me already. I could shove you out in the hall and shut the door in your face with a clear conscience."

"In your position—if I were in it, and I don't say that I could be—my conscience wouldn't be clear."

"All right, conscience! I don't want to discuss my conscience with you," said Leventhal. "It's late."

He took some bedding from the cupboard and, going into the dining room, flung it onto the day bed.

"It's soft," Allbee remarked feeling the mattress.

"Now what else do you need—you want to wash? There's the bathroom."

"I'd like a shower," said Allbee. "It's been a long time since I had one."

Leventhal gave him a towel and found an old bathrobe for him in the closet. He sat down on the bed in his crumpled pajamas and listened disquieted to the water pelting the shower curtain and streaming in the tub. Soon Allbee came out, carrying his clothes. Wet and combed, his yellow hair gave him quite a different look. Leventhal observed his feet with a queer feeling of aversion. The insteps were red, coarse, and swollen, his toes long and misshapen, with heavy nails.

"Amazing, what a shower can do for you," said Allbee.

"I'm going to sleep," Leventhal said. He switched off the bed lamp.

"Good night," said Allbee. "I'm really grateful for this hospitality."

"Okay. There's milk in the refrigerator, if you want something."

"Thanks, I may have a glass." He went toward the dining room. Leventhal covered himself and pulled the pillow into position. The door of the refrigerator clicked open and he thought, "He is taking some." He was already falling asleep when he heard it shut.

14

He slept but he did not rest. His heart beat swiftly and the emotions of the day still filled him. He had an unclear dream in which he held himself off like an unwilling spectator; yet it was he that did everything. He was in a railroad station, carrying a heavy suitcase, forcing his way with it through a crowd the sound of whose shuffling rose toward the flags hanging by the hundreds in the arches. He had missed his train, but the loud-speaker announced that a second section of it was leaving in three minutes. The gate was barely in sight; he could never reach it in time. There was a recoil of the crowd —the guards must have been pushing it back—and he found himself in a corridor which was freshly paved and plastered. It seemed to lead down to the tracks. "Maybe they've just opened this and I'm the first to find it," he thought. He began to run and suddenly came to a barrier, a movable frame resembling a sawhorse. Holding the suitcase before him, he pushed it aside. Two men stopped him. "You can't go through, I've got people working here," one of them said. He wore a business suit and a fedora, and he looked like a contractor. The other man was in overalls. "I must, I've got to get to the tracks," Leventhal said. "There's a gate upstairs. This isn't open to the public. Didn't you see the sign on the door? What door did you come through?" "I didn't come through any door," said Leventhal angrily. "This is an emergency; the train's leaving." The second man appeared to be a thoughtful, sympathetic person, but he was an employee and couldn't interfere. "You can't go back the way you came, either," the contractor told him. "There's a sign up there. You'll have to leave through here." Leventhal turned and a push on the shoulder sent him into an alley.

His face was covered with tears. A few people noticed this, but he did not care about them.

He found himself not awake, precisely, but so nearly awake as to be conscious that he lay in the dark. He had a sense of marvelous relief at the end of the dream. He was, it seemed to him, in a state of great lucidity, and he experienced a rare, pure feeling of happiness. He was convinced that he knew the truth, and he said to himself with satisfaction, "Yes, I do know it, positively. Will I know it in the morning? I do now." For what he thought would have been very strange to his waking mind, difficult to accept if not downright foolish. But why was that? "Why?" he reflected. "Dear God, am I so lazy, so weak, is my soul fat like my body?" His heart was jolting painfully; nevertheless he felt confident and happy. What was it? What did he and others do? Admittedly, like others, he had been in the wrong. That was not so important, either. Everybody committed errors and offences. But it was supremely plain to him that everything, everything without exception, took place as if within a single soul or person. And still—here he was almost tempted to smile at himself—still he suspected, more than suspected, knew, that tomorrow this would be untenable. "I won't be able to hold onto it," he thought. Something would prevent it.

He had a particularly vivid recollection of the explicit recognition in Allbee's eyes which he could not doubt was the double of something in his own. Where did it come from? "Speak of black and white," he mused. Black and white were Mr. Schlossberg's words, to which he frequently returned. Either the truth was simple or we had to accept the fact that we could not know it, and if we could not know it there was nothing to go by. "There's just so much that we can do. What's the use of wearing yourself out for nothing?"

Leventhal said to himself. No, the truth must be something we understand at once, without an introduction or explanation, but so common and familiar that we don't always realize it's around us.

Gripping the pillow, he turned over and shut his eyes. He was too stirred to sleep, however. He could hear Allbee's breathing, and he got up and closed the connecting door.

He had forgotten to set the alarm and he woke up late. The day was gray and hot. Irritated at oversleeping, he dressed and shaved hastily. After he washed off the lather he still looked unshaven. He shook some powder onto a towel, rubbed it on his chin, and slipped a shirt over his head. He had no time to stop for breakfast. In the kitchen he picked up an orange to eat on the way to the subway.

He went into the dining room where Allbee lay face down, closely wrapped in the sheet. His broad calves were bare, his arms thrown forward, one hand touching the chair on which his clothes were heaped. Leventhal pulled at the mattress, but Allbee did not stir, and he was about to shake him but hesitated, nervously and angrily, and decided it would be unwise. For if he got him up now he was liable to lose half the morning in getting him out of the house. Leventhal did not know what to do about him. However—he looked at his watch—there was no time to deliberate now. Full of misgivings, he started for the office.

He almost welcomed his green metal desk with its hundreds of papers. The great, cloud-filled gray space his windows opened on seemed stationary. The activity around him, the swinging of the gates as the girls strode through them, the tremor and shimmer of the long-stemmed fans, had a settling effect on him. He worked hard. By eleven o'clock he had finished a complete set of galleys and he went in to Mr. Beard to discuss a lead article for the next number. Millikan, the son-in-law, was there, sitting beside the old man. He took no part in the conversation. Beard made a few remarks of tentative opposition, merely, Leventhal felt, for the sake of his authority, because he wanted to avoid agreeing at once, not because he had countersuggestions. His eyeshade, dividing his forehead with its white blots from the rest of his face, hid his expression somewhat, but there were indications that he was pretty well satisfied. His mouth and jaw showed it. "Well, can I handle your goddamned job?" Leventhal wanted to ask. He did not say this, he looked casual. Nevertheless a deep quiver of vindication went through him. "Everything is going smoothly," he remarked. Neither of them answered. Leventhal prolonged the silence for nearly a minute, until he forced a nod from Beard, and then he stalked out. He didn't claim to be indispensable; on the other hand, they might admit occasionally, without killing themselves, that he was valuable to them. With all his troubles and distractions, he was still finishing his work well within the deadlines. And Beard realized how efficient he was, that was why he had said that unpleasant thing to Mr. Fay. "What really bothers him," Leventhal thought, "is having to admit that he needs anyone for his business. He wants to be the one, the only, and the all-important. That's not the way a modern concern is run. He'll always be small potatoes."

On the way back to his desk, he encountered Mr. Fay. The fact that Fay had made an effort that day to defend him had led Leventhal to hope for more, a hint as to what had happened, an attempt to warn or advise him. One sign was all that was necessary. It wouldn't hurt to have a friend in the office. Moreover he wanted to thank Fay for putting in a word for him. "Maybe he will talk, one of these days,"

Leventhal told himself. Fay stopped him and mentioned an advertiser who was finishing a new plant that ought to be written up. He had spoken of it before. This time Leventhal was attentive, asked for more of the details, made notes on his pad, and said, "That's easy to fix up." He looked at Fay so expectantly that the latter seemed to think he was going to say more and paused, his dark eyes actively questioning under his graying, short brows and behind the shining circles of his glasses. "Yes," said Leventhal, "I'll get the story for you," and, with a mixture of impressions and, principally, the feeling that Fay was going to disappoint him, he turned away.

The ringing of the phone, reminding him of his sick nephew and of Allbee whom he had left sleeping, brought the blood to his face. He jerked his neck awkwardly as he fixed the receiver between his shoulder and his ear, praying that it might be a business call. With one hand he feverishly worked at the tangled wires.

At first he heard no one and he tried to signal the operator. Presently she broke in casually with, "Somebody by the name of Williston, for you." To restore his self-command, he stopped his breath for an instant. Then he said, "Put him on." He swung slowly back in the leather-backed chair, pulling a drawer open with the tip of his shoe and throwing his leg over it.

"Hello," Williston said.

"Hello, Stan, how've you been?"

"Pretty fair."

"You calling about Allbee?" Leventhal knew perfectly well that this directness was what Williston least wanted; Williston preferred to be roundabout. But why should he permit it?

He did not answer immediately.

"Well, aren't you?"

"I suppose I am. Yes, I am," Williston said, sounding reluctant. "I was wondering if you had seen him."

"Oh, I've seen him. He's been coming around. As a matter of fact, he showed up last night; said he was kicked out of his rooming house. I put him up. He stayed over."

"Kicked out?" Williston doubtfully said.

"What's the matter, you think I'm exaggerating? You haven't seen him. One look at him and it wouldn't sound so impossible."

"What does he aim to do?"

"I wish I could tell, but he probably couldn't say himself. If you want to know, I think he's probably sick. There must be something wrong with him."

Williston seemed to consider this; there was no reply for a while. Then he said, "Hasn't he given you any clue as to what he wants?"

"Too many clues. I can't get any single thing out of him, that's the trouble." He slipped his leg from the drawer and bent over the desk, cradling the phone in both hands. "You should hear him; you'd find out in a hurry there was something wrong."

Williston's voice came back in a drawling laugh. "He's trying to calm me down," thought Leventhal, feeling discouraged. "He thinks I'm overdoing the complaining and wants to kid me out of it."

"Oh, it isn't that bad, is it?" said Williston.

"It's plenty bad. You don't know how bad it is. I tell you, you haven't seen him or heard what he's got to say, what his line is. I did go wrong with Rudiger, I know, and that whole business was unfortunate. I won't try to duck out of it, although I could if I wanted to. But listen, you have no idea what he's like. Probably the thing to do is to get him a job. Whether he'll take it or not is another story. Maybe he doesn't want to work. I can't tell you. He wants everything, and I don't think he wants to do anything. He keeps play acting with me." He stopped and grumbled to himself, "I'll put him straight whether he wants to be put straight or not."

"Oh, now, that's just boyishness," said Williston. Leventhal was unable to decide to which of them the boyishness was attributed. He hunted for words, bluntly bracing his face against the difficulty of carrying on this conversation. It was purposeless, an added burden.

"Well, maybe you can make a useful suggestion, Stan."

"I said I'd do whatever I could." Williston appeared to feel himself accused.

"After all, I'm supposed to be his enemy. You're his friend."

He did not hear all of his answer. He only caught a reference to a "practical step" and understood that Williston was impatient with the way the conversation was going.

"Sure I'm in favor of something practical," he replied. But as soon as the words were out he was aware that he and Williston had swung farther than ever, hopelessly far, from the real issues. Over the telephone the "practical step" was vague enough and when he tried to apply it to Allbee it dissolved into irrelevance. For himself, the practical step was to get rid of the man, and this was not what Williston had in mind. "You think of something," he urged. "You know him. Maybe you can figure out what would satisfy him."

"He must have a definite object. If I could talk to him I might find out."

"How would you get to talk to him? He doesn't want you to know anything about him. He was mad when he found out

I talked to you about him. But I'll suggest it to him and see what happens."

"I'll expect to hear from you, then," said Williston. "You won't forget to call, will you?"

"I'll call you," Leventhal promised. He hung up and, setting the phone on some of his papers as a weight, he made an abstracted survey of his desk, slipped his jacket from the back of the chair, and started out to lunch.

He went down in the elevator amid a crowd of girls from the commercial school upstairs, largely unconscious of the pleasure that he took in their smooth arms and smooth faces. The elevator sank slowly in the musty shaft with a buzz of signals and a sparking of tiny arrowheads. On the street Leventhal bought a paper and glanced through it in the cafeteria. After lunch, he walked toward the river, passing through the sidewalk markets, between the sacks of coffee beans. The roasting odor was mixed with the smell of gas. The occasional piping of a tug or the low blurt of a steamer came through the trample and jamming of trucks, and booms bristled like the spikes of a maguey, dividing the white of the sky as the piers did that of the water.

He was the first to return to the office; the place was empty. A breeze passed over the papers on the desk or left rolled in the typewriters, and shadowed the green linen blinds on the crosspieces of the windows. He stepped out onto the fire escape to finish his cigar, and had just ground it out on the rail and tossed it into the air when one of the phones began to ring. In the violence of his turn, he struck his shoulder on the doorframe and for an instant he could not see—the interior of the office seemed black. The ringing filled the air wildly, coming from all four corners of the room simultaneously. He felt a clutch of horror at his heart, and the thrilling, piercing run of the bell was infinitely faster than

[175]

the flow of his blood. He reached his desk. The call was for him.

"Yes? Who wants me?" he cried to the operator.

It was Villani.

Leventhal closed his eyes. It was what he had been expecting. Mickey was dead. He listened awhile to Villani and then roared out, "Where is my damned brother!"

"He came in last night," said Villani. "He went straight out to the hospital. It was too late already. Poor little boy."

Leventhal put the phone down. He could not restrain the play of muscles in his throat. He held himself off from the edge of the desk, as if about to stand up, and with the sick drop of fuller realization his broad face lost all color and his features grew thick.

After a time he picked up a pad and, printing Mr. Beard's name in large crayon strokes, wrote under it, "Death in the family" and, rising, went to lay it on his desk.

He walked with angry energy to the toilet and began to bathe his head. He had a crushing headache. Over the sink, when his face was wet, he began to cry. He snatched a paper towel from the box and covered his eyes. Then he heard someone approaching and turned blunderingly into a stall. He shut the door and, with his back against it, gradually, with silent effort, brought himself under control.

15

ON THE FERRY there was only a current of brackish air instead of the usual fresh breeze. The boat took the water with a sullen thudding beneath the broad lip of its bow. The air was chalky and the afternoon sun looked pale. One of the deck hands sat with his naked back touching the pilothouse, his head lying on his knees, his big forearms locked about his legs. At the slip, he dragged himself down the ladder to take down the chain, and Leventhal sprang past him and hurried through the shed. His bus was just pulling away from the curb, and he ran alongside and slammed at the door with his open hand. The bus stopped, the door folded open, and he squeezed in among the passengers on the lower step. The driver raised himself in his seat and called out something, stridently. His throat was taut and angry, his gray collar blackened with sweat. No one answered and, after a delay, he ground down the gearshift and they started again. Leventhal was panting. He did not heed the streaming of his face or the stinging of his hand. He was thinking, as he had thought on the boat, that he must expect to be blamed. Elena was bound to blame him and her mother sure to egg her on. He had argued for the hospital, he had brought the specialist; he had meddled. The old lady did not matter, but his dread of Elena was intense. Probably the disease was already in the fatal stage when Denisart took the case. In the hospital Mickey had at least had a chance, and if she had listened to the first doctor's advice he might have been saved. So it was her fault, if anyone's. But it was precisely because of the unreasonableness of the blame that he feared her. Nevertheless he was obliged to face her. He could not stay away now.

He hunted among the rows of bells, found his brother's, rang, and climbed up. The door of the flat was open a few inches. He pushed it and was startled to feel a resisting weight on the inside. Letting the knob go, he retreated a step. It ran swiftly through his mind that it was not a child behind that door, not Philip. And why should Max try to keep him out? Could it be Elena? A hot wave of fright passed over him at the thought that the energy of madness had held back his push. "Who's there?" he said hoarsely. "Who is it?" He went up to the door again. This time, merely at his touch, the door swung open. Elena's mother was in the hallway. He understood at once what had happened. Standing at the hinge to see who was coming she had been caught against the wall in the narrow vestibule.

"What are you doing?" His tone was harsh.

She was silent, and he was baffled by her look; behind its vindictiveness there was something crazily resembling amusement.

"Where is everybody?"

"Go out. I alone," she said in her rough voice. He had never before heard her speak English. It surprised him. As for the amusement, he must have been mistaken about that. It was the concentration of her look that had suggested it. The boy was, after all, her grandson.

"Where did they go?"

Either she did not know or was unable to explain. She uttered a few sounds. Steam was coming from the kitchen; he saw it behind her. Was she cooking dinner?

"Where are they, at the chapel? Is the funeral today?"

She merely shrugged; she refused to answer, and she gave him another of those frightful glances of spite and exultation, as though he were the devil.

"They're going to come home to eat, aren't they—*mangare*? When?"

It was a waste of time. She only wanted to get rid of him. He turned from her and went downstairs.

No one responded to his knock at Villani's. His headache was becoming severer. He frowned and hit at the door despairingly. Then it occurred to him to try the superintendent. He found him in the court, reading the paper in the shade of the furnace room stairs.

"Do you know where I can find my people?" he said. "I'm Max Leventhal's brother."

The superintendent got up. Old and slow, he rested his weight on bent, swollen knuckles.

"Why, the boy's being buried out of Boldi's parlors."

"The old mother-in-law is upstairs, but she wouldn't tell me. Where is this Boldi place?"

"Two blocks down. Turn left when you leave the building. Same side as this. There's a church on the corner." He bent to gather up the paper which had unfolded over his brown felt slippers.

The sun had come round to a clearer portion of the sky and its glare was overpowering. Leventhal took off his jacket. The heat of the pavement penetrated his soles and he felt it in the very bones of his feet. In a long, black peninsular yard a row of scratchy bushes grew, dead green. The walls were flaming coarsely, and each thing—the moping bushes, the face of a woman appearing at a screen, a heap of melons before a grocery—came to him as though raised to a new power and given another quality by the air; and the colors, granular and bloody, black, green, blue, quivered like gases over the steady baselines of shadow. The open door of the grocery was like the entrance to a cave or mine; the cans shone like embedded rocks. He had a momentary impression of being in a foreign city when he saw the church the superintendent had mentioned—the ponderousness, the gorgeousness, the decay of it, the fenced parish house, the garden, and the small fountain thick with white lead and flimsily curtained with water.

He passed through Boldi's office and entered the lounge. There he saw Philip sitting in a wicker chair. His legs were crossed on a footstool and his head rested on his raised shoulder.

"How are you, boy?" Leventhal said quietly.

"Hello, uncle," said Philip. He looked listless.

"I hear your father's back."

"Yes, he came in."

Leventhal caught the flush of candles through the oval windows of the studded leather door. He went into the chapel. It was cool. A master fan murmured somewhere in the building. Beyond the heaped-up, fiery glasses of the altar hung a Christ of human size. Taking off his hat, Leventhal walked up to the coffin. He was struck by the softness of the boy's face, the absence of signs of recoil or fright. He noted the curve of his nose, the texture of his brushed-up hair, the ends of which touched the folds of the satin, the poise of his small chin over his breast and decided, "He was going to turn out like Max and me. A Leventhal." Reflectively he fingered the smooth copper rail with its knot of dark plush and glanced upward. The chapel displeased him. Elena had undoubtedly insisted on a Catholic funeral. That was her right. But from the Leventhals' side, and the boy was one of them, too, it was peculiar, after so many generations, to have this. Prompted by an indistinct feeling, he thought to himself, "Never mind, thanks, we'll manage by ourselves. . . ."

He turned from the rail and encountered his brother.

The sight of him hit Leventhal with a terrible force. He had been prepared to meet him in anger; his very first word was to have been a rebuke. But now, instead of speaking, he took in his brother's appearance, the darkness and soreness of his swollen face, the scar at the corner of his mouth from a cut received in a street fight years ago in Hartford. Outdoor work had weathered him; the loss of several teeth made his jaw longer. His suit—it was a suit such as laborers used to buy in his father's store. His new black shoes were dusty.

"I didn't make it in time," he said.

"I heard, Max."

"I left as soon as the telegram came. I got in about ten minutes late."

"When's the funeral?"

"Four o'clock." Max motioned him to come aside. In the aisle near the wall, clasping Leventhal's hand and stooping over it, he burst into tears. He whispered, but occasionally one of his sobs or half-articulated words broke out of key and reverberated through the place. Leventhal stiffened his arm and supported him. He heard him say, "He was covered up," and bit by bit, through many repetitions, he learned that Max had come into the room unaware that Mickey was dead and found the sheet drawn over his head.

"Awful," he said. "Awful."

He gazed at Max's burly back and his sunburnt neck, and, as his glance moved across the polished rows of benches, he saw Elena sitting between Villani and a priest. The look she gave him was one of bitter anger. Though the light was poor, there was no mistaking it. Her face was white and straining. "What have I done?" he thought; his panic was as great as if he had never foreseen this. He was afraid to let her catch his eye and did not return her look. Helping Max up the aisle, he sat down beside him, still holding his arm. What would he do if then and there—imagining the worst—she began to scream at him, accusing him? Once more she turned her face to him over her shoulder; it seemed to be blazing in its whiteness. She must be mad.

She was mad. He did not allow himself to use the word again. He held it back desperately like a man who is afraid to whisper lest he end by shouting.

He rode out to the cemetery with Villani and the priest, behind the limousine with Max, Elena, Philip, and Mrs. Villani. During the burial he sheltered himself under a tree, hanging back from the others at the graveside in the full blast of the sun. When the shoveling of the earth began he walked back to the car. The chauffeur was waiting on the running board at the edge of the stonedust driveway. The glow of the sun in the locust trees gave a yellowish shine to his uniform. He had white hair, his eyes were bloodshot and his long lips impatiently drawn as he endured the heat moment by moment and breath by breath. Soon Villani and the priest came up. The priest was a Pole, stout and pale. He gave a push to his black Homburg, lit up, drawing deeply, and let the smoke out between his small teeth. Pulling out a handkerchief, he wiped his face and neck and the back of his hands.

"You're a relative, huh?" he said, addressing Leventhal for the first time.

Villani answered for him. "He's the man's brother, Father."

"Ah, yeah, tough deal." His fingers, virtually nailless and curving at the tips, pinched the cigarette. He looked keenly into the sky, creasing the thick white skin of his forehead, and made a remark about the heat. The family were now approaching the cars and the chauffeurs started up the motors.

"Too hot back there for three," said Leventhal, and

climbed into the front seat. He wanted to avoid the priest. Touching the heated metal of the handle, he said mentally, "So long, kid," and peered out of the moving window at the yellow and brown of the large-grained soil and at the two booted men working their shovels. He occasionally saw Max in the back seat of the Cadillac and tried to recall Elena, persistently picturing how she had looked on the way to the grave, walking between Max and Villani, the fullness of her figure in the black dress, the grip of her hands on each arm, the jerking of her head. Poor Max, what was he going to do with her? And what about Philip? "I'd take him in a minute," he thought.

He did not say good-by to the family. It was after sunset when he reached the ferry. The boat went slowly over the sluggish harbor. The splash of a larger vessel reached it and Leventhal caught a glimpse of the murky orange of a hull, like the apparition of a furnace on the water. The searchlight on the bridge passed over it and it was lost in a moment, put out. But its giant wading was still audible seaward in the hot, black air.

After getting off the subway he delayed going home. He stopped in the park. The crowd was extraordinarily thick tonight. The same band of revivalists was on the curb. A woman was singing. Her voice and the accompaniment of the organ were very dim, only a few notes emerging from the immense, interminable mutter. He searched for a long time before he found a seat near the pond where a few half-naked children were splashing. The trees were swathed in stifling dust, and the stars were faint and sparse through the pall. The benches formed a dense, double human wheel; the paths were thronged. There was an overwhelming human closeness and thickness, and Leventhal was penetrated by a sense not merely of the crowd in this park but of innumerable millions, crossing, touching, pressing. What was that story he had once read about Hell cracking open on account of the rage of the god of the sea, and all the souls, crammed together, looking out? But these were alive, this young couple with bare arms, this woman late in pregnancy, sauntering, this bootblack hauling his box by the long strap.

Leventhal fell to thinking that to his father what had happened in Staten Island today would be incomprehensible. In Hartford the old man used to point at the baskets of flowers in the doorways and remark how many foreign children, Italian or Irish, died. He was amazed at the size of the families, at the numbers born and dying. How strange if he could know that his own grandson was one of these, buried in a Catholic cemetery. With flowers, like the others. And baptized. It occurred to Leventhal for the first time that Elena must have had him baptized. And that a son of his was a workingman, indistinguishable from those who came to the store to buy socks, caps, and shirts. He would not have understood it.

Heartsick and tired, Leventhal started home at ten o'clock. He did not think of Allbee till he began to go up, and then quickened his step. Twisting the key, he threw the door back with a bang and turned on the lights. On the couch in the dining room, sheets, bathrobe, and towel were twisted together. There was half a glass of milk on the floor.

He went back to the front room and stretched out on the bed, intending to rest awhile before taking off his clothes and shutting off the lights. He put his hand to his face with a groan. Almost at once he fell asleep.

During the night he heard a noise and sat up. The lights were still burning. Someone was in the flat. He went softly into the dark kitchen. The dining-room door was open, and by the window he saw Allbee undressing. He stood in his underpants, pulling his shirt over his head. The fear that Leventhal felt, though deep, lasted only a second, a single thrust. His indignation, too, was short lived. He returned to the front room and took off his clothes. Switching off the lights, he went toward his bed through the dark, mumbling, "Go, stay—it's all the same to me." He was in a state of indifference akin to numbness, and he lay down more conscious of the heat than of any emotion in himself.

16

MR. MILLIKAN, who attended to make-up at the printer's, was representing the firm at an all-industry conference, and Leventhal, at midday, had to go to the shop in Brooklyn Heights to replace him.

He waited on the subway platform in the dead brown air, feeling spent. He did not know how he was going to get through the day. The train rolled up and he sat down spiritlessly under the slow-wheeling fan that stirred the heat. Again and again he thought about the child's death. So soon closed over, covered up. So soon. He repeated it involuntarily while his head rocked with the bucketing of the cars in the long pull under the river that ended below the St. George Hotel. He left the train and rode up to the street level in the elevator.

Millikan had made up four pages, leaving him four more. The work went slowly; he became drowsy and made mistakes and tedious recounts. Toward four o'clock, he began to drop off. "It's the machine," he thought. The presses were upstairs and they ran without interruption all day. He took time out for a walk. It was curious that he should feel so dull and heavy, and yet at the same time so apprehensive.

He went into a restaurant for a cup of coffee. The chairs were standing on the tables and a boy with a red, bluff head and freckled, rolling shoulders was mopping the tiles. The waitress made a detour of the advancing line of dirty water to ask Leventhal to move out of the way. He drank his coffee at the counter, wiped his mouth on the oblong of a paper napkin he did not bother to unfold, loitered through the lobby of the St. George, examining a few magazines, and returned to the shop. Contemplating the pages with their blank spaces, he sighed and picked up the scissors. The presses had stopped before he was done. At half-past six he pasted his last strip and rubbed his hands clean with a piece of wastepaper.

On his way to dinner, he stopped at his flat to look in the mailbox. There was a note from Mary saying that she was writing a long letter which she expected to mail in a day or two. Disappointed, he slipped the note into his shirt pocket. He did not go upstairs. Near the corner he met Nunez, in his dungarees and straw hat, carrying a webbed market bag full of groceries.

"Eh, eh, hey! How are you, Mr. Leventhal? I see you got yourself some company while your wife is away."

"How do you know?" said Leventhal.

"Us supers, we keep track of everything around a building. We're supposed to be nosey. That's not what it is, you find out even if you don't care. You can't help it. The tenants get surprised. *Brujo*, I see through the wall. They don't know, eh?" He described a spiral with his fingers, enjoying himself greatly. "No. You go out in the morning and then I hear your radio play. This afternoon the dumb-waiter goes up to the fourth floor. Later on, what's in it?— A empty soup can and rye bottle."

"So that's what he's doing?" thought Leventhal. "Guzzling all day. That's what I let him in for." He said to Nunez, "I've got a friend staying with me."

"Oh, I don't care who you got." Nunez gave a suggestive laugh and wrinkled his nose with pleasure, the veins on his forehead puffing out.

"Who do you think I've got?"

"That's okay. The way the dumb-waiter went up, there was no lady pulling on the rope, I know that. Don't worry." He swung the bag with his big-jointed, muscular arm tattooed with a bleeding heart. Leventhal continued toward the restaurant. "No money for rent," he said going down the stairs and bending under the awning. "But for hooch he has it. For hooch he can raise it. Where?" It occurred to him that Allbee had stolen some article from the house and pawned it. But what valuables were there? Mary's sealskin coat was in storage. Spoons? The silver was not worth stealing. Clothing? But a pawnbroker would be running a great risk, seeing how Allbee was dressed, to deal with him. No, hockshops had to think of their licenses. Leventhal did not really fear for his clothes. He had a tweed suit sealed in a mothproof bag in his closet; the rest was not worth pawning. And the suit was a small enough price to pay for getting rid of Allbee. Allbee was certainly clever enough to realize that. Drunks, of course, when they were thirsty enough, desperate enough, turned reckless. "But it isn't the few bucks he's after," Leventhal reasoned. For he had already offered him money. Allbee must have some of his own, since he could afford to buy whisky. Then what about his being evicted, was that an invention? But what of his appearance, that filthy suit of his, his shirt, his long hair? Leventhal tentatively concluded that he kept a little money for whisky by economizing on rent and other things. "But I better lock up the valuables, meanwhile," he told himself.

He ate a small dinner of baked veal overseasoned with thyme, had a glass of iced tea with sandy, undissolved sugar, and lit a cigar. Max and the family had replaced Allbee in his mind. Should he phone? Not just now, not tonight—he busily supplied good excuses, flinching a little at the shadow of his own weakness which lay behind them. He knew it was there. But this was not really the time to call. Later, when things had settled down, Max would soon find out—assuming that Elena's last look in the chapel signified what he thought it did—what he had on his hands. Though perhaps there was nothing so unusual in that look under the circumstances. Perhaps—Leventhal studied the seam in the long ash of his cigar—he had let his imagination run away with him. Grief, overloading of the heart. . . ."Horror, you know," he silently explained. People crying when their faces were twisted might appear to be laughing, and so on. "Well, I hope to God I'm wrong," he said. "I hope I am. And if he can run the old woman out of the house, maybe they can come through." The boy's death ought to bring the family closer together, at least. The old woman's influence on Elena was bad; and now especially she could work round her. For Philip's sake, Max ought to show the old devil the door. With her cooking and housekeeping she might try, at a time like this, to make herself a power in the house. He must impress the danger of this on Max, who might be inclined to let her stay. "Throw her out, don't give her a chance!" Leventhal exclaimed. If Max came to rely on her, why. . . . And he might, if it freed him, go where he liked and leave Philip in her hands. No, she must be pitched out. He sat awhile at his gloomy corner table, his black eyes giving very little evidence of the gloomy anxiety that filled him.

At home he took off his jacket in the vestibule. Through the window, in the clear depth over the wandering brown smoke and the low-lying red of twilight clouds, he saw the evening star. He went through the narrow kitchen into the dining room, which was empty. Coming back to the front room, he was not immediately aware of Allbee's presence. It was only after he had dropped into a chair beside the window that he discovered him sitting between the desk and the corner, and he cried out fiercely, "What's the big idea!"

He shot up and turned on the desk lamp. His hands were shaking.

"I was enjoying the evening."

"My foot, the evening," Leventhal grumbled. "Drunken bastard!"

He was stubbornly silent, after this, determined that All-bee should speak first. The electric clock whirred swiftly. Allbee's head lay on the back of the chair, his large legs were thrown wide apart, their weight supported on his heels. His hands, loose-wristed, were folded on his chest. After some time he moved a little and sighed, "This killing heat, it takes my energy away."

"It couldn't be something besides heat that takes it away, could it?"

"What—?"

"Whisky," Leventhal said. "You're supposed to be look-ing for work. What have you been doing? Sitting here, drink-ing? When you came I understood you were going to get something to do and find yourself a room."

Allbee brought his head forward.

"I don't want to rush into anything," he said beginning to smile. "In any deal—you know that, you must know it by instinct—the worst thing of all is to hurry. Before you make up your mind . . . if you settle for buttons, pea-nuts . . . You have to think things over," he ended with an unsteady, delighted, foolish look of self-congratulation. Was he drunk? Leventhal wondered.

"*You*, a deal," he said contemptuously. "What kind of a deal have you got?"

"Oh, I might have. I might have something."

"Furthermore, how do you get in and out of here? I locked the door last night. I'm sure I locked it."

"I hope you don't mind. There were some keys in the kitchen and one of them fitted."

Leventhal scowled. Had Mary forgotten her key? Or was this an extra? "Originally the agent gave us two," he thought, "and the mailbox keys and the key to the locker in the basement. Or were there three house keys?"

"I wasn't sure I was coming back," said Allbee. "But as long as there was a possibility of it, I thought it would be more convenient to have a key. I tried to call you at your office yesterday, but you weren't in."

"Don't start bothering me at the office," Leventhal said excitedly. "What did you want?"

"I wanted to ask your permission about the key, for one thing. And then there was something else that occurred to me, that on an outside chance there was an opening for someone like me at Beard and Company, and I might apply. You're in a position to help me there."

"At Beard's?—It didn't just occur to you! I don't believe it."

"It did so," Allbee quickly began, but stopped. His large full lips were parted and his loud breathing suggested repressed laughter; he looked at him with comic curiosity. But, seeing him stare back, he started over again, more seriously. "No, it did, it struck me all of a sudden as I was eating breakfast. 'Why shouldn't Leventhal help me get a job at his place?' And it's fair enough, isn't it? I introduced you to Rudiger. We won't count what happened. We'll forget about it. Let's think of it only as a return courtesy. You make an appointment with Mr. Beard for me—does he do the hiring over there in person?—and we'll be square."

"They don't need anybody."

"Let me find that out for myself."

"Anyway, they couldn't give you the type of job you want."

"But you don't care what kind of job I want. It wouldn't make any difference to you, what," he said grinning.

"Whether I became a dish washer or scavenger, or hired myself out as human bait."

"No, it wouldn't, that's true," Leventhal replied.

"Then why should you worry about the type of work they offer me at your place?"

"Didn't I hear you talking about a deal?" said Leventhal. He went to the mantel, fumbled for a cigarette in a jar, and, sitting down, slid his hand across the window sill toward the packet of matches lying in the ash tray. Allbee watched him.

"You know, when I see how your mind works, I actually feel sorry for you," he said finally.

Leventhal pulled deeply at the cigarette; it stuck to his lips and he plucked it away.

"Look, the answer is a straight no. Never mind the discussion. I have plenty of trouble as it is. Skip the discussions." His self-possession was temporary, like a reflection in water that may be wiped out at the first swell.

"I understand. You're afraid I'll turn around and do to you what you did to me at Dill's. You think I want to go there and retaliate by getting you fired. But your introduction isn't necessary. I can make trouble for you without it."

"Go ahead."

"You know I can."

"Well, do!" he began to be shaken by the swells. "You think the job is so valuable to me? I can live without it. So do your worst. Hell with it all!"

"I took Williston's word about you. He said you were all right, so I made the appointment for you with Rudiger. See? I wasn't suspicious. It's not in my make-up, I'm happy to say. I didn't even know who you were, except from seeing you a few times at his parties."

"I feel too low to horse around with you, Allbee. I'm willing to help you out. I told you so already. But as far as having you in the same office where I could see you every day—no! As it is, there are plenty of people over there I don't care to see every day. You'd fit in with them better than I do. I don't have any choice about them. But I do about you. So it's out of the question. No!—and finished. I couldn't stand it."

Allbee seemed to be considering something in Leventhal's words that pleased him, for his smile deepened.

"Yes," he admitted. "You don't have to have me around. And you're right. I think you really are right. You have a choice. I envy you, Leventhal. Because when it came to the important things in my life, I never had the chance to choose. I didn't want my wife to die. And if I could have chosen, she wouldn't have left me. I didn't choose to be stabbed in the back at *Dill's* either."

"Who! I stabbed you in the back?" Leventhal furiously said, making a fist.

"I didn't choose to be fired by Rudiger, do you like that better? Anyway, you're in an independent position and I'm not." He was already falling into that tone of speculative earnestness that Leventhal detested. "Now I believe that luck . . . there really is such a thing as luck and those who do and don't have it. In the long run, I don't know who's better off. It must make things very unreal to have luck all the time. But it's a blessing, in some things, and especially if it gives you the chance to make a choice. That doesn't come very often, does it? For most people? No, it doesn't. It's hard to accept that, but we have to accept it. We don't choose much. We don't choose to be born, for example, and unless we commit suicide we don't choose the time to die, either. But having a few choices in between makes you seem less of an accident to yourself. It makes you feel your life is necessary. The world's a crowded place, damned if it isn't.

[193]

It's an overcrowded place. There's room enough for the
dead. Even they get buried in layers, I hear. There's room
enough for them because they don't want anything. But the
living. . . . Do you want anything? Is there anything you
want? There are a hundred million others who want that
very same damn thing. I don't care whether it's a sandwich
or a seat in the subway or what. I don't know exactly how
you feel about it, but I'll say, speaking for myself, it's hard
to believe that my life is necessary. I guess you wouldn't be
familiar with the Catholic catechism where it asks, 'For whom
was the world made?' Something along that line. And the
answer is, 'For man.' For every man? Yes, for every last
mother's son. Every man. Precious to God, if you please,
and made for His greater glory and given the whole blessed
earth. Like Adam. He called the beasts by their names and
they obeyed him. I wish I could do that. Now that's clever.
For everybody who repeats 'For man' it means 'For me.'
'The world was created for me, and I am absolutely required,
not only now, but forever. And it's all for me, forever.' Does
that make sense?"

He put the question with an unfinished flourish and Leventhal looked at his sweating face and only now realized how
drunk he was.

"Who wants all these people to be here, especially forever? Where're you going to put them all? Who has any
use for them all? Look at all the lousy *me's* the world was
made for and I share it with. Love thy neighbor as thyself?
Who the devil is my neighbor? I want to find out. Yes, sir,
who and what? Even if I wanted to hate him as myself, who
is he? Like myself? God help me if I'm like what I see
around. And as for eternal life, I'm not letting you in on
any secret when I say most people count on dying. . . ."

Leventhal had an impulse to laugh. "Don't be so noisy,"

he said. "I can't help it if the world is too crowded for you, but pipe down."

Allbee also laughed, strenuously, with a staring expression; his entire face was distended. He cried out thickly, "Hot stars and cold hearts, that's your universe!"

"Stop yelling. That's plenty, now. You'd better go to sleep. Go and sleep it off."

"Oh, good old Leventhal! Kindhearted Leventhal, you deep Hebrew. . . ."

"Enough, stop it!" Leventhal interrupted.

Allbee obeyed, though he went on grinning. From time to time he released a pent-up breath and he sank deeper into the armchair.

"Are you really going to do something for me?" he said.

"You've got to stop the tricks, first of all."

"Oh, I don't want to see old man Beard," Allbee assured him. "I won't bother you up there, if that's what you mean."

"You've got to try to do something about yourself."

"But will you really try? You know, use your connections for me?"

"For the love of Mike, I can't do much. And as long as you behave the way you do. . . ."

"Yes, you're right. I've got to get next to myself. I have to change. I intend to. I mean it."

"You see that yourself, don't you?"

"Of course I do. Don't you think I've got any sense at all? I must take myself in hand before everything wriggles away from me . . . get back to what I was when Flora was alive. I feel worthless. I know what I am. Worthless." Delirious tears came to his eyes. "There were good things in me." He struggled and fumbled, half revolting in the fervor of his self-abasement, but half—ah, half you could not help feeling sorry. "Williston will tell you. Flora would if she was here to speak and forgive me. I think she would. She loved me. You can see how I've come down if I talk to you like this. If she were alive, it wouldn't hurt me so much to be a failure."

"Ah, quit—!"

"I'd still be ashamed, but at least I wouldn't have so much to blame myself for."

"You? You hypocrite, you'd never blame yourself in a thousand years. I know your type."

"I am to blame. I know it. My darling!" He put the heel of his hand to his wet forehead, spread his mouth open crudely, and wept.

Leventhal regarded him with a kind of dismayed pity. He rose and stood wondering what to do.

"The thing to do is to make him coffee, I suppose," he decided. He hurried to fill the pot and, striking a match, held it to the burner. The flames spurted up in the star-shaped rows. He tapped the jar with the spoon and measured out the coffee.

When he came back to the front room, Allbee was asleep. He shouted, "Wake up, I'm fixing coffee for you." He clapped his hands and shook him. Finally he lifted one of his lids and looked at his eye. "Passed out," he said. And he thought with grim distaste, "Can I let him stay here like this? He may slide out of the chair and lie on the floor all night." The idea of spending the night like that, with Allbee on the floor and perhaps waking up, frightened him somewhat. Besides, he was beginning to be aware of the disgusting smell of alcohol that came from him. He hauled Allbee from the chair and began to drag him from the room. At the kitchen door he lifted him onto his back, holding him by the wrists, and he carried him to the dining room and dropped him onto the day bed.

17 LABOR DAY was approaching; the coming week was shortened. Press time had been moved back and all copy had to be ready by Friday. Beard called a meeting of the editors to announce this. He was in a talkative mood and he swiveled back and forth, catching the red threads of the carpet in the casters of his chair. At every other sentence he lifted his hand and let it fall slackly. He made it an official occasion because of the holiday. He wouldn't keep them long. They had their work and brevity was the soul of wit. But this had been a good year for the firm, and he wanted the personnel to know how much he appreciated their loyalty and hard work. When you said work you said decency. They went together. So he wasn't thanking his people so much as complimenting them. It was better to wear out than to rust out, as was often quoted. He was a hard worker himself. He lived five miles as the crow flies from the office and he always allowed himself enough time so that if the subway broke down he could still walk the distance before nine o'clock. If a job was worth holding it was worth being loyal to. Life without loyalty was like— Shakespeare said it—a flat tamed piece. Leventhal in his white shirt, his face concealing his somber, weary annoyance, knew this was aimed at him. He kept his eyes on the image of the light striped window shade filling like a sail in the glass of the desk which was already cleared for the holiday.

"Grosser philosoph." Leventhal, walking through the office, repeated his father's phrase with all his father's satire. Of all days to waste time. He got back to work even before the lamp over his papers had come to its full blue radiance. He had promised himself to take a breather today in order to think things over. But he was not really sorry to be too busy.

[197]

Mr. Millikan, his face pale and his nostrils widened, strode through the office carrying galley sheets in each hand. Mr. Fay stopped by to remind Leventhal about his manufacturer who wanted a spread.

"First thing next week, I'll take care of it," Leventhal said. "On Tuesday."

"Say, I'm sorry to hear you had such bad luck in your family—bereavement." Mr. Fay's lips thinned, his tone was formal, and the skin began to gather on his forehead. "Who was it?"

"My brother's kid."

"Oh, a child."

"A little boy."

"That's awfully tough. Beard mentioned it to me." The severity of his lips gave him a look of coldness bordering on suffering. Leventhal understood what caused it.

"Any other children?"

"They have another son."

"That makes it a little easier."

"Yes," Leventhal said.

He let his work drift briefly while he gazed after Mr. Fay. He at least was decent. Beard might have taken a moment off to say something. And Millikan rushed by and didn't even have time to nod. It showed the low quality of the people, their inferiority and meanness. Not that it made any difference to him. This Millikan, when he finally did get around to ask a personal question, never listened to the answer, only seemed to. He was like a shellfish down in the wet sand, and you were the noise of the water to him. Leventhal glanced over his desk—the papers, the glassful of colored pencils, the thick inkstand, the wire letter tray. There were several messages on his spindle and he tore them off. One, dated yesterday, was from Williston; he wanted him to call. Leventhal held the slip of paper in his palm, against his chest, and looked down at it. He thought, "I'll call him when the pressure's off me. It couldn't be so urgent or he would have tried to reach me at the shop or at home, last night."

At noon the receptionist rang to say that there was a man in the waiting room looking for him.

"What's his name?"

"He didn't give any."

"Well, ask him, will you?" The phone went silent. There was no response when he tried to signal her a few minutes later. He walked into the aisle to look at the switchboard. Her place was vacant. He took his straw hat from the hook and put it on. It had been his first guess that the visitor was Max. Max, however, would have given his name. It was probably Allbee. So much for his promise not to bother him at work. The waiting room was deserted. Leventhal, trying to force open the opaque glass slide to see whether she had returned to her switchboard by another entrance, heard her behind him. She was coming through the office door.

"Well, did you locate him?"

"Yes, he's in the corridor, but he doesn't want to give his name or come in." She was laughing, perplexed, and her small eyes seemed to ask Leventhal what was up. He stepped into the corridor.

Allbee was watching the cables and the rising weight at the back of the elevator shaft. He was carrying his jacket wrapped around his arm; his face was yellow and unshaven, his soiled shirt open; he stood loose-hipped, one hand bent against his chest. His shoes were untied. He appeared to have dragged on his clothes as soon as he got out of bed and set out, without losing a second, to see him. No wonder the girl had laughed. But Leventhal was not really disturbed

[199]

either by her laughing or by Allbee himself. The lower half of the red globe above the doors lit up and the elevator sprang to a soft stop. He and Allbee crowded in among the girls from the commercial school upstairs.

"Nice," Allbee whispered. They were forced to stand close. Leventhal could scarcely move his arms. "Nice little tender things. Soon you and I, we'll be too old to take notice." Leventhal was silent. "Last night he was crying for his wife," he was thinking as they sank slowly along the wall.

Allbee followed him through the lobby and into the street.

"I thought you said you weren't going to come around?" said Leventhal.

"You'll notice that I waited outside."

"Well, I don't want you around. I told you that."

Allbee's eyes shone at him with reproachful irony. They were quite clear, considering how drunk he had been. His voice was thick, however. "I promised you I wasn't going to make trouble for you here. Since things are like this between us, you ought to have a little faith in me."

"Yes?" said Leventhal. "How are things between us?"

"Besides, I had a look at the goings-on inside. That's not for me."

"Well, what's on your mind? Make it quick. I have to have lunch and get right back."

Allbee was slow to begin. Could it be, Leventhal wondered, that he was unprepared and improvising something? Or was it part of his game to appear awkward, like this?

"I know you're suspicious of me," he finally said.

"Come on, let's have it."

He wiped his hand over his eyes. There were lines of strain about the root of his nose.

"I've got to get myself in motion."

"What, are you going away?"

[200]

"No, I didn't say I was. Well, yes, as soon as I can. That's understood. I mostly wanted to say. . . ." He reflected. "I was in dead earnest last night; I want to do something about myself. But before I can start there are certain things I'll have to have . . . clean up, make myself look a little more respectable. I can't approach anybody this way."

Leventhal agreed.

"I should get a haircut. And this shirt," he plucked at it. "My suit should be cleaned. Pressed, at least. I need some money."

"You find money for whisky. You don't have any trouble about that."

Allbee's look was earnest and even somewhat impressive, despite the sullen sickliness of his face.

"I suppose you weren't drunk last night. What did you do it on, sink water?"

"That was absolutely the last of Flora's money, the last few dollars. The last connection with her," he uttered the words slowly, "in something tangible."

Leventhal raised his eyes to him skeptically. His gaze contained all the comment he thought necessary. He shrugged and turned his face away.

"I didn't expect you to approve of that or even sympathize. You people, by and large—and this is only an observation, nothing else, take it for what it's worth—you can only tolerate feelings like your own. But this was good-by to my wife. That wasn't sentimental. Just the opposite. To get a haircut or a new shirt with those last few dollars of hers would have been sentimental. Worse. That would have been hypocrisy." His large lips made a burst of disgust. "Hypocritical! The money had to go the way the rest did. It would have been cheap and dishonest to use the last dime differently from the first."

"In other words, it was all for your wife."

"It was. I wasn't going to use a single cent of it to advance myself with. I felt bound to do it that way no matter how much it hurt me. And it did hurt me." He put his hand to his breast. "But this way I've been decent, at least. I didn't become a success at her expense. I didn't become what I wasn't before she died. And consequently I can face myself today." He stood swaying over him, ungainly, his mouth beginning to swell out derisively. "You wouldn't have done that, Leventhal."

"Maybe I wouldn't have to," Leventhal said disgustedly.

"It's easy for you to say. You haven't been touched. Wait till you're touched."

"Pardon?"

"Wait till something happens to your wife."

Leventhal blazed up. "You stop that harping on something happening . . . and that hinting. You've done it before. Damn you, you stop!"

"I don't want anything to happen," Allbee said. "All I've been trying to show is that you've been luckier than I. But you shouldn't forget that luck cuts both ways and be prepared, and when you're in my position—*if* you ever are. That's the whole thing, that *if*." He had recovered his favorite key and he brightened. "*If* swings us around by the ears like rabbits. But *if* . . . ! And you have to square it with yourself, every mistake you ever made, all your sins against her, then maybe you'll admit it isn't so simple. That's all I want to say."

"Oh, now we're on my sins."

"I'm not talking about cheating on your wife. I don't know how it stands, but that's a very unimportant part of it —your cheating on her, or her cheating on you. What I'm talking about holds good regardless. You mustn't forget

[202]

you're an animal. There's where a lot of unnecessary trouble begins. Not that I'm in favor of infidelity. You know how I feel about marriage. But you see a lot of marriages where one partner takes too much from the other. When a woman takes too much from a man, he tries to recover what he can from another woman. Likewise the wife. Everybody tries to work out a balance. Nature is too violent for human ideals, sometimes, and ideals ought to leave it plenty of room. However, we're not monkeys, either, and it's the ideals we ought to live for, not nature. That brings us back to sins and mistakes. I heard of a case. . . ."

Leventhal cried, "Do you think I'm going to stand here and listen to your cases?"

"I thought you might be interested," Allbee said pacifyingly.

"Well, I'm not."

"All right."

Leventhal started toward the restaurant and Allbee walked beside him. The slanting parallels of shadow from the elevated tracks passed over them. The windows and window metals trembled and flashed.

"Where do you eat around here?"

"Down a way."

They came to a corner. "No use going on with you," said Allbee. "I had my coffee before getting on the subway."

"Good-by," Leventhal said indifferently, hardly pausing; he glanced at the traffic light. Allbee hung on, a little to the rear.

"I wanted to ask you—will you lend me a few dollars? Five or so . . . ?"

"To start life over?" said Leventhal, still looking away.

"You offered me some, awhile back."

"Tell me why I should give you anything." Leventhal turned squarely to him.

Allbee met this with an uncertain, puzzled smile while Leventhal, on the other hand, felt more steadily balanced and confident.

"You tell me," he said again.

"You offered it. You'll get it back." Allbee dropped his glance, and there was a curious flicker not only in his lowered lids, over the fullness of his eyeballs, but over his temples—

"Yes, naturally I will," Leventhal said. "You're a man of honor."

"I want to borrow ten bucks or so."

"You raised it. You said five, before, and five is what I'll let you have. But I'll give you notice now that if you show up drunk. . . ."

"Don't worry about that."

"Worry? It's not my lookout."

"I'm not a drunkard. Not a real one."

Leventhal had half a mind to ask what he was, really, what he genuinely thought he was. But he said instead, with casual irony, "And here I believed you when you said you were so reckless." He opened his wallet and took out five singles.

"I appreciate it," said Allbee, folding the money and buttoning it up in his shirt pocket. "You'll get every penny back."

"Okay," Leventhal replied dryly.

Allbee turned away, and Leventhal thought, "If he takes one shot—and he probably thinks he'll have one and quit—he'll take two and then a dozen. That's the way they are."

There was a letter from Mary waiting for him that evening. He pulled it out of the mailbox thankfully. Allbee's hints had bothered him more than he knew. He had brushed

[204]

them aside. What reason did he have to be anxious about her? Nevertheless there were coincidences; things were mentioned and then they occurred. He worked his finger under the flap and tore open the envelope. The letter was thick. He sat down on the stairs and read it in absorption and deep pleasure. It was dated Tuesday night; she had just come back from dinner at her uncle's. She asked for news of Mickey—Leventhal had put off writing about him—and she complained mildly about her mother. It was comical and strange that her mother treated her like a child. She didn't make coffee enough for two in the morning, assuming that her daughter still drank milk, unable to grasp the fact that she was not merely a grown woman but a woman no longer so young. This morning a few gray hairs had showed up. Old! Leventhal smiled, but his smile was touched with solicitude. He turned the page. She had so much time on her hands and so little to do that she had bought yardgoods and was sewing herself some slips, trimming them with lace from old blouses of her mother's, "still in good condition and very pretty as you'll see when I get home." The rest of the letter was about her brother's children. He put it to his mouth as though to cover a cough and touched the paper with his lips.

If she were still in Baltimore, he would have gone down for the holiday. But unless he flew, he could not get back from Charleston by Tuesday. And besides there was her mother in Charleston, recently widowed and no doubt difficult. He would wait and have Mary to himself in a few weeks, when things were quieter. She would make them quieter. He had great faith in her ability to restore normalcy.

The thought of reunion made entering the house all the harder. He listened at the door before going in. He wanted to avoid being taken by surprise again. There were no sounds.

"Let him just come back drunk," Leventhal said to himself. "That's all I ask."

Within a few days the flat had become dirty. The sink was full of dishes and garbage, newspapers were scattered over the front-room floor, the ash trays were spilling over, and the air stank. Depressed, Leventhal opened the windows. Where was Wilma? Didn't she generally come on Wednesdays? Perhaps Mary had forgotten to ask her to continue in her absence. He decided to ask Mrs. Nunez tomorrow to clean the place. Picking up an ash tray, he took it to the toilet to empty. The tiles were slippery. He grasped the shower curtains for support; they were wet. In the dark his foot encountered something sodden and, setting the ash tray in the sink, he bent to the floor and picked up his cotton bathrobe. He took a quick, angry step into the front room and spread the dripping robe to the light. There were shoeprints on it and, around the pocket, pale blue stains that looked like inkstains. He emptied it and found several ads torn from the paper, Jack Shifcart's business card, the one jokingly intended for Schlossberg, and, bent and smeared, the two postcards he had received from Mary a few weeks ago. He hurled the robe furiously into the tub. His face was drawn, his mouth gaping with rage. "The . . . sucking bitch!" he brought out, almost inarticulate and struggling ferociously against a stifling pressure in his throat. He flung aside the chair before his desk, threw the writing leaf down, tore papers out of the pigeonholes and drawers, and began to go through them—as if, in his numbness and blindness, he could tell what was missing. Awkwardly, his hands stiff, he spread them out: letters, bills, certificates, bundles of canceled checks, old bankbooks, recipes that Mary had pasted on cards and put away. Heaping them together again he picked up the blotter, banged up the leaf with his knee, and pushed them, blotter and all, into a drawer. He locked it, put the key in his watch pocket, and sat down on the bed. He still retained the cards and the clippings he had taken from the pocket of the robe. "I'll kill him!" he cried, bringing his fist down heavily on the mattress between his knees; and then he was silent and his large eyes stared as though he were trying to force open an inward blindness with the sharp edge of something actual. He rubbed his fingers thickly on his forehead. Presently he began to read Mary's cards, the words of intimacy meant only for him. There were a few private references and abbreviations that no one else could understand; the drift of the rest was hard to miss. "To carry them around like that, to keep them to look at!" he thought. He felt a drench of shame like a hot liquid over his neck and shoulders. "If that isn't nasty, twisted, bitching dirty!" It sickened him. If Allbee had seen them accidentally . . . that too would have been hateful to him. But it was not accidental; Allbee had gone into his things, his desk— Shifcart's card proved that, for Leventhal was certain he had put it away—and snooped over his correspondence and kept these cards to amuse himself with. And perhaps he had seen Mary's earliest letters, the letters of reconciliation after the engagement was broken. They were in the desk, somewhere. Was that the reason he had made those remarks today about marriage and the rest? He might have made them without knowing, on the chance that he was susceptible. Nearly everyone was. Leventhal thought with a stab of that incident before his marriage and Mary's behavior, which he still did not understand. How could she have done that? But he had long ago decided to accept the fact and stop puzzling about the cause. To Allbee, who might have read the letters, it must have seemed a wonderful opportunity: Mary away, and so why not drop a hint? What he did not know was that Leventhal's old rival was dead. He had died of heart-failure two years ago. Mary's brother had brought the news on his last visit North. It wasn't to be found in a letter.

To himself he said, "A lot a dirty drunk like that would know about a woman like Mary."

18

THE DARK CAME ON. He did not light the bed lamp but sat, still with the cards in his hand, waiting for Allbee, listening for footsteps and hearing instead a variety of sounds from below, the booming of radio music through the floor, mixed voices, the rasping of the ropes in the dumb-waiter; the cries of boys scudding down the street rose above the rest, as distinct as sparks from fire. With the setting of the sun, the colored, brilliant combers of cloud rolled more and more quickly into gray and blue, while red lights appeared on the peaks of buildings, pilot warnings, like shore signals along a coast. The imperfections of the pane through which Leventhal gazed suggested the thickening of water at a great depth when one looks up toward the surface. The air had a salt smell. A breeze had begun to blow; it swayed the curtains and rattled among the papers on the floor.

After a time, Leventhal held his wrist up to the faint, gold bits of light under the window and studied his watch. It was well past eight; he had been sitting for more than an hour. He looked meditatively into the street. His first anger had passed over. From waiting to confront Allbee, he had lapsed gradually into a state of inert rest and now he felt hungry and got up to go to dinner. No use waiting for Allbee, who was probably drinking up the last of the five dollars in some bar and was in that case disposing of himself the quickest way. It was just as well, he reflected, that Allbee had not showed up, for what he obviously wanted was to be taken seriously. Once he had succeeded in this he could work him, Leventhal, as he liked. And that, quite plainly, was his object.

The restaurant was full; there was a crowd around the small bar. He moved to the rear in search of a table. "I got customers next at the bar," the bony, dark waiter said, "but I'll see what I can do for you." He had a cup of coffee in either hand and he hurried away. Leventhal was undecided whether to wait with the others or stand at the kitchen door. It was not very likely that the waiter would give him a table out of turn if he got into the crowd. He continued toward the leaning wall of the kitchen passage. Through the arch he saw one of the cooks beside the brick oven wiping the flour from his arms and waving his apron to cool his face. Leventhal brushed against someone who seemed to have stretched an arm into his path accidentally. Without looking, he said, "Beg your pardon." A man said laughingly, "Why don't you watch?" And though it was peculiar that this should be said with a laugh, he did not turn but merely nodded, and he was going on when he felt his jacket being pulled. It was Williston. Phoebe was with him.

"Well, hello," she said. "Don't you talk to people any more?" It came over Leventhal that she was accusing him of deliberately avoiding them.

"My mind was somewhere else," he said, his cheeks darkening coarsely.

"Sit down. Are you alone?"

"Yes, I am. They promised me a table, so don't let me. . . ."

"Oh, come ahead. Here." Williston pushed back a chair.

Leventhal hesitated, and Phoebe said, "What's the matter, Asa?" in a manner that indicated it was impossible to show reluctance for another moment without offending her.

"Oh, Mary's out of town," he said, "and I don't bother too much about meals. I just run out and grab something. And you're almost through."

"Now sit down, will you?" said Williston.

"What does your wife's being away have to do with it? My Lord!"

Leventhal looked at her dead-white complexion, her thick level eyebrows, and the short, even teeth her smile revealed. The noise of the place cut off their conversation for a moment. He accepted the chair, massively crowding the table as the waiter passed behind him. With an anxious face he struggled up again to catch his attention. He sat down again, telling himself not to be so nervous. Why should they rattle him? He read the menu with his hand to his forehead, feeling the heat and moisture under his fingers, and putting his swarming emotions in order. "What's the matter; can't I stand up to them?" he asked himself. The challenge strengthened him. When he closed the menu he was surer of himself. The waiter came up.

"What's special?" he said.

"Soup, you want bean soup? *Lasagna,* we got tonight."

"I see mussels." He pointed to the shells.

"Very good," said Phoebe.

"*A la possilopo.*" The waiter wrote.

"And a bottle of beer; a plate of soup to start."

"Right up."

"I've been trying to reach you," Williston said.

"Oh?" Leventhal turned to him. "Anything in particular?"

"The same matter."

"I got your message. I was going to call back, but I've been tied up."

"By what?" said Phoebe.

Leventhal considered his answer. He was unwilling to speak of his family; he did not want to appear to be soliciting sympathy, and besides he was incapable of mentioning

Mickey's death conversationally. The thought was repugnant to him.

"Oh, things," he said.

"Labor Day pile-up, eh?" said Williston.

"That and some private things. Mostly work."

"What are you doing with yourself over the week end?" Phoebe asked him. "Planning to go somewhere? We're invited to Fire Island."

"No, I'm not going anywhere."

"Are you facing three days in town alone? You poor man."

"I'm not what you might call alone, exactly." Leventhal glanced at her, speaking quietly. "I have a friend of yours staying with me."

"Of ours?" she cried. He saw that he had her off balance. "You mean Kirby Allbee?"

"Yes, Allbee."

"I wanted to ask you about that," said Williston. "Is he still with you?"

"Still."

"Tell me, how is he?" Phoebe said. "I didn't know you came about him, the other night. I wouldn't have stayed in the kitchen."

"I didn't realize you were so interested."

"Well, now I'd like to know how he is," she said. Leventhal wondered how much of his description Williston had repeated.

"Didn't Stan tell you?"

"Yes, but I want to hear more from you." Her habitual cool, good temper was missing. A faint color appeared below her eyes, and he commented to himself, "Out in the open, for a change." He delayed, thinking that Williston might intervene. The waiter put the black and green mussels before him, and he said, taking up the fork as if to weigh it, "Oh, he's getting around." He began to eat.

"Is he very broken up about Flora?"

"His wife? Yes, he's broken up."

"It must have been terrible for him. I never thought they'd separate. They started out so brilliantly."

"Brilliant?" Leventhal thought. He paused, letting them see that the word had struck him. "What does she mean? That's only the way women talk about marriage. What could be brilliant? He, Allbee, brilliant?" He made an indifferent movement of concession.

"I attended the wedding, if you want to know why it interests me," she said.

"Phoebe and Flora were roommates at school."

"Were they?" said Leventhal, somewhat curious. He poured the beer. "I met her a few times at your house."

"Yes, you must have," Williston said.

Phoebe for a brief moment regained her usual manner. "At the church I remember they were going to have a singer and they didn't on account of his mother. They didn't want to hurt her feelings. Everybody humored her about her singing. She studied in Boston for years and years. She was about sixty, and she might have had a voice once, but she certainly didn't have one then. She sang anyway. She was bound to, at her son's wedding. They couldn't stop her. Poor Kirby. But the old lady was very nice. She told me she had beautiful legs when she was a girl and was so proud of them, wasn't it a shame she had to wear long skirts? She said she was born too soon."

"Excuse me for asking," put in Leventhal, "but was this marriage supposed to be a good thing from his wife's point of view?"

"What do you mean?"

[213]

"Did her family like him?"

"They were suspicious. But I thought he was very promising. Intelligent and charming. So did lots of other people. I always believed he'd outdistance all our friends."

Williston corroborated her. "Yes, he's brainy and well read, too. He used to read an awful lot."

"And suddenly the bottom falls out. I wonder whom you could blame for that." Phoebe sighed and turned her long, handsome, pensive face with its marked, level brows to her husband first and then to Leventhal.

"Why, she wasn't to blame, was she?" said Leventhal. "His wife?"

"No. . . ." Phoebe appeared to be disconcerted. "Why should she be? She loved him."

"Well, if she wasn't to blame, who's left?" asked Leventhal. "She left him, didn't she?"

"Yes, she did. We never learned why. She didn't take it up with me. We saw it from the outside, mostly. It was hard to understand because he was so charming."

"Charming!" Leventhal scornfully repeated to himself. "—Brilliant start!" What could this woman actually have seen with those two eyes of hers? What did she allow herself to see? Could anything that started so well, so promisingly, have ended so badly? There must have been a flaw in the beginning, visible to anyone who wanted to see. But Phoebe did not want to see. And as for Allbee, no wonder he stayed away from the Willistons, they had such a high opinion of him.

He said reservedly, "They say that drinking people usually make a good impression. They're supposed to be likeable."

"Still drinking, eh?" Williston asked in an undertone.

"Still?" Leventhal shrugged, as if to say, "What's the use of asking?"

"No, he was just what I say. Ask Stan. Even before he started drinking. But you haven't told me how he's making out and what he's doing."

"He's doing nothing. And he hasn't told me what he's going to do, either."

"Well, ask him to come over and see us, will you?" Her face was tremulous with hidden resentment.

"With pleasure." Leventhal sounded rather sharp. Williston was turning over a spoon in his short fingers. He had spoken very little realizing, perhaps, that Phoebe was in the wrong, and was afraid to make matters worse by interfering. Leventhal hid his annoyance. They wanted to see Allbee—they could have him altogether, as far as he was concerned—but they didn't say they wanted him to stay with them, only to visit. And why, Leventhal wanted to know, didn't it occur to Phoebe to ask why Allbee was with him rather than with his friends? Logically, they were the ones for him to go to. But it struck him, in examining her white face, that there were certain logical questions she didn't want to ask. She did not want the facts; she warded them off. In a general way she understood them well enough, he was sure. She only wanted to insist that Allbee be taken care of. And chances were that she no more wanted to see him in his present condition than he wanted to see her. She probably knew what he was like. Oh, of course she knew. But she wanted him changed back to what he had been. "My dear lady," Leventhal protested in thought, "I don't ask you to look at things my way, but just to look. That would be enough. Have a look!" However, and he always returned to this, the Willistons had been kind to him; he was indebted to them.— Although what Williston had done for him was nothing compared to what he was being told implicitly to do for Allbee.

Williston roused himself, or so it appeared to Leventhal. "I don't think Kirby wants to see us now, dear," he said. "He would have come before."

"Too bad he hasn't," said Leventhal. He showed more feeling than he had intended, and Phoebe quickly took him up.

"I don't think I understand that, Asa," she said.

"You ought to see him. From the way you're talking about him, I don't think you'd recognize him. I know I don't recognize the same man."

"Well, that may not be my fault." She stopped with a short release of breath. The red began to come out again under her eyes.

"I suppose he has changed," said Williston slowly.

"Believe me, he's not what Phoebe says. I'm telling you." Leventhal tenaciously limited himself to this in order to control his mounting sense of wrong.

"You ought to be more charitable," Phoebe said.

At this he almost lost his head, staring at her while the color spread to her cheeks. He pushed away his plate, muttering, "I can't change myself over to suit you."

"What?" said Williston.

"I said, if I'm not, I'm not!"

"I don't think Phoebe meant what she said, exactly. Phoebe? I think Asa got the wrong impression."

"I see that you misunderstood me," she grudgingly said.

"Well, it doesn't make any difference."

"I didn't mean anything except that Kirby *was* promising, and so on. I wasn't saying anything but that."

What did she know about him? Leventhal thought bitterly. But he was silent.

"I phoned because I wanted to know if I could help out

with a little money," said Williston. "I haven't been able to think of a job for him, but he must need things. I guess he can use a few dollars."

"That's right," Leventhal said.

"I want to give you ten or so. You don't have to tell him where it comes from. He might not want to accept money from me."

"I'll give it to him," said Leventhal. "It's very nice of you."

The Willistons left. Leventhal watched them in the blue mirror of the bar above the massed forms of the bottles. Stan waited while Phoebe stopped to give a touch to her hat and they went up the stairs together, passing under the awning.

19 FROM THE FOYER he saw Mrs. Nunez sitting cross-legged on the divan, putting up her freshly washed hair. She held her chin against her breast, and there were pins in her mouth and others strewn on the brown and white squares of her skirt. He rapped, and she drew her hair back from her eyes but did not change her position or cover her unsymmetrically gartered legs.

"I don't want to disturb you," he said, looking at them. "I was thinking—the flat's pretty dirty. Could you give me a lead about a cleaning woman? Ours hasn't been around."

"Clean? I don't know anybody. If it's straighten, I'll do it for you. I don't do the heavy work."

"Nothing heavy, I just want the place to look a little neater."

"Sure, I'll straighten it for you."

"I'll be much obliged. It's getting to be too much for me."

The look of his front room by lamplight disgusted him. It would have done Phoebe good to see it. He half regretted that he had not invited the Willistons home with him. He set to work gathering up the papers from the floor and spread clean sheets on his bed and laid out a pair of pajamas. In the bathroom he soaked and rinsed the robe and rubbed out the inkstains with a brush and soap powder. Taking it to the roof he wrung it out and spread it on a line. There was a smell of approaching fall in the breeze. Leventhal walked over the pebbles and tar to the parapet. To the east the lights of the two shores joined in a long seam in midriver. Summer would end soon after the holiday and with the start of fall everything would change; Leventhal felt inexplicably convinced of this. The sky was overcast. He looked out awhile and then returned to the staircase, careful of lines and wires in the dark. He touched the robe in passing. It was drying rapidly in the breeze.

On the landing he heard someone coming and glanced below. It was Allbee. Regularly his hand clasped and released the banister as he made his way up. Catching sight of Leventhal at the last turn, he paused and raised his head and seemed to examine him. The low light crossed his face up to the brows and eyes and gave it an expression, most likely accidental, of naked malice. A stir of uneasiness went over Leventhal. He remembered immediately, however, that there were a few things Allbee had to answer to him for. And, to begin with, was he drunk? But he was already quite sure, he could sense that he was sober.

"Well?" he said.

Reaching the landing, Allbee gave him a restrained nod. His hair had been trimmed. Along the sides of his head and down his cheeks there was a conspicuous margin of shaven whiteness. His face shone. He had on a new shirt and a black tie and he carried a paper bag. When he saw Leventhal inspecting him he said, "I picked these up on Second Avenue, in a bargain store."

"I didn't ask you."

"I owe you an accounting," he said matter-of-factly. Leventhal listened for a provocative note in his answer; there was none. He looked at him suspiciously.

"I haven't had a drink today," said Allbee.

"Come in here. There's something I want to find out."

"What is it?"

"Not here; in the house."

Allbee held back. "What's the trouble?" he asked.

Leventhal seized his coat and pulled him forward. Allbee resisted, and he lay hold of him with both hands, and, with a sullen look of determination, his anger rekindled, dragged him into the house and flung the door shut with his foot. He twisted him around. Allbee tried to free himself anew, and Leventhal shouted, "What the hell do you think I'll stand for!"

"What are you talking about?"

"You'll answer me. You won't duck out of it."

He tore his coat out of Leventhal's grasp and swung away. "What's the idea?" he said with a trembling, short laugh, wonderingly. "Have you decided to beat me up?"

"How much do you think I'll take from you!" Leventhal was panting. "Do you think you can get away with everything?"

"Don't lose your head, now." His laugh was gone and he looked at him gravely. "After all, I expect to be treated fairly. I'm in your house, and you have certain advantages over me. . . . Anyway, you ought to tell me what this is all about."

"This is what it's about." Leventhal snatched out the cards. "Going through my desk like a damned crook and blackmailer. That's what it's about."

"Oh, is *that* it?" He swung his hand loosely toward them.

Leventhal's voice broke as he cried, *"That?* Isn't that anything? You followed me around and snooped, before. I let you in here and you get your dirty hands all over my things, my private business, my letters."

"Well, now, that's not true. I haven't touched your letters. I'm not interested in your business."

"Where did I find these!" Leventhal threw the cards down. "In my bathrobe that you were wearing."

"That's where I found them. I don't like to defend myself against such accusations. They're not fair. This is the kind of thing that gets people in trouble."

"Isn't this yours?" Leventhal picked up a clipping from the classified ads.

"Oh, I know what was in that pocket. But some of it was there when I put the robe on. Maybe you object to the fact that I used the robe. I'm sorry, I. . . ."

Leventhal refused to be deflected. "You mean to say that you didn't go through my desk?"

Allbee made a movement of sincere, straightforward denial.

"How about this? Where did you get this?" Leventhal pointed to Shifcart's card.

"I found it on the floor. Now, there I'll admit . . . if I did anything really wrong it was to take that card. It was on the floor near your bed. I had no right to keep it. Perhaps you needed it. I should have asked. But I didn't think of that. I was interested in it. In fact, I was going to bring it up in connection with something I've been thinking about but kept forgetting."

"You're lying."

Allbee was silent. He stood looking at him.

"I didn't put the postcards in the bathrobe," said Leventhal, "and this card of Shifcart's was in the desk."

Allbee answered simply, "If you didn't put them there, then a third party must have. I know I didn't."

"But you read them!" He said this violently, but he wanted to sink away.

"Yes, I did," Allbee dropped his eyes as if to spare him.

"Damn you to hell!" Leventhal shouted in anguish and outrage. "That's not all you read. What else!"

"Nothing."

"You did!"

"No, that was all. I couldn't avoid looking them over. It wasn't intentional. But I took them out of the pocket and so I had to see what they were. It's mostly your wife's fault. She should have put them in an envelope—things like that. I never would have pulled a letter out of an envelope. But I read this before I realized what it was. It's not so serious, is it? What's so special about your cards? Any wife might write like that to a husband, or a husband to a wife. And an old married man like me . . . it's not the same as if a young person, say a young girl, got hold of them. And even then, I wonder if anybody is innocent. And last of all, I don't think it would matter to your wife. This is not the kind of thing for postcards. If she cared, she'd have written it in a letter."

"I still think you're lying."

"Well, if you do, I can't change your mind. But I'm not. Why not keep your desk locked, as long as you don't trust me?"

"It is now."

"You should have locked it sooner. Nobody likes to be jumped on like this. Keep it locked. You have a right to lose your temper when there's definite proof that somebody is monkeying with your private things. It's not very nice. But neither are such accusations. Suppose I did look in your desk, and I absolutely deny it, why should I want to carry the cards around?"

"Why should you? Search me!"

"Like a mental case? Not me, you've got the wrong party."

Leventhal did not know what more to say. Perhaps he was wrong. Except when Allbee spoke of young girls he made sense and even that, fully explained, might not be irrelevant. Besides, the haircut, the shirt and tie, and the fact that he was sober made a difference. It was the haircut, mainly; it gave him a new aspect. His face appeared more solid. Leventhal all at once felt nothing very strongly; he only had a certain curiosity about Allbee. He sat down beside the desk. Allbee sank into the easy chair and stretched his legs out.

After a few minutes of silence he said, "Did you see this morning's paper?"

"Why, what's in the paper?"

"There was an item in it I thought you might have picked up. It's about Rudiger. Really about Rudiger's son, but he was mentioned too. The son's in the army and he was promoted, yesterday. To the rank of major."

"What about it?"

"I just happened to notice. I was in the barber shop looking at the paper and saw the boy's picture. He worked in the office for a while. He's a very ordinary boy. Nice . . . I can't criticize him. Just a college boy; very ordinary, no special spark. It's no business of mine; that is, it can't do me any good or harm. But I'm always interested in the way things work themselves out. Now somebody without influence spends twenty years in the service, first in this hole of a garrison and then in that one, lives with native girls because he can't afford to marry. Maybe he gets a little rank in the end, becomes a second lieutenant. You can't tell me it isn't a matter of influence."

"It probably is," said Leventhal idly.

"Yes. Not that I have anything against him because he happens to be his father's son. Why shouldn't he take advantage of the old man's position? And what else can the old man do for him?" He suddenly changed the subject with a quick laugh. "Notice my haircut?"

"I see."

"I didn't drink, either. That's not what you expected, is it?"

"Go ahead, surprise me."

"No, you thought I'd get looped again."

"Maybe."

"I told you I wasn't that far gone."

"I'm glad to see it."

"Are you?" There was a break of excitement in his hilarity.

"Sure," said Leventhal. He felt a responsive laugh forming in his chest and he held it down. "What do you want, a basket of roses?"

"Why not?"

"A medal?" Leventhal began to smile.

"Yes, a medal." He coughed thickly. "I ought to have one."

"You ought to get one."

"Well, I wasn't even tempted, to be honest about it. I didn't have to fight a yen; not a bit of trouble."

Allbee bent forward and laid his hand on the arm of Leventhal's chair, and for a short space the two men looked at each other and Leventhal felt himself singularly drawn with a kind of affection. It oppressed him, it was repellent. He did not know what to make of it. Still he welcomed it, too. He was remotely disturbed to see himself so changeable. However, it did not seem just then to be a serious fault.

"I had clippers on the sides." Allbee brought the tips of his fingers to his head. "I got into the habit. It's cleaner that way, I've learned. Because of nits. You wouldn't know anything about that, would you?"

Leventhal shrugged.

"Oh, if you got them in your hair, hair like that. . . . Your hair amazes me. Whenever I see you, I have to study it. With some people you sometimes doubt if it's real and you want to see if your man is wearing a wig. But your hair; I've often tried to imagine how it would be to have hair like that. Is it hard to comb?"

[224]

"What do you mean, is it hard?"

"I mean, does it tangle. It must break the teeth out of combs. Say, let me touch it once, will you?"

"Don't be a fool. It's hair. What's hair?" he said.

"No, it's not ordinary hair."

"Ah, get out," Leventhal said, drawing back.

Allbee stood up. "Just to satisfy my curiosity," he said, smiling. He fingered Leventhal's hair, and Leventhal found himself caught under his touch and felt incapable of doing anything. But then he pushed his hand away, crying, "Lay off!"

"It's astonishing. It's like an animal's hair. You must have a terrific constitution."

Leventhal jerked his chair away, wrinkling his forehead in confusion and incipient anger. Then he bawled, "Sit down, you lunatic!" and Allbee went back to his place. He sat forward, ungainly, his hands under his thighs, his jaw slipped to one side, exactly as on the night when he had first confronted Leventhal in the park. The white of his trimmed temples and his shaven face made the blue of his eyes conspicuous.

No further word was spoken for a while. Leventhal was trying to settle his feelings and to determine how to recover the ground he had lost through this last piece of insanity.

"It's hard to have the right mixture of everything," Allbee suddenly began.

"What are you driving at now?" said Leventhal.

"Oh, this about your calling me a lunatic when I give in to an impulse. Nobody can be sure he has the right mixture. Just to give you an example. Lately, a couple of weeks ago, there was a man in the subway, on the tracks. I don't understand how he got there. But he was on the tracks and a train came along and pinned him against the wall. He was bleeding

[225]

to death. A policeman came down and right away forbid anyone to touch this man until the ambulance arrived. That was because he had instructions about accidents. Now that's too much of one thing—playing it safe. The impulse is to save the man, but the policy is to stick to rules. The ambulance came and the man was dragged out and died right away. I'm not a doctor and I can't say whether he had a chance at any time. But suppose he could have been saved? That's what I mean by the mixture."

"Was he yelling for help? What line was that?" Leventhal said with a frown of pain.

"East-side line. Well, of course, when a man is spread-eagled like that. He was filling the tunnel with his noise. And the crowd! The trains were held up and the station was jammed. They kept coming down. People should have pushed the cop out of the way and taken the fellow down. But everybody stood and listened to him. Those are the real trimmers."

"Trimmers?"

"They're not for God and they're not for the Old Scratch. They think they're for themselves but they're not that either."

"What does he tell me this for?" thought Leventhal. "Does he want to work on my feelings? Maybe he doesn't know why himself."

Allbee began to smile. "You should have seen how surprised you looked when I showed up dead sober. You're going to be even more surprised, you know."

"By what?"

"You were joking with me this morning about a new start. You wouldn't take me seriously."

"Do you believe it yourself?"

"Don't you worry," he said confidently. "I know what really goes on inside me. I'll let you in on something. There isn't a man living who doesn't. All this business, 'Know thy-self'! Everybody knows but nobody wants to admit. That's the thing. Some swimmers can hold their breath a long time —those Greek sponge divers—and that's interesting. But the way we keep our eyes shut is a stunt too, because they're made to be open."

"So. You're off again. You can do it without whisky. I thought it was the whisky."

"All right," cried Allbee. "Now let me explain something to you. It's a Christian idea but I don't see why you shouldn't be able to understand it. 'Repent!' That's John the Baptist coming out of the desert. Change yourself, that's what he's saying, and be another man. You must be and the reason for that is that you can be, and when your time comes here you will be. There's another thing behind that 'repent'; it's that we know what to repent. How?" His unsmiling face compelled Leventhal's attention. "*I* know. Everybody knows. But you've got to take away the fear of admitting by a still greater fear. I understand that doctors are beginning to give their patients electric shocks. They tear all hell out of them, and then they won't trifle. You see, you have to get yourself so that you can't stand to keep on in the old way. When you reach that stage—" he knotted his hands and the sinews rose up on his wrists. "It takes a long time before you're ready to quit dodging. Meanwhile, the pain is horrible." He blinked blindly several times as if to clear his eyes of an obstruction. "We're mulish; that's why we have to take such a beating. When we can't stand another lick without dying of it, then we change. And some people never do. They stand there until the last lick falls and die like animals. Others have the strength to change long before. But repent means *now*, this minute and forever, without wasting any more time."

"And this minute has arrived for you already?"

"Yes."

"I don't know whom you're stringing, me or yourself."

"Every word is sincere—sin-cere!" said Allbee inclining his head and gazing at him. He hesitated, his large lips remained parted, the upper, with its long groove, moving a little.

"Go on!" Leventhal abruptly laughed.

"Well, I thought I would *try* to explain it to you." He turned slightly in his chair, resting one shoulder on the cushion, and slowly rubbed the side of his extended leg. "I'm not religious or anything like that, but I know that I don't have to be next year what I was last year. I've been at one end and I can get to the other. There's no limit to what I can be. And even if I should miss being so dazzling, I know the idea of it is genuine."

"We'll see what you are next year."

"You'll be the same, I know. You people. . . ." He shook his head and his cheek brushed his collar.

"If you start that again, you'll be on the steps in a minute." Leventhal began menacingly to rise.

"All right, all right, let's drop it. Only when a man says something serious about himself he likes to be believed," said Allbee. "It makes sense to me that a man can be born again.—I'll take a rain check on the kingdom of heaven, but if I'm tired of being this way I can become a new man. That's all I'm saying." Straightening himself in his chair he was silent and lightly held his big hands together. By the curve of his mouth Leventhal saw that he was very pleased with himself. Indeed the position of his hands spoke of applause rather than rest. The hump of shadow behind him was occasionally extended by the slight stirring of his head. The lamp in its green, watered-silk shade made a second, softer center of brightness in the polish of the desk. A rush of low sounds came up from the street, and a gust of air swelled and separated the curtains; they drifted together again.

At this moment Leventhal felt Allbee's presence, all that concerned him, like a great tiring weight, and looked at him with dead fatigue, his fingers motionless on his thighs. Something would have to happen, something that he could not foresee. Whatever it was, he would be too muddled and fatigued to deal with it. He was played out. His old weakness, his nerves, had never been so bad; he could not concentrate long enough to settle any of his difficulties, and had to wait for the occasion to bring this or that to his attention, and was slow and fitful in his thinking. He ought to have thought of what was going on in Staten Island, if only for Philip's sake, and he should have phoned Max at least once. Max had hung on to him in the chapel; he had no one else to hang on to. And by now he must have decided that he had no one at all. But the reason Leventhal shrank from calling was that he was unable to clarify his thoughts or bring them into focus, and he lacked the energy to continue the effort. And anyway the sparks, the clear spark of Mickey's life, the spark of Elena's sanity, the sparks of thought and courage, even courage as confident as Mary's—how such sparks were chased and overtaken, drowned, put out. Then what good was thinking? His dark, poring face with its full cheeks and high-rising dull hair was hung toward his chest. He drew a deep, irregular breath and raised his hands from his lap in a gesture of exorcism against the spell of confusion and despair. "God will help me out," passed through his mind, and he did not stop to ask himself exactly what he meant by this.

"About the card I picked up," said Allbee. "The business card: is that man a moving-picture agent of some kind? I want to explain why I picked it up. I suppose you know him."

"A little."

"What does he do? What's his line?"

"I think he looks for talent."

"Is he influential? I mean, is he. . . ." But Allbee canceled this question as if it were a mark of his persistent innocence or unworldliness.

"Is he what?"

"Oh . . . on the inside." His lip began to curl; his eyes were distended and humorlessly direct. "I've come to the conclusion that if you want to get along nowadays you have to go along with the powers. It's no use trying to buck them."

"Who told you Shifcart was a power?"

Allbee declined to answer. He lifted his shoulders and looked away disdainfully.

"Who?" Leventhal repeated.

"Let's say he can help me, then, and leave out other considerations."

"Do you want to become an actor?"

"Wouldn't I make a good one?"

"You?"

"Is that so funny?"

A faint smile crossed Leventhal's shadowed face. "I understand your mother thought she was a singer," he said. "And you think you are an actor."

"Oh, you've heard about my mother. Who told you about her, Phoebe?"

"Yes. She sang at your wedding, didn't she?"

"Sensationally," said Allbee in an indeterminate tone; and, after a pause, "No, of course I don't want to act. But I thought with all my experience on magazines that I might be able to get into movie work. I once heard about somebody—an acquaintance of an acquaintance—who was doing

[230]

some preliminary scenario job, looking up stories, and making digests of them, and if I could get into that. . . . Well, maybe your friend can tell me how to do it."

"He's no special friend of mine. How long ago did you hear about this?"

"I don't remember, now. A few years ago."

"Then how do you know you can still get such a job? Why don't you find out from this acquaintance of yours? What have you got to go on? Ask him about it."

Allbee answered quickly, "I couldn't. I wouldn't know where to find him or how to start looking. Besides, he doesn't owe me anything, Leventhal. Why should I go to him?"

"Why? Well, why to me? It makes just as much sense."

His reply tremendously aroused Allbee.

"Why? For good reasons; the best in the world!" He shocked Leventhal by clenching his fists before his breast as if passionately threatening to tear loose from all restraint. "I'm giving you a chance to be fair, Leventhal, and to do what's right. And I want what's right from you. Don't drag anybody else in. This is just between the two of us."

"Don't be crazy."

"Just you and I. Just the two of us."

"I never . . . I never. . . ." Leventhal stammered.

"I can't afford to fool around. The fooling has been kicked out of me. I've been put straight the hard way, the way you pay for with years of your life." He lowered his head and stared at him before continuing. There was a noticeable pulsation in the sides of his face beside his eyes, and in his eyes there was a glint that astounded Leventhal; it resembled nothing in his experience. "Look," said Allbee firmly in a lower voice. "You know that when I say I want an introduction to this man Shifcart it means I am ready to play ball.

I'm offering a settlement. I'm offering to haul down my flag. If he helps me. Do you understand?"

"No, I don't understand," Leventhal said. "I don't even begin to get it. And as long as you keep on talking about settling, I won't lift a finger for you."

"Listen," said Allbee. "I know you want to settle. And so do I. And I know what I'm talking about when I say I'll play ball. The world's changed hands. I'm like the Indian who sees a train running over the prairie where the buffalo used to roam. Well, now that the buffalo have disappeared, I want to get off the pony and be a conductor on that train. I'm not asking to be a stockholder in the company. I know that's impossible. Lots of things are impossible that didn't use to be. When I was younger I had my whole life laid out in my mind. I planned what it was going to be like on the assumption that I came out of the lords of the earth. I had all kinds of expectations. But God disposes. There's no use kidding."

Leventhal, his eyes raised to the ceiling, seemed to ask, "You follow? I don't."

There was a knock at the door.

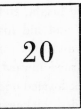

20

IT WAS MAX. He stood before Leventhal with a rolled newspaper under his arm, his shirt open at the throat, the black hair of his chest coming out, and his soft collar pulled over the collar of his coat, the same way Philip's had been on the day of the outing. The suit was the double-breasted one he had worn at the funeral. When the door opened, he seemed to hesitate on the landing, and Leventhal cried out in a cracked voice, "Max! Come in, for heaven's sake."

"You folks in?" Max asked huskily, still hesitant.

It struck Leventhal that his brother was behaving as if he were about to enter a stranger's house. He had never been here before.

"Well, I am, that's sure. I didn't get a chance to tell you the other day. Mary's out of town. But come on in." And he led him over the threshold and turned to the front room, filled with anxiety at his new difficulty. He did not know what to expect from Allbee, what he would say when he learned who Max was. He was already leaning forward inquisitively. Leventhal stood arrested for an instant, incapable of speaking or moving forward. Glancing into the room and seeing Allbee, Max said, apologetically, "Say, you're busy. I'll come back later."

"I'm not," Leventhal whispered. "Come on."

"I should have called up first."

But Leventhal held him by the arm and forced him in. "This is my brother Max. This is Kirby Allbee."

"Your brother? I didn't know you had one."

"Only one."

Reticent and somber, Max looked down, perhaps partly to acknowledge his share in their estrangement.

"I don't know what made me think you were an only

[233]

child, like me." Allbee was conversational and bright, and Leventhal wondered what he was preparing and hid his dread in impassivity. He brought up a chair and Max sat down. The points of his dusty shoes were turned inward. The side of his lowered face and his large neck formed one surface, from the curve of his nose to the padded thickness of his shoulder.

"I often used to wish there were two of us," said Allbee.

"How are things at home, Max?" asked Leventhal.

"Oh," Max said. "You know . . ." Leventhal expected him to finish the sentence, but it tailed off.

Allbee seemed to be commenting to himself smilingly on something in the appearance of the two brothers. Leventhal covertly indicated the door with his head. Allbee's brows curved up questioningly. His whole air said, "Why should I?" Leventhal bent close to him and muttered, "I want to talk to my brother."

"What's the matter?" Allbee spoke out loudly.

Sternly Leventhal made the same sign with his head.

But Max had heard. "Did you ask me what was the matter?" he said.

Allbee looked at Leventhal and shrugged, to confess his slip. He did not reply.

"I guess it must show on me," said Max.

"We had a death in the family recently," Leventhal said. "My youngest son."

An expression went over Allbee's face that Leventhal could not interpret, a cold wrinkling. "Oh, sorry to hear it. When?"

"Four days ago."

"You didn't mention it to me," Allbee said to Leventhal.

"No," Leventhal answered flatly, gazing at his brother.

Allbee came forward swiftly in his chair. "Say, was that the boy . . . the other day?"

"No, not the one that was with me. He means Phil," Leventhal explained to Max. "I took him to the movies awhile back, and we ran into Mr. Allbee."

"Oh, Phil. Knock wood. That's my other son you saw."

"Oh, I see, two children. . . ."

"Are you going?" Leventhal said to him, aside.

"Will you fix it up for me with Shifcart?"

Leventhal fastened his hand on his arm. "Will you go?"

"You said you'd help me."

"We'll take it up later." Leventhal was growing savage with impatience. "Don't think you can hold me up."

"I don't want to interfere with business," said Max.

"What business! There's no business."

Allbee rose and Leventhal went into the hall with him.

"I'll be back for your answer," Allbee said. He looked into Leventhal's face as though he saw something new there. "I'm really surprised. Here this happens to you—your nephew. I'm in the same house and you don't even say a word about it."

"What do I want to talk to you about it for?" Before Allbee could speak again, he had shut the door.

"Who is he?" said Max, when Leventhal came back. "A friend?"

"No, just a guy who keeps coming around."

"He's peculiar looking. . . ." Max checked himself and then said, "I hope I didn't butt in on anything."

"Oh, hell no. I was going to call you up, Max. But I thought I'd better wait awhile."

"I was kind of expecting you to, since you took an interest and came to the funeral, and all."

Max addressed him diffidently, a little formally, feeling his way with a queer politeness, almost the politeness of a stranger. Subdued, worn, and plainly, to Leventhal's eyes,

[235]

tormented, he was making an effort, nevertheless, to find an appropriate tone, one not too familiar. The blood crowded to Leventhal's heart guiltily. He wanted to say something to Max about it. He did not know how and he was afraid of creating a still greater difficulty. How should they talk when they had never, since childhood, spent an hour together? And he surmised also that the flat, the contrast between his upholstered chairs and good rugs and the borax furniture in Staten Island, shabby before half the installments were paid, made Max deferential.

"So how are things going?" he said. He thought Max would speak about Elena. He was in fact certain that the main object of his visit was to discuss her with him.

"I guess as good as I can expect."

"Phil all right?"

"Well, when one kid passes on it's pretty hard on the other one."

"He'll come around."

Max said nothing to this, and Leventhal began to think he was debating whether to mention Elena at all, undecided at the last moment, and struggling with himself.

"Yes, kids come around," Leventhal repeated.

"I wanted to ask you," said Max. "I want to straighten it up with you about the specialist. He says you gave him ten dollars the first visit." His hand dropped inside his coat.

"Oh, no."

But Max opened his wallet and, half rising, laid a ten dollar bill beside the lamp on the desk.

"That's not necessary."

"I want to pay you back. Thanks."

"Now he takes over," was Leventhal's unspoken comment. His original vexation with Max revived and he said, a shade coldly, "You're welcome."

"Not just for the money," said Max. "The rest, **too.**"

Leventhal's temper got the better of him.

"For doing a small part of what you should have been here to do."

Max reflected, raising his rough-skinned, large-jawed face with its high-ridged, freckled nose. "Yes," he said. "I should have been here." He was submissive, seeming to find nothing in himself with which to resist.

Leventhal could not hold back his next question.

"What does Elena say?"

"About what?"

"About me?"

Max appeared surprised.

"What should she say? All she said was that she wondered why you didn't come to the house after the funeral. But she doesn't say much. She's in bed most of the time, crying."

Leventhal had edged forward. The lamplight shone into his hair and over his shoulders.

"Does she give you a lot of trouble, Max?"

"Trouble? You've got to consider. It's a rough deal. She cries. That's pretty natural."

"You might as well be open with me."

Max's surprise grew.

"What's there not to be open about?"

"If you don't know, I don't either. But you've got a chance to talk it out, if you want to. I realize we're not so close. But do you have anyone else to talk to? Maybe you have friends. I didn't notice many at the funeral."

Max said uncertainly, "I don't catch your drift, exactly."

"I asked if Elena gives you trouble."

The blood rose darkly in Max's face under the full mask of his ill-shaven beard. There was a show of fear and bewilderment in his eyes and, reluctantly, he began a motion of denial with his black-nailed hands; he did not finish; he gave it up.

"She's calming down."

"What does she say?"

"All kinds of things," Max said with obvious difficulty, still shunning a direct answer.

But Leventhal did not need a direct answer. He could picture Elena in the brass bed where Mickey had lain, in that terrible room, crying and raging; and Max sitting just as he saw him sitting now, abjectly listening. For what could he do? And Philip had to listen, too. The thought struck into him. But how could the boy be protected? He would have to hear and learn. Leventhal believed what he had said to Max about children coming through. They were mauled in birth and they straightened as they grew because their bones were soft. Mauled again later, they could recover again. She was his mother, so let him see and hear. Was that a cruel view of it? He was full of love for the boy. But it did not do to be soft. Be soft when things were harsh? Not that softness was to be condemned, but there were times when it was only another name for weakness. Softness? Out of the whole creation only man was like that, and he was half harsh.

"Have you had a doctor for her?" he asked.

"What makes you think she needs one?"

"Remember Mamma!"

Max started. "What are you talking about?" he said with a sudden flash of indignation.

"I don't blame you for not wanting it brought up."

"Why do you bring Ma into this? Does she remind you of Ma?"

Leventhal hesitated. "Once in a while, she does. . . . But you admit you have trouble with her."

"What do you expect? She carries on. Sure she carries on. It's a kid, after all. That hits. But she'll be all right. She's getting better already."

"Max, I don't think you understand. People go overboard easily. I guess they're not as strong that way as they used to be and when things get rough they give in. There's more and more of that all the time. Everybody feels it. I do myself, often. Elena was very queer about the kid and the hospital. —That's what she yells about, isn't it? The hospital?" He grew increasingly unsure of himself. "And I thought . . ."

"I remember Ma pretty often, too, and Hartford, and all. You're not the only one."

"No?" Leventhal said. He looked at him searchingly.

"And you're wrong about Elena."

"You don't think I want to be right, do you?"

"The main trouble I'm having with her is that I want to move the family down south. I was looking for a place in Galveston. That was what took so long. I found one and I have a deposit on it. I was going to bring them all down there."

"That's good. The best thing you could do. Take Philip out of New York. It's no place to bring him up."

"But I can't talk Elena into it."

"Why?"

"Maybe I started in too soon after the funeral. But she says she doesn't want to go."

"Tell me, is the old woman around much—her mother?"

"Oh, she's in and out all the time."

"For God's sake, throw her out!"

His vehemence astonished Max.

"She doesn't have anything to do with it."

"Don't let her get a hold. Protect yourself against her."

Max for the first time began to smile.

[239]

"She won't hurt me."

"I'll bet she's telling Elena not to go. How do you know what she tells her? You don't understand what they're saying."

Max's look changed; he became grave again and his mouth sank at the corners. "I understand a little," he said. "I guess you think I should have married a Jewish girl."

"You never heard me say so," Leventhal answered vigorously. Never."

"No."

"You never will. I'm talking about her mother, not Elena. You told me yourself that the old woman hated you, years ago. She'll do you all the harm she can. Maybe you're used to the old devil and don't notice what she's like any more. But I've watched her. It's as clear as day to me that she thinks the baby's death was God's punishment because Elena married you."

Max started and then his lips stiffened, and there was a submerged flaming of indignation beneath his natural darkness and the added darkness of care. "What kind of talk is that!" he said. "I never heard anything so peculiar in all my life. First you've got ideas about Elena and now the old woman."

"You've been away," said Leventhal. "You don't know how she's been acting. She's poison."

"Well, you've sure turned into a suspicious character." Max's face began to soften and he sighed.

"She's full of hate," Leventhal insisted.

"Go on, she's a harmless old woman."

If he were wrong about Elena, thought Leventhal, if he had overshot the mark and misinterpreted that last look of hers in the chapel, the mistake was a terrible and damaging one; the confusion in himself out of which it had risen was

[240]

even more terrible. Eventually he had to have a reckoning with himself, when he was calmer and stronger. It was impossible now. But he was right about the old woman, he was sure. "You must get rid of your mother-in-law, Max!" he said with savage earnestness.

"Ah, what are you talking about?" he said rather wearily. "She's just an old widow, old and cranky. Elena is her only daughter. I can't tell her to stay away. This week she helped, she kept house and cooked for us. I know she doesn't like me. So what? A worn-out old woman. I feel sad, sometimes, when I look at her. No, we'll go to Galveston. Phil will start school there in the fall. He wants to go, and so does Elena. I can talk her into it. She wants to leave New York, only she's still mixed up. But she'll come. I've got to get back to my job, and we don't want to be separated again. I don't see why you're so disturbed about the old woman. If she's the worst I'm ever up against . . ." The large fold of his jacket reached kiltwise almost to his knees on which his hands were set. His unshapely fingers thickened where they should taper and the creases at the joints resembled the threads of flattened screws. "You don't know Elena when there's a tight spot," he resumed. "She's excitable all in pieces before something happens, but usually when it happens she's stronger than I am. During the depression when I was laid up, she went out and peddled stuff from door to door."

"I never heard that you were laid up."

"Well, I was. And then when we were on relief, she has a brother who's a hood and he wanted to take me into a kind of racket he had out in Astoria. I could've seen a little money, but she said no and went all the way out against it, so it was 'No' and we stayed on relief. Another woman would have said, 'Go ahead.'"

[241]

"I see."

"Afterwards things started to pick up and we thought we could add on to the family. Mickey wasn't ever a healthy kid like Phil. And then we must have made mistakes, too. But what can you do? It's not like with God, you know, in the Bible, where he blows his breath into Adam, or whoever. I think I told you that I asked a nurse what room he was in, when I got to the hospital. I went in there and he was lying covered up already. I pulled the sheet off and had a look at him."

"Those fools!" Leventhal exclaimed. "Not to have somebody posted there."

Max excused them with a downward wave of the hand. "All the nurses didn't know. It's a big place." He added, consecutively, "I'm going south with the idea of a new start. I paid a deposit and so on. But to tell the truth, I don't expect much. I feel half burned out already."

Leventhal felt his heart shaken. "Half burned?" he said. "I'm older than you and I don't say that."

Max did not reply. His large trunk was ungainly in the double-breasted jacket.

"There have been times when I felt like that, too," Leventhal went on. "That's a feeling that comes and goes." His brother turned his crude, dark face up to him and his voice died.

They sat together in silence and at last Max stirred and got up. Leventhal went with him to the subway. A heavy mist lay over the street. At the turnstile he dropped two nickels into the slot and Max said over his shoulder, "You don't have to wait with me."

But Leventhal pushed through. They stood at the edge of the platform till the grind of the approaching train reached them.

"If you need me for anything . . ." Leventhal said.

"Thanks."

"I mean it."

"Thank you." He extended his hand. Leventhal clumsily spread his arms wide and clasped him. They felt the concussion of the train, and the streaked face of the lead car with its beam shot toward them in a smolder of dust; the windows ran by. Max returned his embrace. "Call me," Leventhal said hoarsely in Max's ear. The crowd swirled around them at the doors. When the train started, he saw Max gripping a strap and bending over the heads of passengers, peering out.

Pulling out a handkerchief, Leventhal wiped his sweat. He began to labor up the long, steel-striped concrete flights, opening his mouth to assist his breathing. Halfway up he stopped, squeezing against the wall to let others past, looking as if the lack of air maddened him. He felt faint with the expansion of his heart.

Then he continued. The mist had gathered to a light rain. At the top of the stairs he saw an umbrella flung open, like a bat in the chill current of air. The bars of the revolving door raced and clinked. Buttoning his coat, he raised the collar, and his eyes moved from the glare of the cars flowing up in the street to the towering lights that stood far ahead, not quite steady in the immense blackness.

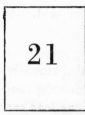

21 IN THE SATURDAY MAIL there was an invitation from Mrs. Harkavy to a party that same evening in honor of her granddaughter's seventh birthday. The postman whom Leventhal encountered in the fog on the outer stairs handed it to him. There was nothing from Mary and he was secretly glad of it, for the truth was that he felt he was stealing away and leaving Allbee in possession of the house. Ostensibly he was going out for coffee. He had risen to find the flat cold, and the windows dripping and gray as tin. Allbee was still asleep in the dining room, his naked arms locked around the narrow mattress, sprawling, uncouth. His clothes lay on the floor and the air was stifling. Leventhal had gone into the kitchen and put on the coffee but, when he pictured himself sitting down in the cheerless front room to drink it, he made a face, shut off the gas, and went down to eat at the Greek's. But he had no intention of coming back after breakfast.

Around Mrs. Harkavy's invitation he half unconsciously and in a complicatedly indirect fashion made out a schedule. He was at first uncertain about attending the party. Should he go so soon after Mickey's death? But, having decided that it would be a good thing for him to be among people, he rode uptown to buy the girl a present. And finding himself near the library at noon, he spent a few hours glancing over some of the trade papers to see what others were doing. So it was nearly evening and he was coming out of a newsreel theatre in Times Square before he realized that behind everything he had contrived to fill this weary day was his unwillingness and inability to deal with Allbee. He had set off purposefully down Broadway, and now something seemed to hinder the steady action of his legs and he faltered and began to go slower.

"All right, I'll send him to Shifcart," Leventhal decided. "What do I care? I'll do it, and if that isn't enough for him, we'll see. Only what will Shifcart think?" But he was already in disfavor with Shifcart, who had looked at him peevishly in the cafeteria when he failed to laugh at his joke. "It would be better to come in cold than with a recommendation from me. But as long as he believes so much in connections let him go and find out for himself."

He stopped at home before dinner to put on a clean shirt. Allbee was out. The dirt and disorder of the place sickened Leventhal. There was rubbish on the kitchen floor and the remains of a meal on the table. "He'd behave better in a flophouse. He's just trying to show me," thought Leventhal. He swept out the kitchen. Bending down with the dust pan, he experienced a curious tightness in the skin of his face. He threw the broom into the corner, washed his hands, and left.

Mrs. Harkavy met him in the entry and she disconcerted him by saying, "I was awfully upset to hear about your nephew." For he had just then, in the elevator, been thinking about Mickey. "Doctor Denisart told me about it. I'm sure he did his best."

Leventhal muttered that he thought so too. Because he was disturbed, he was more conscious than usual of the bracing process he went through on meeting one of the Harkavys. He was fond of them, they were kind, but he had never been able to work out a satisfactory balance with them. Mrs. Harkavy's expression was like her son's, lively and erratic. Yet there was a durable, underlying melancholy in her animation, and occasionally it came uppermost and took him by surprise.

"Someday science will conquer death," she said. "Last

Sunday there was a symposium in the *Times* about it."

Leventhal pulled himself together sufficiently to reply, "I hope. . . ."

"Oh, it looks definite. Then the size of the population will have to be controlled. But science will figure that out, too. There are brains enough for everything. This man discovered something to make the tissues live forever. I don't think we can expect much in our lifetime. It's for future generations. Meanwhile, we have to make the best of it. I think Mr. Banting's father died of diabetes about a year before insulin was discovered. And this Mr. Bogomolets couldn't use his own serum on account of a bad heart, and he died. Asa, how old was the child?"

"Three and a half, four. . . ."

The freakishness seemed to leave her. Only her eyes moved, meeting his own with a familiar, instantaneous significance.

"That's the brother who lives in Queens?"

"Staten Island."

"Asa, sometimes I feel wicked still to be here at my age while children die."

He was at a loss for an answer.

"But I'm not taking it away from anybody," she said, falling back into her eccentricity; it quivered at the corners of her green-ringed eyes.

"Mamma," Julia called.

"The men are in the dining room, Asa. There's wine and liquor on the sideboard." Her face was flushed and she turned away, wide-hipped in her blue dress with its ornamented shoulders.

The guests, none of whom he knew, were playing pinochle. He was disappointed. He had hoped to see Schlossberg or Shifcart.

"Take a hand," said Harkavy.

"No, I don't think I will. Is anybody else coming, Dan?"

"We're expecting a few more people," said Harkavy. He was engrossed in his cards.

Leventhal poured himself a glass of wine and took a diamond-shaped biscuit sprinkled with sugar. Suddenly he remembered the present he had brought and he drank down the wine, tugged the package out of his pocket, and went into the kitchen. There was a cloud over the range. Julia was raising a colander of fried potatoes from the oil, averting her face from the sputter and crying nervously, "Mother, Mother, keep Libbie back."

"Stay away, honey. Julia, don't rush those potatoes. They'll be raw."

Leventhal came forward with his package.

"I brought something for the girl."

"Oh, how thoughtful of you," said Mrs. Harkavy. "With all your own troubles."

Leventhal was impassive.

"Here," he said. "Happy birthday."

There was a gold seal pasted on the tissue paper and Libbie, after one quick glance at him, began picking it off.

"Not even 'thank you, Uncle Leventhal.'" Julia looked furious.

"Julia, it's only shyness, nervousness."

"Say thanks, you little animal."

The girl ran into the hall and Leventhal returned to the dining room. He had a second glass of the sweet wine, and a third.

"Come, sit in," Goldstone said to him.

He shook his head and slouched against the sideboard, leaning on his elbow and sipping. This was his fourth glass and he was beginning to feel a heavy, solvent, milky warmth.

He was conscious of being extremely clear-eyed, of seeing everything, catching every movement as if under extraordinary illumination. As the cards slapped and flicked over the red leather pad, he diverted himself by observing the hands, shuffling, dealing, manipulating the money, the variety of knuckles and fingers. Harkavy's were white, pointed, and simple looking. The hands of the man next to him were strung with veins and overgrown with hair, his thumb was turned back and blackened, perhaps by lead—he might be a printer. The flesh of his palm was red and brutally crosshatched. "Used hard," reflected Leventhal. Yet these hands were limber with coins, and counted and tossed them with the ease of deep familiarity.

Leaving the sideboard he strolled into the dark living room and lit a cigar. He felt the blood at his heart and brain to be a very rich and powerful mixture, for the most part pleasurable. A little painful also. The slight distress, however, was part of the pleasure. He took a sip of wine, licked the base of the glass and wiped it on his wrist to prevent a ring, and set it on a little table. Mrs. Harkavy's voice came down the hall. "Future generations!" he grinned. "My Lord!" He sat down, lame and heavy limbed.

After some time he saw Harkavy come in to the room apparently looking for him. He spoke up from his corner.

"Hey, here!"

"Oh, hiding out, having a quiet cigar. The house is filling up. Mamma and Julia are starting to serve." Leventhal heard the scrape of chairs on the parquet floor of the dining room.

"Say, do you expect Shifcart tonight?"

"I don't think he was asked. What do you want him for?"

"Do you think I made a bad impression on him that day?"

"I know you did on me. I've never seen such an exhibition

of ghetto psychology. The attitude you took toward Disraeli amazed me."

"No, I don't mean that. Did he say anything to you?"

"Nothing. Is this an attack of your old weakness—worrying whether people like you?"

"I wanted to sound him out about something. . . . To see what he'd say. If he'd help me out with someone."

"Who's the favor for?"

"It doesn't matter who, does it?" Leventhal said.

"No, it doesn't. You don't have to tell me." There was already a ring of exasperation in his voice.

"It doesn't make any difference who."

"I asked to be helpful. But I won't play button-button with you. Especially since you have an edge on. I saw you drinking."

"Ah, you could have had a lot of opportunities to be helpful," said Leventhal.

"Why, it must be that what's-his-name that's been bothering you," said Harkavy with a sudden nicker of amused discovery. "That's who, isn't it?"

Leventhal dumbly nodded.

"Then what's the mystery?"

"No mystery," Leventhal muttered.

"Why do you need help with him? What does he want? I don't understand how Shifcart comes into the picture."

"Well, Dan, this Allbee is interested in scenario work and since he once got me an introduction at Dill's he wants me to do the same for him with Shifcart, seeing he's in the movie line. It's mostly for the record that I'm doing it."

"You know Shifcart has nothing to do with scenario. He deals with actors, talent."

"Allbee thought he might have a connection somewhere. I didn't think so, but he asked me, and I thought . . . Well, to tell you the truth, Dan, I didn't know what to think. I had my doubts. But he did get me the interview with Rudiger. So I thought, 'Well, let him go and see Shifcart. Why should I answer for Shifcart? I'll show my good intentions and return the favor,' and so on. That's the story."

"I don't believe it. It seems to me that he's got you on the merry-go-round."

One of Mrs. Harkavy's plants stood behind Leventhal. He felt a leaf graze his hair as he shut his eyes and leaned backwards.

"How did he ever sell you such a bill of goods?" said Harkavy. "Where did he hear of Shifcart?"

"He happened to be at the house and saw a card of Shifcart's."

"So he keeps coming around. You must be encouraging him. I thought we came to the conclusion he was off his nut."

"*You* did!" Blindly roused, Leventhal flung out his arm. "You were the one. That was what you said. You compared him to your aunt."

"Well, you're impetuous tonight. Both of us came to the same conclusion."

"No, no!" Leventhal refused to hear him. "I absolutely deny it. Absolutely!"

"Where did I get it from, if you didn't say it? I can't understand you. I haven't seen the man. Anyhow, what's the odds? Why should that be an issue? I can see you're losing your bearings. Of course, you've got quite a little wine in your system; maybe that partly accounts for your funny behavior. Yes, it is very funny. I always thought you didn't know how to take care of yourself. I can see this man has you eating out of his hand. He comes around, you get excited when you talk about him, you're going to send him to Shifcart. . . ."

"I'd send him anywhere to get rid of him," said Leventhal.

"There, you wouldn't say anything like that unless you were in pretty deep. I can tell that you're keeping back information; don't have to be much of a mindreader to see that. I can't help you any more than to remind you that you're playing for keeps. You're not a boy, any more."

"Dan, you know Shifcart. This has to be done. Tell me . . ." He caught Harkavy's hand.

"Take it up with him yourself."

"Yes, I will, but I want to ask you . . ."

"We'd better go in. They must be waiting for us. We'll discuss this tomorrow when your head is clearer and if you want to be open with me."

The guests, all men, had taken off their jackets and were sitting in the high-backed chairs. In the kitchen door, talking with Mrs. Harkavy, was Mr. Schlossberg who had just arrived and was still wearing his brown topcoat. Leventhal said good evening to him and Schlossberg answered, "How are you?" He did not seem, however, to remember him. "Fourteenth Street a couple of weeks ago," said Leventhal.

"His memory is bad," Harkavy whispered. He drew Leventhal into the row of chairs along the buffet.

Across the table, Leventhal recognized the possessor of the red hands he had watched during the card game. His name was Kaplan and his face, like his hands, was red and creased. He had a sharp blue squint, as though—Leventhal thought—he had made an effort to pierce heaven and distorted his eyes. Just now he was holding up a glass of brandy and saying, "Here's to all."

"Drink up," someone said. "Next year in Jerusalem."

Leventhal heard Julia say, "We had a children's party

last year. It was too nerve racking. This time we decided we would have older people."

"Shall we begin eating?" asked Goldstone.

"We ought to have the cake brought in first," Mrs. Harkavy said. She explained to the company, "They weren't very careful with it at the bakery. Some of the frosting came off with the wax paper. We did our best to repair it."

Julia put the cake with its seven candles on the table. Libbie stood staring into the flames. Her eyes were much like her grandmother's and her uncle's.

"Blow, kiddie," said Harkavy. "Once, that's luckiest."

But Libbie reached out and tried to capture a drop of the melting wax.

"Libbie, dear. . . . " her father urged.

"People are waiting," Julia cried impatiently. "Would you rather be hanging upside down in the closet?"

The child lowered her face to the clear ring of candles. Leventhal saw the liquid image of them in her eyes and on her white forehead. She blew, and the whitish, odorous wax smoke drifted over the table. The guests clapped and cried out.

"Sweet little kid," said Harkavy to Leventhal, who nodded and still gazed heavy eyed at the candles. Julia and her grandmother kissed the girl.

The supper began. Leventhal's clothing, especially his shirt, bound and chafed him, and he opened his collar, grumbling to Harkavy, "It's cutting my neck." But Harkavy had resumed an argument begun earlier in the evening with a Mr. Benjamin who sat between Goldstone and Julia. Leventhal had noticed him in the hall before, clumping on a specially built shoe. He had the complexion of a Hindu, a head of grizzled short curls, and scornful brown-freckled lips; there was a drop of yellow in his wide-set black eyes.

Benjamin sold life insurance, and Harkavy had assailed the insurance companies. "It's all in the Cardozo investigation. Does any more have to be said? The same money that's taken from the customers is used against them." "I don't see, Harkavy," said Mr. Benjamin, "why one business has to be run down more than another. You ought to be against them all. And against government. You're an amateur, Harkavy, an amateur. I've heard your argument from experts. You have to pay for regulation and for order. It's one kind of harness or another. Men need a harness. This is light harness compared to some." "Oh, my dear man, you're as reactionary as they come," said Harkavy. "Are you against all banks and business?" asked Benjamin. "Damn it, certainly I am." Harkavy's voice rose. "Let's hear what kind of a system you're thinking about?" Mr. Benjamin's acerbity almost wiped out his smile.

"Stop the wrangling, Dan, for God's sake," said Goldstone.

"I'll make it easier for you," said Benjamin. "Don't you want to provide for the people you love? Let's not argue about the best system. This one is standing yet."

"It may not be for long. You never know when everything will be swept away overnight." "But meantime . . ." Mrs. Harkavy interrupted. "Daniel, you're just being sensational. I don't like to hear such talk from you." "Mamma, what I say is perfectly true. There have been big organizations before and people who thought they would last forever." "You mean Insull?" said the man on his left. "I mean Rome, Persia, the great Chinese empires!"

Mr. Benjamin shrugged his shoulders. "We have to live today," he said. "If you had a son, Harkavy, you'd want him to have a college education. Who's going to wait for the Messiah? They tell a story about a little town in the

[253]

old country. It was out of the way, in a valley, so the Jews were afraid the Messiah would come and miss them, and they built a high tower and hired one of the town beggars to sit in it all day long. A friend of his meets this beggar and he says, 'How do you like your job, Baruch?' So he says, 'It doesn't pay much, but I think it's steady work.'" There was an uproar at the table. "There's a moral, for you!" cried Benjamin in a suddenly strengthened voice. Leventhal felt himself beginning to smile. "It is!" shouted Mr. Kaplan, laying his hand on Benjamin's shoulder. Mrs. Harkavy, flushing, raised her delighted brows and covered her mouth with her handkerchief.

"Anyway, I don't think it's right," said Harkavy, "to go frightening people the way you do." "Oh? What now?" Harkavy knitted his brows. "I know how you insurance gentlemen work," he said. "You go in to see a prospect. There he is, behind his desk or his counter, still in pretty fair shape, you may say. He has his aches and his troubles, but in general everything is satisfactory. Suddenly you're there to say, 'Have you considered your family's future?' Well and good, every man dies, but you're playing it unfair and hitting where you know it hurts. He thinks about these things alone at night. Most of us do. But now you're undermining him in the daytime. When you've frightened him good he says, 'What'll I do?' And you're ready with the contract and the fountain pen." "Now, Dan," said Goldstone restrainingly. Benjamin glanced at him with his yellow and black eyes as though to say that he needed no defender. "So what," he said. "I do them a favor. Shouldn't they be prepared?"

"Oh, Death!" someone quoted at the far end of the table. "Thou comest when I had thee least in mind." "Yes, that's the thing," Benjamin said lifting himself with a scuff of his heel and pointing. "That's it." "My heavens," said Mrs. Harkavy. "What a morbid thing for a birthday party. With all this food on the table. Can't we find something lighter to talk about?" "The funeral baked meats did furnish forth the marriage feast." "Where the blazes is this poetry coming from?" said Goldstone. "It's Brimberg. His father died and he was able to go to college." Goldstone smiled. "Be serious, down there," he said. "Cousins of mine," he explained to Leventhal, happening to catch his glance. "My mother sewed her own shroud," said Kaplan, raising his distorted shining blue eyes to them. "That's right, it was the custom," said Benjamin. "All the old people used to do it. And a good custom, too, don't you think so, Mr. Schlossberg?" "There's a lot to say for it," Schlossberg replied. "At least they knew where they stood and who they were, in those days. Now they don't know who they are but they don't want to give themselves up. The last funeral I went to, they had paper grass in the grave to cover up the dirt." "So you're on Benjamin's side?" said Harkavy. "No, not exactly," said the old man. "Sure, Benjamin's business is to scare people." "So you're on my side, then?" Mr. Schlossberg looked impatient. "It's not a question of people's feelings," he said. "You don't have to remind them of anything. They don't forget. But they're too busy and too smart to die. It's easy to understand. Here I'm sitting here, and my mind can go around the world. Is there any limit to what I can think? But in another minute I can be dead, on this spot. There's a limit to me. But I have to be myself in full. Which is somebody who dies, isn't it? That's what I was from the beginning. I'm not three people, four people. I was born once and I will die once. You want to be two people? More than human? Maybe it's because you don't know how to be one. Everybody is busy. Every man turns himself

[255]

into a whole corporation to handle the business. So one stockholder is riding in the elevator, and another one is on the roof looking through a telescope, one is eating candy, and one is in the movies looking at a pretty face. Who is left? And how can a corporation die? One stockholder dies. The corporation lives and goes on eating and riding in the elevator and looking at the pretty face. But it stands to reason, paper grass in the grave makes all the grass paper. . . ."

"There's always something new with Schlossberg," said Kaplan. He strangely altered his squint by raising his brows. "What's on his lung is on his tongue."

"Really," Julia broke in. "Mamma is right. What kind of talk is this for a birthday?"

"Never out of place," said Benjamin.

"Out of place?" said Brimberg at the foot of the table. "It depends on your taste. I heard about a French lady of easy virtue who dressed in a bridal veil for her clients."

"Sammy!" came Mrs. Harkavy's scolding scream. And there was more laughter and a hubbub out of which grew a new conversation to which Leventhal, however, did not listen. Harkavy was not watching and he poured himself another glass of wine.

22

BEFORE he was fully awake, Leventhal, on Harkavy's couch where he had spent the night, realized that his head was aching, and, when he opened his eyes, even the gray light of the overcast day was too strong for him and he turned his face to the cushions and hitched the quilt over his shoulder. He was in his undershirt and his feet were bare but he had not taken off his trousers. His belt was tight and he loosened it, and brought his hand out, pressing and kneading the skin of his forehead. Over the arm of the couch he gazed at the period furniture, the ferns, the looped and gathered silk of the unmodish lamps, and the dragons, flowers, and eyes of the rug. He knew the rug. Old Harkavy had gotten it from the estate of a broker who committed suicide on Black Friday.

Occasionally the windows were slammed by a high wind, and when this occurred the curtained French doors shook a little. Steam hissed in the pipes and there was a fall smell of heating radiators. Leventhal's nose was dry. The mohair was rough against his cheek. He did not change his position. Shutting his eyes, he tried to doze away the oppressiveness of his headache.

At a stir behind the French doors he said loudly, "Come!" No one entered, however, and he pushed away the covers. The strap of his watch was loose and it had worked round to the wrong side of his wrist. The lateness of the hour made him frown—it was nearly half-past one. He sat up and leaned forward, his undershirt hanging shapeless over his fat chest. He was about to reach for his shoes and stockings, but his hands remained on his knees and he was suddenly powerless to move and fearfully hampered in his breathing. He had the strange feeling that there was not a single part of him on which the whole world did not press with full weight, on his body, on his soul, pushing upward in his breast and downward in his bowels. He concentrated, moving his lips like someone about to speak, and blew a tormented breath through his nose. What he meanwhile sensed was that this interruption of the customary motions he went through unthinkingly on rising, despite the pain it was causing, was a disguised opportunity to discover something of great importance. He tried to seize the opportunity. He put out all his strength to collect himself, beginning with the primary certainty that the world pressed on him and passed through him. Beyond this he could not go, hard though he drove himself. He was bewilderingly moved. He sat in the same posture, massively, his murky face trained on the ferns standing softly against the gray glass. His nostrils twitched. It came into his head that he was like a man in a mine who could smell smoke and feel heat but never see the flames. And then the cramp and the enigmatic opportunity ended together. His legs quivered as he worked his feet back and forth on the carpet. He walked over to the window and he heard the loud crack of the wind. It was pumping the trees in the small wedge of park six stories below, tearing at the wires on rooftops, fanning the smoke out under the clouds, scattering it like soot on paraffin.

He dressed, feeling a little easier. His shirt cuffs were soiled; he turned them underside up and transferred the links. He stuffed his tie into his pocket; he would put it on after washing. Stripping the couch, he folded up the sheets and the silk quilt and laid them on a chair. When he opened the French doors, he expected to meet Mrs. Harkavy or one of the family in the hall and he wondered why the house was so silent. Harkavy's dark room was open, the bed empty. Leventhal switched on the light and saw trousers hung neatly from the top drawer of the dresser and the suspenders coiled on the floor. An open magazine covered the lamp.

Harkavy was sitting alone in the kitchen. At his elbow the toaster was ticking, and a pot of coffee was warming on the electric heater. He was wearing a corduroy jacket over his pajamas, a belted jacket with large leather buttons. His bare feet were crossed on a chair. His green slippers had fallen to the floor.

"Good morning," Harkavy's look was amused. "The reveler."

"Good morning. Where's the family?"

"Gone to Shifcart senior's for the birthday dinner."

"Why didn't you go?"

"To Long Island City when I have a chance to sleep late? They left at nine."

"I hope you didn't stay here because of me."

"You? No, I wanted to sleep. Holidays are poison if I have to get up early." He stroked the golden-green jacket. "I like a late, peaceful breakfast. Bachelor habits. As long as I'm not married, I've got to stand pat on my advantages."

The kitchen light, reflecting from the tiles and the white refrigerator, was too sharp for Leventhal. He winced away from it slightly.

"How do you feel—not very well?"

"Headache."

"You're not used to drinking."

"No," said Leventhal. The banter annoyed him.

"You were bright-eyed, last night."

He looked rather sullenly at him. "What if I was?"

"Nothing. I'm not blaming you, you understand, for getting a little tight. You probably have good reasons."

"Where's your aspirin?"

"In the bathroom. I'll bring you some." Harkavy started to rise.

"Stay put; I'll find it."

"Have a cup of coffee. It'll do you more good." He removed his feet from the chair. They were very long and white, with toes as slender as fingers.

Leventhal poured himself a cup of black coffee. It was bitter and coated his tongue with a sediment, but he felt it would do him good.

Harkavy sighed. "I'm a little under the weather myself. Not from drinking; the excitement, the arguing, and such. Mamma, though, she was up at seven and got everything in order. What vitality she's got! Her mother—there was another dry old fire for you. She lived to be ninety-four. Do you remember her? Down on Joralemon Street?"

"No." Leventhal, trying to recapture the feeling that had interrupted his dressing, found he retained almost nothing of it.

"I'm a different type," Harkavy said. "The sword that wears out the sheath. But some of these old people. . . . Take Schlossberg, for example, still supporting his family, his good-for-nothing son and his daughters. The old man is a blowhard, sometimes, but you have to hand it to him. With him it's a case of 'touch me and you touch a man,' and these days you can't always be sure what you're touching. I set myself up against him, now and then, because I like a good argument. I don't trust people who won't argue."

Gradually Harkavy's manner underwent a change. He was slouching in his chair, his heels were set wide apart on the linoleum and his arms were hanging over the back of the chair; his hands with their whitish hairs were full veined. Beneath the clear water lines, his lids suddenly appeared flushed and irritated, and when he began again to speak it was with a nervous dodge of the head, as if he were already putting aside an objection.

"Why don't you come clean now on this business we were talking about last night?" he said.

"What's there to come clean about?"

"It baffles me. I've been giving it some thought. After what you said about him, that you should be trying to arrange this. . . ."

Leventhal did not stir his face from the cup. "We went over that yesterday. I told you about *Dill's.*"

"He must have you by the tail."

Leventhal reflected, "This is just curiosity on his part. Why should I satisfy it? That Sunday when he could have helped me out he went away with Goldstone and his friends, and now, because he's itching to know, *I* should talk." He resolved to give him no satisfaction. Nevertheless, the saucer shook in his hand and he held it against his chest, bending his head until folds of skin appeared under his chin and along his jaw. He meditated on his weakness. How weak he was becoming. Even Harkavy could make him tremble.

"How come you changed your mind about him? You said he was loony."

"No, you did."

"On your information. What you told me was all I had to go by. It looks as if he really did a job on you, sold you a bill of goods."

Leventhal doggedly refrained from answering. He kept his head down with a look of worn endurance.

Harkavy persisted. "Didn't he?"

Leventhal drew his lips against his teeth as he wiped his mouth. "I must have wanted to buy," he said.

"It's beyond me. When you came to talk to me about him,

you were mad enough to hang him. He was accusing you of some crime and blaming you for what happened to his wife and what not. Now you want to send him to Shifcart with a reference. And unless I'm mistaken you were fishing for me to help you. I couldn't believe my ears when you asked me about Shifcart. What kind of impression will a man like that make on him? And why do you let him hang around? Didn't you tell me he picked up Shifcart's card at your house? Besides, you know Shifcart can't do anything for him."

"I suppose not."

"And where does he get the idea that Shifcart can help him?"

Though he knew he was making a mistake, Leventhal said, and to some extent it was involuntary, "I think he believes it's all a Jewish setup and Shifcart can pull strings for him. . . . Jews have influence with other Jews."

"No!" Harkavy cried. "No!" His hands flew to his head. "And you're trying to do something for him? You're willing, regardless? Boy, do you know what this does to my opinion of you? Are you in your right mind?"

His horror shook Leventhal.

"Look, Dan, I don't want to go into this any further. Don't push me. I asked you about Shifcart. You told me what you think. . . . Let that be the end of it."

"But how does he do it?" Harkavy's voice rang. "What's he got on you? Is it blackmail? Have you done something?"

"No, nothing. . . . I've been having a lot of trouble. My family—you heard about that. And Mary's away, that's been hard on me, too. My nerves aren't in very good shape. I feel I've been trying to throw something off. You aren't being very helpful. Just let me alone to handle this in my own way." This was a great deal for him to say; it was exorbitant, like a plea. His hands were less steady than ever. He set down the coffee, splashing some of it into the saucer.

"What's between you? How does he work you? First you come to complain about him. Next thing I know he sounds like the Protocols, but it's all right with you." He furiously pounded the metal table, his face and his elongated throat flaming. "Influence with Jews!" he shouted.

Leventhal silently reproached himself. "That was a real mistake. I shouldn't have said that. Why did I let it slip out? I'm not even sure Allbee means that."

To Harkavy, he said, "Don't fly off the handle. I realize it seems bad, but you don't know the facts. I can judge this better than you." He kept his voice low in order to control it.

"The facts? What are you letting this man do to you? Are you going off your rocker?"

"Don't be foolish, Dan," he cried. "I know you mean well, but you're being carried away. And please remember my mother before you say a thing like that. You know about my mother. I told you about her as friend to friend. The meaning of it hasn't sunk in."

This silenced Harkavy briefly. He seemed to scowl. In reality he was clearing his throat. After considering him for a while he said, "Well, you *are* a privileged character. You're the only man living whose mother lost her mind and died." Immediately he changed his tone, clapping his hands sharply. "As friend to friend, what are the facts? This thing about Shifcart is such nonsense it isn't even worth talking about. But you, you must be in a trance. Tell me, what's going on. Just look at you!"

"What's the matter?"

"You look like the devil."

"Do I? Well, I told you. There was the kid's death, first of all."

"You were more honest when you were drunk, last night.

You admitted that you wanted to get the man off your neck. Don't hide behind the child. That's not good. It's dishonest. Wake up! What's life? Metabolism? That's what it is for the bugs. Jesus Christ, no! What's life? Consciousness, that's what it is. That's what you're short on. For God's sake, give yourself a push and a shake. It's dangerous stuff, Asa, this stuff."

Leventhal looked at Harkavy in blank perplexity.

"Well, I'm damned if I can see it," he finally said. "In the first place, when I came to you, you were the one who told me about Williston. . . ."

"And?"

But Leventhal would not continue.

"And? What next?" said Harkavy, sitting forward.

There was a short pause and then Leventhal said, "Say, I've got to have that aspirin." He rose.

"All right, you don't want my help. I can't make you take it. God bless you. You had a chance to unburden yourself and get some advice. How many friends have you got?" He put a slice of bread in the toaster and rammed down the lever.

Among the bottles of lotion and cologne and the powder boxes in Mrs. Harkavy's medicine chest, Leventhal found the aspirin and swallowed a tablet with a sip from the tap. He filled the sink with warm water and pushed back his sleeves; the light green color gave him a kind of pleasure. He dipped in his hands and then glanced at the tub with its thick nickled spout. The linen closet stood open, giving out a dry perfume of soap. Leventhal took a towel and let the metal stopper fall. "I'm going to take a bath, if you don't mind," he called to Harkavy.

"Go ahead."

The faucet ran loudly and Leventhal shut the door and

began to undress. The room grew hot. He sat on the edge of the tub in the roar of the steaming water and lathered his hairy dark body, energetic and all absorbed. The tumult of the faucet relieved him, for some reason. As he lay back in the charge and sway of the water, he observed to himself, as if in compliment, "He didn't get anything out of me." He stroked his chest, releasing tiny bubbles from the hairs. "I'll be better off taking care of things by myself," he thought. He turned off the cold tap and the hot water ran on, green with a white inner shape and a thread of vapor.

He wondered what success Max was having with Elena. He was concerned for him, of course, but he worried mainly about Philip whom, if it turned out that Max was wrong about Elena, he would go to any lengths to save. He postponed thinking about himself. Eventually he would have to —provided that Max was right about Elena and he wrong. The reason for a mistake like that could not be neglected; it had to be dug out. But dug out when he had the strength for the operation, not now. A ring of soap, melting from the bar in his hand, spread over the water.

While he dried himself, his heart beat rapidly. However, his headache was almost gone, and he felt freshened and almost cheerful. He went into the kitchen. Harkavy had set out plates and was scrambling some eggs.

It was not until the meal was nearly over that he suffered a recoil, a raw, painful current through his overtried nerves. He could not continue this way with Allbee. It was enough. It had to be ended. Any day he expected to hear that Mary was coming back. What if she should come back before it was ended? He freed himself from this fear much as one might brush away a clinging insect from one's face. And Allbee might think, because he had not slept at home last night—what might he think, that he was afraid of him? It would give him the confidence to make new demands. He could have the introduction to Shifcart. More than that, no. And he would have to get out of the house. "Enough!" he silently decided. "Enough, enough!" He dropped his fork noisily. Under Harkavy's questioning eyes he looked, as usual, unperturbed; moping somewhat, but steady and calm. He recovered the fork and touched his food with it. But he was unable to swallow another bite.

23

HE STARTED HOME at half-past four. The wind had dropped, the sky was cold and darkening rapidly. In the little park the turned-up rusty shells of leaves scraped in the path and cracked underfoot. Very little green remained in those that streamed raggedly in the trees. A damp warmth, smelling of stone, rose from the subway, and through the gratings Leventhal caught a glimpse of the inert light on the roadbed and of the rails, hard and gray in their simultaneous strike. The close brownstone houses looked autumnal and so did the foot-burnished, steel manhole lids; they were glinting sharply. Summer seemed to have ended prematurely in chill and darkness. The people who had gone out of town for the holiday would be building fires on the beaches, those who were not already crowding the trains into the city.

Leventhal halted on the sidewalk opposite his flat. All the windows in the building were dark. The tiny red lamp in the foyer appeared to be embedded in the fanlight and sent its bloody color into the corners and as far as the polished, florid head of the banister at the rear. Mrs. Nunez' vines, spreading thickly upwards, swayed in a mass on the taut strings. "He's out," said Leventhal to himself. He was exasperated, almost as if Allbee had gone away to thwart him. But actually it was to his advantage to be the first one home, for so far he had not decided how to deal with Allbee. And now, while going up the stairs, he occasionally touched the dust-hung concave of the wall and thought, "What will I do?" He was, however, far too agitated to make any plans. He climbed rapidly, rather struck by the number of landings and, until he recognized a fire bucket with cigarettes buried in the sand, wondering why the place did not look more familiar. Reaching the fourth floor, he put his back against the wall while he felt in both pockets for his key. He brought out a handful of change and keys, and began to pick it over under the weak light. Then it seemed to him that someone was moving in the flat. It could be that Allbee had been sleeping and had just gotten up. That would explain the dark windows. He rapped and put his ear to the panel. He was sure that he heard steps.

He was far from calm when he turned the key in the lock. The door yielded a few inches, and then bumped and held with a rattle. He thrust his hand into the opening and felt the chain. Were there thieves in the house? He was on the point of running down to fetch Nunez or to phone the police when he heard Allbee say, "Is that you?"

"What's the chain up for?" he demanded.

"I'll explain to you later."

"No, you won't, you'll explain it right now."

But the chain remained in place. Leventhal urged himself not to lose his head and an instant later he punched at the door so that it shook and waited, staring at its ancient black trickles and tears of enamel. Then he began to pound again, enraged, shouting, "You! Open!" When he stopped he heard a low sound and, peering into the crack, he saw Allbee's face or rather a segment of his face, his nose, his full lip, and, with the lingering effect of a trance, his eye and the familiar stain beneath it.

"Come on!" he said to him.

"I can't," Allbee whispered. "Come back a little later, will you? Give me about fifteen minutes."

"I'll give you nothing."

"Ten minutes. Be decent."

Leventhal threw himself at the door, whirling around and striking it with the side of his body and his lowered shoulder, his feet gritting on the tiles. He gripped the door posts and pushed. He now heard two voices inside. Again, more desperately, he lunged. The chain broke and he was thrown against the wall of the vestibule. He recovered and rushed into the front room. There Allbee, naked and ungainly, stood beside a woman who was dressing in great haste. He was helping her, handing her stockings and underwear from the heap on the chair beside the bed. She had on her skirt but from the waist up she was bare. Brushing aside his hand with the proffered stockings, she bent to squeeze her foot into a shoe, digging her finger in beside the heel. Her hair covered her face; nevertheless Leventhal thought he recognized her. Mrs. Nunez! Was it Mrs. Nunez? The horror of it bristled on him, and the outcry he had been about to make was choked down.

She stooped toward the light—only the bed lamp was lit and it cast a limited circle over the twisted sheets and the rug—and turned her blouse right side out. Her scared eyes glimmered at him and her breasts hung down heavily as she thrust her arm through the sleeve. Meanwhile, Allbee had hurried to the door and closed it. He came back and put on his shirt, the new shirt he had bought on Second Avenue. The stiff loop of the collar stood off from his neck. Next he drew on his pants, nearly losing his balance as he shifted from foot to foot. Breathing heavily, he looked down and, while he buttoned himself, he said quietly to Leventhal, "At least, go into another room for a while, till she leaves."

"You get out, too."

He dropped his head, and Leventhal could not tell from his expression whether he was entreating or ordering him. He looked at him with anger and contempt, and began to walk toward the kitchen. The woman turned and he saw her plainly. She was straightening her hair, her elbows working quickly above her head. She was a stranger, not Mrs. Nunez; simply a woman. He felt enormously lightened, but at the

[269]

same time it gave him a pang to think of his suspicion. She was a big woman, large hipped; her shoulders were high and the straight lines of her blouse made them appear square. She was tall and her hair was black, and that was all there was to the resemblance. There was an irregularity in the shape of her eyes; one was smaller than the other. It was with the larger, more brilliant eye that she returned his stare. Her smile was unsteady and resentful. He hovered near her a moment, inhaling the strong odor of powder or perfume that emanated from her in the heat of the room. She pushed a white comb into her hair and moved away from him.

He banged the kitchen door and, in the dark, beside the throbbing refrigerator, he waited and heard the low sounds of a conversation. He did not try to follow it. There were footsteps; the tread was the woman's, she was going toward the door. It was for her sake primarily that he had withdrawn, in order to spare her. It wasn't her fault. Probably Allbee had not told her the flat was someone else's. The nerve of him, the nerve! Leventhal nearly cried aloud in revulsion. He distorted his face wildly, stretching his mouth. The nastiness of it! The refrigerator faltered and quivered but always recovered and ran, chaotically and interminably, ran and ran. Its white crown was on a level with his eyes; he could see blue sparks within. The only other thing visible in the room was the pilot light, also blue, a much deeper blue, in the black hollows and spidery bars of the gas range.

The woman's look remained with him. So did her scent; it seemed to cling to the rooms. The voices continued in the vestibule. Leventhal went into the dining room. On the day-bed's crumpled sheets, the pillow gray, almost black, there were newspapers, underclothes, and socks. Between the curtains, on the sill, he discovered a cup of coffee in which drops of mold floated, and crumbs and scraps of food.

The outer door shut and he strode into the front room.

"Look here," said Allbee, as soon as he came through the kitchen door. "I thought you were out of town for the week end. You didn't come home last night. I thought . . ."

"You thought you'd bring a tramp in from the street."

"No . . . now wait." He gave a hasty, somewhat breathless laugh. "I know I have a fallen nature. I never pretended to be anything I wasn't. Why all the excitement? You might have given me a few minutes." He spoke placatingly, with humorous chagrin. He looked sallow and his lips were dry. His smile persisted at the corners covertly, it was boastful.

Leventhal flushed thickly. "In my bed!"

"Well, the day bed is so narrow. No place to take a lady. . . . I wanted a little more space. . . ." He was by no means sure of himself and his voice wavered as he made the joke. "I fail to see what there is to fuss about."

"Oh, you don't see! It gave you a bang to put your whore where I sleep."

The vehemence of his loathing gave a different turn to Allbee's smile; it became jeering, and a yellowish hot tinge came over his bloodshot eyes. Leventhal heard him murmur something about "fastidiousness."

"You hypocrite! I thought you couldn't get over your wife."

"Don't you mention my wife!" Allbee cried.

"Why not, you're always crying about her, aren't you?"

"I say don't! Leave things alone that you can't understand."

"What can't I understand?"

"Not that, for sure!" Allbee said harshly. His face was inflamed; his cheekbones looked as if they had been branded. But he checked himself and slowly the color retreated. Only a few refractory spots remained. He seemed to force himself to make a gesture of retraction. "I mean," he said, "she's dead. What does she have to do with it? I have needs, naturally, the same as anybody else."

"What did she have to do with the other things? You mealymouth, you were using her to work on my feelings. All right, what do I care? Go to hell. But you weren't satisfied that you made this place so filthy I can't stand to come in; you had to bring this woman into my bed."

"But what's there to be so upset about? Where else, if not in bed . . . ?" He looked amused again and blinked his bloodshot eyes. "What do you do? Maybe you have some other way, more refined, different? Don't you people claim that you're the same as everybody else? That's your way of saying that you're above everybody else. I know."

"Go get your stuff in the dining room and clear out. I don't want any more of you."

"You don't care about the woman. You're just using her to make an issue and break your promise to me. Well, and I thought I had seen everything in the way of cynicism. By God, you could give lessons! I never met anyone who could touch you. I guess there's an example in the world of everything a man can imagine, no matter how great or how gruesome. You certainly are not the same as everybody else." He looked at him, keenly, brilliantly, triumphantly insolent. "What do you care about my wife! But your instinct told you where to jab, in the way that insects know where they'll find the most sap."

"You dirty phoney!" Leventhal cried huskily. "You ugly bastard counterfeit. I said it because you're such a liar, with your phoney tears and your wife's name in your mouth, every second word. The poor woman, a fine life she must have had with you, a freak like you, out of a carnival. You don't care what you say. You'll say anything that comes into your head. You're not even human, if you ask me. No wonder she left you."

"It's very interesting that you should take her part. She was like me. What do you think of that? We were alike," he shouted.

"Well, get out! Beat it! I told you to leave when the woman did."

"What about your promise?"

Leventhal pushed him toward the door. Allbee fell back a few steps and, seizing a heavy glass ash tray, he aimed it menacingly and cried, "Keep off me!" Leventhal made a rush at him and knocked the ash tray down. Pinning his arms, he wheeled him around and ran him into the vestibule.

"Let go. I'll leave," he panted.

The door, as Leventhal jerked it open, hit Allbee in the face. He did not resist when Leventhal thrust him out on the landing and, without looking back, he started down the stairs.

Winded, Leventhal stumbled into a chair, pulled at his collar. The sweat ran into his eyes and a pain, starting at his shoulders, passed downward through his chest. Suddenly he thought, "Maybe he's still hanging around. I'd better look." He forced himself up and went to the stairs. Holding the rail, he stared into the shaft. It was silent. He thought as he returned to the flat, "He didn't even have the courage to fight back. As much as he hates me. And he's bigger; he could have killed me." He wondered whether Allbee was stunned by the door when it struck him in the face. The sound of that did not leave him.

He stopped to examine the chain. The staple was only loosened and might have been hamered in. But one of the links had given. He tossed the severed half away. Over the furrows of the rug in the front room there was a long, curving trail of ashes. He wiped his sweat with his sleeve and took in the room, angry, but exultant also; he felt dimly that this disorder and upheaval was part of the price he was obliged to pay for his release.

The radiators were spitting and the room was unendurably hot. He flung up the window and bent out. Instantly he heard the tumultuous swoop of the Third Avenue train rising above the continuous, tidal noise of the street. People were walking among the stripes of light on the pavement, light that came from windows opening on carpeted floors and the shapes of furniture; they passed through the radiance of the glass cage that bulged before the theater and into shadows, tributaries that led into deeper shadows and led, still further on, into mighty holes filled with light and stifled roaring. "Is he around somewhere?" Leventhal asked himself. He doubted that Allbee was near. Certainly he knew he had nothing more to hope for here after tonight. And what he had hoped for in the first place remained a mystery. The idea of an introduction to Shifcart lost all its substance; it was a makeshift demand, improvised. That he was able to see this gave Leventhal the feeling that he was becoming himself again after a long lapse.

The breeze was cooling him too rapidly. He drew his head in, shivering, and sat down, wiping the grit of the sill from his palms. His throat was bitter and raw, and there was a deadening weight in his side. But he sat and rested briefly and soon felt better. When he rose, he began unsystematically to set the flat in order, going slowly and desultorily from task to task.

He stripped the linen from the beds and threw it in the laundry hamper. Then, without taking the trouble to clean out the scraps in the drain, he spilled soap powder over the dishes in the kitchen sink and let the hot water run until the foam boiled up and covered them. He made up his bed with clean sheets, awkwardly shaking the pillows into pillow cases and dragging the bed away from the wall in order to tuck in the blankets. In the dining room, he turned over the mattress of the day bed and forced up the seldom-opened windows. On one of the chairs he found a glossy haberdasher's bag with a Second Avenue address. It contained Allbee's old shirt and a few other articles that he did not examine. He threw the bag into the dumb-waiter, together with the socks and undershirts and the newspapers Allbee had accumulated. Next, in the bathroom, he took down the towels, turned on the shower to rinse the tub, and made an effort to clean the basin. After a few strokes he gave this up and returned the rag to its pipe beneath the sink.

He was moving chairs into place when he saw a comb on the carpet. It must have been the mate to the one the woman had fastened in her hair. Studying it, he could not help breathing its odor. It was a white comb, white bone, its teeth darkened yellow in an uneven fringe. On one side it was decorated with a diamond-shaped piece of glass; on the other, the bit of glass had fallen out of its setting. He did not linger over the comb very long; he let it fall into the waste-basket. He recalled the women in the wrangle he had watched on the corner several weeks back and even reflected that she might have been one of them. She might, easily. After all, where had Allbee picked her up? Probably in a tavern in the neighborhood.

A breeze blew through the flat while he swept the ashes from the rug. It brought the cold and vacancy of the outside into the room. Nevertheless, the smell of the comb occasionally returned, coming over him with some fragment of what had occurred that evening in its wake, like a qualm.

It must have been frightening, sickening for her to hear the crash of the door and then to run out of bed—still another bed. And even granting that she could endure roughness better than another (many a woman would have cried from terror or sheer mortification), he was sorry to have subjected her to it. He found himself regretting the whole incident because of her and almost wished that he had listened to Allbee and gone away. He could have attended to him later. A few impressions of her remained vividly with Leventhal —the heaviness of her figure in the skirt, the way she had crouched to work her foot into the shoe, the look he had received from her queerly shaped eyes. It now struck him that there was more amusement in it than fear, and he could see, too, how with a grain of detachment it was possible for her to find the incident amusing. He began to remember how Allbee had stumbled in pulling up his pants and how comically he had held out the woman's stockings to her. It was low, it was painful, but it was funny. He grinned, his eyes dilated and shone; he gave way explosively to laughter, driving the broom at the floor. "The stockings! Those damn stockings! Standing there without a stitch and passing those stockings!" He broke suddenly into a cough. When he was done laughing and coughing, his face remained unusually expressive. Yes, and he ought not to leave himself out of the picture, glaring at them both. Meanwhile, Allbee was burning, yet trying to keep his head. The woman must have grasped that he did not dare say what he felt. Perhaps he had been boasting to her, telling lies about himself, and that was why his predicament amused her.

But when he sat down for a moment on the bed, all the comedy of it was snatched away and torn to pieces. He was wrong about the woman's expression; he was trying to transform it into something he could bear. The truth was probably far different. He had started out to see what had happened with her eyes and had ended by substituting his own, thus contriving to put her on his side. Whereas, the fact was that she was nearer to Allbee. Both of them, Allbee and the woman, moved or swam toward him out of a depth of life in which he himself would be lost, choked, ended. There lay horror, evil, all that he had kept himself from. In the days when he was clerking in the hotel on the East Side, he had been as near to it as he could ever bear to be. He had seen it face on then. And since, he had learned more about it out of the corner of his eye. Why not say heart, rather than eye? His heart was what caught it, with awful pain and dread, in heavy blows. Then, since the fear and pain were so great, what drew him on?

He picked up the broom and returned to his tasks. As he bent on trembling legs to brush up the ashes, he was thinking, "Maybe I didn't do the right thing. I didn't know what it was. I don't yet. And there had to be a showdown sooner or later. What was I going to do with him? He hated me. He hated me enough to cut my throat. He didn't do it because he was too much of a coward. That's why he was pulling all those stunts instead. He was pulling them on himself as much as on me, and the reason for that was that he hated himself for not having enough nerve, but by clowning he could pass off his own feelings.— All that stuff, the mustard and going on his knees and all that talk. That's what it was for. I had to do something with him. I suppose I handled it badly. Still, it's over; that's the main thing. . . ."

The chairs did not look quite as they did when Mary arranged them; the bed was unevenly made. A swath of ashes still remained on the rug. However, things began to right themselves and it soothed him to be busy. He opened a can of vegetable soup and set it on the stove. While it was heating, he washed the dishes and, for the first time in weeks, turned on the radio simply to hear a voice. The phone rang. It was Max, calling, he said, from a drugstore on Fourteenth Street. He did not want to come unannounced a second time. A good thing, too, Leventhal thought; he would not have answered the doorbell.

He was finishing his soup ten minutes later, when Max arrived. Elena had agreed at last to leave New York. That was his news. He was coming from Pennsylvania Station where he had picked up the reservations. Villani's brother, a secondhand dealer on Bleecker Street, was buying the furniture.

"It'll cost us twice what we're getting to buy new things down there," he said.

"Ah, you don't want this stuff."

"What's the matter with it? Shipping is too high, that's all." Then he smiled at Leventhal. "So . . . ?" he said.

"You mean I was mistaken about Elena."

"I sure do. And about the old lady."

"Oh. Well, you caught me in a bad mood the other night, Max. I'm not always like that. I hope I didn't hurt your feelings."

The lines radiating out from Max's eyes deepened. "Oh, I got a kind of a kick out of the way you built up the old woman," he said.

"I'm glad you finally got Elena to come around. It's going to be all to the good. I'm glad for Phil's sake, especially. When you're settled we'll come down and visit."

"Sure, you'll be welcome. Anytime. Is she going to be back soon?"

Leventhal noticed that Max did not mention Mary by name. Like Elena, he probably did not know what her name was.

"Mary? Just as soon as I can get her to come. I'm going to phone her tonight."

"Your radio's on pretty loud. Got a drive on against spooks?"

They smiled together.

"I guess I really don't know where I'm at when she's away."

Max poured himself a glass of water, declining to sit down for coffee. "Too many things to take care of," he said. He pulled his hat down. His sideburns were long and ill-trimmed, overgrowing his ears.

"I'll see you off," said Leventhal. "When are you leaving?"

"Friday, four o'clock on the Natchez Prince."

"I'll be on hand."

After talking to his wife, Leventhal prepared for bed in a kind of intoxication. He walked up and down the room, undressing, and stopped before her picture on the desk and caressed her face with his thumb over the glass. Under the arch of his chest, he felt a thick, distinct stroke that seemed to him much slower than the actual, remote, jubilant speeding of his heart. His legs were melting with excitement. Mary was probably packing her bags, for she had promised to leave on the earliest train tomorrow. From the way she spoke, he realized that she had been waiting for him to make this call. When he said, "Can you come soon?" she replied, "Tomorrow," with an eagerness that astonished him. She would arrive very early on Tuesday, if the Labor Day crowd did not delay her too much. Meanwhile, he had to attend to the flat; she had to find it as she had left it. Half an hour ago he had thought it passable. Now it looked appallingly dirty. He slipped a coat over his pajamas and was about to go down to see Mrs. Nunez. But he remembered in time that the Nunez' had a telephone and turned back. As usual, he chided himself; the easiest, sensible way came to him last. He found the number in Mary's alphabetized book and dialed it. In a moment he heard her aspirated Spanish " 'Allo?" The thing was quickly arranged: she would be up in the morning. After hanging up, he silently apologized to her for his suspicion. But there was no place in his present mood for penitence or even for thought.

He locked the front door. He ought to have spoken to Nunez about the broken chain while he was on the wire. And for that matter Allbee still had a key; the lock should be changed. He had not retained the number, and he picked up the book again and then decided to let the thing go until morning. Explanations were necessary. Why was the chain broken? Why did a perfectly good lock have to be taken out? He had to have time; he could not invent reasons on the telephone.

He got into bed, piled the pillows against the wall, and sat with a magazine in his lap. He did not read; he had no desire to, and besides nothing took shape before his eyes. Restlessly, he turned the pages and heard the interminable sleepy sigh of the steam in the radiators and the intermittent shock of the subway beneath the house. Finally he threw down the magazine and turned face down on the pillow. His impatience made him groan. He could hardly bear to lie still. Over and over again he saw the station platform, the cars in the tunnel, and made out Mary's face in the crowd of passengers—her hat, her light hair, and last of all her face. He embraced and kissed her, and asked, "Did you have a good trip?" Would that do? He struggled over a choice of greetings. Then once more he imagined himself running on the platform. It was unendurable. He resolved to go to sleep and he turned off the lamp. But as soon as he had done this, he rose—the room was not entirely dark because the light was burning in the bathroom—and dragged the heavy desk chair to the door. He fixed the back of it tightly under the knob and returned to bed. "For God's sake," he muttered, "let me get a night's rest." There was a pallor on the windows; the moon had risen. Standing on the bed, he drew the curtains and dropped down. He pulled the blanket over his head and soon he was asleep.

At first he slept deeply, but after a time he began to stir. He was too warm; he threw some of his covers off; his legs moved as if unwilling to be relaxed, and once or twice he was on the point of jumping up and turning on the lamp. But he held his head down between the pillows obstinately and presently he began to dream.

He was on a boardwalk in broad, open, blue summer weather. The sea was flaring on his right and the shore blackened with bathers. On his left, there was an amusement park with ticket booths, and he saw round yellow and red cars whipping around and bumping together. He entered a place that resembled a hotel—there was a circular veranda where people sat looking at the bay—but proved to be a department store. He was here to buy some rouge for Mary. The salesgirl demonstrated various shades on her own face, wiping off each in turn with a soiled hand towel and bending to the round mirror on the counter to draw a new spot. There was a great, empty glitter of glass and metal around them. What could this possibly be about? Leventhal wondered. For he was perfectly sure he had once seen a chart with all the colors. This work was unnecessary. Nevertheless, he watched her smearing the rouge on her sharp face and did not interrupt her. The odor of the towel had from the beginning seemed familiar. He made so strong an effort to identify it that he half roused himself, aware, all at once, that the odor came from his bed. His eyes were open and his unshaven chin rustled on the pillow. Could the woman's scent have penetrated the slip and the ticking? He raised his head, feeling stifled, and saw the dazzling wall of the bathroom, the yawning clothes hamper, the black fin of the scale. He thought he could hear the steam in the pipes, and yet the room was not warm. He shivered and lit the lamp. His heart nearly burst with fear, for the chair was down and the front door gaping. There were movements in the kitchen. He hunched forward in the gathered bedclothes, listening, and the wires of the spring sang out. His terror, like a cold fluid, like brine, seemed to have been released by the breaking open of something within him. "My God!" he cried to himself. His mouth was parched and the taste of his lips was like that of dried blood. But what if the chair had slid down and the door opened by itself? And what if the kitchen were empty? His nerves again, his sick imagination. But why nerves—as an excuse for his cowardice? So that he would not have to go to the kitchen to investigate? Had he locked the door? He was ready to swear to it. And if it was open now, it was because Allbee, who had a key, had opened it. Leventhal's legs were braced to spring, but he held back, feeling that to be deceived now through his nerves would crush him. But suddenly he rushed from bed, dragging the sheets in which his foot had caught. He kicked free and ran into the kitchen. He collided with someone who crouched there, and a cry came out of him. The air was foul and hard to breathe. Gas was pouring from the oven. "I have to kill him now," he thought as they grappled. He caught the cloth of his coat in his teeth while he swiftly changed his grip, clutching at Allbee's face. He tore away convulsively, but Leventhal crushed him with his weight in the corner. Allbee's fist came down heavily on his neck, beside the shoulder. "You want to murder me? Murder?" Leventhal gasped. The sibilance of the pouring gas was almost deafening.

"Me, myself!" Allbee whispered despairingly, as if with his last breath. "Me . . . !"

Then his head shot up, catching Leventhal on the mouth. The pain made him drop his hands, and Allbee pushed him away and flung out of the kitchen. He stumbled after him down a flight of stairs, trying to shout and bruising his naked feet on the metal edges of the treads. He heard Allbee jump and saw him running into the foyer. Seizing a milk bottle from a neighbor's sill, he threw it. It smashed on the tiles.

He raced back to turn off the gas. He feared an explosion. By the wildly swinging light, he saw a chair placed before the open oven from which Allbee apparently had risen when he ran in.

Leventhal threw open the front-room window and bent out, tears running down his face in the cold air. The long lines of lamps hung down their yellow grains in the gray and blue of the street. He saw no one, not a living thing.

When he had had enough air, he limped to the bathroom. He had bitten his tongue and he rinsed his mouth with peroxide. In spite of the struggle, the revolting sweetness of the gas like the acrid sweetness of sewage, the numbness in his neck, and, now, the sight of blood, he did not seem greatly disturbed. He looked impassive, under the cloud of his hair. He rinsed and spat, washed out the sink, wiped the stains from the mouth of the peroxide bottle, and went to pick up the sheets he had dragged to the floor. By the time he had remade the bed, the flat was nearly free of gas. Though he scarcely thought that Allbee would be back again, he shut the door and barricaded it with the dresser. He

[283]

would sleep undisturbed; he cared about nothing else. Drowsily, he went to check the stove again, to make sure no more gas was escaping. Then he dropped onto the bed. He was still sleeping at eleven o'clock when Mrs. Nunez arrived to start the cleaning. Her repeated knocks woke him.

24

THAT FALL, one of the editors of Harkavy's paper, *Antique Horizons*, went to a national magazine and, through Harkavy, Leventhal got the vacancy. Characteristically, Beard at first declined to meet the offer and then went two hundred dollars higher, but Leventhal left him.

Things went well for him in the next few years. The consciousness of an unremitting daily fight, though still present, was fainter and less troubling. His health was better, and there were changes in his appearance. Something recalcitrant seemed to have left him; he was not exactly affable, but his obstinately unrevealing expression had softened. His face was paler and there were some gray areas in his hair, in spite of which he looked years younger.

And, as time went on, he lost the feeling that he had, as he used to say, "got away with it," his guilty relief, and the accompanying sense of infringement. He was thankful for his job at *Antique Horizons;* he didn't underestimate it; there weren't many better jobs in the trade field. He was lucky, of course. It was understandable that a man suffered when he did not have a place. On the other hand, it was pitiful that he should envy the man who had one. In Leventhal's mind, this was not even a true injustice, for how could you call anything so haphazard an injustice? It was a shuffle, all, all accidental and haphazard. And somewhere, besides, there was a wrong emphasis. As though a man really could be made for, say, Burke-Beard and Company, as though that were true work instead of a delaying maze to be gone through daily in a misery so habitual that one became absentminded about it. This was wrong. But the error rose out of something very mysterious, namely, a conviction or illusion that at the start of life, and perhaps even before, a promise had been made. In thinking of this promise, Leventhal compared it to a ticket, a theater ticket. And with his ticket, a man entitled to an average seat might feel too shabby for the dress circle or sit in it defiantly and arrogantly; another, entitled to the best in the house, might cry out in rage to the usher who led him to the third balcony. And how many more stood disconsolately in the rain and snow, in the long line of those who could only expect to be turned away? But no, this was incorrect. The reality was different. For why should tickets, mere tickets, be promised if promises were being made—tickets to desirable and undesirable places? There were more important things to be promised. Possibly there was a promise, since so many felt it. He himself was almost ready to affirm that there was. But it was misunderstood.

Occasionally he thought about Allbee and wondered whether Williston knew what had happened to him. But he had written to Williston, returning the ten dollars which, for one reason and another, he had failed to give Allbee. In his letter he made a special effort to explain his position, and, realizing that Williston believed he had a tendency to exaggerate, he gave a very careful and moderate account of what had taken place. Allbee, he said, "tried a kind of suicide pact without getting my permission first." He might have added, fairly, "without intending to die himself." For there were reasonable grounds to suspect this. But no reply came from Williston, and Leventhal was too proud to write a second letter; that would be too much like pleading. Perhaps Williston felt that he had kept the money from Allbee out of malice. Leventhal made it as clear as he could that he had had no opportunity to pass it on to him. "Does he think I'm that cheap?" he asked himself resentfully. Repeatedly, he went over all that he had done during those confusing weeks. Hadn't he tried to be fair? Didn't he intend to help him? He considered that he and Allbee were even, by any honest standards. Much difference ten dollars would have made! At first he was deeply annoyed; later he prepared some things to say to Williston if they should meet. But the opportunity never came.

From time to time he heard rumors about Allbee. Invariably, however, he heard them from people who did not know him personally, and he could never be sure that the man to whom they referred actually was Allbee. "Some journalist, from New England, originally, who hit the bottle," etcetera. In three years a dozen or so stories reached him, no two of which agreed. He did not attempt to follow up any of them. Although they always interested him, the truth was that he did not want to know precisely where he was and what he was doing. He believed that he had continued to go down. By now he was in an institution, perhaps, in some hospital, or even already lying in Potter's Field. Leventhal did not care to think too much or too literally about it.

But one night he saw Allbee again.

It happened that a dealer who had furnished some of the antiques for a play that was running on Broadway gave Leventhal two passes. He was reluctant to go; Mary, however, insisted. Mary was pregnant; she was expecting the baby in a month, and she would be tied down, she argued, for a long time to come. Leventhal said that the theater would be very warm—this was early June and prematurely hot—but offered no real opposition. The evening of the play he came home early. (They had moved to the uptown end of Central Park West, closer to the Porto Rican slum than to the blazoned canopies of the Sixties and Seventies.) During dinner he was heavy eyed. But before he had finished his dessert, Mary was clearing the table. He washed, shaved for the second time that day, and put on a Palm Beach suit, breaking it out of the brown paper wrapper in which the cleaner had sealed it eight months ago. The trousers were a little tight and short, for during the preceding winter he had put on weight.

The subway was hot enough; the theater was suffocating. Leventhal sat and endured the play. He had no taste for plays in general, and this was sentimental and untrue— a complicated love affair in a Renaissance palace. He held Mary's hand. In the refulgence of the stage, he saw drops of moisture on her forehead, under the thick loop of her braid, and on her nose. Her skin looked very pure, and his heart rose as he watched her, intent on the play. Presently he brought his eyes back to the stage. His own dark face was damp, and his tight suit was already crumpled; his collar was soaked with sweat.

At the first curtain he quickly got to his feet and guided Mary through the crowd to the lobby. An usher opened the doors to the sidewalk, and they walked out. The tavern adjoining the theater was filling up. Leventhal and Mary lit cigarettes and gazed into the street and upward at the glow of yellow glass that passed into the haze. The afternoon had been almost tropical. A few large drops of rain had fallen; the air was moist, odorous, and black; one felt it like a soft weight. There were night clubs and restaurants in the block, and the traffic was heavy. Suddenly a taxi cut a dangerous curve from the far side of the street and made an abrupt, pitching stop in front of the theater. There was a terrific croaking of horns behind it. The door flung open and a woman was handed out. Something about the queerness of existence, always haunting Leventhal at a short distance, came very close to him when he saw her escort's face over her shoulder in the faint light. The glass slide in the roof of the cab was drawn aside, and the top of a straw hat circled and shone in the opening. The woman left the running board with a little bound, holding her silk scarf to her throat with one hand and gathering her skirt up with the other. Slender and long-legged, she walked with a somewhat free stride, elegant and yet slightly awkward. There were jewels beneath the scarf and on her fingers. Her painted nails looked purple under the frosted light of the marquee. She stood with her back to the street, irritated, holding a small, heavy, glittering bag. The man lingered, for some reason, in the cab.

Mary touched Leventhal's arm.

"Do you recognize her?" she whispered.

But Leventhal was trying to see her companion.

"Isn't that Yvonne Crane?"

"Who?"

"The actress."

"I don't know," he said, looking blankly. "Is it?"

"She's still perfectly beautiful," said Mary with admiration. "How do they stay looking so young?"

The woman, after waiting awhile, turned and said in a low, harsh tone, "Come on. Will you come out of there?"

The man inside shouted quarrelsomely, "He took us the long way around. Does he think I don't know the city? I'm no greenhorn here."

They did not catch the woman's next words, but they heard the driver, laconic and confident, and then the escort, crying out laughingly, "Don't give me that . . . . That's for the visiting fat boys."

The woman opened her purse and threw a bill to the driver.

Leventhal, when he heard the voice, was certain that the

man was Allbee, and, with a rigid face and a look approaching horror in his eyes, he waited for him to appear.

Then Allbee stepped to the curb, saying, "You shouldn't have done that." The cab started away with its open door flapping; the driver, without slowing up, reached back and slammed it.

Leventhal had a close view of Allbee as the two walked into the theater. He was wearing a white dinner jacket. A flower, pinned erratically, swung from his lapel; he pressed his hat under his arm and strode forward, his large shoulders stiffly raised, swaggering and gallant. His cheeks were red and shining. He was laughing into his companion's pretty but nervously severe face. He seemed to be pushing her playfully, and it was evident from the set of her arms that she did not wish to be pushed.

"I don't recognize him," said Mary. "But I'm sure she's Yvonne Crane. I've seen her picture a hundred times. Don't you remember her?"

Throughout the second act, Leventhal peered round at the boxes. He could see no more than the color of a face in the radiance thrown back from the stage, or, occasionally, the black shape of a head rising near the red ball of an exit light, or moving its shadow across the obscure shine of the rails. He thought that they must be sitting in a box. The woman might or might not be Yvonne Crane, though Mary was probably right. She was, in any case, a wealthy woman; and Allbee looked more than moderately prosperous in the dinner jacket and the silk-seamed formal trousers. To say nothing of the flower. The flower struck Leventhal in a very curious way as a mark of something extraordinary, barbaric, rich, even decadent. "Yes, he's gone places," Leventhal mused. "And that woman, whoever she is, he's got that woman under his thumb." None of the rumors had described him as so well off. "And here I had him dead and buried in Potter's Field. Dead. But imagine!" He tugged a handkerchief from his breast pocket and wiped his neck and chin. The lights came to life in the arches, causing him to squint and frown. The curtain was swooping down. There was applause. He had not noticed that the act was ending. The orchestra began a march and, more hurriedly than the first time, he helped Mary rise.

He was lighting her cigarette, looking everywhere for Allbee, when, over her head, he caught sight of him on the stairs. He was alone, and, widening his eyes, he smiled at Leventhal and raised his hand with stiffly spread fingers in a gesture he did not understand. Mary spoke to him. Utterly confused, he answered something. She repeated what she had said. She was asking for her compact, which he had in his pocket. She was going to the ladies' lounge. He hastily got it out and gave it to her. His expression seemed to puzzle her, and she glanced at him sharply before turning away.

As she passed Allbee on the stairs, he gave her pregnant figure an appraising look. Leventhal walked out of the lobby. He was aware that Allbee was coming up to him, but he did not raise his eyes until he heard him speak.

"Hello, Leventhal."

The low, thick voice with its old tone of complicity, the big, obtrusive figure in the white jacket, disturbed him.

"Hello," he answered nervously.

"I saw you when we were coming in."

"I didn't think you did."

"I knew it would be all right with you if I acted like a total stranger, so it's up to me, and I'd feel like a terrible fool if I didn't speak to you. . . . You saw me, didn't you?"

"Yes."

"And who I was with?"

"The actress? My wife recognized her."

"Oh, your wife," he said politely. "Very handsome. Very fetching, even in her condition." He began to smile broadly, displaying his teeth. With his hands on his hips, he bent forward slightly. "Congratulations. I see you're following orders. 'Increase and multiply.'"

Leventhal answered him with a dull, short nod. It seemed to him that Allbee had no real desire to be malicious; he was merely obedient to habit. He might have been smiling at himself and making an appeal of a sort for understanding. On nearer sight, Allbee did not look good. His color was an unhealthy one. Leventhal had the feeling that it was the decay of something that had gone into his appearance of well-being, something intimate. There was very little play in the deepened wrinkles around his eyes. They had a fabric quality, crumpled and blank. A smell of whisky came from him.

"You haven't changed much," said Allbee.

"I wasn't the one that was going to change so much."

"Ah, that. Well, do I still look the same to you?"

"You still drink."

"Ever since I saw you, I've been wondering whether you'd mention that. You're true to form." He grinned, but he was somewhat hurt. "No, I only take it socially because everybody else does."

"You look successful."

"Oh," he said lightly. "Success is a big word. You ought to be careful how you use it."

"What do you do?"

"Just now I'm squiring Miss Crane around. The columnists say we're friends, when they bother to mention her. She's not the drawing card she used to be. You probably know. Well, she doesn't want much public attention now, or she'd be seen with someone more celebrated. But she doesn't care. She's glad all that professional business is over for her and she can live more quietly. She's actually a very intelligent person. We're both a little lost, out there on the Coast."

Leventhal nodded again.

"Oh, yes. She's real nobility. She's really fine. Queenly, if you know what I mean. Some of those women become loathsome when their popularity dies down. They live like criminals. They want to make up for all those years under the public eye, I guess."

"So . . . I congratulate you too," Leventhal murmured.

"She's not Flora, of course. . . . My wife." His continued smile gave a touch of cynicism to the sensational, terrible look of pain that rose to his eyes. Leventhal saw that he could not help himself and pitied him. "She has qualities. . . ."

His last words were lost in the braying of the taxis. Leventhal found nothing to say.

"I want you to know one thing," said Allbee. "That night . . . I wanted to put an end to myself. I wasn't thinking of hurting you. I suppose you would have been. . . . But I wasn't thinking of you. You weren't even in my mind."

Leventhal laughed outright at this.

"You could have jumped in the river. That's a funny lie. Why tell it? Did you have to use my kitchen?"

Allbee glanced around restlessly. The bays that rose into his loose blond hair became crimson. "No," he said miserably. "Well, anyhow, I don't remember how it was. I must have been demented. When you turn against yourself, nobody else means anything to you either." Bitterly shamefaced and self-mocking, he took Leventhal's hand and pressed it. "But I want to say that I owe you something. I was trying to get around it when I talked about trying to kill myself only." He spoke with great difficulty. "I don't want to exaggerate, but I don't want to play it down either. I know I owe you something. I knew it that night when I was standing in your shower. . . ."

Leventhal pulled his hand away.

"What do you do out there, are you an actor?"

"An actor? No, I'm in radio. Advertising. It's a middle-sized job. So you see? I've made my peace with things as they are. I've gotten off the pony—you remember, I said that to you once? I'm on the train."

"A conductor?"

"Conductor, hell! I'm just a passenger." His laugh was short and faint. "Not even first class. I'm not the type that runs things. I never could be. I realized that long ago. I'm the type that comes to terms with whoever runs things. What do I care? The world wasn't made exactly for me. What am I going to do about it?"

"What?" Leventhal smiled at him.

"Approximately made for me will have to be good enough. All that stiffness of once upon a time, that's gone, that's gone."

The crowd was beginning to return. The curtain bell had rung.

"Anyway, I'm enjoying life." Suddenly he looked around and said, "Say, I've got to run. Yvonne will send them out looking for me."

"Wait a minute, what's your idea of who runs things?" said Leventhal. But he heard Mary's voice at his back. Allbee ran in and sprang up the stairs. The bell continued its dinning, and Leventhal and Mary were still in the aisle when the houselights went off. An usher showed them to their seats.

Seize the Day

by

Saul Bellow

with three short stories

and a one-act play

The Viking Press
New York

It is a pleasure to acknowledge
the generous support given me by
the John Simon Guggenheim Foundation,
and its secretary, Mr. Henry Allan Moe.   S.B.

Published in November 1956 by The Viking Press, Inc.,
625 Madison Avenue, New York City

Published on the same day in the Dominion of Canada by
The Macmillan Company of Canada Limited

Acknowledgment is made to Partisan Review, which pub-
lished "Seize the Day," The New Yorker, in which "A
Father-to-Be" appeared, Commentary, which published
"Looking for Mr. Green," Discovery No. 4 for "The
Gonzaga Manuscripts," and to New World Writing 6 for
"The Wrecker."

Library of Congress catalog card number: 56-10686

Printed in the United States of America

Contents

Seize the Day

I

WHEN it came to concealing his troubles, Tommy Wilhelm was not less capable than the next fellow. So at least he thought, and there was a certain amount of evidence to back him up. He had once been an actor—no, not quite, an extra—and he knew what acting should be. Also, he was smoking a cigar, and when a man is smoking a cigar, wearing a hat, he has an advantage; it is harder to find out how he feels. He came from the twenty-third floor down to the lobby on the mezzanine to collect his mail before breakfast, and he believed—he hoped—that he looked passably well: doing all right. It was a matter of sheer hope, because there was not much that he could add to his present effort. On the fourteenth floor he looked for his father to enter the elevator; they often met at this hour, on the way to breakfast. If he worried about his appearance it was mainly for his old father's sake. But there was no stop on the fourteenth, and the elevator sank and sank. Then the smooth door opened and the great dark-red uneven carpet that covered the lobby billowed toward Wilhelm's feet. In the foreground the lobby

3

was dark, sleepy. French drapes like sails kept out the sun, but three high, narrow windows were open, and in the blue air Wilhelm saw a pigeon about to light on the great chain that supported the marquee of the movie house directly underneath the lobby. For one moment he heard the wings beating strongly.

Most of the guests at the Hotel Gloriana were past the age of retirement. Along Broadway in the Seventies, Eighties, and Nineties, a great part of New York's vast population of old men and women lives. Unless the weather is too cold or wet they fill the benches about the tiny railed parks and along the subway gratings from Verdi Square to Columbia University, they crowd the shops and cafeterias, the dime stores, the tearooms, the bakeries, the beauty parlors, the reading rooms and club rooms. Among these old people at the Gloriana, Wilhelm felt out of place. He was comparatively young, in his middle forties, large and blond, with big shoulders; his back was heavy and strong, if already a little stooped or thickened. After breakfast the old guests sat down on the green leather armchairs and sofas in the lobby and began to gossip and look into the papers; they had nothing to do but wait out the day. But Wilhelm was used to an active life and liked to go out energetically in the morning. And for several months, because he had no position, he had kept up his morale by rising early; he was shaved and in the lobby by eight o'clock. He bought the paper and some cigars and drank a Coca-Cola or two before he went in to breakfast with his father. After breakfast—out, out, out to attend to business. The getting out had in itself become the chief business. But he had realized that he could not keep this up much longer, and today he was afraid. He was aware that his routine was about to break up and he sensed that a huge trouble long presaged but till now formless was due. Before evening, he'd know.

Nevertheless he followed his daily course and crossed the lobby.

Rubin, the man at the newsstand, had poor eyes. They may not have been actually weak but they were poor in expression, with lacy lids that furled down at the corners. He dressed well. It didn't seem necessary—he was behind the counter most of the time—but he dressed very well. He had on a rich brown suit; the cuffs embarrassed the hairs on his small hands. He wore a Countess Mara painted necktie. As Wilhelm approached, Rubin did not see him; he was looking out dreamily at the Hotel Ansonia, which was visible from his corner, several blocks away. The Ansonia, the neighborhood's great landmark, was built by Stanford White. It looks like a baroque palace from Prague or Munich enlarged a hundred times, with towers, domes, huge swells and bubbles of metal gone green from exposure, iron fretwork and festoons. Black television antennae are densely planted on its round summits. Under the changes of weather it may look like marble or like sea water, black as slate in the fog, white as tufa in sunlight. This morning it looked like the image of itself reflected in deep water, white and cumulous above, with cavernous distortions underneath. Together, the two men gazed at it.

Then Rubin said, "Your dad is in to breakfast already, the old gentleman."

"Oh, yes? Ahead of me today?"

"That's a real knocked-out shirt you got on," said Rubin. "Where's it from, Saks?"

"No, it's a Jack Fagman—Chicago."

Even when his spirits were low, Wilhelm could still wrinkle his forehead in a pleasing way. Some of the slow, silent movements of his face were very attractive. He went back a step, as if to stand away from himself and get a better look at his shirt. His glance was comic, a comment upon his untidiness. He liked to wear good clothes, but once he had put it on each article appeared to go its own way. Wilhelm, laughing, panted a little; his teeth were small; his cheeks when he laughed and puffed grew round, and he looked much younger than his years. In the old days when he was a college freshman and wore a raccoon coat and a beanie on his large blond head his father used to say that, big as he was, he could charm a bird out of a tree. Wilhelm had great charm still.

"I like this dove-gray color," he said in his sociable, good-natured way. "It isn't washable. You have to send it to the cleaner. It never smells as good as washed. But it's a nice shirt. It cost sixteen, eighteen bucks."

This shirt had not been bought by Wilhelm; it was a present from his boss—his former boss, with whom he had had a falling out. But there was no reason why he should tell Rubin the history of it. Although perhaps Rubin knew—Rubin was the kind of man who knew, and knew and knew. Wilhelm also knew many things about Rubin, for that matter, about Rubin's wife and Rubin's business, Rubin's health. None of these could be mentioned, and the great weight of the unspoken left them little to talk about.

"Well, y'lookin' pretty sharp today," Rubin said.

And Wilhelm said gladly, "Am I? Do you really think so?" He could not believe it. He saw his reflection in the glass cupboard full of cigar boxes, among the grand seals and paper damask and the gold-embossed portraits of famous men, García, Edward the Seventh, Cyrus the Great. You had to allow for the darkness and deformations of the glass, but he thought he didn't look too good. A wide wrinkle like a comprehensive bracket sign was written upon his forehead, the point between his brows, and there were patches of brown on his dark-blond skin. He began to be half amused at the shadow of his own marveling, troubled, desirous eyes, and his nostrils and his lips. Fair-haired hippopotamus!—that was how he looked to himself. He saw a big round face, a wide, flourishing red mouth, stump teeth. And the hat, too; and the cigar, too. I should have done hard labor all my life, he reflected. Hard honest labor that tires you out and makes you sleep. I'd have worked off my energy and felt better. Instead, I had to distinguish myself—yet.

He had put forth plenty of effort, but that was not the same as working hard, was it? And if as a young man he had got off to a bad start it was due to this very same face. Early in the nineteen-thirties, because of his striking looks, he had been very briefly considered star material, and he had gone to Hollywood. There for seven years, stubbornly, he had tried to become a screen artist. Long before that time his ambition or delusion had ended, but through pride and perhaps also through laziness he had remained in California. At last he turned to other things, but those seven years of persistence and defeat had unfitted him somehow for trades and businesses, and then it was too late to go into one of the professions. He had been slow to mature, and he had lost ground, and so he hadn't been able to get rid of his energy and he was convinced that this energy itself had done him the greatest harm.

"I didn't see you at the gin game last night," said Rubin.

"I had to miss it. How did it go?"

For the last few weeks Wilhelm had played gin almost nightly, but yesterday he had felt that he couldn't afford to lose any more. He had never won. Not once. And while the losses were small they weren't gains, were they? They were losses. He was tired of losing, and tired also of the company, and so he had gone by himself to the movies.

"Oh," said Rubin, "it went okay. Carl made a chump of himself yelling at the guys. This time Doctor Tamkin didn't let him get away with it. He told him the psychological reason why."

"What was the reason?"

Rubin said, "I can't quote him. Who could? You know the

way Tamkin talks. Don't ask me. Do you want the *Trib*? Aren't you going to look at the closing quotations?"

"It won't help much to look. I know what they were yesterday at three," said Wilhelm. "But I suppose I better had get the paper." It seemed necessary for him to lift one shoulder in order to put his hand into his jacket pocket. There, among little packets of pills and crushed cigarette butts and strings of cellophane, the red tapes of packages which he sometimes used as dental floss, he recalled that he had dropped some pennies.

"That doesn't sound so good," said Rubin. He meant to be conversationally playful, but his voice had no tone and his eyes, slack and lid-blinded, turned elsewhere. He didn't want to hear. It was all the same to him. Maybe he already knew, being the sort of man who knew and knew.

No, it wasn't good. Wilhelm held three orders of lard in the commodities market. He and Dr. Tamkin had bought this lard together four days ago at 12.96, and the price at once began to fall and was still falling. In the mail this morning there was sure to be a call for additional margin payment. One came every day.

The psychologist, Dr. Tamkin, had got him into this. Tamkin lived at the Gloriana and attended the card game. He had explained to Wilhelm that you could speculate in commodities at one of the uptown branches of a good Wall Street house without making the full deposit of margin legally required. It was up to the branch manager. If he knew you—and all the branch managers knew Tamkin—he would allow you to make short-term purchases. You needed only to open a small account.

"The whole secret of this type of speculation," Tamkin had told him, "is in the alertness. You have to act fast—buy it and sell it; sell it and buy in again. But quick! Get to the window and have them wire Chicago at just the right second. Strike

and strike again! Then get out the same day. In no time at
all you turn over fifteen, twenty thousand dollars' worth of
soy beans, coffee, corn, hides, wheat, cotton." Obviously the
doctor understood the market well. Otherwise he could not
make it sound so simple. "People lose because they are greedy
and can't get out when it starts to go up. They gamble, but
I do it scientifically. This is not guesswork. You must take
a few points and get out. Why, ye gods!" said Dr. Tamkin
with his bulging eyes, his bald head, and his drooping lip.
"Have you stopped to think how much dough people are making in the market?"

Wilhelm with a quick shift from gloomy attention to the
panting laugh which entirely changed his face had said, "Ho,
have I ever! What do you think? Who doesn't know it's
way beyond nineteen-twenty-eight—twenty-nine and still on
the rise? Who hasn't read the Fulbright investigation? There's
money everywhere. Everyone is shoveling it in. Money is—
is—"

"And can you rest—can you sit still while this is going on?"
said Dr. Tamkin. "I confess to you I can't. I think about
people, just because they have a few bucks to invest, making
fortunes. They have no sense, they have no talent, they just
have the extra dough and it makes them more dough. I get
so worked up and tormented and restless, so restless! I haven't
even been able to practice my profession. With all this money
around you don't want to be a fool while everyone else is
making. I know guys who make five, ten thousand a week
just by fooling around. I know a guy at the Hotel Pierre.
There's nothing to him, but he has a whole case of Mumm's
champagne at lunch. I know another guy on Central Park
South— But what's the use of talking. They make millions.
They have smart lawyers who get them out of taxes by a
thousand schemes."

"Whereas I got taken," said Wilhelm. "My wife refused to

sign a joint return. One fairly good year and I got into the thirty-two-per-cent bracket and was stripped bare. What of all my bad years?"

"It's a businessmen's government," said Dr. Tamkin. "You can be sure that these men making five thousand a week—"

"I don't need that sort of money," Wilhelm had said. "But oh! if I could only work out a little steady income from this. Not much. I don't ask much. But how badly I need—! I'd be so grateful if you'd show me how to work it."

"Sure I will. *I* do it regularly. I'll bring you my receipts if you like. And do you want to know something? I approve of your attitude very much. You want to avoid catching the money fever. This type of activity is filled with hostile feeling and lust. You should see what it does to some of these fellows. They go on the market with murder in their hearts."

"What's that I once heard a guy say?" Wilhelm remarked. "A man is only as good as what he loves."

"That's it—just it," Tamkin said. "You don't have to go about it their way. There's also a calm and rational, a psychological approach."

Wilhelm's father, old Dr. Adler, lived in an entirely different world from his son's, but he had warned him once against Dr. Tamkin. Rather casually—he was a very bland old man— he said, "Wilky, perhaps you listen too much to this Tamkin. He's interesting to talk to. I don't doubt it. I think he's pretty common but he's a persuasive man. However, I don't know how reliable he may be."

It made Wilhelm profoundly bitter that his father should speak to him with such detachment about his welfare. Dr. Adler liked to appear affable. Affable! His own son, his one and only son, could not speak his mind or ease his heart to him. I wouldn't turn to Tamkin, he thought, if I could turn to him. At least Tamkin sympathizes with me and tries to give me a hand, whereas Dad doesn't want to be disturbed.

Old Dr. Adler had retired from practice; he had a considerable fortune and could easily have helped his son. Recently Wilhelm had told him, "Father—it so happens that I'm in a bad way now. I hate to have to say it. You realize that I'd rather have good news to bring you. But it's true. And since it's true, Dad— What else am I supposed to say? It's true."

Another father might have appreciated how difficult this confession was—so much bad luck, weariness, weakness, and failure. Wilhelm had tried to copy the old man's tone and made himself sound gentlemanly, low-voiced, tasteful. He didn't allow his voice to tremble; he made no stupid gesture. But the doctor had no answer. He only nodded. You might have told him that Seattle was near Puget Sound, or that the Giants and Dodgers were playing a night game, so little was he moved from his expression of healthy, handsome, good-humored old age. He behaved toward his son as he had formerly done toward his patients, and it was a great grief to Wilhelm; it was almost too much to bear. Couldn't he see—couldn't he feel? Had he lost his family sense?

Greatly hurt, Wilhelm struggled however to be fair. Old people are bound to change, he said. They have hard things to think about. They must prepare for where they are going. They can't live by the old schedule any longer and all their perspectives change, and other people become alike, kin and acquaintances. Dad is no longer the same person, Wilhelm reflected. He was thirty-two when I was born, and now he's going on eighty. Furthermore, it's time I stopped feeling like a kid toward him, a small son.

The handsome old doctor stood well above the other old people in the hotel. He was idolized by everyone. This was what people said: "That's old Professor Adler, who used to teach internal medicine. He was a diagnostician, one of the best in New York, and had a tremendous practice. Isn't he a wonderful-looking old guy? It's a pleasure to see such a fine old scientist, clean and immaculate. He stands straight and understands every single thing you say. He still has all his buttons. You can discuss any subject with him." The clerks, the elevator operators, the telephone girls and waitresses and chambermaids, the management flattered and pampered him. That was what he wanted. He had always been a vain man. To see how his father loved himself sometimes made Wilhelm madly indignant.

He folded over the *Tribune* with its heavy, black, crashing sensational print and read without recognizing any of the words, for his mind was still on his father's vanity. The doctor had created his own praise. People were primed and did not know it. And what did he need praise for? In a hotel where everyone was busy and contacts were so brief and had such small weight, how could it satisfy him? He could be in people's thoughts here and there for a moment; in and then out. He could never matter much to them. Wilhelm let out a long, hard breath and raised the brows of his round and somewhat circular eyes. He stared beyond the thick borders of the paper.

. . . love that well which thou must leave ere long.

Involuntary memory brought him this line. At first he thought it referred to his father, but then he understood that it was for himself, rather. *He* should love that well. "This thou perceivest, which makes *thy* love more strong." Under Dr. Tamkin's influence Wilhelm had recently begun to remember the poems he used to read. Dr. Tamkin knew, or said he knew, the great English poets and once in a while he mentioned a poem of his own. It was a long time since anyone had spoken to Wilhelm about this sort of thing. He didn't like to think about his college days, but if there was one course that now made sense it was Literature I. The textbook was Lieder and Lovett's *British Poetry and Prose,* a black heavy book with thin pages. Did I read that? he asked himself. Yes, he had read it and there was one accomplishment at least he could recall with pleasure. He had read "Yet once more, O ye laurels." How pure this was to say! It was beautiful.

Sunk though he be beneath the wat'ry floor . . .

Such things had always swayed him, and now the power of such words was far, far greater.

Wilhelm respected the truth, but he could lie and one of the things he lied often about was his education. He said he was an alumnus of Penn State; in fact he had left school before his sophomore year was finished. His sister Catherine had a B. S. degree. Wilhelm's late mother was a graduate of Bryn Mawr. He was the only member of the family who had no education. This was another sore point. His father was ashamed of him.

But he had heard the old man bragging to another old man, saying, "My son is a sales executive. He didn't have the patience to finish school. But he does all right for himself. His income is up in the five figures somewhere."

"What—thirty, forty thousand?" said his stooped old friend.

"Well, he needs at least that much for his style of life. Yes, he needs that."

Despite his troubles, Wilhelm almost laughed. Why, that boasting old hypocrite. He knew the sales executive was no more. For many weeks there had been no executive, no sales, no income. But how we love looking fine in the eyes of the world—how beautiful are the old when they are doing a snow job! It's Dad, thought Wilhelm, who is the salesman. He's selling me. *He* should have gone on the road.

But what of the truth? Ah, the truth was that there were problems, and of these problems his father wanted no part.

His father was ashamed of him. The truth, Wilhelm thought, was very awkward. He pressed his lips together, and his tongue went soft; it pained him far at the back, in the cords and throat, and a knot of ill formed in his chest. Dad never was a pal to me when I was young, he reflected. He was at the office or the hospital, or lecturing. He expected me to look out for myself and never gave me much thought. Now he looks down on me. And maybe in some respects he's right.

No wonder Wilhelm delayed the moment when he would have to go into the dining room. He had moved to the end of Rubin's counter. He had opened the *Tribune;* the fresh pages drooped from his hands; the cigar was smoked out and the hat did not defend him. He was wrong to suppose that he was more capable than the next fellow when it came to concealing his troubles. They were clearly written out upon his face. He wasn't even aware of it.

There was the matter of the different names, which, in the hotel, came up frequently. "Are you Doctor Adler's son?" "Yes, but my name is Tommy Wilhelm." And the doctor would say, "My son and I use different monickers. I uphold tradition. He's for the new." The Tommy was Wilhelm's own invention. He adopted it when he went to Hollywood, and dropped the Adler. Hollywood was his own idea, too. He used to pretend that it had all been the doing of a certain talent scout named Maurice Venice. But the scout had never made him a definite offer of a studio connection. He had approached him, but the results of the screen tests had not been good. After the test Wilhelm took the initiative and pressed Maurice Venice until he got him to say, "Well, I suppose you might make it out there." On the strength of this Wilhelm had left college and had gone to California.

Someone had said, and Wilhelm agreed with the saying, that in Los Angeles all the loose objects in the country were collected, as if America had been tilted and everything that wasn't tightly screwed down had slid into Southern California. He himself had been one of these loose objects. Sometimes he told people, "I was too mature for college. I was a big boy, you see. Well, I thought, when do you start to become a man?" After he had driven a painted flivver and had worn a yellow slicker with slogans on it, and played illegal poker, and gone out on Coke dates, he had *had* college. He wanted to try something new and quarreled with his parents about his career. And then a letter came from Maurice Venice.

The story of the scout was long and intricate and there were several versions of it. The truth about it was never told. Wilhelm had lied first boastfully and then out of charity to himself. But his memory was good, he could still separate what he had invented from the actual happenings, and this morning he found it necessary as he stood by Rubin's show-case with his *Tribune* to recall the crazy course of the true events.

I didn't seem even to realize that there was a depression. How could I have been such a jerk as not to prepare for any-thing and just go on luck and inspiration? With round gray eyes expanded and his large shapely lips closed in severity toward himself he forced open all that had been hidden. Dad I couldn't affect one way or another. Mama was the one who tried to stop me, and we carried on and yelled and pleaded. The more I lied the louder I raised my voice, and charged— like a hippopotamus. Poor Mother! How I disappointed her. Rubin heard Wilhelm give a broken sigh as he stood with the forgotten *Tribune* crushed under his arm.

When Wilhelm was aware that Rubin watched him, loitering and idle, apparently not knowing what to do with himself this morning, he turned to the Coca-Cola machine. He swal-lowed hard at the Coke bottle and coughed over it, but he ignored his coughing, for he was still thinking, his eyes upcast and his lips closed behind his hand. By a peculiar twist of habit he wore his coat collar turned up always, as though there were a wind. It never lay flat. But on his broad back, stooped with its own weight, its strength warped almost into deformity, the collar of his sports coat appeared anyway to be no wider than a ribbon.

He was listening to the sound of his own voice as he explained, twenty-five years ago in the living room on West End Avenue, "But Mother, if I don't pan out as an actor I can still go back to school."

But she was afraid he was going to destroy himself. She said, "Wilky, Dad could make it easy for you if you wanted to go into medicine." To remember this stifled him.

"I can't bear hospitals. Besides, I might make a mistake and hurt someone or even kill a patient. I couldn't stand that. Besides, I haven't got that sort of brains."

Then his mother had made the mistake of mentioning her nephew Artie, Wilhelm's cousin, who was an honor student at Columbia in math and languages. That dark little gloomy Artie with his disgusting narrow face, and his moles and self-sniffing ways and his unclean table manners, the boring habit he had of conjugating verbs when you went for a walk with him. "Roumanian is an easy language. You just add a *tl* to everything." He was now a professor, this same Artie with whom Wilhelm had played near the soldiers' and sailors' monument on Riverside Drive. Not that to be a professor was in itself so great. How could anyone bear to know so many languages? And Artie also had to remain Artie, which was a bad deal. But perhaps success had changed him. Now that he had a place in the world perhaps he was better. Did Artie love his languages, and live for them, or was he also, in his heart, cynical? So many people nowadays were. No one seemed satisfied, and Wilhelm was especially horrified by the cynicism of successful people. Cynicism was bread and meat to everyone

And irony, too. Maybe it couldn't be helped. It was probably even necessary. Wilhelm, however, feared it intensely. Whenever at the end of the day he was unusually fatigued he attributed it to cynicism. Too much of the world's business done. Too much falsity. He had various words to express the effect this had on him. Chicken! Unclean! Congestion! he exclaimed in his heart. Rat race! Phony! Murder! Play the Game! Buggers!

At first the letter from the talent scout was nothing but a flattering sort of joke. Wilhelm's picture in the college paper when he was running for class treasurer was seen by Maurice Venice, who wrote to him about a screen test. Wilhelm at once took the train to New York. He found the scout to be huge and oxlike, so stout that his arms seemed caught from beneath in a grip of flesh and fat; it looked as though it must be positively painful. He had little hair. Yet he enjoyed a healthy complexion. His breath was noisy and his voice rather difficult and husky because of the fat in his throat. He had on a double-breasted suit of the type then known as the pillbox; it was chalk-striped, pink on blue; the trousers hugged his ankles.

They met and shook hands and sat down. Together these two big men dwarfed the tiny Broadway office and made the furnishings look like toys. Wilhelm had the color of a Golden Grimes apple when he was well, and then his thick blond hair had been vigorous and his wide shoulders unwarped; he was leaner in the jaws, his eyes fresher and wider; his legs were then still awkward but he was impressively handsome. And he was about to make his first great mistake. Like, he sometimes thought, I was going to pick up a weapon and strike myself a blow with it.

Looming over the desk in the small office darkened by overbuilt midtown—sheer walls, gray spaces, dry lagoons of tar and pebbles—Maurice Venice proceeded to establish his credentials. He said, "My letter was on the regular stationery, but maybe you want to check on me?"

"Who, *me?*" said Wilhelm. "Why?"

"There's guys who think I'm in a racket and make a charge for the test. I don't ask a cent. I'm no agent. There ain't no commission."

"I never even thought of it," said Wilhelm. Was there perhaps something fishy about this Maurice Venice? He protested too much.

In his husky, fat-weakened voice he finally challenged Wilhelm, "If you're not sure, you can call the distributor and find out who I am, Maurice Venice."

Wilhelm wondered at him. "Why shouldn't I be sure? Of course I am."

"Because I can see the way you size me up, and because this is a dinky office. Like you don't believe me. Go ahead. Call. I won't care if you're cautious. I mean it. There's quite a few people who doubt me at first. They can't really believe that fame and fortune are going to hit 'em."

"But I tell you I do believe you," Wilhelm had said, and bent inward to accommodate the pressure of his warm, panting laugh. It was purely nervous. His neck was ruddy and neatly shaved about the ears—he was fresh from the barbershop; his face anxiously glowed with his desire to make a pleasing impression. It was all wasted on Venice, who was just as concerned about the impression *he* was making.

"If you're surprised, I'll just show you what I mean," Venice had said. "It was about fifteen months ago right in this identical same office when I saw a beautiful thing in the paper. It wasn't even a photo but a drawing, a brassière ad, but I knew right away that this was star material. I called up the paper to ask who the girl was, they gave me the name of the advertising agency; I phoned the agency and they gave me the name of the artist; I got hold of the artist and he gave me the number of the model agency. Finally, finally I got her number and phoned her and said, 'This is Maurice Venice, scout for Kaskaskia Films.' So right away she says, 'Yah, so's your old lady.' Well, when I saw I wasn't getting nowhcre with her I said to her, 'Well, miss. I don't blame you. You're a very beautiful thing and must have a dozen admirers after you all the time, boy friends who like to call and pull your leg and give a tease. But as I happen to be a very busy fellow and don't have the time to horse around or argue, I tell you what to do. Here's my number, and here's the number of the Kaskaskia Distributors, Inc. Ask them who am I, Maurice Venice. The scout.' She did it. A little while later she phoned me back, all apologies and excuses, but I didn't want to embarrass her and get off on the wrong foot with an artist. I know better than to do that. So I told her it was a natural precaution, never mind. I wanted to run a screen test right away. Because I seldom am wrong about talent. If I see it, it's there. Get that, please. And do you know who that little girl is today?"

"No," Wilhelm said eagerly. "Who is she?"

Venice said impressively, " 'Nita Christenberry."

Wilhelm sat utterly blank. This was failure. He didn't know the name, and Venice was waiting for his response and would be angry.

And in fact Venice had been offended. He said, "What's the matter with you! Don't you read a magazine? She's a starlet."

"I'm sorry," Wilhelm answered. "I'm at school and don'+ have time to keep up. If I don't know her, it doesn't mean a thing. She made a big hit, I'll bet."

"You can say that again. Here's a photo of her." He handed Wilhelm some pictures. She was a bathing beauty—short, the usual breasts, hips, and smooth thighs. Yes, quite good, as Wilhelm recalled. She stood on high heels and wore a Spanish comb and mantilla. In her hand was a fan.

He had said, "She looks awfully peppy."

"Isn't she a divine girl? And what personality! Not just another broad in the show business, believe me." He had a surprise for Wilhelm. "I have found happiness with her," he said.

"You have?" said Wilhelm, slow to understand.

"Yes, boy, we're engaged."

Wilhelm saw another photograph, taken on the beach. Venice was dressed in a terry-cloth beach outfit, and he and the girl, cheek to cheek, were looking into the camera. Below, in white ink, was written "Love at Malibu Colony."

"I'm sure you'll be very happy. I wish you—"

"I *know*," said Venice firmly, "I'm going to be happy. When I saw that drawing, the breath of fate breathed on me. I felt it over my entire body.'

"Say, it strikes a bell suddenly," Wilhelm had said. "Aren't you related to Martial Venice the producer?"

Venice was either a nephew of the producer or the son of a first cousin. Decidedly he had not made good. It was easy enough for Wilhelm to see this now. The office was so poor, and Venice bragged so nervously and identified himself so scrupulously—the poor guy. He was the obscure failure of an aggressive and powerful clan. As such he had the greatest sympathy from Wilhelm.

Venice had said, "Now I suppose you want to know where you come in. I saw your school paper, by accident. You take quite a remarkable picture."

"It can't be so much," said Wilhelm, more panting than laughing.

"You don't want to tell me my business," Venice said. "Leave it to me. I studied up on this."

"I never imagined— Well, what kind of roles do you think I'd fit?"

"All this time that we've been talking, I've been watching. Don't think I haven't. You remind me of someone. Let's see who it can be—one of the great old-timers. Is it Milton Sills? No, that's not the one. Conway Tearle, Jack Mulhall? George Bancroft? No, his face was ruggeder. One thing I can tell you, though, a George Raft type you're not—those tough, smooth, black little characters."

"No, I wouldn't seem to be."

"No, you're not that flyweight type, with the fists, from a nightclub, and the glamorous sideburns, doing the tango or the bolero. Not Edward G. Robinson, either—I'm thinking aloud. Or the Cagney fly-in-your-face role, a cabbie, with that mouth and those punches."

"I realize that."

"Not suave like William Powell, or a lyric juvenile like Buddy Rogers. I suppose you don't play the sax? No. But—"

"But what?"

"I have you placed as the type that loses the girl to the George Raft type or the William Powell type. You are steady, faithful, you get stood up. The older women would know better. The mothers are on your side. With what they been through, if it was up to them, they'd take you in a minute. You're very sympathetic, even the young girls feel that. You'd make a good provider. But they go more for the other types. It's as clear as anything."

This was not how Wilhelm saw himself. And as he surveyed the old ground he recognized now that he had been not only confused but hurt. Why, he thought, he cast me even then for a loser.

Wilhelm had said, with half a mind to be defiant, "Is that your opinion?"

It never occurred to Venice that a man might object to

stardom in such a role. "Here is your chance," he said. "Now you're just in college. What are you studying?" He snapped his fingers. "Stuff." Wilhelm himself felt this way about it. "You may plug along fifty years before you get anywheres. This way, in one jump, the world knows who you are. You become a name like Roosevelt, Swanson. From east to west, out to China, into South America. This is no bunk. You become a lover to the whole world. The world wants it, needs it. One fellow smiles, a billion people also smile. One fellow cries, the other billion sob with him. Listen, bud—" Venice had pulled himself together to make an effort. On his imagination there was some great weight which he could not discharge. He wanted Wilhelm, too, to feel it. He twisted his large, clean, well-meaning, rather foolish features as though he were their unwilling captive, and said in his choked, fat-obstructed voice, "Listen, everywhere there are people trying hard, miserable, in trouble, downcast, tired, trying and trying. They need a break, right? A break-through, a help, luck, or sympathy."

"That certainly is the truth," said Wilhelm. He had seized the feeling and he waited for Venice to go on. But Venice had no more to say; he had concluded. He gave Wilhelm several pages of blue hectographed script, stapled together, and told him to prepare for the screen test. "Study your lines in front of a mirror," he said. "Let yourself go. The part should take ahold of you. Don't be afraid to make faces and be emotional. Shoot the works. Because when you start to act you're no more an ordinary person, and those things don't apply to you. You don't behave the same way as the average."

And so Wilhelm had never returned to Penn State. His roommate sent his things to New York for him, and the school authorities had to write to Dr. Adler to find out what had happened.

Still, for three months Wilhelm delayed his trip to California.

He wanted to start out with the blessings of his family, but they were never given. He quarreled with his parents and his sister. And then, when he was best aware of the risks and knew a hundred reasons against going and had made himself sick with fear, he left home. This was typical of Wilhelm. After much thought and hesitation and debate he invariably took the course he had rejected innumerable times. Ten such decisions made up the history of his life. He had decided that it would be a bad mistake to go to Hollywood, and then he went. He had made up his mind not to marry his wife, but ran off and got married. He had resolved not to invest money with Tamkin, and then had given him a check.

But Wilhelm had been eager for life to start. College was merely another delay. Venice had approached him and said that the world had named Wilhelm to shine before it. He was to be freed from the anxious and narrow life of the average. Moreover, Venice had claimed that he never made a mistake. His instinct for talent was infallible, he said.

But when Venice saw the results of the screen test he did a quick about-face. In those days Wilhelm had had a speech difficulty. It was not a true stammer, it was a thickness of speech which the sound track exaggerated. The film showed that he had many peculiarities, otherwise unnoticeable. When he shrugged, his hands drew up within his sleeves. The vault of his chest was huge, but he really didn't look strong under the lights. Though he called himself a hippopotamus, he more nearly resembled a bear. His walk was bearlike, quick and rather soft, toes turned inward, as though his shoes were an impediment. About one thing Venice had been right. Wilhelm was photogenic, and his wavy blond hair (now graying) came out well, but after the test Venice refused to encourage him. He tried to get rid of him. He couldn't afford to take a chance on him, he had made too many mistakes already and lived in fear of his powerful relatives.

Wilhelm had told his parents, "Venice says I owe it to my-self to go." How ashamed he was now of this lie! He had begged Venice not to give him up. He had said, "Can't you help me out? It would kill me to go back to school now."

Then when he reached the Coast he learned that a recom-mendation from Maurice Venice was the kiss of death. Venice needed help and charity more than he, Wilhelm, ever had. A few years later when Wilhelm was down on his luck and work-ing as an orderly in a Los Angeles hospital, he saw Venice's picture in the papers. He was under indictment for pandering. Closely following the trial, Wilhelm found out that Venice had indeed been employed by Kaskaskia Films but that he had evidently made use of the connection to organize a ring of call girls. Then what did he want with me? Wilhelm had cried to himself. He was unwilling to believe anything very bad about Venice. Perhaps he was foolish and unlucky, a fall guy, a dupe, a sucker. You didn't give a man fifteen years in prison for that. Wilhelm often thought that he might write him a letter to say how sorry he was. He remembered the breath of fate and Venice's certainty that he would be happy. 'Nita Christenberry was sentenced to three years. Wilhelm recognized her although she had changed her name.

By that time Wilhelm too had taken his new name. In California he became Tommy Wilhelm. Dr. Adler would not accept the change. Today he still called his son Wilky, as he had done for more than forty years. Well, now, Wilhelm was think-ing, the paper crowded in disarray under his arm, there's really very little that a man can change at will. He can't change his lungs, or nerves, or constitution or temperament. They're not under his control. When he's young and strong and impulsive and dissatisfied with the way things are he wants to rearrange them to assert his freedom. He can't overthrow the government or be differently born; he only has a little scope and maybe a foreboding, too, that essentially you can't change. Nevertheless, he makes a gesture and becomes Tommy Wilhelm. Wilhelm had always had a great longing to be Tommy. He had never, however, succeeded in feeling like Tommy, and in his soul had always remained Wilky. When he was drunk he reproached himself horribly as Wilky. "You fool, you clunk, you Wilky!" he called himself. He thought that it was a good thing perhaps that he had not become a success as Tommy since that would not have been a genuine success. Wilhelm would have feared that not he but Tommy had brought it off, cheating Wilky of his birthright. Yes, it had been a stupid thing to do, but it was his imperfect judgment at the age of twenty which should be blamed. He had cast off his father's name, and with it his father's opinion of him. It was, he knew it was, his bid for liberty, Adler being in his mind the title of the species, Tommy the freedom of the person. But Wilky was his inescapable self.

In middle age you no longer thought such thoughts about free choice. Then it came over you that from one grandfather you had inherited such and such a head of hair which looked like honey when it whitens or sugars in the jar; from another, broad thick shoulders; an oddity of speech from one uncle, and small teeth from another, and the gray eyes with darkness diffused even into the whites, and a wide-lipped mouth like a statue from Peru. Wandering races have such looks, the bones of one tribe, the skin of another. From his mother he had gotten sensitive feelings, a soft heart, a brooding nature, a tendency to be confused under pressure.

The changed name was a mistake, and he would admit it as freely as you liked. But this mistake couldn't be undone now, so why must his father continually remind him how he had sinned? It was too late. He would have to go back to the pathetic day when the sin was committed. And where was that day? Past and dead. Whose humiliating memories were these? His and not his father's. What had he to think back on that he could call good? Very, very little. You had to forgive. First, to forgive yourself, and then, general forgiveness. Didn't he suffer from his mistakes far more than his father could?

"Oh, God," Wilhelm prayed. "Let me out of my trouble. Let me out of my thoughts, and let me do something better with myself. For all the time I have wasted I am very sorry. Let me out of this clutch and into a different life. For I am all balled up. Have mercy."

II

The mail.

The clerk who gave it to him did not care what sort of appearance he made this morning. He only glanced at him from under his brows, upward, as the letters changed hands. Why should the hotel people waste courtesies on him? They had his number. The clerk knew that he was handing him, along with the letters, a bill for his rent. Wilhelm assumed a look that removed him from all such things. But it was bad. To pay the bill he would have to withdraw money from his brokerage account, and the account was being watched because of the drop in lard. According to the *Tribune*'s figures lard was still twenty points below last year's level. There were government price supports. Wilhelm didn't know how these worked but he understood that the farmer was protected and that the SEC kept an eye on the market and therefore he believed that lard would rise again and he wasn't greatly worried as yet. But in the meantime his father might have offered to pick up his hotel tab. Why didn't he? What a selfish old man he was! He saw his son's hardships; he could so easily help him. How little it would mean to him, and how much to Wilhelm! Where was the old man's heart? Maybe, thought Wilhelm, I was sentimental in the past and exaggerated his kindliness—warm family life. It may never have been there.

Not long ago his father had said to him in his usual affable, pleasant way, "Well, Wilky, here we are under the same roof again, after all these years."

Wilhelm was glad for an instant. At last they would talk over old times. But he was also on guard against insinuations. Wasn't his father saying, "Why are you here in a hotel with me and not at home in Brooklyn with your wife and two boys? You're neither a widower nor a bachelor. You have brought me all your confusions. What do you expect me to do with them?"

So Wilhelm studied the remark for a bit, then said, "The roof is twenty-six stories up. But how many years has it been?"

"That's what I was asking you."

"Gosh, Dad, I'm not sure. Wasn't it the year Mother died? What year was that?"

He asked this question with an innocent frown on his Golden Grimes, dark-blond face. *What year was it!* As though he didn't know the year, the month, the day, the very hour of his mother's death.

"Wasn't it nineteen-thirty-one?" said Dr. Adler.

"Oh, was it?" said Wilhelm. And in hiding the sadness and the overwhelming irony of the question he gave a nervous shiver and wagged his head and felt the ends of his collar rapidly.

"Do you know?" his father said. "You must realize, an old fellow's memory becomes unreliable. It was in winter, that I'm sure of. Nineteen-thirty-two?"

Yes, it was age. Don't make an issue of it, Wilhelm advised himself. If you were to ask the old doctor in what year he had interned, he'd tell you correctly. All the same, don't make an issue. Don't quarrel with your own father. Have pity on an old man's failings.

"I believe the year was closer to nineteen-thirty-four, Dad," he said.

But Dr. Adler was thinking, Why the devil can't he stand

still when we're talking? He's either hoisting his pants up and down by the pockets or jittering with his feet. A regular mountain of tics he's getting to be. Wilhelm had a habit of moving his feet back and forth as though, hurrying into a house, he had to clean his shoes first on the doormat.

Then Wilhelm had said, "Yes, that was the beginning of the end, wasn't it, Father?"

Wilhelm often astonished Dr. Adler. Beginning of the end? What could he mean—what was he fishing for? Whose end? The end of family life? The old man was puzzled but he would not give Wilhelm an opening to introduce his complaints. He had learned that it was better not to take up Wilhelm's strange challenges. So he merely agreed pleasantly, for he was a master of social behavior, and said, "It was an awful misfortune for us all."

He thought, What business has he to complain to *me* of his mother's death?

Face to face they had stood, each declaring himself silently after his own way. It was: it was not, the beginning of the end—*some* end.

Unaware of anything odd in his doing it, for he did it all the time, Wilhelm had pinched out the coal of his cigarette and dropped the butt in his pocket, where there were many more. And as he gazed at his father the little finger of his right hand began to twitch and tremble; of that he was unconscious, too.

And yet Wilhelm believed that when he put his mind to it he could have perfect and even distinguished manners, outdoing his father. Despite the slight thickness in his speech— it amounted almost to a stammer when he started the same phrase over several times in his effort to eliminate the thick sound—he could be fluent. Otherwise he would never have made a good salesman. He claimed also that he was a good listener. When he listened he made a tight mouth and rolled his eyes thoughtfully. He would soon tire and begin to utter short, loud, impatient breaths, and he would say, "Oh yes . . . yes . . . yes. I couldn't agree more." When he was forced to differ he would declare, "Well, I'm not sure. I don't really see it that way. I'm of two minds about it." He would never willingly hurt any man's feelings.

But in conversation with his father he was apt to lose control of himself. After any talk with Dr. Adler, Wilhelm generally felt dissatisfied, and his dissatisfaction reached its greatest intensity when they discussed family matters. Ostensibly he had been trying to help the old man to remember a date, but in reality he meant to tell him, "You were set free when Ma died. You wanted to forget her. You'd like to get rid of Catherine, too. Me, too. You're not kidding anyone"—Wilhelm striving to put this across, and the old man not having it. In the end he was left struggling, while his father seemed unmoved.

And then once more Wilhelm had said to himself, "But man! you're not a kid. Even then you weren't a kid!" He looked down over the front of his big, indecently big, spoiled body. He was beginning to lose his shape, his gut was fat, and he looked like a hippopotamus. His younger son called him "a hummuspotamus"; that was little Paul. And here he was still struggling with his old dad, filled with ancient grievances. Instead of saying, "Good-by, youth! Oh, good-by those marvelous, foolish wasted days. What a big clunk I was—I *am*."

Wilhelm was still paying heavily for his mistakes. His wife Margaret would not give him a divorce, and he had to support her and the two children. She would regularly agree to divorce him, and then think things over again and set new and more difficult conditions. No court would have awarded her the amounts he paid. One of today's letters, as he had expected, was from her. For the first time he had sent her a postdated check, and she protested. She also enclosed bills for the boys' educational insurance policies, due next week. Wilhelm's mother-in-law had taken out these policies in Beverly Hills, and since her death two years ago he had to pay the premiums. Why couldn't she have minded her own business! They were his kids, and he took care of them and always would. He had planned to set up a trust fund. But that was on his former expectations. Now he had to rethink the future, because of the money problem. Meanwhile, here were the bills to be paid. When he saw the two sums punched out so neatly on the cards he cursed the company and its IBM equipment. His heart and his head were congested with anger. Everyone was supposed to have money. It was nothing to the company. It published pictures of funerals in the magazines and frightened the suckers, and then punched out little holes, and the customers would lie awake to think out ways to raise the dough. They'd be ashamed not to have it. They couldn't let a great company down, either, and they got the scratch. In the old days a man was put in prison for debt, but there were subtler things now. They made it a shame not to have money and set everybody to work.

Well, and what else had Margaret sent him? He tore the envelope open with his thumb, swearing that he would send any other bills back to her. There was, luckily, nothing more. He put the hole-punched cards in his pocket. Didn't Margaret know that he was nearly at the end of his rope? Of course. Her instinct told her that this was her opportunity, and she was giving him the works.

He went into the dining room, which was under Austro-Hungarian management at the Hotel Gloriana. It was run like a European establishment. The pastries were excellent, especially the strudel. He often had apple strudel and coffee in the afternoon.

As soon as he entered he saw his father's small head in the sunny bay at the farther end, and heard his precise voice. It was with an odd sort of perilous expression that Wilhelm crossed the dining room.

Dr. Adler liked to sit in a corner that looked across Broadway down to the Hudson and New Jersey. On the other side of the street was a supermodern cafeteria with gold and purple mosaic columns. On the second floor a private-eye school, a dental laboratory, a reducing parlor, a veteran's club, and a Hebrew school shared the space. The old man was sprinkling sugar on his strawberries. Small hoops of brilliance were cast by the water glasses on the white tablecloth, despite a faint murkiness in the sunshine. It was early summer, and the long window was turned inward; a moth was on the pane; the putty was broken and the white enamel on the frames was streaming with wrinkles.

"Ha, Wilky," said the old man to his tardy son. "You haven't met our neighbor Mr. Perls, have you? From the fifteenth floor."

"How d'do," Wilhelm said. He did not welcome this stranger; he began at once to find fault with him. Mr. Perls carried a heavy cane with a crutch tip. Dyed hair, a skinny forehead—these were not reasons for bias. Nor was it Mr. Perls's fault that Dr. Adler was using him, not wishing to have breakfast with his son alone. But a gruffer voice within Wilhelm spoke, asking, "Who is this damn frazzle-faced herring with his dyed hair and his fish teeth and this drippy mustache? Another one of Dad's German friends. Where does he collect all these guys? What is the stuff on his teeth? I never saw such pointed crowns. Are they stainless steel, or a kind of silver? How can a human face get into this condition. Uch!" Staring with his widely spaced gray eyes, Wilhelm sat, his broad back stooped under the sports jacket. He clasped his hands on the table with an implication of suppliance. Then he began to relent a little toward Mr. Perls, beginning at the teeth. Each of those crowns represented a tooth ground to the quick, and estimating a man's grief with his teeth as two per cent of the total, and adding to that his flight from Germany and the probable origin of his wincing wrinkles, not to be confused with the wrinkles of his smile, it came to a sizable load.

"Mr. Perls was a hosiery wholesaler," said Dr. Adler.

"Is this the son you told me was in the selling line?" said Mr. Perls.

Dr. Adler replied, "I have only this one son. One daughter. She was a medical technician before she got married—anesthetist. At one time she had an important position in Mount Sinai."

He couldn't mention his children without boasting. In Wilhelm's opinion, there was little to boast of. Catherine, like Wilhelm, was big and fair-haired. She had married a court reporter who had a pretty hard time of it. She had taken a professional name, too—Philippa. At forty she was still ambitious to become a painter. Wilhelm didn't venture to criticize her work. It didn't do much to him, he said, but then he was no critic. Anyway, he and his sister were generally on the outs and he didn't often see her paintings. She worked very hard, but there were fifty thousand people in New York with paints and brushes, each practically a law unto himself. It was the Tower of Babel in paint. *He* didn't want to go far into this. Things were chaotic all over.

Dr. Adler thought that Wilhelm looked particularly untidy this morning—unrested, too, his eyes red-rimmed from excessive smoking. He was breathing through his mouth and he was evidently much distracted and rolled his red-shot eyes barbarously. As usual, his coat collar was turned up as though he had had to go out in the rain. When he went to business he pulled himself together a little; otherwise he let himself go and looked like hell.

"What's the matter, Wilky, didn't you sleep last night?"

"Not very much."

"You take too many pills of every kind—first stimulants

and then depressants, anodynes followed by analeptics, until the poor organism doesn't know what's happened. Then the luminal won't put people to sleep, and the Pervitin or Benzedrine won't wake them. God knows! These things get to be as serious as poisons, and yet everyone puts all their faith in them."

"No, Dad, it's not the pills. It's that I'm not used to New York any more. For a native, that's very peculiar, isn't it? It was never so noisy at night as now, and every little thing is a strain. Like the alternate parking. You have to run out at eight to move your car. And where can you put it? If you forget for a minute they tow you away. Then some fool puts advertising leaflets under your windshield wiper and you have heart failure a block away because you think you've got a ticket. When you do get stung with a ticket, you can't argue. You haven't got a chance in court and the city wants the revenue."

"But in your line you have to have a car, eh?" said Mr. Perls.

"Lord knows why any lunatic would want one in the city who didn't need it for his livelihood."

Wilhelm's old Pontiac was parked in the street. Formerly, when on an expense account, he had always put it up in a garage. Now he was afraid to move the car from Riverside Drive lest he lose his space, and he used it only on Saturdays when the Dodgers were playing in Ebbets Field and he took his boys to the game. Last Sunday, when the Dodgers were out of town, he had gone out to visit his mother's grave.

Dr. Adler had refused to go along. He couldn't bear his son's driving. Forgetfully, Wilhelm traveled for miles in second gear; he was seldom in the right lane and he neither gave signals nor watched for lights. The upholstery of his Pontiac was filthy with grease and ashes. One cigarette burned in the ashtray, another in his hand, a third on the floor with maps and other waste paper and Coca-Cola bottles. He dreamed at the wheel or argued and gestured, and therefore the old doctor would not ride with him.

Then Wilhelm had come back from the cemetery angry because the stone bench between his mother's and his grandmother's graves had been overturned and broken by vandals. "Those damn teen-age hoodlums get worse and worse," he said. "Why, they must have used a sledge-hammer to break the seat smack in half like that. If I could catch one of them!" He wanted the doctor to pay for a new seat, but his father was cool to the idea. He said he was going to have himself cremated.

Mr. Perls said, "I don't blame you if you get no sleep up where you are." His voice was tuned somewhat sharp, as though he were slightly deaf. "Don't you have Parigi the singing teacher there? God, they have some queer elements in this hotel. On which floor is that Estonian woman with all her cats and dogs? They should have made her leave long ago."

"They've moved her down to twelve," said Dr. Adler.

Wilhelm ordered a large Coca-Cola with his breakfast. Working in secret at the small envelopes in his pocket, he found two pills by touch. Much fingering had worn and weakened the paper. Under cover of a napkin he swallowed a Phenaphen sedative and a Unicap, but the doctor was sharp-eyed and said, "Wilky, what are you taking now?"

"Just my vitamin pills." He put his cigar butt in an ashtray on the table behind him, for his father did not like the odor. Then he drank his Coca-Cola.

"That's what you drink for breakfast, and not orange juice?" said Mr. Perls. He seemed to sense that he would not lose Dr. Adler's favor by taking an ironic tone with his son.

"The caffeine stimulates brain activity," said the old doctor. "It does all kinds of things to the respiratory center."

"It's just a habit of the road, that's all," Wilhelm said. "If you drive around long enough it turns your brains, your stomach, and everything else."

His father explained, "Wilky used to be with the Rojax Corporation. He was their northeastern sales representative for a good many years but recently ended the connection."

"Yes," said Wilhelm, "I was with them from the end of the war." He sipped the Coca-Cola and chewed the ice, glancing at one and the other with his attitude of large, shaky, patient dignity. The waitress set two boiled eggs before him.

"What kind of line does this Rojax company manufacture?" said Mr. Perls.

"Kiddies' furniture. Little chairs, rockers, tables, jungle gyms, slides, swings, seesaws."

Wilhelm let his father do the explaining. Large and stiff-backed, he tried to sit patiently, but his feet were abnormally restless. All right! His father had to impress Mr. Perls? He would go along once more, and play his part. Fine! He would play along and help his father maintain his style. Style was the main consideration. That was just fine!

"I was with the Rojax Corporation for almost ten years," he said. "We parted ways because they wanted me to share my territory. They took a son-in-law into the business—a new fellow. It was his idea."

To himself, Wilhelm said, Now God alone can tell why I have to lay my whole life bare to this blasted herring here. I'm sure nobody else does it. Other people keep their business to themselves. Not me.

He continued, "But the rationalization was that it was too big a territory for one man. I had a monopoly. That wasn't so. The real reason was that they had gotten to the place where they would have to make me an officer of the corporation. Vice presidency. I was in line for it, but instead this son-in-law got in, and—"

Dr. Adler thought Wilhelm was discussing his grievances much too openly and said, "My son's income was up in the five figures."

As soon as money was mentioned, Mr. Perls's voice grew eagerly sharper. "Yes? What, the thirty-two-per-cent bracket? Higher even, I guess?" He asked for a hint, and he named the figures not idly but with a sort of hugging relish. Uch! How they love money, thought Wilhelm. They adore money! Holy money! Beautiful money! It was getting so that people were feeble-minded about everything except money. While if you didn't have it you were a dummy, a dummy! You had to excuse yourself from the face of the earth. Chicken! that's what it was. The world's business. If only he could find a way out of it.

Such thinking brought on the usual congestion. It would grow into a fit of passion if he allowed it to continue. Therefore he stopped talking and began to eat.

Before he struck the egg with his spoon he dried the moisture with his napkin. Then he battered it (in his father's opinion) more than was necessary. A faint grime was left by his fingers on the white of the egg after he had picked away the shell. Dr. Adler saw it with silent repugnance. What a Wilky he had given to the world! Why, he didn't even wash his hands in the morning. He used an electric razor so that he didn't have to touch water. The doctor couldn't bear Wilky's dirty habits. Only once—and never again, he swore—had he visited his room. Wilhelm, in pajamas and stockings had sat on his bed, drinking gin from a coffee mug and rooting for the Dodgers on television. "That's two and two on you, Duke. Come on—hit it, now." He came down on the mattress—bam! The bed looked kicked to pieces. Then he drank the gin as though it were tea, and urged his team on with his fist. The smell of dirty clothes was outrageous. By the bedside lay a quart bottle and foolish magazines and mystery stories for the hours of insomnia. Wilhelm lived in worse filth than a savage. When the Doctor spoke to him about this he answered, "Well, I have no wife to look after my things." And who— *who!*—had done the leaving? Not Margaret. The Doctor was certain that she wanted him back.

Wilhelm drank his coffee with a trembling hand. In his full face, his abused bloodshot gray eyes moved back and forth. Jerkily he set his cup back and put half the length of a cigarette into his mouth; he seemed to hold it with his teeth, as though it were a cigar.

"I can't let them get away with it," he said. "It's also a question of morale."

His father corrected him. "Don't you mean a moral question, Wilky?"

"I mean that, too. I have to do something to protect myself. I was promised executive standing." Correction before a stranger mortified him, and his dark-blond face changed color, more pale, and then more dark. He went on talking to Perls but his eyes spied on his father. "I was the one who opened the territory for them. I could go back for one of their competitors and take away their customers. *My* customers. Morale enters into it because they've tried to take away my confidence."

"Would you offer a different line to the same people?" Mr. Perls wondered.

"Why not? I know what's wrong with the Rojax product."

"Nonsense," said his father. "Just nonsense and kid's talk, Wilky. You're only looking for trouble and embarrassment that way. What would you gain by such a silly feud? You have to think about making a living and meeting your obligations."

Hot and bitter, Wilhelm said with pride, while his feet moved angrily under the table, "I don't have to be told about my obligations. I've been meeting them for years. In more than twenty years I've never had a penny of help from anybody.

I preferred to dig a ditch on the WPA but never asked anyone to meet my obligations for me."

"Wilky has had all kinds of experiences," said Dr. Adler.

The old doctor's face had a wholesome reddish and almost translucent color, like a ripe apricot. The wrinkles beside his ears were deep because the skin conformed so tightly to his bones. With all his might, he was a healthy and fine small old man. He wore a white vest of a light check pattern. His hearing-aid doodad was in the pocket. An unusual shirt of red and black stripes covered his chest. He bought his clothes in a college shop farther uptown. Wilhelm thought he had no business to get himself up like a jockey, out of respect for his profession.

"Well," said Mr. Perls. "I can understand how you feel. You want to fight it out. By a certain time of life, to have to start all over again can't be a pleasure, though a good man can always do it. But anyway you want to keep on with a business you know already, and not have to meet a whole lot of new contacts."

Wilhlem again thought, Why does it have to be me and my life that's discussed, and not him and his life? He would never allow it. But I am an idiot. I have no reserve. To me it can be done. I talk. I must ask for it. Everybody wants to have intimate conversations, but the smart fellows don't give out, only the fools. The smart fellows talk intimately about the fools, and examine them all over and give them advice. Why do I allow it? The hint about his age had hurt him. No, you can't admit it's as good as ever, he conceded. Things do give out.

"In the meantime," Dr. Adler said, "Wilky is taking it easy and considering various propositions. Isn't that so?"

"More or less," said Wilhelm. He suffered his father to increase Mr. Perls's respect for him. The WPA ditch had brought the family into contempt. He was a little tired. The spirit, the peculiar burden of his existence lay upon him like an accretion, a load, a hump. In any moment of quiet, when sheer fatigue prevented him from struggling, he was apt to feel this mysterious weight, this growth or collection of nameless things which it was the business of his life to carry about. That must be what a man was for. This large, odd, excited, fleshy, blond, abrupt personality named Wilhelm, or Tommy, was here, present, in the present—Dr. Tamkin had been putting into his mind many suggestions about the present moment, the here and now—this Wilky, or Tommy Wilhelm, forty-four years old, father of two sons, at present living in the Hotel Gloriana, was assigned to be the carrier of a load which was his own self, his characteristic self. There was no figure or estimate for the value of this load. But it is probably exaggerated by the subject, T. W. Who is a visionary sort of animal. Who has to believe that he can know why he exists. Though he has never seriously tried to find out why.

Mr. Perls said, "If he wants time to think things over and have a rest, why doesn't he run down to Florida for a while? Off season it's cheap and quiet. Fairyland. The mangoes are just coming in. I got two acres down there. You'd think you were in India."

Mr. Perls utterly astonished Wilhelm when he spoke of fairyland with a foreign accent. Mangoes—India? What did he mean, India?

"Once upon a time," said Wilhelm, "I did some public-relations work for a big hotel down in Cuba. If I could get them a notice in Leonard Lyons or one of the other columns it might be good for another holiday there, gratis. I haven't had a vacation for a long time, and I could stand a rest after going so hard. You know that's true, Father." He meant that his father knew how deep the crisis was becoming; how badly he was strapped for money; and that he could not rest but would be crushed if he stumbled; and that his obligations would destroy him. He couldn't falter. He thought, The money! When I had it, I flowed money. They bled it away from me. I hemorrhaged money. But now it's almost all gone, and where am I supposed to turn for more?

He said, "As a matter of fact, Father, I am tired as hell."

But Mr. Perls began to smile and said, "I understand from Doctor Tamkin that you're going into some kind of investment with him, partners."

"You know, he's a very ingenious fellow," said Dr. Adler. "I really enjoy hearing him go on. I wonder if he really is a medical doctor."

"Isn't he?" said Perls. "Everybody thinks he is. He talks about his patients. Doesn't he write prescriptions?"

"I don't really know what he does," said Dr. Adler. "He's a cunning man."

"He's a psychologist, I understand," said Wilhelm.

"I don't know what sort of psychologist or psychiatrist he may be," said his father. "He's a little vague. It's growing into a major industry, and a very expensive one. Fellows have to hold down very big jobs in order to pay those fees. Anyway, this Tamkin is clever. He never said he practiced here, but I believe he was a doctor in California. They don't seem to have much legislation out there to cover these things, and I hear a thousand dollars will get you a degree from a Los Angeles correspondence school. He gives the impression of knowing something about chemistry, and things like hypnotism. I wouldn't trust him, though."

"And why wouldn't you?" Wilhelm demanded.

"Because he's probably a liar. Do you believe he invented all the things he claims?"

Mr. Perls was grinning.

"He was written up in *Fortune,*" said Wilhelm. "Yes, in *Fortune* magazine. He showed me the article. I've seen his clippings."

"That doesn't make him legitimate," said Dr. Adler. "It might have been another Tamkin. Make no mistake, he's an operator. Perhaps even crazy."

"Crazy, you say?"

Mr. Perls put in, "He could be both sane and crazy. In these days nobody can tell for sure which is which."

"An electrical device for truck drivers to wear in their caps," said Dr. Adler, describing one of Tamkin's proposed inventions. "To wake them with a shock when they begin to be drowsy at the wheel. It's triggered by the change in blood-pressure when they start to doze."

"It doesn't sound like such an impossible thing to me," said Wilhelm.

Mr. Perls said, "To me he described an underwater suit so a man could walk on the bed of the Hudson in case of an atomic attack. He said he could walk to Albany in it."

"Ha, ha, ha, ha, ha!" cried Dr. Adler in his old man's voice. "Tamkin's Folly. You could go on a camping trip under Niagara Falls."

"This is just his kind of fantasy," said Wilhelm. "It doesn't mean a thing. Inventors are supposed to be like that. I get funny ideas myself. Everybody wants to make something. Any American does."

But his father ignored this and said to Perls, "What other inventions did he describe?"

While the frazzle-faced Mr. Perls and his father in the unseemly, monkey-striped shirt were laughing, Wilhelm could not restrain himself and joined in with his own panting laugh. But he was in despair. They were laughing at the man to whom he had given a power of attorney over his last seven hundred dollars to speculate for him in the commodities market. They had bought all that lard. It had to rise today. By ten o'clock, or half-past ten, trading would be active, and he would see.

III

Between white tablecloths and glassware and glancing silver-ware, through overfull light, the long figure of Mr. Perls went away into the darkness of the lobby. He thrust with his cane, and dragged a large built-up shoe which Wilhelm had not included in his estimate of troubles. Dr. Adler wanted to talk about him. "There's a poor man," he said, "with a bone condition which is gradually breaking him up."

"One of those progressive diseases?" said Wilhelm.

"Very bad. I've learned," the doctor told him, "to keep my sympathy for the real ailments. This Perls is more to be pitied than any man I know."

Wilhelm understood he was being put on notice and did not express his opinion. He ate and ate. He did not hurry but kept putting food on his plate until he had gone through the muffins and his father's strawberries, and then some pieces of bacon that were left; he had several cups of coffee, and when he was finished he sat gigantically in a state of arrest and didn't seem to know what he should do next.

For a while father and son were uncommonly still. Wilhelm's preparations to please Dr. Adler had failed completely, for the old man kept thinking, You'd never guess he had a clean upbringing, and, What a dirty devil this son of mine is. Why can't he try to sweeten his appearance a little? Why does he want to drag himself like this? And he makes himself look so idealistic.

Wilhelm sat, mountainous. He was not really so slovenly as his father found him to be. In some aspects he even had a certain delicacy. His mouth, though broad, had a fine outline, and his brow and his gradually incurved nose, dignity, and in his blond hair there was white but there were also shades of gold and chestnut. When he was with the Rojax Corporation Wilhelm had kept a small apartment in Roxbury, two rooms in a large house with a small porch and garden, and on mornings of leisure, in late spring weather like this, he used to sit expanded in a wicker chair with the sunlight pouring through the weave, and sunlight through the slug-eaten holes of the young hollyhocks and as deeply as the grass allowed into small flowers. This peace (he forgot that that time had had its troubles, too), this peace was gone. It must not have belonged to him, really, for to be here in New York with his old father was more genuinely like his life. He was well aware that he didn't stand a chance of getting sympathy from his father, who said he kept his for real ailments. Moreover, he advised himself repeatedly not to discuss his vexatious problems with him, for his father, with some justice, wanted to be left in peace. Wilhelm also knew that when he began to talk about these things he made himself feel worse, he became congested with them and worked himself into a clutch. Therefore he warned himself, Lay off, pal. It'll only be an aggravation. From a deeper source, however, came other promptings. If he didn't keep his troubles before him he risked losing them altogether, and he knew by experience that this was worse. And furthermore, he could not succeed in excusing his father on the ground of old age. No. No, he could not. I am his son, he thought. He is my father. He is as much father as I am son —old or not. Affirming this, though in complete silence, he sat, and, sitting, he kept his father at the table with him.

"Wilky," said the old man, "have you gone down to the baths here yet?"

"No, Dad, not yet."

"Well, you know the Gloriana has one of the finest pools in New York. Eighty feet, blue tile. It's a beauty."

Wilhelm had seen it. On the way to the gin game you passed the stairway to the pool. He did not care for the odor of the wall-locked and chlorinated water.

"You ought to investigate the Russian and Turkish baths,

and the sunlamps and massage. I don't hold with sunlamps. But the massage does a world of good, and there's nothing better than hydrotherapy when you come right down to it. Simple water has a calming effect and would do you more good than all the barbiturates and alcohol in the world."

Wilhelm reflected that this advice was as far as his father's help and sympathy would extend.

"I thought," he said, "that the water cure was for lunatics."

The doctor received this as one of his son's jokes and said with a smile, "Well, it won't turn a sane man into a lunatic. It does a great deal for me. I couldn't live without my massages and steam."

"You're probably right. I ought to try it one of these days. Yesterday, late in the afternoon, my head was about to bust and I just had to have a little air, so I walked around the Reservoir, and I sat down for a while in a playground. It rests me to watch the kids play potsy and skiprope."

The doctor said with approval, "Well, now, that's more like the idea."

"It's the end of the lilacs," said Wilhelm. "When they burn it's the beginning of summer. At least, in the city. Around the time of year when the candy stores take down the windows and start to sell sodas on the sidewalk. But even though I was raised here, Dad, I can't take city life any more, and I miss the country. There's too much push here for me. It works me up too much. I take things too hard. I wonder why you never retired to a quieter place."

The doctor opened his small hand on the table in a gesture so old and so typical that Wilhelm felt it like an actual touch upon the foundations of his life. "I am a city boy myself, you must remember," Dr. Adler explained. "But if you find the city so hard on you, you ought to get out."

"I'll do that," said Wilhelm, "as soon as I can make the right connection. Meanwhile—"

His father interrupted, "Meanwhile I suggest you cut down on drugs."

"You exaggerate that, Dad. I don't really— I give myself a little boost against—" He almost pronounced the word "misery" but he kept his resolution not to complain.

The doctor, however, fell into the error of pushing his advice too hard. It was all he had to give his son and he gave it once more. "Water and exercise," he said.

He wants a young, smart, successful son, thought Wilhelm, and he said, "Oh, Father, it's nice of you to give me this medical advice, but steam isn't going to cure what ails me."

The doctor measurably drew back, warned by the sudden weak strain of Wilhelm's voice and all that the droop of his face, the swell of his belly against the restraint of his belt intimated.

"Some new business?" he asked unwillingly.

Wilhelm made a great preliminary summary which involved the whole of his body. He drew and held a long breath, and his color changed and his eyes swam. "New?" he said.

"You make too much of your problems," said the doctor. "They ought not to be turned into a career. Concentrate on real troubles—fatal sickness, accidents." The old man's whole manner said, Wilky, don't start this on me. I have a right to be spared.

Wilhelm himself prayed for restraint; he knew this weakness of his and fought it. He knew, also, his father's character. And he began mildly, "As far as the fatal part of it goes, everyone on this side of the grave is the same distance from death. No, I guess my trouble is not exactly new. I've got to pay premiums on two policies for the boys. Margaret sent them to me. She unloads everything on me. Her mother left her an income. She won't even file a joint tax return. I get stuck. Etcetera. But you've heard the whole story before."

"I certainly have," said the old man. "And I've told you to stop giving her so much money."

Wilhelm worked his lips in silence before he could speak. The congestion was growing. "Oh, but my kids, Father. My kids. I love them. I don't want them to lack anything."

The doctor said with a half-deaf benevolence, "Well, naturally. And she, I'll bet, is the beneficiary of that policy."

"Let her be. I'd sooner die myself before I collected a cent of such money."

"Ah yes." The old man sighed. He did not like the mention of death. "Did I tell you that your sister Catherine—Philippa —is after me again."

"What for?"

"She wants to rent a gallery for an exhibition."

Stiffly fair-minded, Wilhelm said, "Well, of course that's up to you, Father."

The round-headed old man with his fine, feather-white, ferny hair said, "No, Wilky. There's not a thing on those canvases. I don't believe it; it's a case of the emperor's clothes. I may be old enough for my second childhood, but at least the first is well behind me. I was glad enough to buy crayons for her when she was four. But now she's a woman of forty and too old to be encouraged in her delusions. She's no painter."

"I wouldn't go so far as to call her a born artist," said Wilhelm, "but you can't blame her for trying something worth while."

"Let her husband pamper her."

Wilhelm had done his best to be just to his sister, and he had sincerely meant to spare his father, but the old man's tight, benevolent deafness had its usual effect on him. He said, "When it comes to women and money, I'm completely in the dark. What makes Margaret act like this?"

"She's showing you that you can't make it without her,"

said the doctor. "She aims to bring you back by financial force."

"But if she ruins me, Dad, how can she expect me to come back? No, I have a sense of honor. What you don't see is that she's trying to put an end to me."

His father stared. To him this was absurd. And Wilhelm thought, Once a guy starts to slip, he figures he might as well be a clunk. A real big clunk. He even takes pride in it. But there's nothing to be proud of—hey, boy? Nothing. I don't blame Dad for his attitude. And it's no cause for pride.

"I don't understand that. But if you feel like this why don't you settle with her once and for all?"

"What do you mean, Dad?" said Wilhelm, surprised. "I thought I told you. Do you think I'm not willing to settle? Four years ago when we broke up I gave her everything—goods, furniture, savings. I tried to show good will, but I didn't get anywhere. Why when I wanted Scissors, the dog, because the animal and I were so attached to each other—it was bad enough to leave the kids—she absolutely refused me. Not that she cared a damn about the animal. I don't think you've seen him. He's an Australian sheep dog. They usually have one blank or whitish eye which gives a misleading look, but they're the gentlest dogs and have unusual delicacy about eating or talking. Let me at least have the companionship of this animal. Never." Wilhelm was greatly moved. He wiped his face at all corners with his napkin. Dr. Adler felt that his son was indulging himself too much in his emotions.

"Whenever she can hit me, she hits, and she seems to live for that alone. And she demands more and more, and still more. Two years ago she wanted to go back to college and get another degree. It increased my burden but I thought it would be wiser in the end if she got a better job through it. But still she takes as much from me as before. Next thing she'll want to be a doctor of philosophy. She says the women in her family live long, and I'll have to pay and pay for the rest of my life."

The doctor said impatiently, "Well, these are details, not principles. Just details which you can leave out. The dog! You're mixing up all kinds of irrelevant things. Go to a good lawyer."

"But I've already told you, Dad. I got a lawyer, and she got one, too, and both of them talk and send me bills, and I eat my heart out. Oh, Dad, Dad, what a hole I'm in!" said Wilhelm in utter misery. "The lawyers—see?—draw up an agreement, and she says okay on Monday and wants more money on Tuesday. And it begins again."

"I always thought she was a strange kind of woman," said Dr. Adler. He felt that by disliking Margaret from the first and disapproving of the marriage he had done all that he could be expected to do.

"Strange, Father? I'll show you what she's like." Wilhelm took hold of his broad throat with brown-stained fingers and bitten nails and began to choke himself.

"What are you doing?" cried the old man.

"I'm showing you what she does to me."

"Stop that—stop it!" the old man said and tapped the table commandingly.

"Well, Dad, she hates me. I feel that she's strangling me. I can't catch my breath. She just has fixed herself on me to kill me. She can do it at long distance. One of these days I'll be struck down by suffocation or apoplexy because of her. I just can't catch my breath."

"Take your hands off your throat, you foolish man," said his father. "Stop this bunk. Don't expect me to believe in all kinds of voodoo."

"If that's what you want to call it, all right." His face flamed and paled and swelled and his breath was laborious.

"But I'm telling you that from the time I met her I've been a slave. The Emancipation Proclamation was only for colored people. A husband like me is a slave, with an iron collar. The churches go up to Albany and supervise the law. They won't have divorces. The court says, 'You want to be free. Then you have to work twice as hard—twice, at least! Work! you bum.' So then guys kill each other for the buck, and they may be free of a wife who hates them but they are sold to the company. The company knows a guy has got to have his salary, and takes full advantage of him. Don't talk to me about being free. A rich man may be free on an income of a million net. A poor man may be free because nobody cares what he does. But a fellow in my position has to sweat it out until he drops dead."

His father replied to this, "Wilky, it's entirely your own fault. You don't have to allow it."

Stopped in his eloquence, Wilhelm could not speak for a while. Dumb and incompetent, he struggled for breath and frowned with effort into his father's face.

"I don't understand your problems," said the old man. "I never had any like them."

By now Wilhelm had lost his head and he waved his hands and said over and over, "Oh, Dad, don't give me that stuff, don't give me that. Please don't give me that sort of thing."

"It's true," said his father. "I come from a different world. Your mother and I led an entirely different life."

"Oh, how can you compare Mother," Wilhelm said. "Mother was a help to you. Did she harm you ever?"

"There's no need to carry on like an opera, Wilky," said the doctor. "This is only your side of things."

"What? It's the truth," said Wilhelm.

The old man could not be persuaded and shook his round head and drew his vest down over the gilded shirt, and leaned back with a completeness of style that made this look, to any-one out of hearing, like an ordinary conversation between a middle-aged man and his respected father. Wilhelm towered and swayed, big and sloven, with his gray eyes red-shot and his honey-colored hair twisted in flaming shapes upward. In-justice made him angry, made him beg. But he wanted an understanding with his father, and he tried to capitulate to him. He said, "You can't compare Mother and Margaret, and neither can you and I be compared, because you, Dad, were a success. And a success—is a success. I never made a success."

The doctor's old face lost all of its composure and became hard and angry. His small breast rose sharply under the red and black shirt and he said, "Yes. Because of hard work. I was not self-indulgent, not lazy. My old man sold dry goods in Williamsburg. We were nothing, do you understand? I knew I couldn't afford to waste my chances."

"I wouldn't admit for one minute that I was lazy," said Wilhelm. "If anything, I tried too hard. I admit I made many mistakes. Like I thought I shouldn't do things you had done already. Study chemistry. You had done it already. It was in the family."

His father continued, "I didn't run around with fifty women, either. I was not a Hollywood star. I didn't have time to go to Cuba for a vacation. I stayed at home and took care of my children."

Oh, thought Wilhelm, eyes turning upward. Why did I come here in the first place, to live near him? New York is like a gas. The colors are running. My head feels so tight, I don't know what I'm doing. He thinks I want to take away his money or that I envy him. He doesn't see what I want.

"Dad," Wilhelm said aloud, "you're being very unfair. It's true the movies was a false step. But I love my boys. I didn't abandon them. I left Margaret because I had to."

"Why did you have to?"

"Well—" said Wilhelm, struggling to condense his many reasons into a few plain words. "I had to—I had to."

With sudden and surprising bluntness his father said, "Did you have bed-trouble with her? Then you should have stuck it out. Sooner or later everyone has it. Normal people stay with it. It passes. But you wouldn't, so now you pay for your stupid romantic notions. Have I made my view clear?"

It was very clear. Wilhelm seemed to hear it repeated from various sides and inclined his head different ways, and listened and thought. Finally he said, "I guess that's the medical standpoint. You may be right. I just couldn't live with Margaret. I wanted to stick it out, but I was getting very sick. She was one way and I was another. She wouldn't be like me, so I tried to be like her, and I couldn't do it."

"Are you sure she didn't tell *you* to go?" the doctor said.

"I wish she had. I'd be in a better position now. No, it was me. I didn't want to leave, but I couldn't stay. Somebody had to take the initiative. I did. Now I'm the fall guy too."

Pushing aside in advance all the objections that his son would make, the doctor said, "Why did you lose your job with Rojax?"

"I didn't, I've told you."

"You're lying. You wouldn't have ended the connection. You need the money too badly. But you must have got into trouble." The small old man spoke concisely and with great strength. "Since you have to talk and can't let it alone, tell the truth. Was there a scandal—a woman?"

Wilhelm fiercely defended himself. "No, Dad, there wasn't any woman. I told you how it was."

"Maybe it was a man, then," the old man said wickedly.

Shocked, Wilhelm stared at him with burning pallor and dry lips. His skin looked a little yellow. "I don't think you know what you're talking about," he answered after a moment. "You shouldn't let your imagination run so free. Since you've been living here on Broadway you must think you understand life, up-to-date. You ought to know your own son a little better. Let's drop that, now."

"All right, Wilky, I'll withdraw it. But something must have happened in Roxbury nevertheless. You'll never go back. You're just talking wildly about representing a rival company. You won't. You've done something to spoil your reputation, I think. But you've got girl friends who are expecting you back, isn't that so?"

"I take a lady out now and then while on the road," said Wilhelm. "I'm not a monk."

"No one special? Are you sure you haven't gotten into complications?"

He had tried to unburden himself and instead, Wilhelm thought, he had to undergo an inquisition to prove himself worthy of a sympathetic word. Because his father believed that he did all kinds of gross things.

"There is a woman in Roxbury that I went with. We fell in love and wanted to marry, but she got tired of waiting for my divorce. Margaret figured that. On top of which the girl was a Catholic and I had to go with her to the priest and make an explanation."

Neither did this last confession touch Dr. Adler's sympathies or sway his calm old head or affect the color of his complexion.

"No, no, no, no; all wrong," he said.

Again Wilhelm cautioned himself. Remember his age. He is no longer the same person. He can't bear trouble. I'm so choked up and congested anyway I can't see straight. Will I ever get out of the woods, and recover my balance? You're never the same afterward. Trouble rusts out the system.

"You really *want* a divorce?" said the old man.

"For the price I pay I should be getting something."

"In that case," Dr. Adler said, "it seems to me no normal person would stand for such treatment from a woman."

"Ah, Father, Father!" said Wilhelm. "It's always the same thing with you. Look how you lead me on. You always start out to help me with my problems, and be sympathetic and so forth. It gets my hopes up and I begin to be grateful. But before we're through I'm a hundred times more depressed than before. Why is that? You have no sympathy. You want to shift all the blame on to me. Maybe you're wise to do it." Wilhelm was beginning to lose himself. "All you seem to think about is your death. Well, I'm sorry. But I'm going to die too. And I'm your son. It isn't my fault in the first place. There ought to be a right way to do this, and be fair to each other. But what I want to know is, why do you start up with me if you're not going to help me? What do you want to know about my problems for, Father? So you can lay the whole responsibility on me—so that you won't have to help me? D'you want me to comfort you for having such a son?" Wilhelm had a great knot of wrong tied tight within his chest, and tears approached his eyes but he didn't let them out. He looked shabby enough as it was. His voice was thick and hazy, and he was stammering and could not bring his awful feelings forth.

"You have some purpose of your own," said the doctor, "in acting so unreasonable. What do you want from me? What do you expect?"

"What do I expect?" said Wilhelm. He felt as though he were unable to recover something. Like a ball in the surf, washed beyond reach, his self-control was going out. "I expect *help!*" The words escaped him in a loud, wild, frantic cry and startled the old man, and two or three breakfasters within hearing glanced their way. Wilhelm's hair, the color of whitened honey, rose dense and tall with the expansion of his face, and he said, "When I suffer—you aren't even sorry. That's because you have no affection for me, and you don't want any part of me."

"Why must I like the way you behave? No, I don't like it." said Dr. Adler.

"All right. You want me to change myself. But suppose I could do it—what would I become? What could I? Let's suppose that all my life I have had the wrong ideas about myself and wasn't what I thought I was. And wasn't even careful to take a few precautions, as most people do—like a woodchuck has a few exits to his tunnel. But what shall I do now? More than half my life is over. More than half. And now you tell me I'm not even normal."

The old man too had lost his calm. "You cry about being helped," he said. "When you thought you had to go into the service I sent a check to Margaret every month. As a family man you could have had an exemption. But no! The war couldn't be fought without you and you had to get yourself drafted and be an office-boy in the Pacific theater. Any clerk could have done what you did. You could find nothing better to become than a GI."

Wilhelm was going to reply, and half raised his bearish figure from the chair, his fingers spread and whitened by their grip on the table, but the old man would not let him begin. He said, "I see other elderly people here with children who aren't much good, and they keep backing them and holding them up at a great sacrifice. But I'm not going to make that mistake. It doesn't enter your mind that when I die—a year, two years from now—you'll still be here. I do think of it."

He had intended to say that he had a right to be left in peace. Instead he gave Wilhelm the impression that he meant it was not fair for the better man of the two, and the more useful, the more admired, to leave the world first. Perhaps he meant that, too—a little; but he would not under other circumstances have come out with it so flatly.

"Father," said Wilhelm with an unusual openness of appeal. "Don't you think I know how you feel? I have pity. I want you to live on and on. If you outlive me, that's perfectly okay by me." As his father did not answer this avowal and turned away his glance, Wilhelm suddenly burst out, "No, but you hate me. And if I had money you wouldn't. By God, you have to admit it. The money makes the difference. Then we would be a fine father and son, if I was a credit to you— so you could boast and brag about me all over the hotel. But I'm not the right type of son. I'm too old, I'm too old and too unlucky."

His father said, "I can't give you any money. There would be no end to it if I started. You and your sister would take every last buck from me. I'm still alive, not dead. I am still here. Life isn't over yet. I am as much alive as you or anyone. And I want nobody on my back. Get off! And I give you the same advice, Wilky. Carry nobody on your back."

"Just keep your money," said Wilhelm miserably. "Keep it and enjoy it yourself. That's the ticket!"

IV

Ass! Idiot! Wild boar! Dumb mule! Slave! Lousy, wallowing hippopotamus! Wilhelm called himself as his bending legs carried him from the dining room. His pride! His inflamed feelings! His begging and feebleness! And trading insults with his old father—and spreading confusion over everything. Oh, how poor, contemptible, and ridiculous he was! When he remembered how he had said, with great reproof, "You ought to know your own son"—why, how corny and abominable it was.

He could not get out of the sharply brilliant dining room fast enough. He was horribly worked up; his neck and shoul-

ders, his entire chest ached as though they had been tightly
tied with ropes. He smelled the salt odor of tears in his nose.

But at the same time, since there were depths in Wilhelm
not unsuspected by himself, he received a suggestion from
some remote element in his thoughts that the business of life,
the real business—to carry his peculiar burden, to feel shame
and impotence, to taste these quelled tears—the only important
business, the highest business was being done. Maybe the making of mistakes expressed the very purpose of his life and the
essence of his being here. Maybe he was supposed to make them
and suffer from them on this earth. And though he had raised
himself above Mr. Perls and his father because they adored
money, still they were called to act energetically and this was
better than to yell and cry, pray and beg, poke and blunder and
go by fits and starts and fall upon the thorns of life. And finally
sink beneath that watery floor—would that be tough luck, or
would it be good riddance?

But he raged once more against his father. Other people
with money, while they're still alive, want to see it do some
good. Granted, he shouldn't support me. But have I ever
asked him to do that? Have I ever asked for dough at all,
either for Margaret or for the kids or for myself? It isn't the
money, but only the assistance; not even assistance, but just the
feeling. But he may be trying to teach me that a grown man
should be cured of such feeling. Feeling got me in dutch at
Rojax. I had the *feeling* that I belonged to the firm, and my
feelings were hurt when they put Gerber in over me. Dad
thinks I'm too simple. But I'm not so simple as he thinks. What
about his feelings? He doesn't forget death for one single
second, and that's what makes him like this. And not only is
death on his mind but through money he forces me to think
about it, too. It gives him power over me. He forces me that
way, he himself, and then he's sore. If he were poor, I could care
for him and show it. The way I *could* care, too, if I only

had a chance. He'd see how much love and respect I had in me. It would make him a different man, too. He'd put his hands on me and give me his blessing."

Someone in a gray straw hat with a wide cocoa-colored band spoke to Wilhelm in the lobby. The light was dusky, splotched with red underfoot; green, the leather furniture; yellow, the indirect lighting.

"Hey, Tommy. Say, there."

"Excuse me," said Wilhelm, trying to reach a house phone. But this was Dr. Tamkin, whom he was just about to call.

"You have a very obsessional look on your face," said Dr. Tamkin.

Wilhlem thought, Here he is, Here he is. If I could only figure this guy out.

"Oh," he said to Tamkin. "Have I got such a look? Well, whatever it is, you name it and I'm sure to have it."

The sight of Dr. Tamkin brought his quarrel with his father to a close. He found himself flowing into another channel.

"What are we doing?" he said. "What's going to happen to lard today?"

"Don't worry yourself about that. All we have to do is hold on to it and it's sure to go up. But what's made you so hot under the collar, Wilhelm?"

"Oh, one of those family situations." This was the moment to take a new look at Tamkin, and he viewed him closely but gained nothing by the new effort. It was conceivable that Tamkin was everything that he claimed to be, and all the gossip false. But was he a scientific man, or not? If he was not, this might be a case for the district attorney's office to investigate. Was he a liar? That was a delicate question. Even a liar might be trustworthy in some ways. Could he trust Tamkin— could he? He feverishly, fruitlessly sought an answer.

But the time for this question was past, and he had to trust him now. After a long struggle to come to a decision, he had given him the money. Practical judgment was in abeyance. He had worn himself out, and the decision was no decision. How had this happened? But how had his Hollywood career begun? It was not because of Maurice Venice, who turned out to be a pimp. It was because Wilhelm himself was ripe for the mistake. His marriage, too, had been like that. Through such decisions somehow his life had taken form. And so, from the moment when he tasted the peculiar flavor of fatality in Dr. Tamkin, he could no longer keep back the money.

Five days ago Tamkin had said, "Meet me tomorrow, and we'll go to the market." Wilhelm, therefore, had had to go. At eleven o'clock they had walked to the brokerage office. On the way, Tamkin broke the news to Wilhelm that though this was an equal partnership he couldn't put up his half of the money just yet; it was tied up for a week or so in one of his patents. Today he would be two hundred dollars short; next week, he'd make it up. But neither of them needed an income from the market, of course. This was only a sporting proposition anyhow, Tamkin said. Wilhelm had to answer, "Of course." It was too late to withdraw. What else could he do? Then came the formal part of the transaction, and it was frightening. The very shade of green of Tamkin's check looked wrong; it was a false, disheartening color. His handwriting was peculiar, even monstrous; the e's were like i's, the t's and l's the same, and the h's like wasps' bellies. He wrote like a fourth-grader. Scientists, however, dealt mostly in symbols; they printed. This was Wilhelm's explanation.

Dr. Tamkin had given him his check for three hundred dollars. Wilhelm, in a blinded and convulsed aberration, pressed and pressed to try to kill the trembling of his hand as he wrote out his check for a thousand. He set his lips tight, crouched with his huge back over the table, and wrote with crumbling, terrified fingers, knowing that if Tamkin's check bounced his own would not be honored either. His sole cleverness was to set the date ahead by one day to give the green check time to clear.

Next he had signed a power of attorney, allowing Tamkin to speculate with his money, and this was an even more frightening document. Tamkin had never said a word about it, but here they were and it had to be done.

After delivering his signatures, the only precaution Wilhelm took was to come back to the manager of the brokerage office and ask him privately, "Uh, about Doctor Tamkin. We were in here a few minutes ago, remember?"

That day had been a weeping, smoky one and Wilhelm had gotten away from Tamkin on the pretext of having to run to the post office. Tamkin had gone to lunch alone, and here was Wilhelm, back again, breathless, his hat dripping, needlessly asking the manager if he remembered.

"Yes, sir, I know," the manager had said. He was a cold, mild, lean German who dressed correctly and around his neck wore a pair of opera glasses with which he read the board. He was an extremely correct person except that he never shaved in the morning, not caring, probably, how he looked to the fumblers and the old people and the operators and the gamblers and the idlers of Broadway uptown. The market closed at three. Maybe, Wilhelm guessed, he had a thick beard and took a lady out to dinner later and wanted to look fresh-shaven.

"Just a question," said Wilhelm. "A few minutes ago I signed a power of attorney so Doctor Tamkin could invest for me. You gave me the blanks."

"Yes, sir, I remember."

"Now this is what I want to know," Wilhelm had said. "I'm no lawyer and I only gave the paper a glance. Does this give Doctor Tamkin power of attorney over any other assets of mine—money, or property?"

The rain had dribbled from Wilhelm's deformed, transparent raincoat; the buttons of his shirt, which always seemed tiny, were partly broken, in pearly quarters of the moon, and some of the dark, thick golden hairs that grew on his belly stood out. It was the manager's business to conceal his opinion of him; he was shrewd, gray, correct (although unshaven) and had little to say except on matters that came to his desk. He must have recognized in Wilhelm a man who reflected long and then made the decision he had rejected twenty separate times. Silvery, cool, level, long-profiled, experienced, indifferent, observant, with unshaven refinement, he scarcely looked at Wilhelm, who trembled with fearful awkwardness. The manager's face, low-colored, long-nostriled, acted as a unit of perception; his eyes merely did their reduced share. Here was a man, like Rubin, who knew and knew and knew. He, a foreigner, knew; Wilhelm, in the city of his birth, was ignorant.

The manager had said, "No, sir, it does not give him."

"Only over the funds I deposited with you?"

"Yes, that is right, sir."

"Thank you, that's what I wanted to find out," Wilhelm had said, grateful.

The answer comforted him. However, the question had no value. None at all. For Wilhelm had no other assets. He had given Tamkin his last money. There wasn't enough of it to cover his obligations anyway, and Wilhelm had reckoned that he might as well go bankrupt now as next month. "Either broke or rich," was how he had figured, and that formula had encouraged him to make the gamble. Well, not rich; he did not expect that, but perhaps Tamkin might really show him how to earn what he needed in the market. By now, however, he had forgotten his own reckoning and was aware only that he stood to lose his seven hundred dollars to the last cent.

Dr. Tamkin took the attitude that they were a pair of gentlemen experimenting with lard and grain futures. The money, a few hundred dollars, meant nothing much to either of them. He said to Wilhlem, "Watch. You'll get a big kick out of this and wonder why more people don't go into it. You think the Wall Street guys are so smart—geniuses? That's because most of us are psychologically afraid to think about the details. Tell me this. When you're on the road, and you don't understand what goes on under the hood of your car, you'll worry what'll happen if something goes wrong with the engine. Am I wrong?" No, he was right. "Well," said Dr. Tamkin with an expression of quiet triumph about his mouth, almost the suggestion of a jeer. "It's the same psychological principle, Wilhelm. They are rich because you don't understand what goes on. But it's no mystery, and by putting in a little money and applying certain principles of observation, you begin to grasp it. It can't be studied in the abstract. You have to take a specimen risk so that you feel the process, the money-flow, the whole complex. To know how it feels to be a seaweed you have to get in the water. In a very short time we'll take out a hundred-per-cent profit." Thus Wilhelm had had to pretend at the outset that his interest in the market was theoretical.

"Well," said Tamkin when he met him now in the lobby, "what's the problem, what is this family situation? Tell me." He put himself forward as the keen mental scientist. Whenever this happened Wilhelm didn't know what to reply. No matter what he said or did it seemed that Dr. Tamkin saw through him.

"I had some words with my dad."

Dr. Tamkin found nothing extraordinary in this. "It's the eternal same story." he said. "The elemental conflict of parent and child. It won't end, ever. Even with a fine old gentleman like your dad."

"I don't suppose it will. I've never been able to get anywhere with him. He objects to my feelings. He thinks they're sordid. I upset him and he gets mad at me. But maybe all old men are alike."

"Sons, too. Take it from one of them," said Dr. Tamkin. "All the same, you should be proud of such a fine old patriarch of a father. It should give you hope. The longer he lives, the longer your life expectancy becomes."

Wilhelm answered, brooding, "I guess so. But I think I inherit more from my mother's side, and she died in her fifties."

"A problem arose between a young fellow I'm treating and his dad—I just had a consultation," said Dr. Tamkin as he removed his dark gray hat.

"So early in the morning?" said Wilhelm with suspicion.

"Over the telephone, of course."

What a creature Tamkin was when he took off his hat! The indirect light showed the many complexities of his bald skull, his gull's nose, his rather handsome eyebrows, his vain mustache, his deceiver's brown eyes. His figure was stocky, rigid, short in the neck, so that the large ball of the occiput touched his collar. His bones were peculiarly formed, as though twisted twice where the ordinary human bone was turned only once, and his shoulders rose in two pagodalike points. At midbody he was thick. He stood pigeon-toed, a sign perhaps that he was devious or had much to hide. The skin of his hands was aging, and his nails were moonless, concave, clawlike, and they appeared loose. His eyes were as brown as beaver fur and full of strange lines. The two large brown naked balls looked thoughtful—but were they? And honest—but was Dr. Tamkin honest? There was a hypnotic power in his eyes, but this was not always of the same strength, nor was Wilhelm convinced that it was completely natural. He felt that Tamkin tried to make his eyes deliberately conspicuous, with studied art, and that he brought forth his hypnotic effect by an exertion. Occasionally it failed or drooped, and when this happened the sense of his face passed downward to his heavy (possibly foolish?) red underlip.

Wilhelm wanted to talk about the lard holdings, but Dr. Tamkin said, "This father-and-son case of mine would be instructive to you. It's a different psychological type completely than your dad. This man's father thinks that he isn't his son."

"Why not?"

"Because he has found out something about the mother carrying on with a friend of the family for twenty-five years."

"Well, what do you know!" said Wilhelm. His silent thought was, Pure bull. Nothing but bull!

"You must note how interesting the woman is, too. She has two husbands. Whose are the kids? The fellow detected her and she gave a signed confession that two of the four children were not the father's."

"It's amazing," said Wilhelm, but he said it in a rather distant way He was always hearing such stories from Dr. Tamkin. If you were to believe Tamkin, most of the world was like this. Everybody in the hotel had a mental disorder, a secret history, a concealed disease. The wife of Rubin at the newsstand was supposed to be kept by Carl, the yelling, loud-mouthed gin-rummy player. The wife of Frank in the barbershop had disappeared with a GI while he was waiting for her to disembark at the French Lines pier. Everyone was like the faces on a playing card, upside down either way. Every public figure had a character neurosis. Maddest of all were the businessmen, the heartless, flaunting, boisterous business class who ruled this country with their hard manners and their bold lies and their absurd words that nobody could believe. They were crazier than anyone. They spread the plague. Wilhelm, thinking of the Rojax Corporation, was inclined to agree that many businessmen were insane. And he supposed that Tamkin, for all his peculiarities, spoke a kind of truth and did some people a sort of good. It confirmed Wilhelm's suspicions to hear that there was a plague, and he said, "I couldn't agree with you more. They trade on anything, they steal everything, they're cynical right to the bones."

"You have to realize," said Tamkin, speaking of his patient, or his client, "that the mother's confession isn't good. It's a confession of duress. I try to tell the young fellow he shouldn't worry about a phony confession. But what does it help him if I am rational with him?"

"No?" said Wilhelm, intensely nervous. "I think we ought to go over to the market. It'll be opening pretty soon."

"Oh, come on," said Tamkin. "It isn't even nine o'clock, and there isn't much trading the first hour anyway. Things don't get hot in Chicago until half-past ten, and they're an hour behind us, don't forget. Anyway, I say lard will go up, and it will. Take my word. I've made a study of the guilt-aggression cycle which is behind it. I ought to know *something* about that. Straighten your collar."

"But meantime," said Wilhelm, "we have taken a licking this week. Are you sure your insight is at its best? Maybe when it isn't we should lay off and wait."

"Don't you realize," Dr. Tamkin told him, "you can't march in a straight line to the victory? You fluctuate toward it. From Euclid to Newton there was straight lines. The modern age analyzes the wavers. On my own accounts, I took a licking in hides and coffee. But I have confidence. I'm sure I'll out-guess them." He gave Wilhelm a narrow smile, friendly, calming, shrewd, and wizardlike, patronizing, secret, potent. He saw his fears and smiled at them. "It's something," he remarked, "to see how the competition-factor will manifest itself in different individuals."

"So? Let's go over."

"But I haven't had my breakfast yet."

"I've had mine."

"Come, have a cup of coffee."

"I wouldn't want to meet my dad." Looking through the glass doors, Wilhelm saw that his father had left by the other exit. Wilhelm thought, He didn't want to run into me, either. He said to Dr. Tamkin, "Okay, I'll sit with you, but let's hurry it up because I'd like to get to the market while there's still a place to sit. Everybody and his uncle gets in ahead of you."

"I want to tell you about this boy and his dad. It's highly absorbing. The father was a nudist. Everybody went naked in the house. Maybe the woman found men *with* clothes attractive. Her husband didn't believe in cutting his hair, either. He practiced dentistry. In his office he wore riding pants and a pair of boots, and he wore a green eyeshade."

"Oh, come off it," said Wilhelm.

"This is a true case history."

Without warning, Wilhelm began to laugh. He himself had had no premonition of his change of humor. His face became warm and pleasant, and he forgot his father, his anxieties; he panted bearlike, happily, through his teeth. "This sounds like a horse-dentist. He wouldn't have to put on pants to treat a horse. Now what else are you going to tell me? Did the wife play the mandolin? Does the boy join the cavalry? Oh, Tamkin, you really are a killer-diller."

"Oh, you think I'm trying to amuse you," said Tamkin. "That's because you aren't familiar with my outlook. I deal in facts. Facts always are sensational. I'll say that a second time. Facts *always!* are sensational."

Wilhelm was reluctant to part with his good mood. The doctor had little sense of humor. He was looking at him earnestly.

"I'd bet you any amount of money," said Tamkin, "that the facts about you are sensational."

"Oh—ha, ha! You want them? You can sell them to a true-confession magazine."

"People forget how sensational the things are that they do. They don't see it on themselves. It blends into the background of their daily life."

Wilhelm smiled. "Are you sure this boy tells you the truth?"

"Yes, because I've known the whole family for years."

"And you do psychological work with your own friends? I didn't know that was allowed."

"Well, I'm a radical in the profession. I have to do good wherever I can."

Wilhelm's face became ponderous again and pale. His whitened gold hair lay heavy on his head, and he clasped uneasy fingers on the table. Sensational, but oddly enough, dull, too. Now how do you figure that out? It blends with the background. Funny but unfunny. True but false. Casual but laborious, Tamkin was. Wilhelm was most suspicious of him when he took his driest tone.

"With me," said Dr. Tamkin, "I am at my most efficient when I don't need the fee. When I only love. Without a financial reward. I remove myself from the social influence. Especially money. The spiritual compensation is what I look for. Bringing people into the here-and-now. The real universe. That's the present moment. The past is no good to us. The future is full of anxiety. Only the present is real—the here-and-now. Seize the day."

"Well," said Wilhelm, his earnestness returning. "I know you are a very unusual man. I like what you say about here-and-now. Are all the people who come to see you personal friends and patients too? Like that tall handsome girl, the one who always wears those beautiful broomstick skirts and belts?"

"She was an epileptic, and a most bad and serious pathology, too. I'm curing her successfully. She hasn't had a seizure in six months, and she used to have one every week."

"And that young cameraman, the one who showed us those movies from the jungles of Brazil, isn't he related to her?"

"Her brother. He's under my care, too. He has some terrible tendencies, which are to be expected when you have an epileptic sibling. I came into their lives when they needed help desperately, and took hold of them. A certain man forty years older than she had her in his control and used to give her fits by suggestion whenever she tried to leave him. If you only knew one per cent of what goes on in the city of New York! You see, I understand what it is when the lonely person begins to feel like an animal. When the night comes and he feels like howling from his window like a wolf. I'm taking complete care of that young fellow and his sister. I have to steady him down or he'll go from Brazil to Australia the next day. The way I keep him in the here-and-now is by teaching him Greek."

This was a complete surprise! "What, do you know Greek?"

"A friend of mine taught me when I was in Cairo. I studied Aristotle with him to keep from being idle."

Wilhelm tried to take in these new claims and examine them. Howling from the window like a wolf when night comes sounded genuine to him. That was something really to think about. But the Greek! He realized that Tamkin was watching to see how he took it. More elements were continually being added. A few days ago Tamkin had hinted that he had once been in the underworld, one of the Detroit Purple Gang. He was once head of a mental clinic in Toledo. He had worked with a Polish inventor on an unsinkable ship. He was a technical consultant in the field of television. In the life of a man of genius, all of these things might happen. But had they happened to Tamkin? Was he a genius? He often said that he had attended some of the Egyptian royal family as a psychiatrist. "But everybody is alike, common or aristocrat," he told Wilhelm. "The aristocrat knows less about life."

An Egyptian princess whom he had treated in California, for horrible disorders he had described to Wilhelm, retained him to come back to the old country with her, and there he had

had many of her friends and relatives under his care. They turned over a villa on the Nile to him. "For ethical reasons, I can't tell you many of the details about them," he said— but Wilhelm had already heard all these details, and strange and shocking they were, if true. *If* true—he could not be free from doubt. For instance, the general who had to wear ladies' silk stockings and stand otherwise naked before the mirror— and all the rest. Listening to the doctor when he was so strangely factual, Wilhelm had to translate his words into his own language, and he could not translate fast enough or find terms to fit what he heard.

"Those Egyptian big shots invested in the market, too, for the heck of it. What did they need extra money for? By association, I almost became a millionaire myself, and if I had played it smart there's no telling what might have happened. I could have been the ambassador." The American? The Egyptian ambassador? "A friend of mine tipped me off on the cotton. I made a heavy purchase of it. I didn't have that kind of money, but everybody there knew me. It never entered their minds that a person of their social circle didn't have dough. The sale was made on the phone. Then, while the cotton shipment was at sea, the price tripled. When the stuff suddenly became so valuable all hell broke loose on the world cotton market, they looked to see who was the owner of this big shipment. Me! They investigated my credit and found out I was a mere doctor, and they canceled. This was illegal. I sued them. But as I didn't have the money to fight them I sold the suit to a Wall Street lawyer for twenty thousand dollars. He fought it and was winning. They settled with him out of court for more than a million. But on the way back from Cairo, flying, there was a crash. All on board died. I have this guilt on my conscience, of being the murderer of that lawyer. Although he was a crook."

Wilhelm thought, I must be a real jerk to sit and listen to such impossible stories. I guess I am a sucker for people who talk about the deeper things of life, even the way he does.

"We scientific men speak of irrational guilt, Wilhelm," said Dr. Tamkin, as if Wilhelm were a pupil in his class. "But in such a situation, because of the money, I wished him harm. I realize it. This isn't the time to describe all the details, but the money made me guilty. *Money* and *Murder* both begin with *M*. *Machinery*. *Mischief*."

Wilhelm, his mind thinking for him at random, said, "What about *Mercy*? *Milk-of-human-kindness*?"

"One fact should be clear to you by now. Money-making is aggression. That's the whole thing. The functionalistic explanation is the only one. People come to the market to kill. They say, 'I'm going to make a killing.' It's not accidental. Only they haven't got the genuine courage to kill, and they erect a symbol of it. The money. They make a killing by a fantasy. Now, counting any number is always a sadistic activity. Like hitting. In the Bible, the Jews wouldn't allow you to count them. They knew it was sadistic."

"I don't understand what you mean," said Wilhelm. A strange uneasiness tore at him. The day was growing too warm and his head felt dim. "What makes them want to kill?"

"By and by, you'll get the drift," Dr. Tamkin assured him. His amazing eyes had some of the rich dryness of a brown fur. Innumerable crystalline hairs or spicules of light glittered in their bold surfaces. "You can't understand without first spending years on the study of the ultimates of human and animal behavior, the deep chemical, organismic, and spiritual secrets of life. I am a psychological poet."

"If you're this kind of poet," said Wilhelm, whose fingers in his pocket were feeling in the little envelopes for the Phenaphen capsules, "what are you doing on the market?"

"That's a good question. Maybe I am better at speculation because I don't care. Basically, I don't wish hard enough for money, and therefore I come with a cool head to it."

Wilhelm thought, Oh, sure! That's an answer, is it? I bet that if I took a strong attitude he'd back down on everything. He'd grovel in front of me. The way he looks at me on the sly, to see if I'm being taken in! He swallowed his Phenaphen pill with a long gulp of water. The rims of his eyes grew red as it went down. And then he felt calmer.

"Let me see if I can give you an answer that will satisfy you," said Dr. Tamkin. His flapjacks were set before him. He spread the butter on them, poured on brown maple syrup, quartered them, and began to eat with hard, active, muscular jaws which sometimes gave a creak at the hinges. He pressed the handle of his knife against his chest and said, "In here, the human bosom—mine, yours, everybody's—there isn't just one soul. There's a lot of souls. But there are two main ones, the real soul and a pretender soul. Now! Every man realizes that he has to love something or somebody. He feels that he must go outward. 'If thou canst not love, what art thou?' Are you with me?"

"Yes, Doc, I think so," said Wilhelm listening—a little skeptically but nonetheless hard.

" 'What art thou?' Nothing. That's the answer. Nothing. In the heart of hearts—Nothing! So of course you can't stand that and want to be Something, and you try. But instead of being this Something, the man puts it over on everybody instead. You can't be that strict to yourself. You love a *little*. Like you have a dog" (*Scissors!*) "or give some money to a charity drive. Now that isn't love, is it? What is it? Egotism, pure and simple. It's a way to love the pretender soul. Vanity. Only vanity is what it is. And social control. The interest of the pretender soul is the same as the interest of the social life, the society mechanism. This is the main tragedy of human life. Oh, it is terrible! Terrible! You are not free. Your own betrayer is inside of you and sells you out. You have to obey him like a slave. He makes you work like a horse. And for what? For who?"

"Yes, for what?" The doctor's words caught Wilhelm's heart. "I couldn't agree more," he said. "When do we get free?"

"The purpose is to keep the whole thing going. The true soul is the one that pays the price. It suffers and gets sick, and it realizes that the pretender can't be loved. Because the pretender is a lie. The true soul loves the truth. And when the true soul feels like this, it wants to kill the pretender. The love has turned into hate. Then you become dangerous. A killer. You have to kill the deceiver."

"Does this happen to everybody?"

The doctor answered simply, "Yes, to everybody. Of course, for simplification purposes, I have spoken of the soul; it isn't a scientific term, but it helps you to understand it. Whenever the slayer slays, he wants to slay the soul in him which has gypped and deceived him. Who is his enemy? Him. And his lover? Also. Therefore, all suicide is murder, and all murder is suicide. It's the one and identical phenomenon. Biologically, the pretender soul takes away the energy of the true soul and makes it feeble, like a parasite. It happens unconsciously, unawaringly, in the depths of the organism. Ever take up parasitology?"

"No, it's my dad who's the doctor."

"You should read a book about it."

Wilhelm said, "But this means that the world is full of murderers. So it's not the world. It's a kind of hell."

"Sure," the doctor said. "At least a kind of purgiatory. You walk on the bodies. They are all around. I can hear them cry *de profundis* and wring their hands. I hear them, poor human beasts. I can't help hearing. And my eyes are open to it. I have to cry, too. This is the human tragedy-comedy."

Wilhelm tried to capture his vision. And again the doctor looked untrustworthy to him, and he doubted him. "Well," he said, "there are also kind, ordinary, helpful people. They're— out in the country. All over. What kind of morbid stuff do you read, anyway?" The doctor's room was full of books.

"I read the best of literature, science and philosophy," Dr. Tamkin said. Wilhelm had observed that in his room even the TV aerial was set upon a pile of volumes. "Korzybski, Aristotle, Freud, W. H. Sheldon, and all the great poets. You answer me like a layman. You haven't applied your mind strictly to this."

"Very interesting," said Wilhelm. He was aware that he hadn't applied his mind strictly to anything. "You don't have to think I'm a dummy, though. I have ideas, too." A glance at the clock told him that the market would soon open. They could spare a few minutes yet. There were still more things he wanted to hear from Tamkin. He realized that Tamkin spoke faultily, but then scientific men were not always strictly literate. It was the description of the two souls that had awed him. In Tommy he saw the pretender. And even Wilky might not be himself. Might the name of his true soul be the one by which his old grandfather had called him—Velvel? The name of a soul, however, must be only that—soul. What did it look like? Does my soul look like me? Is there a soul that looks like Dad? Like Tamkin? Where does the true soul get its strength? Why does it have to love truth? Wilhelm was tormented, but tried to be oblivious to his torment. Secretly, he prayed the doctor would give him some useful advice and transform his life. "Yes, I understand you," he said. "It isn't lost on me."

"I never said you weren't intelligent, but only you just haven't made a study of it all. As a matter of fact you're a profound personality with very profound creative capacities but also disturbances. I've been concerned with you, and for some time I've been treating you."

"Without my knowing it? I haven't felt you doing anything. What do you mean? I don't think I like being treated without my knowledge. I'm of two minds. What's the matter, don't you think I'm normal?" And he really was divided in mind. That the doctor cared about him pleased him. This was what he craved, that someone should care about him, wish him well. Kindness, mercy, he wanted. But—and here he retracted his heavy shoulders in his peculiar way, drawing his hands up into his sleeves; his feet moved uneasily under the table—but he was worried, too, and even somewhat indignant. For what right had Tamkin to meddle without being asked? What kind of privileged life did this man lead? He took other people's money and speculated with it. Everybody came under his care. No one could have secrets from him.

The doctor looked at him with his deadly brown, heavy, impenetrable eyes, his naked shining head, his red hanging underlip, and said, "You have lots of guilt in you."

Wilhelm helplessly admitted, as he felt the heat rise to his wide face, "Yes, I think so too. But personally," he added, "I don't feel like a murderer. I always try to lay off. It's the others who get me. You know—make me feel oppressed. And if you don't mind, and it's all the same to you, I would rather know it when you start to treat me. And now, Tamkin, for Christ's sake, they're putting out the lunch menus already. Will you sign the check, and let's go!"

Tamkin did as he asked, and they rose. They were passing the bookkeeper's desk when he took out a substantial bundle of onionskin papers and said, "These are receipts of the transactions. Duplicates. You'd better keep them as the account is in your name and you'll need them for income taxes. And here is a copy of a poem I wrote yesterday."

"I have to leave something at the desk for my father," Wilhelm said, and he put his hotel bill in an envelope with a note. *Dear Dad, Please carry me this month, Yours, W.* He watched the clerk with his sullen pug's profile and his stiff-necked look push the envelope into his father's box.

"May I ask you really why you and your dad had words?" said Dr. Tamkin, who had hung back, waiting.

"It was about my future," said Wilhelm. He hurried down the stairs with swift steps, like a tower in motion, his hands in his trousers pockets. He was ashamed to discuss the matter. "He says there's a reason why I can't go back to my old territory, and there is. I told everybody I was going to be an officer of the corporation. And I was supposed to. It was promised. But then they welshed because of the son-in-law. I bragged and made myself look big."

"If you was humble enough, you could go back. But it doesn't make much difference. We'll make you a good living on the market."

They came into the sunshine of upper Broadway, not clear but throbbing through the dust and fumes, a false air of gas visible at eye level as it spurted from the bursting buses. From old habit, Wilhelm turned up the collar of his jacket.

"Just a technical question," Wilhelm said. "What happens if your losses are bigger than your deposit?"

"Don't worry. They have ultramodern electronic book-keeping machinery, and it won't let you get in debt. It puts you out automatically. But I want you to read this poem. You haven't read it yet."

Light as a locust, a helicopter bringing mail from Newark Airport to La Guardia sprang over the city in a long leap.

The paper Wilhelm unfolded had ruled borders in red ink. He read:

MECHANISM VS FUNCTIONALISM
ISM VS HISM

If thee thyself couldst only see
Thy greatness that is and yet to be,
Thou would feel joy-beauty-what ecstasy.
They are at thy feet, earth-moon-sea, the trinity.

Why-forth then dost thou tarry
And partake thee only of the crust
And skim the earth's surface narry
When all creations art thy just?

Seek ye then that which art not there
In thine own glory let thyself rest.
Witness. Thy power is not bare.
Thou art King. Thou art at thy best.

Look then right before thee.
Open thine eyes and see.
At the foot of Mt. Serenity
Is thy cradle to eternity.

Utterly confused, Wilhelm said to himself explosively, What kind of mishmash, claptrap is this! What does he want from me? Damn him to hell, he might as well hit me on the head, and lay me out, kill me. What does he give me this for? What's the purpose? Is it a deliberate test? Does he want to mix me up? He's already got me mixed up completely. I was never good at riddles. Kiss those seven hundred bucks good-by, and call it one more mistake in a long line of mistakes— Oh, Mama, what a line! He stood near the shining window of a fancy fruit store, holding Tamkin's paper, rather dazed, as though a charge of photographer's flash powder had gone up in his eyes.

But he's waiting for my reaction. I have to say something to him about his poem. It really is no joke. What will I tell him? Who is this King? The poem is written *to* someone. But who? I can't even bring myself to talk. I feel too choked and strangled. With all the books he reads, how come the guy is so illiterate? And why do people just naturally assume that you'll know what they're talking about? No. I don't know, and nobody knows. The planets don't, the stars don't, infinite space doesn't. It doesn't square with Planck's Constant or anything else. So what's the good of it? Where's the need of it? What does he mean here by Mount Serenity? Could it be a figure of speech for Mount Everest? As he says people are all committing suicide, maybe those guys who climbed Everest were only trying to kill themselves, and if we want peace we should stay at the foot of the mountain. In the here-and-now. But it's also here-and-now on the slope, and on the top, where they climbed to seize the day. Surface narry is something he can't mean, I don't believe. I'm about to start foaming at the mouth. "Thy cradle . . ." *Who* is resting in his cradle—in his glory? My thoughts are at an end. I feel the wall. No more. So ——k it all! The money and everything. Take it away! When I have the money they eat me alive, like those piranha fish in the movie about the Brazilian jungle. It was hideous when they ate up that Brahma bull in the river. He turned pale, just like clay, and in five minutes nothing was left except the skeleton still in one piece, floating away. When I haven't got it any more, at least they'll let me alone.

"Well, what do you think of this?" said Dr. Tamkin. He gave a special sort of wise smile, as though Wilhelm must now see what kind of man he was dealing with.

"Nice. Very nice. Have you been writing long?"

"I've been developing this line of thought for years and years. You follow it all the way?"

"I'm trying to figure out who this Thou is."

"Thou? Thou is you."

"Me! Why? This applies to *me?*"

"Why shouldn't it apply to you. You were in my mind when I composed it. Of course, the hero of the poem is sick humanity. If it would open its eyes it would be great."

"Yes, but how do I get into this?"

"The main idea of the poem is *con*struct or *de*struct. There is no ground in between. Mechanism is *de*struct. Money of course is *de*struct. When the last grave is dug, the gravedigger will have to be paid. If you could have confidence in nature you would not have to fear. It would keep you up. Creative is nature. Rapid. Lavish. Inspirational. It shapes leaves. It rolls the waters of the earth. Man is the chief of this. All creations are his just inheritance. You don't know what you've got within you. A person either creates or he destroys. There is no neutrality . . ."

"I realized you were no beginner," said Wilhelm with propriety. "I have only one criticism to make. I think 'why-forth' is wrong. You should write 'Wherefore then dost thou . . .' " And he reflected, So? I took a gamble. It'll have to be a miracle, though, to save me. My money will be gone, then it won't be able to destruct me. He can't just take and lose it, though. He's in it, too. I think he's in a bad way himself. He must be. I'm sure because, come to think of it, he sweated blood when he signed that check. But what have I let myself in for? The waters of the earth are going to roll over me.

v

Patiently, in the window of the fruit store, a man with a scoop spread crushed ice between his rows of vegetables. There were also Persian melons, lilacs, tulips with radiant black at the middle. The many street noises came back after a little while from the caves of the sky. Crossing the tide of Broadway traffic, Wilhelm was saying to himself, The reason Tamkin lectures me is that somebody has lectured him, and the reason for the poem is that he wants to give me good advice. Everybody seems to know something. Even fellows like Tamkin. Many people know what to do, but how many can do it?

He believed that he must, that he could and would recover the good things, the happy things, the easy tranquil things of life. He had made mistakes, but he could overlook these. He had been a fool, but that could be forgiven. The time wasted—must be relinquished. What else could one do about it? Things were too complex, but they might be reduced to simplicity again. Recovery was possible. First he had to get out of the city. No, first he had to pull out his money. . . .

From the carnival of the street—pushcarts, accordion and fiddle, shoeshine, begging, the dust going round like a woman on stilts—they entered the narrow crowded theater of the brokerage office. From front to back it was filled with the Broadway crowd. But how was lard doing this morning? From the rear of the hall Wilhelm tried to read the tiny figures. The German manager was looking through his binoculars. Tamkin placed himself on Wilhelm's left and covered his conspicuous bald head. "The guy'll ask me about the margin," he muttered. They passed, however, unobserved. "Look, the lard has held its place," he said.

Tamkin's eyes must be very sharp to read the figures over so many heads and at this distance—another respect in which he was unusual.

The room was always crowded. Everyone talked. Only at the front could you hear the flutter of the wheels within the board. Teletyped news items crossed the illuminated screen above.

"Lard. Now what about rye?" said Tamkin, rising on his toes. Here he was a different man, active and impatient. He parted people who stood in his way. His face turned resolute, and on either side of his mouth odd bulges formed under his mustache. Already he was pointing out to Wilhelm the appearance of a new pattern on the board. "There's something up today," he said.

"Then why'd you take so long with breakfast?" said Wilhelm.

There were no reserved seats in the room, only customary ones. Tamkin always sat in the second row, on the commodities side of the aisle. Some of his acquaintances kept their hats on the chairs for him.

"Thanks. Thanks," said Tamkin, and he told Wilhelm, "I fixed it up yesterday."

"That was a smart thought," said Wilhelm. They sat down.

With folded hands, by the wall, sat an old Chinese businessman in a seersucker coat. Smooth and fat, he wore a white Vandyke. One day Wilhelm had seen him on Riverside Drive pushing two little girls along in a baby carriage—his grandchildren. Then there were two women in their fifties, supposed to be sisters, shrewd and able money-makers, according to Tamkin. They had never a word to say to Wilhelm. But they would chat with Tamkin. Tamkin talked to everyone.

Wilhelm sat between Mr. Rowland, who was elderly, and Mr. Rappaport, who was very old. Yesterday Rowland had told him that in the year 1908, when he was a junior at Harvard, his mother had given him twenty shares of steel for his birthday, and then he had started to read the financial news and had never practiced law but instead followed the market for the rest of his life. Now he speculated only in soy beans, of which he had made a specialty. By his conservative method, said Tamkin, he cleared two hundred a week. Small potatoes, but then he was a bachelor, retired, and didn't need money.

"Without dependents," said Tamkin. "He doesn't have the problems that you and I do."

Did Tamkin have dependents? He had everything that it was possible for a man to have—science, Greek, chemistry, poetry, and now dependents too. That beautiful girl with epilepsy, perhaps. He often said that she was a pure, marvelous, spiritual child who had no knowledge of the world. He protected her, and, if he was not lying, adored her. And if you encouraged Tamkin by believing him, or even if you refrained from questioning him, his hints became more daring. Sometimes he said that he paid for her music lessons. Sometimes he seemed to have footed the bill for the brother's camera expedition to Brazil. And he spoke of paying for the support of the orphaned child of a dead sweetheart. These hints, made dully as asides, grew by repetition into sensational claims.

"For myself, I don't need much," said Tamkin. "But a man can't live for himself and I need the money for certain important things. What do you figure you have to have, to get by?"

"Not less than fifteen grand, after taxes. That's for my wife and the two boys."

"Isn't there anybody else?" said Tamkin with a shrewdness almost cruel. But his look grew more sympathetic as Wilhelm stumbled, not willing to recall another grief.

"Well—there was. But it wasn't a money matter."

"I should hope!" said Tamkin. "If love is love, it's free. Fifteen grand, though, isn't too much for a man of your intelligence to ask out of life. Fools, hard-hearted criminals, and murderers have millions to squander. They burn up the world —oil, coal, wood, metal, and soil, and suck even the air and the sky. They consume, and they give back no benefit. A man like you, humble for life, who wants to feel and live, has trouble— not wanting," said Tamkin in his parenthetical fashion, "to exchange an ounce of soul for a pound of social power—he'll never make it without help in a world like this. But don't you worry." Wilhelm grasped at this assurance. "Just you never mind. We'll go easily beyond your figure."

Dr. Tamkin gave Wilhelm comfort. He often said that he had made as much as a thousand a week in commodities.

Wilhelm had examined the receipts, but until this moment it had never occurred to him that there must be debit slips too; he had been shown only the credits.

"But fifteen grand is not an ambitious figure," Tamkin was telling him. "For that you don't have to wear yourself out on the road, dealing with narrow-minded people. A lot of them don't like Jews, either, I suppose?"

"I can't afford to notice. I'm lucky when I have my occupation. Tamkin, do you mean you can save our money?"

"Oh, did I forget to mention what I did before closing yesterday? You see, I closed out one of the lard contracts and bought a hedge of December rye. The rye is up three points already and takes some of the sting out. But lard will go up, too."

"Where? God, yes, you're right," said Wilhelm, eager, and got to his feet to look. New hope freshened his heart. "Why didn't you tell me before?"

And Tamkin, smiling like a benevolent magician, said, "You must learn to have trust. The slump in lard can't last. And just take a look at eggs. Didn't I predict they couldn't go any lower? They're rising and rising. If we had taken eggs we'd be far ahead."

"Then why didn't we take them?"

"We were just about to. I had a buying order in at .24, but the tide turned at .26¼ and we barely missed. Never mind. Lard will go back to last year's levels."

Maybe. But when? Wilhelm could not allow his hopes to grow too strong. However, for a little while he could breathe more easily. Late-morning trading was getting active. The shining numbers whirred on the board, which sounded like a huge cage of artificial birds. Lard fluctuated between two points, but rye slowly climbed.

He closed his strained, greatly earnest eyes briefly and

nodded his Buddha's head, too large to suffer such uncertainties. For several moments of peace he was removed to his small yard in Roxbury.

He breathed in the sugar of the pure morning.

He heard the long phrases of the birds.

No enemy wanted his life.

Wilhelm thought, I will get out of here. I don't belong in New York any more. And he sighed like a sleeper.

Tamkin said, "Excuse me," and left his seat. He could not sit still in the room but passed back and forth between the stocks and commodities sections. He knew dozens of people and was continually engaging in discussions. Was he giving advice, gathering information, or giving it, or practicing—whatever mysterious profession he practiced? Hypnotism? Perhaps he could put people in a trance while he talked to them. What a rare, peculiar bird he was, with those pointed shoulders, that bare head, his loose nails, almost claws, and those brown, soft, deadly, heavy eyes.

He spoke of things that mattered, and as very few people did this he could take you by surprise, excite you, move you. Maybe he wished to do good, maybe give himself a lift to a higher level, maybe believe his own prophecies, maybe touch his own heart. Who could tell? He had picked up a lot of strange ideas; Wilhelm could only suspect, he could not say with certainty, that Tamkin hadn't made them his own.

Now Tamkin and he were equal partners, but Tamkin had put up only three hundred dollars. Suppose he did this not only once but five times; then an investment of fifteen hundred dollars gave him five thousand to speculate with. If he had power of attorney in every case, he could shift the money from one account to another. No, the German probably kept an eye on him. Nevertheless it was possible. Calculations like this made Wilhelm feel ill. Obviously Tamkin was a plunger. But how did he get by? He must be in his fifties. How did he support himself? Five years in Egypt; Hollywood before that; Michigan; Ohio; Chicago. A man of fifty has supported himself for at least thirty years. You could be sure that Tamkin had never worked in a factory or in an office. How did he make it? His taste in clothes was horrible, but he didn't buy cheap things. He wore corduroy or velvet shirts from Clyde's, painted neckties, striped socks. There was a slightly acid or pasty smell about his person; for a doctor, he didn't bathe much. Also, Dr. Tamkin had a good room at the Gloriana and had had it for about a year. But so was Wilhelm himself a guest, with an unpaid bill at present in his father's box. Did the beautiful girl with the skirts and belts pay him? Was he defrauding his so-called patients? So many questions impossible to answer could not be asked about an honest man. Nor perhaps about a sane man. Was Tamkin a lunatic, then? That sick Mr. Perls at breakfast had said that there was no easy way to tell the sane from the mad, and he was right about that in any big city and especially in New York—the end of the world, with its complexity and machinery, bricks and tubes, wires and stones, holes and heights. And was everybody crazy here? What sort of people did you see? Every other man spoke a language entirely his own, which he had figured out by private thinking; he had his own ideas and peculiar ways. If you wanted to talk about a glass of water, you had to start back with God creating the heavens and earth; the apple; Abraham; Moses and Jesus; Rome; the Middle Ages; gunpowder; the Revolution; back to Newton; up to Einstein; then war and Lenin and Hitler. After reviewing this and getting it all straight again you could proceed to talk about a glass of water. "I'm fainting, please get me a little water." You were lucky even then to make yourself understood. And this happened over and over and over with everyone you met. You had to translate and translate, explain and explain, back and forth, and it was the punishment of hell itself not to understand or

be understood, not to know the crazy from the sane, the wise
from the fools, the young from the old or the sick from the
well. The fathers were no fathers and the sons no sons. You
had to talk with yourself in the daytime and reason with yourself at night. Who else was there to talk to in a city like New
York?

A queer look came over Wilhelm's face with its eyes turned
up and his silent mouth with its high upper lip. He went
several degrees further—when you are like this, dreaming that
everybody is outcast, you realize that this must be one of the
small matters. There is a larger body, and from this you cannot
be separated. The glass of water fades out. You do not go
from simple *a* and simple *b* to the great *x* and *y*, nor does it
matter whether you agree about the glass but, far beneath such
details, what Tamkin would call the real soul says plain and
understandable things to everyone. There sons and fathers are
themselves, and a glass of water is only an ornament; it makes
a hoop of brightness on the cloth; it is an angel's mouth. There
truth for everybody may be found, and confusion is only—
only temporary, thought Wilhelm.

The idea of this larger body had been planted in him a few
days ago beneath Times Square, when he had gone downtown
to pick up tickets for the baseball game on Saturday (a double-
header at the Polo Grounds). He was going through an underground corridor, a place he had always hated and hated more
than ever now. On the walls between the advertisements were
words in chalk: "Sin No More," and "Do Not Eat the Pig,"
he had particularly noticed. And in the dark tunnel, in the
haste, heat, and darkness which disfigure and make freaks and
fragments of nose and eyes and teeth, all of a sudden, unsought,
a general love for all these imperfect and lurid-looking people
burst out in Wilhelm's breast. He loved them. One and all, he
passionately loved them. They were his brothers and his sisters.
He was imperfect and disfigured himself, but what difference

did that make if he was united with them by this blaze of love? And as he walked he began to say, "Oh my brothers—my brothers and my sisters," blessing them all as well as himself.

So what did it matter how many languages there were, or how hard it was to describe a glass of water? Or matter that a few minutes later he didn't feel anything like a brother toward the man who sold him the tickets?

On that very same afternoon he didn't hold so high an opinion of this same onrush of loving kindness. What did it come to? As they had the capacity and must use it once in a while, people were bound to have such involuntary feelings. It was only another one of those subway things. Like having a hard-on at random. But today, his day of reckoning, he consulted his memory again and thought, I must go back to that. That's the right clue and may do me the most good. Something very big. Truth, like.

The old fellow on the right, Mr. Rappaport, was nearly blind and kept asking Wilhelm, "What's the new figure on November wheat? Give me July soy beans too." When you told him he didn't say thank you. He said, "Okay," instead, or, "Check," and turned away until he needed you again. He was very old, older even than Dr. Adler, and if you believed Tamkin he had once been the Rockefeller of the chicken business and had retired with a large fortune.

Wilhelm had a queer feeling about the chicken industry, that it was sinister. On the road, he frequently passed chicken farms. Those big, rambling, wooden buildings out in the neglected fields; they were like prisons. The lights burned all night in them to cheat the poor hens into laying. Then the slaughter. Pile all the coops of the slaughtered on end, and in one week they'd go higher than Mount Everest or Mount Serenity. The blood filling the Gulf of Mexico. The chicken shit, acid, burning the earth.

How old—old this Mr. Rappaport was! Purple stains were

buried in the flesh of his nose, and the cartilage of his ear was twisted like a cabbage heart. Beyond remedy by glasses, his eyes were smoky and faded.

"Read me that soy-bean figure now, boy," he said, and Wilhelm did. He thought perhaps the old man might give him a tip, or some useful advice or information about Tamkin. But no. He only wrote memoranda on a pad, and put the pad in his pocket. He let no one see what he had written. And Wilhelm thought this was the way a man who had grown rich by the murder of millions of animals, little chickens, would act. If there was a life to come he might have to answer for the killing of all those chickens. What if they all were waiting? But if there was a life to come, everybody would have to answer. But if there was a life to come, the chickens themselves would be all right.

Well! What stupid ideas he was having this morning. Phooey!

Finally old Rappaport did address a few remarks to Wilhelm. He asked him whether he had reserved his seat in the synagogue for Yom Kippur.

"No," said Wilhelm.

"Well, you better hurry up if you expect to say *Yiskor* for your parents. I never miss."

And Wilhelm thought, Yes, I suppose I should say a prayer for Mother once in a while. His mother had belonged to the Reform congregation. His father had no religion. At the cemetery Wilhelm had paid a man to say a prayer for her. He was among the tombs and he wanted to be tipped for the *El molai rachamin*. "Thou God of Mercy," Wilhelm thought that meant. *B'gan Aden*—"in Paradise." Singing, they drew it out. *B'gan Ay–den*. The broken bench beside the grave made him wish to do something. Wilhelm often prayed in his own manner. He did not go to the synagogue but he would occasionally perform certain devotions, according to his feelings. Now he reflected, In Dad's eyes I am the wrong kind of Jew. He doesn't like the way I act. Only he is the right kind of Jew. Whatever you are, it always turns out to be the wrong kind.

Mr. Rappaport grumbled and whiffed at his long cigar, and the board, like a swarm of electrical bees, whirred.

"Since you were in the chicken business, I thought you'd speculate in eggs, Mr. Rappaport." Wilhelm, with his warm, panting laugh, sought to charm the old man.

"Oh. Yeah. Loyalty, hey?" said old Rappaport. "I should stick to them. I spent a lot of time amongst chickens. I got to be an expert chicken-sexer. When the chick hatches you have to tell the boys from the girls. It's not easy. You need long, long experience. What do you think, it's a joke? A whole industry depends on it. Yes, now and then I buy a contract eggs. What have you got today?"

Wilhelm said anxiously, "Lard. Rye."

"Buy? Sell?"

"Bought."

"Uh," said the old man. Wilhelm could not determine what he meant by this. But of course you couldn't expect him to make himself any clearer. It was not in the code to give information to anyone. Sick with desire, Wilhelm waited for Mr. Rappaport to make an exception in his case. Just this once! Because it was critical. Silently, by a sort of telepathic concentration, he begged the old man to speak the single word that would save him, give him the merest sign. "Oh, please— please help," he nearly said. If Rappaport would close one eye, or lay his head to one side, or raise his finger and point to a column in the paper or to a figure on his pad. A hint! A hint!

A long perfect ash formed on the end of the cigar, the white ghost of the leaf with all its veins and its fainter pungency. It was ignored, in its beauty, by the old man. For it was beautiful. Wilhelm he ignored as well.

Then Tamkin said to him, "Wilhelm, look at the jump our rye just took."

December rye climbed three points as they tensely watched; the tumblers raced and the machine's lights buzzed.

"A point and a half more, and we can cover the lard losses," said Tamkin. He showed him his calculations on the margin of the *Times*.

"I think you should put in the selling order now. Let's get out with a small loss."

"Get out now? Nothing doing."

"Why not? Why should we wait?"

"Because," said Tamkin with a smiling, almost openly scoffing look, "you've got to keep your nerve when the market starts to go places. Now's when you can make something."

"I'd get out while the getting's good."

"No, you shouldn't lose your head like this. It's obvious to me what the mechanism is, back in the Chicago market. There's a short supply of December rye. Look, it's just gone up another quarter. We should ride it."

"I'm losing my taste for the gamble," said Wilhelm. "You can't feel safe when it goes up so fast. It's liable to come down just as quick."

Dryly, as though he were dealing with a child, Tamkin told him in a tone of tiring patience, "Now listen, Tommy. I have it diagnosed right. If you wish I should sell I can give the sell order. But this is the difference between healthiness and pathology. One is objective, doesn't change his mind every minute, enjoys the risk element. But that's not the neurotic character. The neurotic character—"

"Damn it, Tamkin!" said Wilhelm roughly. "Cut that out. I don't like it. Leave my character out of consideration. Don't pull any more of that stuff on me. I tell you I don't like it."

Tamkin therefore went no further; he backed down. "I meant," he said, softer, "that as a salesman you are basically an artist type. The seller is in the visionary sphere of the business function. And then you're an actor, too."

"No matter what type I am—" An angry and yet weak sweetness rose into Wilhelm's throat. He coughed as though he had the flu. It was twenty years since he had appeared on the screen as an extra. He blew the bagpipes in a film called *Annie Laurie*. Annie had come to warn the young Laird; he would not believe her and called the bagpipers to drown her out. He made fun of her while she wrung her hands. Wilhelm, in a kilt, barelegged, blew and blew and blew and not a sound came out. Of course all the music was recorded. He fell sick with the flu after that and still suffered sometimes from chest weakness.

"Something stuck in your throat?" said Tamkin. "I think maybe you are too disturbed to think clearly. You should try some of my 'here-and-now' mental exercises. It stops you from thinking so much about the future and the past and cuts down confusion."

"Yes, yes, yes, yes," said Wilhelm, his eyes fixed on December rye.

"Nature only knows one thing, and that's the present. Present, present, eternal present, like a big, huge, giant wave—colossal, bright and beautiful, full of life and death, climbing into the sky, standing in the seas. You must go along with the actual, the Here-and-Now, the glory—"

. . . chest weakness, Wilhelm's recollection went on. Margaret nursed him. They had had two rooms of furniture, which was later seized. She sat on the bed and read to him. He made her read for days, and she read stories, poetry, everything in the house. He felt dizzy, stifled when he tried to smoke. They had him wear a flannel vest.

> Come then, Sorrow!
> Sweetest Sorrow!
> Like an own babe I nurse thee on my breast!

Why did he remember that? Why?

"You have to pick out something that's in the actual, immediate present moment," said Tamkin. "And say to yourself here-and-now, here-and-now, here-and-now. 'Where am I?' 'Here.' 'When is it?' 'Now.' Take an object or a person. Anybody. 'Here and now I see a person.' 'Here and now I see a man.' 'Here and now I see a man sitting on a chair.' Take me, for instance. Don't let your mind wander. 'Here and now I see a man in a brown suit. Here and now I see a corduroy shirt.' You have to narrow it down, one item at a time, and not let your imagination shoot ahead. Be in the present. Grasp the hour, the moment, the instant."

Is he trying to hypnotize or con me? Wilhelm wondered. To take my mind off selling? But even if I'm back at seven hundred bucks, then where am I?

As if in prayer, his lids coming down with raised veins, frayed out, on his significant eyes, Tamkin said, " 'Here and now I see a button. Here and now I see the thread that sews the button. Here and now I see the green thread.' " Inch by inch he contemplated himself in order to show Wilhelm how calm it would make him. But Wilhelm was hearing Margaret's voice as she read, somewhat unwillingly,

> Come then, Sorrow!
>
> .   .   .   .
>
> I thought to leave thee,
> And deceive thee,
> But now of all the world I love thee best.

Then Mr. Rappaport's old hand pressed his thigh, and he said, "What's my wheat? Those damn guys are blocking the way. I can't see."

VI

Rye was still ahead when they went out to lunch, and lard was holding its own.

They ate in the cafeteria with the gilded front. There was the same art inside as outside. The food looked sumptuous.

Whole fishes were framed like pictures with carrots, and the salads were like terraced landscapes or like Mexican pyramids; slices of lemon and onion and radishes were like sun and moon and stars; the cream pies were about a foot thick and the cakes swollen as if sleepers had baked them in their dreams.

"What'll you have?" said Tamkin.

"Not much. I ate a big breakfast. I'll find a table. Bring me some yogurt and crackers and a cup of tea. I don't want to spend much time over lunch."

Tamkin said, "You've got to eat."

Finding an empty place at this hour was not easy. The old people idled and gossiped over their coffee. The elderly ladies were rouged and mascaraed and hennaed and used blue hair rinse and eye shadow and wore costume jewelry, and many of them were proud and stared at you with expressions that did not belong to their age. Were there no longer any respectable old ladies who knitted and cooked and looked after their grandchildren? Wilhelm's grandmother had dressed him in a sailor suit and danced him on her knee, blew on the porridge for him and said, "Admiral, you must eat." But what was the use of remembering this so late in the day?

He managed to find a table, and Dr. Tamkin came along with a tray piled with plates and cups. He had Yankee pot roast, purple cabbage, potatoes, a big slice of watermelon, and two cups of coffee. Wilhelm could not even swallow his yogurt. His chest pained him still.

At once Tamkin involved him in a lengthy discussion. Did he do it to stall Wilhelm and prevent him from selling out the rye—or to recover the ground lost when he had made Wilhelm angry by hints about the neurotic character? Or did he have no purpose except to talk?

"I think you worry a lot too much about what your wife and your father will say. Do they matter so much?"

Wilhelm replied, "A person can become tired of looking

himself over and trying to fix himself up. You can spend the
entire second half of your life recovering from the mistakes of
the first half."

"I believe your dad told me he had some money to leave
you."

"He probably does have something."

"A lot?"

"Who can tell," said Wilhelm guardedly.

"You ought to think over what you'll do with it."

"I may be too feeble to do anything by the time I get it. If
I get anything."

"A thing like this you ought to plan out carefully. Invest
it properly." He began to unfold schemes whereby you bought
bonds, and used the bonds as security to buy something else
and thereby earned twelve per cent safely on your money. Wilhelm failed to follow the details. Tamkin said, "If he made
you a gift now, you wouldn't have to pay the inheritance taxes."

Bitterly, Wilhelm told him, "My father's death blots out all
other considerations from his mind. He forces me to think
about it, too. Then he hates me because he succeeds. When I
get desperate—of course I think about money. But I don't
want anything to happen to him. I certainly don't want him
to die." Tamkin's brown eyes glittered shrewdly at him. "You
don't believe it. Maybe it's not psychological. But on my word
of honor. A joke is a joke, but I don't want to joke about stuff
like this. When he dies, I'll be robbed, like. I'll have no more
father."

"You love your old man?"

Wilhelm grasped at this. "Of course, of course I love him.
My father. My mother—" As he said this there was a great
pull at the very center of his soul. When a fish strikes the
line you feel the live force in your hand. A mysterious being
beneath the water, driven by hunger, has taken the hook and

rushes away and fights, writhing. Wilhelm never identified what struck within him. It did not reveal itself. It got away.

And Tamkin, the confuser of the imagination, began to tell, or to fabricate, the strange history of *his* father. "He was a great singer," he said. "He left us five kids because he fell in love with an opera soprano. I never held it against him, but admired the way he followed the life-principle. I wanted to do the same. Because of unhappiness, at a certain age, the brain starts to die back." (True, true! thought Wilhelm) "Twenty years later I was doing experiments in Eastman Kodak, Rochester, and I found the old fellow. He had five more children." (False, false!) "He wept; he was ashamed. I had nothing against him. I naturally felt strange."

"My dad is something of a stranger to me, too," said Wilhelm, and he began to muse. Where is the familiar person he used to be? Or I used to be? Catherine—she won't even talk to me any more, my own sister. It may not be so much my trouble that Papa turns his back on as my confusion. It's too much. The ruins of life, and on top of that confusion—chaos and old night. Is it an easier farewell for Dad if we don't part friends? He should maybe do it angrily— "Blast you with my curse!" And why, Wilhelm further asked, should he or anybody else pity me; or why should I be pitied sooner than another fellow? It is my childish mind that thinks people are ready to give it just because you need it.

Then Wilhelm began to think about his own two sons and to wonder how he appeared to them, and what they would think of him. Right now he had an advantage through baseball. When he went to fetch them, to go to Ebbets Field, though, he was not himself. He put on a front but he felt as if he had swallowed a fistful of sand. The strange, familiar house, horribly awkward; the dog, Scissors, rolled over on his back and barked and whined. Wilhelm acted as if there were nothing irregular, but a weary heaviness came over him. On the way to Flatbush he would think up anecdotes about old Pigtown and Charlie Ebbets for the boys and reminiscences of the old stars, but it was very heavy going. They did not know how much he cared for them. No. It hurt him greatly and he blamed Margaret for turning them against him. She wanted to ruin him, while she wore the mask of kindness. Up in Roxbury he had to go and explain to the priest, who was not sympathetic. They don't care about individuals, their rules come first. Olive said she would marry him outside the Church when he was divorced. But Margaret would not let go. Olive's father was a pretty decent old guy, an osteopath, and he understood what it was all about. Finally he said, "See here, I have to advise Olive. She is asking me. I am mostly a freethinker myself, but the girl has to live in this town." And by now Wilhelm and Olive had had a great many troubles and she was beginning to dread his days in Roxbury, she said. He trembled at offending this small, pretty, dark girl whom he adored. When she would get up late on Sunday morning she would wake him almost in tears at being late for Mass. He would try to help her hitch her garters and smooth out her slip and dress and even put on her hat with shaky hands; then he would rush her to church and drive in second gear in his forgetful way, trying to apologize and to calm her. She got out a block from church to avoid gossip. Even so she loved him, and she would have married him if he had obtained the divorce. But Margaret must have sensed this. Margaret would tell him he did not really want a divorce; he was afraid of it. He cried, "Take everything I've got, Margaret. Let me go to Reno. Don't you want to marry again?" No. She went out with other men, but took his money. She lived in order to punish him.

Dr. Tamkin told Wilhelm, "Your dad is jealous of you."

Wilhelm smiled. "Of *me?* That's rich."

"Sure. People are always jealous of a man who leaves his wife."

"Oh," said Wilhelm scornfully. "When it comes to wives he wouldn't have to envy me."

"Yes, and your wife envies you, too. She thinks, He's free and goes with young women. Is she getting old?"

"Not exactly old," said Wilhelm, whom the mention of his wife made sad. Twenty years ago, in a neat blue wool suit, in a soft hat made of the same cloth—he could plainly see her. He stooped his yellow head and looked under the hat at her clear, simple face, her living eyes moving, her straight small nose, her jaw beautifully, painfully clear in its form. It was a cool day, but he smelled the odor of pines in the sun, in the granite canyon. Just south of Santa Barbara, this was.

"She's forty-some years old," he said.

"I was married to a lush," said Tamkin. "A painful alcoholic. I couldn't take her out to dinner because she'd say she was going to the ladies' toilet and disappear into the bar. I'd ask the bartenders they shouldn't serve her. But I loved her deeply. She was the most spiritual woman of my entire experience."

"Where is she now?"

"Drowned," said Tamkin. "At Provincetown, Cape Cod. It must have been a suicide. She was that way—suicidal. I tried everything in my power to cure her. Because," said Tamkin, "my real calling is to be a healer. I get wounded. I suffer from it. I would like to escape from the sicknesses of others, but I can't. I am only on loan to myself, so to speak. I belong to humanity."

Liar! Wilhelm inwardly called him. Nasty lies. He invented a woman and killed her off and then called himself a healer, and made himself so earnest he looked like a bad-natured sheep. He's a puffed-up little bogus and humbug with smelly feet. A doctor! A doctor would wash himself. He believes he's making a terrific impression, and he practically invites you to take off your hat when he talks about himself; and he thinks he has an imagination, but he hasn't, neither is he smart.

Then what am I doing with him here, and why did I give him the seven hundred dollars? thought Wilhelm.

Oh, this was a day of reckoning. It was a day, he thought, on which, willing or not, he would take a good close look at the truth. He breathed hard and his misshapen hat came low upon his congested dark-blond face. A rude look. Tamkin was a charlatan, and furthermore he was desperate. And furthermore, Wilhelm had always known this about him. But he appeared to have worked it out at the back of his mind that Tamkin for thirty or forty years had gotten through many a tight place, that he would get through this crisis too and bring him, Wilhelm, to safety also. And Wilhelm realized that he was on Tamkin's back. It made him feel that he had virtually left the ground and was riding upon the other man. He was in the air. It was for Tamkin to take the steps.

The doctor, if he was a doctor, did not look anxious. But then his face did not have much variety. Talking always about spontaneous emotion and open receptors and free impulses, he was about as expressive as a pincushion. When his hypnotic spell failed, his big underlip made him look weak-minded. Fear stared from his eyes, sometimes, so humble as to make you sorry for him. Once or twice Wilhelm had seen that look. Like a dog, he thought. Perhaps he didn't look it now, but he was very nervous. Wilhelm knew, but he could not afford to recognize this too openly. The doctor needed a little room, a little time. He should not be pressed now. So Tamkin went on, telling his tales.

Wilhelm said to himself, I am on his back—his back. I gambled seven hundred bucks, so I must take this ride. I have to go along with him. It's too late. I can't get off.

"You know," Tamkin said, "that blind old man Rappaport—he's pretty close to totally blind—is one of the most interesting personalities around here. If you could only get him to tell his true story. It's fascinating. This is what he told me. You often hear about bigamists with a secret life. But this old man never hid anything from anybody. He's a regular patriarch. Now, I'll tell you what he did. He had two whole families, separate and apart, one in Williamsburg and the other in the Bronx. The two wives knew about each other. The wife in the Bronx was younger; she's close to seventy now. When he got sore at one wife he went to live with the other one. Meanwhile he ran his chicken business in New Jersey. By one wife he had four kids, and by the other six. They're all grown, but they never have met their half-brothers and sisters and don't want to. The whole bunch of them are listed in the telephone book."

"I can't believe it," said Wilhelm.

"He told me this himself. And do you know what else? While he had his eyesight he used to read a lot, but the only books he would read were by Theodore Roosevelt. He had a set in each of the places where he lived, and he brought his kids up on those books."

"Please," said Wilhelm, "don't feed me any more of this stuff, will you? Kindly do not—"

"In telling you this," said Tamkin with one of his hypnotic subtleties, "I do have a motive. I want you to see how some people free themselves from morbid guilt feelings and follow their instincts. Innately, the female knows how to cripple by sickening a man with guilt. It is a very special *de*struct, and she sends her curse to make a fellow impotent. As if she says, 'Unless I allow it, you will never more be a man.' But men like my old dad or Mr. Rappaport answer, 'Woman, what art thou to me?' You can't do that yet. You're a halfway case. You want to follow your instinct, but you're too worried still. For instance, about your kids—"

"Now look here," said Wilhelm, stamping his feet. "One thing! Don't bring up my boys. Just lay off."

"I was only going to say that they are better off than with conflicts in the home."

"I'm deprived of my children." Wilhelm bit his lip. It was too late to turn away. The anguish struck him. "I pay and pay. I never see them. They grow up without me. She makes them like herself. She'll bring them up to be my enemies. Please let's not talk about this."

But Tamkin said, "Why do you let her make you suffer so? It defeats the original object in leaving her. Don't play her game. Now, Wilhelm, I'm trying to do you some good. I want to tell you, don't marry suffering. Some people do. They get married to it, and sleep and eat together, just as husband and wife. If they go with joy they think it's adultery."

When Wilhelm heard this he had, in spite of himself, to admit that there was a great deal in Tamkin's words. Yes, thought Wilhelm, suffering is the only kind of life they are sure they can have, and if they quit suffering they're afraid they'll have nothing. He knows it. This time the faker knows what he's talking about.

Looking at Tamkin he believed he saw all this confessed from his usually barren face. Yes, yes, he too. One hundred false-hoods, but at last one truth. Howling like a wolf from the city window. No one can bear it any more. Everyone is so full of it that at last everybody must proclaim it. It! It!

Then suddenly Wilhelm rose and said, "That's enough of this. Tamkin, let's go back to the market."

"I haven't finished my melon."

"Never mind that. You've had enough to eat. I want to go back."

Dr. Tamkin slid the two checks across the table. "Who paid yesterday? It's your turn, I think."

It was not until they were leaving the cafeteria that Wilhelm remembered definitely that he had paid yesterday too. But it wasn't worth arguing about.

Tamkin kept repeating as they walked down the street that there were many who were dedicated to suffering. But he told Wilhelm, "I'm optimistic in your case, and I have seen a world of maladjustment. There's hope for you. You don't really want to destroy yourself. You're trying hard to keep your feelings open, Wilhelm. I can see it. Seven per cent of this country is committing suicide by alcohol. Another three, maybe, narcotics. Another sixty just fading away into dust by boredom. Twenty more who have sold their souls to the Devil. Then there's a small percentage of those who want to live. That's the only significant thing in the whole world of today. Those are the only two classes of people there are. Some want to live, but the great majority don't." This fantastic Tamkin began to surpass himself. "They don't. Or else, why these wars? I'll tell you more," he said. "The love of the dying amounts to one thing; they want you to die with them. It's because they love you. Make no mistake."

True, true! thought Wilhelm, profoundly moved by these revelations. How does he know these things? How can he be such a jerk, and even perhaps an operator, a swindler, and understand so well what gives? I believe what he says. It simplifies much—everything. People are dropping like flies. I am trying to stay alive and work too hard at it. That's what's turning my brains. This working hard defeats its own end. At what point should I start over? Let me go back a ways and try once more.

Only a few hundred yards separated the cafeteria from the broker's, and within that short space Wilhelm turned again, in measurable degrees, from these wide considerations to the problems of the moment. The closer he approached to the market, the more Wilhelm had to think about money.

They passed the newsreel theater where the ragged shoeshine kids called after them. The same old bearded man with his bandaged beggar face and his tiny ragged feet and the old press clipping on his fiddle case to prove he had once been a concert violinist, pointed his bow at Wilhelm, saying, "You!" Wilhelm went by with worried eyes, bent on crossing Seventy-second Street. In full tumult the great afternoon current raced for Columbus Circle, where the mouth of midtown stood open and the skyscrapers gave back the yellow fire of the sun.

As they approached the polished stone front of the new office building, Dr. Tamkin said, "Well, isn't that old Rappaport by the door? I think he should carry a white cane, but he will never admit there's a single thing the matter with his eyes."

Mr. Rappaport did not stand well; his knees were sunk, while his pelvis only half filled his trousers. His suspenders held them, gaping.

He stopped Wilhelm with an extended hand, having some-how recognized him. In his deep voice he commanded him, "Take me to the cigar store."

"You want me—? Tamkin!" Wilhelm whispered, "You take him."

Tamkin shook his head. "He wants you. Don't refuse the old gentleman." Significantly he said in a lower voice. "This minute is another instance of the 'here-and-now.' You have to live in this very minute, and you don't want to. A man asks you for help. Don't think of the market. It won't run away. Show your respect to the old boy. Go ahead. That may be more valuable."

"Take me," said the old chicken merchant again.

Greatly annoyed, Wilhelm wrinkled his face at Tamkin. He took the old man's big but light elbow at the bone. "Well, let's step on it," he said. "Or wait—I want to have a look at the board first to see how we're doing."

But Tamkin had already started Mr. Rappaport forward. He was walking, and he scolded Wilhelm, saying, "Don't leave me standing in the middle of the sidewalk. I'm afraid to get knocked over."

"Let's get a move on. Come." Wilhelm urged him as Tamkin went into the broker's.

The traffic seemed to come down Broadway out of the sky, where the hot spokes of the sun rolled from the south. Hot, stony odors rose from the subway grating in the street.

"These teen-age hoodlums worry me. I'm ascared of these Puerto Rican kids, and these young characters who take dope," said Mr. Rappaport. "They go around all hopped up."

"Hoodlums?" said Wilhelm. "I went to the cemetery and my mother's stone bench was split. I could have broken somebody's neck for that. Which store do you go to?"

"Across Broadway. That La Magnita sign next door to the Automat."

"What's the matter with this store here on this side?"

"They don't carry my brand, that's what's the matter."

Wilhelm cursed, but checked the words.

"What are you talking?"

"Those damn taxis," said Wilhelm. "They want to run everybody down."

They entered the cool, odorous shop. Mr. Rappaport put away his large cigars with great care in various pockets while Wilhelm muttered, "Come on, you old creeper. What a poky old character! The whole world waits on him." Rappaport did not offer Wilhelm a cigar, but, holding one up, he asked, "What do you say at the size of these, huh? They're Churchill-type cigars."

He barely crawls along, thought Wilhelm. His pants are dropping off because he hasn't got enough flesh for them to stick to. He's almost blind, and covered with spots, but this old man still makes money in the market. Is loaded with dough, probably. And I bet he doesn't give his children any. Some of them must be in their fifties. This is what keeps middle-aged men as children. He's master over the dough. Think—just think! Who controls everything? Old men of this type. Without needs. They don't need therefore they have. I need, therefore I don't have. That would be too easy.

"I'm older even than Churchill," said Rappaport.

Now he wanted to talk! But if you asked him a question in the market, he couldn't be bothered to answer.

"I bet you are," said Wilhelm. "Come, let's get going."

"I was a fighter, too, like Churchill," said the old man. "When we licked Spain I went into the Navy. Yes, I was a gob that time. What did I have to lose? Nothing. After the battle of San Juan Hill, Teddy Roosevelt kicked me off the beach."

"Come, watch the curb," said Wilhelm.

"I was curious and wanted to see what went on. I didn't have no business there, but I took a boat and rowed myself to the beach. Two of our guys was dead, layin' under the American flag to keep the flies off. So I says to the guy on duty, there, who was the sentry, 'Let's have a look at these guys. I want to see what went on here,' and he says, 'Naw,' but I talked him into it. So he took off the flag and there were these two tall guys, both gentlemen, lying in their boots. They was very tall. The two of them had long mustaches. They were high-society boys. I think one of them was called Fish, from up the Hudson, a big-shot family. When I looked up, there was Teddy Roosevelt, with his hat off, and he was looking at these fellows, the only ones who got killed there. Then he says to me, 'What's the Navy want here? Have you got orders?' 'No, sir,' I says to him. 'Well, get the hell off the beach, then.' "

Old Rappaport was very proud of this memory. "Everything he said had such snap, such class. Man! I love that Teddy Roosevelt," he said, "I love him!"

Ah, what people are! He is almost not with us, and his life

is nearly gone, but T. R. once yelled at him, so he loves him. I guess it is love, too. Wilhelm smiled. So maybe the rest of Tamkin's story was true, about the ten children and the wives and the telephone directory.

He said, "Come on, come on, Mr. Rappaport," and hurried the old man back by the large hollow elbow; he gripped it through the thin cotton cloth. Re-entering the brokerage office where under the lights the tumblers were speeding with the clack of drumsticks upon wooden blocks, more than ever resembling a Chinese theater, Wilhelm strained his eyes to see the board.

The lard figures were unfamiliar. That amount couldn't be lard! They must have put the figures in the wrong slot. He traced the line back to the margin. It was down to .19, and had dropped twenty points since noon. And what about the contract of rye? It had sunk back to its earlier position, and they had lost their chance to sell.

Old Mr. Rappaport said to Wilhelm, "Read me my wheat figure."

"Oh, leave me alone for a minute," he said, and positively hid his face from the old man behind one hand. He looked for Tamkin, Tamkin's bald head, or Tamkin with his gray straw and the cocoa-colored band. He couldn't see him. Where was he? The seats next to Rowland were taken by strangers. He thrust himself over the one on the aisle, Mr. Rappaport's former place, and pushed at the back of the chair until the new occupant, a red-headed man with a thin, determined face, leaned forward to get out of his way but would not surrender the seat. "Where's Tamkin?" Wilhelm asked Rowland.

"Gee, I don't know. Is anything wrong?"

"You must have seen him. He came in a while back."

"No, but I didn't."

Wilhelm fumbled out a pencil from the top pocket of his coat and began to make calculations. His very fingers were numb, and in his agitation he was afraid he made mistakes with the decimal points and went over the subtraction and multiplication like a schoolboy at an exam. His heart, accustomed to many sorts of crisis, was now in a new panic. And, as he had dreaded, he was wiped out. It was unnecessary to ask the German manager. He could see for himself that the electronic bookkeeping device must have closed him out. The manager probably had known that Tamkin wasn't to be trusted, and on that first day he might have warned him. But you couldn't expect him to interfere.

"You get hit?" said Mr. Rowland.

And Wilhelm, quite coolly, said, "Oh, it could have been worse, I guess." He put the piece of paper into his pocket with its cigarette butts and packets of pills. The lie helped him out—although, for a moment, he was afraid he would cry. But he hardened himself. The hardening effort made a violent, vertical pain go through his chest, like that caused by a pocket of air under the collar bones. To the old chicken millionaire, who by this time had become acquainted with the drop in rye and lard, he also denied that anything serious had happened. "It's just one of those temporary slumps. Nothing to be scared about," he said, and remained in possession of himself. His need to cry, like someone in a crowd, pushed and jostled and abused him from behind, and Wilhelm did not dare turn. He said to himself, I will not cry in front of these people. I'll be damned if I'll break down in front of them like a kid, even though I never expect to see them again. No! No! And yet his unshed tears rose and rose and he looked like a man about to drown. But when they talked to him, he answered very distinctly. He tried to speak proudly.

". . . going away?" he heard Rowland ask.

"What?"

"I thought you might be going away too. Tamkin said he was going to Maine this summer for his vacation."

"Oh, going away?"

Wilhelm broke off and went to look for Tamkin in the men's toilet. Across the corridor was the room where the machinery of the board was housed. It hummed and whirred like mechanical birds, and the tubes glittered in the dark. A couple of businessmen with cigarettes in their fingers were having a conversation in the lavatory. At the top of the closet door sat a gray straw hat with a cocoa-colored band. "Tamkin," said Wilhelm. He tried to identify the feet below the door. "Are you in there, Doctor Tamkin?" he said with stifled anger. "Answer me. It's Wilhelm."

The hat was taken down, the latch lifted, and a stranger came out who looked at him with annoyance.

"You waiting?" said one of the businessmen. He was warning Wilhelm that he was out of turn.

"Me? Not me," said Wilhelm. "I'm looking for a fellow."

Bitterly angry, he said to himself that Tamkin would pay him the two hundred dollars at least, his share of the original deposit. "And before he takes the train to Maine, too. Before he spends a penny on vacation—that liar! We went into this as equal partners."

VII

I was the man beneath; Tamkin was on my back, and I thought I was on his. He made me carry him, too, besides Margaret. Like this they ride on me with hoofs and claws. Tear me to pieces, stamp on me and break my bones.

Once more the hoary old fiddler pointed his bow at Wilhelm as he hurried by. Wilhelm rejected his begging and denied the omen. He dodged heavily through traffic and with his quick, small steps ran up the lower stairway of the Gloriana Hotel with its dark-tinted mirrors, kind to people's defects. From the lobby he phoned Tamkin's room, and when no one answered he took the elevator up. A rouged woman in her fifties with a mink stole led three tiny dogs on a leash, high-strung creatures with prominent black eyes, like dwarf deer, and legs like twigs. This was the eccentric Estonian lady who had been moved with her pets to the twelfth floor.

She identified Wilhelm. "You are Doctor Adler's son," she said.

Formally, he nodded.

"I am a dear friend of your father."

He stood in the corner and would not meet her glance, and she thought he was snubbing her and made a mental note to speak of it to the doctor.

The linen wagon stood at Tamkin's door, and the chambermaid's key with its big brass tongue was in the lock.

"Has Doctor Tamkin been here?" he asked her.

"No, I haven't seen him."

Wilhelm came in, however, to look around. He examined the photos on the desk, trying to connect the faces with the strange people in Tamkin's stories. Big, heavy volumes were stacked under the double-pronged TV aerial. *Science and Sanity,* he read, and there were several books of poetry. The *Wall Street Journal* hung in separate sheets from the bed-table under the weight of the silver water jug. A bathrobe with lightning streaks of red and white was laid across the foot of the bed with a pair of expensive batik pajamas. It was a box of a room, but from the windows you saw the river as far uptown as the bridge, as far downtown as Hoboken. What lay between was deep, azure, dirty, complex, crystal, rusty, with the red bones of new apartments rising on the bluffs of New Jersey, and huge liners in their berths, the tugs with matted beards of cordage. Even the brackish tidal river smell rose this high, like the smell of mop water. From every side he heard pianos, and the voices of men and women singing scales and opera, all mixed, and the sounds of pigeons on the ledges.

Again Wilhelm took the phone. "Can you locate Doctor

Tamkin in the lobby for me?" he asked. And when the operator reported that she could not, Wilhelm gave the number of his father's room, but Dr. Adler was not in either. "Well, please give me the masseur. I say the massage room. Don't you understand me? The men's health club. Yes, Max Schilper's—how am I supposed to know the name of it?"

There a strange voice said, "Toktor Adler?" It was the old Czech prizefighter with the deformed nose and ears who was attendant down there and gave out soap, sheets, and sandals. He went away. A hollow endless silence followed. Wilhelm flickered the receiver with his nails, whistled into it, but could not summon either the attendant or the operator.

The maid saw him examining the bottles of pills on Tamkin's table and seemed suspicious of him. He was running low on Phenaphen pills and was looking for something else. But he swallowed one of his own tablets and went out and rang again for the elevator. He went down to the health club. Through the steamy windows, when he emerged, he saw the reflection of the swimming pool swirling green at the bottom of the lowest stairway. He went through the locker-room curtains. Two men wrapped in towels were playing Ping-pong. They were awkward and the ball bounded high. The Negro in the toilet was shining shoes. He did not know Dr. Adler by name, and Wilhelm descended to the massage room. On the tables naked men were lying. It was not a brightly lighted place, and it was very hot, and under the white faint moons of the ceiling shone pale skins. Calendar pictures of pretty girls dressed in tiny fringes were pinned on the wall. On the first table, eyes deeply shut in heavy silent luxury lay a man with a full square beard and short legs, stocky and black-haired. He might have been an orthodox Russian. Wrapped in a sheet, waiting, the man beside him was newly shaved and red from the steambath. He had a big happy face and was dreaming. And after him was an athlete, strikingly muscled, powerful and young, with a strong white curve to his genital and a half-angry smile on his mouth. Dr. Adler was on the fourth table, and Wilhelm stood over his father's pale, slight body. His ribs were narrow and small, his belly round, white, and high. It had its own being, like something separate. His thighs were weak, the muscles of his arms had fallen, his throat was creased.

The masseur in his undershirt bent and whispered in his ear, "It's your son," and Dr. Adler opened his eyes into Wilhelm's face. At once he saw the trouble in it, and by an instantaneous reflex he removed himself from the danger of contagion, and he said serenely, "Well, have you taken my advice, Wilky?"

"Oh, Dad," said Wilhelm.

"To take a swim and get a massage?"

"Did you get my note?" said Wilhelm.

"Yes, but I'm afraid you'll have to ask somebody else, because I can't. I had no idea you were so low on funds. How did you let it happen? Didn't you lay anything aside?"

"Oh, please, Dad," said Wilhelm, almost bringing his hands together in a clasp.

"I'm sorry," said the doctor. "I really am. But I have set up a rule. I've thought about it, I believe it is a good rule, and I don't want to change it. You haven't acted wisely. What's the matter?"

"Everything. Just everything. What isn't? I did have a little, but I haven't been very smart."

"You took some gamble? You lost it? Was it Tamkin? I told you, Wilky, not to build on that Tamkin. Did you? I suspect—"

"Yes, Dad, I'm afraid I trusted him."

Dr. Adler surrendered his arm to the masseur, who was using wintergreen oil.

"Trusted! And got taken?"

"I'm afraid I kind of—" Wilhelm glanced at the masseur but he was absorbed in his work. He probably did not listen to conversations. "I did. I might as well say it. I should have listened to you."

"Well, I won't remind you how often I warned you. It must be very painful."

"Yes, Father, it is."

"I don't know how many times you have to be burned in order to learn something. The same mistakes, over and over."

"I couldn't agree with you more," said Wilhelm with a face of despair. "You're so right, Father. It's the same mistakes, and I get burned again and again. I can't seem to—I'm stupid, Dad, I just can't breathe. My chest is all up—I feel choked. I just simply can't catch my breath."

He stared at his father's nakedness. Presently he became aware that Dr. Adler was making an effort to keep his temper. He was on the verge of an explosion. Wilhelm hung his face and said, "Nobody likes bad luck, eh Dad?"

"So! It's bad luck, now. A minute ago it was stupidity."

"It is stupidity—it's some of both. It's true that I can't learn. But I—"

"I don't want to listen to the details," said his father. "And I want you to understand that I'm too old to take on new burdens. I'm just too old to do it. And people who will just wait for help—must *wait* for help. They have got to stop waiting."

"It isn't all a question of money—there are other things a father can give to a son." He lifted up his gray eyes and his nostrils grew wide with a look of suffering appeal that stirred his father even more deeply against him.

He warningly said to him, "Look out, Wilky, you're tiring my patience very much."

"I try not to. But one word from you, just a word, would

go a long way. I've never asked you for very much. But you are not a kind man, Father. You don't give the little bit I beg you for."

He recognized that his father was now furiously angry. Dr. Adler started to say something, and then raised himself and gathered the sheet over him as he did so. His mouth opened, wide, dark, twisted, and he said to Wilhelm, "You want to make yourself into my cross. But I am not going to pick up a cross. I'll see you dead, Wilky, by Christ, before I let you do that to me."

"Father, listen! Listen!"

"Go away from me now. It's torture for me to look at you, you slob!" cried Dr. Adler.

Wilhelm's blood rose up madly, in anger equal to his father's, but then it sank down and left him helplessly captive to misery. He said stiffly, and with a strange sort of formality, "Okay, Dad. That'll be enough. That's about all we should say." And he stalked out heavily by the door adjacent to the swimming pool and the steam room, and labored up two long flights from the basement. Once more he took the elevator to the lobby on the mezzanine.

He inquired at the desk for Dr. Tamkin.

The clerk said, "No, I haven't seen him. But I think there's something in the box for you."

"Me? Give it here," said Wilhelm and opened a telephone message from his wife. It read, "Please phone Mrs. Wilhelm on return. Urgent."

Whenever he received an urgent message from his wife he was always thrown into a great fear for the children. He ran to the phone booth, spilled out the change from his pockets onto the little curved steel shelf under the telephone, and dialed the Digby number.

"Yes?" said his wife. Scissors barked in the parlor.

"Margaret?"

"Yes, hello." They never exchanged any other greeting. She instantly knew his voice.

"The boys all right?"

"They're out on their bicycles. Why shouldn't they be all right? Scissors, quiet!"

"Your message scared me," he said. "I wish you wouldn't make 'urgent' so common."

"I had something to tell you."

Her familiar unbending voice awakened in him a kind of hungry longing, not for Margaret but for the peace he had once known.

"You sent me a postdated check," she said. "I can't allow that. It's already five days past the first. You dated your check for the twelfth."

"Well, I have no money. I haven't got it. You can't send me to prison for that. I'll be lucky if I can raise it by the twelfth."

She answered, "You better get it, Tommy."

"Yes? What for?" he said. "Tell me. For the sake of what? To tell lies about me to everyone? You—"

She cut him off. "You know what for. I've got the boys to bring up."

Wilhelm in the narrow booth broke into a heavy sweat. He dropped his head and shrugged while with his fingers he arranged nickels, dimes, and quarters in rows. "I'm doing my best," he said. "I've had some bad luck. As a matter of fact, it's been so bad that I don't know where I am. I couldn't tell you what day of the week this is. I can't think straight. I'd better not even try. This has been one of those days, Margaret. May I never live to go through another like it. I mean that with all my heart. So I'm not going to try to do any thinking today. Tomorrow I'm going to see some guys. One is a sales manager. The other is in television. But not to act," he hastily added. "On the business end."

"That's just some more of your talk, Tommy," she said. "You ought to patch things up with Rojax Corporation. They'd take you back. You've got to stop thinking like a youngster."

"What do you mean?"

"Well," she said, measured and unbending, remorselessly unbending, "you still think like a youngster. But you can't do that any more. Every other day you want to make a new start. But in eighteen years you'll be eligible for retirement. Nobody wants to hire a new man of your age."

"I know. But listen, you don't have to sound so hard. I can't get on my knees to them. And really you don't have to sound so hard. I haven't done you so much harm."

"Tommy, I have to chase you and ask you for money that you owe us, and I hate it."

She hated also to be told that her voice was hard.

"I'm making an effort to control myself," she told him.

He could picture her, her graying bangs cut with strict fixity above her pretty, decisive face. She prided herself on being fair-minded. We could not bear, he thought, to know what we do. Even though blood is spilled. Even though the breath of life is taken from someone's nostrils. This is the way of the weak; quiet and fair. And then smash! They smash!

"Rojax take me back? I'd have to crawl back. They don't need me. After so many years I should have got stock in the firm. How can I support the three of you, and live myself, on half the territory? And why should I even try when you won't lift a finger to help? I sent you back to school, didn't I? At that time you said—"

His voice was rising. She did not like that and intercepted him. "You misunderstood me," she said.

"You must realize you're killing me. You can't be as blind as all that. Thou shalt not kill! Don't you remember that?"

She said, "You're just raving now. When you calm down it'll be different. I have great confidence in your earning ability."

"Margaret, you don't grasp the situation. You'll have to get a job."

"Absolutely not. I'm not going to have two young children running loose."

"They're not babies," Wilhelm said. "Tommy is fourteen. Paulie is going to be ten."

"Look," Margaret said in her deliberate manner. "We can't continue this conversation if you're going to yell so, Tommy. They're at a dangerous age. There are teen-aged gangs—the parents working, or the families broken up."

Once again she was reminding him that it was he who had left her. She had the bringing up of the children as her burden, while he must expect to pay the price of his freedom.

Freedom! he thought with consuming bitterness. Ashes in his mouth, not freedom. Give me my children. For they are mine too.

Can you be the woman I lived with? he started to say. Have you forgotten that we slept so long together? Must you now deal with me like this, and have no mercy?

He would be better off with Margaret again than he was today. This was what she wanted to make him feel, and she drove it home. "Are you in misery?" she was saying. "But you have deserved it." And he could not return to her any more than he could beg Rojax to take him back. If it cost him his life, he could not. Margaret had ruined him with Olive. She hit him and hit him, beat him, battered him, wanted to beat the very life out of him.

"Margaret, I want you please to reconsider about work. You have that degree now. Why did I pay your tuition?"

"Because it seemed practical. But it isn't. Growing boys need parental authority and a home."

He begged her, "Margaret, go easy on me. You ought to. I'm at the end of my rope and feel that I'm suffocating. You don't want to be responsible for a person's destruction. You've got to let up. I feel I'm about to burst." His face had expanded. He struck a blow upon the tin and wood and nails of the wall of the booth. "You've got to let me breathe. If I should keel over, what then? And it's something I can never understand about you. How you can treat someone like this whom you lived with so long. Who gave you the best of himself. Who tried. Who loved you." Merely to pronounce the word "love" made him tremble.

"Ah," she said with a sharp breath. "Now we're coming to it. How did you imagine it was going to be—big shot? Everything made smooth for you? I thought you were leading up to this."

She had not, perhaps, intended to reply as harshly as she did, but she brooded a great deal and now she could not forbear to punish him and make him feel pains like those she had to undergo.

He struck the wall again, this time with his knuckles, and he had scarcely enough air in his lungs to speak in a whisper, because his heart pushed upward with a frightful pressure. He got up and stamped his feet in the narrow enclosure.

"Haven't I always done my best?" he yelled, though his voice sounded weak and thin to his own ears. "Everything comes from me and nothing back again to me. There's no law that'll punish this, but you are committing a crime against me. Before God—and that's no joke. I mean that. Before God! Sooner or later the boys will know it."

In a firm tone, levelly, Margaret said to him, "I won't stand to be howled at. When you can speak normally and have something sensible to say I'll listen. But not to this." She hung up.

Wilhelm tried to tear the apparatus from the wall. He ground his teeth and seized the black box with insane digging fingers and made a stifled cry and pulled. Then he saw an elderly lady staring through the glass door, utterly appalled by him, and he ran from the booth, leaving a large amount of change on the shelf. He hurried down the stairs and into the street.

On Broadway it was still bright afternoon and the gassy air was almost motionless under the leaden spokes of sunlight, and sawdust footprints lay about the doorways of butcher shops and fruit stores. And the great, great crowd, the inexhaustible current of millions of every race and kind pouring out, pressing round, of every age, of every genius, possessors of every human secret, antique and future, in every face the refinement of one particular motive or essence—*I labor, I spend, I strive, I design, I love, I cling, I uphold, I give way, I envy, I long, I scorn, I die, I hide, I want.* Faster, much faster than any man could make the tally. The sidewalks were wider than any causeway; the street itself was immense, and it quaked and gleamed and it seemed to Wilhelm to throb at the last limit of endurance. And although the sunlight appeared like a broad tissue, its actual weight made him feel like a drunkard.

"I'll get a divorce if it's the last thing I do," he swore. "As for Dad— As for Dad— I'll have to sell the car for junk and pay the hotel. I'll have to go on my knees to Olive and say, 'Stand by me a while. Don't let her win. Olive!' " And he thought, I'll try to start again with Olive. In fact, I must. Olive loves me. Olive—

Beside a row of limousines near the curb he thought he saw Dr. Tamkin. Of course he had been mistaken before about the hat with the cocoa-colored band and didn't want to make the same mistake twice. But wasn't that Tamkin who was speaking so earnestly, with pointed shoulders, to someone under the canopy of the funeral parlor? For this was a huge funeral. He looked for the singular face under the dark gray, fashionable hatbrim. There were two open cars filled with flowers, and a policeman tried to keep a path open to pedestrians. Right at the canopy-pole, now wasn't that that damned Tamkin talking away with a solemn face, gesticulating with an open hand?

"Tamkin!" shouted Wilhelm, going forward. But he was pushed to the side by a policeman clutching his nightstick at both end, like a rolling pin. Wilhelm was even farther from Tamkin now, and swore under his breath at the cop who continued to press him back, back, belly and ribs, saying, "Keep it moving there, please," his face red with impatient sweat, his brows like red fur. Wilhelm said to him haughtily, "You shouldn't push people like this."

The policeman, however, was not really to blame. He had been ordered to keep a way clear. Wilhelm was moved forward by the pressure of the crowd.

He cried, "Tamkin!"

But Tamkin was gone. Or rather, it was he himself who was carried from the street into the chapel. The pressure ended inside, where it was dark and cool. The flow of fan-driven air dried his face, which he wiped hard with his handkerchief to stop the slight salt itch. He gave a sigh when he heard the organ notes that stirred and breathed from the pipes and he saw people in the pews. Men in formal clothes and black homburgs strode softly back and forth on the cork floor, up and down the center aisle. The white of the stained glass was like mother-of-pearl, with the blue of a great star fluid, like velvet ribbon.

Well, thought Wilhelm, if that was Tamkin outside I might as well wait for him here where it's cool. Funny, he never mentioned he had a funeral to go to today. But that's just like the guy.

But within a few minutes he had forgotten Tamkin. He stood along the wall with others and looked toward the coffin and the slow line that was moving past it, gazing at the face of the dead. Presently he too was in this line, and slowly, slowly, foot by foot, the beating of his heart anxious, thick, frightening, but somehow also rich, he neared the coffin and paused for his turn, and gazed down. He caught his breath when he looked at the corpse, and his face swelled, his eyes shone hugely with instant tears.

The dead man was gray-haired. He had two large waves of gray hair at the front. But he was not old. His face was long, and he had a bony nose, slightly, delicately twisted. His brows were raised as though he had sunk into the final thought. Now at last he was with it, after the end of all distractions, and when his flesh was no longer flesh. And by this meditative look Wilhelm was so struck that he could not go away. In spite of the tinge of horror, and then the splash of heartsickness that he felt, he could not go. He stepped out of line and remained beside the coffin; his eyes filled silently and through his still tears he studied the man as the line of visitors moved with veiled looks past the satin coffin toward the standing bank of lilies, lilacs, roses. With great stifling sorrow, almost admiration, Wilhelm nodded and nodded. On the surface, the dead man with his formal shirt and his tie and silk lapels and his powdered skin looked so proper; only a little beneath so—black, Wilhelm thought, so fallen in the eyes.

Standing a little apart, Wilhelm began to cry. He cried at first softly and from sentiment, but soon from deeper feeling. He sobbed loudly and his face grew distorted and hot, and the tears stung his skin. A man——another human creature, was what first went through his thoughts, but other and different things were torn from him. What'll I do? I'm stripped and kicked out. . . . Oh, Father, what do I ask of you? What'll I do about the kids—Tommy, Paul? My children. And Olive? My dear! Why, why, why—you must protect me against that devil who wants my life. If you want it, then kill me. Take, take it, take it from me."

Soon he was past words, past reason, coherence. He could not stop. The source of all tears had suddenly sprung open within him, black, deep, and hot, and they were pouring out and convulsed his body, bending his stubborn head, bowing his shoulders, twisting his face, crippling the very hands with which he held the handkerchief. His efforts to collect himself were useless. The great knot of ill and grief in his throat swelled upward and he gave in utterly and held his face and wept. He cried with all his heart.

He, alone of all the people in the chapel, was sobbing. No one knew who he was.

One woman said, "Is that perhaps the cousin from New Orleans they were expecting?"

"It must be somebody real close to carry on so."

"Oh my, oh my! To be mourned like that," said one man and looked at Wilhelm's heavy shaken shoulders, his clutched face and whitened fair hair, with wide, glinting, jealous eyes.

"The man's brother, maybe?"

"Oh, I doubt that very much," said another bystander. "They're not alike at all. Night and day."

The flowers and lights fused ecstatically in Wilhelm's blind, wet eyes; the heavy sea-like music came up to his ears. It poured into him where he had hidden himself in the center of a crowd by the great and happy oblivion of tears. He heard it and sank deeper than sorrow, through torn sobs and cries toward the consummation of his heart's ultimate need.

A Father-to-Be

THE strangest notions had a way of forcing themselves into Rogin's mind. Just thirty-one and passable-looking, with short black hair, small eyes, but a high, open forehead, he was a research chemist, and his mind was generally serious and dependable. But on a snowy Sunday evening while this stocky man, buttoned to the chin in a Burberry coat and walking in his preposterous gait—feet turned outward—was going toward the subway, he fell into a peculiar state.

He was on his way to have supper with his fiancée. She had phoned him a short while ago and said, "You'd better pick up a few things on the way."

"What do we need?"

"Some roast beef, for one thing. I bought a quarter of a pound coming home from my aunt's."

"Why a quarter of a pound, Joan?" said Rogin, deeply annoyed. "That's just about enough for one good sandwich."

"So you have to stop at a delicatessen. I had no more money."

He was about to ask, "What happened to the thirty dollars

I gave you on Wednesday?" but he knew that would not be right.

"I had to give Phyllis money for the cleaning woman," said Joan.

Phyllis, Joan's cousin, was a young divorcée, extremely wealthy. The two women shared an apartment.

"Roast beef," he said, "and what else?"

"Some shampoo, sweetheart. We've used up all the shampoo. And hurry, darling, I've missed you all day."

"And I've missed you," said Rogin, but to tell the truth he had been worrying most of the time. He had a younger brother whom he was putting through college. And his mother, whose annuity wasn't quite enough in these days of inflation and high taxes, needed money, too. Joan had debts he was helping her to pay, for she wasn't working. She was looking for something suitable to do. Beautiful, well educated, aristocratic in her attitude, she couldn't clerk in a dime store; she couldn't model clothes (Rogin thought this made girls vain and stiff, and he didn't want her to); she couldn't be a waitress or a cashier. What could she be? Well, something would turn up, and meantime Rogin hesitated to complain. He paid her bills —the dentist, the department store, the osteopath, the doctor, the psychiatrist. At Christmas, Rogin almost went mad. Joan bought him a velvet smoking jacket with frog fasteners, a beautiful pipe, and a pouch. She bought Phyllis a garnet brooch, an Italian silk umbrella, and a gold cigarette holder. For other friends, she bought Dutch pewter and Swedish glassware. Before she was through, she had spent five hundred dollars of Rogin's money. He loved her too much to show his suffering. He believed she had a far better nature than his. She didn't worry about money. She had a marvelous character, always cheerful, and she really didn't need a psychiatrist at all. She went to one because Phyllis did and it made her curious.

She tried too much to keep up with her cousin, whose father had made millions in the rug business.

While the woman in the drugstore was wrapping the shampoo bottle, a clear idea suddenly arose in Rogin's thoughts· Money surrounds you in life as the earth does in death. Superimposition is the universal law. Who is free? No one is free. Who has no burdens? Everyone is under pressure. The very rocks, the waters of the earth, beasts, men, children—everyone has some weight to carry. This idea was extremely clear to him at first. Soon it became rather vague, but it had a great effect nevertheless, as if someone had given him a valuable gift. (Not like the velvet smoking jacket he couldn't bring himself to wear, or the pipe it choked him to smoke.) The notion that all were under pressure and affliction, instead of saddening him, had the opposite influence. It put him in a wonderful mood. It was extraordinary how happy he became and, in addition, clear-sighted. His eyes all at once were opened to what was around him. He saw with delight how the druggist and the woman who wrapped the shampoo bottle were smiling and flirting, how the lines of worry in her face went over into lines of cheer and the druggist's receding gums did not hinder his kidding and friendliness. And in the delicatessen, also, it was amazing how much Rogin noted and what happiness it gave him simply to be there.

Delicatessens on Sunday night, when all other stores are shut, will overcharge you ferociously, and Rogin would normally have been on guard, but he was not tonight, or scarcely so. Smells of pickle, sausage, mustard, and smoked fish overjoyed him. He pitied the people who would buy the chicken salad and chopped herring; they could do it only because their sight was too dim to see what they were getting—the fat flakes of pepper on the chicken, the soppy herring, mostly vinegar-soaked stale bread. Who would buy them? Late risers, people living alone, waking up in the darkness of the afternoon, finding their refrigerators empty, or people whose gaze was turned inward. The roast beef looked not bad, and Rogin ordered a pound.

While the storekeeper was slicing the meat, he yelled at a Puerto Rican kid who was reaching for a bag of chocolate cookies, "Hey, you want to pull me down the whole display on yourself? You, *chico,* wait a half a minute." This storekeeper, though he looked like one of Pancho Villa's bandits, the kind that smeared their enemies with syrup and staked them down on anthills, a man with toadlike eyes and stout hands made to clasp pistols hung around his belly, was not so bad. He was a New York man, thought Rogin—who was from Albany himself—a New York man toughened by every abuse of the city, trained to suspect everyone. But in his own realm, on the board behind the counter, there was justice. Even clemency.

The Puerto Rican kid wore a complete cowboy outfit—a green hat with white braid, guns, chaps, spurs, boots, and gauntlets—but he couldn't speak any English. Rogin unhooked the cellophane bag of hard circular cookies and gave it to him. The boy tore the cellophane with his teeth and began to chew one of those dry chocolate discs. Rogin recognized his state—the energetic dream of childhood. Once, he, too, had found these dry biscuits delicious. It would have bored him now to eat one.

What else would Joan like? Rogin thought fondly. Some strawberries? "Give me some frozen strawberries. No, raspberries, she likes those better. And heavy cream. And some rolls, cream cheese, and some of those rubber-looking gherkins."

"What rubber?"

"Those, deep green, with eyes. Some ice cream might be in order, too."

He tried to think of a compliment, a good comparison, an

endearment, for Joan when she'd open the door. What about her complexion? There was really nothing to compare her sweet, small, daring, shapely, timid, defiant, loving face to. How difficult she was, and how beautiful!

As Rogin went down into the stony, odorous, metallic, captive air of the subway, he was diverted by an unusual confession made by a man to his friend. These were two very tall men, shapeless in their winter clothes, as if their coats concealed suits of chain mail.

"So, how long have you known me?" said one.

"Twelve years."

"Well, I have an admission to make," he said. "I've decided that I might as well. For years I've been a heavy drinker. You didn't know. Practically an alcoholic."

But his friend was not surprised, and he answered immediately, "Yes, I did know."

"You knew? Impossible! How could you?"

Why, thought Rogin, as if it could be a secret! Look at that long, austere, alcohol-washed face, that drink-ruined nose, the skin by his ears like turkey wattles, and those whiskey-saddened eyes.

"Well, I did know, though."

"You couldn't have. I can't believe it." He was upset, and his friend didn't seem to want to soothe him. "But it's all right now," he said. "I've been going to a doctor and taking pills, a new revolutionary Danish discovery. It's a miracle. I'm beginning to believe they can cure you of anything and everything. You can't beat the Danes in science. They do everything. They turned a man into a woman."

"That isn't how they stop you from drinking, is it?"

"No. I hope not. This is only like aspirin. It's super-aspirin. They call it the aspirin of the future. But if you use it, you have to stop drinking."

Rogin's illuminated mind asked of itself while the human

tides of the subway swayed back and forth, and cars linked and
transparent like fish bladders raced under the streets: How
come he thought nobody would know what everybody couldn't
help knowing? And, as a chemist, he asked himself what kind
of compound this new Danish drug might be, and started thinking about various inventions of his own, synthetic albumen, a
cigarette that lit itself, a cheaper motor fuel. Ye gods, but he
needed money! As never before. What was to be done? His
mother was growing more and more difficult. On Friday night,
she had neglected to cut up his meat for him, and he was
hurt. She had sat at the table motionless, with her long-suffer-
ing face, severe, and let him cut his own meat, a thing she
almost never did. She had always spoiled him and made his
brother envy him. But what she expected now! Oh, Lord,
how he had to pay, and it had never even occurred to him
formerly that these things might have a price.

Seated, one of the passengers, Rogin recovered his calm,
happy, even clairvoyant state of mind. To think of money was
to think as the world wanted you to think; then you'd never
be your own master. When people said they wouldn't do something for love or money, they meant that love and money
were opposite passions and one the enemy of the other. He
went on to reflect how little people knew about this, how they
slept through life, how small a light the light of consciousness
was. Rogin's clean, snub-nosed face shone while his heart was
torn with joy at these deeper thoughts of our ignorance. You
might take this drunkard as an example, who for long years
thought his closest friends never suspected he drank. Rogin
looked up and down the aisle for this remarkable knightly
symbol, but he was gone.

However, there was no lack of things to see. There was a
small girl with a new white muff; into the muff a doll's head
was sewn, and the child was happy and affectionately vain of
it, while her old man, stout and grim, with a huge scowling

nose, kept picking her up and resettling her in the seat, as if he were trying to change her into something else. Then another child, led by her mother, boarded the car, and this other child carried the very same doll-faced muff, and this greatly annoyed both parents. The woman, who looked like a difficult, contentious woman, took her daughter away. It seemed to Rogin that each child was in love with its own muff and didn't even see the other, but it was one of his foibles to think he understood the hearts of little children.

A foreign family next engaged his attention. They looked like Central Americans to him. On one side the mother, quite old, dark-faced, white-haired, and worn out; on the other a son with the whitened, porous hands of a dishwasher. But what was the dwarf who sat between them—a son or a daughter? The hair was long and wavy and the cheeks smooth, but the shirt and tie were masculine. The overcoat was feminine, but the shoes—the shoes were a puzzle. A pair of brown oxfords with an outer seam like a man's, but Baby Louis heels like a woman's—a plain toe like a man's, but a strap across the instep like a woman's. No stockings. That didn't help much. The dwarf's fingers were beringed, but without a wedding band. There were small grim dents in the cheeks. The eyes were puffy and concealed, but Rogin did not doubt that they could reveal strange things if they chose and that this was a creature of remarkable understanding. He had for many years owned De la Mare's *Memoirs of a Midget*. Now he took a resolve; he would read it. As soon as he had decided, he was free from his consuming curiosity as to the dwarf's sex and was able to look at the person who sat beside him.

Thoughts very often grow fertile in the subway, because of the motion, the great company, the subtlety of the rider's state as he rattles under streets and rivers, under the foundations of great buildings, and Rogin's mind had already been strangely stimulated. Clasping the bag of groceries from which there

rose odors of bread and pickle spice, he was following a train
of reflections, first about the chemistry of sex determination, the
X and Y chromosomes, hereditary linkages, the uterus, afterward about his brother as a tax exemption. He recalled two
dreams of the night before. In one, an undertaker had offered
to cut his hair, and he had refused. In another, he had been
carrying a woman on his head. Sad dreams, both! Very sad!
Which was the woman—Joan or Mother? And the undertaker—his lawyer? He gave a deep sigh, and by force of habit
began to put together his synthetic albumen that was to revolu-
tionize the entire egg industry.

Meanwhile, he had not interrupted his examination of the
passengers and had fallen into a study of the man next to
him. This was a man whom he had never in his life seen
before but with whom he now suddenly felt linked through all
existence. He was middle-aged, sturdy, with clear skin and blue
eyes. His hands were clean, well formed, but Rogin did not
approve of them. The coat he wore was a fairly expensive blue
check such as Rogin would never have chosen for himself.
He would not have worn blue suède shoes, either, or such a
faultless hat, a cumbersome felt animal of a hat encircled by
a high, fat ribbon. There are all kinds of dandies, not all of
them are of the flaunting kind; some are dandies of respectabil-
ity, and Rogin's fellow passenger was one of these. His straight-
nosed profile was handsome, yet he had betrayed his gift,
for he was flat-looking. But in his flat way he seemed to warn
people that he wanted no difficulties with them, he wanted
nothing to do with them. Wearing such blue suède shoes, he
could not afford to have people treading on his feet, and he
seemed to draw about himself a circle of privilege, notifying
all others to mind their own business and let him read his
paper. He was holding a *Tribune,* and perhaps it would be
overstatement to say that he was reading. He was holding it.

His clear skin and blue eyes, his straight and purely Roman

nose—even the way he sat—all strongly suggested one person to Rogin: Joan. He tried to escape the comparison, but it couldn't be helped. This man not only looked like Joan's father, whom Rogin detested; he looked like Joan herself. Forty years hence, a son of hers, provided she had one, might be like this. A son of hers? Of such a son, he himself, Rogin, would be the father. Lacking in dominant traits as compared with Joan, his heritage would not appear. Probably the children would resemble her. Yes, think forty years ahead, and a man like this, who sat by him knee to knee in the hurtling car among their fellow creatures, unconscious participants in a sort of great carnival of transit—such a man would carry forward what had been Rogin.

This was why he felt bound to him through all existence. What were forty years reckoned against eternity! Forty years were gone, and he was gazing at his own son. Here he was. Rogin was frightened and moved. "My son! My son!" he said to himself, and the pity of it almost made him burst into tears. The holy and frightful work of the masters of life and death brought this about. We were their instruments. We worked toward ends we thought were our own. But no! The whole thing was so unjust. To suffer, to labor, to toil and force your way through the spikes of life, to crawl through its darkest caverns, to push through the worst, to struggle under the weight of economy, to make money—only to become the father of a fourth-rate man of the world like this, so flat-looking, with his ordinary, clean, rosy, uninteresting, self-satisfied, fundamentally bourgeois face. What a curse to have a dull son! A son like this, who could never understand his father. They had absolutely nothing, but nothing, in common, he and this neat, chubby, blue-eyed man. He was so pleased, thought Rogin, with all he owned and all he did and all he was that he could hardly unfasten his lip. Look at that lip, sticking up at the tip like a little thorn or egg tooth. He wouldn't give anyone the time of day. Would this perhaps be general forty years from now? Would personalities be chillier as the world aged and grew colder? The inhumanity of the next generation incensed Rogin. Father and son had no sign to make to each other. Terrible! Inhuman! What a vision of existence it gave him. Man's personal aims were nothing, illusion. The life force occupied each of us in turn in its progress toward its own fulfillment, trampling on our individual humanity, using us for its own ends like mere dinosaurs or bees, exploiting love heartlessly, making us engage in the social process, labor, struggle for money, and submit to the law of pressure, the universal law of layers, superimposition!

What the blazes am I getting into? Rogin thought. To be the father of a throwback to *her* father. The image of this white-haired, gross, peevish old man with his ugly selfish blue eyes revolted Rogin. This was how his grandson would look. Joan, with whom Rogin was now more and more displeased, could not help that. For her, it was inevitable. But did it have to be inevitable for him? Well, then, Rogin, you fool, don't be a damned instrument. Get out of the way!

But it was too late for this, because he had already experienced the sensation of sitting next to his own son, his son and Joan's. He kept staring at him, waiting for him to say something, but the presumptive son remained coldly silent though he must have been aware of Rogin's scrutiny. They even got out at the same stop—Sheridan Square. When they stepped to the platform, the man, without even looking at Rogin, went away in a different direction in his detestable blue-checked coat, with his rosy, nasty face.

The whole thing upset Rogin very badly. When he approached Joan's door and heard Phyllis's little dog Henri barking even before he could knock, his face was very tense. "I won't be used," he declared to himself. "I have my own right to exist." Joan had better watch out. She had a light way of bypassing grave questions he had given earnest thought to. She always assumed no really disturbing thing would happen. He could not afford the luxury of such a carefree, debonair attitude himself, because he had to work hard and earn money so that disturbing things would *not* happen. Well, at the moment this situation could not be helped, and he really did not mind the money if he could feel that she was not necessarily the mother of such a son as his subway son or entirely the daughter of that awful, obscene father of hers. After all, Rogin was not himself so much like either of his parents, and quite different from his brother.

Joan came to the door, wearing one of Phyllis's expensive housecoats. It suited her very well. At first sight of her happy face, Rogin was brushed by the shadow of resemblance; the touch of it was extremely light, almost figmentary, but it made his flesh tremble.

She began to kiss him, saying, "Oh, my baby. You're covered with snow. Why didn't you wear your hat? It's all over its little head"—her favorite third-person endearment.

"Well, let me put down this bag of stuff. Let me take off my coat," grumbled Rogin, and escaped from her embrace. Why couldn't she wait making up to him? "It's so hot in here. My face is burning. Why do you keep the place at this temperature? And that damned dog keeps barking. If you didn't keep it cooped up, it wouldn't be so spoiled and noisy. Why doesn't anybody ever walk him?"

"Oh, it's not really so hot here! You've just come in from the cold. Don't you think this housecoat fits me better than Phyllis? Especially across the hips. She thinks so, too. She may sell it to me."

"I hope not," Rogin almost exclaimed.

She brought a towel to dry the melting snow from his short black hair. The flurry of rubbing excited Henri intolerably, and Joan locked him up in the bedroom, where he jumped persistently against the door with a rhythmic sound of claws on the wood.

Joan said, "Did you bring the shampoo?"

"Here it is."

"Then I'll wash your hair before dinner. Come."

"I don't want it washed."

"Oh, come on," she said, laughing.

Her lack of consciousness of guilt amazed him. He did not see how it could be. And the carpeted, furnished, lamplit, curtained room seemed to stand against his vision. So that he felt accusing and angry, his spirit sore and bitter, but it did not seem fitting to say why. Indeed, he began to worry lest the reason for it all slip away from him.

They took off his coat and his shirt in the bathroom, and she filled the sink. Rogin was full of his troubled emotions; now that his chest was bare he could feel them even more distinctly inside, and he said to himself, I'll have a thing or two to tell her pretty soon. I'm not letting them get away with it. "Do you think," he was going to tell her, "that I alone was made to carry the burden of the whole world on me? Do you think I was born just to be taken advantage of and sacrificed? Do you think I'm just a natural resource, like a coal mine, or oil well, or fishery, or the like? Remember, that I'm a man is no reason why I should be loaded down. I have a soul in me no bigger or stronger than yours.

Take away the externals, like the muscles, deeper voice, and so forth, and what remains? A pair of spirits, practically alike. So why shouldn't there also be equality? I can't always be the strong one."

"Sit here," said Joan, bringing up a kitchen stool to the sink. "Your hair's gotten all matted."

He sat with his breast against the cool enamel, his chin on the edge of the basin, the green, hot, radiant water reflecting the glass and the tile, and the sweet, cool, fragrant juice of the shampoo poured on his head. She began to wash him.

"You have the healthiest-looking scalp," she said. "It's all pink."

He answered, "Well, it should be white. There must be something wrong with me."

"But there's absolutely nothing wrong with you," she said, and pressed against him from behind, surrounding him, pouring the water gently over him until it seemed to him that the water came from within him, it was the warm fluid of his own secret loving spirit overflowing into the sink, green and foaming, and the words he had rehearsed he forgot, and his anger at his son-to-be disappeared altogether, and he sighed, and said to her from the water-filled hollow of the sink, "You always have such wonderful ideas, Joan. You know? You have a kind of instinct, a regular gift."

Looking for Mr. Green

Whatsoever thy hand findeth to do, do it with thy might. . . .

Hard work? No, it wasn't really so hard. He
wasn't used to walking and stair-climbing, but the physical
difficulty of his new job was not what George Grebe felt most.
He was delivering relief checks in the Negro district, and although he was a native Chicagoan this was not a part of the
city he knew much about—it needed a depression to introduce
him to it. No, it wasn't literally hard work, not as reckoned in
foot-pounds, but yet he was beginning to feel the strain of it,
to grow aware of its peculiar difficulty. He could find the streets
and numbers, but the clients were not where they were supposed to be, and he felt like a hunter inexperienced in the
camouflage of his game. It was an unfavorable day, too—fall,
and cold, dark weather, windy. But, anyway, instead of shells
in his deep trenchcoat pocket he had the cardboard of checks,
punctured for the spindles of the file, the holes reminding him
of the holes in player-piano paper. And he didn't look much
like a hunter, either; his was a city figure entirely, belted up
in this Irish conspirator's coat. He was slender without being
tall, stiff in the back, his legs looking shabby in a pair of old

135

tweed pants gone through and fringy at the cuffs. With this stiffness, he kept his head forward, so that his face was red from the sharpness of the weather; and it was an indoors sort of face with gray eyes that persisted in some kind of thought and yet seemed to avoid definiteness of conclusion. He wore sideburns that surprised you somewhat by the tough curl of the blond hair and the effect of assertion in their length. He was not so mild as he looked, nor so youthful; and nevertheless there was no effort on his part to seem what he was not. He was an educated man; he was a bachelor; he was in some ways simple; without lushing, he liked a drink; his luck had not been good. Nothing was deliberately hidden.

He felt that his luck was better than usual today. When he had reported for work that morning he had expected to be shut up in the relief office at a clerk's job, for he had been hired downtown as a clerk, and he was glad to have, instead, the freedom of the streets and welcomed, at least at first, the vigor of the cold and even the blowing of the hard wind. But on the other hand he was not getting on with the distribution of the checks. It was true that it was a city job; nobody expected you to push too hard at a city job. His supervisor, that young Mr. Raynor, had practically told him that. Still, he wanted to do well at it. For one thing, when he knew how quickly he could deliver a batch of checks, he would know also how much time he could expect to clip for himself. And then, too, the clients would be waiting for their money. That was not the most important consideration, though it certainly mattered to him. No, but he wanted to do well, simply for doing-well's sake, to acquit himself decently of a job because he so rarely had a job to do that required just this sort of energy. Of this peculiar energy he now had a superabundance; once it had started to flow, it flowed all too heavily. And, for the time being anyway, he was balked. He could not find Mr. Green.

So he stood in his big-skirted trenchcoat with a large envelope in his hand and papers showing from his pocket,
wondering why people should be so hard to locate who were
too feeble or sick to come to the station to collect their own
checks. But Raynor had told him that tracking them down
was not easy at first and had offered him some advice on how
to proceed. "If you can see the postman, he's your first man to
ask, and your best bet. If you can't connect with him, try the
stores and tradespeople around. Then the janitor and the
neighbors. But you'll find the closer you come to your man the
less people will tell you. They don't want to tell you anything."

"Because I'm a stranger."

"Because you're white. We ought to have a Negro doing
this, but we don't at the moment, and of course you've got
to eat, too, and this is public employment. Jobs have to be
made. Oh, that holds for me too. Mind you, I'm not letting
myself out. I've got three years of seniority on you, that's all.
And a law degree. Otherwise, you might be back of the desk
and I might be going out into the field this cold day. The same
dough pays us both and for the same, exact, identical reason.
What's my law degree got to do with it? But you have to pass
out these checks, Mr. Grebe, and it'll help if you're stubborn,
so I hope you are."

"Yes, I'm fairly stubborn."

Raynor sketched hard with an eraser in the old dirt of his
desk, left-handed, and said, "Sure, what else can you answer
to such a question. Anyhow, the trouble you're going to have
is that they don't like to give information about anybody. They
think you're a plain-clothes dick or an installment collector,
or summons-server or something like that. Till you've been seen
around the neighborhood for a few months and people know
you're only from the relief."

It was dark, ground-freezing, pre-Thanksgiving weather;

the wind played hob with the smoke, rushing it down, and Grebe missed his gloves, which he had left in Raynor's office. And no one would admit knowing Green. It was past three o'clock and the postman had made his last delivery. The nearest grocer, himself a Negro, had never heard the name Tulliver Green, or said he hadn't. Grebe was inclined to think that it was true, that he had in the end convinced the man that he wanted only to deliver a check. But he wasn't sure. He needed experience in interpreting looks and signs and, even more, the will not to be put off or denied and even the force to bully if need be. If the grocer did know, he had got rid of him easily. But since most of his trade was with reliefers, why should he prevent the delivery of a check? Maybe Green, or Mrs. Green, if there was a Mrs. Green, patronized another grocer. And was there a Mrs. Green? It was one of Grebe's great handicaps that he hadn't looked at any of the case records. Raynor should have let him read files for a few hours. But he apparently saw no need for that, probably considering the job unimportant. Why prepare systematically to deliver a few checks?

But now it was time to look for the janitor. Grebe took in the building in the wind and gloom of the late November day —trampled, frost-hardened lots on one side; on the other, an automobile junk yard and then the infinite work of Elevated frames, weak-looking, gaping with rubbish fires; two sets of leaning brick porches three stories high and a flight of cement stairs to the cellar. Descending, he entered the underground passage, where he tried the doors until one opened and he found himself in the furnace room. There someone rose toward him and approached, scraping on the coal grit and bending under the canvas-jacketed pipes.

"Are you the janitor?"

"What do you want?"

"I'm looking for a man who's supposed to be living here. Green."

"What Green?"

"Oh, you maybe have more than one Green?" said Grebe with new, pleasant hope. "This is Tulliver Green."

"I don't think I c'n help you, mister. I don't know any."

"A crippled man."

The janitor stood bent before him. Could it be that he was crippled? Oh, God! what if he was. Grebe's gray eyes sought with excited difficulty to see. But no, he was only very short and stooped. A head awakened from meditation, a strong-haired beard, low, wide shoulders. A staleness of sweat and coal rose from his black shirt and the burlap sack he wore as an apron.

"Crippled how?"

Grebe thought and then answered with the light voice of unmixed candor, "I don't know. I've never seen him." This was damaging, but his only other choice was to make a lying guess, and he was not up to it. "I'm delivering checks for the relief to shut-in cases. If he weren't crippled he'd come to collect himself. That's why I said crippled. Bedridden, chair-ridden—is there anybody like that?"

This sort of frankness was one of Grebe's oldest talents, going back to childhood. But it gained him nothing here.

"No suh. I've got four buildin's same as this that I take care of. I don' know all the tenants, leave alone the tenants' tenants. The rooms turn over so fast, people movin' in and out every day. I can't tell you."

"Then where should I ask?"

The janitor opened his grimy lips but Grebe did not hear him in the piping of the valves and the consuming pull of air to flame in the body of the furnace. He knew, however, what he had said.

"Well, all the same, thanks. Sorry I bothered you. I'll prowl around upstairs again and see if I can turn up someone who knows him."

Once more in the cold air and early darkness he made the short circle from the cellarway to the entrance crowded between the brickwork pillars and began to climb to the third floor. Pieces of plaster ground under his feet; strips of brass tape from which the carpeting had been torn away marked old boundaries at the sides. In the passage, the cold reached him worse than in the street; it touched him to the bone. The hall toilets ran like springs. He thought grimly as he heard the wind burning around the building with a sound like that of the furnace, that this was a great piece of constructed shelter. Then he struck a match in the gloom and searched for names and numbers among the writings and scribbles on the walls. He saw WHOODY-DOODY GO TO JESUS, and zigzags, caricatures, sexual scrawls, and curses. So the sealed rooms of pyramids were also decorated, and the caves of human dawn.

The information on his card was, TULLIVER GREEN—APT 3D. There were no names, however, and no numbers. His shoulders drawn up, tears of cold in his eyes, breathing vapor, he went the length of the corridor and told himself that if he had been lucky enough to have the temperament for it he would bang on one of the doors and bawl out "Tulliver Green!" until he got results. But it wasn't in him to make an uproar and he continued to burn matches, passing the light over the walls. At the rear, in a corner off the hall, he discovered a door he had not seen before and he thought it best to investigate. It sounded empty when he knocked, but a young Negress answered, hardly more than a girl. She opened only a bit, to guard the warmth of the room.

"Yes suh?"

"I'm from the district relief station on Prairie Avenue. I'm looking for a man named Tulliver Green to give him his check. Do you know him?"

No, she didn't; but he thought she had not understood anything of what he had said. She had a dream-bound, dream-blind face, very soft and black, shut off. She wore a man's jacket and pulled the ends together at her throat. Her hair was parted in three directions, at the sides and transversely, standing up at the front in a dull puff.

"Is there somebody around here who might know?"

"I jus' taken this room las' week."

He observed that she shivered, but even her shiver was somnambulistic and there was no sharp consciousness of cold in the big smooth eyes of her handsome face.

"All right, miss, thank you. Thanks," he said, and went to try another place.

Here he was admitted. He was grateful, for the room was warm. It was full of people, and they were silent as he entered —ten people, or a dozen, perhaps more, sitting on benches like a parliament. There was no light, properly speaking, but a tempered darkness that the window gave, and everyone seemed to him enormous, the men padded out in heavy work clothes and winter coats, and the women huge, too, in their sweaters, hats, and old furs. And, besides, bed and bedding, a black cooking range, a piano piled towering to the ceiling with papers, a dining-room table of the old style of prosperous Chicago. Among these people Grebe, with his cold-heightened fresh color and his smaller stature, entered like a schoolboy. Even though he was met with smiles and good will, he knew, before a single word was spoken, that all the currents ran against him and that he would make no headway. Nevertheless he began. "Does anybody here know how I can deliver a check to Mr. Tulliver Green?"

"Green?" It was the man that had let him in who answered.

He was in short sleeves, in a checkered shirt, and had a queer, high head, profusely overgrown and long as a shako; the veins entered it strongly from his forehead. "I never heard mention of him. Is this where he live?"

"This is the address they gave me at the station. He's a sick man, and he'll need his check. Can't anybody tell me where to find him?"

He stood his ground and waited for a reply, his crimson wool scarf wound about his neck and drooping outside his trenchcoat, pockets weighted with the block of checks and official forms. They must have realized that he was not a college boy employed afternoons by a bill collector, trying foxily to pass for a relief clerk, recognized that he was an older man who knew himself what need was, who had had more than an average seasoning in hardship. It was evident enough if you looked at the marks under his eyes and at the sides of his mouth.

"Anybody know this sick man?"

"No suh." On all sides he saw heads shaken and smiles of denial. No one knew. And maybe it was true, he considered, standing silent in the earthen, musky human gloom of the place as the rumble continued. But he could never really be sure.

"What's the matter with this man?" said shako-head.

"I've never seen him. All I can tell you is that he can't come in person for his money. It's my first day in this district."

"Maybe they given you the wrong number?"

"I don't believe so. But where else can I ask about him?" He felt that his persistence amused them deeply, and in a way he shared their amusement that he should stand up so tenaciously to them. Though smaller, though slight, he was his own man, he retracted nothing about himself, and he looked back at them, gray-eyed, with amusement and also with a sort of courage. On the bench some man spoke in his throat, the words impossible to catch, and a woman answered with a wild, shrieking laugh, which was quickly cut off.

"Well, so nobody will tell me?"

"Ain't nobody who knows."

"At least, if he lives here, he pays rent to someone. Who manages the building?"

"Greatham Company. That's on Thirty-ninth Street."

Grebe wrote it in his pad. But, in the street again, a sheet of wind-driven paper clinging to his leg while he deliberated what direction to take next, it seemed a feeble lead to follow. Probably this Green didn't rent a flat, but a room. Sometimes there were as many as twenty people living in an apartment; the real-estate agent would know only the lessee. And not even the agent could tell you who the renters were. In some places the beds were even used in shifts, watchmen or jitney drivers or short-order cooks in night joints turning out after a day's sleep and surrendering their beds to a sister, a nephew, or perhaps a stranger, just off the bus. There were large numbers of newcomers in this terrific, blight-bitten portion of the city between Cottage Grove and Ashland, wandering from house to house and room to room. When you saw them, how could you know them? They didn't carry bundles on their backs or look picturesque. You only saw a man, a Negro, walking in the street or riding in the car, like everyone else, with his thumb closed on a transfer. And therefore how were you supposed to tell? Grebe thought the Greatham agent would only laugh at his question.

But how much it would have simplified the job to be able to say that Green was old, or blind, or consumptive. An hour in the files, taking a few notes, and he needn't have been at such a disadvantage. When Raynor gave him the block of checks he had asked, "How much should I know about these people?" Then Raynor had looked as though he were preparing to accuse him of trying to make the job more important than it was. He smiled, because by then they were on fine terms, but nevertheless he had been getting ready to say something like that when the confusion began in the station over Staika and her children.

Grebe had waited a long time for this job. It came to him through the pull of an old schoolmate in the Corporation Counsel's office, never a close friend, but suddenly sympathetic and interested—pleased to show, moreover, how well he had done, how strongly he was coming on even in these miserable times. Well, he was coming through strongly, along with the Democratic administration itself. Grebe had gone to see him in City Hall, and they had had a counter lunch or beers at least once a month for a year, and finally it had been possible to swing the job. He didn't mind being assigned the lowest clerical grade, nor even being a messenger, though Raynor thought he did.

This Raynor was an original sort of guy and Grebe had taken to him immediately. As was proper on the first day, Grebe had come early, but he waited long, for Raynor was late. At last he darted into his cubicle of an office as though he had just jumped from one of those hurtling huge red Indiana Avenue cars. His thin, rough face was wind-stung and he was grinning and saying something breathlessly to himself. In his hat, a small fedora and his coat, the velvet collar a neat fit about his neck, and his silk muffler that set off the nervous twist of his chin, he swayed and turned himself in his swivel chair, feet leaving the ground; so that he pranced a little as he sat. Meanwhile he took Grebe's measure out of his eyes, eyes of an unusual vertical length and slightly sardonic. So the two men sat for a while, saying nothing, while the supervisor raised his hat from his miscombed hair and put it in his lap. His cold-darkened hands were not clean. A steel beam passed through the little makeshift room, from which machine belts once had hung. The building was an old factory.

"I'm younger than you; I hope you won't find it hard taking

orders from me," said Raynor. "But I don't make them up, either. You're how old, about?"

"Thirty-five."

"And you thought you'd be inside doing paper-work. But it so happens I have to send you out."

"I don't mind."

"And it's mostly a Negro load we have in this district."

"So I thought it would be."

"Fine. You'll get along. *C'est un bon boulot.* Do you know French?"

"Some."

"I thought you'd be a university man."

"Have you been in France?" said Grebe.

"No, that's the French of the Berlitz School. I've been at it for more than a year, just as I'm sure people have been, all over the world, office boys in China and braves in Tanganyika. In fact, I damn well know it. Such is the attractive power of civilization. It's overrated, but what do you want? *Que voulez vous?* I get *Le Rire* and all the spicy papers, just like in Tanganyika. It must be mystifying, out there. But my reason is that I'm aiming at the diplomatic service. I have a cousin who's a courier, and the way he describes it is awfully attractive. He rides in the *wagon-lits* and reads books. While we— What did you do before?"

"I sold."

"Where?"

"Canned meat at Stop and Shop. In the basement."

"And before that?"

"Window shades, at Goldblatt's."

"Steady work?"

"No, Thursdays and Saturdays. I also sold shoes."

"You've been a shoe-dog, too. Well. And prior to that? Here it is in your folder." He opened the record. "St. Olaf's College, instructor in classical languages. Fellow, University of

Chicago, 1926-27. I've had Latin, too. Let's trade quotations
—'*Dum spiro spero.*' "

" '*Da dextram misero.*' "

" '*Alea jacta est.*' "

" '*Excelsior.*' "

Raynor shouted with laugher, and other workers came to
look at him over the partition. Grebe also laughed, feeling
pleased and easy. The luxury of fun on a nervous morning.

When they were done and no one was watching or listening,
Raynor said rather seriously, "What made you study Latin in
the first place. Was it for the priesthood?"

"No."

"Just for the hell of it? For the culture? Oh, the things people
think they can pull!" He made his cry hilarious and tragic.
"I ran my pants off so I could study for the bar, and I've
passed the bar, so I get twelve dollars a week more than you
as a bonus for having seen life straight and whole. I'll tell you,
as a man of culture, that even though nothing looks to be real,
and everything stands for something else, and that thing for
another thing, and that thing for a still further one—there
ain't any comparison between twenty-five and thirty-seven dollars a week, regardless of the last reality. Don't you think that
was clear to your Greeks? They were a thoughtful people, but
they didn't part with their slaves."

This was a great deal more than Grebe had looked for
in his first interview with his supervisor. He was too shy to
show all the astonishment he felt. He laughed a little, aroused,
and brushed at the sunbeam that covered his head with its
dust. "Do you think my mistake was so terrible?"

"Damn right it was terrible, and you know it now that you've
had the whip of hard times laid on your back. You should
have been preparing yourself for trouble. Your people must
have been well off to send you to the university. Stop me, if
I'm stepping on your toes. Did your mother pamper you? Did

your father give in to you? Were you brought up tenderly, with permission to go out and find out what were the last things that everything else stands for while everybody else labored in the fallen world of appearances?"

"Well, no, it wasn't exactly like that." Grebe smiled. *The fallen world of appearances!* no less. But now it was his turn to deliver a surprise. "We weren't rich. My father was the last genuine English butler in Chicago—"

"Are you kidding?"

"Why should I be?"

"In a livery?"

"In livery. Up on the Gold Coast."

"And he wanted you to be educated like a gentleman?"

"He did not. He sent me to the Armour Institute to study chemical engineering. But when he died I changed schools."

He stopped himself, and considered how quickly Raynor had reached him. In no time he had your valise on the table and all your stuff unpacked. And afterward, in the streets, he was still reviewing how far he might have gone, and how much he might have been led to tell if they had not been interrupted by Mrs. Staika's great noise.

But just then a young woman, one of Raynor's workers, ran into the cubicle exclaiming, "Haven't you heard all the fuss?"

"We haven't heard anything."

"It's Staika, giving out with all her might. The reporters are coming. She said she phoned the papers, and you know she did."

"But what is she up to?" said Raynor.

"She brought her wash and she's ironing it here, with our current, because the relief won't pay her electric bill. She has her ironing board set up by the admitting desk, and her kids are with her, all six. They never are in school more than once a week. She's always dragging them around with her because of her reputation."

"I don't want to miss any of this," said Raynor, jumping up. Grebe, as he followed with the secretary, said, "Who is this Staika?"

"They call her the 'Blood Mother of Federal Street.' She's a professional donor at the hospitals. I think they pay ten dollars a pint. Of course it's no joke, but she makes a very big thing out of it and she and the kids are in the papers all the time."

A small crowd, staff and clients divided by a plywood barrier, stood in the narrow space of the entrance, and Staika was shouting in a gruff, mannish voice, plunging the iron on the board and slamming it on the metal rest.

"My father and mother came in a steerage, and I was born in our own house, Robey by Huron. I'm no dirty immigrant. I'm a US citizen. My husband is a gassed veteran from France with lungs weaker'n paper, that hardly can he go to the toilet by himself. These six children of mine, I have to buy the shoes for their feet with my own blood. Even a lousy little white communion necktie, that's a couple of drops of blood; a little piece of mosquito veil for my Vadja so she won't be ashamed in church for the other girls, they take my blood for it by Goldblatt. That's how I keep goin'. A fine thing if I had to depend on the relief. And there's plenty of people on the rolls —fakes! There's nothin' *they* can't get, that can go and wrap bacon at Swift and Armour any time. They're lookin' for them by the Yards. They never have to be out of work. Only they rather lay in their lousy beds and eat the public's money." She was not afraid, in a predominantly Negro station, to shout this way about Negroes.

Grebe and Raynor worked themselves forward to get a closer view of the woman. She was flaming with anger and with pleasure at herself, broad and huge, a golden-headed woman who wore a cotton cap laced with pink ribbon. She was barelegged and had on black gym-shoes, her hoover apron was open and her great breasts, not much restrained by a man's undershirt, hampered her arms as she worked at the kid's dress on the ironing board. And the children, silent and white, with a kind of locked obstinacy, in sheepskins and lumberjackets, stood behind her. She had captured the station, and the pleasure this gave her was enormous. Yet her grievances were true grievances. She was telling the truth. But she behaved like a liar. The look of her small eyes was hidden, and while she raged she also seemed to be spinning and planning.

"They send me out college case-workers in silk pants to talk me out of what I got comin'. Are they better'n me? Who told them? Fire them. Let 'em go and get married, and then you won't have to cut electric from people's budget."

The chief supervisor, Mr. Ewing, couldn't silence her and he stood with folded arms at the head of his staff, bald, bald-headed, saying to his subordinates like the ex-school principal he was, "Pretty soon she'll be tired and go."

"No she won't," said Raynor to Grebe. "She'll get what she wants. She knows more about the relief even than Ewing. She's been on the rolls for years, and she always gets what she wants because she puts on a noisy show. Ewing knows it. He'll give in soon. He's only saving face. If he gets bad publicity, the Commissioner'll have him on the carpet, downtown. She's got him submerged; she'll submerge everybody in time, and that includes nations and governments."

Grebe replied with his characteristic smile, disagreeing completely. Who would take Staika's orders, and what changes could her yelling ever bring about?

No, what Grebe saw in her, the power that made people listen, was that her cry expressed the war of flesh and blood, perhaps turned a little crazy and certainly intensely ugly, on this place and this condition. And at first, when he went out, the spirit of Staika somehow presided over the whole district for him, and it took color from her; he saw her color, in the spotty curb-fires, and the fires under the El, the straight alley of flamey gloom. Later, too, when he went into a tavern for a shot of rye, the sweat of beer, association with West Side Polish streets, made him think of her again.

He wiped the corners of his mouth with his muffler, his handkerchief being inconvenient to reach for, and went out again to get on with the delivery of his checks. The air bit cold and hard and a few flakes of snow formed near him. A train struck by and left a quiver in the frames and a bristling icy hiss over the rails.

Crossing the street, he descended a flight of board steps into a basement grocery, setting off a little bell. It was a dark, long store and it caught you with its stinks of smoked meat, soap, dried peaches, and fish. There was a fire wrinkling and flapping in the little stove, and the proprietor was waiting, an Italian with a long, hollow face and stubborn bristles. He kept his hands warm under his apron.

No, he didn't know Green. You knew people, but not names. The same man might not have the same name twice. The police didn't know, either, and mostly didn't care. When somebody was shot or knifed they took the body away and didn't look for the murderer. In the first place, nobody would tell them anything. So they made up a name for the coroner and called it quits. And in the second place, they didn't give a goddam anyhow. But they couldn't get to the bottom of a thing even if they wanted to. Nobody would get to know even a tenth of what went on among these people. They stabbed and stole, they did every crime and abomination you ever heard of, men and men, women and women, parents and children, worse than the animals. They carried on their own way, and the horrors passed off like a smoke. There was never anything like it in the history of the whole world.

It was a long speech, deepening with every word in its fantasy and passion and becoming increasingly senseless and terrible: a swarm amassed by suggestion and invention, a huge, hugging, despairing knot, a human wheel of heads, legs, bellies, arms, rolling through his shop.

Grebe felt that he must interrupt him. He said sharply, "What are you talking about! All I asked was whether you knew this man."

"That isn't even the half of it. I been here six years. You probably don't want to believe this. But suppose it's true?"

"All the same," said Grebe, "there must be a way to find a person."

The Italian's close-spaced eyes had been queerly concentrated, as were his muscles, while he leaned across the counter trying to convince Grebe. Now he gave up the effort and sat down on his stool. "Oh—I suppose. Once in a while. But I been telling you, even the cops don't get anywhere."

"They're always after somebody. It's not the same thing."

"Well, keep trying if you want. I can't help you."

But he didn't keep trying. He had no more time to spend on Green. He slipped Green's check to the back of the block. The next name on the list was FIELD, WINSTON.

He found the back-yard bungalow without the least trouble; it shared a lot with another house, a few feet of yard between. Grebe knew these two-shack arrangements. They had been built in vast numbers in the days before the swamps were filled and the streets raised, and they were all the same—a boardwalk along the fence, well under street level, three or four ball-headed posts for clotheslines, greening wood, dead shingles, and a long, long flight of stairs to the rear door.

A twelve-year-old boy let him into the kitchen, and there the old man was, sitting by the table in a wheel chair.

"Oh, it's d' government man," he said to the boy when Grebe drew out his checks. "Go bring me my box of papers." He cleared a space on the table.

"Oh, you don't have to go to all that trouble," said Grebe

But Field laid out his papers: Social Security card, relief certification, letters from the state hospital in Manteno, and a naval discharge dated San Diego, 1920.

"That's plenty," Grebe said. "Just sign."

"You got to know who I am," the old man said. "You're from the government. It's not your check, it's a government check and you got no business to hand it over till everything is proved."

He loved the ceremony of it, and Grebe made no more objections. Field emptied his box and finished out the circle of cards and letters.

"There's everything I done and been. Just the death certificate and they can close book on me." He said this with a certain happy pride and magnificence. Still he did not sign; he merely held the little pen upright on the golden-green corduroy of his thigh. Grebe did not hurry him. He felt the old man's hunger for conversation.

"I got to get better coal," he said. "I send my little gran'son to the yard with my order and they fill his wagon with screening. The stove ain't made for it. It fall through the grate. The order says Franklin County egg-size coal."

"I'll report it and see what can be done."

"Nothing can be done, I expect. You know and I know. There ain't no little ways to make things better, and the only big thing is money. That's the only sunbeams, money. Nothing is black where it shines, and the only place you see black is where it ain't shining. What we colored have to have is our own rich. There ain't no other way."

Grebe sat, his reddened forehead bridged levelly by his close-cut hair and his cheeks lowered in the wings of his collar—the caked fire shone hard within the isinglass and iron frames but the room was not comfortable—sat and listened while the old man unfolded his scheme. This was to create one Negro millionaire a month by subscription. One clever, good-hearted young fellow elected every month would sign a contract to use the money to start a business employing Negroes. This would be advertised by chain letters and word of mouth, and every Negro wage-earner would contribute a dollar a month. Within five years there would be sixty millionaires.

"That'll fetch respect," he said with a throat-stopped sound that came out like a foreign syllable. "You got to take and organize all the money that gets thrown away on the policy wheel and horse race. As long as they can take it away from you, they got no respect for you. Money, that's d' sun of human kind!" Field was a Negro of mixed blood, perhaps Cherokee, or Natchez; his skin was reddish. And he sounded, speaking about a golden sun in this dark room, and looked, shaggy and slab-headed, with the mingled blood of his face and broad lips, the little pen still upright in his hand, like one of the underground kings of mythology, old judge Minos himself.

And now he accepted the check and signed. Not to soil the slip, he held it down with his knuckles. The table budged and creaked, the center of the gloomy, heathen midden of the kitchen covered with bread, meat, and cans, and the scramble of papers.

"Don't you think my scheme'd work?"

"It's worth thinking about. Something ought to be done, I agree."

"It'll work if people will do it. That's all. That's the only thing, any time. When they understand it in the same way, all of them."

"That's true," said Grebe, rising. His glance met the old man's.

"I know you got to go," he said. "Well, God bless you, boy, you ain't been sly with me. I can tell it in a minute."

He went back through the buried yard. Someone nursed a candle in a shed, where a man unloaded kindling wood from a sprawl-wheeled baby buggy and two voices carried on a high conversation. As he came up the sheltered passage he heard the hard boost of the wind in the branches and against the house fronts, and then, reaching the sidewalk, he saw the needle-eye red of cable towers in the open icy height hundreds of feet above the. river and the factories—those keen points. From here, his view was unobstructed all the way to the South Branch and its timber banks, and the cranes beside the water. Rebuilt after the Great Fire, this part of the city was, not fifty years later, in ruins again, factories boarded up, buildings deserted or fallen, gaps of prairie between. But it wasn't desolation that this made you feel, but rather a faltering of organization that set free a huge energy, an escaped, unattached, unregulated power from the giant raw place. Not only must people feel it but, it seemed to Grebe, they were compelled to match it. In their very bodies. He no less than others, he realized. Say that his parents had been servants in their time, whereas he was not supposed to be one. He thought that they had never done any service like this, which no one visible asked for, and probably flesh and blood could not even perform. Nor could anyone show why it should be performed; or see where the performance would lead. That did not mean that he wanted to be released from it, he realized with a grimly pensive face. On the contrary. He had something to do. To be compelled to feel this energy and yet have no task to do—that was horrible; that was suffering; he knew what that was. It was now quitting time. Six o'clock. He could go home if he liked, to his room, that is, to wash in hot water, to pour a drink, lie down on his quilt, read the paper, eat some liver paste on crackers before going out to dinner. But to think of this actually made him feel a little sick, as though he had swallowed hard air. He had six checks left, and he was determined to deliver at least one of these: Mr. Green's check.

So he started again. He had four or five dark blocks to go, past open lots, condemned houses, old foundations, closed schools, black churches, mounds, and he reflected that there must be many people alive who had once seen the neighborhood rebuilt and new. Now there was a second layer of ruins; centuries of history accomplished through human massing. Numbers had given the place forced growth; enormous numbers had also broken it down. Objects once so new, so concrete that it could never have occurred to anyone they stood for other things, had crumbled. Therefore, reflected Grebe, the secret of them was out. It was that they stood for themselves by agreement, and were natural and not unnatural by agreement, and when the things themselves collapsed the agreement became visible. What was it, otherwise, that kept cities from looking peculiar? Rome, that was almost permanent, did not give rise to thoughts like these. And was it abidingly real? But in Chicago, where the cycles were so fast and the familiar died out, and again rose changed, and died again in thirty years, you saw the common agreement or covenant, and you were forced to think about appearances and realities. (He remembered Raynor and he smiled. Raynor was a clever boy.) Once you had grasped this, a great many things became intelligible. For instance, why Mr. Field should conceive such a scheme. Of course, if people were to agree to create a millionaire, a real millionaire would come into existence. And if you wanted to know how Mr. Field was inspired to think of this, why, he had within sight of his kitchen window the chart, the very bones of a successful scheme—the El with its blue and green confetti of signals. People consented to pay dimes and ride the crash-box cars, and so it was a success. Yet how absurd it looked; how little reality there was to start with. And yet Yerkes, the great financier who built it, had known that he could get people to agree to do it. Viewed as itself, what a scheme of a scheme it seemed, how close to an appearance. Then why wonder at Mr. Field's idea? He had grasped a principle. And then Grebe remembered, too, that Mr. Yerkes had established the Yerkes Observatory and endowed it with millions. Now how did the notion come to him in his New York museum of a palace or his Aegean-bound yacht to give money to astronomers? Was he awed perhaps by the success of his bizarre enterprise and therefore ready to spend money to find out where in the universe being and seeming were identical? Yes, he wanted to know what abides; and whether flesh is Bible-grass; and he offered money to be burned in the fire of suns. Okay, then, Grebe thought further, these things exist because people consent to exist with them—we have got so far—and also there is a reality which doesn't depend on consent but within which consent is a game. But what about need, the need that keeps so many vast thousands in position? You tell me that, you *private* little gentleman and *decent* soul— he used these words against himself scornfully. Why is the consent given to misery? And why so painfully ugly? Because there *is something* that is dismal and permanently ugly? Here he sighed and gave it up, and thought it was enough for the present moment that he had a real check in his pocket for a Mr. Green who must be real beyond question. If only his neighbors didn't think they had to conceal him.

This time he stopped at the second floor. He struck a match and found a door. Presently a man answered his knock and Grebe had the check ready and showed it even before he began. "Does Tulliver Green live here? I'm from the relief."

The man narrowed the opening and spoke to someone at his back.

"Does he live here?"

"Uh-uh. No."

"Or anywhere in this building? He's a sick man and he can't come for his dough." He exhibited the check in the light, which was smoky—the air smelled of charred lard—and the man held off the brim of his cap to study it.

"Uh-uh. Never seen the name."

"There's nobody around here that uses crutches?"

He seemed to think, but it was Grebe's impression that he was simply waiting for a decent interval to pass.

"No, suh. Nobody I ever see."

"I've been looking for this man all afternoon," Grebe spoke out with sudden force, "and I'm going to have to carry this check back to the station. It seems strange not to be able to find a person to *give* him something when you're looking for him for a good reason. I suppose if I had bad news for him I'd find him quick enough."

There was a responsive motion in the other man's face. "That's right, I reckon."

"It almost doesn't do any good to have a name if you can't be found by it. It doesn't stand for anything. He might as well not have any," he went on, smiling. It was as much of a concession as he could make to his desire to laugh.

"Well, now, there's a little old knot-back man I see once in a while. He might be the one you lookin' for. Downstairs."

"Where? Right side or left? Which door?"

"I don't know which. Thin face little knot-back with a stick."

But no one answered at any of the doors on the first floor. He went to the end of the corridor, searching by matchlight, and found only a stairless exit to the yard, a drop of about six feet. But there was a bungalow near the alley, an old house like Mr. Field's. To jump was unsafe. He ran from the front door, through the underground passage and into the yard. The place was occupied. There was a light through the curtains, upstairs. The name on the ticket under the broken, scoop-shaped mailbox was Green! He exultantly rang the bell and pressed against the locked door. Then the lock clicked faintly and a long staircase opened before him. Someone was slowly coming down—a woman. He had the impression in the weak light that she was shaping her hair as she came, making herself presentable, for he saw her arms raised. But it was for support

that they were raised; she was feeling her way downward, down
the walls, stumbling. Next he wondered about the pressure of
her feet on the treads; she did not seem to be wearing shoes.
And it was a freezing stairway. His ring had got her out of bed,
perhaps, and she had forgotten to put them on. And then he
saw that she was not only shoeless but naked; she was entirely
naked, climbing down while she talked to herself, a heavy
woman, naked and drunk. She blundered into him. The contact
of her breasts, though they touched only his coat, made him
go back against the door with a blind shock. See what he had
tracked down, in his hunting game!

The woman was saying to herself, furious with insult, "So I
cain't ——k, huh? I'll show that son-of-a-bitch kin I, cain't I."

What should he do now? Grebe asked himself. Why, he
should go. He should turn away and go. He couldn't talk to this
woman. He couldn't keep her standing naked in the cold. But
when he tried he found himself unable to turn away.

He said, "Is this where Mr. Green lives?"

But she was still talking to herself and did not hear him.

"Is this Mr. Green's house?"

At last she turned her furious drunken glance on him. "What
do you want?"

Again her eyes wandered from him; there was a dot of blood
in their enraged brilliance. He wondered why she didn't feel the
cold.

"I'm from the relief."

"Awright, what?"

"I've got a check for Tulliver Green."

This time she heard him and put out her hand.

"No, no, for *Mr.* Green. He's got to sign," he said. How was
he going to get Green's signature tonight!

"I'll take it. He cain't."

He desperately shook his head, thinking of Mr. Field's precautions about identification. "I can't let you have it. It's for him. Are you Mrs. Green?"

"Maybe I is, and maybe I ain't. Who want to know?"

"Is he upstairs?"

"Awright. Take it up yourself, you goddam fool."

Sure, he was a goddamned fool. Of course he could not go up because Green would probably be drunk and naked, too. And perhaps he would appear on the landing soon. He looked eagerly upward. Under the light was a high narrow brown wall. Empty! It remained empty!

"Hell with you, then!" he heard her cry. To deliver a check for coal and clothes, he was keeping her in the cold. She did not feel it, but his face was burning with frost and self-ridicule. He backed away from her.

"I'll come tomorrow, tell him."

"Ah, hell with you. Don' never come. What you doin' here in the nighttime? Don' come back." She yelled so that he saw the breadth of her tongue. She stood astride in the long cold box of the hall and held on to the banister and the wall. The bungalow itself was shaped something like a box, a clumsy, high box pointing into the freezing air with its sharp, wintry lights.

"If you are Mrs. Green, I'll give you the check," he said, changing his mind.

"Give here, then." She took it, took the pen offered with it in her left hand, and tried to sign the receipt on the wall. He looked around, almost as though to see whether his madness was being observed, and came near believing that someone was standing on a mountain of used tires in the auto-junking shop next door.

"But are you Mrs. Green?" he now thought to ask. But she was already climbing the stairs with the check, and it was too late, if he had made an error, if he was now in trouble, to undo the thing. But he wasn't going to worry about it. Though she might not be Mrs. Green, he was convinced that Mr. Green was upstairs. Whoever she was, the woman stood for Green, whom he was not to see this tine. Well, you silly bastard, he said to himself, so you think you found him. So what? Maybe you really did find him—what of it? But it was important that there was a real Mr. Green whom they could not keep him from reaching because he seemed to come as an emissary from hostile appearances. And though the self-ridicule was slow to diminish, and his face still blazed with it, he had, nevertheless, a feeling of elation, too. "For after all," he said, "he *could* be found!"

The Gonzaga Manuscripts

Buttoned to the throat in a long, soft over-coat, dark green, Clarence Feiler got off the Hendaye Express in the Madrid station. It was late afternoon and it was raining, and the station with its throng and its dim orange lights seemed sunken under darkness and noise. The gaunt horselike Spanish locomotives screamed off their steam and the hurrying passengers struggled in the narrow gates. Porters and touts approached Clarence, obviously a foreigner by his small blond beard, blue eyes, almost brimless hat, long coat and crepe-soled shoes. But he carried his own bag and had no need of them. This was not his first visit to Madrid. An old limousine took him to the Pension La Granja, where he had a room reserved. This limousine probably had run on the boulevards of Madrid before Clarence was born but it was mechanically still beautiful. In the spacious darkness of the back seat the windows were like the glass of an old cabinet, and he listened happily to the voice of the wonderful old motor. Where could you get another ride like this, on such an evening, through such a place? Clarence loved Spanish cities, even the poorest and barrenest, and the capitals stirred his heart as no other places did. He had first come as an undergraduate, a mere kid, studying Spanish literature at the University of Minnesota; and then he had come again and seen the ruins of the Civil War. This time he came not as a tourist but on a quest. He had heard from a Spanish Republican refugee in California, where he now lived, that there were more than a hundred poems by Manuel Gonzaga somewhere in Madrid. Not a single Spanish publishing house could print them because they were so critical of the Army and the state. It was hard to believe that poems by one of the greatest of modern Spanish geniuses could be suppressed, but the refugee gave Clarence reliable proof that it was so. He showed him letters to one of Gonzaga's nephews from a man named Gúzman del Nido, Gonzaga's friend and literary executor, with whom he had served in North Africa, admitting that he had once had the poems but had given them up to a certain Countess del Camino since most of them were love poems addressed to her. The countess had died during the war, her home had been looted, and he didn't know what had become of the poems.

"Perhaps he doesn't care, either," said the refugee. "He's one of these people who think everything has come to an end anyway, and they might as well live comfortably. Gúzman del Nido lives very comfortably. He's rich. He is a member of the Cortes."

"Money doesn't have to do that to you," said Clarence, who had a little money himself. He was not exactly a rich man, but he didn't have to work for a living. "He must have a bad character not to care about his friend's work. And such work! You know, I was just killing time in graduate school till I came across Gonzaga. The year I spent doing my thesis on *Los Huesos Secos* was the first good year I had had since I was a boy. There hasn't been anything like it since. I'm not much on modern poetry in English. Some of it is very fine, of course, but it doesn't express much wish to live. To live as a creature, that is. As if it were not good enough. But the first time I opened Gonzaga I read:

> These few bits of calcium my teeth are,
> And these few ohms my brain is,
> May make you think I am nothing but puny.
> Let me tell you, sir,
> I am like any creature—
> A creature.

I felt right away and in spite of this ironical turn that I was in touch with a poet who could show me how to go on, and what attitude to take toward life. The great, passionate poems carried me away, like 'The Poem of Night,' which I still know by heart from beginning to end and which often seems like the only thing I really have got—" Clarence was sometimes given to exaggerating. "Or take the poem called 'Confession,' the one that goes:

> I used to welcome all
> And now I fear all.
> If it rained it was comforting
> And if it shone, comforting,
> But now my very weight is dreadful . . .

When I read that, Gonzaga made me understand how we lose everything by trying to become everything. This was the most valuable lesson of my life, I think. Gosh! There should be someone trying to find those posthumous poems. They ought not to be given up. They must be marvelous."

He felt, suddenly, as if he had been thrown into a race, terribly excited, full of effort, feverish—and profoundly grateful. For Clarence had not found his occupation and had nothing to do. He did not think it right to marry until he had found something and could offer a wife leadership. His beard was grown not to hide weaknesses but as a project, to give his life shape. He was becoming an eccentric; it was all he could do with his good impulses. As yet he did not realize that these impulses were religious. He was too timid to say he believed in God, and he couldn't think that it would matter to anyone what he believed. Since he was weak, it would be said, he must have some such belief. However, he was really enthusiastic about Gonzaga, and to recover this inspired Spaniard's poems was something that mattered. And "Does it really matter?" was always the test question. It filled Clarence with secret pleasure to know that he was not indifferent, at bottom pretending. It *did* matter, and what mattered might save him. He was in Madrid not to perform an act of cultural piety but to do a decent and necessary thing, namely, bring the testimony of a great man before the world. Which certainly could use it.

As soon as he arrived at the Pension La Granja and the lamps were lit in his room, a comfortable large room with balconies facing the trees of the Retiro, Madrid's biggest park, Clarence called for the porter and sent off two letters. One was addressed to Gúzman del Nido, Gonzaga's comrade-in-arms of the Moroccan War and literary executor, and the other to a Miss Faith Ungar on García de Paredes Street. This Miss Ungar was an art student, or rather student of art history; her fiancé was an airline pilot who brought in cheaper pesetas from Tangiers. Clarence disliked black-marketing, but the legal rate of exchange was ridiculous; he was prepared to pay a lot of money for those manuscripts and at eighteen to one he might spend a small fortune.

His landlady came to welcome him to the pension—a pale, big woman with a sort of turban of hair wound spirally to a point. She came also to collect his passport and other travel papers for police inspection and to give him a briefing on her guests. A retired general was the oldest. She had also some people from British Shell and the widow of a Minister and six members of a Brazilian trade delegation, so the dining room was full. "And are you a tourist?" she said, glancing at the *triptico,* the elaborate police document all travelers have to carry in Spain.

"In a way," said Clarence, guardedly. He didn't like to be thought of as a tourist, and yet secrecy was necessary. Gonzaga's poems, though unpublished, would probably come under the head of national treasures.

"Or have you come to study something?"

"Yes, that's it."

"There's a great deal here to interest people from a country as new as yours."

"There certainly is," he said, his rosy beard-lengthened face turned to her, seeming perfectly sincere. The color of his mouth was especially vivid in the lamplight. It was not yet full evening and the rain was stopping. Beyond the trees of the Retiro the sky was making itself clear of clouds, and a last yellow daylight pierced the water-gray. Trolley sparks scratched green within the locust trees.

A bell rang, an old handbell, announcing dinner. A maid passed, ringing it proudly, her shoulders thrown back.

The guests were eating soup in the dining room, an interior room, not very airy, with dark red, cloth-covered walls. The Brazilians were having a lively conversation. The old general, feeble-headed, eyes nearly extinct, was bothering the soup with his spoon but not eating. Doña Elvia seated Clarence with a hefty British lady; he knew he must expect to have trouble with her. She was in a bad way. Her face was heavily made up; she thought she was a person of charm, and she did have a certain charm, but her eyes were burning. Tresses of dark-reddish hair fought strongly for position on her head.

"If you came here with the intention of having fun, you won't have it in Madrid. I've been here twenty years and never had any," she said. "By now I'm so tired out I don't even look for any. I don't read any books, I don't go to the cinema, and I can just barely stand to read *Coyote* and look at the funnies. I can't understand why so many Americans want to come here. They're all over the place. One of your bishops was arrested at Santander for bathing without the top of his costume."

"Really?"

"They're very strict in Spain about dress. I suppose if they had known he was a bishop they would have let him alone. However, in the water . . ."

"It's strange," said Clarence. "Well, anyway, he's not one of *my* bishops. I have no bishops."

"You do have Congressmen, though. Two of those had their pants stolen while taking a nap on the Barcelona Express. The thieves reached into the compartment from the roof. It happened in broad daylight. They carried about two thousand dollars each. Don't they have pocketbooks? Why do they carry so much money in their pockets?"

Clarence frowned. "Yes, I read about that," he said. "I can't tell you why they carry so much money in their trouser pockets. Maybe that's the custom down South. It's none of my business, though."

"I'm afraid I'm annoying you," she said. She was not afraid at all; a bold look of enjoyment had entered her eyes. She was trying to bait him. Why? he wondered; he found no ready answer.

"You're not annoying me."

"If I am," she said, "it's not absolutely my fault. You know Stendhal once wrote there was a secret principle of unhappiness in the English."

"Is that so?" he said. He looked at her with deep interest. What a busted-up face; full of unhappy vigor and directionless intelligence. Yes, she was astonishing. He felt sorry for her and yet lucky to have met her, in spite of everything.

"He may have been right. You see, I used to read widely

once. I was a cultivated person. But the reason for it was sex, and that went."

"Oh, come, I wouldn't say—"

"I shouldn't be talking like this. It's partly the weather. It's been raining so hard. It isn't supposed to rain like this in the summer. I've never seen so much damned rain. You people may be to blame for that."

"Who people? Which people?"

"It could be because of the atom bomb," she said. "The weather has never been normal since the atom thing started. Nobody can tell what this radioactive stuff is doing. Perhaps it's the beginning of the end."

"You make me feel very strange," said Clarence. "But why are the American bombs the dangerous ones? There are others."

"Because one always reads of the Americans exploding them. They do it under water. Holes are torn in the ocean bottom. The cold water rushes in and cools the core of the earth. Then the surface shrinks. No one can tell what will happen. It's affected the weather already."

Clarence's color grew very high and he looked dazed. He paid no attention to his broiled meat and french-fried potatoes. "I don't keep up much with science," he said. "I remember I did read somewhere that industry gives off six billion tons of carbon dioxide every year and so the earth is growing warmer because the carbon dioxide in the air is opaque to heat radiation. All that means that the glaciers won't be coming back."

"Yes, but what about Carbon Fourteen? You Americans are filling the air with Carbon Fourteen, which is very dangerous."

"I don't know about it. I am not all Americans. You are not all the English. You didn't lick the Armada, I didn't open the West. You are not Winston Churchill, I am not the Pentagon."

"I believe you are some sort of fanatic," she announced.

"And I believe you're a nasty old bag!" he said, enraged. He left the table and went to his room.

Half an hour later she knocked at his door. "I'm terribly sorry," she said. "I suppose I did go too far. But it's all right, we're friends now, aren't we? It does you so much good to be angry. It really is good." She did, now, look very friendly and happy.

"It's all right. I'm sorry too," he said.

After all, how would feuding with this Englishwoman help him with his quest? And then there were wrong ways and right ways of going about it. Gonzaga's poems should be recovered in the spirit of Gonzaga himself. Otherwise, what was the use?

Considering it all next morning, he saw that this Miss Walsh, the Englishwoman, had done him a service by baiting him. Unwittingly, she offered a test of his motive. He could not come to Spain and act badly, blindly. So he was deepened in his thought and in his purpose, and felt an increased debt to Gonzaga and to those poems.

He was in a hurry next morning to get to a bookstore and see what Gonzaga items there were in print. Impatiently he turned himself out of the comfortable bed, pulled on his underpants, dealt nervously with his cuff-buttons, washed at his little sink with the glass shelves and pointed faucets, and combed his hair and whiskers with his palms. Odors of soil and flowers came from the Retiro across the freshly watered street. The morning was clear, still and blue. He took one bite of the brick bits of toast the maid brought, sipped from the immense cup of bitter café-au-lait, and then rushed out to find a bookstore.

At Bucholz's he found only a single volume he had not seen before, a collection of letters from Gonzaga to his father. The frontispiece showed Gonzaga in his lieutenant's uniform— a small man, by Clarence's standard—sitting up straight at the keyboard of an old-fashioned piano, his large eyes opened directly into the camera. Underneath he had noted, "Whenever I am lucky enough to come upon a piano in one of these Moroccan towns, I can, after playing for ten or fifteen minutes, discover how I really feel. Otherwise I am ignorant." Clarence's face colored with satisfaction as he stooped and looked. What a man this Gonzaga was—what a personality! On the very first page was an early version of a poem he had always admired, the one that began:

> Let me hear a sound
> Truly not my own;
> The voice of another,
> Truly other. . . .

The book engrossed him entirely until eleven o'clock. With a sort of hungry emotion, he sat at a café table and read it from cover to cover. It was beautiful. He thanked God for sending him the Republican refugee who had given him the idea of coming to Spain.

Reluctantly he left the café and took a cab to García de Paredes Street, where Miss Ungar lived. He hated to do it, but he needed the pesetas, and it was unavoidable.

Again he was lucky. She was not at all the kind of person you would have expected a black-marketing art student to be; she was young and unusually attractive with a long, intelligent white face. Her hair was drawn tightly back over her elongated head and tied off in an arched, sparkling tail. Her eyes were extremely clear. Clarence was greatly taken with her. Even the fact that her teeth, because of the contrast with her very fair skin, were not too bright, impressed him. It proved to him that she was genuine. On a ribbon round her neck she wore a large silver medal.

"Is that a religious thing you're wearing?"

"No. Do you want to look at it?" She bent forward so that it

swung free. He picked up the warm piece of silver and read:
Helena Waite Award for Historical Studies.

"You won it?"

"Yes."

"Then why are you in this kind of business?"

"And what did you come here for?" she said.

"I need pesetas."

"And we need dollars. My fiancé and I want to buy a
house."

"I see."

"Besides, it's a way of meeting a lot of people. You'd be
surprised how few interesting people an American woman in
Madrid can meet. I can't spend all my time in the Prado or
at the Library. The embassy people are about as interesting
as a plate of cold cuts. My fiancé only gets here twice a month.
Are you on a holiday?"

"Sort of."

She didn't believe him. She knew he had come with a definite
purpose. He could not say why, but this pleased him.

"How do you like the Granja?"

"It's all right. An Englishwoman there lammed into me
last night, first about the atom bomb and then saying that I
must be a fanatic. She thought I was peculiar."

"Everybody has to make it as he can," she said.

"That's exactly the way I feel about it."

He had thought that the kind of woman who became engaged to an airline pilot might look down on him. She didn't,
not in the least. Soon he was wondering how that sort of man
could interest her.

"If you have no other plans, why don't you come to lunch
with me," he said, "and save me from that Miss Walsh?"

They went out to eat. Though the day had grown hot, she
stopped in the courtyard to put on a pair of net gloves; women
without gloves were considered common in Madrid. For his

part Clarence thought the momentary grasp of her fingers as she worked them into the gloves was wonderful; what a lot of life she had! Her white face gave off a pleasant heat. As they walked, she told him she couldn't give him many pesetas just yet; she'd pay whatever rate was quoted in the *Tribune* on the day the money arrived. That day, Clarence reflected, would also be the day on which her pilot arrived; he had no business to be disturbed by that, and yet it did disturb him.

Near the Naval Ministry they were stopped by a procession. Priests with banners led it, and after them came a statue of the Virgin carried by four men. A group of barefooted widows followed in their mourning with black mantillas. Old women passed, carrying tapers. Most of these appeared to be old maids, and the flames made a clear additional light near each face. A band played Beethoven's Funeral March. Above the walls of the ministry trees shot their leaves; there was the same odor of flowers and soil that Clarence had smelled that morning, of graves, of summer pines. Across the square, on the car tracks, a welding arc hummed and scalded. The dazzling mouths of the horns were carried past and the fires in the daylight moved away, but it was the bare white feet of the widows treading on the dusty asphalt paving that Clarence watched, and when they were gone he said to Miss Ungar, "Wasn't that splendid? I'm glad I'm here."

His brows had risen; his face was so lively that Miss Ungar laughed and said, "You take it big. I like the way you take it. You ought to be sure to visit Toledo. Have you ever been there?"

"No."

"I go often. I'm doing a study. Come with me next time I go. I can show you lots of things there."

"There's nothing I'd like better. When do you go next?"

"Tomorrow."

He was disappointed. "Oh, I'm sorry, I can't make it tomorrow," he said. "I arrived yesterday and I'm going to be very busy for a while. Just give me a rain-check, will you? I'll hold you to this. But there is something special I came to do— you guessed it, I suppose—and I can't take the time to go anywhere now. I'm all keyed up."

"Is this mission of yours a secret?"

"In a way. There's an illegal side to it, probably. But I don't think you'd tell on me, and I'm so full of it I'm willing to talk. Have you ever heard of a poet named Gonzaga?"

"Gonzaga? I must have. But I don't think I ever read his poems."

"You should read them. He was very great, one of the most original of modern Spanish poets, and in the class of Juan Ramón Jiménez, Lorca, and Machado. I studied him at school and he means a lot to me. To understand what he did, you have to think first of modern literature as a sort of grand council considering what mankind should do next, how they should fill their mortal time, what they should feel, what they should see, where they should get their courage, how they should love, how they should be pure or great, and all the rest. This advice of literature has never done much good. But you see God doesn't rule over men as he used to, and for a long time people haven't been able to feel that life was firmly attached at both ends so that they could stand confidently in the middle and trust the place where they were. That kind of faith is missing, and for many years poets have tried to supply a substitute. Like 'the unacknowledged legislators' or 'the best is yet to be,' or Walt Whitman saying that whoever touched him could be sure he was touching a man. Some have stood up for beauty, and some have stood up for perfect proportion, and the very best have soon gotten tired of art for its own sake. Some took it as their duty to behave like brave performers who try to hold down panic during a theater fire. Very great ones have quit, like Tolstoi, who became a reformer, or like Rimbaud, who went to Abyssinia, and at the end of his life was begging of a priest, '*Montrez-moi. Montrez . . .* Show me something.' Frightening, the lives some of these geniuses led. Maybe they assumed too much responsibility. They knew that if by their poems and novels *they* were fixing values, there must be something wrong with the values. One man can't furnish them. Oh, he may try, if his inspiration is for values, but not if his inspiration is for words. If you throw the full responsibility for meaning and for the establishing of good and evil on poets, they are doomed to go down. However, the poets reflected what was happening to everyone. There are people who feel that they are responsible for *everything*. Gonzaga is free from this, and that's why I love him. Here. See what he says in some of these letters. I found this marvelous collection this morning."

His long hands shaking, he pressed flat the little book on the table of the restaurant. Miss Ungar's quiet face expressed more than intellectual interest. "Listen. He writes to his father: 'Many feel they must say it all, whereas all has been said, unsaid, resaid so many times that we are bound to feel futile unless we understand that we are merely adding our voices. Adding them when moved by the spirit. Then and then only.' Or this: 'A poem may outlive its subject—say, my poem about the girl who sang songs on the train—but the poet has no right to expect this. The poem has no greater privilege than the girl.' You see what kind of man he was?"

"Impressive—really!" she said. "I see that."

"I've come to Spain to find some of his unpublished poems. I have some money, and I've never really been able to find the thing that I wanted to do. I'm not original myself, except in some minor way. Anyhow, that's why I'm here. Lots of people call themselves leaders, healers, priests, and spokesmen for God, prophets or witnesses, but Gonzaga was a human being who spoke only as a human being; there was nothing spurious about him. He tried never to misrepresent; he wanted to see. To move you he didn't have to do anything, he merely had to be. We've made the most natural things the hardest of all. Unfortunately for us all, he was killed while still young. But he left some poems to a certain Countess del Camino, and I'm here to locate them."

"It's a grand thing. I wish you luck. I hope people will help you."

"Why shouldn't they?"

"I don't know, but don't you expect to run into trouble?"

"Do you think I ought to expect to?"

"If you want my honest opinion, yes."

"I may get the poems—why, just like that," he said. "You never can tell."

"Started, by God!" he said when he received an answer from Gúzman del Nido. The member of the Cortes invited him to dinner. All that day he was in a state, and the weather was peculiarly thick, first glaring sunshine, then explosive rains. "See what I told you," said Miss Walsh. But when Clarence went out late in the afternoon, the sky was clear and pale again and the Palm Sunday leaves braided in the ironwork of balconies were withering in the sunlight. He walked to the Puerta del Sol with its crowd of pleasure-seekers, beggars, curb-haunters, wealthy women, soldiers, cops, lottery-ticket and fountain-pen peddlers, and priests, humble door-openers, chair-menders, and musicians. At seven-thirty he boarded a streetcar, following directions; it seemed to take him to every other point of the city first. Finally, with the wisp of trolley paper still in his hand, he got off and mounted a bare stony alley at the top of which was the del Nido villa. Suddenly there was another cloudburst—*una tormenta* was what the Madrileños called it. No doorway offered cover and he was drenched. At the gate he had to wait a long while for the porter to answer his ring, perhaps five minutes in the hard rain. This would probably give comfort to the English-woman with her atomic theories. His nervous long eyes seemed to catch some of the slaty blue of the pouring rain-cloud; his blond beard darkened, and he pulled in his shoulders. The tall gate opened. The porter held out an umbrella in his brown fist. Clarence walked past him to the door of the house. The rain stopped when he was halfway up the path.

So he was at a disadvantage when Gúzman del Nido came forward to meet him. He walked clumsily in his sodden wool suit. It had a shameful smell, like wet dog.

"How do you do, Señor Feiler. What a shame about the rain. It has ruined your suit but it gives your face a fine color."

They shook hands, and it came over Clarence with a thrill as he looked at the high-bridged nose and dark, fine-textured skin of del Nido that he was in touch with Gonzaga himself —this round-shouldered man in his linen suit, bowing his sloping head, smiling with sharp teeth, with his hairless hand and big-boned wrist and his awkward fanny, he had been Gonzaga's friend and belonged within the legend. Clarence at once sensed that he would make him look foolish if he could, through the irony of his very complete manners. He also realized that del Nido was the sort of person who cut everyone down to size, Gonzaga included; precisely the sort of man to whom Gonzaga had written: *"Go away! You have no holy ones."*

"The letter I sent you—" Clarence managed to begin. They were hurrying toward the dining room; other guests were waiting.

"We can discuss it later."

"I understand you gave certain poems to the Countess del Camino," he said.

But del Nido was speaking with another guest. The candles were lit and the company sat down.

Clarence had no appetite.

He was sitting between an Italian Monsignore and an Egyptian lady who had lived in New York and spoke a very slangy English. There was a German gentleman, too, who headed some insurance company; he sat between Señora del Nido and her daughter. From his end of the table, del Nido with his narrow sleek head and his forward-curved teeth shining with valuable crowns, dominated the conversation. About his eyes the skin was twisted in curious laugh-wrinkles. Impressed, appalled, too, Clarence asked himself again and again how Gonzaga could have trusted such a person. A maker of witticisms, as Pascal had said, a bad character. When these words of Pascal came into his head, Clarence turned to the Monsignore as a man to whom this might make sense. But the Monsignore was interested mostly in stamp-collecting. Clarence was not, so the Monsignore had nothing further to say to him. He was a gloomy, fleshy man whose hair grew strongly and low over the single deep wrinkle of his forehead.

Gúzman del Nido kept on talking. He talked about modern painting, about mystery stories, about old Russia, about the movies, about Nietzsche. Dreamy-looking, the daughter seemed not to listen; his wife expanded some of his remarks. The daughter stared with close-set eyes into the candle flames. The Egyptian lady was amused by the strong smell of Clarence's rain-shrinking clothes. She made a remark about wet wool. He was grateful for the absence of electric lights.

"An American was arrested in Córdoba," said Gúzman del Nido. "He stole the hat of a *Guardia Civil* for a souvenir."

"Isn't that unusual!"

"He'll find the jail smaller than the jails at home. I hope you won't mind if I tell a story about Americans and the size of things in Spain."

"Why should I mind?" said Clarence.

"Splendid. Well, there was an American whose Spanish host could not impress him. Everything was larger in America. The skyscrapers were bigger than the palaces. The cars were bigger.

The cats were bigger. At last his host placed a lobster between his sheets and when the horrified American saw it his host said, 'This is one of our bedbugs. I don't think you can beat that.' "

For some reason this fetched Clarence more than it did the others. He uttered a bark of laughter that made the candle-lights bend and flutter.

"Perhaps you'll tell us an American story," said del Nido.

Clarence thought. "Well, here's one," he said. "Two dogs meet in the street. Old friends. One says, 'Hello.' The other answers, 'Cock-a-doodle-do!' 'What does that mean? What's this cock-a-doodle-do stuff?' 'Oh,' says he, 'I've been studying foreign languages.' "

Dead silence. No one laughed. The Egyptian lady said, "I'm afraid you laid an egg." Clarence was angry.

"Is this story told in English or in American?" del Nido asked.

That started a discussion. Was American really a sort of English? Was it a language? No one seemed sure, and Clarence at last said, "I don't know whether or not it is a language, but there is *something* spoken. I've seen people cry in it and so forth, just as elsewhere."

"We deserved that," said del Nido. "It's true, we're not fair to Americans. In reality the only true Europeans left are Americans."

"How so?"

"The Europeans themselves do not have the peace of mind to appreciate what's best. Life is too hard for us, society too unstable."

Clarence realized that he was being shafted; del Nido was satirizing his quest; he undoubtedly meant that Clarence could not comprehend Gonzaga's poems. An ugly hatred for del Nido grew and knotted in his breast. He wanted to hit him, to strangle him, to trample him, to pick him up and hurl him at the wall. Luckily del Nido was called to the phone, and Clarence stared out his rage at the empty place, the napkin, the silver, the crest of the chair. Only Señorita del Nido seemed aware that he was offended.

Once more Clarence told himself that there was a wrong way to go about obtaining the poems, a way contrary to their spirit. That did much to calm him. He managed to get down a few spoonfuls of ice cream and mastered himself.

"Why are you so interested in Gonzaga?" said del Nido to him later in the garden, under the date palms with their remote leaves.

"I studied Spanish literature in college and became a Gonzagian."

"Wasn't that rather strange, though? You must forgive me, but I see my poor old friend Gonzaga, who was Spanish of the Spanish, in that terrible uniform we used to wear, and our hands and faces bruised and baked and chapped by the desert sun, and I ask myself why he should have had an effect . . ."

"I don't know why. I'd like to understand it myself; but the fact that he did is what you start with."

"I have made an interesting observation about poets and their lives. Some are better in real life than in their work. You read bitter poems and then you find the poet is personally very happy and good-tempered. Some are worse in their personality than you would guess from their work. They are luckier, in a way, because they have a chance to correct their faults and improve themselves. Best of all are the ones who are exactly the same inside and out, in the spoken word and the written. To be what you seem to be is the objective of true culture. Gonzaga was of the second type."

"Was he?" It occurred to Clarence that del Nido was trying to make himself more interesting to him than Gonzaga could be, to push Gonzaga out.

"I think I can tell you one reason why Gonzaga appeals to

me," said Clarence. "He got away from solving *his* own problem. I often feel this way about it: a poem is great because it is absolutely necessary. Before it came silence. After it comes more silence. It begins when it must and ends when it must, and therefore it's not personal. It's 'the sound truly not my own.' " Now he was proving to del Nido that he *could* comprehend; at the same time he knew that he was throwing away his effort. Gúzman del Nido was fundamentally indifferent. Indifferent, indifferent, indifferent! He fundamentally did not care. What can you do with people who don't fundamentally care! "But you know why I came to you. I want to know what became of Gonzaga's last poems. What were they like?"

They were superb love poems. But I don't know where they are now. They were dedicated to the Countess del Camino and I was supposed to hand them on to her. Which I did."

"There aren't any copies?" said Clarence, trembling as del Nido spoke of the poems.

"No. They were for the countess."

"Of course. But they were also for everyone else."

"There's plenty of poetry already, for everyone. Homer, Dante, Calderón, Shakespeare. Have you noticed how much difference it makes?"

"It should make a difference. Besides, Calderón wasn't your friend. But Gonzaga was. Where's the countess now? The poor woman is dead, isn't she? And what happened to those poems? Where do you think the poems can be?"

"I don't know. She had a secretary named Polvo, a fine old man. A few years ago he died, too. The old man's nephews live in Alcalá de Henares. Where Cervantes was born, you know. They're in the civil service, and they're very decent people, I hear."

"You never even asked them what happened to your friend's poems?" cried Clarence, astonished. "Didn't you want to find them?"

"I thought eventually I'd try to trace them. I'm sure the countess would have taken good care of her poems."

This was where the discussion stopped, and Clarence was just as glad that it couldn't continue; he sensed that Gúzman del Nido would have liked to give him the dirt on Gonzaga— revelations involving women, drunkenness and dope-taking, bribery, gonorrhea, or even murder. Gonzaga had escaped into the army; that was notorious. But Clarence didn't want to hear del Nido's reminiscences.

It's natural to suppose, because a man is great, that the people around him must have known how to respond to greatness, but when those people turn out to be no better than Gúzman del Nido you wonder what response greatness really needs.

This was what Clarence was saying to Miss Ungar several days later.

"He's glad he doesn't have the poems," said Miss Ungar. "If he had them he'd feel obliged to do something about them, and he's afraid of that because of his official position."

"That's right. Exactly," said Clarence. "But he did me one favor anyway. He put me on to the countess's secretary's nephews. I've written to them and they've invited me to Alcalá de Henares. They didn't mention the poems but maybe they were just being discreet. I'd better start being more discreet myself. There's something unpleasant going on, lately."

"What is it?"

"I think the police have an eye on me."

"Oh, come!"

"I do. I'm serious. My room was searched yesterday. I know it was. My landlady didn't answer one way or another when I asked her. She didn't even bother."

"It's too peculiar for anything," Miss Ungar said, laughing in amazement. "But why should they search? What for?"

"I suppose I just inspire suspicion. And then I made a mistake with my landlady the day after my visit to del Nido. She's a very patriotic character. She has a retired general in the pension, too. Well, she was talking to me the other morning and among other things she told me how healthy she was, strong as a rock—*una roca*—a sort of Gibraltar. And like a dumbbell I said, without even thinking, '*Gibraltar Español!*' That was an awful boner."

"Why?"

"During the war, you see, when the British were taking such a pounding there was a great agitation for the return of Gibraltar to Spain. The slogan was *Gibraltar Español!* Of course they don't like to be reminded that they were dying for the British to get it good and hot from Germany. Well, she probably thinks I'm a political secret somebody. And she was just plain offended."

"But what difference does it really make, as long as you don't do anything illegal?"

"When you're watched closely you're bound sooner or later to do *something*," he said.

He went out to Alcalá on a Sunday afternoon and met the two nephews of Don Francisco Polvo and their wives and daughters.

They proved to be a family of laughers. They laughed when they spoke and when you answered. You saw nothing in the town but sleepy walls, and parched trees and stones. The brothers were squat, sandy-haired, broad-bellied men.

"We're having tea in the garden," said Don Luis Polvo. He was called "the Englishman" by the others because he had lived in London for several months twenty years ago; they addressed him as "My Lord," and he obliged them by acting like an *Inglés*. He even owned a scotch terrier named *Duglas*. The family cried to him, "Now's your chance to speak English, Luis. Speak to him!"

"Jolly country, eh?" Luis said. That was about all he could manage.

"Very."

"More, more!"

"Charing Cross."

"Go on, Luis, say more."

"Piccadilly. And that's all I can remember."

The tea was served. Clarence drank and sweltered. Lizards raced in the knotty grapevines and by the well. . . . The wives were embroidering. The laughing daughters were conversing in French, obviously about Clarence. Nobody appeared to believe what he said. Lanky and pained he sat in what looked to be a suit made of burlap, with his tea. Instead of a saucer, he felt as though he were holding on to the rim of Saturn.

After tea they showed him through the house. It was huge, old, bare, thick-walled and chill, and it was filled with the portraits and the clothing of ancestors—weapons, breastplates, helmets, daggers, guns. In one room where the picture of a general in the Napoleonic Wars was hung, a fun-making mood seized the brothers. They tried on plumed hats, then sabers, and finally full uniforms. Wearing spurs, medals, musty gloves, they went running back to the terrace where the women sat. Don Luis dragged a sword, his seat hung down and the cocked hat sagged broken, opening in the middle on his sandy baldness. With a Napoleonic musket, full of self-mockery, he performed the manual-at-arms to uproarious laughter. Clarence laughed, too, his cheeks creased; he couldn't explain however why his heart was growing heavier by the minute.

Don Luis aimed the musket and shouted, *"La bomba atómica! Poum!"*

The hit he scored with this was enormous. The women shrieked, swiveling their fans, and his brother fell on his

behind in the sanded path, weeping with laughter. The terrier
Duglas leaped into Don Luis's face, fiercely excited.

Don Luis threw a stick and cried, "Fetch, fetch, *Duglas!
La bomba atómica! La bomba atómica!*"

The blood stormed Clarence's head so furiously he heard
the strange noise of it. This was another assault on him. Oh! he
thought frantically, the things he had to bear! The punishment he had to take trying to salvage those poems!

As if in the distance, the voice of Don Luis cried, "Hiro-
shima! Nagasaki! Bikini! Good show!" He flung the stick and
the dog bounded on taut legs, little *Duglas,* from the diminished
figure of his master and back—the tiny white and brown animal, while laughter incessantly pierced the dry air of the
garden.

It was not a decent joke, even though Don Luis in that
split hat and the withered coat was mocking the dead military
grandeur of his own country. That didn't even the score. The
hideous stun of the bomb and its unbearable, death-brilliant
mushroom cloud filled Clarence's brain. This was not right.

He managed to stop Don Luis. He approached him, laid a
hand on the musket, and asked to speak with him privately.
It made the others laugh. The ladies started to murmur about
him. An older woman said, *"Es gracioso";* the girls seemed to
disagree. He heard one of them answer, *"Non, il n'est pas
gentil."* Proudly polite, Clarence faced it out. "Damn their
damn tea!" he said to himself. His shirt was sticking to his
back.

"We did not inherit my uncle's papers," said Don Luis.
"Enough, *Duglas!*" He threw the stick down the well. "My
brother and I inherited this old house and other land but if
there were papers they probably went to my cousin Pedro
Alvarez-Polvo who lives in Segovia. He's a very interesting
fellow. He works for the *Banco Español* but is a cultivated

person. The countess had no family. She was fond of my uncle. My uncle was extremely fond of Alvarez-Polvo. They shared the same interests."

"Did your uncle ever speak of Gonzaga?"

"I don't recall. The countess had a large number of artistic admirers. This Gonzaga interests you very much, doesn't he?"

"Yes. Why shouldn't I be interested in him? You may some day be interested in an American poet."

"I? No!" Don Luis laughed, but he was startled.

What people! Damn these dirty laughers! Clarence waited until Don Luis's shocked and latterly somewhat guilty laughter ended, and his broad yap, with spacious teeth, closed—his lips shook with resistance to closing, and finally remained closed.

"Do you think your cousin Alvarez-Polvo would know . . ."

"He would know a lot," said Don Luis, composed. "My uncle confided in him. *He* can tell you something definite, you can count on him. I'll give you a letter of introduction to him."

"If it's not too much trouble."

"No, no, the pleasure is mine." Don Luis was all courtesy.

After returning to Madrid on the bus through the baking plain of Castile, Clarence phoned Miss Ungar. He wanted her sympathy and comfort. But she didn't invite him to come over. She said, "I can give you the pesetas tomorrow." That was her tactful way of informing him that the pilot had landed, and he thought she sounded regretful. Perhaps she was not really in love with her fiancé. Clarence now had the impression that the black-marketing was not her idea but the pilot's. It embarrassed her, but she was too loyal to admit it to him.

"I'll come by later in the week. There's no hurry," he said. "I'm busy anyway."

It would hurt him to do it, but he'd cash a check at the

American Express tomorrow at the preposterous legal rate of exchange.

Disappointed, Clarence hung up. *He* should have a woman like that. It passed dimly over his mind that a live woman would make a better quest than a dead poet. But the poet was already *there;* the woman not. He sent a letter to Alvarez-Polvo, washed all over, and lay reading Gonzaga by a buzzing light under the canopy of his bed.

He arrived in Segovia early one Sunday morning. It was filled with sunlight, the clouds were silk-white in the mountain air. Their shadows wandered over the slopes of the bare sierra like creatures that crept and warmed themselves on the soil and rock. All over the old valley were convents, hermitages, churches, towers, the graves of San Juan and other mystical saints. At the highest point of Segovia was the Alcázar of Isabella the Catholic. And passing over the town with its many knobby granite curves that divided the sky was the aqueduct, this noble Roman remnant, as bushy as old men's ears. Clarence stood at the window of his hotel and looked at this conjured rise of stones that bridged the streets. It got him, all of it— the ancient mountain slopes worn as if by the struggles of Jacob with the angel, the spires, the dry glistening of the atmosphere, the hermit places in green hideaways, the sheep bells' clunk, the cistern water dropping, while beams came as straight as harpwires from the sun. All of this, like a mild weight, seemed to press on him; it opened him up. He felt his breath creep within him like a tiny pet animal.

He went down through the courtyard. There the cistern of fat stone held green water, full of bottom-radiations from the golden brass of the faucets. Framed above it in an archway were ladies' hair styles of twenty years ago—a brilliantine advertisement. Ten or so beautiful señoritas with bangs, shingles, and windswept bobs smiled like various priestesses of love. Therefore Clarence had the idea that this cistern was the Fountain of Youth. And also that it was something Arcadian. He said, " 'Ye glorious nymphs!' " and burst out laughing. He felt happy—magnificent! The sun poured over his head and embraced his back hotly.

Smiling, he rambled up and down the streets. He went to the Alcázar. Soldiers in German helmets were on guard. He went to the cathedral. It was ancient but the stones looked brand-new. After lunch he sat at the café in front of the aqueduct waiting for Alvarez-Polvo. On the wide sloping sidewalk there were hundreds of folding chairs, empty, the paint blazed off them and the wood emerging as gray as silverfish. The long low windows were open, so that inside and outside mingled their air, the yellow and the sombre, the bar brown and the sky clear blue. A gypsy woman came out and gave Clarence the eye. She was an entertainer, but whether a real gypsy or not was conjectural. In the phrase he had heard, some of these girls were *Gitanas de miedo,* or strictly from hunger. But he sat and studied the aqueduct, trying to imagine what sort of machinery they could have used to raise the stones.

A black hearse with mourners who trod after it slowly, and with all the plumes, and carvings of angels and death-grimacers, went through the main arch to the cemetery. After ten minutes it came galloping back with furious lashing of the horses, the silk-hatted coachman standing, yacking at them. Only a little later the same hearse returned with another procession of mourners who supported one another, weeping aloud, grief pushing on their backs. Through the arch again. And once more the hearse came flying back. With a sudden tightness of the guts Clarence thought, Why all these burials at once? Was this a plague? He looked at the frothy edge of his glass with horror.

But Alvarez-Polvo set his mind at rest. He said, "The hearse was broken all week. It has just been repaired."

He was a strange-looking man. His face seemed to have been worked by three or four diseases and then abandoned. His nose swelled out and shrunk his eyes. He had a huge mouth, like his cousin Don Luis. He wore a beret, and a yellow silk sash was wound around his belly. Clarence often had noticed that short men with big bellies sometimes held their arms ready for defense as they walked, but at heart expected defeat. Alvarez-Polvo, too, had that posture. However, his brown, mottled, creased, sunlit face with kinky gray hair escaping from the beret seemed to declare that he had a soul like a drum. If you struck, you wouldn't injure him. You'd hear a sound.

"You know what I've come for?" said Clarence.

"Yes, I do know. But let's not start talking business right away. You've never been in Segovia before, I assume, and you must let me be hospitable. I'm a proud Segoviano—proud of this ancient, beautiful city, and it would give me pleasure to show you the principal places."

At the words "talking business" Clarence's heart rose a notch. Was it only a matter of settling the price? Then he had the poems! Something in Clarence flapped with eager joy, like a flag in the wind.

"By all means. For a while. It is beautiful. Never in my life have I seen anything so gorgeous as Segovia."

Alvarez-Polvo took his arm.

"With me you will not only see, you will also understand. I have made a study of it. I'm a lover of such things. I seldom have an opportunity to express it. Wherever I take my wife, she is interested only in *novelas morbosas*. At Versailles she sat and read Ellery Queen. In Paris, the same. In Rome, the same. If she lives to the end of time, she will never run out of *novelas morbosas*."

From this remark, without notice, he took a deep plunge into the subject of women, and he carried Clarence with him. Women, women, women! All the types of Spanish beauty. The Granadinas, the Malagueñas, the Castellanas, the Catalunas. And then the Germans, the Greeks, the French, the Swedes! He tightened his hold on Clarence and pulled him close as he boasted and complained and catalogued and confessed. He was ruined! They had taken his money, his health, his time, his years, his life, women had—innocent, mindless, beautiful, ravaging, insidious, malevolent, chestnut, blond, red, black. . . . Clarence felt hemmed in by women's faces, and by women's bodies.

"I suppose you'd call this a Romanesque church, wouldn't you?" Clarence said, stopping.

"Of course it is," said Alvarez-Polvo. "Just notice how the Renaissance building next to it was designed to harmonize with it."

Clarence was looking at the pillars and their blunted faces of humorous, devil-beast humanities, the stone birds, demon lollers, apostles. Two men carried by a spring and mattress in a pushcart. They looked like the kings of Shinar and Elam defeated by Abraham.

"Come, have a glass of wine," said Alvarez-Polvo. "I'm not allowed to drink since my operation, but you must have something."

When could they begin to talk about the poems? Clarence was impatient. Gonzaga's poems would mean little if anything to a man like this, but in spite of his endless gallant bunk and his swagger and his complaints about having broken his springs in the service of love and beauty, he was probably a very cunning old fuff. He wanted to stall Clarence and find out what the poems were worth to him. And so Clarence gazed, or blinked, straight ahead, and kept a tight grip on his feelings.

In the *bodega* were huge barrels, copper fittings, innumerable bottles duplicated in the purple mirror, platters of *mariscos,* crawfish bugging their eyes on stalks, their feelers cooked into various last shapes. From the middle of the floor rose a narrow spiral staircase. It mounted—who-knew-where? Clarence tried to see but couldn't. A little torn-frocked beggar child came selling lottery tickets. The old chaser petted her; she wheedled; she took his small hand and laid her cheek to it. Still talking, he felt her hair. He stroked his fill and sent her away with a coin.

Clarence drank down the sweet, yellow Malaga.

"Now," said Alvarez-Polvo, "I will show you a church few visitors ever see."

They descended to the lower part of town, down littered stairways of stone, by cavelike homes and a lot where runty boys were passing a football with their heads, and dribbling and hooking it with their boots.

"Here," Alvarez-Polvo said. "This wall is of the tenth century and this one of the seventeenth."

The air inside the church was dark, cool, thick as ointment. Hollows of dark red and dark blue and heavy yellow slowly took shape, and Clarence began to see the altar, the columns.

Alvarez-Polvo was silent. The two men were standing before a harshly crowned Christ. The figure was gored deeply in the side, rust-blooded. The head-cover of thorns was too wide and heavy to be borne. As he confronted it, Clarence felt that it threatened to scratch the life out of him, to scratch him to the heart.

"The matter that interests us both . . ." Alvarez-Polvo then said.

"Yes, yes, let's go somewhere and have a talk about it. You got the poems among your uncle's papers. Do you have them here in Segovia?"

"Poems?" said Alvarez-Polvo, turning the dark and ruined face from the aisle. "That's a strange word to use for them."

"Do you mean they're not in that form? What are they, then? What are they written in?"

"Why, the usual legal language. According to law."

"I don't understand."

"Neither do I. But I can show you what I'm talking about. Here. I have one with me. I brought it along." He drew a document from his pocket.

Clarence held it, trembling. It was heavy, glossy and heavy. He felt an embossed surface. Yes, there was a seal on it. What had the countess done with the poems? This paper was emblazoned with a gilt star. He sought light and read, within an elaborate border of wavy green, *Compañia de Minas, S.A.*

"Is this— It can't be. You've given me the wrong thing." His heart was racing. "Look in your pocket again."

"The wrong thing?"

"It looks like shares of stock."

"Then it isn't the wrong thing. It's what it's supposed to be, mining stock. Isn't that what you're interested in?"

"Of course not! Certainly not! What kind of mine?"

"It's a pitchblende mine in Morocco, that's what it is."

"What in the name of anything do I want with pitchblende!" Clarence shouted.

"What any sensible man would want. To sell it. Pitchblende has uranium in it. Uranium is used in atom bombs."

Oh, dear God!

"Claro. Para la bomba atómica."

"What have I to do with atom bombs? What do I care about atom bombs! To hell with atom bombs!" Clarence cried out, furious.

"I understood you were a financier."

"Me? Do I look like one?"

"Yes, of course you do. More English than American, I thought. But a financier. Aren't you?"

"I am not. I came about the poems of Gonzaga, the poems

owned by the Countess del Camino. Love poems dedicated to her by the poet Manuel Gonzaga."

"Manuel? The soldier? The little fellow? The one that was her lover in nineteen-twenty-eight? He was killed in Morocco."

"Yes, yes! What did your uncle do with the poems?"

"Oh, that's what you were talking about. Why, my uncle did nothing with them. The countess did, herself. She had them buried with her. She took them to the grave."

"Buried! With her, you say! And no copies?"

"I doubt it. My uncle had instructions from her, and he was very loyal. He lived by loyalty. My uncle—"

"Oh, damn! Oh, damn it! And didn't he leave you anything in that collection of papers that has to do with Gonzaga? No journals, no letters that mention Gonzaga? Nothing?"

"He left me these shares in the mine. They're valuable. Not yet, but they will be if I can get capital. But you can't raise money in Spain. Spanish capital is cowardly, ignorant of science. It is still in the Counter-Reformation. Let me show you the location of this mine." He opened a map and began to explain the geography of the Atlas Mountains.

Clarence walked out on him—ran, rather than walked. He had to get out of Segovia. Quickly. Immediately. Panting, enraged, choking, he clambered from the lower town.

As soon as he entered his room at the hotel he knew that his valise had been searched. Storming, he slammed it shut and dragged it down the stairs, past the cistern, and into the lobby.

He called in a shout to the manager, "Why must the police come and turn my things upside down?"

White-faced and stern, the manager said, "You must be mistaken, señor."

"I am not mistaken. Why must the police bother foreign visitors?"

A man rose angrily from a chair in the lobby. He wore an old suit with a mourning band on the arm.

"These Englishmen!" he said with fury. "They don't know what hospitality is. They come here and enjoy themselves, and criticize our country, and complain about police. What hypocrisy! There are more police in England. The whole world knows you have a huge jail in Liverpool, filled with Masons. Five thousand Masons are *encarcelados* in Liverpool alone."

Clarence couldn't reply. He stared. Then he paid his bill and left. All the way to Madrid he sat numb and motionless in his second-class seat.

As the train left the mountains, the heavens seemed to split; a rain began to fall, heavy and sudden, boiling on the wide plain.

He knew what to expect from that redheaded Miss Walsh at dinner.

The Wrecker

A One-act Play

Cast

A HUSBAND

A WIFE

A MOTHER-IN-LAW

A CITY EMPLOYEE

SCENE: *The living room of a railroad flat on the East Side in New York. Chesterfield suite, ribbon plants, rubber plants, all the cherished objects of the woman's temple, the man's asylum. At curtain wife and mother-in-law are discovered packing fragile articles into a barrel, wrapping them in paper.*
Suddenly, a huge crash backstage.

MOTHER-IN-LAW (*gives a shriek, suppresses it, asks angrily*): How can you stand it!

WIFE (*looks concerned; she leans forward slightly against the barrel, not daring to look in the direction of the noise*): I've been standing it since yesterday. I'll probably get used to it. They say you get used to any kind of noise.

MOTHER-IN-LAW: You should never have let him start.

WIFE: I held him back till yesterday, when the people down-stairs moved. They were the last.

MOTHER-IN-LAW: The place is spooky. An empty building, and you on the third floor. They all left their trash on the stairs. It shows how inconsiderate people are. As long as there's a single tenant in the house they shouldn't have cluttered the staircase. I could hardly pass by.

WIFE (*sorrowfully patient with her mother*): I'm sorry, Mother, but it's the last time you'll be visiting me here anyway.

MOTHER-IN-LAW (*another rumbling noise offstage rear; she turns towards it*): I suppose he fought with all the neighbors enough. You shouldn't be sorry to leave this—this dump. It ought to have been condemned years ago.

WIFE: Oh, I'm not exactly sorry. After fifteen years in the same place, though, you stop criticizing it. You never think whether it's a bad place or a good one.

MOTHER-IN-LAW: Nonsense. You ought to be happy to move into an elevator building. And get rid of the old dumbwaiter. And have white woodwork. And a toilet where you don't have to pull the chain. Things a person needs for her self-respect.

WIFE: It was good enough when I was a bride. (*Teary, thinking of the past*): I was proud of it. And Albert used to be so kind about it. He helped me paper the walls . . .

MOTHER-IN-LAW: Sarah, he's a neurotic.

WIFE: Oh, Mother! You don't have to sound like a doctor.

Terrible crash offstage.

MOTHER-IN-LAW: Would any person in his right mind be doing that? Have you moved out the breakables?

WIFE: I took a lot of things over to the new apartment yester-day.

MOTHER-IN-LAW: I suppose you're trying to save money by doing the moving yourself. I'm positively disgusted. Why, on the bonus the city is offering you could have it all done for you while you went to Atlantic City or even Virginia Beach and took a rest. You'd come back to a clean house. He turns down the bonus the city's giving for moving a few days before the lease is up so they can start their work. He keeps you here, and you let him. Oh, it's maddening. A husband like that is maddening. I predict that on this very spot, in this very space, when the school is built they'll be teaching about men like him in the abnormal psychology course. Why, think what you could do with a thousand dollars. You could get a new coat.

WIFE: We could pay our debts.

MOTHER-IN-LAW: And last year he let his insurance policy lapse because of a hundred-dollar premium. He's of unsound mind. Don't try to tell me he's not.

WIFE (*mildly*): He say he doesn't believe in life insurance.

MOTHER-IN-LAW: I don't know where he gets his thoughts.

Husband enters, pulling a mirror on casters, an oval mirror. He is wearing dusty overalls, a painter's cap, and carries a hammer on his hip, a hatchet on the other side. He holds a short crowbar.

HUSBAND: I thought I'd better get this out of the way.

MOTHER-IN-LAW (*sarcastic*): Why not smash it. Break all the furniture too, while you're at it. It would be good for your temperament.

HUSBAND (*turning*): Oh, it's you. For once I'm glad to see you. Last night I dreamed you were here—like the bird of prey at the battle. Welcome to the last of my house! (*He is very enthusiastic. To wife*): Baby, I knocked out the pantry wall, and do you know what? now you can go from the kitchen to the dining room without turning corners. It was thrilling to knock a hole in that wall. Oh! Wow, what excitement!

MOTHER-IN-LAW: Pretty expensive amusement.

HUSBAND: What do you mean, amusement!

MOTHER-IN-LAW: A thousand-dollar amusement. Do you give

any thought to what you could do with that money? Have you taken even five minutes off to sit down quietly in a corner and concentrate on what you could do? Your thoughts are always on the move, like the bottom of the sea.

HUSBAND: I have thought. With a thousand dollars I could pay off a lot of people who have never done anything except make me unhappy, and strengthen their hand so they make me and others like me still more unhappy. Installments! For a lot of stuff I never really needed!

MOTHER-IN-LAW: Like meat.

HUSBAND: Food I pay for. Those are debts of honor. But the other stuff. Huh!

MOTHER-IN-LAW: Like insurance.

HUSBAND: If I have to die, what will happen? The less secure Sarah is the more she'll feel my death. You want to be able to mourn for me, don't you, darling?

WIFE: Of course.

HUSBAND: There. And if I leave her too comfortable she won't feel my death acutely enough. Why should things be better when I die? The city is full of unhappy old women whose husbands left them well-off. It is like revenge from the grave. There lies the husband in the earth. With probably a telephone beside him—they say there is one beside Mary Baker Eddy. A monument to his wife's security. And now she goes shopping—she doesn't need anything. She goes to Schrafft's. She pesters the elevator starter to find her an Irish Sweepstakes ticket. She buys magazines and doesn't know what to do with herself.

MOTHER-IN-LAW (*snaps her fingers*): That! for you and your philosophy. A man who has no respect for a thousand dollars isn't intelligent. You're ascared to do better in life.

HUSBAND: I'm getting a thousand dollars' worth out of it. More. (*Shakes his crowbar like a spear.*) Oh, what am I wasting words on you for! Today I'm a man of deeds, like a hero out of Homer, like a man who does something for civilization.

WIFE: This is what he keeps saying.

HUSBAND: Where there's no demolition there's no advancement. The old must go down. You only see what is built. You forget what had to be taken away, and yet it is the same process. Man does not wait for time to do his work for him. He makes an end; he begins again. (*Pounds the floor with the butt of his crowbar. A picture falls from the wall.*)

WIFE: Look what you've done!

MOTHER-IN-LAW: If you have to tear down walls, why don't you go downstairs and do it. They've moved out and nobody'll care. Then you'd have the bonus and your fun.

HUSBAND: It shows how little you understand. The neighbors' walls do not interest me. It was right here that everything happened to me. Here I was out of work, and looked at the walls. And here I was sick, and looked at the walls. And here I was blue, and here I cursed the world. And here maybe I learned my own limitations—oh, yes, the realization that I wasn't all I thought I was. It all took place within these walls. It went into them. And you ask me what I've got against them? *Plenty!* I *know* them. Oh, I've made a long study of them. There's a long history between us. And now that they have to come down why shouldn't I put my hand to the work? Who has a better right—a more sacred right? Why should I leave it to anyone? I will do it. Myself, I'll tear holes out. I'll see the East River through the dining room. I'll have the satisfaction myself, and get my revenge for all those terrible times. What good will the walls downstairs do me? I want to take it out on my own walls. I know every lump, every blister, every face in the cracks of the ceiling. Now I'm going to see what this place is made of, what the walls are like inside. I'm going to tear out the laths and get behind all the swellings—like the brows, eyes, landscapes, and so on. I'll find all the rats' nests and see if there are any treasures or bones. You can never tell what you'll find in an old building.

WIFE (*to mother*): You see how overexcited he is?

MOTHER-IN-LAW: I see he's passing up an opportunity to make your life easier because he wants to play like a boy. Treasures! People ought to be forced to be their age. What if he put on a sailor suit and told you he was going to sail his little boat in Central Park pond? What a sex the males are! It's a miracle how anything ever works out.

HUSBAND: I am excited! I feel like Samson in the Temple of Gaza! (*So poses in the doorway.*) Take cover, ye Philistines, your oppression is ended. My strength has come back to me. Though you took my hair and put out my eyes and bound me in your mill your walls are doomed! Doomed!

MOTHER-IN-LAW (*a little frightened*): He's off his rocker.

HUSBAND (*rousing himself*): I am not. (*Points at her with the crowbar; says seriously*): Beware of diagnosing those near to you. You should never do that. Not even when it's true. At your age you should know better. What do you think is lunacy is just happiness. You aren't used to it, probably haven't seen it in a long time. You've forgotten what it looks like.

WIFE: You are happy.

HUSBAND: Tremendously. Can't you see how happy I am? I'm a new man. And that's why I snap my fingers at the thousand-dollar bonus. If I were as usual I'd need that thousand to help me stand it.

WIFE: Is it as bad as that to be as usual? (*She is wounded.*)

HUSBAND: My dear, don't you take the blame for that. A daily life is a strange thing, and what are a husband and wife to do? They must live it together. Nobody is to blame. But these last two days I have carried a marvelous feeling in my heart. Like a poet. I have welcomed each night's sleep and blessed every morning's rising. I have been like a young boy reading a wonderful book who must put it down at night and says to himself, Just close your eyes a while and when you open them again it will be morning and you can go on with it. And in the morning, which comes soon, it's very sweet; his book is still wonderful; it doesn't disappoint him. This is how my days have been since I started wrecking this apartment.

WIFE (*pathetic*): I didn't know you hated it so.

MOTHER-IN-LAW: All I can say is that I hope it will pass over before it gets to the Bellevue stage.

A ring at the door. Wife answers and admits the city employee. He has a portfolio under his arm—cardboard—and his double-breasted suit is chalkstriped. An eater of clams and drinker of beer. Seeing ladies, he takes the toothpick from his mouth and with same hand removes his hat.

CITY EMPLOYEE: It gets kind of peculiar in a building when everybody—

WIFE: Oh, it's the man from the city.

MOTHER-IN-LAW (*best manners*): How do you do.

WIFE: It is spooky, isn't it? Yesterday as I was cooking supper it was the first time I could remember that there was no radio program downstairs at Pellegrinis', and nobody playing the piano. It was just like the last days of some poor old widow.

CITY EMPLOYEE: I come to open this bonus situation again. You understand, there's people waiting to start operations, the wrecking crew, the excavators, contractors. It's not exactly playing the game when everybody else has taken the bonus and moved out.

HUSBAND: My lease runs for three weeks yet.

CITY EMPLOYEE: You could be evicted with eminent domain.

HUSBAND: It still would take weeks. Try it.

CITY EMPLOYEE: It's no good trying to hold the city up for more dough, if that's your idea.

HUSBAND: So, you think my idea is to get dough out of you?

MOTHER-IN-LAW: I wish I thought he was that smart.

CITY EMPLOYEE: Well, you don't want to put the city on the spot like this.

HUSBAND: What do I care about the city? It never did me a favor in all my life.

CITY EMPLOYEE: What are you talkin'. There's invisible benefit all over. The sidewalks, the sewers, the water, the bridges, the garbage, the police—

HUSBAND: The police are no invisible benefit. (*Swings his crowbar over his shoulder, turns about limberly, and marches away.*)

City employee stands amazed. A great crash is heard. Staggering.

CITY EMPLOYEE: What's that—what's he doin'?

MOTHER-IN-LAW: Can't you guess?

WIFE: Mother!

MOTHER-IN-LAW: Do you think you can keep it a secret? He's wrecking the house.

WIFE: Mother, that's downright disloyal.

CITY EMPLOYEE: Is he nuts or something? (*Slams hat against thigh.*) Who said he could? This is bought by the city. He's on m'nicipal property. Why, it ain't legal anyhow. (*Another crash. City employee shouts down corridor.*) Hey! (*No answer. City employee exits, rear.*)

MOTHER-IN-LAW: Now maybe we'll get somewhere with that stubborn man.

WIFE: Now he's in trouble.

MOTHER-IN-LAW: He deserves it.

WIFE: No, he doesn't. You don't understand him.

MOTHER-IN-LAW: If I had to live with him fifteen years to understand him it wouldn't be worth it.

City employee re-enters, covered with white dust, quivering with anger. He shouts down corridor, rear.

CITY EMPLOYEE: Who the hell do you think *you* are! (*Another crash.*) Who gave you the right? (*Sound of chopping.*) Lady, your husband better not carry this any further. I'm tellin' you for your own good. He's poundin' chunks out of the walls with a sledgehammer. This just is not allowed, and that's all.

WIFE: Why not? It's his right. Isn't a man's home his castle?

CITY EMPLOYEE (*startled, wiping his face*): He can have it for his castle, but not for his loony bin. Besides, it ain't his. The city bought it and they can get him for damaging municipal property.

WIFE: They've got their nerve. We paid enough rent before the city even heard of it.

MOTHER-IN-LAW: The way you stand up for him!

WIFE: Of course I do. Ain't I the man's wife? I know what he's been through if you don't, and if he wants his revenge on the place it's his by right.

CITY EMPLOYEE (*feels his ear*): Do I understand, lady, that he's passin' up the bonus just to do the wreckin' job on this place himself? (*Hears the husband hammering within. His face passes through wonder, outrage, envy, and finally stops at an expression of law violated.*) It's not only crazy but illegal. It's real bad. For this he can go to jail. (*Draws forth notebook, looks about, makes notes.*) He don't even have a permit.

MOTHER-IN-LAW: I knew all along it was something fundamental.

WIFE: I don't understand why.

CITY EMPLOYEE: Lady, for one thing wrecking is a licensed occupation. You can't just go wreck. You have to know how. You must realize it's a profession like any other and you have to qualify for it. How does he know what to do about electricity, gas, water? Can he take out the bathtub or the toilet—any fixtures? He'd be shocked, suffocated, or drowned. And what about the street? You have to protect your pedestrians. Where's your scaffold? Where's your dumping? He can get the book thrown at him.

Thunderous crash. Husband enters, carrying framed wedding picture.

HUSBAND: I think this wedding picture got jarred, dear. No real harm. Better put it away.

WIFE (*catches breath*): You're starting on the bedroom! (*She takes picture from him, holds it tightly.*)

HUSBAND: I thought I might do a little work in there later today.

WIFE: The bedroom.

CITY EMPLOYEE: Listen, bud, you're heading into all kinds of trouble.

WIFE (*from a different viewpoint*): Yes, Albert, you are.

HUSBAND: The city wants to have this place torn down, doesn't it? It wants a school built here, doesn't it? Suppose I volunteered my help in tearing down my own apartment? They'd never accept it. I'd have to see people and fill forms and answer questions and in the end I wouldn't get in on it. So I'm independently contributing my labor. What's wrong with that? (*Hooks crowbar into mantlepiece and wrenches off top. Bric-a-brac goes flying.*)

WIFE (*wildly*): Oh, my things! The sea-shells! The little jug from Vermont! The little cups! (*Goes on hands and knees. Mother-in-law, muttering, helps.*)

HUSBAND: Oh, it's nothing, Sarah. I'll get you new knickknacks. These are about worn out. Look at that grand cockroach. If it isn't the oldest resident in person! He's not even disturbed. What presence. This is what you call aristocracy. Fifteen years

we've been his vassals. He's never done a lick of work, I'll bet.
Why should he?

MOTHER-IN-LAW (*to city employee*): You see what's happening? But it's probably just temporary. You ought to give him till tomorrow to decide. He'll most likely come back to his senses.

CITY EMPLOYEE: He's off his control, all right, I can see that.

HUSBAND: See what a difference the point of view makes. I never was better. I am a magician. This joint is enchanted, you see. I'm getting rid of a lot of past life, dangerous to the soul. The past, you understand, is very dangerous if you don't deal with it. If I had a warehouse I could put this harmful past life into, or if I could take it to sea in a scow and dump it, let the seagulls have it, I'd be satisfied. You can't drag your heavy, heavy history around with you. Suppose the hummingbird had to keep remembering that in the ancient past it was a snake?

CITY EMPLOYEE (*touching his forehead*): Oh, man! (*He goes out.*)

MOTHER-IN-LAW: I'd better talk to him. Maybe I can make him hold off a while. You'd better reason with *him* meanwhile and please God his mentality will return. (*Exit.*)

WIFE (*broken cup in hand*): Albert—

HUSBAND: Yes, darling?

WIFE: Isn't there anything—anything here you don't hold a grudge against?

HUSBAND (*speculative*): I suppose there is.

WIFE: You suffered in every room?

HUSBAND: Well, you carry it around from room to room, you see.

WIFE: The bedroom, too.

HUSBAND (*uneasy*): No more than the others, probably.

WIFE: Isn't there anything you'd like to save instead of wreck? You might remember something that made your life worth while.

HUSBAND: Of course. You want to be fair about it.

WIFE (*with light irony*): The kitchen, perhaps, in memory of good meals. (*He shrugs. Wife changes tone.*) Albert, I have tried to make you a home. We've had many bad times, that's true. But didn't I comfort you? That time you came in and said your paycheck was stolen?

HUSBAND (*feebly*): It was, too.

WIFE: The time you were knocked down by the cab on Lexington Avenue and I brought you home from the hospital in a cab, and when you woke up at night I had to go and make tea for you and stay awake with you. And what about the time the furniture company wanted to repossess the living-room suite?

HUSBAND: Yes, I remember.

WIFE: And what about the time we came back from Jones Beach that afternoon, and—

HUSBAND: Sure, sure, that was great. That was a wonderful afternoon, wasn't it?

WIFE: What about all those good things?

HUSBAND: We haven't forgotten. Did I say we should? But let's not get sentimental, old girl. Because when you come right down to it, you can't check off every grievance against a happy time. You can't have happy times if you have to swallow all the grievances. Anyhow, this is too much like bookkeeping. Why do you have to pretend to me that you're not sore at this joint, too. It never bored you? Didn't it ever make you want to yell? Didn't you ever feel here that you were in a cage? Didn't these walls ever look at you with yellow foreheads and their lousy, dull eyes? Don't kid me.

WIFE (*hesitant*): Sometimes, of course.

HUSBAND (*hands her a hatchet*): What are you waiting for, then? Be honest. Pitch in.

WIFE (*decisively rejects hatchet*): No, I'm not going to. I papered and painted these walls myself, and washed the floors and the woodwork.

HUSBAND: And swore at the landlord.

WIFE: Never mind the landlord. We lived here.

HUSBAND: We suffered here.

WIFE: That would have happened to you anywhere.

HUSBAND: Sometimes you ought to give in to your violent feelings, Sarah. It's great to be angry. Anger is beautiful. It gives you a sense of honor. It brings back your self-respect.

WIFE: All right, then. I am angry.

HUSBAND: About what?

WIFE: It's the bedroom I'm angry about. You haven't been happy, and this is your way of saying it.

HUSBAND (*without enough emphasis*): Yes, I have been. Well, look here, Sarah old girl. Let's not act in bad faith. I mean—you know. If it isn't always what it should be, at least you don't have to think you're protecting the home by pretending. Most likely it all clears up in the end—

WIFE: You don't love me.

HUSBAND (*indignant*): Of course I love you. Do you think I'm wrecking this joint for myself? Every other hole I pound in the wall is for you. I say, "This is for Sarah. This is where she bowed her head. This is where she heard bad news. This is where she scalded her foot. Where we argued—"

WIFE: But the bedroom, Albert, the bedroom.

HUSBAND: Well, come and help me bust up the dining room and we can discuss the bedroom later. It's only another room.

WIFE: It isn't. And if you touch it—

HUSBAND: Threats?

WIFE: You can't expect me to be overjoyed.

HUSBAND: And you can't expect me to be superhuman like you. If you can forgive everything, that's your good luck. But if I did it I'd be acting in bad faith. Things always should be nice, that's for sure. But tell me, why is it so glorious to tear this house down? Why is it ecstasy to see the ceilings fall, and chopping I feel like dancing, and the smell of dust makes my heart float with joy, like the smell of flowers, and I never feel tired?

WIFE: Have I tried to stop you? Did I insist about the thousand dollars? Did I complain at having to pack all the things myself?

HUSBAND: All that is true. Still, you should be glad I have found something that cries aloud to be done, an object—

WIFE: Yes, I should be delighted that you don't knock me down; I should be pleased you don't batter me on the head with your ax, like the pantry shelves.

HUSBAND: Sweetheart, please understand. An object—

WIFE: —is a substitute for me. Because I've had you in a trap. Was this your home or was it the Bastille? Did it mean nothing to you? Did you have to lie down each night worried that animals might bite you in your sleep, or people run in to attack you? You have no gratitude in your makeup. I often go back to where I used to live when I was a girl. The lot is vacant and nobody I know is there. I ask myself, Where is everything that meant so much to me? I'd bring it back if I could. Next year there'll be a school here, and children sitting where we used to—

HUSBAND: They'll be studying history.

WIFE: And where will we be?

HUSBAND: In the new apartment.

WIFE: No, I'm speaking of the lives we used to lead here. Where will they be?

HUSBAND: And where will the lives the schoolchildren will lead on this spot be later on? You say this was the Bastille for me. Don't you mean that you want it to be a museum?

WIFE: Albert, I don't think I've made you a bad wife.

HUSBAND: Of course not.

WIFE: I've given in to your impulses and you always had my first consideration. I've never stood in your way. You want to wreck the house? Go ahead, wreck it!

HUSBAND: Angel!

WIFE: Only, if you wreck the bedroom, you'll be moving into the new apartment by yourself.

HUSBAND: You don't mean it!

WIFE: I'll leave you. It was you who told me anger was wonderful.

HUSBAND: You wouldn't do that.

WIFE: I will. And what else can I do? You force me to it.

HUSBAND: I am convinced now. Only the most ordinary men should become husbands. Whatever they may dream of, when you come right down to it women want their husbands to be ordinary and to make no trouble. Husbands are not heroes: heroes are not husbands. That's all there is to it.

WIFE: Do you call what you're doing heroism? (*She laughs.*)

HUSBAND: Amuse yourself if you like. It shows you never applied your mind to this subject. Does it say anywhere that Achilles ever built anything? Or Ulysses? They tore down Troy and killed everyone in it. Who were the heroes of the war? The fellows who dropped bombs on cities. A hero destroys the links with the past when they bother him. He frees himself from what other men have done before him.

WIFE: Other men before him? Are you trying to say—(*Indignant*): What other men have ever been in that bedroom? You're accusing me!

HUSBAND: No, no, no. Why do you have to be so damned literal. Besides—you don't have to protest so much. You'll make me think I'm missing up on something. Is it some other bedroom I should be thinking of tearing down? Is that it?

WIFE (*startled at first, then reproachful*): How can you allow yourself to say such things! Oh, Albert!

HUSBAND: I always mean well, but my mind betrays me. Ah, Sarah, come along. (*Active again*): Try it. When you've tried you'll understand what I've been driving at. You have to prime yourself sometimes. Take one sock at a wall. Just one.

See how different you'll feel. (*Hands her his hatchet.*) You don't realize what you'll get out of it.

WIFE: No. I've already told you what I'd do.

HUSBAND: Come, free yourself, Sarah.

WIFE: No, that's not what I call freeing myself. It's ingratitude.

HUSBAND: You're not big, but you sure are obstinate. And also because it was *your* house it was wonderful. That's how vain you are.

WIFE: Now I will leave. It's a lucky thing I thought of opening a bank account of my own.

HUSBAND: You're far too rigid—far, far. You have to learn to be more flexible. It's a practical matter. For the sake of your health.

WIFE (*sighs and shakes her head*): How many ideas you have. Do you want me to believe that what you're doing you're doing for your health's sake?

HUSBAND: Of course it's for my health. (*To audience*): I'm dead serious. (*To wife*): Now why else do you think I'm being so truthful? It's risky. If I say too much you'll get sore. But if I don't do it I feel sick. (*Puts backs of hands to eyes and brings hands away with a whisking motion.*) Let's wipe out some of the falsehood. Let's admit what our souls tell us is true and stop denying it for the sake of keeping the peace or preserving the marriage and the home. Yes, just because of health. So the old bedroom will be destroyed, but maybe then the new one will be fit for princes and queens. Maybe it will make the roses bloom from the plaster and daisies from the rug.

WIFE (*half swayed*): Oh, Albert, do you really think so?

HUSBAND: Yes, yes. So come. We'll take some of the doors off the hinges and set them up. Have you noticed how pretty it is when the wreckers are working, with blue doors and pink doors standing outside? And you know how the plaster was always falling into the bathtub, well now we can fill the tub with plaster. Rip up the old linoleum. Tear up the floors. Go through the place like a hurricane. Come on.

WIFE (*steels herself*): No.

HUSBAND (*turning*): You won't?

WIFE: I told you what I'd do.

HUSBAND: It's the bedroom?

WIFE: Yes, I'll leave.

HUSBAND (*furious*): All right, go then. Go. Damn! Take your shells and your damn precious female breakables, your Vermont jugs and your slave-chains of china, and get out of here. I'll wreck the joint myself. I'll demolish it; I'll raze it; I'll tear it to pieces; I'll level it down to the ground. (*Smites ceiling with crowbar. Chandelier falls and hits him on the head. He drops.*)

WIFE (*rushing to him*): Oh, he's fractured his skull. Albert, baby. Oh, sweetheart, what have you done? Mother! Mama! Oh, help. (*Kisses him, rubs his hands, examines his head, listens to his heart.*) It must be a concussion. I'll never forgive myself if it is. If he had to do it, at least I could have stuck by him and made him do it in a safer way. Oh, my little sweetheart. Little bright-thought. (*As he revives*): You stood right up to me. Oh, honey, you were so right. Let's never quarrel. How does it feel? (*He groans, hold his head, starts to sit up.*)

HUSBAND: If it was any heavier it would have killed me. I bit my tongue.

WIFE: Albert, darling; Albert, look at me! (*She takes the hatchet and starts delicately to chip at the walls.*) Albert, you see? I've got the idea. It's just as you said. It really is glorious. (*Finds bulb and throws it down. Is slightly shocked by noise and own daring.*) Oh, Albert, how slow I am to learn anything. If I didn't have you to show me the way I'd be just a timid, conservative, poky creature, worrying like a mole. Imagine how it would be to live a whole life without doing anything big. (*Chips away at the fireplace.*)

HUSBAND: Just about knocked my brains out. What are you doing? (*Watches.*)

WIFE: Doing? Why, what you tried to convince me to do, for my own good. And I couldn't agree with you more.

HUSBAND (*doesn't look happy about it*): Wait a minute.

WIFE (*still chipping*): Why, what's the matter? Is it the noise?

HUSBAND: Now hold on a minute.

WIFE: But you've convinced me—

HUSBAND: Yes, but I'm not so sure. On you it doesn't look so good.

WIFE: Why not, I'd like to know? Now you want to stop me? Just as I've discovered what you meant? I know you didn't expect me to, but I have found out and you (*shakes her head*) don't want me to?

HUSBAND (*rising, uncomfortable*): It's not that exactly.

WIFE: How's your head?

HUSBAND: All right, I guess.

WIFE: You don't feel dizzy?

HUSBAND: Not very. It's a miracle.

WIFE (*hands him crowbar*): Then you can go back to work. (*Kisses him.*)

HUSBAND: I do think I need a little rest first.

WIFE: But not for long. I suddenly feel such strength in me. As soon as I picked up the hatchet it just poured into my hands. An hour ago they felt so feeble I couldn't have peeled a potato. Rest, dear, and then we can start on the bedroom together.

HUSBAND: The bedroom?

WIFE: Of course, the bedroom.

HUSBAND (*thinking*): You—

WIFE: Of course, I. Now that I understand what you meant.

HUSBAND: Well, Sarah (*haltingly*), is it really—I mean from your standpoint—such a good idea?

WIFE: You don't want to wreck it? I do, now when I think

of some of the things that happened, all of a sudden I want to express what I never dared—

HUSBAND (*reprovingly*): Sarah!

WIFE: Well, I want to admit what's true, too. You have nothing against that, have you? There are a few places on the ceiling that just burn me up when I think of them. I've only now become conscious of it all.

HUSBAND: Sarah, don't you feel— Are you sure?

WIFE: Why, darling, you surprise me. Have you changed your mind about the bedroom? Why, silly, didn't you tell me a daily life was a strange thing, and what were husband and wife to do about it—they have to live it together?

HUSBAND: Yes, yes, of course. But—

WIFE: And don't you want to wreck the house?

HUSBAND: Yes, but all at once you want to start with the bedroom. Tell me something—

WIFE: What is there to tell? Do I have to draw pictures?

HUSBAND: Please, Sarah.

WIFE (*once more offers him the crowbar*): Are you with me or not? Are you going to back down or will you come along?

HUSBAND: All right. (*He is very reluctant.*)

WIFE: Better fetch a stepladder. I'm mad to get at that ceiling. (*Grips hatchet and laughs exultantly.*) Something has just entered my mind.

HUSBAND: What?

WIFE: That maybe the best way to preserve the marriage is to destroy the home. (*Embraces him.*)

HUSBAND (*mildly*): It may well be.

Curtain. After which, a thunderous crash.